with *Revenge*

comes *Terror*

a jihadist attack on America

a novel

by **S.P. Grogan**

with Revenge comes Terror
  a jihadist attack on America

© 2016 by S.P. Grogan
ISBN: 978-0-9801164-8-9

Notes: In this story both *al-Qaida* and *al-Qaeda* are correct and may be used interchangeably.

Look to back of this book for Author's Final Note, Time Line, and Cast of Characters.

For more information, visit: www.spgrogan.com and read author's other works, *Vegas Die*, *Captain Cooked*, and *Atomic Dreams at the Red Tiki Lounge*

Addison & Highsmith Publishing
840 S. Rancho Drive, Suite 337
Las Vegas, NV 89106
Email: *Addisonhighsmith@gmail.com*

Author's Comment:

In November, 2014, I released the Ebook, "Terror and Revenge", which dealt with a fictionalized radical jihadist attack on the United States as seen through two perspectives: one, the view of a glory-seeking terrorist and, the second, actions by certain bored and ambivalent 'stars' of our modern pop culture.

A year later, recent terrorist attacks world-wide again raises the alarm that 'credible threats' may soon result in mayhem and fear in America. Writing an updated version, I felt it my responsibility to keep knocking on the public door, raising warnings of possibilities, seeking heroic responses. Please read this mini epic on past historical events interwoven into a fictional story and if concerned as I am please pass it on to your friends.

Being prepared and vigilant is my only goal.

SPG

In memory to those innocents who lost their lives to terrorism
may they be remembered...and avenged

Table of Contents

Episode 1

Headline from *Washington Times* – December 23, 2010

Osama bin Laden is Dead

Is bin Laden dead or alive? Nobody seems to know for sure, or, if anybody does, he isn't saying.

The White House's Afghanistan-Pakistan Review this month didn't even mention him despite an ongoing, decade-long manhunt.... Al-Qaeda wants America and the world to believe bin Laden is alive. His image is a specter of the horrors of September 11, helping build public support for everything from troop surges a globe away to warrantless wiretaps. But the image of bin Laden is getting moldy, and there's little reason for his ghost to scare anyone anymore. If al-Qaeda wants America to believe bin Laden is alive, it should put up or shut up.... [Column written by Robert Weiner, former Clinton White House spokesman]

1.

2010   Somewhere in Northern Pakistan

"And that is the last of your reports?"

"Yes, beloved Sheik. Well, there is an odd one. It should be dismissed for its silliness, but it does pertain to you."

"Irrelevance to you or the Council may, to me, have importance."

"Various media outlets report they are mobilizing another team to find you."

"For five years we have been safe. Corrupt governments cannot smite we who are righteous to a just cause; again, as all others, they will fail."

"As you say, but they are not government agents. It is an American television show.

"What?"

"From Hollywood."

"Khalaf, that is insufferable. Allah watch over us from such decadent gnats. You were right; think no more of what is doomed. Let our plan proceed. After all these years, we have heard from the Scientist. The time is coming. Go to al-Awlaki and tell him to awaken the Professor from his long slumber. When all is in place I shall authorize, and only by my command, the launching of *Crimson Scimitar*."

"Yes, sire. Once again, an assured victory to the Faithful."

"Indeed. When we shall succeed with *Scimitar*, and that day is near, then the world will have television worth watching. Allah be praised."

With a nod of his esteemed leader's head, the man known only as Khalaf was dismissed.

Sitting, he leaned over and bowed reverently. Then he rose and kissed the older man on the cheek, noticing the tiredness in his taut face.

Khalaf left the large room on the third floor and went down the stairs past the second floor where he stayed overnight on occasion, for reasons of both exhaustion and safety. He walked out into the hard-packed dirt compound of the ground level, filled with running children and women at domestic work. A tethered milk cow grazed on a small hay pile.

His emotions were mixed. His meeting with his mentor and leader, Sheik Osama bin Laden, had gone extremely well. It was his fourth meeting since being elevated to primary contact between the leader of al-Qaeda and the Supreme Council, who, on rubber-stamped consensus, then forwarded its leader's commands out to the jihadist network. Khalaf's position as a special courier required him to make a physical appearance before the other ruling members of the Council, all of them secreted throughout various countries, his messages designed to avoid any chance of telecommunication eavesdropping. He accepted the truth of his posting, for such travel occurred when grandiose plans were in play. If he was caught, or placed in a compromising position, it was understood that death must come swiftly from his own hand.

Recently his thoughts were jumbled and caused by his ambition, which he acknowledged to himself, this knowing desire that he wished to achieve more. Gratified, yes: he had been singled out for his past success in infiltrating the Muslim Brotherhood in Cairo, creating a small cadre of followers who, though swearing fidelity to a conservative strain of Islam, all swore in secrecy the blood oath to the Caliphate of al-Qaeda, a true belief in the coming new power in the region, superior to all current weak governments in the Middle East. Their mantra was eons old: *Death to all unbelievers*. Sheik Osama bin Laden was destined by Allah to be the first emir, and Khalaf challenged himself, eager in his determination to one day be sitting next to the holy throne.

He watched a goat being brought into the compound. Life around him seemed normal, Khalaf mused, but still this place of high walls seemed more a prison than refuge. Osama's son, the one called Khalid, stepped to his side.

"Where is he sending you this time?"

"Yemen. To speak to our brothers al-Wahishi and al-Awlaki." Khalaf did not trust the cleric, Anwar al-Awlaki. He held suspicion against everything of the West, and al-Awlaki came from America, born and raised. But bin Laden seemed to hold trust in the young spokesperson of al-Qaeda, and Khalaf acquiesced to his supreme commander. Still....

"Will the 'Sword of the Just' be there?"

"Yes, I expect so. This is a major meeting concerning our activities in the West." Saif al-Adel, known as the 'Sword of the Just,' had been appointed, last month, November 2010, by Khalid's father "as new commander to spearhead al-Qaeda's offensive of operations in the West," stated an English-language New Delhi newspaper.

"It must be nice to see the world," said Khalid, his eyes observing the cloudless sky. "I   would like to see Paris some time. Photographs in the magazines are quite elegant. Did you bring us any new books or magazines?"

"One book only, sad to say." Khalaf knew they all suffered from various forms of cloistered stress. He smiled at the 22-year-old, expressing encouragement to the son of his leader, perhaps someday an heir-apparent – though another son, Hamza bin Laden, a year younger, had the reputation and name of 'Crown Prince of Terror.' Khalaf understood that one must make many friends to have a few worthy allies.

"The books have been quite helpful."

"Yes," said Khalaf, believing that bin Laden's son did not know how much these books had come to assist the cause. "Read them again, for they will improve your reading of English."

"The tongue of dogs," laughed Khalid. They watched as one of the women slit the bleating goat's throat, while another caught its flowing blood in a cooking pot. The woman holding the red-drenched knife looked up. She smiled to Khalaf and went back to her work, next slitting the goat's belly. From his recent visits, Khalaf had been accepted as a distant cousin to the Sheik. It was not true, yet it gave him stature in a world based on tribes held taut by the   strict Koran code of family obedience and blood honor.

"Ahmed," Khalaf called out. A man, looking disheveled, as if he had just arisen from sleep, approached. He smelled of sweat and greasy food, but then Khalaf considered the whole compound ripe with nefarious odors, stale and, at the same time, pungent like old garbage not yet discarded.

He held out his hand. "From the emir. He wants it sent out today; now, if you could."

Khalaf's voice was determined, as if to set the pecking order – that he was not a mere runner but a higher up. The other man took the small work-stick, a thumb-sized flash drive that was their method of conveying messages to the outside world.

Ibrahim Saeed Ahmed and his brother, Abrar, were couriers who made trips to local coffee shops and made the Internet connection with others across the globe in the al-Qaeda network. It was simple and effective against the risks. Khalaf glanced up, more of a twitch in his afterthought. The Americans, NATO, they had too many eyes in the sky. Were they, he wondered, at this moment, spying on him?

2.

Indeed, they were watching, but they were in a whitewashed building only four hundred yards away. On its second floor, two men, dark-skinned with unshaven faces, were taking turns at observation, one watching from the shadows with binoculars, the other resting on a metal framed bed, a Nikon camera with telescopic scope, lay on the table next to him.

"The gate is opening." The man adjusted his 10x42mm Swarovski Optik binoculars and focused.

The other man grabbed the camera and moved quickly to his post.

Half of the large green gate door had swung open.

A gray-bearded man with hunched shoulders walked out carrying gardening tools and a ragged sack in the other hand.

"Their occasional gardener. The local weed whacker." Both men spoke English with Middle Eastern accents. Eyes went back to the opened gate. "Wait. Here comes Scooter."

Ibrahim Ahmed exited on an aged Vespa, exhaust smoking.

"Wish we could follow him," the photographer said, clicking digital pics of Abu. He turned his view back to the closing gate, saw no one else, and noted that the gardener had disappeared around a corner.

"Can't blow our cover. Just log occurrence, date and time," said the man with the binoculars, scanning the high walls and the land surrounding. Nothing out of the ordinary, everything as usual, and usual included the butchering of the goat in the corner of the compound.

"Someone else up the food chain will tell us what we are doing here."

"Do we even know who or what we are looking at?"

"No idea. But someone thinks ho-hum Pakistani suburban life is worth cataloguing. And we informed them of that one occupant we rarely see, our 'Tall Man' as being of interest."

"You do have to admit it's strange that a group of hired help have run of the place."

"Squatters, my guess." They returned to their routine, one observing, and the other lying on the bed resting.

Shouldering his field implements of hoe and rake, Khalaf maintained his disguise for the half-mile walk past potato fields to his predetermined niche between two large houses, unseen from the roadway. Leaning the gardening tools against the wall, he stripped off his robe, tugged away his false beard, then rifled through the sack and emerged from the shadows a captain in the Pakistan military. It was a logical choice because of the close proximity of their compound to the Pakistan Military Academy in Kakul. This disguise would have few questioning him, his forged papers leaving no doubt as to his reassignment and posting down to Karachi. What set him apart, and gave him a no-nonsense need for saluted response, is that he wore the green ribbon of Sitarae-Jurat (Star of Courage), the third highest military award in the country. Any authority to challenge him would be awed away by his seething contempt at their bothering a hero. It was enough aloofness to get him to the airport in Islamabad, where his next disguise would turn him into the traveling computer salesman for IBM Egypt. Two flight stops and he would be in Yemen for his meeting with al-Qaida leadership in the Arabian Peninsula. Khalaf would deliver the message on **Crimson Scimitar**, that bin Laden said to stand ready, activation to soon follow.

More importantly, Khalaf wanted to have a one-on-one with Naser Al-Wahishi and better still with al-Adel to build up support for Khalaf joining the **Scimitar** campaign, in what he knew would be al-Qaida's greatest triumph against the United States.

3.

December 2010 Las Vegas, Nevada

Halibut with a mango avocado salsa sounded enticing, a treat that even his kids might appreciate from their old man. In recent years, he had become quite the gourmet, addicted to experimenting off the foodie websites and television food networks. Tonight, fish sounded right for a healthy menu. As he pushed his grocery cart down the aisle of the gourmet market, he stopped to pick up a bottle of northern California virgin olive oil for a light brushing on the fish that he would grill outside. What else? Mixed spring greens sounded good, with a Balsamic vinegar dressing. Only the best for Marcie and the kids. Thinking of his children reminded him that it was another hour before he would need to arrive at the soccer field and pick up the youngest for the drive home.

He did not see the dark-haired man with the ponytail approach, likewise pushing a grocery cart, staring at shelves as if seeking a hidden food item. As they slowly passed each other, the man leaned over and whispered, "On the day of victory no one is tired." In Arabic!

The family man, the cook and chauffeur of children, froze at those words of a distant memory. He turned in shock that was tinged with fear, aware that the world as he knew it had just been altered.

"Do you mind, that jar of pickles behind you, the sweet gherkins, could you hand it to me? ...Professor Rogers."

The Professor noted that the stranger peered from beneath a ball cap bearing the number 51 of the local baseball farm team. The man was clean-shaven, with light olive skin that could pass for a suntan, and seemed like an ordinary shopper unless one looked closely, as the Professor did. The ball cap pulled down, scraggly raven-dark and greased hair poking out, hid what he finally realized as the oddity. The man's right ear was missing. Barely visible, half covered by his hair, a nub bump of flesh with a dark hole, like an enlarged but deformed bellybutton. The stranger spoke again, an unknown accent barely discernible. "And do you have something to say to me?"

Hesitation first, then, as if by a mute who had just found his lost voice, scratchy and strained, came the English response: "Days will show what we were ignorant of; and news will come that you have not sent." He paused, glanced either way to be assured of being alone in the shopping aisle with this man, the messenger, knowing he was about to reveal a deep mystery.

In Arabic, he whispered, "In the name of Allah, the Benevolent, the Merciful."

"Very good, Professor." The smile seemed innocent as between friends, but the stranger's severe tone showed otherwise. "Had you not said those words, I would have had to kill you on the spot, and your Marcie would be a grieving widow. Unless I decided to visit your home tonight and slit her throat and those of your children. Too messy, I have found, and what with all that new carpeting in your bedrooms."

The Professor felt the blood drain from his face, both with mortified fear for his family, but more because of knowing the truth. James Rogers, the Professor, was not the man others in this community knew. Long before his wife and children, before the house in the Las Vegas Summerlin suburbs, his soul had gone over to a darker cause.

"What do you want of me?"

"Are you prepared? Are they ready?"

"Yes, but they will be as surprised I am. Such a day seemed like it would never come."

The man sneered and leaned close, venom coming from his lips. "You are fated to play your part. Prepare your people. Look for a man who calls himself a scientist, perhaps within the next month, or within several months. He will say the words, 'Scimitar.' You will learn more from him. I will return with your supplies. If you have any issue, however minor, that might put our plan at risk, contact me immediately. Here is a telephone number. Memorize it. Let it ring five times, then hang up. I will contact you and see what can be done about your problem.

Goodbye, Professor." With a casual air, the messenger sauntered to the end of the aisle, abandoned his cart, and disappeared around the corner.

For the longest time, the Professor could not move. Memories flooded back, bitter tasting ones. His stomach soured and his heart went cold.

4.

10 years earlier Las Vegas

The Report of the National Commission on Terrorist Attacks Upon the United States would give the specific date as of June 29th, 2001. The Professor remembered that night quite clearly, especially the meeting place, a strip club called Olympic Gardens. A young, idealistic jihadist back then, mostly due to brazen thoughts forged by a personal history demanding his private revenge, he sought contact with like minds and had a passion for action. In his recruitment during his Middle East tour in the early 1990s, they allowed him to sidestep the training camps, to preserve anonymity, and he became known, only to Osama bin Laden and the Supreme Council, as *The Professor*. This code name was bestowed because at that time, in his early career, he struggled as a low-paid teaching assistant in the International Affairs department at the University of Nevada-Las Vegas, UNLV.

He could have arranged the meeting for their motel room at the EconoLodge on Las Vegas Boulevard. But no, they were being careful, and later, on national news after the attacks, he understood why. All four men were tightly wound, which was visible only by eye-darting paranoia, and skittish towards an assignment of which they told him nothing and dropped no hints. He admired their minimal speech of caution, seeing them as they were, True Believers, Defenders of the Faith, unquestioning soldiers, focused, and absorbed by details towards Execution of the plan. For two days, disguised as awed tourists, they cruised Sin City ridiculing all they saw as being the heart of the Great Satan. Or so they told him.

Dance music blared while women in negligee costumes circulated, pitching their wares of 20-dollar lap dances or for that extra something, more in the back VIP room. The music covered their conversation. Three of the men kept the women from approaching too closely by the subterfuge of pretending to be enamored by enhanced breasts, leering at the pandering pasty, perfumed beauties, the men liberal in paying the harlots to press against their crotches with swaying friction. The Professor noticed, by the men's sarcastic smiles, that they did not mind suggestive banter with the strippers, and in fact enjoyed testing in conversation the cover stories they were using while traveling the United States.

"Are you committed?" their leader asked into the Professor's ear.

"My parents died in Lebanon by Israeli war planes, planes made in the U.S. dropping U.S. bombs." It was not quite a true story, but his hatred for his adopted homeland was real and surged from deeply buried aggravations.

"Can the heat of your anger remain fired years from now when you are called to your destiny?"

"I pledged with my dripping blood to Allah, to the brotherhood of al-Qaeda. There is no turning back."

"You may rejoice that we will first strike a magnificent blow, and you may watch with pride as this government run by drunken cowboys quakes and quivers in fear. That will be the beginning of their undoing, and then later, and I do not know the details, your task may be even greater. But you must wait and control your desire for revenge.

Patience must be your wife. Someday the call will come."

"I am ready. What must I do?"

"You must create three cells of four members each, no cell to know of the other, all to live quiet lives until they are called upon. And best that they look more like you, faceless, the typical common-looking white man, rather than like us, like Saudi exchange students with limited visas."

"It will be done."

"Consider several years, if not longer. Beyond that I know nothing more, except when from a stranger you hear the words in Arabic, 'On the day of victory no one is tired.'"

He handed over a scrap of paper. "Memorize this and respond to your messenger."

The Professor repeated the code words with deep emotion, his eyes closed as if he had heard a command from heaven, and when he recovered his senses the young men were gone and he was left, jostled in the midst of parading flesh, to pay their bar tab. Maybe one lap dance would not hurt, he considered, a reward for the distinction they had tendered and how they must value him. Eyeing an attractive blonde who wiggled his way, he pulled out $40. My pledge is sacrosanct, he thought in affirmation, feeling himself harden. Playing with her breasts will not compromise my assignment.

From that date of the strip club meeting, only two months remained before 9/11 and the burning, imploding towers. Those men, those heroes he had met, did change the world, but the Professor did not think such change was to the benefit of his people, his faith. Transgressions continued. The Unfaithful still occupied his people's land. His own call to duty would not arrive until more than 10 years later, to this day, when this severe Messenger of Allah in the supermarket had awoken his other self. Success or failure, the implied message had been delivered: be prepared to succeed or die. He breathed deeply and finished his shopping. Yes, fish tonight. If he hurried, perhaps he still had time to watch his son's soccer game.

5.

December 2010 Afghanistan

There is the old war movie cliché that if your buddy, sharing the foxhole with you, shows you his worn photo of his wife and baby from back home, then he or both of you are doomed to the sniper's bullet or the falling mortar round.

E-4 rated Shawn Pacheco of Navy SEAL Team Four hadn't gone that far in believing he had jinxed his buddies, but in his platoon, the night before the mission, he felt odd man out, uncomfortable, sensing they looked at him with unspoken expressions of distain.

Everyone knew of his earlier Skype telephone call with Janet, his fiancée, making wedding plans, she waiting for him in Cleveland, Ohio. In the mess tent he had boasted optimism of love and honeymooning, of going home soon. Just like in a war movie. Fated.

There were feather-stepped shuffles across the light snow. They were stalking their quarry, or so they thought. No words were exchanged; it was all hand signals as they approached the cave, gray-etched outlines over the eastern mountains in the Pachir Wa Agam District of Nangarhar Province. In another half hour they would not need their night vision goggles, so the push was on to move quickly, silently, with stealth. Pacheco, a member of the elite SEAL Team Four, was proud to be part of the unit, expecting greater recognition when his paperwork would be approved for a new status as an expert in explosives. He assumed this was the reason they put him on point, further field work, that from his knowledge they expected him to spot nuances in the landscape – disturbances that might be telltale signs of planted IEDs.

This mission was to engage Taliban combatants thought to be located in or near this cave location, in hopes that a high-valued target might be present.

Though his squad said little in prepping, their hopes buoyed and there were little exchanges of ribbing and joking. They wished that any target might be the Big Guy himself, Osama bin Laden, or even his second-in-command, The Doctor, al-Zawahiri, so they could go home, away from this damn, cold country. And Shawn back to Ohio and to Janet, his promised bride.

The cave, with its small squat entrance, was shallow, with little depth, and empty. Its litter showed habitation from at least two months ago. It was bad intel, more usual than not these days if you got your information from local villager scuttlebutt. Anxiety waned and fingers on triggers relaxed, but only slightly. Several team members were pissed, and cursed at limestone walls, less about the mission's failure than about a lack of action, which cemented a SEAL Team's honed training into the élan expected of them.

In single file, they backtracked down the narrow trail, hearing distant choppers returning to the LZ for embarkation. Tensions eased more. The first slivers of sunlight hit mountaintops, and daylight moved down toward the valley below. When the trail opened up, Pacheco's best friend, Reyes Montoya, gave him a friendly nudge to the side and moved to the front of the small column.

On a switchback turn, Montoya spotted an old juice can sticking out of the snow.

Probably recalling his high school soccer days, he made a move at playing, rushing the net with the winning kick. It was a mental mistake and a fatal one, because what looked benign in this godforsaken land never was.

A thin wire attached to the juice can tripped the detonator on the PMA-2 mine. 'Goal, he scores' whispered Montoya. It was loud enough that Pacheco knew in that second what was about to occur. He could do nothing but turn his head and accept the blast.

When he awoke in the base hospital, he discovered he had been concussed, bruised, and scattered wounds stitched up. He still had all his limbs though, and he felt himself damn lucky. The doctors later told him that the bone and gristle removed from his chest and arms had been Montoya's.

To SEAL Team Four, all blame could not be affixed without collective guilt about a stupid mistake by a dead friend, and it wasn't a mistake since SEAL members did not make such errors in judgment. Except maybe guilt on Pacheco, who should have maintained point position, instead of Montoya. Would he have done the same, would he have kicked the juice can, or would he been more cautious, he wondered? The latter, he knew, but it mattered little.

To his comrades, Shawn, they groused, failed at his assignment to watch out for all of them, steer them away from booby traps, and to take the explosion himself if it had come to that. He came out of the hospital to find himself a Jonah and a pariah; shunned. Personal grief made him accept his fellow SEAL members' silent accusations, and he began to believe he had killed Montoya himself.

And perhaps it was he who should have died instead of his friend? Physically he recovered quickly, but the mental damage ate at his conscience like a cancer. He did not talk to Janet for a month, and when he did the conversation seemed one-sided, stilted. Talk of pre-wedding parties had lost their allure.

6.

January 2011 New York City

"Should not creativity be used for a higher moral purpose?"

She zapped him, tore into his mind-set, just at the climax where Starfighter Hugh Fox began, at the 20th Level, destroying the headquarters of MegaToth Command and Control. The woman's voice had brought him from the galactic unworldly back to a familiar reality of a chattering cocktail crowd.

He dropped his cosmic beam weapon away from the movie theater-sized flat screen and turned to the crowd of the imbibing inquisitive, all well-heeled and attired formally for the charity evening. His avatar, looking like Hugh Fox himself and programmed by his company, Skilleo Game Technology, to offer human-styled expressive emotions, turned to say 'what the –' but not finishing the surprise of abandonment, it was blasted instead into jellied gore by one of the thousand MegaToth NucleoDisseminators the game master had thus far defeated. "You are history," came the programmed voice as game play went into stasis, waiting for the Starfighter game player to reboot.

Hugh's eyes turned to his audience, seeking out his presumed critic. Those in the small group surrounding him were not fans, but consumers, the parents of fans who had so far made "MegaToth Doomslayer V" the top-selling electronic game of the last holiday season, and winner of this year's *Achievement Interactive Awards*. He was here tonight, at an uppity charity event for cancer research, where he would offer a lucky bidder, at the celebrity auction following dinner, the right to put his or her name, character and personality into his next Skilleo game as the evil OverLord. Among gamesters, this would be on par with Marvel Comics creating an action hero based on one's own image. He expected frenzied bidding that night by indulgent parents who were pressured by their precocious children to purchase a rare and personalized piece of the Hugh Fox Skilleo Empire.

Hugh spotted her in the crowd. She dressed stylishly in expensive and tasteful clothes and she was quite attractive—for an older woman, maybe near thirty years old, he guessed. He found most of the society crowd were older than his twenty three and still growing age.

She seemed alone.

He passed his weapon baton to J-Q, his PA, personal assistant, and highly paid go-fer. J-Q, ultimate in loyalty to his boss, was nicknamed 'J' after the Men in Black movie character and 'Q' for James Bond's weapons supplier. He worked mostly for the fun of hanging around a corporate atmosphere that was based on imaginary realms that offered unknown, mindboggling surprises.

When J-Q picked up the weapon and resumed the demonstration, the computer game downloaded all of J-Q's stored play habit information, based both on fingerprint recognition and also his hand grip's strength pressure. The game began anew with J-Q's avatar fighting MegaToths at Level 7. Only Hugh Fox, two lab engineers, and three walled-in game junkies scattered around the world had ever played Level 20, *Ender's Game Platform* as it was called by those joy-stick pilgrims who, with admiration and reverence, seek the ultimate video game high.

Hugh ignored those who pointed him out in low whispers, and didn't care that by tomorrow's editions, the tabloids would describe his blue jeans and black corduroy tux jacket with no tie as his usual, slovenly nerd image. He was quite comfortable with himself, and as a gentleman might, he guided the woman away from the game he had fantasized, nurtured, and brought into being with the support of his 1,600 loyal employees and fellow thrill geekers.

"You say I am not using my creative juices properly?"

"No, one can certainly see that genius must have its outlets, and it certainly seems you have found your calling." Her voice trilled lightly, easily and melted with mild laughter.

With a slight shrug of his shoulders he replied, "I'm no genius." He truly believed that, though his intelligence and success suggested otherwise.

"Not according to how *The Journal* and *Forbes* and all the business bloggers go on about you. Founded Skilleo at 18, your first billion dollars in sales by 21. Privately owned, you and only a few venture capital firms, which I might add, makes you master of your domain. I just wonder if you could do more with your creative spirit to help, you know, mankind."

Even though she was smiling, Hugh felt he was being lectured to. The implication seemed to be that he was still a young man of potential, but one handicapped by immaturity. His feathers bristled.

"I am here tonight for a worthy cause," he said with serious inflection. "My company does have a foundation that contributes generously. Its primary focus is challenge grants and scholarships for science and math education in the public schools." He had his litany down pat.

"Yes, but Mr. Fox," she said, and she leaned in. Her perfume enhanced her closeness; his brain computed an orange scent and his vision snapped the outlines of a shapely body within a sleek black dress. He studied her face and expressions – freckles, a deep purple eye shadow drawing out fathomless aquamarine eyes, and a singular skin color. Not that old, he decided, as she continued, "I do not find fault in your corporate benevolence. But are you maximizing all of that talent within? You have made money, yes, but are you sure you could not do more? Instead of other people using your money for a greater good, you and your ideas could directly solve a problem with worldly magnitude. Self-satisfaction in its purest form."

It was one of those moments, a long pause during which silent communication was in process, intense yet undefined. She reached out and touched his arm—not electricity, nor a tingle, but--then someone called out and she turned, her touch drifting away.

"Samantha. There you are." An elegant gentleman, Armani-tuxed and coiffed in a weathered commodore look, with a slight gray sanding to his thick hair, appeared with an extra glass of champagne, which he handed over. "Thought I'd lost you."

"I wandered over to see Mr. Fox's display," she said. "It's quite exceptional – if one is into destroying NucleoDisseminators." She smiled at him, a disarming tease. Hugh put a look of surprise on his face, brightened that this lady knew details of his game. She introduced the gentleman and Hugh filed away his name, somewhere unimportant, after noting that Samantha called the man her "escort for the evening," in a kind, solicitous fashion so as not to offend. It left a lot said unsaid, he thought. He was not a boyfriend or she would not have said "escort," nor was he a fiancé – though she would make a great trophy wife at this sort of event, he thought, recognizing his callousness.

The couple excused themselves and went to find their table, as the non-profit festivities of the hotel-catered meal were beginning. He, himself, sat with an assortment of Fortune 100 CEOs and their spouses, where talk weaved and flowed over government intrusion into business by taxes and burdensome oversight, of fabled golf games, and of nightmare remodels of second and third homes on the ski slopes and at the beach.

Hugh smiled and indulged the genial table conversations, mostly as a listener since the others did not know on what level and on what subject they could easily discourse with him.

After the salad plates were removed, and while waiting for the entrée, he glanced through the evening's program, and there she was.

Samantha Carlisle. Of course! *That* Samantha, the one known to the world for SammyC Fashions, well branded for her spritzy clothing lines. One of her couture lines was called *Provac*, short for 'provocative.' Every teen girl, those adolescent caterpillars morphing into coquettish butterflies, had a closet rack dedicated to SammyC labels. Mature women seeking to imply naughty ways through their fashion wore Jimmie Chu and Gucci accessories, but dazzled in SammyC's *Kling* for night-on-the-town/next-morning outfits.

He did not know this firsthand, introverted bachelor that he was, wedded only to the design table and computer screen. He knew it because of his speed scanning of news sources to stay on pace with youth marketing, and track the fickleness of cultural fads as they might eventually arise in one of his games.

Tonight, his curiosity did one better. He pulled out his personalized handheld, the walkabout computer designed by his engineers to be larger than an iPhone but less intrusive than an iPad; to be something inoffensive but expected of any multi-tasked executive, especially someone like himself who was known as the Gadgets Guy. He put on his WiFi earplug and as the dinner buzzed around him like a distant hum, he pulled up a Google-Nexus search. As his finger scrolled across a sentence, it was translated into vocalized speech in his ear, and automatically archived to a file for future reference. As he smiled and exchanged comments with his dinner companions, he was also being educated.

In minutes, Hugh knew her bio and all her public secrets.

According to SEC filings, Samantha Carlisle could boast, having achieved multimillionaire status in her own right. At the height of a rebounding stock market, she had sold her fashion house to an Italian public conglomerate for $400 million in cash and stock.

That information counterbalanced his insecurities about why she had made a play for him at the party. She hadn't. As an unattached, now wealthy woman, she did not need him (nor any man) for her bliss and financial security. Burned in past surface encounters with women who wanted his credit card and not his heart, he realized their meeting showed her true character: She was merely being friendly, engaging in banter, and with that he found parity with Ms. Carlisle.

He found her a fresh, kindred spirit.

The evening's ceremony launched into speeches for the cause and touting of the upcoming auction, which would give its proceeds to charity and included a list of special high-end and glamorous bid items from personally prepared dinners for 10 by top chefs to yacht cruises off the Bahamas.

Hugh read that Samantha Carlisle was offering her own donation to the cause: *A Ten-Day African Photographic Safari including a personal tour of the SammyC Save Our Wildlife Refuge in Kenya.* It was all-inclusive, featuring catered meals and private jet access – hers – and the private tour would be hosted by the refuge's namesake.

Interesting, he thought. His capsulated research had revealed that she was active in many charities. There was social column chatter of her attendance at highbrow functions where she was seen with various escorts. Then it hit him, and he replayed their brief conversation, beginning with her opening line: "Should not creativity be used for a higher moral purpose?"

That was it. She was not talking about him; she was talking about herself. At the pinnacle of what everyone else would laud as success, Samantha Carlisle was probably bored; not neces-sarily with the functions and responsibilities of daily fashion design or charity boards, but because she lacked a true-life purpose. She was searching for that pizzazz of significance.

Just like him.

At the appropriate time, he raised his hand and outbid everyone else. At the back of the room, J-Q made a note in his PDA:

SammyC's Save Our Wildlife Refuge — ask date, plan trip – and wrote a Skilleo Foundation check to the charity for $150,000, the highest of all the bid items that evening. Hugh Fox never carried cash or credit cards.

7.

January 2011 São Paulo, Brazil

From the balcony, Carlita 'Callie' Cardoza watched her computer screen, which featured five small boxes in matrix showing live camera feeds. CAM ONE, the videographer, was aimed at the front of the deluxe apartment complex. CAM TWO, another camera carrying staffer, peered across the street, scanning light auto and pedestrian traffic. CAM THREE was at the airport, on standby, prepared for their arrival if everything went right. It was a big "if." Cameras Four and Five were head cams, located in ball caps, one inside the van down the street on the driver and the other inside an apartment on the ground level, waiting for the appropriate rushed exit.

"Heads up," she spoke into her headset's microphone. "Lights just went out from the penthouse. He's on the move. Everyone alert." She slammed closed her computer, threw it into her backpack, swung it to her shoulder, tore off down the hall and took the staircase in bounds.

She had previously timed her exit. She had 20 seconds before the Target would reach the ground floor and exit the elevator.

On the street, giving a few huffs from her sprint, she positioned herself across from the two guards at the front door. The men picked up on her presence, noted her fine form, and began some undercurrent of smutty dialogue between them. Good, she thought; they are distracted. She glanced up the street and saw the black van, with the detachable 'Floristas' sign on its side, begin its slow acceleration.

"Here he comes," she said into her ear bud mike. "One guard."

Timing made a blur of the snatch.

Target and his bodyguard exited the front door, nodded to the guards on either side, and turned to walk down the street. Callie knew, from his habits, that he was heading to his favorite nightclub. Not tonight, or thereafter, she thought.

Following right behind the Target, coming out from the dummy apartment they had rented weeks earlier, Colonel Richard 'Storm' King smiled at the armed doormen, then brought his hands from his pockets and zapped them both with 5 million volts from Streetwise Blackout stun guns. In his next motion, he dropped the stun guns and whipped out two black bags. He jerked the bags over the men's heads as they quivered on the ground, and pulled the plastic tie cuffs so they locked tight to the neck. There were breathing holes, but even if the guards could pull their weapons, now they could not see what to shoot at. It was a King invention for tactical advantage.

In the same few seconds, the side door of the onrushing black van flew open, and another stun gun shot out electrical wires, as the bodyguard standing next to the Target turned to see what the commotion was at the apartment entrance. As he fell, a large muscular man jumped from the van, collared the Target and tossed him like a sack of garbage into the van.

The bodyguard, better trained than the rent-a-cop door guards, was pulling his revolver just as Callie stepped on his wrist. She wrenched the weapon from his hand and drew another black bag, shoving the blindness over the man's head. She was covered by King, who had taken down the apartment guard duo and had now drawn a semi-automatic Walther P99. Both Cardoza and King jumped into the van, yanking the door shut as the vehicle burned squealing rubber away from the curb, dodging late night traffic on its way to Sao Paulo's Guarulhos International Airport.

A stationary min-cam and microphone inside the van picked up Callie, and one of the ball cap cams gave a close-up.

To the Target, she said, "Welcome, Mr. Pettigrew, to your worst nightmare," and then administered the hypodermic, with its cocktail solution of chloral hydrate and haloperidol.

"Night-night," said King, "you motherfucker." They would later bleep out that explicative.

Back at the room where moments ago Callie had watched the apartment, a man stood with his own headset communicator on. He watched the three, head-bagged men writhing on the ground in neuron pain. He saw the black van speed away with the Target.

"Cut," said the Director. "That's a wrap on this end."

8.

January 2011 Silicon Valley, California

End of the day. Hugh Fox let the sweat run from his gritting face, a feel-good sense of accomplishment. He punched in a higher setting on the treadmill: *Climb the Mountain* mode.

After their respective assistants had compared calendars, the photo safari tour to Africa had been set for next week, and Hugh felt himself needing to take stock of his physical condition. He did not think this trip would be strenuous, but nevertheless he wanted to upgrade his cardio and have his bodily fluids balanced to take the African heat and offset the required infusion of medical immunizations. Even his corporation's in-house insurance section and his private doctor made provisions for possible scenarios of travel emergencies, from kidnappings to Ebola infections.

Today, in the Skilleo company gym, an optional job benefit, fellow employees groaned and grunted to their own health maintenance programs. Running in place allowed Hugh's mind to wander, checking off priorities, thinking in multi-dimensional levels, still falling back to his social introduction to Samantha Carlisle. He was not so much attracted to her, or so he told himself, as haunted by the thread of that lingering conversation. Had he indeed given his all to a goal beneficial to others? Her words nagged. He felt them thrown back on him like a challenge.

Yes, he could up the dollars of his foundation gifts, but to where? Bill and Melinda already had world health covered. Most movie stars publicized their own importance to a specific charity, or went out of their way to adopt an underprivileged waif. Didn't Brangelina have a baker's dozen of little critters? Not for him. He already spent too much of his life in the daily grind of trying to guess what were in the buying minds of a young audience, the finicky –the never satisfied.

Whatever extra effort he could afford, he didn't want to be seen as a me-too sort of grandstander. Most of his corporate giving was generous but under the radar, a package of gifts to United Way-type 501(c)(3) charities. Even Jerry's Kids (now sans Jerry) received a donation, though not during telethon season.

His corporate giving philosophy mirrored his personality; there was a shyness that downplayed his presence.

Gaining attention was not his norm, except as adjunct to promoting his games sales. He would leave headline grabbing to Virgin's Branson and to Trump. As he climbed to the treadmill's first plateau, he watched the multiple television screens before him, their sound muted: sports, market and business news. Such silence, the seeing but not hearing, compartmentalized his mood: he was good at what he did, which was turning creative thinking into popular game design. How could that skill be put to specific use – as this woman, acting as catalyst, called "for the benefit of mankind?"

A news feature caught his attention, and he turned up the sound. A law firm was being chastised for placing newspaper ads seeking to represent 9/11 victims regarding the disbursement of monies by the federal government's *Victim Benefit Relief Fund.* The ad used stock footage of a fireman, placing him before a grainy image of the aftermath of the Twin Tower destruction.

The fire helmet was photo shopped out, and placed in his hands instead some sort of marketing plaque. Tacky. It had since been learned that the fireman had not been at the World Trade Center that tragic day, nor had he even been a fireman yet on that historic date.

The television's talking head critics were yelling at the insensitivity of the ambulance chasing shysters. They shouted that 9/11 should never be forgotten, should never be commercialized in any way. 9/11, they said, should always be a wake-up call for the innocent, a reminder that there are very evil people in the world who have no compassion and will kill anyone to achieve their aims, one specific goal being the fall and destruction of the United States.

September 11, 2001. The terrorist attacks on Washington, D.C. and New York City, and a burning, cratered field in Pennsylvania impacted the psyche of American citizens and changed their way of living forever. Hugh admitted to himself that he had not thought about that tragedy in a long time, nor even given it any serious thought in recent years. As the televised news item ended, he agreed with a survivor being interviewed, who bemoaned that we all should be reminded we are still under attack and that complacency is this country's greatest weakness.

He felt his running pace picking up. Weren't they building a memorial in New York?

Maybe his foundation could be useful in some way. He went one step further. Had they caught all the perpetrators of this evil? Hadn't he heard that they were prosecuting some of the 9/11 plotters in a military court? But that didn't include all of them, right? No, it didn't. Not all of the alleged masterminds had been brought to justice. He turned to J-Q, who was off to the side and on his back, 200 pounds of weights hoisted above his head.

"Have they ever caught – what's his name, Osama...something?"

Episode 2

By **James Wolcott** Vanity Fair, December 2009

The influence of Reality TV has been insidious, pervasive. It has ruined television, and by ruining television it has ruined America.... The voyeurism of Reality TV, the viewer's passivity is kept intact, pampered and massaged and force-fed Chicken McNuggets of carefully edited snippets that permit him or her to sit in easy judgment and feel superior at watching familiar strangers make fools of themselves. Reality TV looks in only one direction: down....

9.

January 2011 Burbank, California

Five Aces Studioz

INTEROFFICE MEMO: Private and Confidential
(*Summary of Final Script: Route from Production to
Edit Department—Work from my notes*)
Show: <u>King's Retribution</u>
Season Final Episode: *Grandma Mary's Gift*

<u>Opening Scene</u>: Colonel King and his second-in-command, Carlita 'Callie' Cardoza, arrive at the Midwest home of Mary Branch, a widow in her mid-60s. Exterior shot shows quiet, unassuming neighborhood of mature trees, clean yards and blooming gardens.

<u>Interior</u>: Mary's living room is maintained with family photos [close-up of deceased husband photo], collectible china bells and glass paperweights [close up].

<u>Talent</u>: Mary explains that she invested $55,000 of her husband's insurance money into the Peregrine Fund, after her stockbroker sent a prospectus saying that this investment would provide the best return, provide for her during her lifetime, and then act as a tax-free estate gift to her two grandchildren. When the Fund stopped paying interest she called, only to discover that the Manager of the Fund, touted Wall Street bizwhiz Matthew Pettigrew, had looted all the funds' assets under his control and fled the country, disappearing with more than $85 million dollars.

VOICE OVER: Hundreds of investors were robbed, and Grandma Mary lost everything she invested. Her home's mortgage is at risk. That's the house she's lived in for more than 40 years, [she is crying at this point; CUT to Callie who looks teary-eyed] and which she wanted to leave as a legacy for her grandchildren.

[Trademark King voice, holding Mary's hand: "Mr. Pettigrew will face the King's Retribution."

SHOW LOGO—arrow flying into Pettigrew's target face] [dub Music] <<Break>>

Scene: Collage of bits and news snippets, narrated by King. History of Pettigrew, his fund, and the theft of fund assets. Typical Ponzi scheme, then as house of cards falls, he flees the U.S. to hide out and enjoy his spoils.

Scene: Office of New York City Prosecutor's Office, Securities Division. Meeting with Storm, Callie and a Federal Bureau of Investigation prosecutor and agent.

Meeting highlights [cut and paste]: Charges are filed and Pettigrew is wanted. FBI believes he is in South America, there's one clue pointing to Brazil, but Brazil has no fast extradition policy.

Agent bemoans how long it would take to get Pettigrew back to the States; even longer if he has high-priced attorneys. Prosecutor mentions there is a $1 million award for his capture and return for prosecution. [CUT TO: Callie] "This is our sort of case." Usual disclaimer: Warning from FBI agent not to take action into one's own hands. That Pettigrew could have bodyguards and be dangerous. [CUT TO: Storm smiling at Callie] <<BREAK>>

Scene: Flying Squad Headquarters. Back and forth shots [STORM RECOMMENDS PICKING UP SEQUENCE SPEED]. Callie on computer tracking last payment Pettigrew made to his attorney before services terminated. From mid-town, First Federal. Show criminal's time line.

Show payment made after Pettigrew left country. Callie fakes out bank with a verification notice.

Funds wired from bank in São Paulo, Brazil.

Storm, with Clayton and Bennie, discusses travel itinerary and extraction method. Callie shows off snatch equipment. Callie and Bennie will be point team to locate Pettigrew in São Paulo, Brazil. [STORM SAYS MAKE POINT OF NEEDLE IN HAYSTACK. THIS IS 6th LARGEST POPULATED CITY IN WORLD, 11 MILLION.] <<BREAK >>

SCENE: Pick up archival film on São Paulo: airplane landing, city view, etc.

Shot of street, patch in fast graphics, cut-aways of target apartment house. We have grainy footage of Pettigrew walking the street with bodyguard [CUT: back to old photo; his hair is now dyed and he has beard].

Hotel Room: Strategy Session—Three Days—show anxious faces, plenty of them. Callie will use the bank ploy, say there is a problem with Pettigrew's wire account, and can he come in personally and re-sign forms. [PUT IN VERBAL FIGHT BETWEEN CALLIE AND STORM.

ONCE AGAIN SHE WANTS FIELD ACTION AND NOT ALWAYS TO BE ON LOGISTICS]

SCENE: Grab off the street. Van used. Tased bodyguard—black bag to all including apartment door guards [Setting up cameras was harder on this than last; used FIVE locations. CAMERA ONE, roving: Three head caps on Storm, Callie and Bennie. CAMERA TWO, stationary. If we missed the right spot for the grab, the whole thing would have been blown and we'd have had to use post-event junk.]

Street: [STORM SAYS SHOW HE AND CLAYTON CHECKING GUNS—THAT'S A NEW ONE, USUALLY IT'S TASERS, AND ONLY CLAYTON WITH LOW LOAD SHOTGUN—BUT DO IT] Fast action take down. (Storm is the man—great action shots). Van driving away.

<<BREAK>>

WRAP: Jet landing, closed limo to Halls of Justice, prosecutor and police take custody. (We invited news channels to shoot it all; use some of their footage as source).

FINAL SCENE: Grandma Mary's house. Storm hands her a check for $55,000, hugs all around.

Find it, but she does say, 'What a wonderful gift'. <<END>> (Source: $55,000 as usual from our production fund while we are waiting for reward payment. Probably will take the other Peregrine Fund investors years to get their monies back. Jeez, don't the viewers know we wouldn't have even shot the Grandmommy segment if we had not first apprehended Pettigrew?!

As Storm says, no glory for failure. By the way, be forewarned, a first: Storm wants to view the post edit. Has a bug up his ass, guess he wants to give this show a little goosing. Hope it's not a new Stormin' norm. Don't forget wrap party next week. Like to see rough-cut by then. –

Confidential, do not distribute — Hope this helps us for next season's renewal. Remember we have two projects floating, six months out in research. In May or June, another snatch and grab to film for the pipeline. Hope it's not the last. Ciao. – b/a

10.

February 2011 Late night

Sky Bar at Mondrian Hotel, West Hollywood

The private party bounced and weaved, and even with a Gestapo-like bouncer at the door the terrace was sprinkled with crashers and wannabes, interspersed with front office executives of the Five Aces Studioz production company and their guests. Not the A-List; it was more of a B-gathering, gentrified enough to have a few paparazzi hanging out downstairs, their cameras poised. Just in case, Lindsay (drunk and wearing a monitoring bracelet) or Gaga (naked, but painted in day-glo colors) dropped by.

Callie stood near the bar, a glass of champagne in her hand as a defense mechanism, warding off groupie handshakes and hugs from the front office personnel. "Great year for *King's Retribution*," they all seemed to say while snarfing down free cocktails and buffet canapés. She replied stiffly, accepting their congratulations with a forced smile, and listening to advice given by people who knew nothing about how the show could be made better, and reminiscences of certain shows that seemed to stand out, or she was informed.

The staff crew visited among themselves in whispers, morose; the next season was unannounced, and they were worried about their futures. The two cameras, CAM ONE and CAM TWO, were present, as usual, and in operating mode. The contracts they had signed meant that at all public functions, as well as on set, they had to be unobtrusively filming, so video of the stars was candid, not showing actors playing to the camera. CAM TWO was stationary, to the side of the entry door, most certainly focused, Callie thought, on Storm's grand celebrity entrance. CAM ONE wandered the crowd fringes, picking up snatch shots; perhaps for a future documentary in the making, or maybe a requiem, or planning for the sales pitch video to be used later for syndication.

"You gonna get drunk and slug someone?" This came from the show's on-camera muscle, Clayton Briggs. He took the empty glass from her hand and replaced it with more bubbly.

"He hasn't arrived, and I am sober, dammit."

"Hey, it's not that he has all the control. Scriptwriters and production suits have put our little pegs in the holes." He stood over her, looking down. Clayton, an ex-NFL linebacker, was Storm's shadow when the grabs were made, more pushing and shoving than fists flying.

After two years in close proximity, Storm and Callie knew Clayton's secrets, even the one his former wife had been unaware during eight years of a turbulent marriage. Callie saw him glance over and above the imbibing, giggling young women on the bar couch who thought his stares were for them, his eyes fell on the thin young man nattily dressed in Polo garb. Quick smiles about the in-joke flashed between the men. In Hollywood, career positioning for second banana hunks required remaining in the closet.

"Your agent has you booked off-season?" asked Clayton. The strong man had a good side business appearing in television ads for a national chain of health clubs.

"Nothing lucrative per se. A guest appearance on *Ellen* prior to the Grandmother Mary episode." Not sipping, she chugged at the champagne. "Storm will do Leno."

"That's it?"

"Negotiating for a mobile phone app commercial. Guess I'm just not in the league of Paris, Snookie, or a Kardashian yet." Callie enjoyed her minor stardom, and wished for more recognition, but did not begrudge the heightened world of other television stars in reality world entertainment, the ones who pulled down $5-10 million a year from someone else writing their tell-all fashion and health hint books, and hosting raucous birthday parties at Vegas night club venues. There was a public demand for the unique to amuse people during their daily drudge, in these days when they could create stars out of even pawnshop employees. *King's Retribution* seemed more respectable than the outlandish or trite formulas with *Retribution's* audience Nielsen ratings in proximity to *Cops* and *48 Hours,* and it definitely ranked higher than storage war auctions and car repo shows.

Reviewers had niched this television action show. One critic wrote: "*King's Retribution* is where bounty hunters meet U.S. Marshalls, tinged with Mission Impossible tech, spiced up with a little A-Team humor thrown in." Callie these days found no humor in her employment at all.

Growing applause drew their attention. Colonel (Ret.) David 'Storm' King, star of the reality television show *"King's Retribution,"* made his entrance, hitting invisible cue spots, shaking hands and accepting praise for a season well done. He worked the room, a consummate politician knowing whose ego needed to be stroked.

His walk of fame brought him to Callie, her expression set strong, heat emanating, ember tinder to the powder keg. He ignored her temper with a forehead kiss, and in turn was ignored by her; she looked away.

"You aren't going to make a scene here tonight? A few low-life paparazzi are stalking the sidewalks outside, eager for your flare-up." He talked through his bared teeth, so his face seemed locked in a grin.

"There will be plenty of time to make my sentiments known. Of course, you know them already."

"They are not going to replace Clayton, or even Bennie, the wheelman, with you.

Strength is required, and you know it. Give yourself credit – you're designated as the Beauty-with-Brains-Babe. Everyone admits to that. Once an army colonel, I play the director general of ops now. And you're a co-star: can you ask for more than that?" He threw a few beguiling nods to passing fans.

Callie seethed.

"I have worked hard, and I could do more. You know that. I'm an ex-policewoman. I have the creds."

"Yes, my dear, but a policewoman, even if once the head of the computer section of the San Diego Police Department, does not make you a ball buster for hand-to-hand fisticuffs with criminals."

"I didn't do too bad with the bodyguard in Brazil. And I've stayed in shape, even on that one show where I ran the FBI field course at Quantico. I held my own."

"Indeed." He gave her a leering tug to his eyebrow. "And am I to assume I will see more of that tonight? Exertion, that is?"

"Is there a choice? Just don't show up at my place drunk. And I am not in the mood of you bringing along some stray bimbo for a three-way."

"Tonight is a celebration, and tipsy might be an acceptable outcome. Besides, the Five Aces Studioz front office a-holes set you and me up with a business luncheon tomorrow. I need my special relaxation program in order to bring my A-game." He gave her that Storm smolder look, a mixture of desire and testosterone.

He did have that animalism. After the show's debut season, their star pairing, she with her Spanish ancestry's hot blood, and his insecurities, which required constant propping of his manliness, drew them together, collided more like it, two moths sucked into the candle of rutting passion. What they both knew, though did not admit, was that at this juncture in their careers, they needed and used each other for stability, to keep out all that was bad in the Hollywood scene; the temptations and leeches that could drag down their mini-stardom by the wrong interview or an ill-timed photo.

Not ready to admit she was at a dead-end in their relationship, she capitulated with gruffness. "Don't be too late." And star and co-star went their separate ways in the continued frenzy of the wrap party.

11.

King stood naked before the window that flung the entire lights of the city of L.A. at him.

Mixed within the lights, his own reflection stood out and bounced back from a soft light glow emanating from the bathroom. He couldn't sleep. Callie could and was nestled under the covers, deep in another world of peace. Good for her, he thought.

His mind buzzed from alcohol and the ramifications of his recent memo to the Post- Production editor. King usually did not exercise his contract clause for overseeing final editing but in this case there was justification, known only to him. He prayed that the television crew and later the viewing public did not understand the crises as he did.

The season finale was in the can, it following the proven story-line formula of a successful hunt and capture of the bad guy. This Pettigrew creep. King needed to subtly direct the editor to tweak, and add revised cliffhanger flourishes at each commercial break. Maybe no one else saw it like he did, nor felt the mellow vibes he felt while shooting the last bit of location footage. The spark and magic the show had in the past was not evident, and the tight-paced action did not match up to the military-style precision he sought in each script.

His on-camera cast members, the "Flying Squad," each of them with their own expertise, seemed lethargic now, merely marching to the repetitive cadence of the first two successful seasons. Not having grit in your stomach, nor the fervor to live each dangerous moment in a war zone, would leave you a mangled corpse on the battlefield, and in the Reality TV world theresults were similar, as in fatal, with show cancellation being the deadly bullet.

They could blame the inattentiveness on the uncertainty and on the undertone of gossip in the last few weeks: Would *King's Retribution* be picked up for a third season? Cast and crew members were updating their curriculum vitae, just in case, and scanning *The Hollywood Reporter* and *Variety* for job opportunities in the more current reality shows with their hip, scatological, sex-texting voyeurism. Where was the next *Housewives Of...*? The next Jersey den of sin tableaux? All Reality TV was manufactured to whore before the gods of commercial revenue, anointed by audience measured ratings. And, King would admit, but only to himself, he was among those tarnished zealots: The paycheck was too good.

When the last season episode aired in two months, viewers probably wouldn't see the lifelessness, the plodding. The audience would view the standard formula, the hunt and capture, and would certainly applaud this particular outcome. *King's Retribution* succeeded by appealing to a wide range of demographics. Women viewers, and many gay men, tuned in, hoping, as they had come to expect, that Storm King would somehow, for whatever reason, be able to take his shirt off and flex his well-toned abs and muscles, whether he was lighting an explosive fuse or swimming in shark-infested waters.

Demographics showed that straight men in the 16-30 age group enjoyed the macho aspect though most of the dangerous work, except for the actual grabbing of the culprits, was staged by the Special Effects coordinator, Hiram Abbas, but it was not all fakery. Storm had the talent on his resume, including the U.S. Army's Silver Star. True hero status did not hurt the rep.

As Season Two ended, athletic moves before the cameras were not coming easily to King. He increased his morning exercise regimen to rid himself of creaking knee pops. Pain pills and a few bracer cocktails masked the aches in his lower back, where micro shrapnel fragments lay dangerously close to his spine. Certified healthy by the production company's doctor, he was good for a few more years of gung-ho acting. His swagger made him look fierce, with the intensity of a rogue killer, and the audience, caught up in the chase and catch, forgot that the show never had killed a fugitive.

Maybe, he mused, that was a negative for the violence-acclimated media masses – the lack of blood spatter. Most injuries to the apprehension team were the fault of misstep and bad luck, nothing too serious. Leave the jackass moves to cretins. Meticulous planning; that was the key. Avoid risks.

The future dogged King's thoughts. The television show, in the right time slot, had its loyal fan base and should be picked up by the network, but King feared fatal stagnancy, and this doubt made a soldier vulnerable. There needed to be an infusion of new ideas. Some brainstorm to make everyone take notice.

These were his thoughts as King gargled the last of his warm scotch. More recently, trying to maintain his bravado image he felt a couple of drinks here and there would reinforce his hard living rep, and found a Dean Martin comfort with a cocktail glass in hand.

He glanced at the sleeping Callie, unsure of where they were heading. Too many uncertainties. And then there was this lunch tomorrow. He didn't even know whom they were meeting with, or what sort of game face he should wear. Certainly fake optimism would have to be plastered onto the expected King caricature, not as a soldier but as a media star. That was a role he could handle well.

12.

February 2011　Bagram Airbase, Afghanistan

He saluted. His SEAL commander opened a file in front of him. Shawn remained at attention and realized there was another man in the small office.

"How are you healing, Pacheco?"

"Fine, sir. Ready to go back active."

"Good." His commander glanced into a file folder. "Records indicate you finished your SO [Special Warfare Operations] Training. Your skill set, I see, is explosives. High marks.

Know your stuff, sailor?"

His commander gave him a throw-off smile. It was an inside joke. SEALS were of the Navy, Delta Force of the Army. The officer closed the file.

Shawn did not like where this was going and was unsure of his response, but nevertheless puffed up his chest.

"Yes, sir. I feel I am quite qualified at anything those terrorists throw at us, or bury on the roadways." He did not mean to say all that. The words surged beyond his usual control.

"The leader of your platoon says you took it very hard when you lost a friend in the field?" Shawn, caught off guard, froze for a second as bad memories of brilliant flashes in his face resurfaced.

The man in the corner added, "Losing someone that close can cloud your decision making. A booby trap going off can make a SEAL over-cautious the next time."

Pacheco now understood. The other man was a Navy shrink. They had flown in a psychiatrist, specifically to sideline him and take him out of the action. No way. His answer had to be to their psyche, not his. He had to hide his torn feelings, and erase Montoya's smile, which came to him most nights in his dreams as a haunting.

"A SEAL has to go on. He can't compromise his training or put those around him at risk.

"Sir, it is sad to lose anyone. But the job is foremost."

"And you think you can perform your duties, and be the explosives expert you were trained to be?"

"Yes, Sir!"

"That's what I thought too. A few scrapes can't stop a SEAL." The commander reached inside his drawer and handed over a small black insignia patch. It was a SO badge, an anchor crossed horizontally by a trident, and diagonally by a flintlock pistol.

Pacheco could not hold back a smile. All the concentrated work, the long hours, had paid off.

"Don't thank me too soon. You're not going to be sewing that on quite yet. I've just signed papers to transfer you."

"Sir?" Suddenly, bile stood in his throat. Did his fellow SEAL team members not want him around? Was there a conspiracy to trade him off? Stateside, perhaps?

"It's an official request order. You are going over to SEAL Team Six. One of their ordinance SOs came down with appendicitis, bad luck for him, and they are in need of back up.

"That's you. Six is being called up, and is training on an operation. I have no details."

"Does that suit you?"

He wasn't being asked for input. At least it sounded temporary – out on loan, a fill-in job, and then they might send him back. A team was a team. Four was not Six, and he knew he would be treated as an outsider until he showed his stuff. But it was no different from the vibes he was getting around here.

"I'm ready, Sir."

"Pack it in. You're going to a special camp Six is setting up. Leaving tomorrow at 0900. Orders are outside and cut for you. Dismissed."

Pacheco saluted and departed.

The commander looked to the Navy doctor, waiting for an opinion.

"What can I tell you? He's combat stressed, but aren't all those kids? Does he have a breaking point? Is he at it? Yes, and maybe, but it's buried deep. I couldn't see anything from looking at him. His medicals show me nothing. And as for all this 'black cat jinx crap' coming out of his unit, that's what it is. Pure shit."

"Everything else about Pacheco is top-rated. I don't want to lose a good SEAL."

"He won't be productive, nor will his comrades, if they're all looking over their shoulders at him. Yeah, the transfer might solve most of the problems, providing the Six operation is nothing too explosive, pardon the pun."

13.

February 2011

Yemen, at a village north of the city of Sayyan

Khalaf had not made that entire trip to watch an execution.

From the moment he landed in Sana'a, Yemen's capital, he found himself in a war zone, surrounded by citizens teetering on civil war. His escort guide met him at the airport and then deposited Khalaf into a rusted bus filled with people going in his planned direction. Soldiers in military trucks rushed down streets, and the closer he got to the city's edge, the more armed men were in civilian clothes. All along his route he heard scattered gunfire.

Precautions were essential and there was safety in feigning innocence. Everyone was nervous about what group, government or anti-government, might erect roadblocks, and randomly rob or shoot the passengers, or both. During the three-hour trip, with its many stops to load and unload passengers, the bus baked from the heat to the point that interior shade was no help. Nor did the desert breeze make a difference, with its light dusting as the bus growled along.

The roadway leaving the capital was surreal, with refugees trudging along pushing carts or driving overburdened cars and trucks, making their way on both sides of the road heading both directions – into the city, toward the safety of government forces, and out into the desert towns, seeking safe harbor among the revolutionary tribes. Near the coast, al-Qaeda maintained strength and vied to be a major player. Because of this, the meeting had been scheduled in the opposite direction, away from any disputing factions.

For this journey Khalaf styled himself as a relief aid worker, wearing a red crescent armband, a variation of the West's Red Cross. He would not hide himself in traditional garb. He wore jeans, covered loosely by a short-sleeved, white cotton shirt, and secreted in his waistband a German-made Heckler & Koch, a P2000 9 mm, a lighter pistol nevertheless quite deadly. His disguise was designed to confuse any questioner, who would not easily guess which side he belonged to. If any rifle pointed their way, he and his guide, a young Yemen boy barely 16, would take control of the bus and shoot and kill whomever impeded their journey.

He abhorred this method of crowded, bumpy transportation. His presence deserved more consideration: He was a diplomat at the behest of bin Laden, with important messages.

And, as he felt, they tried to put him in his place, at the end of his arduous trip; he did not like to be "invited" to stand under the broiling sun, waiting for the prisoner to be led out.

Shahin orchestrated this show, which was certainly timed for Khalaf's benefit. The men had met several times since 2005, and always it was as if they were competitors in one upsmanship games, suggestive, though never anything overt. It was merely role playing; strutting.

Khalaf had bin Laden's confidence. Shahin basked in recognition from the Supreme Council.

By bearing witness, the inference was obvious – he must carry back, to their leader in Pakistan, the fervor shown, by the Islamic fighters in Yemen, unwavering to Jihad. Narrow faced, with a pointed, reddish-black beard, Shahin, the hawk for al-Awkari, motioned to his men.

They dragged a beaten man out of mud-plastered building and thrown before a crumbling wall. The prisoner was black-skinned, not of Arabic origin. Khalaf could hear the man's wails, certainly crying out his innocence, and mumbling shouted prayers. The men surrounded this unfortunate, laughing at his discomfort and it was apparent to Khalaf they could not understand what the man said. They slung their weapons carelessly, smoking cigarettes as they glanced at the offender on the ground. He did not cower, but writhed in pained laminations from a broken leg and arm.

"You have been found guilty against Islam. You are a spy!" shouted Shahin.

The man muttered indecipherable incantations, certainly reciting his prayers.

"Accept your fate."

The man began to shake out words of anguished woe, and Khalaf realized he recognized the words, but held his tongue to silence. To intercede would be to invite confrontation and an awkward showdown with meaningless consequences. Khalaf had more important goals to accomplish, and they were more valuable than a stranger's destined doom.

One of his nearby supporters handed Shahin an ornate sword, an antique called a scimitar. He took aim and swung the sword. The executioner's grunting effort sliced the man's head clean; it made a thudding sound, and pumping arteries spewed the victim's neck blood, spurting first a small hose stream, then easing as the pressure of life ebbed and like a dripping faucet crimson drops fell onto darkening sand.

Shahin wiped the sword against the man's clothes and then strode over to Khalaf, who gave an impassive stare, showing no emotion, especially not the disgust he harbored.

"You see what we do with spies, Khalaf. The man was caught with a pickup full of ammunition boxes heading towards the capital."

"The evidence was overwhelming as to his guilt I presume, even if you do not have a confession?"

"Yes, indeed, it was apparent."

"You realize the last words the man uttered were: 'I am innocent, as Allah knows'? Plus, he spoke a few words from the Koran."

"And the language he spoke, you recognized it? No doubt some form of Yemen dialect.

"We could not afford him to join the government against our revolutionary brothers."

Khalaf shook his head at the haughty ignorance. "Brother Shahin, he prayed in a dialect of Sudanese, from a small tribe in southern Sudan that is totally cut-off from the rest of the world. Not only does that tribe ascribe to the holy words of Islam, but it is said the prophet Mohammed himself went to that region to bring the sword and to convert the people to Allah. I read about them when I attended Cairo University, and listened to their recorded lyrical prayers.

"That man probably is, or rather *was*, more pure in the original Faith than you or I. He was probably traveling to join his fellow Followers of the Faith, not the government. But you would not have known that, having graduated from the University of Virginia."

"Still, he was not one of us." Shahin shrugged indifference. Hatred among Moslems existed as old as the Koran, tribal schisms out of the blood of Mohammad, split apart by whose interpretation of the Koran was the True Word. Al-Qaeda sprung from Sunni doctrine and all other sects, whether Shia or Sufis, were heretics, *takfir* (unbelievers), subject to destruction.

Brute slaughter did not impress Khalaf. He turned and walked towards the building where the al-Qaeda leaders were waiting. Behind him, Shahin reminded his followers of the justice done, and warned them what befalls those who do not follow the True Path. Again and again, they all shouted, "Allah's will" and "Allah's is Great".

14.

"Thanks to our benevolent leader and his supporters world-wide," said Naser Abdel Karim al-Wahishi, "especially those who are technologically equal to our Western enemies, we have approximately three hours before satellites focus on this sector of the desert and we must all go our separate ways."

He spoke from experience. Only last December, two American missiles had been fired on a militant camp at the Ghulam Khan sub-district of North Waziristan in Pakistan, wounding al-Wahishi in the arm. Two years before there had been a similar meeting in Yemen, which al-Awlaki attended, and hours after its ending, government jets directed by a U.S. communication plane circling overhead, pounded the buildings killing innocents who had unknowingly reoccupied the space.

Here, today, the most imposing target of all, the greatest brain trust strength of the al-Qaeda movement in the Arab world, excepting the absence of bin Laden and al-Zawahiri.

Fifteen men sat in this room sipping coffee or ginger tea, several munching on *bint as-sahn,* the honey-covered puff pastry. Greetings of " مالسلا مكيلع Aslamualikom" and " فيـك مكلاح kayf halukom" coursed around the room. Khalaf was formally recognized by al-Wahishi, and a cooler nod of the head from the American, Anwar al Awlaki.

Fahd Mohammed Ahmed al-Quso, one of the collaborators on the *USS Cole* bombing, motioned Khalaf to take a cushion near him. Khalaf recognized Ibrahim Hassan Al Asiri, the Yemen Bomber, sitting in a corner, eating flatbread and fried eggplant as if he had not had a good meal in some time. Asiri, angrier and more blindly fanatical than anyone else in attendance, had tried to destroy cargo planes using PETN bombs disguised as copier machine parts. Similar bomb ingredients of his were used by the Underwear Bomber when he tried to blow up an America-bound commercial airliner.

Asiri had agreed to supply the destructive equipment for the Crimson Scimitar operation. Shahin would oversee its delivery into America to a man known only as *The Professor.* Khalaf knew this much from the verbal messages he delivered between bin Laden and leaders of the Supreme Council. Of the operation's specifics, he knew little.

Discussions began, and it was like a corporate board meeting, with each attendee offering his report on various ongoing operations; after all, al-Qaeda boasted followers, commanders and cells in more than 25 countries.

Ali al-Shihri, deputy commander of al-Qaeda in Yemen and former Guantánamo detainee, gave an overview of the build-up of armed al-Qaeda soldiers and other affiliated militants, and their plan to make incursions against the Yemen southern coastal city of Zinjibar, seeking a softness in the underbelly of the government's defense forces.

Next, they heard from a courier who came from Northern Pakistan as a representative of Ilyas Kashmiri, the regional operations chief for al-Qaeda and its forays into Afghanistan. When not crossing the border, his soldiers and martyr bombers mounted attacks in Pakistan against Pakistanis, the goal to undermine the American-stooge government. His report was positive and all smiled. The American military had been publicly announcing drawdowns of troops in Afghanistan, with a total evacuation by 2012, or 2013 at the latest. Kashmiri, under bin Laden's direction, worked in the midst of formulating plans to coordinate with the Taliban in order to help capture regional towns in districts where the central government did not maintain effective control. The Supreme Council members gave their blessing, which reaffirmed bin Laden's titular power to give operational plan direction to all beneath him.

When the time arrived to present bin Laden's messages, Khalaf spoke sparingly and concisely, giving all the news that bin Laden wanted imparted, especially the ramping up of the Crimson Scimitar operation. He stressed that his master wanted final say and that he demanded personal control for making the launch decision, and wanted full progress reports relayed to him for his opinions.

"We have heard your report, brother Khalaf," said al-Wahishi, "and we are pleased that Crimson Scimitar is going forward. We will do our part. With the anniversary of our holy brothers' martyrdom in America, we will launch our own attacks."

Al-Awlaki spoke. "I feel our individual efforts, what we call the Lone Wolves, will bother the West more than your attempt at a master stroke."

Opinions of strategies differed within the ranks. The al-Awlaki contingent, which was younger and more technologically savvy, did not like the 9/11 attacks. A sleeping giant, the United States and its Western allies, had awakened and thrown its military power to suppress the earlier gains, such as the Taliban's expulsion from power.

Before websites of al-Awlaki were dismantled by Western authorities, they had more than 200,000 hits. His most famous utterance was "If one killing upsets them so much, then we should have 700 followers killing 700 Americans." As recently as November 2010, he had posted a video calling for Muslims around the world to kill Americans "without hesitation."

His loyalty to the cause unassailable, Anwar al-Awlaki's teachings and personal encouragement caused the actions of the Fort Hood shooter, and he was the personal recruiter and handler of Umar Farouk Abdulmutallab, the attempted Northwest Airlines Flight bomber who tried to set off explosives in his underwear on Christmas Day 2009. Al-Awlaki, an American of Yemen ancestry, believed individual attacks – Lone Wolves – would be the most effective at undermining the security of Western countries. America was the priority target –

"The party of devils."

Osama bin Laden believed 9/11 to have been a success, and had told Khalaf that another attack, greater than the Twin Towers, would be required to move the United States out of the Middle East, and force them to abandon Israel. Hence, *Crimson Scimitar*. It was interesting that though al-Awlaki and bin Laden had never met, the Emir, in playing his politics, would give over the running of this operation to the young Iman and his trusted deputy Shahin. That did bother Khalaf.

As young as al-Awlaki, Khalaf believed in what the Iman espoused, for he thought of himself as an avowed fundamentalist, but he was also utterly loyal to bin Laden and that was where his future of advancement lay. He did not have to like al-Awlaki nor Shanin his protégé, yet Khalaf well understood his position, and his ranking in this august meeting, a mere courier, one of four to his superior. Cautious, after everyone had given their opinions, he answered, "All attacks should be welcomed to keep our enemies in confusion."

"Yes," agreed al-Wahishi. "We support our leader in his goals to sow the greatest damage by his brilliant planning."

Khalaf felt this might be his opportunity.

"Whether it is your Lone Wolf attacks, or **Crimson Scimitar**, it is my hope to go to America and lead one of the attacks."

"But it is not the wishes of your leader?"

"He need only listen to your agreement, and I will join with the others."

"It is well and good," said al-Awlaki, speaking in English, the common language of all who sat on the floor in the meeting which represented several nationalities. To Khalaf, it seemed unclean that al-Awlaki's casual speech used American idioms and analogies to basketball and rock & roll stars.

"Such loyalty is appreciated," continued al-Awlaki, "but this is an operation in the United States, and our most exalted leader has decided that what will bring success is our strategy of attacking our enemies using home-grown martyrs. It has been very carefully planned for a decade, and to make alterations will lead to mistakes."

The courier knew what was coming. It would be the orchestration of re-affirming the on-the-scene operational leader of Crimson Scimitar, this news for Khalaf to report back to bin Laden. And there at the door was Shahin.

"I am ready to serve and will depart when the word is given." Khalaf expected this choice. Not only was Shahin educated in America, but he was also a prized student from the Virginia mosque that al-Awlaki once led as Iman. Ten years ago, the acolyte Shahin had provided several stolen credit cards to be used by the martyrs of 9/11. And as the ultimate irony, Shahin had even accompanied the religious leader al-Awlaki when he was invited to the White House, immediately after 9/11 to offer bereavement prayers for Moslem government employees.

"I will carry the word," said Khalaf, masking his disappointment, "plus the list of Lone Wolf attacks you have planned. Allah be praised for your efforts." In this he was sincere, and he listened to the news from all who spoke, cataloguing with a sharp memory of what he must take back to Pakistan and to his future Emir of the First al-Qaeda Caliphate.

Plans were coming together. The current destabilization in the region would help their cause in rebuilding new regimes under al-

Qaeda rule. The world would accept them as the formidable lion, there to receive the people's fealty, but only if America were to be humbled.

Crimson Scimitar would be the knife stroke to the neck against the weak and defenseless, just as Shahin had so adeptly demonstrated. So be it, accepted Khalaf.

It was Shahin's smugness of speech that Khalaf could not bear listening to. The operational commander gave only minimal details of **Crimson Scimitar**, speaking as though it were his own invention and not bin Laden's decade-old Master Plan of Attack, unknowing that by Khalaf's own suggestions certain aspects of the operational plan had been modified. He might not know plan specifics but the greater scheme bore Khalaf's own imprint, and this rose above being a mere courier.

What happened after the meeting was the ultimate slap in Khalaf's face.

"A donkey?" He stared at the scraggly, emaciated beast of burden.

"Only a few miles, to the pick-up point," grinned Shahin. "We must convey to the skywatchers that nothing of significance took place. Some of the Council will move to a school, among the children, and others will depart by fast jeep."

As Khalaf swayed and bounced over rocky terrain, a guide in lead, he swore that his embarrassment would be avenged. He saw Shahin as the culprit – not a hawk, but a crow.

15.

February 2011 Aberdare National Park, Kenya

"That's a growl I'm hearing? Out there, close by?"

"Yes, and sounds like it's getting closer," said Samantha, not moving. She sipped her unfiltered 2006 Chardonnay, personally bottled for her by the de Wetshof Estate winery of South Africa.

If she was not going to look concerned, Hugh would act accordingly, and his face slipped on an ambivalent mask.

They sat on the veranda of a tree house overlooking the watering hole, the luxurious private hotel hundreds of yards behind them, near the crest of a hill. The serving staff had cleared their dinner plates and properly absented themselves. Now the deep heart of Africa, the darkness of the savannah night, lay outside the ring of spotlights which allowed both of them, Hugh Fox in curious excitement, to watch wildebeests, hyenas, giraffes, and antelopes trek to the muddy watering hole for an evening drink.

Now predators were approaching. Hugh pulled his camera to his side, ready for another telescopic masterpiece, knowing he would have to remodel a room in his house in a Dark Continent motif using the results of his weeklong trip.

It had been an exciting trip; everything he could have asked for. His lovely guide was the best part of the tour, and he felt their personalities mesh. They were two intelligent people always interested in learning more about the world around them, about each other. *Copacetic*, that was a good word. Tomorrow would be the tour of the Refuge and of the animal hospital she founded, and then back to civilization.

Perhaps the moment was right – with the dinner afterglow, and the nocturnal noises sounding like a jungle meditation tape, though real. Why not?

"I have an idea I am pursuing, and would welcome your opinion."

She curled up in her canvas chair.

"I wouldn't be good at analyzing a video game concept," she said, "unless you wished me to advise you on color coordination, or interior design of space stations. But you have me here, or I have you here, rather, the night is young, and I am quite lucid. Pray, go on. I appreciate mind stimulation in any form."

They exchanged comfortable smiles. On previous nights, their dinner conversations had been enlightening, refreshing. They learned they were two intellectuals who could maintain discourses without seeming condescending to the other. Friendly banter.

Hugh Fox dove in.

"Excluding natural disasters that we have no control over, what is the greatest threat to our civilization?"

"If this were a set-up for the unanswerable, I would plead ignorance. But knowing you, I would guess 'nuclear misadventure' would definitely impact everyone in the world, and threaten the existence of human civilization. Chernobyl, and more recently, Japan. Radiation, once loose, is impossible to stick back in the genie bottle."

"True. Now, if I rephrased the question: '*Who* would be the greatest threat?'"

Sipping her wine, and mulling over her thoughts, she answered, "Rogue governments. Dictators out of control, though most seem contained, or at least only interested in their own backyards."

"Nine-eleven. The attack on the U.S. by Islamic fundamentalists – what does that conjure in your mind?" he asked. "Definitely out of control, blinded-by-religion fanaticism. They spout, 'No one can go to heaven except me and mine, everyone else is consigned to damnable hellfire'."

"And you are correct at your first guess. Did you know that these al-Qaeda operatives originally targeted nuclear power plants on the East Coast? Later they changed their targets to symbols of America: the Trade Center, the Pentagon, and the last presumed to be Congress, the U.S. Capitol. The targets were only changed because the terrorist leaders could not guarantee where on a nuclear plant would be the most sensitive point to hit to do the maximum damage."

"But didn't I read that the U.S. is prosecuting the conspirators, the masterminds in 9/11, by holding military trials at Guantanamo? I read that in the <u>Times</u>, on my way to the Fashion section."

"Mere appendages of a multi-headed snake, but not the head itself."

"Hugh, what are *you* thinking? I have the feeling your mind is several steps ahead of anyone else's."

He looked straight at her. "I am going to capture Osama bin Laden, the titular head of al Qaeda, the directing force behind the 9/11 attacks."

"The U.S. has tried, the CIA, and other government security forces. Isn't he hiding in Afghanistan?"

"Governments have tried, yes, but they've not succeeded. From personal experience, I have more faith in the power of private enterprise. I believe I could put together a team, supported with the latest technology and energized with the right motivation."

"Motivated to bring evil to justice?" He expected to see her laugh at him, but she did not.

"There is a coincidence. I founded my company in New York City, and it was fledgling and struggling back in 2001. Cherisee Fortier worked for me as a fabric buyer. Her two young nieces were in town from Iowa that day, and she took them to an early lunch at the restaurant Windows of the World on top of the World Trade Center. I can't tell you all our anguish and heartache.

"Just my own thoughts of Cherisee, smart as a whip, shepherding her two nieces towards the rooftop, believing helicopters would save them – and, from what I've read, finding the doors bolted shut. No escape, no hope." Samantha's voice cracked and tears welled.

"I can assure you my goal is noble – justice – but for others, the $10 million reward that's on the head of the leader of Al Qaeda, dead or alive, should be incentive enough for the mercenary types. I might even add my own funds to the reward kitty.

"Let me show you something." He pulled out his ever-present, pencil-thin, hand-held computer and punched a few buttons.

He nodded at it. "I got an insider to get me this before its release and had my crew cut out superfluous background plotting."

He moved to sit next to her and she leaned into his shoulder, and placed her hand on his thigh – to steady her balance, he presumed. He played the short version of "Grandmother Mary's Gift" from the *King's Retribution* television show, produced by Five Aces Studioz. When it was over, he beamed as might a student who knew he had all the answers and would breeze through his SAT exams with high scores; as he, indeed, did in high school, entering college a year early.

Samantha Carlisle searched the young man's features, trying to delve deep into his makeup, her eyes curious about what she accepted as intense energy unbundling. His excitement seemed contagious; stimulation for others to latch onto.

"You are very serious. And what are these actors for?"

"They would be the nucleus of my team. They have spent two years, 30 televised shows, analyzing the workings of criminals and figuring out how to locate and capture crooks. A terrorist is just a crook with a political alibi. I will supplement them with funds and the support of my brightest tech gurus.

"I can make them more efficient and – ."

His fast talk and enthusiasm was interrupted by a sharp, guttural scream, followed by a lingering banshee cry that sounded like a baby in distress. It was close, near the watering hole.

"That's not the cry of a big cat hunting," said Samantha. "That's pain." She arose and went to a large flat suitcase off to the side of the expansive deck. She took out a leather case, and from that a long rifle. She started putting the barrel and stock together, efficiently, and at the barrel end she inserted a lethal-looking arrow stub, needle-thin with a feather attached.

"My god," was Hugh's response.

"Pneu-Dart X Caliber rifle. It can put 1 to 10 ccs of knock-out drugs into an animal from a great distance."

Samantha walked to the railing with the rifle under her arm. Calling into a walkie-talkie she picked up from a table top, speaking patois of an African language – it was somewhat of an English pidgin so far as Hugh could determine – she directed the listener to be prepared with a holding box. At the balcony railing, they strained their eyes into the darkness. Another scream had them both looking to the left of the water hole. The last of the animals, two miniature gazelles, bolted from their drinking place and disappeared.

"Suspicious critter, circling. Not looking for dinner but definitely needing to get to the water." Out of a backpack she pulled a large, scope-like object bearing irregular optics; one end larger than the other.

She intrigued him with her sudden metamorphous from the anthropologist Jane Goodall to the white huntress Calamity Jane. It was somewhat sexy with its connotations of impassioned violence: hunter facing prey. It was like what he had been thinking about all along but had not yet visualized, what was missing as he put his idea into concept – the passion of the hunt. He hoped Colonel King would provide such a missing element. He watched her professionally add the device to the rifle.

"Sniper Scope?"

"It's something of my own invention. An adaptation of a golf course range finder, but with night vision capabilities. One of the problems animal naturalists have in capturing animals with sedatives is gauging the right combination of ketamine and medetomidine in a 10 cc dart.

"Too much and they die, but too little and they run off, sick and vulnerable to carnivores. What I do when I am siting the rifle is have the scope data chip determine what type of animal, and the weight, and make an immediate dosage calculation to remix in the dart if necessary. And then I can put the animal asleep safely and quickly."

"There it is," cried Hugh, excited. "It's a leopard. It's limping."

"Actually, a cheetah. And look at its side. See that blood? The cat wants to roll in the mud and cover the wound, but that's not a gash. It's not a tusk or clawing wound. It looks like a bullet hole. It went in the side, most likely hit the ribs and then out the hip. Damn poachers!"

She brought the rifle to bear, sited it, made an adjustment, let out her breath, stilled and fired. The bright feather appeared on the flank of the cheetah, and the animal screamed in new pain. It bared its fangs, stood a moment, wavered, and then slowly crouched to the ground, and in a minute, it rolled to its side.

From nowhere, a group of workers appeared, pushing a large box. One checked the animal's vital signs, and soon the creature was loaded and carted off.

"You will see our new patient tomorrow."

"I am impressed; a woman who puts her rifle where her convictions are."

"Poachers are driving African animals to extinction," she said. "We try to stop them, and try to repopulate species in zoos, but zoos are not a natural environment to maintain the wild instincts. Whether it's due to poverty or revolutions, local poachers sneak in here to kill for pelts to wrap a fashionable woman. I never use fur in my designs.

"Then there are the poachers of horn and tusk used for illegal aphrodisiacs, which, of course, are like snake oil liniment. Superstition and totally unproven."

"Would you say the extinction of the world's nature deserves to be saved?" he asked.

"Of course." She broke down the rifle and laid it aside.

"You can see my point, then, of tracking down evil. My focus is only on one evil person.

"Capture him, and the morale and strength of the entire beast is depleted. I believe there might be a chance for success by bringing new perspectives to bear on the hunt. Using that analogy, what I want is to design a specialized and modified rifle, by using new technology, so to speak, to track down the human prey."

She picked up her wine glass, and he refilled it. Her drink was to calm rushed adrenaline, her thrill of pulling the trigger, the power of release; yes, of the hunt, the capture without killing.

She stared, her eyes locked into his, and raised her glass.

"I salute you, Hugh. You have set a noble quest. More power to you, but it lacks one important asset."

"It does?" His mind raced; he thought he had allowed for all contingencies.

"It's missing my presence. I intend to join you. Child killers first, and animal slaughterers next. Helping you will be a progression, with my own goals in mind."

"Sam, this could be dangerous."

"Yes, it could be," she said. "We shouldn't waste time. Let's go and talk more about your plans."

"Go?"

"To the hotel, my bedroom. If we are to be fellow travelers, I want to learn more about the man behind the idea." She gave him a slow, warm kiss, letting her fingers trace his face.

Hugh followed, giving no response except curious acquiescence.

16.

February 2011 Los Angeles

Smoldering, a slow, angry fire burning inside her, left Callie hot flashing. She was mad at King for being an insensitive prick, for dumping her at the wrap party and then coming to her drunk, the sex more groping and pawing. She could analyze all that, and see the man insecure about being a star and afraid of commitment. Easy for him to wake to see a new face each week, and then when remorse set in, run back to her as the only stable force in his life.

What galled her even more was that now he sat across from her, nibbling on bruschetta, giving off no warmth, no charm; no indications that she was someone special. Men!

Dammit, it was really her own fault, she conceded. Her needs were screwed up, and avoiding shallow "Hal" types putting the moves on her drove her into a self-imposed cloister, rationalizing acceptance of the man sitting across from her, the star of *King's Retribution.*

The scheduled luncheon meeting found them both at the Asian-fusion restaurant *Katsuya*, on Hollywood Boulevard, where they were surrounded by the mover-and-shaker crowd. She was not privy to the topic of the meeting, and despised blind agendas. She had just been told to show up, a star required to make a showing, the luncheon blessed by the heads of Five Aces Studioz, their production company. Five Aces owned and produced King's reality show, as well as a couple of mediocre sitcoms. Several years back, they'd had a string of hit, low-budget slasher movies, reruns on late night cable, where Callie feared her own career might be headed.

"I'll ask the writers to enlarge your part next season," said King. It was his tactless way of asking forgiveness.

She was having none of the bullshit. "That's how the fight started, you may recall. I don't need my role as the show's 'Hooters Tactician' expanded. I want to do field work, so if you're sincere about helping my career, re-design me as a Lady Rambo."

"You saw how the Pettigrew grab went down. That bodyguard could have shot me. What would you have done if he pulled a gun on you?"

"Shot him in the leg. And, as you'll recall, I did help disarm the asshole."

It wasn't what King wanted to hear. She was Rambo alright, very much like Sly's movie character: off-kilter, the loner. He did not come out and tell Callie, though she certainly had guessed, the show's producers hired her because of her curvaceous body, her pixy-tease face.

She was typecast as a Sandra Bullock Spanish-Mexican actress, and her sexual salsa allure was a balance for Retribution's masculinity. Too bad she smoldered as much off-screen as on screen, thought King, dismissing her concerns as he wondered who the studio was sending over for them to schmooze.

Callie arched her back like a spitting she-cat, looking around the table for the messiest thing to throw in his face if needed. Sushi seemed to be the fare of choice, but she stopped as two limousines pulled up in front of *Katsuya* and paparazzi positioned their camera cannons. A staged arrival, which was not unusual in Tinsel Town, where restaurants like *The Ivy*, *Bazzar*, or *Michael Mina's XIV* were the places to be seen at, to be caught unaware, (yeah, right). Most diners turned their heads, wondering who would alight from the opening limos.

The buzz began.

"Hugh Fox and Samantha Carlisle," Callie whispered aloud more to her own hearing than for King's benefit. Stars can be star-struck and though a television personality where she had her own public recognition, she accepted she was not on any 'A' List. "People Magazine reported they are an item. Quite close for the last two weeks, I read."

"I see you're into deep literature."

"This from a man who quotes Rush Limbaugh as the gospel?" She watched as the two beautiful, and extremely nouveau riche, gave directions to their assistants. Their mutual bodyguard, a hefty, broad-shouldered wrestler in a sports coat, moved unobtrusively into nearby shadows.

"I wonder what they're doing here?" Callie had spoken too soon.

"Colonel King and Miss Cardoza," beamed Hugh Fox, walking their way and extending his hand. His other hand rested gently on Samantha Carlisle's back. Touching tenderly, Callie noted; not so much guiding.

Rising to meet them, both Callie and Storm reacted to this honor with mild shock, soaking in the people-watchers near their table and wondering themselves what was going on.

After cordial greetings were exchanged, the lunch menu was perused and food orders – rock shrimp tempura and miso-marinated black cod – were placed. Awkward silence infused the high profile foursome. Nothing left to do but get down to the business at hand, thought King with a Scotch neat in his blood-stream, and being an ex-military aggressor, he took the lead.

"I had no idea the show's producers wanted us to meet with you. Wish I had been forewarned."

"I am a recent fan," said Samantha, smiling at both of the TV personalities. "In fact, in the last two weeks I have studied all your episodes. Miss Cardoza, I think you are sitting on a lot of unexpressed talent."

Callie could not help but beam, and shot a quick glance at King that said, 'See? Told you so.'

"I wonder how you go about selecting your show's topics, your quarry?" Hugh gave off an inquisitive sincerity, and King felt it his duty to illuminate his honored hosts, assuming one of them would pick up the check.

"Well, the producers have a research team that scours news-papers, gets tip reports from prosecutors' offices, or even from bail bondsmen who handle high priority cases. With our show's popularity, sometimes there are anonymous contacts to our office with a lead or a story line to pursue."

"What comes next?" asked Samantha, showing her own inter-est, but also studying Colonel King with an apprising intensity. The King's Retribution star, his co-star knew oh so well liked being the center of attention.

"They start a priority system, using the information they have so far. Who's on the run, and where might they be hiding? Then our writers have a bull session with Research and see which story is best to develop. Several of our story projects are two years out."

"And when you do select a target, you seem to catch the crim-inal."

"Teamwork we can be proud of." King gave a nodding kudo to Callie, trying to mend fences. Callie hoped these mega-rich realized that many shows were scrubbed, either because the crook was caught, or because the bad guy went to ground without a single clue to give direction.

A lot of the show's camera work never saw the light of day.

The luncheon courses started and between bites, Hugh and Samantha tagged teamed with questions about the show and its personnel to a point that Callie realized something was in play.

These two multi-millionaires knew too much and their questions were not naïve. They were confirming what they already knew.

"I notice that the networks, and nearly all cable channels, has one or more of its own reality shows," said Samantha.

"COPS, on Fox, debuted in 1989, won the 1993 American Television Award for best reality show, and it is still tops in its time slot. Fans seem to really get into reality crime shows like *King's Retribution.*" Callie kicked at King under the table, but the flattery smothered his senses over her warning.

Hugh Fox asked, "Do you see reality shows like yours fostering stereotypes about criminals? Most are minorities, aren't they?"

"I have read those editorials," answered King, "but we're different. We go after smart criminals who think they can get away with it. Most of our criminals are Anglo, whereas pure cop shows, like *48 Hours*, are inner city and do have a higher percentage of urban minority. We would go after any fugitive, though."

"I find some reality shows demeaning," said Samantha. "They speak to our lower base values. They're all about television executives going for ratings. And they exploit the participants' hunger for attention, their eagerness to publicly parade any lack of moral integrity.

"Why can't a show hit for a greater moral target, try to benefit mankind?"

Callie saw Fox hide a chuckle as he put a piece of sushi into his mouth.

King felt he had to defend his livelihood. "I would agree there are shows aiming at a young audience and do pander to sexual stupidity, but again look at *King's Retribution*. People, audiences, want to see good prevail. That has always been my – our – objective."

Hugh Fox looked at Samantha Carlisle with a smile that acknowledged silent agreement.

"What if we had an idea for a story?" asked Hugh. "Someone to pursue and capture; would that be of interest to you?"

Colonel King finally saw the trap. He had accepted the flattery, when in truth he was being set up to read a fledgling, wannabe author's script. He maintained his graciousness, though, rocking back in his chair, a little more suspect. Callie gave him a subtle, "You're on your own, buster" look.

"The show's producers would be open to any great plot line," responded King, always the soldier-statesman. "Especially from you, of course. But they make the final decisions." He spoke quick, correcting an error relating to his ego. "Naturally, my opinion is heard when I see any of our action elements missing. And the prize, the evil doer, must have the panache to catch the audience's attention, and draw them in from crime to capture."

Callie saw Hugh Fox beam. It was a surprising trait, she thought. Child-like; a kid on Christmas morning. His looks, she thought, leaned to cute, boyish. He was an adult youngster having fun; not someone wearing a masculine mask like Storm King.

"I'm glad to hear you say that," said Hugh. "Indeed, I have an evil fugitive in mind. And the research required and qualified apprehension team not only fits well with your television show, but we both have decided that you are the people to bring it about."

Callie had a feeling of foreboding and sensed trouble.

"Who is this felon you're after?" King heated up, in spite of who their luncheon guests were. "Some ex-employee who defrauded you?" His voice got a little bit sarcastic. "I don't think we can create a solid hour around an executive's personal vendetta."

Hugh paused a good ten seconds before answering.

"Osama bin Laden."

"What?"

"Who, rather," corrected Samantha. "Osama bin Laden, the terrorist war criminal."

"Bin Laden." King scoffed and gave a laugh. "The U.S. Government, with all its spy and satellite tools, has not even gotten close since they botched up his capture in the Tora Bora Mountains of Afghanistan. That was the last known sighting. Some say he's dead."

"And he may be which would be glad news for the world. However, my initial research indicates that he is still alive. But the question is: if you were given an infusion of logistical support, additional funding and enough research personnel to accomplish an intense investigation as to his location, would you undertake searching for, and if possible, capturing Osama bin Laden?"

King began a silent staring contest around the table as his mind clicked. Fast comprehension, like a military field decision, data in, assessment risk—Yet, when he really came down to an answer he felt he would go no farther than lip service, and he knew he could fake interest. His 10-second decision took in television viewer statistics. Maybe *King's Retribution* could build the storyline's intrigue over a two-show segment, generate a media circus with

History Channel flair. Touting the chasing of a terrorist as a season opener, even if they didn't catch him, would guarantee high ratings and a third season. He also saw the downside. A program like this, attempting to capture a world-famous terrorist, he thought, would certainly fail to reach its objective, and perhaps end in ridicule like when the mustached hypester-journalist Geraldo opened mobster Capone's safe only to discover it empty. Yes, that captured a large viewer audience, but Geraldo had come off as a cliché for sensationalist and poor investigative journalism.

"Yes, I would be interested. But I don't see the producers going along. They like safe formats, outcomes assured, and all packaged up sweetly."

"I don't think you have to worry about your production company being in opposition," Samantha said. She was all business, folding her napkin on her plate as if the meeting were at an end. "Hugh and I bought Five Aces Studioz last week. We're your new bosses. And we want you to capture Osama bin Laden."

Episode 3

Before you embark on a journey of revenge, dig two graves.
-- Confucius

17.

March 2011 Miami, Florida

They were ten years in the making, and *The Professor* was somewhat proud of his three attack cells. Two of them unfortunately were criminal in composition requiring money to be exchanged to gain uncertain loyalty, while the third cell gave blind faith being made up of disillusioned, idealistic former students, culled over the years and nurtured into his personal sphere of dissatisfaction mixed with fanatical fatalism.

The criminal cells had no idea they were being used, nor that their final tasks would be nothing like what they had been told were their philosophical objectives. The Professor believed that al-Qaeda leadership—the emir, bin Laden, himself—had imparted the ultimate, 9/11 outcome information only to Commander Atta and the other chosen pilots. The rest of the attack cells that day thought they were going to hijack planes, not crash them into buildings. It did not matter if a few of the foot soldiers were misinformed. Ignorance for sacrifice – if it assures success – is always a worthy tenet.

It was his Florida cell, if you could call it that, which gave him the most trouble. Its members acted more like "weekend warriors." They came in contact with the authorities in haphazard circumstances, and risked falling apart by arrest or internal disloyalty.

Hiding behind the excuse of another university conference on foreign policy, he found himself in an industrial section of Miami, seeking out the motorcycle repair shop. He had dressed down, slovenly, in dirty jeans and a plain t-shirt without logos. He parked his rental car several blocks away, and his walk in the humidity added a layer of sweat to his grimy appearance.

The repair shop, with only one BMW motorcycle up on a bay rack, looked more like a parts warehouse--probably because it was an illegal chop shop for stolen motorcycles, hefted from other areas in Florida and nearby states.

The Professor's contact, Mike 'Gator' Donaldson, was the shop owner and primary mechanic. He was a stocky man with bad teeth and sharp incisors that gave him his nickname while his physique portrayed him as a walking advertisement for a tattoo parlor, his tats having been poorly crafted in prison. His alma mater was the correctional institution called Glades.

Gator knew nothing about what was going on in the Middle East, but after an abusive upbringing and other sociological baggage, he hated all races and all religions. Outside of the occasional, stereotyped racist epithet, he did not give politics much thought. More than anything else, he hated the Federal Government. Pick some initials and he hated them. DEA for his drug busts, IRS for his surprise audits, FBI for stings he got caught up in. Local cops for expired license tags. He had no greater passion, outside of straight Tequila shots and big-breasted biker chicks, than wanting to stick it big time to the government. This intensity provided the blind rage that drove him into conspiracy, where the Professor gave him the specific, destructive scheme to vent and destroy.

"Are the other clubs still in on this?"

"Just three of them, and again I can't name names. They hate the Feds as much as you do." The Professor passed himself off as a Cuban biker with an ax to grind, the ringleader from an outlaw club based out of Tallahassee.

"The more there are to help us, the bigger the body count," grinned Gator displaying the vulgarity of his tobacco-stained teeth.

"The other clubs will join you with their targets. Kill some, great. But we will achieve just as much by showing them as screw-up assholes when they can't catch us."

Walking from the garage into a fenced storage yard, Gator opened the door to a large aluminum shed, flipped a light switch, and pulled up a trapdoor that had been hidden beneath an oil-soaked tarp. Inside, the Professor saw about four wooden shipping crates piled atop each other.

"This came in last week as bike parts. Wherever you got this firepower, it's enough to blow up the entire Federal Judicial Center." Gator gave a gargled, congestive laugh. "Up until now, we've been practicing, playing around with dynamite that went missing from a construction company four years ago. You know, like blowing up stumps and fish in the swamp. But your stuff's gonna work like hot shit."

"In a couple of months I'll get you word on the target."

The Professor saw Gator grimace.

"What's the problem?"

"It's Kettering. Busted on a meth charge. He's up for trial in a month. I'm afraid he might cut a deal—you know, and talk about our little blow-up escapades. Just like me, he doesn't know what government building we're hitting. He might crap us out for holding unlicensed federal explosives. So far he hasn't said nothing, but I know they're gonna put the heat on. He might be a good guy, you know, loyal, and a friend, but he's in a three strikes situation when he goes before a judge."

Complications as they approached the Crimson Scimitar launch were unacceptable.

"Not good. We don't need a screw-up this late. We need at least three of you on this job.

And I'll be sending you one of my Cubans with explosive knowledge, but you guys are the soldiers, and you do want to send a message to the Feds, don't you?"

"Yeah, I know. So I've been thinking. There's a buddy of mine, just out this week on Murder Two. Thinks it was a bum rap. Someone else pulled the trigger but, you know, he was there when it went down so they bundled them all up, and he got 15 years, but he was out in five because of a prison overcrowding release program. Still, he's more pissed than me. We're tight and he'll keep his mouth shut. I can depend on him. Doesn't even have to know much."

"And your buddy Kettering?"

"I can move this junk to a storage unit I got. No one knows about it. Over there, until your Cuban buddy shows up, I can start making the bomb packages to the specs you gave me.

Kettering won't have anything to snitch about."

"I don't like loose ends. I know a guy.... "

"Whatever." Gator glanced away in dismissal, his friendship with his buddy Kettering not so important as to derail blowing up the System.

"Yeah, whatever. You'll hear from me. The time is fast approaching."

"Can't wait to rock 'n roll," said Gator, locking away the explosives.

The Professor found the repair shop owner's statement ironic. A 9/11 passenger, one of several that tried to save their aircraft from crashing in Washington, D.C., only to then crater in a

Pennsylvania cornfield, said similar words. Rock 'n roll is a party, a rock in the highway, an impediment.

Professor Rogers looked for a gas station to change clothes, ready to rip off his t-shirt and use it to wipe off the day's sweltering mugginess.

Turning his car air conditioning on full blast, he placed a coded call, one he never thought he would have to make. He left a message for Mr. Fix-it, as he called him, the one-eared man whose name was Razzor Hassim. No rocky bumps for Crimson Scimitar.

18.

March 2011 Washington, D.C.

Inside the hallowed marble halls of Congress, the closed session of the Appropriations Subcommittee for the U.S. Senate Select Committee on Intelligence had adjourned for the day.

Ronald Givens, Assistant Deputy Director of the Central Intelligence Agency, and several of his staffers were gathering up their presentation papers, having underwhelmed three of the five U. S. Senator committee members in attendance and sent them into nodding dozes with their data soaked presentation: "Assessment of economic risk and estimated financial aid support required to countries impacted by the Arab Spring."

"Arab Spring" was the new speaking point nomenclature out of the White House and State Department, defined as recent events of populace agitation against single political party regimes. The word "totalitarian" was thought unwise to impart in public speechmaking; it was better said that the U.S. sought, as an end result, a hybrid form of democracy. That, too, was unspoken, usually by lifers out of the State Department who saw more anarchy in the Mediterranean and Middle East news, with a tilt towards Islamic radicalism overpowering the democratic dissi-dents. After all, Lenin's communism consumed Imperial Russia, and they were but one of many minority parties vying for power. All history with qualified variations repeats itself, or so said the smartest analysts within the government.

"Do you have a moment, Ron?"

Givens was closing his briefcase over the documents stamped 'Top Security, Do Not Distribute.' He looked up to see the fash-ionable and very powerful senior Senator from California smiling. "Of course, Senator."

They found seats at the back of the empty meeting chamber. Ronald Givens was in his mid-forties and dressed pinstriped conservative with the proper power tie and patriotic flag lapel pin. He felt at ease in his present rank he had reached within the Agency, and was optimistic about his future. Expecting the President to win re-election next year, he envisioned that senior

Administration officials would start resigning in the mid-term to accept high-paying, private sector executive or consultant employment. A few valuable posts should become available, priming his ascendency; perhaps to head up the CIA—or on a grander scale, why not a Cabinet post? One part of his strategy of finesse and working the angles required paying careful attention to U.S. Senators.

"Senator Crandall, sorry for the dry numbers. At this time we can only speculate. Any full-fledged revolution will require point-ed infusion of aid for the new government. We just don't know at what point we can determine if they are our friends or not."

"No problem. I'm used to hocus-pocus and smoke and mirror budgets. After all, I am from California." U.S. Senator Lucy Crandall drew a deep breath, collecting her thoughts and weighing the political chits this conversation might cost her.

"Mr. Givens, I have an odd request, but one I think you and the Agency might be able to help with." She paused, and then plunged forth. "I have one constituent, a young man, who through his charitable foundation has been a major supporter to several of the environmental causes I publicly champion. Speak-ing candidly, and confidentially, so far he has not made any huge contributions to my re-election campaign. Nor, I should point out, to the President's reelection finance committee. I believe if I can halfway deliver on his interesting request, it might kick him loose to be generous to our party's Political Action Committees."

And, through them, trickle down to her own future re-election coffers, thought Givens. He did not like playing the favors game unless it benefitted his career, but this was Washington, D.C., and his boss, the Agency Director, and above the Director, all those surrounding the President of the United States, were adept at it. They knew how best to disperse election promises, offering them first as tensile steel – which then, after post-vote counts, disappeared like confetti in a windstorm.

"Well, let's see what we can reasonably do, Senator." Always equivocate, he thought, mindful of the exit strategy. He heard her sigh.

"The young man I'm speaking of is Hugh Fox."

"Fox, of that skilly video games empire? My two kids are ad-dicted, to the point they even have his games downloaded as phone apps."

"The same. Somehow, in his idealistic fervor, Mr. Fox wants to go hunting for real-life Islamic radical terrorists. His corporate lobbyist contacted me several days ago, starting a push to see if I can use my position to gain friends and allies in the intelligence community. They want expertise that might point them in the right direction."

"The kid must have let one of his games override his brain. If you're asking whether the Agency can open its files to some doobie-smoking geek, you know the answer would have to be a firm 'no.'

"I feel the same way, except for what I would call 'ramifications.' It seems Mr. Fox has hired, or otherwise secured the services of, Colonel Storm King."

"Colonel King, of that fugitive manhunt TV show?"

"Yes. And from my perspective this means publicity, and maybe not the best for the Administration. The new super-duo's first target is none other than Osama bin Laden."

Ronald Givens showed surprise, which he quickly smothered.

"Crap, and pardon my French, Senator. That has to be headline hunting."

"No doubt, but you would agree that your agency hasn't caught the bastard. I don't want, and I'm sure your boss doesn't want, the perception of this inability to catch bin Laden paraded out in the media as a failure, and maybe even comparing us to the last Administration's lack of success."

"I wouldn't say this in public, Senator, but bin Laden is a non-event. As you know, there are more lethal groups out there with fanatical hate-America agendas. Besides, we have dispersed or killed most of the higher-ups in al-Qaeda." He'd just told the Senator an outright fabrication and sensed she could see through his spy doublespeak.

"But the Supreme Council of al-Qaeda still functions, even if bin Laden is dead, or if he's alive and incapacitated some day. As you can see, I do read the intelligence assessment reports you copy to the committee.

"What I am seeking, Mr. Givens, is a semblance of providing assistance, without necessarily opening up any state secrets. This ambitious crusade, if one may call it that, will probably gain them a few pages of early publicity, but once their search goes nowhere, fans and the rest of us will get bored and change channels. Your department does not need to overtly assist, but you should be aware, and if the press asks, perhaps not come off with a negative response, but with guarded caution. Wish them well, while saying one ought to leave the fight against terrorism to the professionals."

"I grant you, if handled wrong it could become a dicey public relations issue. That wouldn't be welcomed. Our opponents, as you well know, seek any political issue to improve their polling numbers."

"Exactly my concern."

Givens saw himself being manipulated by a politician; damned if you do, damned if you don't.

"Senator, it's very kind of you to let me know what might be coming. I will have our staff formulate a response. As a token of our limited cooperation, very limited, you can hint to Mr. Fox and Colonel King, off channels, that we will see what we can do to aid these 'volunteers.' I might be able to find a few non-classified White Papers with general background on al-Qaeda to toss them, as the proverbial bone."

"It's all I can ask. Thank you." The Senator rose and departed. The Assistant Deputy Director of the CIA pulled out his cell, punched in a highly restricted number and made immediate contact: the bin Laden Desk at Langley. In the public's eye, the search for bin Laden had waned since 9/11, and it had taken a back seat to major events, as today's report on Arab Spring demonstrated. Syria. Libya. Egypt. Even rich Bahrain. All were in play and at risk.

Governments in dangerous flux went to the top of the priority list, well in front of brainwashed vest bombers seeking virgins in heaven by vaporizing themselves into red mist gore.

"Anything knew on Geronimo?" It was the Agency's code name for bin Laden.

The man on the other end of the line responded, "Perhaps. As I told you and everyone in the Eyes Only Clearance, including the President, we are tracking a courier who has a history running errands for Geronimo. He's living in Pakistan, close to Islamabad, and still seems to be a message runner. We think he's staying at an al-Qaeda safe house. Even with no confirmation of Geronimo's presence, we have your Director's and the President's approval to prepare military contingency plans. That's all I have at the moment. In a nutshell, though we have a warm trail, we have no confirmation as to whether we've found a High Priority Target, al-Qaeda or Taliban or even this newly announced Islamic State of Iraq and Syria (ISIS)."

Next Givens called his boss, who also had been updated on this high value lead.

"Yes, I agree it's worth a look-see," said the CIA Director, "but I told the Section Ops, 'Let's not let our allies in on the intelligence quite yet'."

Givens concurred. Twenty years in the spook business, including seven years in backwater hellholes as a field agent, Givens did not trust any ally of America. They didn't bleed red, white and blue. He got to the point. "Nothing major, sir; just a nuisance glitch." He abbreviated his conversation with Senator Crandall. Hearing no immediate response to the Senator's request, he continued, "I believe that, without fanfare, I can find a way to sidetrack them. We don't need gungho cameras filming a 'Great Chase' across the sands of Arabia." Givens, in his mind, started formulating a response to the Senator's request. He would kill two birds; no, better yet, *stuff* two dead-on-arrival birds with one response.

He ended the call pleased with himself. He received no firm verbal authorization from his boss to proceed, but rather a decentralized affirmation through silence. Givens took the conversation as good enough to take quick action. After all, this posse plan by a Gameboy brat and a drunk ex-soldier cowboy (he recalled hearing somewhere King liked his whiskey) were a nonissue, anyway; they were petty players, a waste of his time.

There were more critical issues to confront in this unsafe world. The Japanese earthquake and resulting tsunami were examples of the critical need for contingency planning. Ronald Givens had been appointed to an intra-governmental taskforce to deal with potential future catastrophic nuclear power plant failures within U.S. borders, whether by natural or terrorist causes, and to develop new protection safeguards to deal with damaged nuclear plants from atmospheric fuel leakage, cooling fuel rods and emergency radioactive storage disbursement.

Representing the CIA on the taskforce, he believed was a plum assignment. It was a privilege to be part of greater events in these nervous, historic times, instead of consorting with reality TV trash.

Givens found himself once more contemplating the Senator's request and realized how to stifle the yo-yo stunt. Can't act too overt, can't even be seen to have presence. It was better to toss cold water on it, artfully finessed, with sensitivity to the players. As a first step, he needed to find out what those jokers were up to, gathering intel on the ground, and in California of all places. He needed to establish an anonymous agency presence; someone to "look and report."

Who could he choose for this babysitting operation?

The name came to him quickly: Wendell Holmes. He knew Holmes was on his way out, about to be shoved through the door into early retirement with a Twenty-Five Year Service Badge. There were only a few months left before they turned him out to pasture – and in Given's mind it was good riddance. It was a perfect ending to Wendell Holmes's muddled career. Givens felt pleased with his choice.

His course of action selected, he phoned in his command call, wondering if Holmes would realize the reassignment came from his former field partner as a last gotcha. He suddenly thought less of the Senator's situation, not caring if the solution – Wendell Holmes on the scene – solved anything. Givens straightened his tie, tugged his shirt cuffs out from his suit jacket to their proper length at the wrist, retrieved his briefcase and headed back to his office, where there were true issues of world turmoil.

19.

March 2011 Miami

Kettering's head was rolling with a beer buzz, and he wanted to give his statement to the detectives and get it over with. With his testimony, he could avoid being found habitual and possibly avoid doing thirty to life. He just needed to hand them someone else, other than himself, and his friend Gator seemed the perfect mark. Make the deal, his attorney pushed him, or you are in deep shit and they slam the door behind you – that door with the bars and without a key.

He had been in with Gator and Lewis and enjoying all their antics for at least five years.

It was mostly small potato stuff, dealing drugs and motorcycle thefts. Cops had left them alone for the most part, seeing them as small fish, more like middlemen. Until he screwed up, that is.

He itched around his ankle where the monitor bracelet held snug. Glancing out the window, he saw the patrol car at the curb and knew that on the hour they would knock on his door to collect him. He had to make his story sound colorful. Not dynamiting in the swamps – building bombs-- sounded better and that should get their attention. The Feds would go ape shit and make a big deal about the information. Maybe they'd stage a high visibility bust, and call Gator and Lewis Aryan Nation skinheads who were going to blow up banks because of the mortgage bust; whatever. Whatever got the evening news headlines. Whatever got him off the hook.

Kettering threw his empty at the trash, missed and grabbed another beer from the fridge. The television suddenly went to snow fuzz. Damn. He had been watching a rerun of *King's Retribution*. Not a bad show, he thought, and for a dishonest man like him, it provided insight regarding what to do if he ever went on the run. He enjoyed seeing how the bad guys got caught, and the mistakes they made. He'd yell at the screen about how dumb some of the wealthiest crooks were.

His favorite TV show focused on straight-laced business jerk-offs who had their hand in the till and then went on the run. Television had its educational moments. He could learn to be smarter, know where to hide and know how not to avoid their stupid errors. It was the same with the other cop shows. You could learn a lot about how not to get caught by educating yourself at someone else's expense; by being a couch slug. Like this one show about how they investigate homicides. Maybe like today's interview. Kettering mulled over his possible "tattle tale confession" and decided that if the cop in the interview room comes up and put his hand on his, and said for him to look into his heart and find God to do the right thing, then that would mean they're trying to do that bonding thing and make him slip up. He'd have to be careful with them.

Focus on Gator and the dynamite. The D.A. would give him a break for that, his attorney said, and cut him slack on the other charge. He should have been smarter and not put his meth lab in his garage where it smelled up the place. His sense of smell had been destroyed by meth chemicals. He should tell one of those television cop show producers that smells stinking up the neighborhood can trip you up. He heard tapping on glass. Someone was knocking at the back door. He stretched himself up, glanced into the kitchen, and saw some repair guy in uniform. Oh, yeah, the cable for the television. Must be down in the entire neighborhood.

Taking wobbly steps, he opened the door, and said to the repair man, "Fucking thing won't work. Can't see my shows."

"Yeah. We know. It's an area-wide outage but should have been fixed. This won't take a minute. I'll check your connection at the set and then to the house. Sorry for the inconvenience."

Kettering laughed, more about whom they were hiring these days. It was like those Ethiopian guys who drove the cabs and worked the corner convenience stores. It used to be Cubans, then Chinks moved in and now Sand Niggers. And this guy was strange; no doubt a foreigner. Even with his cable repair cap, you could that odd thing about him, see that his ear was missing.

Wondering if they give you a handicapped parking pass for having no ear, Kettering turned to point the way to the living room and was too slow to react when the needle plunged into his neck. A bee sting, but no pain, merely a surprise he could not speak of. He found he could not speak and all motion drained from his limbs. The repairman eased him down on the floor, saying, "Scimitar will not fail."

What's "scimitar?" "What's a 'scimitar'?" Kettering had no idea. And why couldn't he move?

He did have his vision still. His eyeballs rolled, bug-eyed in their sockets, staring and then trying to blink as the repairman pulled an explosives package from his work bag, put it on the floor next to the motionless man, and set a timer.

"You might as well be useful as a distraction," said Razzor Hassim.

Kettering noticed, too late, that the man was wearing gloves. He should have been more suspicious. He had never seen that on television. He could not move to save himself and watched as color maps and photographs were scattered around the living room. And after the repairman exited the back door, shutting it quietly as if being careful not to wake anyone, a funny thing happened: The television rebooted and regained its clarity. *King's Retribution* flared back on with fast sequences of a chase scene. Kettering realized he had seen that episode before and wanted to laugh, but a bright light erased his confused thoughts and ended his wicked life.

20.

March 2011 Santa Monica, California

Callie's first view of the War Room impressed her. Hugh Fox had leased half of the top floor office building at the corner of Third Street and Washington Avenue in Santa Monica.

Formerly offices for a stock brokerage firm, the layout held open workspace cubicles, surrounded by VIP glassed-in offices. Moving quickly, a dozen or so youth-hip worker bees were plugged into computers, clicking away. Doing what? Callie could only guess they were siphoning off data on the "enemy" and running the information through a filtering program, created most certainly by some Skilleo Game engineering nerd. Three of them hunched over their keyboards, staring into the screens, and looked like "exchange student" types. One woman worker wore a hajib head covering, and Callie assumed she could probably read Arabic script.

Callie observed this activity from the boardroom, where the principals had gathered for their first formal strategy meeting. J-Q acted as meeting secretary. As though it were a labor negotiation, Hugh and Samantha sat on one side of the table, and Storm and Callie at the other. J-Q was at one end of the table, and *Retribution's* muscle, Clayton Briggs, was at the other end.

King started things off with a basic question:

"Okay, where do we begin?" His voice was dismissive, like he would go along with this joke but just for a while.

Fox beamed, caught up in the project, and where the others sought common ground regarding what their purpose was, Fox exuded clarity.

"We start by excluding areas where bin Laden is not to be found. We are analyzing his most recent emails to give us direction. For example, heavy flooding occurred in Pakistan last summer. Bin Laden put out a softer-toned down video calling for a new Muslim relief agency to assist flood-victims. From that, can we infer that he is perhaps in or around Pakistan, versus anywhere else?"

Samantha offered her endorsement of the possibility.

"It sounds like what you might hear from a neighbor to his friends," she said. "Trying to be the good ol' boy politician showing concern for his constituency."

"It's just as likely," offered King, "that he's shaved his beard and is working on a tan at the Royal Savoy at Sharm El Sheikh." That was an Egyptian beach resort in the Sinai Peninsula.

The night before, King had confided to Callie that if they were going to go on a wild goose chase, it should be to a five-star hideout.

Fox ignored the apparent lack of confidence about his cause. Even he might have agreed that the task before them seemed daunting. "I can assure you," he said, "that the people we have working on bin Laden's biography and personal habits" – he motioned to the works stations beyond the conference room – "are united in consensus that bin Laden will always be a fanatic, that he has an image to uphold to his base, his fans, and that this requires him to be near the action; not on a working vacation."

"It would help," said Clayton Briggs, slurping at a power drink, two empty cans on the table before him, "if the government would give us a hand. I mean, we all are on the same team.

Let them send us a couple of James Bonds."

"Bond is English, and fictional, but nevertheless it's a worthy observation," agreed Fox.

This meeting was called as an organizational gathering, but Fox wanted just as much to delve more into the personalities he'd asked to assist. "In fact, I have made some overtures through my sources, and have been given an assurance that we can expect a 'volunteer' with expertise in the Middle East. But you cannot expect them to bless our project too openly."

"One would expect not," came King's dry comment, and everyone at the table understood who would take on the role of the Project's skeptic.

Samantha spoke up. She disliked formal meetings without agendas, and was noting that Hugh's corporate style was of a free-for-all bull session. She preferred chop-chop bullet point decisions. "I think we need to take the general topics of our research, each of us pick a specific subject, and then Hugh can assign a researcher to our ideas."

"Even 'bin Laden is dead' theories?" asked King.

"Even those." Fox turned his eyes to the other television star.

"What guesswork do you think we should concentrate on, Miss Cardoza? You've been very quiet."

Callie saw all eyes in the room fall upon her, and cast her own gaze back to Hugh Fox.

The intensity in his face made him almost glow. For the first time, she saw beyond his aura of public success and saw instead a young man asking a serious question. He was not pandering to her own fame, and was treating her neither better, nor less, but on equal terms, in accordance with her own value. Samantha Carlisle was a lucky woman to have him.

"Okay," she said. "We should accept that the government is constantly monitoring all communications. At their disposal, they have billions of dollars and technological resources we do not have. And that they are not going to share is a given. Still, they might be overwhelmed with too much information, and true clues may be missed. We therefore have as good a chance as anyone to find this murderer."

She brought them back to the truth – that this was not an adventurous lark, but a quest mystery to find a boasting killer. As they pondered that sobering fact, she continued.

"I would like to work on tracking down the bin Laden family. As one man, he could hide in his cave and never be found. But he is a family man, with multiple wives and many children.

With such a large, extended family, one of them is bound to make a slip, and with good luck, may even lead us directly to him."

Silence followed.

"Yes, I like that," said Samantha. "We know the spook agencies are run by alpha males.

Probably none of them thought of looking at the women around bin Laden."

Fox nodded approval, his attention on Callie. "Your suggestion, your investigation. Go for it. After the meeting, I'll pull in some people to build your team. Now, let's parcel up the jobs, assign staff, and in a week we'll see what proverbial sweet nuggets we shake loose from the date palms."

They talked for another half hour, taking on assignments. After the meeting broke up, Fox took them around to each of the cubicles and introduced the Hunt Team, as they called themselves, to all of his employees, brought in from his own company, and calling themselves the Discovery Team. Callie marveled at the expensive computer equipment Fox had at his disposal. The government's equipment was from the lowest bidder, where Fox apparently owned the latest, all of it top shelf. She started to look forward to seeing what systems and downloads he had amassed, and to use her own expertise in computer programming. It got her excited about starting her own research project: The bin Laden family tree. This could be fun escapism for a month or so, she considered, after all, she had nothing better to do, and did not relish making the public relations swings to play politics with next season's future, especially following in King's shadow.

Perhaps, though, the bin Laden "Hunt Team" should have addressed one further issue – that of secrecy. King himself was a man who usually said yes to any headline, all publicity being somehow favorable, but he would not have wanted the world to hear of this crazy project prematurely, before he could spin it to his benefit. He would keep his own counsel and say nothing overtly.

However, as the day wound down, someone at their work station, diseased with that social addiction of one who must say anything rather than nothing, tweeted to a friend:

@#sweetnewjob#CapturebinLadenhunt#Hunters-r-StormKing&HughFox#.

There are two universal truths: That the world is connected, and that there are no secrets in La La Land.

21.

March 2011 Miami

"You're from Homeland Security?"

They shook hands.

Wendell Holmes's cover story was only partly true. He handed his business card to the FBI agent, and at the same time showed a photo ID badge, ridiculous since the laminated photo revealed a much younger self, taken many years ago.

"We are called in from time to time to determine if any incidents reach the threshold of concerns for greater response, you know, with international implications," he said. "I show up, look around and write a report."

He did not say that he was on loan to Homeland Security from the CIA nor that he thought that with this recent assignment he had been relegated to the generic title of Field Inspector and banished to the hinterland.

"Well, the police called us in," said the young FBI agent Harry Curtis. "For about the same purpose. You know, explosives, and wondering if there is some sort of national conspiracy.

"Better safe, with more eyes on the ground, than horribly sorry."

"I agree."

Both men were staring at what was once the home of the late meth dealer Kettering. After the walls blew out, the structure had caught fire, even though the police sitting right outside the door. Their police car was heavily damaged, but they were still able to quickly direct the fire department to the scene, and most of the blaze damage had been contained.

"What is the police theory, and yours?" Holmes asked as he crossed the crime scene tape, making Curtis follow and wonder if this was acceptable protocol.

"A homemade bomb gone wrong. Police are going to raid a repair shop where they think the explosives are being stored. Today, in fact, if you want to tag along. So far, we have not officially been called in. Locals think it should stay local. Except for the materials found, we would have said yes."

Holmes stepped carefully through the blackened debris.

"And the kitchen here is blast center?"

"Not much left of Mr. Kettering."

"The police report said the bomb he was working on contained French-made plastique explosives."

"Yes, that's a little strange because Kettering was telling the locals that the explosives he had seen first-hand stored were boxes of dynamite."

"Think he was going more sophisticated?"

"Don't know. But you think a guy who could build a meth lab would be a little more careful when he's building an exotic bomb. They did find a few fragments of what we think is the timer mechanism. And oddly, pink paper bits, when pasted back together like a puzzle, you could visualize black scraggly lines like thunder bolts. We think it wrapped the explosives.

"We're checking with foreign manufacturers."

"On the timer, maybe he got a.m. mixed up with p.m." From the burned wood kitchen remnants, Holmes walked into a smoke- and water-soiled living room, taking quick looks into the bed-rooms. Police were good at finding the big clues, like a burned, fragmented body in the aftermath of an explosion. Holmes had a good cataloguing memory for what he saw, intuitive enough to absorb small details. Short of a photographic memory, he cap-tured brief observational moments with his iPhone for later review.

He didn't say it, but something seemed strange, off kilter. He wasn't sure what it was. Couldn't quite define it.

"Yes, I would like to be in on the raid. And you said you had those materials found in the house?"

He let Agent Curtis drive while he reviewed the file.

The raid was a bust, no dynamite, no bomb-making materials on the premises. Holmes surmised that many of the motorcycle parts in the shop were stolen, but the warrant narrowed the search scope to defined particulars and the U.S. Drug Enforce-ment Agency, with local Miami cops and their bomb squad and the SWAT unit on standby, called the shots as they rushed the building.

Holmes hung back from the proceedings, watching the shop owner and another employee glare at the invasive toss apart, each biker throwing nasty thoughts with acid-laser stares, grum-bling under their breaths and they weren't reciting poetry. Holmes saw a mind-set he knew well, – hatred from a class of people who kept alive feeding on soul-eating maggot anger. He hoped local cops would keep these guys on their radar. This type that might have already graduated from petty theft to higher classes of violence and mayhem. He felt they were primed to toss a Molotov cocktail for mindless new thrills.

Excitement rose from the good guys when the bomb-sniffing dog hit on a storage trailer and tugged at his leash and howled. Under a tarp on the floor, they found a trap door, and the DEA-Miami Police strike force thought they had scored. When it was opened, out came a small box of fireworks, pop bottle rockets and sparkling cone fountains. Holmes saw a curled smile on the repair shop owner's face, a small twinge of gotcha; them vs. the cops, and *them* won this round. To the CIA agent, with his years observing human nature, he saw the shop owner basically admit, without words, that there was more to what went on today. Holmes filed away everything he saw.

FBI Agent Curtis joined him, and they watched the DEA and the SWAT teams pack it in and leave.

"You have an opinion?" asked Curtis.

"More curiosity than theory."

"Think Kettering wanted to be another Timothy McVey?" McVey was the Oklahoma City bomber and mass murderer of hundreds of innocents, executed as an American-grown terrorist.

The file folder that Holmes reviewed on the drive over contained partially burned photographs of a Miami building, and maps associated with its location.

The David W. Dyer Federal Building and U.S. Courthouse

"Possibly. Looks like he picked out a target."

"Local police say Kettering and this Gator and all his cronies are very anti-government.

But search warrants on their homes turned up nothing. So far the police see this as a one-man show, prematurely cancelled."

"Keep digging, if your office can. I have strange vibes about this one. Maybe it's too much incoming, unfiltered data on this old brain of mine. Take the photos, for example. The ones you recovered. If this was to be a planned attack, planting a bomb, you think there would be more of a surveillance of the building. The shots in these photos are only of the front, basically taken, as it seems, by someone taking snapshots from his car while driving by, not side shots or rear views of the building."

"Maybe they burned up in the fire."

"Maybe. Another observation. Unless he had just developed the photos, there are no pin marks, no thumbtack holes on any of the corners. Again, if he was going to be a diligent planner, you'd think he would have put the photos on a wall, created a storyboard of his attack plans, and it wouldn't be in his kitchen. More likely a bedroom."

"There was nothing like that."

"Something else is odd. It was just the bomb? No other bomb-making materials?"

"The police detectives told me that none were found here. You think it might have been made elsewhere and delivered to him to hide, but he started fiddling with it, or shook it wrong, and ker-plooie!?"

"That's as good a scenario as any. But... what started all this was him being arrested for the meth lab in his garage, which Miami police hauled off. You'd think they might have discovered any other unusual equipment, not for meth but for bomb making. And why build a bomb at all with the police sitting outside your house?"

"Maybe meth fried his brain. I'll check with the locals and their evidence lockers and see if bomb makings components were mixed in with the meth equipment."

"Please do. But what brought me here in the first place are the French origin of the explosives. The make-up is just too exotic for a meth-head." Holmes filed away all this information to be reconstituted later in his official summary report. He saw nothing for Homeland Security or CIA interest, no clue towards a foreign power that was now in league with biker gangs.

His cell phone played the James Bond theme.

"You gotta be kidding!" Curtis laughed.

"An early-retirement indulgence." He answered, listened, and then hung up.

"New assignment. California and right away, so I can't hang around and snoop. Please keep me in the loop on this. It just doesn't feel right."

On the ride back to pick up his rental, he mused on his bringing up the subject of retirement to the Fibber. He was nearing the end of his career, and Holmes had no idea what he would do after he received his symbolic gold watch. He wasn't even that old; had his teeth, his hair, and could get it up whenever candlelight and soft music set the mood, though he had for stimulus backup a prescription for blue 'energy' pills. As to the unknown tomorrows, he hadn't made any plans and had hardly even contemplated any. Always on the go, even though his more recent assignments smelled more of paper pushing bureaucracy than of hot gunpowder and saving wayward damsels. He had no vocations, and the only hobby if you counted it, was an occasional short story he might write during field down time, a release to let his mind wander into imaginary worlds. At his apartment a large box in a closet held his scribblings, gathering dust, dismissed the minute they were created.

He had no idea what he would do when he was out on the street, and that scared him more than facing armed mobs. For the final countdown months until his retirement, they, the unknown powers above, let him work out of his one-bedroom condo in Alexandria, Virginia. The scuttlebutt was that they did not want him office-based at Langley. They gave him the title of Field Inspector and loaned him off to Homeland Security, where his assignment was to travel the U.S. and do follow-up reports on local law enforcement cases that might garner CIA interest. If one was flagged as "threat potential," then of course the investigation would be transferred to other agents. Holmes accepted the direction, kept his face to the work ahead, fearful about his pending retirement, and diligently filed his reports. The report to Homeland on the self-bombing in Miami, copied to the CIA computers, would be classified "no further investigation warranted." Let the locals do their job. Still, it was a curious death.

His mind shifted to tonight's expected phone briefing from Langley. He had no idea why they needed him in California. Another police investigation? Maybe, he pondered, they found a backwater assignment to park him for a few months until they kicked him out.

22.

Late March Camp Pendleton, California

"Go! Go!" The shouted words blared into his headset, and he and the rest of his squad team repelled from both sides of the hovering helicopter into the darkness of the night. Rotor wash kicked up plumes of dust and dried out their mouths with the taste of dirt. The others carried light loads, as the intervention attack force, but Pacheco and his partner bore the heavy weight of explosive charges. Pacheco's gloved hands heated up as he carried himself with a rush to the ground. After hitting with a bouncing thud, he was off and running towards the gates. They had been rebuilt since the last practice run.

Shawn Pacheco, lately of the war zone in Afghanistan, had been, he would later say, "thrown" across the globe to unite with his new teammates of SEAL Team Six, located temporarily at Camp Pendleton, north of San Diego and west of Fallbrook in a giant training reserve used primarily for the Marines. His transfer paperwork said his placement fell under the Naval Special Warfare Development Group ("NEVGRU") of the Joint Special Operations Command.

He had definitely felt the jet lag when he reached the base camp a week earlier. Since then there had been two night operations of helicopters rushing over hills, barely scraping the coastal sage. His tasks were defined with precision. He and his partner, a SEAL operator named Marco Vitali, rushed the gate, set the charges, moved to cover, and detonated the satchel charge.

Vitali returned to the helicopter, taking up a security perimeter, while Pacheco would speed around the walled building area, something the old men of multiple Iraq tours called a "middle class *al-qasr* [castle]." His secondary job was to be prepared, if called upon, to throw another charge against the gate on the other side of the target al-qasr. And he was to keep his eyes open and prevent any escapes from the buildings.

Tonight, he had heard, this would be the last exercise at this location, with a planned deployment – again, a rumor – to Afghanistan. Pacheco had the smarts to realize the mission meant an extraction; attacking this building that was definitely highly fortified, and extract a person or persons. The SEALs had a history of this type of operation. The most recent and notable was in the Indian Ocean in 2009 when SEAL snipers took out, at a range of 75 yards from a rolling ship, two pirate kidnappers of hostage Captain Phillips.

Failed operations do not receive the same media notice, but nevertheless became teaching tools, as tragic as they might be – especially when errors are made by members of a SEAL Team.

In October 2010, SEAL Team Six made an early morning raid on a mountain Taliban hideout to rescue a Scottish aid worker held prisoner. In the midst of the raid, as kidnappers were being killed, a fragmentation grenade thrown by a SEAL mortally wounded the woman hostage. The exploding grenade had not been necessary, and, worse, the SEAL initially denied using it, the first report blaming a suicide vest. It was all caught on helmet cameras – the truth came out and the sailor was disciplined leaving the team's morale in a bad funk. Pacheco, accepting his outsider status, felt the underlying current when he was in casual B.S. chatter. He noticed a consensus that most of those he was now working with hoped that this new mission, whatever it was, would vindicate them for their mistaken killing of an inno-cent woman. Thinking about the death of Montoya, Shawn Pacheco agreed with that word: "vindication." It sounded nobler than "retaliation," but not by much.

To Pacheco, several factors gave weight to the importance of the upcoming operation.

The best clue: the civilians involved. Pacheco did not talk to any of them, but by their silent presence and whispering actions, these people definitely were not acting like they were under the direction of the military. To the contrary, the civilians were providing intelligence on who and what was to be attacked. Shawn knew they were handlers from the Central Intelligence Agency.

The planned attack created its own curiosity. After the as-saulting force neutralized the opposition, one team would be deployed to handle prisoners, suggesting that a great number of people might be detained. A third SEAL group would consist of the CIA with its own 3-member team, those bearing only side arms – yet as he viewed them, in these ops exercises, they came running in with empty duffel bags, even a box of heavy-duty garbage bags. So, he thought, it was to be a rescue and then picking up and bagging...what?

And not to forget the military dog trained not to bark in the middle of the night, even with the simulated weapon fire popping up to garner realism. A dog in its own Kevlar to do what? For control, tracking? If a sniffer, nosing around, to uncover...what? Digging a Taliban Saddam Hussein out of his hidey-hole? Shawn Pacheco reached his conclusion – something big was coming down.

A flare went off into the night sky, and at the same time a voice came into his ear: "Stand down. Return to breaching point." He heard the reduction of the helicopter rotor noise. It was mission assessment time and he hustled to join his comrades near the gate that he and Vitali had, moments earlier, surgically removed.

In their post-op briefing, where they gave assessments of this commando course of action (COA), the commander field judges said that everyone hit their tasked goals. Minor criticisms were heard, but there was no bawling out of any member like at boot camp. SEALS knew what to do. Mistakes, as he well knew, were deadly. Give me the job and it will get done. The only thing of bother was timing, they said. We need to bring down the in-and-out to less than an hour, and we can't achieve this with a lean-to facsimile. You will soon be joining other members of this special force, and all of you will train on a realistic mock-up. Within the next few days. Be prepared to ship out tomorrow. Regulated good-byes only.

He knew what that meant. When he was in Afghanistan, the higher-ups monitored his email to Janet. "Being deployed on mission. Will be unable to communicate for some time. Will talk to you as soon as I can. Love, Shawn." He wanted to say more, longed to see her, to hold her and seek her comfort. The emptiness from Montoya's death still hovered in his mind as a curse.

He hoped someday she would understand this turmoil, and believe in him, as he was unable to do for himself.

Episode 4

America is a great power possessed of tremendous military might and a wide-ranging economy, but all this is built on an unstable foundation which can be targeted, with special attention to its obvious weak spots. If America is hit in one hundredth of these weak spots, God willing, it will stumble, wither away and relinquish world leadership.
--Osama bin Laden

23.

Late March 2011 Los Angeles

SnoopOnline, the media gossip consolidator for the tabloids, broke the story in the early morning hours and it was immediately picked up by all the interbred tattler sheets. The news went viral before noon, with the bloggers disseminating their opinions. It received its final blessing of "validity" from the television networks in the evening news hour.

In those brief, attention-grabbing television seconds, the public heard this:

TV Show to Hunt Bin Laden

The popular television reality show "King's Retribution," which tracks down and captures criminals, will next focus its attention on trying to discover the whereabouts of international terrorist Osama bin Laden, and bringing him to justice.

Retribution's star, retired Army Colonel David 'Storm' King, said, "We have a successful track record focusing on criminals from the U.S. Who says we can't go after evil wherever it is to be found? As I see it, bin Laden is top of the list as the world's most diabolical murderer."

A theorem about publicity says that any public notice designed to be positive will garner an untold number of dispelling negatives.

Reeling from media inquisition about the leaked information, Callie and Storm discovered that the publicity onslaught's downside was ridicule. Talk show comedians skewed the news with jokes of capturing bin Laden but having to do so between commercial breaks; and comedians said that instead of torturing bin Laden by waterboarding, the same effect could be achieved by forcing him to watch American television reruns of "The Bachelor" or locking him in a cell where he had to listen to "Achy Breaky Heart" and "The Macarena."

News pundits criticized what they called the crassness of Tinsel Town making a game out of capturing a mass killer, and said that the true hunt should be left to government experts.

Ensconced in its cubicles, the Discovery Team found itself inundated with well intentioned (or not) citizens calling to offer their insights as to under which rock bin Laden had hidden his miserable self. Much of the information seemed miraculous in origin, whether by tarot cards, Ouija board, or dartboard guesses. Email at the *King's Retribution* fan site crashed, and a phone tip line put callers on perpetual hold.

Good news, though, was still good news, it seemed. That was the take from Hugh Fox, and in presiding over one of the group's "sessions of progress," handed a fax to King who read it and announced, with a growing smile, "The network has renewed us for a third season, providing we launch the new season with our bin Laden hunt. Briggs, go and notify the rest of the crew. I'll work with the PR department later for a public news release."

Storm King accepted that hunting the terrorist and the resulting television show – with or without a capture – would drive viewers to the season's premiere, and ratings should soar. And in the process, King believed he would become an even more recognized personage, a face for the magazine covers, the go-to expert for the court session talk shows. He decided to text his agent about sniffing out possible action movie roles, especially with Schwarzenegger on the outs.

King could see himself as a Harrison Ford or Sean Connery, though younger and on the cusp of being a strong, maturing character. To King's current way of thinking, capturing bin Laden was secondary to staging the process and managing the perception. If they came back empty-handed, as he expected, the show could be focused with al Qaeda history as backstory, and then a stock footage travelogue to the Middle East. Any search sequence could be televised with dramatic license – quick shots in and among empty buildings, dark alleys, maybe a cave or two.

The idea proposed by this small news story – that someone, government or a private resource like the *King's Retribution* might capture Osama bin Laden and return him to the United States for trial – resonated throughout the country with various results.

The Northern California Attorneys' Association and the Law Club at the University of California at Berkeley jointly announced a mock trial, which would be held to try Osama bin Laden 'for crimes against humanity'. The subtext from the liberal-leaning hosts was a question of whether he could ever get a fair trial under American jurisprudence? They extended an invitation for King to act as an actor-witness in the script, as if he had already captured bin Laden.

Publicity like this could not be declined, and King accepted, inviting everyone on the Hunt Team to accompany him, including Callie, Hugh Fox, and Samantha Carlisle. King would bask in the glory of a hero yet crowned.

24.

Late March   Battleford, Georgia

Samuel Tate, pastor of the Church of True Believers, held his rural congregation of fifty parishioners in thrall. They saw their God as the only God, and believed the Bible was the only word from God, not open to interpretation – except by Pastor Tate. When the topic would arise, he preached against the presence of Anti-Christ bin Laden as a prisoner on American soil, which must be condemned as blasphemous. A show trial, he preached, even one that was a pretense, would draw too much attention to the Devil and his accursed followers. Pastor Tate conveniently fainted and revived with the revelation that he alone must bring the message to the masses: Only those who joined the Church of True Believers would enter heaven; and there was no place in such celestial for those who did not believe in God or the crucifixion and arising of Jesus Christ, as extolled through Pastor Tate's teachings.

Jubilant with the Holy Spirit for having given him these thoughts, Pastor Tate asked his travel agent to book him a flight to San Francisco so he could attend the staged legal trial of Osama bin Laden. Then he called his publicist and told him to put out a press release saying that Pastor Samuel Tate would appear at UC Berkeley, birth site of the Free Speech Movement in the '60s, to announce before the cameras, and thus the world, that he would burn a Koran in protest.

When the press release hit the Arabic-language television news network known as *al Jazeera*, stating that an infidel would burn a Qur'an, the book holding the religious treatises of Islam, a mob rioted in Algeria and three people were killed. At an ethnic newsstand in Chicago upon reading about Pastor Tate's one-man book burning, Razzor Hassim told himself that somebody should stop anyone who might attempt to desecrate the holy words, words from God himself that were told to Muhammad through the archangel Gabriel.

Hassim had an appointment to meet *The Professor* in Los Angeles. It would be no inconvenience that he could take a detour and travel by way of San Francisco and observe this sacrilege that sought to condemn his spiritual leader.

Americans were crazy for stunts, he thought, and it was so ridiculous; no one would ever catch Osama bin Laden. The al-Qaeda Supreme Council and the Emir were inviolate. And by dedicated association, wrapped in the same cause of imparting political retaliation, Hassim considered himself equally invincible. And he would act as a tool of Allah's to smite evil.

25.

End of March 2011 The White House

The President of the United States glanced through the updated memo entitled "Anatomy of a Lead," which had been prepared by the deputy chief of the Pakistan-Afghanistan Department of the CIA.

"Do you think bin Laden is at this house in Abbottabad? Says here it's a few hundred yards from Pakistan's West Point military academy. You got to be kidding!"

"Perhaps it's a protective shield for whoever is at that location. As you have been briefed, much of their Intelligence Agency is compromised with fundamentalists," replied the CIA Director. "If bin Laden is there, it's certain he is under someone's protective umbrella. If we go forward, we can't let the Pakistani government get wind of any planned operation, or it will for certain filter down the chain of command. It's happened before. As to our 'Lead' report, it has been constantly upgraded with new data, and though on-the-ground surveillance has no confirmation of who's in that compound, as you might have read, it's my staff's firm opinion that it is an al-Qaeda sanctuary for some high value target. The prime choices are down to bin Laden or al Zawahiri. Either one, and we must take action."

"If we have confirmation of the target, especially if it's 'Geronimo,' a drone missile would be the safest response," came the answer from the Chairman of the Joint Chiefs.

"We've been through this before," stated the CIA Director. "We have to capture the son-of- a-bitch. Bits and pieces of body parts won't satisfy the public or the press, I might add."

Yes, I concur," said the President. "Where are we in initiating an operation?"

"Per your last instructions, our SEAL Team Six and my field personnel have been in training on the East and West coasts, and as we speak they are being brought together and sent over to Bagram for final assault practice on a replica of the compound."

"Timing?"

"If nothing changes within the target location, our strike force will be ready by mid-May.

With the latest and final intelligence assessment we can give you a window for a final decision."

"Okay. Apprise me of any new details. Trying to move troops out of Iraq and Afghanistan is a balancing act as it is. Ending up like Carter's failure at rescuing the Tehran embassy hostages is not an option."

"I agree, Mr. President. This operation is designed to be surgical, swift, clean. In-out."

"It had better be. And what's this I hear, and Michelle has to tell me, about some television cop show going after bin Laden?"

"Hot air, Mr. President. Headline seekers."

"We don't need any interference that could tip our hand as to how close we might finally be."

"Yes, and in that vein, I have made sure that we have someone in the field who can keep a lid, if need be, on any cowboy antics."

"Good," said the President, and he opened another briefing folder to another world crises needing to be dealt with.

If required, those *King's Retribution* yokels would be misdirected, the CIA Director said to himself. He understood the wall of plausible deniability he had to create for the President; not that this was at any level of national security.

He had agreed with Assistant Deputy Givens that putting soon-to-retire agent Wendell Holmes out among the Hollywood nuts was a perfect "kick-out-the-door" assignment. Holmes could be a thorn, so the farther away he was, the better. The Director of the CIA could recall in his own experience that back in 1998, after he had left the White House as Clinton's Chief of Staff but remained as one of Clinton's private brain trust advisors, the name Wendell Holmes had surfaced in what became known as *Operation Infinite Reach*. It was a memory not pleasing to the Clinton White House, the Director distinctly remembered.

26.

August 20, 1998 Khartoum, North Sudan

As they had approached the factory, the two men in flowing black robes hugged the buildings, obscured by the night's deepest shadows. Both men, with their white skin, would be out of place at any time of the day, so their faces were wrapped in cloth with eyes peering from slits, each man burdened with a backpack.

At the warehouse door, one of them began jimmying an archaic lock. Within 15 seconds it clicked, and the door opened with a creaking squeak. They froze. From an earlier reconnaissance, they knew a night watchman walked through the building at odd hours. The two men eased in, skirting piles of boxes marked in Arabic: "Urgent: Medical Supplies."

The name on the building said *Al-Shifa*, the Arabic word for 'healing.'

At the CIA, early data-gathering suggested this pharmaceutical plant might not be making medicine, but processing the deadly nerve agent VX, the ingredient that would, in later years, be known as a primary component for WMD, weapons of mass destruction.

The two men went to their separate tasks. The younger agent crept over to what looked like waste disposal barrels and began scraping refuse into a test tube vial. Then he quickly scrambled to another part of the warehouse, near the rolling assembly line of boxing products.

He crawled under the conveyor system and gathered caking samples of dried sludge.

Wendell Holmes, the older agent by seven years, had set himself the task of seeking out the small testing laboratory. He threw his robe over some cabinets, and under the cloth covering he snapped flash photos of the bottles and labels with an old Pentax camera. He took a selective sampling of bottles from dispensary shelves and off the quality control tables, examined the Arabic-language labels, and placed bottles in his backpack, in specially segmented Styrofoam pockets to protect them from breaking.

When he rejoined his associate, he found him between boxes running litmus test strips on his gathered vials. He was using an

eye-dropper to add saline solution, and then checking the chemically altered strips against a color chart.

"I found it," whispered the younger man, excited. "EMPTA, for
sure." It was the chemical base used in the VX nerve agent.

"Where did you find it? Maybe we can find some bottles to
confirm."

Glancing at the vial in question, the young man shrugged.

"This came from the soil sample I pulled from outside."

"Outside?" Holmes's voice was hoarse with incredulity. "Not in
the plant?"

Near the street, but it must be tied to this building."

You think so? In a busy industrial section of Khartoum? All I
found were medicine bottles, all labeled properly, with shipping
manifests going out to hospitals and clinics in this country.
Nothing being shipped to Iraq."

"Well, I called it in when I had a positive sample." With a
snobby attitude, the younger agent pointed to his sat phone.

"You did what?" Holmes bristled and his voice rose above a
whisper to exasperated shock.

"The strike. We have enough. That terrorist, what's his name,
Osama whatever, we've been told he's the financial angel behind
this factory."

Holmes knew that the Agency had made this a major push for
clarification; they were seeking some "retaliation" target for recent
embassy bombings in Africa, those taking responsibility being a
new Islamic terrorist group called al-Qaeda or al-Qaida. The
Clinton Administration wanted to show the world that no one
escaped this superpower's wrath; that they could retaliate with
an "infinite reach."

But this clandestine incursion had been to gain evidence,
nothing more, and had now been compromised and pointed
toward a deadly conclusion. Holmes regretted he had been stuck
with such a high-strung newbie.

"Ronnie, you idiot! Didn't you read the rough intel? The man's
name is Osama bin Laden, and that was someone's guess. It's
unverified! Shit! How much time do we have?"

"They acknowledged immediate launch. We should get going."
The young man spoke nervously. Suddenly, playing Secret Agent
had become a little tenuous, because a cruise missile had been
called in on his location, on his head – by him.

Regardless of his partner's stupidity, Holmes agreed it was time to hustle.

But then a flashlight shone in the young man's face, and they heard a startled, Arabic voice. Holmes, off to the side, launched a fist and knocked the watchman, senseless, to the ground. Taking advantage of his partner's quick response, the younger man ran as fast as he could toward the door they had first entered. Holmes shook his head to realize that the boy's style of bravery meant 'save self first.' He bent down and slung the watchman over his shoulder, balancing the backpack on his other shoulder. Then he, too, moved as quickly as he could. Move ass and avoid the incoming, he thought.

Exiting onto the roadway, he crossed the street and lowered the factory worker to the ground. He could see his fellow agent leaning against a building a block away. Suddenly, the watchman jumped to his feet and tore back across the street, yelling as loud as he could, "Thieves!"

In Arabic, Holmes shouted a warning that made no sense: "Bombs are falling." The watchman did not understand, or else did not hear. Familiar only with his job's routine, he ran back into the factory, seeking a phone to call the authorities.

Holmes walked down the street. In disgust, he watched his partner retch out his fear.

"You asshole! Did you really have to start an international incident based only on one glob of dirt?"

Agent Ronnie Givens gave no reply. Night turned to day and the Al-Shifa Pharmaceutical Plant, and its dutiful watchman, ceased to exist in an explosion of fire and rubble.

27.

1998 to 1999 Washington, D.C.

Holmes filed the internal CIA field report, and he minced no words. The destruction of the pharmaceutical plant and the killing of a factory employee had been initiated by a premature analysis of one only soil sample taken from outside the plant, not within the building as requested.

Though Givens was named in the report, Holmes did not specifically draw attention to the ineptitude of the sampling conclusions. The implication of who was at fault was clear, leaving Holmes with an enemy for life.

At that time, and in announcing the single missile attack in Sudan, the Clinton government cited the following evidence as justifying its actions: (1) Contact between plant officials and Iraqi chemical weapons experts, who were thought to be using the EMPTA ingredient in their VX production. (2) Ties between the al-Shifa plant and the Islamist al-Qaeda group of Osama bin Laden, which was believed to be behind various bomb attacks on African embassies.

A report written in 1999 by the U.S. State Department Bureau of Intelligence and Research questioned the attack on the factory, suggesting the evidence offered was "weak." Bin Laden, who had been a resident in Khartoum in the 1980s, had left Sudan by 1996.

The connection with Iraq turned out to be a $199,000 order for veterinary medicines. One critic of the attack questioned: "What was the hurry to bomb? The factory could not be folded up like a tent and spirited away. The U.S. had diplomatic relations with Sudan.... Perhaps instead someone [the inference meant Clinton] needed to look 'Presidential.'

The Clinton Administration sought to distance itself from the intra-agency turmoil generated by Holmes's known "report of doubt." In 2000, Holmes found himself "reassigned," as they say, to the embassy staff in Outer Mongolia. Supporting Holmes and his report was an in-house CIA analyst who also voiced doubts, and who had questioned the evidence requiring a bombing response even before the power to launch a strike had been given to Ronald Givens. In 2006, that analyst was fired based on her outspoken opinion. Not wishing to admit to faulty intelligence, or even more insidious, a Wag the Dog fabrication, the CIA Boy's Club closed ranks to silence and denial. And the benefactor? Ronald Givens was promoted; it was the first of many upward moves.

In 2001, the al-Shifa plant owner sued the United States for more than $50 million, the owner saying he had explicit records of what the factory had actually produced and that it was medicine, not chemical weapons. He demanded a formal apology from the United States. The Sudanese government continued to keep the factory "as is," in its destroyed condition, indefinitely, asking the U.S. to come in, investigate and prove its case. The U.S. government never responded.

As in many international incidents, the side stories were lost in the shuffle to what seemed more important on the world stage. One result had far-reaching consequences no one at the time noted. The medicines destroyed at the al-Shifa pharmaceutical plant never made it to the people in the countryside, and after 1998, an increasing number of sick Sudanese citizens died for want of treatment. Many of those who survived bore a hatred for the most powerful country in the world, and in seeking justice, some turned to al-Qaeda, which was thereafter funded in part by wealthy Sudanese, which in a turn, was one of al-Qaeda's monetary contribution sources that led to 9/11/2001.

Holmes thereafter believed there was a correlation, a thin thread binding al-Shifa and the Twin Towers; and wondered whether Ronald Givens ever understood his small action was the catalyst, that he, the spark, to the international powder keg, of why all things are in such a rotten mess today.

28.

First week of April, 2011 Santa Monica, California

In hindsight, Hugh Fox didn't exactly know why he decided to drop by the War Room at around 11 p.m., instead of going back to his hotel suite. It was one of those fortuitous events that moves a person along a different current in the stream.

He had finished up a late night dinner at the French-American restaurant *Melisse* on Wilshire Boulevard, sitting at a private table with a small group of venture capitalists and film producers who were going home pretty well zonked on assorted Napa reds. Earlier in the evening, they had been at their best doing their "Luv ya, baby" pitch to him. What they sought were the film rights to one of his most successful video games in the Skilleo Games catalogue, *Galaxy Slaughter*.

At this point in the industry, most comic superhero characters were already optioned out, with films in production or already released and seeking theatergoer buzz, and fingers crossed for a surge of interest that would guarantee a sequel and a branding franchise of recurring royalties. The new idea pickings had been slim at Comic-Con the previous year, and the studio money seemed to be moving back into video game themes, even old board games like 'Battleship'.

What impressed the moneymen and the mini moguls was that Skilleo didn't just create a game but it also patented the "art of game play," developed around the patents' innovative methods to attract player interaction. Where Pixar had triumphed with digital clarity in the cartoon format, Skilleo held the edge in gamesmanship technology. 3-D, as example, seemed to be reaching a peak in movie ticket sales; initial curiosity had leveled off since viewers had come to expect only jump-out-of-the-screen action. 3D advancement created a niche audience to be drawn into the experience. Skilleo, out of their labs, had a large, prototype IMAX-size movie screen in a theater where moviegoers could sit with high-intensity, spectral beam "guns," and at the appointed sequence cue, could join the hero and blast away at the flesh-eating, bloodsucking, inter-galactic androids with actual screen response from the shooter's weapon. Aim, fire, bad critter evaporated. It was incredible; another leap for the entertainment of mankind and also for Skilleo. The checkbooks were open and Fox was asked to fill in the amount. He left them drooling, and hanging out to dry, without an immediate answer.

His restive spirit had brought him here to his current, hands-on project. In the silent, dark War Room, Fox saw a single globe of light within one of the cubicles and walked over to find Callie Cardoza punching away at a computer keyboard. Her black hair pulled back into a casual bun, she was engrossed in the display screen and oblivious to his arrival.

"Late night?"

Whoa!" She jumped at his voice.

"Sorry. I wanted to see who was putting in overtime. Should have guessed it was one of the boss ladies, and not any worker bee."

"Hardly a boss," said Callie, turning to watch him take a chair next to her. "And speaking of which, where is the boss lady, Ms. Carlisle?"

"She's in New York for some sort of Fashion Week. And your Colonel King?"

"He's certainly not 'mine.' We are, how would they say, 'close acquaintances.' Working at close quarters on a set can do that to you."

They looked at each other during an awkward silence, both perhaps realizing that, oddly, they had each qualified where their significant other was as a prelude to conversation.

"And what are you working on?" Hugh asked. Her body seemed to emote the fervor of the hunt he had sought to impress on his staff and cohorts.

"Bin Laden's family tree." She turned her screen so he could see a diagram of multiple lines listing family relationships. She scrolled down several pages. "Over 600 *closely-related* family members."

"Amazing. I guess if he were Christian, the Christmas card mailing list would bankrupt him."

"Naw, he could afford it. His family's company, Saudi Bin-Laden Group, is one of the largest construction firms in the Islamic world, with offices internationally. They gross about US $5 billion annually."

"The Saudi rich boy has time on his hands, so why not a little terrorism for fun?"

"Interesting, he's not a pure Saudi. His grandfather was a tribesman from Yemen and his father was born in Yemen and then settled in Saudi Arabia before World War II. He started a small construction company that blossomed when he came to the notice of and fell under the benefice of the Saud family."

"As in King Saud of Saudi Arabia?"

"The same, but still confusing. To track the bin Laden progeny, I have had to break it into groupings based on the wives' nationalities: Saudi, Syrian, Lebanese, Egyptian. Osama is one of 25 children of his father, Muhammed bin Laden, by his tenth wife. So I categorized our buddy into the Syrian group."

"That's quite a lot of due diligence to go searching through every single name and background."

"Agreed. So we have to do some assumptions that a computer program filtering system might not have the capabilities to run."

"My engineers could certainly create anything you required."

"Sorry, but they could never duplicate the old stand-by 'women's intuition.'"

"Indeed, I hear it's a mystery of the centuries, if not eons." Their smiles met. "So, how do your female hunches beat out a Cray or an IBM supercomputer?"

"Think as a man might, then out-think him."

"Now I'm worried."

"Seriously, bin Laden has five wives and about 22 known children, 18 of the children surviving. He looks to the children as his legacy, but when it comes to his personal needs – and certainly all men, including priests, have some form of libido – I am going to make the nonscientific assumption that he wants warmth and comfort from his latest wives, from his wife Siham Sabar, and his last wife, Amal al-Sadah, a.k.a. Amal Ahmed Abdul Fatah."

"There seems to be sense to that reasoning. But I never could understand, regardless of culture, how a man could handle more than one woman."

"You are a wise man."

"Though maintaining a short-term harem might have its merits."

"Ah, a typical male response, but a surprise from you. I thought for kinky needs you would merely create digital avatar groupies and then program them to whisper sweet algorithms."

Fox accepted that this ex-cop had smarts and he enjoyed her sharp-witted personality, but this banter had drifted toward flirty. It wasn't a bad feeling, but unsettling. He did have a girlfriend of sorts, or at least a bed partner.

"So how does Mr. bin Laden getting his rocks off with Wife 5 help us?"

Safely back on track.

"It is not so much bin Laden's proclivity, as it is learning the character of his latest wife, Amal Ahmed Abdul Fatah. We know they married when she was 17 years old, and that she came from Yemen as a gift from a powerful Yemeni family. What I read is that it was an arranged marriage to strengthen bin Laden's ties back to his ancestral home country. So, like a mail-order bride she was taken out of her comfort zone, and her husband has her tucked away somewhere.

"Maybe with him, maybe alone. She and Osama have had children, all young still, so they are with her.

"I'm betting she has pangs of homesickness, missing old friends and family. Actual members of his direct family, the older wives and children, know he's in hiding, and they know not to contact him, and he will contact them only in an emergency. But it's *her* family I want to concentrate on – to discover if they have made any unusual trips out of their homeland, and where to. That may be the lead we need.

"And there is one other element that might be the catalyst."

"And that is?"

"At 29, she's the youngest wife. There could be a jealousy factor among the older wives causing marriage dissension, or she could just be bored hiding out with him, thus cranky. Or if not, anxious to be with him, thus horny. I'm counting on one of these elements of disharmony to be the key to identifying his location."

She leaned back and sighed, looking to him for a confirmation of her train of thought. At this point, if she were in a discussion with Storm, he would have found something wrong with her concept. He was unable to offer any form of compliment.

But Hugh mulled over the machinations to her logic.

"It's a theorem to be proved, but strong on the equation. Yes, I like it, but how are you going to track her family?"

"Well, I've already been able to pull her tribal records, and I found passports issued to five family members: two uncles, an aunt, and two of her sisters."

"Passports? How?"

"There is the Europol database, which tags passports from countries that are defined as 'hotspots.' I'm sure the CIA and the U.S. State Department through Homeland Security have something similar."

He straightened up, alert.

"What? You hacked into the International Police database? Callie, that could have ramifications. That could backfire on us!"

She caught the fact he called her by her first name. It was a first, even if it was in agitation.

"No worries, I think."

"You think? Please don't stress me out."

"I went back into my old job's computer at the San Diego Police Department. When the latest system upgrade happened, I was there and left a few back doors open, so any request to Europol would come from the Police Department email box, and into a blind account I could access. And all I asked Europol to do is put us into an alert system on this group of family members, and when they are on the move across international borders."

"Telling them what? A reality TV show wanted to be kept informed?"

"I built a story about several Arab family members being sought for forced female genital mutilation of a girl under 15 years of age. Given most of their computer data input clerks are probably women I believe my request will gain some priority, perhaps some internal eyes on my targets."

"I am impressed." And he was, paying her a little more attention and wondering more about her.

"I am also impressed," came a gravel voice from the blackness. Hugh and Callie jumped and she grabbed Hugh's hand.

A man came out of the darkness like a ghost forming in the shallow light. He was an older man, maybe late forties; what made him look old were touches of grey to his sideburns and leathered wrinkles to a craggy, outdoors face.

"I don't mean to interrupt, but the door downstairs was open and the office door was unlocked."

"Unlocked? I don't think so." Hugh felt Callie release his hand and saw her hand inch towards the large purse at the side of her computer. It was a reactive response from an ex-cop, but not a good ending for someone else and Hugh found himself sandwiched between both.

"Unlocked," said the man, his statement firm and unyielding.

"And what can I do for you this late at night?" Fox sought to diffuse the situation, warily eyeing Callie as she pulled the purse to her side and snapped it open.

"Mr. Fox, I presume? My name is Wendell Holmes. I have been assigned to your group, team or whatever you're calling your operation, as a 'Field Tour Guide.'"

"Assigned by whom?" Fox relaxed only slightly. He did not presume that this was a mugging, an irate fan or anything more sinister, because the man had come into the full light of the desk with his hands to his side, empty, his palms strangely turned outward. Hugh put his hand gently on top of Callie's as her fingers were edging into the depths of the purse. Her eyes were focused on the man, gauging his distance, his bulk and target points.

"If you recall, you had your public relations and your lobbyists seek experts who might be able to help if and when you left the U.S. on your search. I am the one selected to be your, as we are calling my position, field guide." The man called Holmes snickered with humor at his own title.

"What makes you an expert to be guiding us?" Callie voiced direct suspicion. She was always cautious when she worked alone at night in an office complex. She knew both doors were locked, and there was no way Hugh Fox would have left them unlocked on his entry. B&E, breaking and entering, were not bona fide credentials they required as they pursued their bin Laden caper.

Wendell Holmes gave them a disarming smile, knowing that less is more and too much, indeed, is distrust.

"Let's see. You, we, are all leaving tomorrow on Mr. Fox's plane to Oakland for the legal forum Colonel King will be participating in."

Fox saw the game. No resume would be offered. It was a test. A verbal duel, so to speak.

"That's common knowledge. There was a news story in today's *L.A. Times*."

"True, but are you aware that Colonel King is at the Zanzibar night club as we speak, fortifying himself with courage?"

"That's not that unusual," said Callie, irritated again at King. Not that unusual for a vain man trying to drink himself young, she thought.

"With this project, we shouldn't be talking about bar hopping," Fox said. "I expect this to be dangerous."

"Then you're holding hands with the right person." His words caught Callie and Hugh off guard. They looked at each other, glanced down and then moved their hands from a warm touch both were unconsciously enjoying.

"Coming from the background of having been an office-based computer policewoman, one would be surprised to learn you are proficient in firearms, Ms. Cardoza, having actually shot someone," the mysterious man named Holmes said, applying a fatherly smile.

Hugh glanced at Callie. Before he went forward on this project, he had had his research staff run in-depth dossiers on the two stars of *King's Retribution*, but this was news to him.

Callie, surprised herself at hearing the ancient history, recovered and gave this Mr. Holmes a smirk, acknowledging that the man had his sources.

More to Hugh she said, "Many years back, a drunk boyfriend, 'ex' for sure, came at me with a knife. It was right when I graduated from the Police Academy. But the incident got expunged from my record as self-defense."

"'Expunged' is such a subjective word," responded Holmes. "Would it be more accurate to point out that the ex-boyfriend can never have children, and that the police report was 'expunged' only after you were promoted to the computer section? A coincidence?

"And while we're on the subject, I assume you gave up your regulation firearm upon leaving the San Diego Police Department. Their standard issue, I believe, is a Glock 22 .40 caliber. You have certainly downsized to something more feminine, yet still lethal, like a Beretta Tomcat. Yes, I could see you with that one. It's easy to hide in a purse."

This was too much, and her anger flared.

"How did you…?"

"Here are the bullets." Holmes dropped the live ammunition on a desk across from them.

Hugh and Callie were stunned at this trespasser.

"What the – ? I went to the restroom over an hour ago, you son-of-a…."

"Two more points are in my favor." Wendell Holmes, immensely enjoying this moment, turned his back and began disappearing into the shadows.

"Language. I speak passable Arabic, plus a smidge of pidgin tourist Urdu and Farsi. If that's the part of the world to which we're headed."

There was silence. Fox smiled and begrudgingly accepted the man as a player – but playing for whose team? And he had to ask, as if it were sealing the deal.

"And the other point?"

"I have met Osama bin Laden. Several times, in fact."

Somewhere in the War Room they heard a door open and close, but they saw nothing.

29.

First week of April, 2011 London

The apartment's panoramic view took in the Parliament building across the Thames, and he could also see the revolving Ferris
wheel known as the London Eye, with its 800 riders per revolution all unaware that soon their world might change to more fear
and uncertainty. They could only blame themselves, thought
Khalaf. What could you expect when the Imperialist British trod
across the Trans-Jordan and carved up the Ottoman Empire,
solely to suit the desires of allies that could be properly kept
subservient to the Western need of oil to fuel their battleships?
And added fuel to the fire, issued the cursed Balfour Resolution
creating the State of Israel, founded by terrorist Zionists.

"How long since you have been here?" asked the older man,
sitting on the couch, enjoying his tea service. Kahlaf likewise
sipped. It was a silver tip Darjeeling tea, he had been told. He
gave the man's question a few seconds of consideration. Had time
moved that fast?

"About seven years. I did graduate-level Economics studies
here in the city for two years, but I never finished the degree. The
Brotherhood brought me back to Cairo to help form student
protests against Mubarak."

"And, as you see, a seed planted becomes a flowering garden."

"Yes, Mubarak is gone. It's not so much flowers blooming
these days as it is weeds springing forth, and some of them need
to be ripped out by their roots."

"Will you ever go back to Egypt?"

Kahlaf knew the answer, but pondering the question left an
impression that such a door might be open. It wasn't. He had
cast his fate with al-Qaeda, been recruited by Mullah Omar
himself, and reported directly to bin Laden, which was a great
honor.

"The Emir requires my presence."

"Future Emir. Bin Laden requires at least one country to affix
his star and create his caliphate."

"That time is coming. Crimson Scimitar will define his great-
ness, his power, and we will either regain Afghanistan when the

Americans leave, or Sudan or Yemen could come under our power."

"You mean 'his' power?"

"Of course, I am speaking collective to our organization, with the Emir as supreme ruler."

The older man smiled. He had been around many years, and had seen so many youths spout rabid slogans, only to settle into the comfort of the system when age gave them the wisdom that the world could not be conquered; that one vest bomber sworn to Allah's cause would not alter governments.

"More tea?"

"Will your associate be arriving shortly?"

"Yes, any time."

"Then, yes please, two cups is my limit. It is very good."

The man, a banker by the name of Taher Abboud, poured for him and both drank silently, each in contemplation.

Banker Abboud finally offered, "Your English is quite excellent," turning the conversation trivial. "No trace of a Middle Eastern accent. Very Oxford in lilt. And your dress to visit me is certainly not that of a man of the desert, or high mountain caves, or wherever our illustrious leader is now ensconced."

A test for him to slip and mention where bin Laden might be? Khalaf saw the sly humor in the smile of the financial man who was also a devout fundamentalist. The banker was hidden in the elegant dress code of suit and tie worn by those who do daily transactions with the Bank of England and its various correspondent banks. Kahlaf dressed for this occasion in a late winter tweed sport coat and white turtleneck, trendier than what his staid conspirator chose as his business uniform.

"Yes, while attending school I went out of my way to blend in. I thought it might be useful at some future date." Khalaf had trimmed his beard before flying to Great Britain by way of the Emirates, and then allowed a barbershop on Mill Street in Mayfair to sculpt and trim him, close-cut, into fashion. People might see him as 'foreign' but they would not be able to identify a nationality.

"I heard from another source, one of our brethren involved in Crimson Scimitar, that it was you who conceived this phase of the operation, on your own. It is very brilliant, I might add."

Khalaf accepted the praise as his due and felt good that his talents were recognized. His recent trip to Yemen and his meeting with several members of the Supreme Council had not been as complimentary, nor as rewarding, as he had hoped.

"Let us just say that learning from our enemies led me to the concept. But indeed I was blessed that the Emir approved and asked you to finish the structuring. If it is brilliant and succeeds, it will be because we both see the value."

"Yes, and 'value' is a key word." The doorbell rang and the banker Abboud rose to answer.

A young man, Arabic in looks, entered carrying two large suitcases and they exchanged greetings. In the business world he went by Zia Johnson, but his birth name was Ziad Mahoummed Barakat, and he worked as a stockbroker at one of the large brokerage firms in London. It was located in the Canary Wharf financial district, with offices strategically located in New York and Chicago.

Khalaf listened in silence as Abboud the banker outlined the role of Johnson/Barakat the stockbroker. The young man gave a sheepish smile, realizing he was in the presence of a direct link to the head of al-Qaeda, which was an extreme privilege. Abboud finished by saying, "And he will leave for New York within a week before the launch of Crimson Scimitar, so as to be in place on the attack date."

"Good. Thank you, Zia, for volunteering. Not all of us can serve as martyrs to our just cause, but believe me that I will pass word of your deeds, when accomplished, back to the Emir."

"I am most grateful," said the young stockbroker with an expression of joy. "I have longed to be a participant in the battle of the Faith."

Abboud walked him to the door and Zia Johnson left, hesitant, clearly preferring to stay and know more about all that would come to pass.

The banker took the suitcases to the dining room table. Khalaf followed and saw that they were filled with money: English pounds, and other Euro currency.

"Taher, how much does this give us?"

"There are nearly two million Muslims in the United Kingdom, my friend. Our population grows at 10 times the number of the Anglo-Saxon race. There are 1,500 mosques and 20 percent of the Imams within those mosques are our supporters and say so indirectly when they can in Friday prayers. But as president of the Islamic Benevolent Foundation, I can tell you that almost all of them have contributed to us to assist the less fortunate. When I bank this delivery, our balance will be about $4 million in ready funds. And at the appointed time, I will make the transfer."

"And we can count on Barakat? Everything has to be timed so accurately."

"He is my wife's nephew. I saw his passion at an early age and directed it well. But realize he is more anti-Zionist than he is one of your al-Qaeda indoctrinates, those habitually unemployable and left only to cast hatred on others due to their own misfortune. Ziad is sharp.

He's a good choice."

"You do not need to defend him. If he is your recommendation, I am satisfied and will report back as such."

"Thank you, Maulawi Jan." The man mentioned a name Kahlaf had gone by several years earlier. It was a birth name dropped for a one word *nom de guerre* more in tune with a holy revolution.

Khalaf walked back to the window and the London skyline before him wondering if any of the al-Qaeda sponsored cells, the ones he knew nothing about, would be launching their own attacks on the anniversary of 9/11. The word had gone out for such attacks; he had delivered the message himself to various regional al-Qaeda commanders with supporters in Western countries.

Would the London Eye be such a target? It was so visible, and offered so many possible deaths and injuries. Maybe attacks on the Summer Olympics in 2012? No, not his concern. He brought his mind back to his duties. The United States came first and would feel the might of Crimson Scimitar. If only bin Laden would give the word.

He said aloud, as more reinforcement to his commitment, "Abboud, we shall succeed.

The infidel Americans saw 9/11 as one attack, yet there were several simultaneous operations consisting of four planes. Crimson Scimitar is an octopus of many tentacles. If, by bad fortune, they cut one tentacle off, other arms will be out grabbing and strangling.

"Above all," he said, "the Emir, the head, is inviolate and will always be lord over us."

30.

First week in April, 2011 San Francisco Airport

Razzor Hassim knew that Fate had blessed him and shown him that he was to be an instrument of Allah's will. It could not be more obvious.

He had just arrived from Chicago on a flight that was delayed forty-five minutes when the pilot refused to let two white-turbaned men remain on the flight. Their protestations of innocence, of their religious freedoms being violated, carried no weight with the pilot, Lord of the Commercial Skies. He was an extremely stupid man, thought Hassim, a poor excuse for a worldly, educated man if he did not even realize that these two men were not Muslims at all, nor Islamic clerics, but were of the Sikh religion from India. A pilot who can't tell Indians from Persians visibly demonstrated the shortcomings of their culture, where they praise what a wonderful place America is as the melting pot of the world. Hypocrites.

Hassim, wearing a Chicago Cubs baseball cap, sat in his window seat and continued to read a Western cowboy sheriff mystery by author Craig Johnson. No one bothered him. No one paid him attention at all, except to ask what sort of beverage he would like to drink. "Diet coke," he said, and "Thank you" when it was delivered.

As he walked the terminal he looked at the overhead signage to find his way to Baggage Claim. As he proceeded, he saw two separate mobs of people coming his way.

Photographers and cameramen were pressing against Pastor Samuel Tate, and Hassim could hear the man ranting.

"I will be protesting outside the meeting tonight. It is an abomination against the Lord Almighty to even give this ungodly evil called bin Laden any sort of guise of respectability or humanity. The man wants to kill us all and supplant our blessed Christ with the addled words of a mere camel trader, a desert brigand. It shall not happen! Tonight after the gathering, for all to see, I will burn this false book of theirs."

He raised his arms to the airport ceiling, as he brought his voice to higher octave.

"It is not for true believers, men or women, to make their choice in the affairs if God and His apostle decree otherwise. He that disobeys God and His apostle strays far indeed."

A reporter took advantage of the Pastor catching his breath and interjected: "And did you bring a Koran to burn? Can you show us what you intend to burn?"

Pastor Tate found himself coming down from his spiritual high to practicalities requiring some thought.

"I would not sully my luggage with such perdition. I will search out a bookstore and see if they have a copy. This town, based on sin and carnal pleasure with those of the same sex, certainly promotes such foul teachings." He paused. "And yes, I must buy a can of gasoline to anoint and sanctify this purging."

He took off down the corridor, his pulled suitcase inadvertently bumping into Hassim, an act the pastor ignored and did not look back. Several news reporters and their camera team fell away, their story gathering complete, and confronted the second mob: An approaching gaggle of paparazzi falling in step with Colonel King of *King's Retribution*.

King stopped, allowing everyone to catch up with him and causing travelers to slow down to see who was attracting so much media attention, what famous personage who seemed to glow in the recognition. Knowing his publicity people were coordinating his arrival, King had pressured Fox to offload his party at the main public ramps and concourse instead of at the more discreet corporate-based operations terminal.

Behind King, at a safe distance in order to stay out of the limelight, were Hugh Fox, Samantha Carlisle, Callie Cordoza, who was incognito in scarf and sunglasses, as well as the minor players of the entourage, Clayton Briggs and J-Q. Behind them and off to the side was the interloper, Wendell Holmes; uninvited on the Skilleo corporate jet, but not disinvited. They had all found him a man of few words, pleasant when responding but otherwise quiet. To Fox, the presence of Holmes offered the Hunt Team legitimacy. There was among them at least one person who seemed to be a professional, though he still had not offered written or confirmed credentials; his demeanor was his calling card. Fox appreciated the understated and the man's lack of boasting, which was refreshing in his world.

The camera lights on and microphones thrust into his face, Colonel King pontificated for his fans.

"I'm pleased with this invitation to represent *King's Retribution*, with the premise that we will be the ones to bring Osama bin Laden to justice." He made certain his smile and features moved left to right, in order to meet all the cameras recording.

"To understand the importance of the role I will play, you all must come tonight to this mock trial. You'll see further proof that evil cannot escape the best system of justice in the world. And to Mr. bin Laden, wherever you are, I will only say, 'You can hide, but not from *King's Retribution*. We are coming to get you.'"

With a regal air, he led the way, forcing the coterie of press to catch up with him as he strutted and tossed out pithy platitudes and homilies of benign significance.

"Will you write a book of your experiences in tracking down bin Laden?" asked a puffing, out-of-breath reporter.

"In catching bin Laden," bellowed King, "I shall make history, not write it."

From a respectful if not wished for distance, Samantha turned to Hugh. "Our hero seems even larger than the celluloid time slot he inhabits."

From the back of the group, Wendell Holmes put in his own two cents.

"The only thing necessary for the triumph of evil is for good men to do nothing."

"Yes, that is why we are here," Fox beamed. "Thank you, Mr. Holmes."

"Those were the words of Edmund Burke, English member of Parliament, who voiced opposition to England's war with the American colonist revolutionaries," said Holmes.

Unable to keep up to the military fast-walk cadence, the reporters slowed, and looking around, finally understood that Storm King had formed a partnership with one of the richest 'couples' in the country. They descended upon Fox and Carlisle and also the seductive Callie Cardoza, now recognized, and King found himself alone, signing an autograph for a small child, who looked at him in worshipful awe.

Choices, choices. Hassim beamed at his good fortune. They must be attacked, taught a lesson and destroyed. But who first?

His eyes fell on a man wearing sunglasses inside the terminal and standing off to the side, away from the press. He must have arrived with the retinue of the *King's Retribution* group, and he was standing with two or three others watching the interviews taking place, except –Suddenly unnerved, Hassim realized the man was staring at him, and immediately, as he looked around, it became clear that people were passing him by and only he stood in the middle of the terminal: set apart, conspicuous. Damn. He turned and hustled. What a foolish mistake.

And why had that man directed his attention at him? He was probably just a bodyguard to the stars, like the large man who stood near him. That was it. Just doing his job and identifying potential threats. Hassim looked over his shoulder, seeing no one suspicious, he relaxed and slowed his exiting pace.

Well, yes, he was a threat. The sooner, the better, since he had to meet *The Professor* in Los Angeles in two days. Again, he came back to the dilemma: Choices. Who first?

Episode 5

**6 Studies That Prove Reality TV Is Causing the
Apocalypse
by Luke McKinney
March 12, 2011**

#6. People Watch Reality TV For Horrifying Reasons
Excerpt: *The study found that those who watched reality TV
were far more concerned with social status and vengeance, and
significantly less motivated by idealism, morality or honor...*
#5. It Actively Damages Civilizations
#4. Mere Exposure to Reality TV Makes You a Worse Person
Excerpt: *A survey of first-time plastic surgery patients found
that 78 percent were influenced by reality television, and 57
percent of all first-time patients were "high-intensity" viewers of
cosmetic surgery reality TV.*
#3. There Is More Reality TV Than Science (And We) Can
Handle
#2. It Even Manages to Make the Internet Dumber
#1. The One Way Reality TV Seems to Be Useful
Excerpt...*Reality TV is making a lot of money, thanks to the
fact that a real TV show costs over a million dollars to make,
while a reality show costs around $100,000.*

31.

April 7, 2011 California Desert

Pacheco lay on his belly tasting the local dirt as small arms fire crackled all around him.

Mostly they were fake rounds, with a few coordinated bursts of live ammunition to signify urban battlefield conditions. Sweat grimed his hands. His fingers stretched and scraped two colored wires out of the dirt, and his upper body inch-crawled to the hidden IED. A bad snip of the wire might set off a simulated explosion, or might not, or an "insurgent" hiding on a floor above could use his cell phone to arc a signal to the explosive. Shit. Practice or not, he had the internal shakes, hoping his squad unit backed up behind him in the narrow street didn't notice his timing reflex lagging a few seconds.

From training at Camp Pendleton on the California coast they had been ferried by a C-130 cargo jet over to the Twentynine Palms military base, located 175 miles northeast of San Diego. This base was more than 900 square miles, but the two selected squads of SEAL Team Six were destined to its mini desert metropolis, unknown to the public, which was mocked up with 1,500 buildings and designed to resemble an Afghan city. Team Six was inserted within a training exercise involving Camp Pendleton's 2nd Battalion, 4th Marine Regiment, which was preparing for an August deployment to Afghanistan. Over three days, Marine trainers would run the SEAL Team members through an exhaustive, alternative regimen to their planned objective, which was still to be revealed. It was basically an "If everything goes ape shit, what are the options?" backup scenario.

In the anticipated raid, or assault, or whatever was planned for SEAL Team Six, imaginary helicopters were to have malfunctioned or been shot down after landing them, and the SEAL Teams would need to extract themselves through highly contested city blocks. That scenario gave Pacheco a little hint into the job ahead: It was in a city, not countryside. He could fight under any circumstances. His whole career had been shaped for him to react as a soldier facing a violent, merciless enemy, but he preferred to battle in hilly terrain, as opposed to inside a village where everyone hated you and they were possibly all armed to the teeth, including the women; the gooks just ready to take their potshots at you.

Shawn snipped the wire, without an explosion, and yelled out 'Clear.' The squad rushed past him, leapfrogging down the street, rifles swinging side to side at unseen dangers.

"Brace. Controlled det!" shouted a "coyote," one of the marine trainers and exercise referees.

Suddenly, a rattling explosion shook the buildings, vibrating the ground. Even though it was mock practice, team personnel walked warily. Simulated war could be just as dangerous.

A fellow demolition squad member ran to Pacheco's side, out of breath, and took a look at what Pacheco had faced in defusing the bomb. He gave an approving nod.

"If we get through these next few days," said the huffing SEAL, Pacheco's bomb tech grunt partner Vitali, "I hear we're primed to launch out of here."

"Any word?"

"Naw, but I think they want us to go back and run sequences on that big white house at Pendleton. New intel, I think. Whatever it is, pretty sure we're going to be hitting it hard."

"About time," grumbled Pacheco, easing himself against the wall, wiping his face, and then starting to follow the others down the street, where two SEAL members fired as an "enemy combatant" appeared in an upstairs window. His right hand shook. That IED disconnect went too damn slow. If this fakery had been live and hot, he thought, he would have been dead. Not a good confidence builder, and when he caught a glance of a fellow SEAL across the street, for just a moment he thought he saw Montoya's face, and that dopey grin he gave just before he kicked the can, literally, and disappeared in that red mist.

His reality was stilted and he shook his head. Gathering up his skewed senses, he rejoined his fellow SEALS as they sought to escape the imaginary city.

32.

April 11, 2011 Silicon Valley, California

The caravan of limousines drifted south along Highway 280, away from the airport, veering off at Los Altos Hills and then winding its way west to the five-acre Skilleo Game Technology campus, nestled against the Palo Alto Foothills Park. Stretching her legs upon exiting the limo, Callie took in the environment. By now, sunlight had burned away most of the coastal sea fog, yet there was still a smell of cool distant ocean carried by a feathery breeze to moderate the late spring weather. Before her, up a dozen steps on a small rise, lay three buildings, each four stories tall and each curved in a wide arc, spaceships designed of brushed aluminum glinting with a chrome shine, and accented with wide swaths of dark green glass.

Looking full circle, she saw hazy mountains in the distance, while to the south, on the grounds of Hugh Fox's corporate headquarters, there stood a phalanx of wind turbines of varying dimensions, and to the north, an array of solar panels. California "politically correct," she mused.

King had been right to guess the place would be an enviro hangout, with "greens" trying to balance good deeds with acceptable levels of greed. What also caught her attention was that the offices overlooked an immense, landscaped garden not of thorn roses or gentle petunias, but boasting an elaborate maze of high hedges worthy of "The Shining." Not menacing so much as a siren song to draw one in with curiosity. For Hugh Fox, even nature must have its game play, she thought.

The tour group consisted of Fox, Skilleo's majority owner, leading the way and exchanging small laughs of conversation with Samantha Carlisle, who was at his side. Storm King took second position in stride, puffing out his chest, his face critical as if looking for a fault to point out. Callie could guess that King's attitude, previously braced by limo cocktails, held less awe at the man's success and more festering jealousy that youth was being so obscenely rewarded.

Perhaps King envied that the upbeat games inventor walked with a beautiful woman, and one not as attractive as Callie thought of herself, she thought as she compared their attributes.

Such insecurity put her in a dour mood and she walked alone; or so she thought, until she realized that the mysterious new addition to the team, this Wendell Holmes if that was his name, opened the door for her. He wore a neutral smile, and throughout the tour did not speak except once.

The visual videographers, CAM ONE and CAM TWO were ever present, cameras always on.

Something would be made from all the film they were amassing. A documentary, a reality show within a reality show; no one had told them what they were making, or what to tape. Tasked without tasks, required to be their own creator, One and Two said nothing and did their best to blend into the scenery in order to gain their best shots, still close enough that their directional microphones gained the best voice quality even during casual conversation.

Last to enter the building and receive the requisite Guest IDs was the bodyguard Clayton Briggs, looking less "muscle man" in a sport coat, and Bennie, the *King's Retribution* getaway driver. A small-framed man, balding and nervous, Bennie bore a weasel-narrow face with out-of-style tortoise glasses constantly pushed back on his nose. He and Briggs took their status as the show's filler character actors, and knew their best talent was shying away from others' limelight.

Paychecks for their limited acting skills kept them thankful for jobs others could have easily filled.

The tour lasted two hours. Everyone participating retained a specific memory after seeing all the wondrous, high-tech gadgets and the smiled "hellos" from each employee they met in the labs or saw in the wide hallways, including those who skateboarded or roller-skated by.

Samantha Carlisle commented approvingly on Skilleo's day care center for employees' children, and was amazed that the company operated a medical clinic offering preventative advice on carpal tunnel syndrome, exercise regimens for computer finger tendonitis, and offered desk side neck massages and break areas with vibrating chairs near work stations.

The alpha males King, Briggs, and Bennie had to be dragged away from the Testing Laboratory, a basketball court sized, carpeted, living room with TV screens mounted on the walls everywhere, and serious employee testers sitting and playing games, or standing in participatory action screen games of golf, baseball or bowling. The three men each picked a game, not yet released to the public, and were excited that they could tell stories of what new Skilleo games the Christmas season would find under the tree (in departing, everyone received a swag bag of the latest games).

King played "Infamy 2," portraying a superhero with the power to remove evil scum by striking them with bursts of electricity, ice, and other elemental ammo. The game was set in an imaginary city similar to a hurricane-ravaged New Orleans, where thugs and radiated swamp monsters needed to be obliterated. Bennie put on 3-D game goggles and played the baseball game "Triple Play," and kept exclaiming how realistic the hitting and pitching seemed as he took wild swings. Clayton's choice was "Vegas Noire," a detective TV series-type game in which crimes are solved and the player role-plays required guesses during gruesome CSI-type autopsies.

Callie noted that Samantha deferred from choosing an action game, and, in fact, looked away as if there were a horror to such masculine excitement, whether it was sports or action brutality. Callie likewise begged off. Seeking to say something positive, Samantha did offer a comment to Hugh, "I have heard of your educational brands, that kids can learn cognitive skills by interplay."

Callie saw Hugh beam at the praise. She tried the same, pointing to a game that several second-grade testing subjects were animated about. "Is that one of your educational games? Those children definitely are enjoying it."

"A prototype game, 'Angry Turtles.' The kids are using the computer mouse to skip upside down turtles across a lake into the mouths of alligators to gain points. We will quiz players afterward and analyze their responses as to satisfaction levels." He gave thought as if processing the entire program, the kids were yelling in glee about. "I am not that thrilled about the design in the violence."

Callie noted a genuine smile slip from his face as Samantha turn away and exit the room. Did he see disappointment in her expression? That children were absorbed with cruelty as much as gratuitous violence of a play game?

Animation returned to Hugh's features, which Callie found herself enjoying, as Hugh Fox took over from the personable, yet serious, tour guide as they entered the Research Lab. He went through the process of game creation, from idea germination to outsourced manufacturing. "The fertile mind of an individual dictates what the public eventually sees as their own tastes," he said, showing them a room – comfort again the priority – where in one corner a group of people tossed out brainstorming concepts, in friendly and rollicking banter; in another part of the room, researchers huddled over laptops. "We ask them to scroll to search the Internet universe and see what else is being communicated out there in the world. A disjointed fragment of an interesting idea might be given over to the brainstorming section of this department."

The bodyguard Clayton Briggs noticed a woman circling the floor in an enclosed booth, presumably soundproofed and with one-way glass. She seemed distracted, her arms waving, and muttering to herself. "What's she doing?" he asked.

"Oh, we take some of our smartest people, as volunteers, and have them enter what we call the Escape Room on a rotating basis. They speak about whatever comes to their mind, which we record and then sift for any germ of an idea."

Callie had seen this sort of behavior before. On the street.

"She's tripping." Callie frowned, but relented at Hugh's direct smile.

"Only mild hallucinogenics, I assure you. Some of the world's greatest art, literature, and scientific ideas were created by people involved in chemically induced incidents that led to their creativity. Writer Aldous Huxley on LSD, the artist Van Gogh with absinthe addiction, scientist Carl Sagan tripping out on pot. Baudelaire wrote in opium hazes, and Hemingway and F. Scott Fitzgerald had alcohol as their temptress muse."

Bennie, looking into another glass-partitioned room, asked, "And is this gentleman on druggie withdrawal?"

They all peered in to see a young man, the epitome of a surfer dude, laid out on a tilted psychiatrist's couch, his head wired.

"That's our Dream Room," explained Fox casually. "We're trying to record a person's brain waves as he sleeps; trying to capture a dream sequence. And as he comes out of deep sleep perhaps he'll start talking and we can compare the sentence fragments, and perhaps someday be able to look into a real dream, and there, capture an essential, pure, virgin idea."

They all stared at him, not knowing if they were present among the most genius of geniuses, or in Dr. Frankenstein's chop shop.

"You have to understand," Fox went on, seeing their reactions. "In order to compete in a crowded world of products, creation and delivery of any product must be totally unique for it to survive, though luck and timing are also important elements to a game release. It takes us three to four years to go from idea generation in this laboratory to the product being on a toy store shelf. In that time, public fickleness or new technology can make our product obsolete. We cannot waste resources being wrong. Skilleo must always be ahead of the techno market curve."

For the first time, Wendell Holmes spoke up.

"There seems to be a gentleman over in the corner talking only to himself. And he is finger shooting. I presume he's playing a game but he's talking to no one. I expect, as your rooms of Dreams and Escape exist, one would find the best subjects for ideas might be from the delusional, schizos and psychotics." They all turned to the finger shooter and saw the man involved in a western shoot 'em up. Fast draw, dip and turn to shoot – it was like an old arcade game of hidden pop-up targets of villainous desperados. Callie accepted that to the Skilleo mindset, shooting red man savages was unacceptable.

Curious, they all gravitated in the player's direction as Fox explained.

"Another prototype in testing mode. It's two or three years from the market. As you all may be aware, the participant game player has moved from a joystick to a data-accepting handheld device, like a tennis racket. We're now to the point where the game computer can view the player's action and accordingly mimic the action. That's the new standard. We are adding a modification. Voice command.

"The man is speaking into a Bluetooth device," offered King, with a skeptical squint, "but I don't see it. Have you miniaturized it?"

"You can't see it, because the device is embedded in his jaw." Fox saw disbelievers. "No, really. Where iPhones are moving towards voice-activated responses to word association in order to discern a variety of questions, in the future we might be able to dispense with the earplug, or having to push a button to activate a device. You might say, 'Car Turn On,' and the action would occur without a key. But since we are game play oriented, the central game box, again in the near future, will be able to record your voice tangents, and recognize you in the midst of group game play. Installation in the jaw might someday be a common, outpatient procedure, not harmful and less effort than getting a tattoo, and with more application use."

Shaking their heads and accepting that they must be Neanderthal Luddites, they moved on. Some of them, amazed, brainstormed aloud about what uses such a jaw-implanted device might have. Callie saw that the last of them to exit the room was Holmes, who had walked up to the talking game player, and, after some deep eye contact, ran his hand along both sides of the man's jaw, seeking a bump or a blemish that showed where the device lay hidden under the skin.

He, too, was impressed.

Callie's stand-out memory of the day's tour was the walkthrough of Hugh Fox's private office. Like a person's library or medicine cabinet, one's office revealed the subtleties of its occupant's mind and style; supplied clues that, in this case, laid open the personal myths to this supposed "introvert genius." She scanned the office in detective mode. To say the place bore a minimalist coldness, with its utilitarian furniture and lack of bric-a-brac, would be incorrect.

Even saying that "functionalism" pervaded the style did not properly convey the work environment.

Callie, who had been invited to many stars' abodes on the party circuit, did not see boasting, or flaunted wealth or executive arrogance. Fox's furniture, of post-modern Swedish construction, was comfortable. His smoked, cracked-glass conference table was oval, a sign of equality in body placement. She saw no wall of fame, with photos that celebrated the boss standing with prominent politicians or sports figures. There were no family photos, and most particularly, no desk photo of Samantha Carlisle. Callie found that telling, though she could not for the life of her decide what Carlisle's photogenic absence revealed.

The top of his desk lay vacant, clean of daily toil, if any such paper bureaucracy tedium ever did find its way to the steel and glass work area. Three wafer-thin computer screens were mount-ed on one side of his circular desk, and a large, mounted TV screen – more a movie screen – took up one side of an office wall. A floor-to-ceiling glass wall behind his desk overlooked the gar-den maze. Callie wondered: If Hugh ever looked in that direction, would he then sit quietly, contemplating the puzzle garden, and could he trace a correct path from entrance to exit? Was he that kind of man?

Another long wall was bare except for three paintings – small, ink sketches in ornate gold frames. It took Callie a minute to recognize the significance of these three art pieces, styled from the same artist, being the only items in such a large, empty space. She knew her silent guess was correct. *Leonardo da Vinci.* Originals, no doubt, and worth dollar signs of a million or two.

A hidden meaning? Perhaps it was acknowledgement or praise from one inventor to another; or, perhaps, daily inspiration.

Callie knew Storm King's thoughts were not on the host's fas-cinating character, which was intertwined in his personal pres-ence, his office, his corporate style, of Skilleo Games and its amazing technology. Obvious glances at his watch made it clear that King wanted to go prep for the night's event, the pretend trial of Osama bin Laden *in absentia.* And, as in times past, Storm-King's diligence meant lubrication at the hotel's mini bar.

They waited for the limousines to appear for the ride to San Francisco's Stanford Court Hotel. It was as close to UC Berkeley as King wanted to be. "The den of yuppie commies," he had intoned in a bass voice, as if his pronouncement was pure truth.

Wendell Holmes stood next to Callie and gazed back up at the fourth floor window of the executive office they had just left.

"Don't you find it interesting?" he started.

"What's that?" She did not dislike him, but she didn't know him, and felt it prudent to be cautious of whomever he might really be working for. A man with an agenda is always more dangerous, because his interests are not for the good of the whole.

He continued. "That if you scan the pages of the game cata-logue of Skilleo Games Technology, there are multiple choices for addictive game customers, but no war games. Yes, there are bloody, explosive battles with crooks and aliens, but not one of Marines or SEALS battling turbaned, dark-skinned terrorists."

"And you are implying what? He's a liberal, sympathetic to Islamic interests?"

"No, not at all. Mr. Fox is a sincere young man in what he does well, which is create.

"Like most, his core beliefs are sub-surface, not deep commitments. Future experience, outside of his Skilleo cave, will bring him the knowledge that will shape him. Perhaps Mr. Fox is smart enough to realize he needs enlightenment, and that has piqued my curiosity."

"You're referring to this crazy hunt to find bin Laden? Are you saying it's a quest for Mr. Fox's personal, as you say, 'enlightenment?'"

"Let me put it this way. It's curious that instead of having his game engineers draw up a storyboard of World War II battles, or fighting nasty North Koreans, or yes, even Arabic-looking terrorists, that Mr. Fox might be personally, by his own hand, creating a new game. And not in his mind, per se, but one of reality, actual war experiences, and field tested under his own observations."

"I don't consider myself a pawn in anyone's game." Callie's eyes followed Wendell Holmes' stare to Fox's office, where they had left Hugh and Samantha in a tête-à-tête. Were they up there for a quickie on that conference table? The woman's ass imprinted on the glass for the cleaning crew to wonder about? Callie shook the imagery. She did wonder about ulterior motives: What were those rich folks up to? Putting her into a game? Risking her life?

"No one is going to use me," she reiterated with a growl that was as aimed much to herself as to Holmes; and it was less about Fox's motives than it was in consideration of her current relationship with Storm King.

33.

Afternoon, April 11 Department of Energy
Washington, D.C.

Ronald Givens didn't like it when he was relegated to a lesser seat at the conference table, his presence required merely to be sure the CIA had been noticed. He already knew his pat answer to the invariable question.

"Our agency has no valid report of any foreign group, from any chatter we have so far analyzed, that would be a threat to your planned transportation operation."

Others had their own intelligence statement ready to put forth. Around the table were representatives from the Department of Energy, U.S. Atomic Energy Commission, National Regulatory Agency, Homeland Security, Federal Bureau of Investigation as well as the CIA, represented by Assistant Deputy Director Givens.

The task force's point person, a take-no-prisoner woman scientist from the National Regulatory Agency passed around a photocopied clipping.

"As you can see, pursuant to the Department Energy mandate and the approval of your agencies, we have started low-key practice runs. Our first hot run is scheduled for later in the year when all contingencies are in place."

Givens picked up the paper and read a cut-and-copied Associated Press news article:

Las Vegas *Review Journal*, February 2011

Low-level nuclear waste to be shipped through Nevada

San Clemente, Calif. – A 192-wheel trailer will make four trips hauling old generator parts considered to be low-level nuclear waste from California through Nevada and to Utah for disposal.

Officials from Southern California Edison's San Onofre Nuclear Generating Station said the levels of radiation from the old parts pose no risk to the public, but that "they hope the public won't come out to see the lumbering trailer."

Its departure date was not released for security reasons.

The FBI committee representative piped up from the end of the table.

"Going from California to Utah by way of Nevada is not like going from the East Coast reactor to a Nevada depository site?"

"You have had a chance to look over the Environmental Assessment Report," said the scientist/chairperson, pointing to a large, stuffed, six-inch thick binder. Each member had one before him or her, and each binder would be gathered up after the meeting as it was "for your eyes only."

"The route is straight interstate, for the most part," she said, "until we cross into Nevada then we can use less traveled highways. The head of each state's highway patrol will receive four hour advance notice of the trailer's passing over their state lines. Each governor has received a letter of notification, and there is so far no negative political response by any of them."

"Of course the manifest description," said Givens in his put-down voice, "still says low level radiation canisters, when in fact the cargo is high-level toxins."

Coming from the field of science, where fact is indisputable truth and there is no equivocation, she never did like politicians, and this CIA administrator assigned to the working panel proved her case. She felt Givens added nothing to the discussion, but rather just strutted his prominence. She was about to speak when the key technocrat from the Department of Energy, and her immediate boss, gave the final word.

"All this has been debated, Mr. Givens, and you and your agency of course voted for this direction. The time has come to test the operation. And you know, as well as I, that multiple redundant fail-safes have been built into this project. I assume that you have nothing new to report from your sources?"

Givens gave a clenched-teeth smile and responded with his pat answer – that from an international security survey, there were no concerns that put this truck carrier operation at risk.

The FBI rep gave his expected answer, that from their sources of information there were no valid internal threats, and that all existing home-grown terrorist groups had been identified and infiltrated and none held designs on a truck supposedly bearing generator parts of low level radiation.

The committee members had previously approved the operation, which came about after the tragic, March 9th earthquake-tsunami that wiped out Japan's Fukushima Daiichi nuclear plant and caused the world's worst nuclear accident since Chernobyl. In the U.S., there was political breast pounding by alarmists in and out of Congress that forced federal agencies to revisit contingency plans for disaster scenarios from earthquakes to terrorist breaches. It was a massive safety review, since the U.S. had 104 nuclear power reactors in 31 states. Many plants were old systems, with the first built in 1960 and the last having opened in 1996. With rampant environmental and anti-nuclear opposition after Japan's disaster, the next plants would not come on line until 2020, if ever.

The most pressing issue – less than an internal meltdown and equal to a natural disaster – was that of nuclear waste, the spent fuel rods and other highly radioactive by-products that needed a resting place for permanent warehousing for a thousand years. In emergency conditions, when a major incident began, systems in nuclear plants would shut down automatically and there were back-up systems of manual turn-off buttons. However, nuclear waste protection was minimal at best and there were no long-range, publicly approved and vetted plans in place. The rising public clamor for more stringent protection led the federal government to begin testing possibilities, and as it always has done in crisis mode it turned within, conducting secretive discussions framed with tinges of paranoia.

This ex parte committee, formed for the betterment of everyone's security, had devised a test plan for a delivery system that would bring highly dangerous nuclear waste to a central depository. The first action step, before it went public, was a successful test run.

"What's the timetable for the first shipment?" asked Givens, trying a conciliatory voice and not giving a damn about the importance of what was occurring, seeing merely another meeting to be checked off of his busy schedule.

"September or August, maybe later," replied the Atomic Energy scientist, returning a weak smile.

"I suggest it not be on September 11th. Bad luck ramifications."

"We will take that under advisement, of course. A good thought." And the group turned to the mundane matters of implementation, with group concurrence that the first truckload would be generated from the New York power plant.

To reinforce that their committee selection had been correct, another news story was circulated at the table, this one dated three weeks earlier on March 16.

What's the most at-risk U.S. nuclear power plant?

(*CBS News*)

The Nuclear Regulatory Commission recently provided MSNBC with an updated list of the American nuclear power plants at highest risk of core damage (which can lead to meltdowns and radiation release) in the event of an earthquake. What parts of the country are most at risk?

You may be surprised.

Most might assume that California plants, built around the turbulent San Andreas Fault line, might be the most dangerous. Actually, the most at-risk plant isn't even on the West Coast – it's the Indian Point Energy Center on the Hudson River. With a 1 in 10,000 chance of core breach, that's right on the edge of what the NRC calls "immediate concern regarding adequate protection."

The article continued, but it drew a quick response from the FBI spokesperson, who was not a friend of the media.

"We don't need some investigative reporter starting to snoop around when we announce a 'low level radiation shipment' to an undisclosed destination."

"No, we don't," said Homeland Security, "and I can assure you we are moving as quickly as possible to get this first run operation up and completed. We must be prepared to move more quickly if it is required sooner, yet we must not act precipitously and put the secrecy we have so far achieved at risk of media disclosure."

And they all agreed. Secrecy was essential.

They just didn't know that national security had already been breached.

34.

April 11 New York State

As they had their *Professor*, they called this one, "The Scientist," and he did not like the moniker. After all, he was the Assistant Operations Manager of the Indian Points Energy Center, which was operated by a private corporation under National Regulatory supervision. And he thought it a joke that he must now report to an unknown person known as 'The Professor.' But the news was good for the cause. When he secured the date for the trucks leaving his facility, everything would be put in place. He would know that date and have enough time to relay the information, and that would set Crimson Scimitar on the road to its destiny.

The manager's name was Brahma Singh, and by a quirk in genetic features he had passed as an Indian Sikh, though his ancestry came from the valley region of Kashmir. Before the 1948 U.N. boundary settlement in the First Indio-Pakistani War of 1947, the family name of his small shopkeeping family had been Khan. That was before his displaced family found itself trapped by the ceasefire in the town of Kotli.

New boundaries shifted their identifications and ability to survive the economics, and with the need to assimilate to the conquering culture as well, they didn't find it easy to suddenly be impoverished refugees back in Moslem Pakistan. He'd grown up giving lip service as a Sikh, yet a closet Islamic, and became politicized when attending graduate school in nuclear physics at the Indian Institute of Technology in Kanpur. A tourist trip to Pakistan when he was a youth further radicalized him under the mind control of the Lal Masjid mosque in Islamabad and its many calls of jihad against Westerners. His education and some good luck brought him into the nuclear energy industry, and he was determined to protect his beliefs by striking out at India and its allies who supported military control of his parents' home of Pakistan – the underlying enemy, namely, the United States.

He hid well behind his public façade as a Sikh. He found humorous how the wearing of the dastar (turban) confused Protestant and Catholic faiths and while the disguise left him faking another religion he seemed modify his own beliefs to fit the circumstances at hand, that in being more the nationalistic spy and saboteur than the irrational religious extremist.

Brahma Singh knew that Crimson Scimitar was likely to succeed. And he relished the role he played, supplying, by happenstance, the main ingredient: High yield radiation.

Indian Point supplied nearly 30 percent of New York State's electricity, but Singh knew that he could not, by himself, sabotage it. Since 9/11, all power plants had safeguards aimed at preventing terrorism. When he heard about the transportation plan from the Atomic Energy Commission, he decided that his best opportunity would be to send a ticking time bomb somewhere else in order to maximize damage. With Crimson Scimitar, al-Qaeda could achieve more than a small nuclear plant 'accident', but by its design could wipe out a much larger swath of the American economy.

The main 'spreading epidemic' component of Crimson Scimitar would be poisonous nuclear waste. Indian Point stored its spent fuel rods submerged under 27 feet of water within 40 foot deep pools, each made of four to six foot wide concrete walls and with liners that had half inch thick stainless steel. The problem was that they had run out of pool storage for spent fuel rods. After five years in those pools, the spent rods should be moved to "dry storage casks," which again were supposed to be impervious from floods, tornadoes and projectiles. A nonnuclear explosion in the main transformer on November 7, 2010 triggered the debate over moving the spent fuel rods to a safe sanctuary elsewhere. After the March 11, 2011 Tohoku earthquake, political fears hastened a quick decision to make the move as soon as possible.

On the morning after the April 11 committee meeting in Washington, Singh's boss called him in and told him the spent fuel rods would move across the country in September or October.

Taking a long lunch break away from the plant, Singh went into the nearby Buchanan Public Library and joined an online discussion forum about his favorite team, the New York Jets.

"Can't wait to see the Jet Big Boys winning in September or October of the season," he typed.

"Yes," came a reply 15 minutes later. "Jet Big Boys victories sound good to me," typed *The Professor* from his home computer in Las Vegas, adding, "Any specific Jet Big Boys game and date you will be rooting on?"

"Let me think on that, will keep you informed about the Big Boys," typed Singh, who then went off for his own pleasure and started looking at game stats and fantasy match-ups. After all, the Jets were expected to have a pretty good fall season.

That evening, making a special trip to UNLV, *The Professor* accessed a computer in the faculty's Administration Office and joined a forum site about the Blackburn Rovers, an English professional football association in the Premier League. Transposing the Scientist's football vernacular into soccer speak, he posted: "Hope to get tickets to the Big Boy Rovers games in September-October, but no specific date yet."

The cut-out at this point, the London banker Taher Abboud responded, "I will look to receive your specific game date and ask around about Big Boy Rover tickets. All is well here."

On the next morning, April 14, messenger Ibrahim Ahmed sat on one of the old public computers in an Islamabad coffee shop and looked at the forum discussion in the Urdu language about the Pakistan national cricket team. One member asked if there would be a September-October charity test match, as he had heard. Ahmed printed out the communication.

As this trail of news circled the Earth, low-orbit satellite feeds streamed trillions of sentences written in that 24-hour period down to the multi-Cray computers, owned and run by the CIA and housed in a concrete bunker under a Virginia hillside. Hundreds of program filters, designed to discover specific-sequence alarm words and instantaneously set these worrisome fragments aside in an alert folder of "grey intelligence worthy of further review," were unperturbed by multiple uses, in different languages, of the phrase "Big Boy." Had American alliteration and interpretive context scopes been in place – to define not what was there as is but what might be interpretive, such as aspects of coded black humor – filters might have noted that *Little Boy* was the first atomic bomb exploded over Hiroshima, in August 1945. Its opposite, *Big Boy*, might suggest much worse. On his smoke-sputtering moped, messenger Ibrahim Ahmed chugged the latest report back to the whitewashed compound in Abbottabad.

The main recipient of the good news, Osama bin Laden, in turn gave various command instructions to the returning Khalaf to share with the other attack team members regarding the approximate timetable of Crimson Scimitar. No one could know that this would be the last attack he would plan against the United States, or, in fact, against any people. But would this attack, these multiple attacks be launched? Osama bin Laden had less than two weeks to live.

35.

April 11, evening University of California at Berkeley

Osama bin Laden, rather, the look-alike, sat at the defense table, alive and well. The pre-mock trial organizers immediately went into separate camps. The "prosecuting team" sought to have the actor bin Laden dress in Guantanamo orange, or a coat and tie with trimmed beard, while the "defense" argued that its client was a known religious leader and hence had the right to wear an Imam sort of dress. The "judge," actually a retired federal court judge, agreed with the defense; besides, he said, the actor looked more like Osama in his white tunic and turban, and it would play better to the television cameras.

Over 1,200 people crammed into the U of Cal auditorium in Berkeley, with hundreds more outside waving placards of support or opposition to the trial, *U.S. vs. Osama bin Laden* – including the railing Pastor Samuel Tate of the Church of True Believers, standing on his own soapbox-like pedestal across the street from the auditorium. Passing cameras took quick shots of him as the outtake-oddity, waving his Bible in one hand and a Koran in the other. He said, vaguely, "Later," when asked when he was going to burn the Koran, requiring more media coverage before he would light a match. He did not want to be upstaged by the shouting, positioning and other goings on within the Star Chamber.

"Call your first witness," intoned the judge, his gavel banging the audience's noise level down to a low hum.

"The State calls Colonel David King."

All eyes were focused on Storm King as he strode to the witness stand, holding his "cheat sheet" so he might better play his part as the capturing agent of the "alleged" terrorist. In the second row, where cameras had earlier clicked away in a paparazzi frenzy, Hugh Fox sat next to Samantha Carlisle. King sat on the other side of Samantha, and Callie Cardoza was next to him.

Barely fitting next to Callie was the bodyguard Clayton and then Bennie. Another *King's Retribution* crew member, the show's special effects coordinator Hiram Abbas, sat in the next seat, and because of his Middle Eastern looks, the press was speculating

whether or not he was a "mystery character witness" there to cast
bin Laden in a favorable light. Several rows back, lodged between
students texting gossip or iPadding their school work, sat Wendell
Holmes who took in the circus atmosphere, seeing no value to the
evening except that it perhaps would further King's plugs of his
television show.

"Let us qualify our witness to his lengthy history of service to
his country, and his expertise in tracking down wanted felons."

King started into his early military background but was soon
interrupted by the defense attorney. He was a partially bearded,
high-strung man who did look somewhat like the criminal defense attorney Alan Dershowitz, the expert on death penalty
cases, which might have significance, depending on the verdict.

"We accept Colonel 'Storm' King's credentials and expertise as
an ex-military officer," said the defense, stretching the word
'Storm' to bring titters from the audience.

"And you are now the star of a television show called 'King's
Retribution,'" which is known for finding and capturing wanted
criminals?"

"Objection. Calls for speculation. Our client has not been
proven as a criminal, nor does any document thus far produced
show that he is wanted."

"Sustained," said the Judge. "Facts not yet in evidence. Rephrase your question, counselor."

The Prosecution chose to move on, leaving King somewhat
flustered and angry that he had not been able to extol the high
points of *King's Retribution.*

"You captured the defendant, Osama bin Laden, did you not?"

"Yes, I did." In the audience, Callie smirked. King didn't mention it would have taken his entire team to make such a capture,
and as usual, the star witness was not handing out any laurels to
others.

"And where did this take place?"

"He was found on the island of Mindanao in the Philippines."

"And you transported him to Berkeley for this trial?"

The Philippines had a large Moslem population, and the
scriptwriters felt it would be better to move away from Middle
Eastern inferences, as well as not suggesting that the Federal
Government had taken control and transported bin Laden to

Cuba's Guantanamo prison, which would open up another whole evening of arguing the constitutionality of that prison.

After several more predictable questions to advance the reasons for being here this evening, the State prosecutor passed the witness to the defense. This part was unrehearsed, in order to keep the tension heightened and gain unfettered responses.

"You, meaning your television show personnel, captured the supposed most wanted criminal in the world?"

"Yes, King's Retribution, with new episodes this fall." The audience laughed, and King mistook the mood as being favorable to him.

"You did not so much capture Sheik bin Laden as you kidnapped him, is that correct?"

"What?"

"Did you have the permission of the Philippine government to extradite the defendant?"

"Well, no." King did not like the man's tenor and the way this seemed to be going.

"Did you have a warrant for his arrest?"

"No." He thought he had the right answer. "But everyone knew the U.S. Government wanted him for 9/11."

"But you had no actual authority to take him from his home and sneak him away. Isn't that kidnapping, when it goes against a person's will?"

"It was an international arrest."

"But you had no international sanction, either from the UN or from the International Court in The Hague."

"America wanted him brought to justice for 9/11."

"You mention 9/11. But do you have any evidence that he was the mastermind behind 9/11?"

King sputtered, "In one of his tapes he said so."

"Is that true? Is it not a fact that, as monstrous as 9/11 might have been to U.S. citizens, the defendant merely acknowledged approval of the actions? Being a supporter of a political or religious group, where certain members of a wide-based organization take action into their own hands, does not make one a direct participant in an alleged crime. Perhaps not even an accessory after the fact."

"Objection. Move to strike. Our learned defense is testifying, not the witness."

"9/11 was not an *alleged* crime," blurted King, upset that he himself could not offer an opinion.

"Objection," cried the Defense, and the two attorneys began to hurl various posturing legalities at the court, as the Judge banged the gavel.

King was dragged through several more lines of dogged questions, including the defense's insinuation that *King's Retribution* had made the kidnapping to secure the $25 million reward and had tortured its prisoner and subjected him to cruel conditions of incarceration, holding him in a Motel 6 prior to the trial without a working television or access to his attorneys.

King was sweating, finding himself reduced to being the jib of buffoonery, and left the witness stand cranky and complaining that it wasn't what he thought it would be like. He realized the whole spectacle was rigged, something his cadre of friends and supporters had known early on and sought to give him a warning.

The trial continued for another hour and half. The prosecution entered a list of bin Laden's crimes, not only 9/11 atrocities but also bombings he directed across the Middle East, on the continent of Africa and even nightclub destruction in Indonesia. That Osama bin Laden, cried the prosecution, was the mastermind of an evil criminal organization that hid behind religious extremist slogans to prey on and enlist gullible followers.

Osama bin Laden's defense laid a strong foundation for freeing its client. If there were to be a real trial, it proffered, it should be under the World Court, not U.S. jurisdiction where its client could not gain a fair trial – not in any courthouse in America. That bringing bin Laden to any American court would be illegal because habeas corpus would not be in place, and chances were the U.S. Government would place bin Laden at Guantanamo. And as proven by other alleged combat belligerents, he would not have access to an attorney, nor be allowed to defend himself under the American jurisprudence system, as opposed to in a military court. And even if a kangaroo court convicted him, the defense said, he would most likely be executed quickly without opportunity of the appeal process. Finally, to King's chagrin, the defense again argued that its client had been maliciously kidnapped by "bounty hunting ruffians" and that there was no legal basis for such detention.

Both sides gave flowery summations, and to speed along the outcome the judge instructed the jury, made up of students and professors, to cast ballots there in their seats. The verdict: *Not guilty.* This brought cheers from one side of the audience, and hoots and boos from the other, with many of those shouting, "Hang him like Saddam!"

Now, late in the evening, the audience began breaking up, leaving small cliques still arguing damning evidence against the "trampled rights" of the accused. Post-jury remarks made it clear that the majority felt bin Laden should be tried in the World Court for crimes against humanity. Liberal pre-law activists ranted that bin Laden would not get a fair trial in the U.S., and that it was American fairness that held sway above and beyond the crime, even a heinous one, that someone was accused of committing.

After all, they cried out to make their point, then-lawyer and future president John Adams defended British redcoats for murder (and got them acquitted)! Elsewhere, supporters of the "hang 'em" school of justice crowded around King dispensing anger at the verdict and praising him for his actions and testimony, which mollified the television star and reassured him that going on a search for bin Laden would lead to improved show ratings.

36.

Viewing the departing audience, Callie saw the show's newest member – or rather the bin Laden hunt facilitator, Wendell Holmes – sitting by himself and tapping out a text message with his large thumbs. She smiled in surprise, not thinking of him as tech-savvy, and she would have been incredulous if she'd seen what he was sending out.

Holmes had been singularly impressed, but for a far different reason than listening to stimulating forensic debate. He was impressed not so much by the final verdict but by the passionate confetti of political logic that led to that outcome. Could not the Agency and the White House see what he had just witnessed?

It took Holmes considerable trial and effort to tap out this note on his iPhone; he was all thumbs and not a man in love with make-life-easy tech devices. Tonight's entertainment proved the point – that a donnybrook would occur if bin Laden were to be matriculated through U.S. courts, and that there was a chance, though slim, that he could be found less than responsible for the actions of others. Yes, he would be found guilty – the man-in-the-street mob sentiment was still strong – but the death penalty might not happen. Bin Laden wanted martyrdom, and sensing this, a mixed jury might think they were punishing him by sticking the SOB in the basement of a hellhole prison; life without parole. But in response, this would only incite every card-carrying al-Qaeda member around the world to highjack planes or ships loaded with American passengers in order to barter for their leader's freedom. No, he had defined the thorny problem correctly and knew he had to forcefully enunciate, and move the White House to see this dilemma.

If the U.S. captured bin Laden and moved him to Guantanamo Bay, it then, because of current law, could not move him to U.S. soil, not even to stand trial. The President remained committed to closing that prison, and if that happened, both bin Laden and second-in-command Zawahiri, already indicted, would stand trial in New York City. Again, it would be a jurisdictional tug-of-war by myriad federal agencies, and Holmes was certain it would take 10 years of legal motions and two-step appeal wrangling before a trial even commenced. The current Administration was poles apart in the discussion. Holmes's boss at the CIA, in dis-

cussion before a Senate committee on worldwide threats, had
hypothetically suggested that if bin Laden were captured he'd be
interrogated at Bagram Airfield in Afghanistan and "eventually"
sent to Guantanamo Bay. Holmes knew from past direct
knowledge that this meant waterboarding, for information that
uncovered the whereabouts of other al-Qaeda operatives – while
the U.S. left leaning press, and its cohorts in the Administration,
would cry torture, and families of 9/11 victims would demand bin
Laden be answerable to the U.S. court system.

A clusterfuck, Holmes thought again, and he hit the Send button.

Holmes comfortable in his assessment, rose and followed the
audience out into the night.

37.

Late evening April 11   University of California at Berkeley

When they heard the curdled scream, they were on the steps of the auditorium, awaiting the limos for the trip back to the hotel. Glancing around, they thought they saw two figures on the sidewalk across the street. Callie took off running, with Holmes a step behind.

Hugh Fox turned to Samantha. "Stay here, call the police."

King, who was still at the door signing autographs, barely looked up. Fox hurried down the steps, more at a fast, wary pace than running, concerned about what sort of disgruntled and perhaps crazed spectators were having a fistfight.

Someone took off running down a shadowed alleyway, his footsteps fading.

Callie and the CIA agent hovered over the man on the ground, listening to his moaning and his gurgled crying, and noticed blood on the ground. Fox arrived and bent over the injured man.

"Good God, call an ambulance!" he said. "His eyes have been gouged out!"

"It's that church nut," said Holmes, seeing strewn posters around them and regarding the bloodied, eyeless face. "The preacher at the airport. The one burning the Koran."

Callie had pulled her pistol out of her evening purse and started after the attacker when Hugh caught up to her and grabbed her arm.

"Callie, no. You have no back-up and there's a lunatic with a knife, maybe his own gun, out there in the dark."

She looked into his eyes, saw concern, and relented. They heard sirens drawing closer, and saw a curious crowd surging toward them. They turned back to blinded Pastor Samuel Tate, whose head was rolling side to side in excruciating pain. Samantha was here, on her knees with blood soaking her dress, holding the man's grasping hands away from his face. The injured man sought feebly to restore his own sight to empty eye sockets, like some kind of desperate miracle.

"From what I can see," said Holmes, returning from his own survey of the attack ground and not realizing his poor choice of words, "there was no Koran burning tonight, because I don't see a Koran. But I did find one of these...." He held up a bloody eyeball. "We need a cup of ice. I doubt it can be saved, but maybe there's a prayer of a chance."

38.

CIA Headquarters   Washington, D.C.

The night staffer at the al-Qaeda desk at Langley received the clear text message, recorded it, and placed it queue for morning review and action, if any. They knew who Holmes was, and his entry code and his Middle East background. After all, he was still one of them.

By the next morning, April 12, the message had been sanitized, Holmes's name removed since many knew of his muddy reputation within Langley. On April 13th, it reached the desk of Ronald Givens, who was preparing the day's briefing report for the Director of the CIA, who would be giving a worldview intelligence summary to the President at a mid-morning briefing.

The message read:

"It is my recommendation, upon recent analysis of legal circumstances within the U.S., that apprehension of Geronimo is not conducive to a favorable resolution for all concerned, and that better circumstances would be the action taken of extreme prejudice."

Givens wrote 'Concur' under the message, and initialed the report. He had no reasoning in his sign-off, no knowledge that the author was the one man whose career he wanted to see tank, and had done his utmost to push the man down the stairs and out the Agency door. Givens just felt it would do him no harm to support a finding for the termination of a terrorist.

With the critical information in the world reduced to bullet points for the Leader of the Free World, the Director of the CIA, reading from his notes, said simply, "Our legal and field analysts believe it best that, should any combat situation be initiated, that Geronimo not survive."

The President of the United States had recently heard his own Attorney General state that he hoped the U.S. would capture and interrogate bin Laden, but that they did not expect the al-Qaeda leader to be taken alive. Not knowing that a CIA agent had used the term "clusterfuck" to describe the legal situation in a jailed bin Laden, the President of the United States, saw the world through politically tinted glasses, a reelection campaign lay ahead, and this was a moral issue not requiring national debate.

"Do we still believe we have him located?"

"Yes," came the reply. "Our assessment is that there is a 50 percent probability he is in that house. If he's not there, it's at least a command center and a target of the upper echelon."

The President turned to the three military men in the Oval Office.

"Are we ready to launch?" he asked.

"Training is being completed. Two more weeks at the most."

"Keep me informed at all times. When your people are in place, I will make a 'Go or not go' decision. We cannot make a mistake."

"Yes, Mr. President," said the military men. The President turned to the CIA Director.

"I am relying on your assessments being accurate."

"Yes, Mr. President."

Later, the Director of the CIA stopped at Givens's office.

"The Man accepted your position."

"I'll pass the word." Down the chain of command this word circulated, until the SEAL Commander informed the selected Attack Squad leader: "If he's there we've been ordered to kill the bastard."

Episode 6

Should there be cameras everywhere in outdoor streets? My personal view is having cameras in inner cities is a very good thing. In the case of London, petty crime has gone down. They catch terrorists because of it. And if something really bad happens, most of the time you can figure out who did it.
-- Bill Gates

39.

April 13, 2011 San Diego, California

Rows of concrete warehouses spread across the horizon, drab and dusty looking, like a maze of stubby monoliths where some god had press-punched out repetitive ugliness. Professor James Rogers turned off Highway 905 where it met Siempre Viva Road and drove down a large alleyway road between a pod of buildings, reading signs until he found the D-2000 complex and the office/warehouse #2025, labeled "Johnson Fresh Produce." Informed by his cell that Hassim had just arrived at Lindbergh Field from San Francisco, he parked and awaited his 2 p.m. appointment.

He left the car running for its weak, blowing air though it offered little relief from the heat. Leaning his head back he closed his eyes, his body heavy with exhaustion. He had arrived at this warehouse complex south of San Diego after a long, early morning drive from Las Vegas.

Five hours in travel, perhaps a one-hour meeting, and then five hours back with no one the wiser.

He even paid for his gas with cash.

He cleared his mind and willed himself to nod off for a few minutes. It surprised him that over the last month he had become both eager and nervous in anticipation of Crimson Scimitar, a risk that, if successful, would mean satisfied revenge. Thinking about this as he drifted into a semi-conscious slumber dredged up the history that brought him to this day and its unfolding plot.

James Rodgers had not been born with that name. His mother was a Lebanese nurse and his father, a French Algerian doctor. His parents had in common a revolutionary fervor for aiding the underdog, and in time found themselves working side by side at the Palestinian Ain al-Hilweh refugee camp in Lebanon, where they spent laborious hours tending to the undernourished and ill, performing operations with scant medical supplies. For the first nine years of his life, their son played with Palestinian children in the rubble of destroyed villages.

They were watched over by Yasser Arafat's Fatah militia, who patrolled the children's playgrounds and, after dark, drove their rocket pickup trucks toward the battle lines of the First Lebanon

War, often taking along 13- or 14-year-old boys, who stood in the truck beds carrying the smaller rocket-propelled grenades. Their son watched the firework trails of the large rockets lifting off, red ribbons streaking skyward, in clapping glee. Sometimes he heard a distant boom and was told another kibbutz must have been destroyed. All his friends would cheer, but he did not understand. The drifting smell of gunpowder in the air became intoxicating to the impressionable youngster.

One day the rockets came back, deadly projectiles hurling in his direction, fired from contrail jets high above. And as he watched, the jeeps disintegrated, and the men and boys who had smiled at him vaporized before his eyes. As if it were comforting, he was later told that the attack was expected, a required response for some atrocity one side did to the other, the original offense long forgotten. In press releases, military strikes were always called "precision," except for this one time when the errant rocket fizzled in trajectory and found the refugee camp's hospital. By the time the boy arrived, the dead were being carried out, unrecognizable, his parents among them.

He was not an orphan for long. A representative of UNESCO that had known his parents in the camp rescued the shell-shocked boy who was found wandering aimlessly. The boy carried his Superman backpack filled with few clothes and a tattered copy of the Koran, the only surviving artifact of his mother's memory. The rescuing aid worker's name was Rogèt, with the French pronunciation, and the boy was brought back into the UNESCO camp, where the common language among the humanitarian workers was English. He caught onto the language quickly.

A year later, an aid volunteer teacher from Alberta, Canada decided a good deed for her own peace of mind was to rescue at least one refugee, and that it should be the attractive little boy who spoke her language. He seemed bright and they called him Jacques Rogèt, which she later Anglicized to "James Rogers," James being the first name of her deceased second husband.

James Rogers acclimated to his new mother figure, had a growth spurt, and accepted – as curious youth might do to repress violent nightmares – the good life of a suburb in Quebec, Canada, where both his English and nearly forgotten French could be nurtured.

If he had not run into an Arabic-speaking boy at his private boarding school one day, he might have grown into someone staid and boring. He began to question his life, dragging from his repressed memories his early life circumstances, seeing before him the violence of his parents' death, and feeling he could smell the burned flesh that seared his nostrils. As he questioned his background, challenging his birthright and purpose, he picked up his mother's Koran and began to read with intensity. Eventually he sought out a local mosque.

Above all, in reliving his parents' death he recalled who had flown the jets (the Israelis), and more importantly to him, who had made the bombs and the jets – the American capitalists.

This knowledge did not take him down the road of understanding and forgiveness, but instead down a darker road, where anger festered, became putrid and turned into a hunger to seek revenge. To understand his enemy he had to learn about them, and his schooling led him into political science courses and eventually, because the job market stronger, found him settling in the United States.

Crimson Scimitar was payback for his nom de guerre, *The Professor*, but his dream of revenge had a nightmare aspect. In the many passed years, he had also grown comfortable in suburban life raising a family. His nightmare was seeing his children as orphans, as he once was.

With a start, he awoke as knuckles tapped on the car window next to his head. The visage of Razzor Hassim stared down at him, causing him to shiver as if he saw Death, cold and unsympathetic to his own desires in life.

"Professor, follow me." Rogers did so, following Hassim into the Johnson Fresh Produce building. An older lady, looking like a withered piece of fruit, sat at the front desk reading a Mexican movie magazine. She clicked them in through a secured door. Near the loading dock, two workers loaded boxes of lettuce onto a flatbed truck. Hassim led him to the back of the warehouse, behind crates of food products and plastic sheets into a cold room where fresh fruit was stacked on pallets. Hassim entered a small office and shut the door behind them. On a side wall, storage boxes were piled on a metal rack. He pulled the rack aside, revealing a closed, hidden door.

What time do you have?" asked Hassim, or The Enforcer or Mr. FixIt, as Rogers called him behind his back, replied, "2:15."

"As do I." He pulled out a cell phone and placed a call. "Buenos Días, Manuel. Nostros estamos aqui."

For five minutes, they said nothing. Apparently they were waiting.

The hidden door finally opened and a young man peered out warily, his automatic pistol pointed at their chests.

"Señor Smith," the man said, and he lowered the pistol slightly.

"Luis, ¿Qué pasa?" young man eyed the Professor, and the pistol eased up. "¿Quien es?"

"Mi amigo, Señor Jones. El pago port tu trabajo." *My friend. He paid for your work.*

He turned to the Professor. "And this is Luis Delgado, one of the best. A fierce man."

Peligroso hombre, si? People down here fear his reputation."

The pistol went to the man's side, and he smiled. The door swung back, open.

The Enforcer and the Professor descended a long ramp and found themselves in a tunnel.

Rogers was amazed. Electric light bulbs hung from the ceiling going down the corridor, a far distance. Dual rails lay flush with the floor, a mini-railroad track. The air felt sticky but tolerable, and Rogers felt a slight breeze and heard the hum of an electric motor signaling a cooling system in use.

They walked for five minutes, standing up; it was not a small tunnel. When they passed a red painted slash on the tunnel's ceiling, Hassim turned to him and said, "Mexico." They arrived at another ramp and went up. They were in a storage warehouse, mostly storage shelves piled in disarray with boxes of parts that seemed to be used appliances. The young Mexican brought them to an open area surrounded by crates that was a meeting area with several chairs and a dilapidated couch with uneven cushions. A man, Rogers guessed was in his late thirties sat there, dressed in slacks and a floral shirt.

"Señor Smith, welcome," he said in rough English, and he bade them to join him. The younger man went to a cooler and came back offering cans of Jarritos sodas, and Rogers felt he should not decline. Hassim, or "Señor Smith," made introductions. No hands were shaken, but there were nods of satisfaction. Rogers was introduced with his own alias, "Jones," and the man in charge had introduced himself as "Alvarez."

"Señor Jones, what do you think of what we built for you?"

"I am impressed, and thank you for your work." Hassim had prompted *The* Professor earlier that the less said, the better.

"Your payments to us have been timely and appreciated. We built this like we would an American highway, but with our own builders who never knew where they were. Each night we picked them up and brought them here blindfolded. But my question is: When can we expect our last payment, and does your offer hold true as to our own use?"

"Soon, within three months or so," said Rogers, "you can expect one major delivery to your warehouse, which is to be sent over to us. If our property arrives intact, with no problems, then after that the tunnel will be turned over for your full use, and our obligations will end."

Hassim spoke slowly, so his words and meaning would be understood. "Until that time, this tunnel will not be used at all."

"It is a valuable commodity," said Alvarez, "and should be used as soon as possible. Any time it could be discovered."

"Did you not show us your plans to string perpendicular piping near the surface to mislead their ground sensor sweepers?" Hassim gave him a serious stare down.

"Sí," Alvarez shrugged. "I hope your shipment comes soon."

Hassim ignored him.

"And how are you doing on the people we asked for?"

"Sí, sí. Per your instructions, we have, how do you say it, 'subcontracted' out for five drug soldiers from the Sinaloa Cartel based in Tijuana. These are men without remorse who like your money and will do as you say. We told them it will be some sort of attack on a DEA meeting in the U.S. They are eager to strike back for the losses they have been taking."

"And they will bring the fire power we asked for?"

"Yes. It's a strange request, but they would rather act tomorrow than months from now."

"Well, you have paid them well, for us, to be on standby. They will see action; that we can promise."

"I have decided to place Luis in charge of them. They will obey him, and he will obey me."

"And they will follow our direction, and understand we are going to attack the Norte Americano Federales?"

"Your money has been good, and they can expect a large bonus when they are successful, is that correct?"

"Our goal is success. They will be rich, and you will have your tunnel. And we will be gone, and you will never say we were here." Hassim's voice was clear and slow. His intent was clear.

Alvarez looked at both men and accepted that their agenda, these secret plans, would not be made known to him. He had accepted Hassim's earlier visits and funding for the tunnel, knowing the man was a foreigner. Just as they were, when they were in the United States.

Outsiders. And after several actions of vetting this strange man with one ear, Alvarez was confident, as well as he could be, that this was no gringo sting. What purpose would it serve?

No, he would not kill them and take their tunnel, though his men had pushed for such action.

There was money still to be made, and frankly, though he was a brave man, he feared the man who called himself the false name of Señor Jones. Alvarez feared that if something happened to

Jones, others would follow to take revenge on him, his men and even their families. He believed the others could be as ruthless and merciless as the cartels to which he acted as middleman. And yes, if they were going to help kill DEA agents that was not such a bad thing. And if it all failed, Alvarez knew he could recruit other soldiers for his personal needs, including a new lieutenant.

Luis Delgado, they all were, expendable. There were more mercenaries out there, all greedy, all wishing to advance, with guns and blood, a proven resumè for the cartels.

The three of them inspected the delivered crate. Hassim exchanged a glance with Alvarez and checked to make sure the seals were in place. He left the box unopened as a test of Alvarez's curiosity. Hassim had his own exit plan, mopping up, including killing the man and all tracks of their visit would be erased, but he would have to wait until the dust settled on the fallout from the reaction of the Crimson Scimitar attacks. The tunnel was the planned retreat and it must remain in his control, until then end, then he had other plans that Alvarez would not like.

"Yes, this can be sent over to the other side and stored in that warehouse whenever you have the time. Expect a few more crates."

"Bueno. It will let us practice with the carrier system. A lot of merchandise can move quickly down this tunnel." Alvarez paused and smiled with an open mouthed grin that revealed a grave robber's prayer: multiple gold teeth. "We will control a strategic money maker when we have control of the tunnel."

"In time. I will notify you when the major shipment will arrive."

"Esta bien, nosotros estarenios preparados." *Good, we shall be ready.*

Professor James Rogers said nothing as they walked down the tunnel, back to the U.S. side, and saw that the lights in the underground corridor were switched off. Hassim secured the door and put the metal storage rack back in place.

At their respective cars, the Enforcer spoke.

"That tour was for your benefit. They needed confirmation of higher authority. It gives them further comfort, if they trust anyone to begin with. And if something were to happen to me, you must be here to carry out the first steps of Crimson Scimitar."

"I thought my goal was to provide the three cells, which I have done. Sadly, with this one I have had to buy their services."

"If I am killed, because that is the only reason I would not make our timetable, you would have to be at this location to receive the 'shipments' across the border. Beyond that, all attacks will flow to their own simultaneous execution. Nevada determines the timing of both California and Florida."

Hassim changed the subject, removing his ball cap and wiping his forehead.

"Have you heard from the Scientist?" Having a direct conversation between them was better than risking computer or phone communications.

"Yes, they have put their plans in motion for two months from now. The exact date is being held confidential until the truck convoy can be put in place. But we will know for certain, since he is one of the project coordinators."

"Good. I am glad this attack is ready to be launched. It will be a spectacular success that every one of our followers can rejoice in."

"We can only hope so." Rogers hadn't meant to dampen his enthusiasm, and knew the Enforcer would pick up on it.

"You have doubts?"

"Not really. There just seems to be more headlines drawing attention to, as they call them, 'terrorist sightings.' Did you notice a nut Christian religious leader tried to burn a Koran and someone blinded him? And it was at some event where a television show is promoting itself to capture bin Laden. We do not need the public or the authorities to be on guard."

"Do you wish me to destroy those television stars?"

"No, of course not. I just wish we had the complacency that existed on 9/10/01." It struck Rogers that Hassim had been in traveling in San Francisco, which was near the location of the blinding attack.

"You were just in San Francisco, weren't you?" Suddenly he felt he knew the truth and it produced a phlegm of fear in Roger's throat. He swallowed away sour bile.

"Only passing through. But you are right that we must be vigilant. Hopefully, no more accidents like happened to that unfortunate biker in Florida. Make sure your people are in line and faithful to our cause. Martyrs will be required for the glory of Crimson Scimitar."

With that, Hassim departed for Allah knew where, and that left the Professor uncomfortable. He realized that until this attack was successful he would live on the edge, agitated. He had picked up a new habit of looking over his shoulder and expecting to see this killer with one ear.

40.

April 15   Santa Monica, California

Exuberance about the last month of the chase for real or imagined terrorists had waned, and the mood in the conference room was a 'blah' funk. The attack on the minister at the Oakland mock trial had left them all in a stupor. What had happened? What was their relationship to all this? They were certainly no longer on the periphery of national events; now *King's Retribution* was an indirect catalyst of the violence, with several critics even calling them agitators.

The headlines, which mostly King noticed via his clipping service, portrayed the television show, *King's Retribution,* as stoking the fires of religious intolerance, and causing the fringe elements to ride along on the show's coattails for publicity's sake. Gone, misplaced from the public's clamoring view, was the honorable quest to capture an international mass murderer.

In the past several days, online and media pundits from both the left and right of the political spectrum decried their insensitivity, or worse, made them seem like ignorant grandstanders. It didn't make them feel better to hear on the news that though Pastor Samuel Tate was recovering, blind in one eye. The eye, contrary to Holmes's observation, had been "miraculously" reattached thanks to the advancements of modern ocular surgery. Fanning the flames of his notoriety from his hospital bed, Pastor Tate, now a cyclops martyr, filled the airwaves with venom-laced press releases fomenting cries for a heavenly crusade against Islamic devils. No perpetrator had been arrested regarding the pastor's attack, and rumors abounded on what it all meant.

A new flurry of hate mail dripped into the Five Aces Studioz offices, which set the tone when they all reassembled in Santa Monica to refocus on the task at hand.

The quiet team consisted of Hugh, Samantha, Storm, and *King's Retribution* staff members Clayton Briggs and Bennie. J-Q kept meeting notes. Callie Cardoza excused herself to answer an international telephone call. CAM ONE and TWO roamed, omnisciently present seeking ignored invisibility.

Wendell Holmes, their alleged advisor, sat not at the conference table but off in a corner.

His position might have seemed subordinate, but his aloofness from the gathering gave off more mysterious vibes. No one had the brazen courage to ask him: Who did he report to? What did he bring to the table as his expertise? Samantha Carlisle, who made it her career to study the human body, to see how to best wardrobe a body's nuances to accent and draw out the best in character, found herself at a loss as to how to define the man. Not unlike Storm King, Holmes looked rugged, yet he gave off a more sublime countenance; less military aggression than King. She almost wanted to say it was a false beatitude, one that could easily mask a sub-surface violence.

His smile reminded her of a coiling viper, a bush cobra or maybe a corporate raider. She had met both, in different circumstances, and dispatched both in her own lethal fashion.

Holmes gave Samantha a nod, his mouth curling slightly upward. To others, the gesture might have been interpreted as a smile, perhaps meant to be disarming. Samantha, though, saw the man's enigma – alluring but not revealing. She shifted, uncomfortable, and turned her gaze back to the table, back to the security of Hugh Fox's defined personality of exuberance with fringe benefits of occasional raw sex the dividend. Today, she needed to give him her support, and for that she was content.

The Team waded through various staff presentations of gathered information and condensed world news reports by various anti-terrorist consultants. Analyst/employees came and left bearing investigative reports. By the end of the two-hour session, a large pile of folders lay in front of Fox.

"And the consensus of what we have uncovered so far?" Fox asked the conference gatherers.

"We don't know where bin Laden is, any more than our own government does," King said, his voice gravely with sarcasm.

"I think we can be more specific on where we don't think he is," said Samantha, who had been paying attention and taking notes. "I would accept the premise, based on his past actions, that bin Laden is still directing from behind the scenes, not hiding, and more active than just giving out occasional sound bites to Al Jazeera television. So he needs his followers close at hand, and an atmosphere where his followers can support or help hide him."

"Considering 22 percent of the world's population practices the Islamic faith, and they are on every continent, we might be able to reduce the search grid by 10 percent." King sipped from a plastic cup, and by now everyone accepted that his drink of the day held spiked octane proof.

Trying to be helpful, the show's get-away driver Bennie said, "I say he's not in South America or Australia or New Zealand."

"I don't think he's hiding in North America," said Clayton, who wanted to demonstrate that his mind had not been impacted by lifetime use of bodybuilding steroids. "He has this persona to project. He's not going to shave his beard and dress outdoorsy and escape to Canada.

Like you said, Ms. Carlisle, he's still the main honcho. He needs a stage to perform on."

King glanced up, bristling, believing one of his own had just put in a dig against him, but before he could snipe about it, the door opened and they all turned and saw Callie.

"I may have something," she said.

"We only accept good news today," said Fox, trying to move the group's downcast attitude into a more positive one. It was the way he led – moving beyond negatives.

"If you recall, I had some feelers out through the international police database about bin Laden's extended family."

"And?" cued King, skeptically.

"Well," she said, and a smile spread across her face. She held it for a few seconds, to drawn them into the anticipation.

"A week ago, Ali Tameni Fatah, who is an uncle of bin Laden's last wife, Amal Ahmed Abdul Fatah, was granted a visa from Yemen to Egypt and then to Pakistan, returning by way of Saudi Arabia and Mecca. He could be on his haji, his pilgrimage to the holy city. But what is more interesting is that he is taking along a woman, not his wife. And more importantly, her age and the birthdate on her passport match the age range of this Amal Fatah's older sister."

"But she is not the sister of this bin Laden wife?" Samantha asked, seeking the significance.

"I'm guessing it's a fake name on the passport. Could be a mistress, yes, but my hunch is it would be too flagrant for him to display a girlfriend that openly in their sort of Yemeni culture."

"So, if that's true, what do you think these bin Laden relatives are up to?"

"Could be anything, but why to Pakistan on this itinerary? Well, it does fit if he's making a swing of holy cities. Islamabad, the capital of Pakistan, is home of the Faisal Mosque, the largest mosque in South Asia and the sixth largest mosque in the world. If he is flying under that cover story, maybe we can take the jump and say that bin Laden's fifth wife might awaiting a visit from her Yemeni sister."

"Okay," said Fox, nodding and noting Callie's seriousness. He saw her building momentum toward a resurgence of interest in the hunt, and the spark they had all been missing these last several days. "Okay, since we have no other lead of substance to date, let's say that you're on the right track. If bin Laden's favorite wife of the moment is having family visitors, it should follow that bin Laden must be nearby."

"Why not land in Pakistan, and then they drive to a cave in Afghanistan for a family reunion?" King was not ready to be convinced so easily.

Fox answered. "Possibly, but I can't see any bin Laden family member, especially the women, wanting to make a social visit in an active war zone. Nor do I see bin Laden cowering in a cave. We are not giving the man credit for the deviousness and survival skills that have gotten him this far."

"I've got more about where the uncle and his female companion are going." Callie wanted to be the center of the discussion; this was her scoop, something that put her above the fray. She wasn't seeking stardom, but recognition of her worth. As she began to speak, though, it suddenly hit her: Who was she trying to impress? Not King. That ship already sailed. He would never recognize her talent. Nor did she need to impress Samantha Carlisle; they were in totally different worlds of achievement. As she began to speak, she focused on Hugh Fox before moving her eyes around the table, so as not to betray any listener preference.

"When I heard that this uncle might end up in Pakistan, I set up a team here to begin monitoring hotels where they might stay, both in Karachi and Islamabad. If they stayed with friends, then we would have no chance, but I was hoping that perhaps the uncle was not traveling on his own nickel but as a guest of the bin Laden family's generosity. If so, the uncle might want to travel in Arabic first class and enjoy a taste of the good life."

And?" said King, a little more interested. His brain cells were grinding out the potentials of a new script plot.

"An hour ago we had a hit. That was the call I took. A reservation was booked under the uncle's name for two rooms in a small boutique hotel, in a suburb just outside of Islamabad."

"I assume your source is accurate?" said the previously silent Wendell Holmes. They all looked at him. The Sphinx talked. "Just asking; we've been down a lot of false trails."

Callie exuded confidence, and her smile was just shy of a smirk. "My information is from international police computers and their filter programs. I flagged several family names in the system, which lists outstanding warrants for genitalia maiming of young girls. I assume my search matrix might be as solid as the ones you rely on." She raised her eyebrows. Holmes did not respond, but waved his hand as if to say, "Go on, it's your show."

"Not in Islamabad, but outside?" asked Samantha.

"A small town called Abbottabad."

"I've heard of it," King said. "That's where they have their version of our West Point.

"No, I can't see it. A wanted fugitive hiding among the police?" He drained the last of his drink, and tossing his cup at the wastebasket, a missed rim shot.

"Wait a second! Wait a second!" Fox jumped up, excited and tearing at the stack of folders before him. "I saw something here. Hold on." They all watched as the centi-billionaire tore through binders and piles of research like a kid searching Christmas morning presents for his Daisy air rifle, or more like, an iPad upgrade.

"Amazing! Here it is." He scanned it to make sure, and then read aloud: "On January 25th (of this year), Pakistani intelligence, the ISI, raided a house in Abbottabad and captured the Indonesian and al-Qaeda-linked militant Umar Patek, on the run from a US $1 million bounty for allegedly helping mastermind the 2002 suicide bombings of nightclubs in Bali that killed 202 people."

"What's an Indonesian terrorist doing in Pakistan?" asked the bodyguard Clayton Briggs.

As if to finish the thought, Bennie said, "If not to confer on tactics with his superior boss."

"But here's where it gets better," Fox said, rifling through more papers. "The Associated Press says that earlier in January, two French al-Qaeda members, one of them of Pakistani origin, were caught in Lahore *after leaving* Abbottabad. It was suggested they were trying to reach Taliban leaders in North Waziristan. But then on January 23rd, Pakistani ISI arrested their contact, a clerk in the local post office. Guess where? He worked in Abbottabad. Too many damn coincidences."

"From what I've read," said Callie, presenting her conclusion, "the Taliban has been strong in the region just north of Abbottabad. The town of Buner, 30 miles from Abbottabad, fell to the Taliban in 2009, and they had an active training camp close to the town of Mansehr. That's only a few miles from Abbottabad."

"Why didn't we hear about this capture of the Indonesian terrorist before?" King asked, scolding no one in particular. "Or of these other captures? Certainly that suggests a concentration of gooks that would be glad to hide bin Laden. Or to visit and pay him homage."

"Like relatives paying a social call," said Callie, emphasizing what had originally brought the current threads together.

"It is interesting to note," Fox said, studying the research notes in his hand, "that although Umar Patek was captured on January 25th, the news was not made public until March 30th, less than fifteen days ago. And only then, the columnist writes, as a slip to the Associated Press. And guess when the information about the capture of the two French nationals and the Pakistani postal clerk, Tahir Shehzad, were made public?"

"Surprise us," said Samantha, her voice adding humor to his upbeat charm.

"April 14th. Yesterday. What do you make of that?"

Callie gave it her best shot. "The intelligence communities are keeping the public from knowing about these captures, and probably providing disinformation to the terrorist network, trying not to tip their hand. But they must be closing in on the quarry."

"Osama 'The Skunk' bin Laden," said King. He swiveled in his chair in order to glare at Wendell Holmes, who sat passive, betraying no emotion. It seemed to grate on the ex-soldier.

"Let's hightail it to Islamabad, and I mean pronto. We'll take a day trip to this Abbottabad and kick some raghead butt." King psyched himself up. This could be the real deal, and he wanted to

be the point man before the cameras. After the Oakland court-
room debacle and the attack on that minister, King needed to
regain the high ground.

Though they didn't match King's earthy response, the others
found their collective spirits soar with agreement. All the facts
seemed too coincidental, all closing in on that one town. Only

J-Q, the boss's facilitator and go-to guy, had questions.

"How do you quickly fly to a terror-prone country and get past
the airport and national security, when they know your publicized job is to capture one of their folk heroes? And just where
exactly is Osama bin Laden? I assume this town is not just a
couple of desert tents, but a city with many possible hiding
places."

"We found the town," said King, rising and cinching up his
belt as though to emphasize his readiness. "Locating the hide-out
is one of *King's Retribution's* specialties. That's why I'm here, and
I am going. Are you all coming, or are you going to stay in Cali-
fornication like a bunch of wusses?" With a dramatic flourish, he
swept out of the room.

Callie had to groan about the display of King's massive ego.
This might not be a cruise on "The Love Boat," but she had to
agree, even if hesitantly, that doing something was better than
sitting on their rear ends. And she did believe all the evidence
pointed toward a specific geographic location.

*What was the least that could happen? Bad intel and a bad
choice of a vacation spot.*

"I think I might have a way to get us all there under the radar," said Samantha Carlisle with an expression of smug conspiracy.

"The game's afoot," said Hugh Fox, laughing, and the rest
joined in to the infectious merriment. Except for Wendell Holmes.

Amateurs, he thought. *They're headed for trouble, and I'm the
designated baby sitter.*

41.

April 19   The White House   Washington, D.C.

The President of the United States cursed and his face shook in disbelief.

"They are going where?" He was in the Oval Office, which was filled to standing room only with all the key players: CIA, Homeland Security, Secretary of State, the Vice President, the Chairman of the Joint Chief of Staff, and core military commanders, who were keyed in to the upcoming raid preparations, including the Admiral in charge of the SEAL insertion. This was their fourth meeting of operational planning with all the power players present.

"They've decided Abbottabad is where bin Laden is hiding," said the CIA Director, realizing his boss was pissed. He felt the same way; and worse, he hated being the messenger.

"Do we have a leak? Is this operation compromised?"

"We think they figured it out on their own, with their own resources. We have an agent in the field. In fact, right in the middle of their camp. He is out of our agency's loop, and has no idea what we are up to. He conveyed that information innocently, in a daily report saying they were on their way to Pakistan via a few other countries."

"But this Abbottabad town..." The President shook his head, exasperated. "Can't we stop these Hollywood Rambos at the airport? Halt them at customs? The Pakistani government surely is not going to allow a vigilante group to go traipsing around their countryside."

"Zoos," said the Secretary of State.

"What?"

"Their travel request is for an official visit to Middle East zoos, tied to the SammyC Wildlife Foundation. The ploy, and a smart one, I might add, is to give each zoo they visit a grant to acquire modernized veterinarian equipment. Their press release went out already. If we find a way to cancel their trip, we will have a good-will debacle with key allies. *Arab* allies."

"Good Lord."

"We can neutralize their trip," said the Navy Admiral who oversaw SEAL team deployment. Everyone looked at him in shock, wondering how the military man defined the word "neutralize."

"We can launch Operation Neptune Spear earlier than expected. Our intelligence has not changed. The last report shows daily life as usual. What we do know is that someone big is living there."

"Bin Laden? Any confirmation?"

The CIA Director felt that the direct truth was necessary. "I am now at about 55 percent 'yes' in our assessment."

"But that's not as comforting as a sure thing. Okay, around the room, what are your opinions? Let's have frank talk, go or no go?"

Most nodded assent in a wary fashion. The Vice President said, "I'm a more cautious man. I wouldn't launch until we were 100% certain bin Laden was the 'Tall Man' the observers have seen in the compound."

The President gave pause as he took in more one word opinions, reviewing them all on a mental slate.

"Alright, caution is a wise practice, but I don't know if that's true in this terror war." He turned to the Admiral. "How soon can we move up the operation's jump-off schedule?"

"Alternatives scenarios have been prepared for, and instead of mid-May I can have our people in place by month end. Interdiction and boots on the ground by April 30, or May 1, no later." The admiral sought to convey firm confidence. He knew firsthand that the SEAL Teams had reached prime operational effectiveness a week before.

"Okay, give me a daily briefing as you get into place. I need 24 hours for a final review of all intelligence and our troop preparedness. And I will be the one making the final decision. Is that clear?"

Around the room came the affirmation on who was Commander-in-Chief.

"And you say we have a spy in their camp? I'm talking about the TV show people."

"Yes, he's accepted as an expert advisor. We were about ready to retire him and thought this was a quiet pasture to park him. But he will follow orders." Recalling who he had in this position, the CIA Director thought to himself, dismayed:

Holmes is a cowboy that follows orders as he interprets them, but sometimes you have to play the cards that are dealt.

"Well," said the President of the United States, "see if your inside snoop can disrupt their schedule; and hear my words, nothing overt or harmful. Just slow them down. I am trying to exact justice for the American people for 9/11, and I won't find this government outmaneuvered for television ratings."

"Yes, Mr. President," said the CIA Director. He wondered what sabotage directive the Agency should convey to Holmes. He thought, *certainly this bunch of celluloid bounty hunters couldn't screw up an op sanctioned by the head of the Free World and undertaken by the might of the U.S. military. Or could they?*

42.

April 22   Bagram Air Base   Parwan Province, Afghanistan

The wheels of the Boeing C-17 Globemaster III military transport aircraft thudded heavy on the runway.

Here I am, back again, thought SEAL Six member Shawn Pacheco, watching moist condensation hiss from the overhead as the cabin's depressurized air absorbed itself into the desert's dry heat. And this was supposed to be springtime.

Whatever the assignment is this time, it'll be big. I don't dare speculate. The briefing will be soon enough. Tonight, maybe.

My part is small. 1-2-3-4. Repel from the helicopter. Blow a hole in the house wall, help secure the perimeter, search for arms caches. Jump back on helicopter. I can do the job in my sleep, what could go wrong?

43.

April 28 in transit, 30,000 feet over the south Atlantic

Hugh Fox prodded, in a friendly manner. "Now that we have you trapped with only a parachute exit, and a captured audience needing mid-flight diversion, let me ask. You mentioned meeting Osama bin Laden once?"

"Three times."

That perked everybody up, as they sprawled in the leather seats of Fox's Embraer corporate jet as comfortably as they could. Samantha, Callie, Storm made up the remainder of the passenger list. J-Q had remained behind as Hugh's corporate alter ego at Skilleo Game Technology headquarters.

A second executive jet, Samantha's, held Clayton, Bennie, Hiram and CAM ONE and TWO and trailed 30 miles behind. The leadership had decided that a camcorder need not capture all moments, and that privacy aboard Fox's jet would allow some candid conversation.

"We're waiting," said Samantha, putting down her *Women's Wear Daily* trade journal.

"I expect we'll get the sanitized, Freedom of Information story?"

Holmes had really not given much support to the fugitive hunt, and Callie was still suspicious of his agenda.

"Yeah, tell us about the son-of-a-bitch," said King. A steward replaced King's empty Scotch glass with a refresher.

Holmes put down his e-reader and removed his ear buds. Later he would continue listening to "The Life of Washington;" there were enough hours of historical biographical audio left to cover all anticipated and unforeseen travel spots in this entire adventure.

Their first fuel stop had been Miami and next the Canaries. Then the first stop on their itinerary would be Cairo, and a visit to the zoo at Giza. Then they'd go on to their covert destination in Islamabad as the guests of the director of the Islamabad Zoo, which was located at the base of the Margalla Hills.

"The Osama bin Laden I first met in January of 1980 was friendly; shy even."

"Bullshit," said King, tepidly.

"No interruptions." Samantha scolded him lightly, and King gave off a low, feral growl.

"One has to keep in mind the historical context. In December 1979, the Soviets invaded Afghanistan. Bin Laden was only 22 then, and he showed up several weeks later, full of idealism. At that stage, he was not radicalized, and he was extremely loyal to the Saud family, from whence his family fortune had sprung. In fact, when I met him he was known as a construction executive for the bin Laden family interests.

"We crossed paths when I was sent as a youngster to Pakistan to gather information on the situation of who was helping, and could we help, as we defined it: aiding the Afghan *Mujahedeen* in its resistance to the Soviet occupation of Afghanistan. This was still the Cold War, and Jimmy Carter was president."

"You said 'we,'" said Callie. Fox gave her a stare that said, "Do not dig too deep," and Holmes continued.

"I met Osama in Lahore. We were about the same age, he a few years older, and we were both determined to shape the world. We were loyal to our home countries, he to Saudi Arabia, and myself to the red, white and blue. We were doing similar work when we crossed paths. He was collecting funds from Gulf Coast countries and funneling them to the Afghan fighters, and I was doing the same from another direction. Right after the Soviet invasion, President Carter started arming the mujahedeen with cast-off U.S. supplies. Several times, bin Laden and I had to coordinate logistics, making sure the right equipment flowed to the tribes who were going to be the best fighters. It was heavy political balancing, for both him and me."

"I saw the movie *Charlie Wilson's War*," interrupted Fox, "with Tom Hanks and Julia Roberts. That was *you* somewhere in that story? Amazing!"

"Please. I was a young grunt in the trenches. More a supply clerk, whereas Osama bin Laden already was demonstrating leadership talent, and he was a problem solver. And as he used funds to buy weapons, he also established hospitals for the guerrilla wounded and bombed villagers, and brought candy and treats to the widows and orphans. While we wanted to beat the Soviets through a proxy war and send them home with a bloody nose, bin Laden was building friendship networks."

"Is it true that we armed bin Laden and gave the Taliban an open door to take over Afghanistan after the Soviets left?" Samantha was trying to understand the mess called the Middle East.

"Not then, and not directly. What we left was a vacuum of leadership. The Soviets evacuated and we left a leadership gap, and created a civil war."

"So you two were friends?" King didn't like this story. "I thought bin Laden hated Westerners."

"Not in 1980. And yes, for a couple of years, we were dark coffee-sipping buds, respectful of our mutual goals. It wasn't until 1986, when he fell under the influence of the Islamic scholar Sheikh Abdullah Azzam that his thoughts turned to the concept of world jihad.

"You might recall that in late 1979, radical Islamists captured the Grand Mosque in Mecca, espousing liturgical epitaphs that bin Laden would mimic years later. But at that time, he supported the ruling al Saud family to come in, under religious fatwas, to allow soldiers to recapture the mosque, using firepower in the sacred shrine and being supported by French military advisors."

They heard a change in the pitch of the plane's engines and could feel the beginning of a slow descent.

"It would have saved the world, and the U.S., a lot of grief," said King, "if the Commies had killed the bastard back in the 1980s." He drained his glass.

"That almost happened. In 1982, bin Laden was trapped with a small contingent of Arab guerrilla volunteers near Jaji, in Paktia Province. They were under bombardment by a Russian mechanized battalion, heavy field howitzers and under aerial bombardment and strafing by a MIG fighter."

On the intercom, the pilot gave landing instructions to his VIP passengers.

Holmes picked up his e-book.

"Well, what happened?" demanded Samantha Carlisle. She was intrigued; caught up in the telling.

Holmes stuck in the ear buds. "I saved his life." He closed his eyes and tuned into the audio chapter about 22-year-old George Washington's fiasco as a military man at the surrender of Fort Necessity at the Great Meadows.

They all stared at the unassuming man.

44.

April 28 outside the Abbottabad Compound

"The old gardener has returned," said the observer, lowering his binoculars.

"How long has he been gone?" The other watcher turned to a notebook, written in coded notations, and thumbed back through the pages.

"About two weeks this time, unless we missed him coming in the evenings."

"No, that is not his routine. He comes when the weeds need whacking, stays a few days, and then he's gone."

"Where do you think he goes?"

"Probably has a poppy field to tend. He would make a lot more money cultivating opium than running a lawn care business."

Standing at the window, back in the shadows, the observer resurveyed the compound as best he could, with only a small visual angle of the grounds.

"Did you hear anything back from the vaccinations the doctor took at the residence?"

"They're not saying much, just there are a lot of the same family members there, and mostly they are women and children all related."

"A good trick, getting DNA encoded for future comparisons."

The other man began to write in his notebook.

"Okay, they want another count of the residents."

"The requests for information are picking up. Something's in the wind, I think."

"We are not paid to think, but to watch and observe and report. I count no changes from last time except for the gardener's arrival. That makes four men in the compound, plus the Tall Man, who you only saw once. Plus the women and children – there haven't been any changes.

I don't know how we can make the 'status quo' sound exciting."

"Just write it up and report it. I wonder how long we're going to have to stay here?"

"Not long, I say. This all has to mean something."

45.

April 28 inside the Abbottabad Compound

"Are you rested?"

"Thank you for concern, my Sheik."

"Is it true, what I hear about our brother Umar Patek?"

"Yes, the government shot him when they raided one of our follower's homes. Patek was taken away injured, along with his wife."

"I am sorry that we did not have a chance to meet. What was your impression of him, Khalaf? You were my intermediary."

"Sadly, he seemed like a man on the run, too harried to be a sharp thinker. I think he wanted to see you in order to rebuild his confidence, to go back to Jakarta and plan more worthwhile attacks on the government."

"You do not think his capture will come back to haunt us here?"

"I am sure they will be tortured, but no. I was very cautious in my meeting with him.

They did not know who I was, and I made a major effort to cover my trail. Besides, as you know, I traveled to see The Doctor."

"And how is our leader?" Khalaf knew that bin Laden had the habit of minimizing his importance and portraying others in al-Qaeda as more worthy.

"He sends you his prayers for long life. Like all of us, he awaits your command to launch Crimson Scimitar."

"If I could, I would do it this minute. It is indeed frustrating that we must await the capitalistic system of the Americans to overproduce their nuclear waste products. The Scientist reports that they are preparing their shipment, but it is still several months off."

Khalaf said nothing. He felt a little jealous that he was not totally immersed in the planning of what would be al-Qaeda's greatest triumph, and angered that his fellow jihadist, Shahin, was at that moment mobilizing in Yemen, poised to lead the main assault.

Bin Laden likewise held silent, as if pondering.

"I am disappointed that all other associations of our followers are not achieving great success; that those in Yemen and Somalia believe Lone Wolf attacks will lead to victory. And I am sadden we are losing so many good soldiers to the enemy. We must again regain the offensive." Bin Laden sipped at tea that had grown cold.

"I am considering," said the future Emir, of the planned al-Qaeda caliphate, "that if we are successful with Crimson Scimitar, it may be time for us to approach the West and tell them I would be willing to put aside my 1996 declaration of war on the United States if they will accept two of my six Articles of Demands. And I may ask you to head the delegation to approach their leaders."

Khalaf leaned back in shock, overwhelmed.

"What a great honor you bestow, my beloved Sheik. I know by heart your tenets. They have been my faith for the struggle. Which ones do you believe will be achievable?"

Osama bin Laden stroked his beard with a satisfying tug. Kahlaf thought he looked worn and tired, though he never left his third floor residence in the compound.

"I think we have achieved one goal by the Americans making their misplaced demands against tyrannical Muslim governments, with their catch phrase of 'Arab Spring.' That is a joke, and so typical of their need to reduce great philosophies into short slogans. Their demands for democracy underscore that we of profound faith will soon be in control of governments using elected Islamic majorities – Libya, Egypt, Yemen and eventually Syria. When we gain such strength, then, like Iran's Ayatollahs, we shall ask for our own Pan Moslem union, but it shall be the Caliphate."

"Yes, in my travels I have seen the disillusioned masses of the faith, ready to rise. I am sure they seek a single voice."

"Crimson Scimitar will reduce America economically, and for fear of another such attack I shall demand, first, the removal of all Western military from the Prophet's homeland on the Arabian Peninsula."

"Your nemesis, the al Saud family, is being undermined by this *Arab Spring* movement.

They will certainly fall if the U.S. Fleet is sent home."

"Exactly. You are, as I have always believed, an apt pupil and a future leader."

Khalaf bowed his head reverently, and asked, "And what of your second demand regarding their retreat?"

"Yes. I want to control OPEC, and raise oil prices to all the Western nations. I hear an economic recession is building across the world. Now is the time to foment increased energy prices. With the fall of the Sauds, we can pressure the Gulf States and our brothers in Iraq to raise their prices. If the American economy fails, then perhaps they will cut back their economic spending on foreign aid, especially to Israel. And that will be a holy quest for another attack, something the Iranians, who I deeply mistrust, still might be willing to initiate with a nuclear sword."

Khalaf heard the renewed fervor in the sheik's voice of his great plans. Over the last days of his presence in the compound he had heard only a disgruntled voice, complaints of followers who did not follow the Sheik's desires. Here was the active man of years past: the Caliphate again a true possibility.

"What do you ask of me? What can I do now to advance our cause?"

"I have sorely missed good conversation. The television reception is poor and when I hear the news, it is not what it should be. There is much to plan in preparing to reach the Americans once Crimson Scimitar has succeeded. Let us talk and strategize, and then I will send you with messages to all our commanders for new battle plans, as well as to select a delegation to visit Washington, D.C. It will be time to bait the lion in his den."

"Who might join me on this mission?" Khalaf wished to purge one name from a planned delegation.

"Al-Rahman will decline I am sure. In fact, I wish to see him become my true second-incommand."

To Khalaf this suggested al-Zawahari might serve in a lesser role, this was a surprise. The Sheik must be thinking in terms of a massive re-organization in the ranks. With the success of Crimson Scimitar, no one would question his leader's commands. Khalaf felt he must force the issue so as not to be undermined by the others appointed.

"And what about brother al-Awlaki? If I may be as bold, I met with him recently, and did not see a man of great vision."

"His American upbringing does not sit well with me. If he were to take a sword and rush into battle, I would praise him and have no doubts. But I do have doubts; he may be too ambitious."

Khalaf had his answer and felt relieved.

"Again, I thank you for such an honor. Allah be praised and guide such our blade to be true and swift, crimson with blood of the non-believers."

Sheik bin Laden gave a weary smile, pleased to hear a positive voice.

"Join me in prayer this evening. Today is the twenty-eighth, and I want you on the road no later than the third of May. By then, I shall have outlined the demands for the Americans to quit the Middle East altogether."

"I am humbled," whispered Kahlaf, "and by your command I shall serve you and our cause to my death." His head touched the floor and tears welled in his eyes. His body surged with newfound energy. Finally, he had his calling. Soon he would be a leader, a statesman within al-Qaeda. His dream of power, of sitting next to the Caliphate throne, would become a great event. And all this new life would begin on May 3rd, when he would carry his mantle of new duties and authority, blessed holy by Osama bin Laden, to all followers of al-Qaeda and then the world itself. Nothing could stop his ascendency; he would never again be known as Maulawi Abd al-Khaliq Jan. As bin Laden had proclaimed, he had the name of a "future leader:" *Kahlaf.*

Nothing could stop him.

46.

April 29th 8:20 a.m. The White House

The President of the United States moved quickly across the lawn to the waiting presidential transportation, call sign *Marine One*, a sleek VH-3D Sea King Marine helicopter.

One of the Marine military liaison stood at attention at the foot of the steps prepared to offer the customary salute to the office, the power, and the man who now held it just over two years into his Administration. Today much weighed on his mind. He was going to Andrews Air Force base to board Air Force One, flying to Alabama to tour storm-ravaged counties. Later, they will say, he looked serious but unperturbed, simply fulfilling those duties calling for a presidential presence to offer comfort to those now homeless. His cabinet and his security advisors know otherwise.

There are many events that define one's legacy in this office, political decisions which might backfire and lead to humiliated downfall and ignominious resignation or a stewardship where accomplished legislation defines the future of American character, like The New Deal or The Great Society. The President knew he was at that momentous decision with options weighed and a myriad of opinions sorted, where the percentage of confidence to a successful outcome still hovered around 51% odds; nevertheless, it came down to the simple two choices of being wrong with the aftermath of downplaying the error as minor in the scheme of daily international events, or being by luck making the right decision and becoming the Avenger, restoring pride by action to a neurotic and uncertain world power as was the United States this crisp April morning.

On the steps of the helicopter he turned to make the obligatory wave to the few staff and press onlookers, and to the photo-clicking tourists beyond the fence. The time had arrived. He motioned over his chief National Security Advisor.

"Tell them it's a 'go'."

The next night, the 30th, put him in one of those ironic moments of playing the consummate actor. At the White House Press Correspondent's Dinner, Host Comedian Seth Meyers cracked the joke: "People think Bin Laden is hiding out in the

Hindu Kush, but did you know that every day from 4-5 he hosts a show on CSPAN?" The President of United States laughed along with the audience.

Episode 7

We love death. The U.S. loves life. That is the difference between us two.
--Osama bin Laden

47.

April 30th   evening Giza, Egypt

His arms eased around her, crossing, and his hands rubbed over her silk nightgown, grasping her small and firm breasts, perfect handfuls. He buried his face in her freshly washed hair with its scent of lemon and hint of mint. She leaned into him with a pleased moan as her hands grasped the elastic in his boxers, pulled and slipped her fingers inside, rubbing and teasing him erect, hard and eager.

"A million dollars for your thoughts," Hugh whispered against Samantha's ear. He exhaled a warm breath and felt her excitement as her hands increased their play.

"I want you to buy me one of those," she said, her head nodding beyond the open balcony of the Presidential Suite, on top of the Mena House Oberoi in Giza. *The Churchill Suite.* The great man himself had stayed at this five-star hotel in 1914, but probably had not enjoyed the hands-on moment quite as they were doing.

Fox looked at the magnificent view of the massive Pyramid of Cheops, outlined by a red stained evening sky.

"One or all three? I might get a better rate on shipping if they come as a package deal."

"Do we have to go on?" queried Samantha, half serious. "Couldn't we stay in this idyllic setting for a week, ride camels across the desert and have sweaty sex on a magic carpet?"

Hugh responded in kind humor. "Perhaps go down to Tahrir Square on Friday nights and join the mob of 20,000 students and the Moslem Brotherhood demanding a new Islamic constitution based on Sharia law?"

"You certainly know how to take the romance out of a girl's wet dream of wanting to be deflowered by a Sheik of Araby."

He nibbled on the nape of her neck and continued the light banter.

"After today, I have the feeling you would rather be seduced next to a water hole with animals looking on, seeing if your screams can out blast lions' roars and the yipping of hyenas."

"Wasn't that a fun zoo tour today? Seeing the North Sahara species of cheetahs and Dorcas gazelles?"

"The zoo officials were certainly appreciative of the grant you gave to initiate a state-of-the-art breeding facility."

"Speaking of breeding...." She purred and turned into him, releasing one hand, but the other hand still stroking him. "I don't want to go, and I bet I can make you agree."

"The Islamabad Zoo is expecting us tomorrow afternoon. There's a long morning of flight ahead, but...." His kiss was strong. His tongue entered her mouth and flicked at hers.

When they came up for air, he gave his own rendition of a feral growl. "Let's see if we can cause an earthquake that will topple the pyramids with stronger tremors than destroyed the Lighthouse of Alexandria."

He eased her to the bed and raised her nightgown. He found her nerve endings easily, but she wanted the moments to last and rolled to his rocking motion. She kissed and tugged at his lower lip and felt the heat of her insides, where her muscles held him tight and brought the momentum of his power to her building climax of shudders and hoarse shouts. At the height of their released sensuality, she grabbed his hair in both hands and pulled back his face to stare into his eyes. She felt a warmth surge from him as he filled her. They were both satiated and breathing hard, their bodies glistening with salty moisture. He fell to her side and she lay a leg across him with her head on his chest, and felt the throbbing as it ebbed away.

She did not love him, and he knew it. His feelings were likewise at odds – the passion was eager, yet the tug of his heart was not so certain; uncommitted. They enjoyed each other's company and spoke the same intelligent language. It felt like they'd had to take their companionship to the ultimate conclusion, copulation, in order to satisfy their curiosity, explore, and revel in bringing each other pleasure. They were people of compassion and caring, yet they could not bring about those emotions between themselves and forge a bond of total loving, of opening themselves up and asking the other to absorb their essence; of making two into one.

They were having a good time during their adventure of trying to do the right thing, and sex was a beneficial byproduct. They seemed to have the perfect relationship for two Type A, bicoastal business tycoons. Passion fusion when they met, business-like text and emails when apart.

Hugh spoke to this situation, but only in a roundabout way and in analogous terms.

"If you lived 3,000 years ago, in the age of the pharaohs, you would be high priestess of the cult of Imhotep, who became known as the Healer." She responded in kind.

"You might not have been a pharaoh back then, because you would not be able to stand the palace intrigue. I think I see you as the Architect, the one who builds the Great Pyramid."

"So I would have 30,000 workers at my command, and it would take 80 years to complete? That's a lot of 1099 forms to file, and I hope the project is a non-union shop."

"You'd find a way to build the greatest pyramid." She toyed with his chest hairs, playfully braiding. "But better, you'd find a way to build a replica all miniature, so all the citizens of Thebes and Luxor could afford their own backyard pyramid. And then you'd bring out Versions 2 and 3, and mint many Egyptian piastres." They both laughed and rolled among the satin sheets.

His hold on her was gentle and caressing. He mulled something over, and he was more serious when he spoke.

"The ancient Egyptians were actually correct in their religion in three instances. Far more realistic than what we have today. As befitting you, they believed that animals could be gods.

Second, they once created a monotheistic religion based on the Sun as the only god--Aten; and they were correct, for without that god, we are all nonexistent." Except for their matched breathing, silence drifted through the room, but street sounds came in from outside the window.

"So far, you are indeed astute. What is the third tenet of your new faith?"

He laughed.

"They had their worldly goods buried with them when they departed their mortal coil.

They held to a religion that believed you could take it with you. Today that would solve a lot of material hassling among relatives and rid us of estate planners completely."

She gave him a supportive chuckle before she turned serious herself. Unexpectedly, she asked, "What do you think of Wendell Holmes? Is he for real? Did he know Osama bin Laden like he said, and even saved his life once?"

"I have no reason to doubt it. On tomorrow's flight junket, he will be forced to relay that tidbit. We are all too anxious. To think that by failing to let a basic stranger die, the future would have been altered and 9/11 would never had occurred; the 'what ifs' are mind-blowing."

"I find him interesting," she said, and there was momentary silence.

"'More than me,' asks the jealous lover?"

"Of course not, silly. It's just that he's a quantity; yet undefined in this mission we're on."

"I would hate that the worldly older man is more of an attraction than youth and indurance."

Samantha leaned up on her arm and looked at the handsome, clean-lined face with wet, stringy hair across its forehead. Then she crawled up on him and moved over his hips. She rubbed against him, bringing a desire visibly back to life.

"A youthful cock prevails every time," she said, shifting to turn her back toward his prone position; anticipating, as she knelt across him.

"I have found the tomb!" his mock cry of thrill. "And to its soft darkness, I bring the Mighty Obelisk!"

48.

April 31st Early morning
Mena House Oberoi Hotel, Giza

Holmes dropped off his single bag with the concierge. He would have breakfast on the terrace, he thought, while waiting for the others to arrive for the limousine ride back to the airport. He bought the latest faxed copy of the *New York Times*, and also the Egyptian-English written *Al-Ahram Weekly*. A quick scan bore nothing that would hinder their plans to arrive in Pakistan early in the afternoon. Local headlines screamed for prosecution and the death penalty for the deposed Egyptian president Mubarak. *Sic semper tyrannis*. Death to tyrants.

Though, he thought, Muhammad Hosni El Sayed Mubarak had been one of America's more supportive bureaucratic rulers with a 30-year run in power, toppled only two months ago.

What had been unleashed? How could the U.S. administration praise the rise of democracy in Egypt when the Middle East desk knows the strength building in the Moslem Brotherhood? They will take control, he surmised from his own experiences. Islamic law will stifle outside tourism, internecine anarchy will bleed out, and dictatorial theocracy will take over – slaying the innocent, like the Coptic Christians, and then the moderates. It'll be Iran all over. From his experience he wondered if the Egyptian military would let their power be defused, place them under the thumbs of the Mullahs, take away their perks.

Dominos tumbling and a more violent world at the precipice. Being shown the exit of his career, should he even care? He laughed to himself: Do I have such an ego that I feel I really could do something about the world's turmoil?

He returned his key to the front desk, knowing that his room had been covered by the Fox-Carlisle Traveling Circus or however they were billing this farce. He had his instructions: tag along and take notes. And in terms of that request, he had performed admirably and had even a free around-the-world trip with barely any effort.

The clerk at the front desk took note of his key number and smiled.

"You have a message, Mr. Holmes," he said. He handed over a printed phone message.

He half expected a change in plans; a decision to abandon this wild goose chase, or maybe turn the jets towards South Africa. The attractive and personable Ms. Carlisle was definitely a "Protect the Wildlife" enthusiast, and he admired that she put her resources behind her commitment. The Egyptian Zoo was definitely a zoo, with its unique 40 acres of lushness, but he viewed Samantha more in the big picture, where she could make a difference. Providing opportunities to send new stock of animals into the wild to replenish wilderness habitats, maybe, or at least what was left out there. Still, he wondered on a ridiculous paradox: If fur stoles came back into fashion, would she rationalize that a mink farm was not the same as stocking the jungles with wild and snarling creatures? No, only for the short time he knew her, he believed she had a good heart. But like him, could she make such a difference, save the world, her world of wild animals from man's slaughter?

He glanced at the note and then grimaced. How in the hell? How, with all their technology, did they send a phone message that could easily have missed him? And how did they expect him to accomplish what they asked? He wadded up the note and tossed it into the nearest trashcan, and then stalked off for a hearty, five-star breakfast. Maybe his last, he thought, before his meals become Pashtu cuisine.

Perspiring and with her t-shirt soaked, Callie Cardoza entered the hotel from her standard five-mile run. This one, though, was a little outlandish: she ran the base of one of the pyramids, and then around the Sphinx and back. This would be her closest she got to the attractions as a tourist, since what was on the schedule now was a shower and packing for the airport. Next time, if there was a chance, she would return as the casual tourist. No, probably not.

From across the lobby, she watched as Wendell Holmes wadded up and threw some paper away. Her curiosity was piqued. There was no real reason for her interest, except her wariness of Holmes altogether, including his most recent tale, puffery that was highly implausible. She had decided the man was a tag-along of no value to this project. Yet, though she was not a detective she was a former cop, and her past experience in the computer field service required intelligence.

And most important of all, she was a woman with intuition.

After Holmes's departure, when she could not see him anymore, she went over and retrieved what turned out to be a phone message. It puzzled her, for all it said was: *Delay meeting until May 2. L.P.* What was that about? She mused over the contents and turned the paper over in her hand. She didn't know any meetings that were set up by either Hugh or Samantha. Was it one Holmes was supposed to arrange? With all his fake buffoonery, was he finally going to be of use to them? And who, or what, was 'L.P.?'

Whatever.

Callie Cardoza would not believe anything Wendell Holmes told them anyway.

49.

April 31st morning Bagram Airbase, Afghanistan

He was a sailor-soldier, part of unit, part of a greater operation, but his training, his focus had been to one task, and other than a mission yet undefined, Pacheco knew little except rumor, until the Commander stood before the assembled group of 70 assorted SEAL specialists, and confirmed, "We think we found Osama bin Laden, and your job is to kill him." The serious looking young men broke out into a cheer.

The curtain was pulled back from the wall displaying photos of what looked like a rural farm neighborhood, and a tarp was yanked off a table showing a scale mock-up of a house. *The House.* As Pacheco could see, as he stood off to the side in the crowded military ready room, this was the house exactly to the life size cut-out they had practiced on in the California desert, as other SEALS had trained on a similar façade building in Pakistan at a place called Camp Alpha.

It now became clear about the civilians who were now giving their report. C.I.A. He and his comrades would be storming this house based on CIA intelligence. Hope the damn place wasn't empty, Pacheco worried. The CIA men didn't identify themselves as spooks, merely 'intelligence collectors'. From them he heard the operation called *'Operation Neptune Spear'*, something he knew, the trident being a part of the Navy Special Warfare insignia. Yet, he had heard the name 'Geronimo' bantered about between two SEALS not in his attack squad, and just within his eavesdropping.

As he listened they were given the overview of the operation, not just a segment, but now heard how it all would come together.

Tonight, the operation would begin, offering little moonlight. The 160th Special Operations Aviation Regiment (SOAR) would provide two modified Black Hawk helicopters.

Pacheco heard the word 'stealth' and thought it ridiculous that you could make a helicopter quiet.

Larger Chinook helicopters would be placed on the ground half-way between Jalalabad in Afghanistan and Abbottabad, sitting on a dry stream bed, poised with back-up fuel or to be there if the operation went sour, to evacuate the survivors or to interdict with Pakistani forces if they were in league with bin Laden and tried to interfere with force. Another SEAL team would sit in a Chinook just inside Afghanistan likewise ready to ride to the rescue.

Pacheco was to be in the first helicopter, Razor One, his sole job to run to the side of the house and detonate the wall for entry, even if the front door seemed to be unblocked. Once the demolition charge did the trick, then he was to do a quick check of the perimeter walls, and look at the outbuildings for booby-traps or hidden weapon caches. Report back to the helicopter to be on stand-by and ready for embarkation. Quick and easy.

Those in the assault force inside the compound were handed out plastic tie-on handcuffs.

Prisoners were expected: five to six men inside, the rest, about twenty or so, women and children. Check women for weapons, secure them all. Two SEALS identified themselves as the detainee section, and it was pointed out where all the captured non-combatants were to be held, so the interpreters could conduct on-the-spot interrogations.

Sitting on its haunches like a soldier at parade rest, Pacheco spotted 'Cairo', the Belgian Malinois dog, trained to sniff out any hidey-holes for Sadaam Hussein type characters, or run down any escapees.

We are taking no chances, he considered, and whoever was in that building was going to be ours by morning. Pacheco grinned to a fellow SEAL, and got a conspiratorial waving Hawaiian shaka, 'all's great bro.'

"Okay," finished the Commander after the thirty minute overview was laid out. "Break into your designated assault teams for your last verbal walk through. Fall out formation tonight at 21:00. Lift off at 22:00. Religious services three buildings to the west available to all after you are dismissed."

Pacheco walked to the front of the room and viewed all the daytime photos posted on the wall. So this was Abbottabad, Pakistan. Looks peaceful enough. Rural farm-like. How does that perspective help? It's going to be past midnight and no moon. Pitch dark, and probably gooks shooting back at us. Maybe they will be shooting off flares and it will be sort of macabre daylight and we will be sitting ducks. Oh, well, considered Pacheco, 'ours is to do or die' and he started listening to the assignment tasking of Razor One for the umpteenth time, still wondering, "Will bin Laden have the light on and the welcome mat out?" Fuck him if he opens the door.

Two hours later, the report came down; cloudy weather obscured the strike zone. The bubble of anticipation burst among the SEALS casting a somber pall, not bitter, just disappointment. Neptune Spear postponed, rescheduled for tomorrow night, the 1st of May. Just great, was Pacheco's assessment: Murphy's Law at work in the guise of Mother Nature.

50.

April 31st   early afternoon over Pakistani airspace

Wendell Holmes's inflight story:

We have demonized the man, and on the world stage, certainly for good reason. But back in the1980's the young man, as I met and knew him, was the construction executive under a dominating family, trying to set himself apart from multiple brothers and sisters, to find himself both for vocation and his beliefs. This led him to be vulnerable to many outside influences, the most telling were the Islamic radicals who shaped their religion to fit the political goals to gain power.

So it was in the winter of 1983, after the Soviet invasion when bin Laden decided he wanted to be an Arab mujidheen, tired of being a Crescent relief worker and supplier of funds to the Afghans battling the athiest Red Menace. As in our history we had 'volunteer' brigades, like Chennault's Air Force against the Japanese, or the Abraham Lincoln Brigade to fight against Fascist Franco. Bin Laden saw romance believing he could form an Arab Brigade to become Afghan Freedom fighters.

He soon had a cadre of a dozen enthusiasts from Yemen, Egypt, and Saudi Arabia that wished to follow him as he went into Afghanistan to set up a guerrilla base camp. I think at this date he was a little naïve and premature, but then so were the Soviets in the war they fought. Bin Laden rushed out to become a guerilla leader without a supply line of logistics, just as the Soviets were saturating the country side with bulky mechanized military equipment. Two wrongs came to blows in the wrong valley.

I was going in country with a supply donkey team consisting of two proto-type Stinger shoulder launch SAMs, the FIM-92B, new and approved over the 'B' model. Also, we carried a couple of heavy machine guns, and related ammunition and repair equipment. Tools were as valuable as bullets. Sand and dust could jam any of this equipment and a good supply of machine oil, and even a battery hand-held vacuums were worth their weight in gold while out in the field.

Bin Laden was leading his Dirty Dozen to reconnoiter a base of operation outside Jaji in Afghanistan and we all happened, as coincidences go, to meet on the same smuggler's trail, and felt our numbers more secure in joining forces. My mujahedeen contact would meet me in two days, and the rendezvous point would be three clicks from where bin Laden had his objective.

The first night in bivouac, as was his nature, he tried to convince my pack carriers to abandon doing the Western Imperialist lackey's job and join, with of course all my military stores, his cause of righteousness. It was not so much Islamic slogans he espoused as battle of good versus evil. The blessings of his cause by Mohammad would come in 1986.

That night we had a friendly argument, my warning him off to leave my job and my people alone. In the end we reached a mutual truce and drank bitter cold coffee, nibbled on stale wheat bread, and slept without tents. The next morning the Soviet observers found us crossing a ridge line, and all hell broke loose. In the Soviet invasion, we tend to forget that the Russians actually did create a viable Afghan military force, and within those people, there were local citizens that kept their eyes out for invaders, us, coming in from Pakistani borders. Once the forward observers saw our line of march they radioed in both for air support, as well as to a military unit with mounted howitzer cannons one valley over.

One minute the crisp morning air is silent, except a bird screech echoing down below on the valley floor, and next the ridge above us explodes, a sun bursting with fireball and concussion. Military measurement by the forward observers, capable but not brilliant with head math, made the error when they computed their trajectory fire, putting our coordinates where we had just been and not where we had just hiked to, and that mistake saved our lives.

The phrase 'sitting ducks' comes to mind as the world around you goes to shit. And although there was no specific trail leading off the ridge line, we did start scrambling down, and the next wave of fire did again hit right where we had been. Rocks and chip shards flying everywhere.

Bin Laden lost one man with granite chunk shrapnel to the head.

The exploding shells became an orange fiery beacon to the overhead MiG 21 Fishbed jet zeroing in on its bombing run. Had the Soviets flown down on us with a slower prop plane with their napalm or with a Hind Mi 24 helicopter gunship we would have been Swiss cheese on toast since the pilot would actually have seen our rattled teeth. As it was the jet's first run dropped his ordinance on the lip of where the cannon fire on the hill still was smoking, and with luck, the napalm ran to the other side, but not before vaporizing two of bin Laden's soldiers, too late off the top path, into crispy critters.

I knew a second strike both of howitzer fire—and these were most probably the Soviets D-130s throwing 122m shell-- and another MiG bombing run were in the cards, and here is when I made the command decision, the gut call, the famous 'under-fire-in-the-trench-cures all forms of atheism'. I told everyone to run back up to the path, and go up. We did this running, trying to hold on to skittish braying donkeys. I had recalled further up the trail, I had seen some sort of cut in the rock, like a wild goat trail, leading down, not the valley we wanted, since this new direction was toward the Soviet mechanized artillery, but it would have to do since we still had targets pinned on our backs. Stumbling down a cliff is as scary as seeing the jet over your shoulder make its arc turn for another run. We could only pray, in several languages, and by the grace of luck, prayer, Jehovah and Allah, the pilot assumed like I hoped that the spotters were again calling in on us being where we had just left. I can tell you napalm heat is BBQ searing when that sort of lighter fuel spreads across the ground even several hundred yards away from our position.

All of bin Laden's remaining cadre were shitting bricks, a couple of them shell shocked. They were volunteers from universities of textbook, their reading limited to ancient authors spouting political science theory, and only with the smoke, heat and smell of death could they comprehend there is no glory when you see a buddy holding his guts. I speak metaphorically for the moment. That happened about five seconds later to one of his folks when the howitzers decided to carpet shell the entire ridge line. We had run out of time and positioning, and in the open, just had to hunker down as shells rained like a volcano eruption with exploding rocks and blossoming lava, but the view from inside the volcano. I had thrown myself down and found indirectly had done so on top of his mightiness, Mr. Osama bin Laden; seems we both were calling dibs on the same overhang of a small ledge. Two more of his men met Allah, and I lost one porter and a donkey bleeding itself out.

When there was a moment's respite as we knew they were reloading, and the jet making another turn, I yelled, 'Screw this shit!' into bin Laden's ear. We had no choice, nowhere really to scramble without tumbling down, and they had our position. No more running left, right, up, or down. I ran to one of the donkeys and hauled the boxes to the ground, and with my trusty Buck Hunter knife opened the box up and pulled out the proto-type Stinger. I couldn't do anything about the howitzers, but the MiG 21 still was a flying thorn, probably on a strafing run with its twin barrel 23 mm machine guns, hoping to skew us into shish-kabob.

I crawled over to bin Laden and said, though he was probably half deaf as I was, "Want a battlefield lesson on the benefits of the upgraded Stinger FIM-92B. I'll give you guys one if we survive! And then loudly, I went through the memorized manual of use, it requires two to operate. I made him shoulder the launcher, but I leaned over him to do all the work. And in a nick of time, we fired at the screaming MiG.

WOOSH! It is a beautiful sight to see the white trail take off, waggle before acquiring target. Back in 1983 the Soviets had not converted all their jets and helicopters to anti- ground missile electronics. The MiG pilot probably received the signal of incoming, and I saw his evasion tactic. Too late. They never did learn anything by studying air tactics from the Vietnam War, mainly since the North Vietnam SAMs weren't aimed at their allies, but at us. The Russkie almost made it, but he was in too close and the Stinger at its rated speed of Mach 2.2 hit the plane's tail. The explosion shook him for a few seconds, he tried to save his ship, but the plane's tail fell off. I guess he ejected. Never heard. But I think the crew on the Soviet howitzer tank artillery batteries had followed the rocket action because we gained a quick silence in the bombardment. Now, the cannon commanders in charge had to start thinking they might be facing more firepower than a throw-back rifle squad of British Empire sharpshooters with old Enfield rifles.

Immediately, I had to find the next target, the spotter team, whether Soviet or Afghan, and had to believe they were on the higher mountain top across the valley, and with field glasses I finally spotted them, a rock embattlement, several soldiers, looking right back at me. This time, I had to do all the work. I had to reconfigure the directional gizmos not to seek out a heat or air-frame registry but to fire innate like a big bazooka. I was never a great marksman, but the projectile did hit right below them, giving them a piss-in-the-pants scare, and sending them running to a safer spot. This blinded the artillery for targeting and that was enough time for us to regroup with our survivors, two of them critical with wounds, and make the trek back the way we had come, back across the Pakistan border, and for me to get drunk soaking in a tepid bath.

Bin Laden gained a good dose of education on that adventure. It wasn't until late 1985 he came back to establish a working camp, on that same mountain top where the spotters had been located and this time brought along hundreds of wannabe hero martyrs. From the battle of Jaji in 1987 to the battle of Jalalabad in 1989 he kept learning by his mistakes to establish himself as a battle field leader which stoked his reputation among his growing followers. To second guess him as a tactician would be a grave error. 9/11 sadly proved the error of our leaders discounting his concept of a world jihad. It is very real threat today as it was ten years ago.

"Did you ever hook up with him again," asked Hugh Fox, looking at the window, seeing the land of Pakistan reach up to meet them as they approached the airport in Islamabad.

Holmes shrugged. "Once or twice more, strictly business negotiations. He couldn't handle a Western Imperialist saving him from becoming kosher fried bacon. Definitely put me out of his rolodex. No, after that we went our separate ways, though in 1991 his fledgling al-Qaeda tried to blow me up and the U.S Military Attaché in Karachi with a truck bomb. Tit for tat, in 2000 my friends sent Afghan tribal guerrillas to assassinate him, but that came to naught. But those are stories for another time, if they can be told at all." Wendell Holmes gave himself a satisfied nod in dredging up those memories, bittersweet, fading. He caught himself and glanced around at them all. Samantha wondered about the mystery of the man, while Callie did not believe his story's veracity except as a tall tale. Storm King had passed out an hour earlier and only woke up when the plane bounced and jerked unceremoniously down the runway in Islamabad.

Exiting through customs, a guide approached holding a sign 'U.N. Wildlife Federation', their cover story, and followed him with all porter-carried luggage out to their assigned Range Rovers, *gansta ghetto* power vehicles, each with darkened windows, each with an armed driver, and a front seat bodyguard from an international private security company; One of the drivers asked for and was directed to Samantha and handed her a note.

Her face showed disappointment.

"What?" Asked Hugh, concerned.

"From the Zoo director. Asked that our tour be postponed until tomorrow. Unavoidable conflict, he says."

"Tomorrow, it is. Not the end of the world. I'm sure most of us are travel weary." His cheery smile, his arm around her shoulders, edged her back to accepting the delay. Her anticipation returned. She hated when someone else's schedule did not follow her schedule. She returned a half-way nod, yes, tomorrow would be fine, and all those around her gave re-assuring smiles, except the one from Holmes. His twist of his lip bore the satisfaction that his call from Cairo, before their flight departed, to his agency station contact in Islamabad, another career man named Henry Kane, brought the required result. Holmes would have to think on what would give him two more days of stalling before *King's Retribution* certainly would take the drive to Abbottabad. Tomorrow was the 1st ...He was struck with a sudden idea as his glance fell on Colonel King (Retired), and retiring, wobbling, to his designated vehicle for the trip to their hotel. Not a bad idea, thought Holmes, easy to implement with no one the wiser.

51.

May 1st   9 a.m.   Serena Hotel—Islamabad

The two of them walked the stone pathway within the Jasmine Gardens of the Serena Hotel.

King's Retribution, aka the U.N. Wildlife Federation, had taken over the top floor of the hotel. When Holmes had walked the corridor on his way to his meeting he had passed the open room where Callie Cardoza, Clayton Briggs, and Bennie were unpacking their travel boxes of computer and surveillance equipment. CAM ONE was positioned over in the corner covering the scene as well panning to the fashion modeling Hiram Abbas, their special effects and disguise makeup artist, who had gone native and paraded around showing off his mufti outfit, more Arabian desert than street Pakistani. The man would be laughed at unless the locals assumed he was an Arab foreigner. It might work. The hotel's location was in the Embassy district.

As they strolled the grounds the C.I.A.'s station chief, Henry Kane, queried, "What's the word as you've heard it?" He was a man of middle age appearance, early fifties, premature graying hair, wearing black rim glasses with thick bottle lenses. He dressed local business casual in a white short-sleeve cotton shirt, with black thin tie, and carried a morning newspaper in his hand, downplaying his role as a mid-level office worker or an English-speaking manager of a telephone service center.

"I was going to ask you the same thing," responded Holmes. People walking the garden were few, admiring the flowers, doing sniffs of the floral aromas, or fast paces with the determination to be somewhere; all look liked they belonged. To Holmes wandering glances, nothing suspicious, though he expected a select few of the hotel staff were in the pay of the government as informants.

"Something is going down," said Kane, in a whisper, "the Ambassador has been notified to be on call this evening." Kane worked at the American Embassy as a passport official, his public face job. "And all essential personnel were asked to be in their offices by 7 a.m. tomorrow morning. Want to take a stab; you were usually pretty good at deductive assessment?"

Holmes mulled over what information he could ponder, bits and pieces, nothing concrete.

"From what you are telling me, it might be a regional operation that could have blowback. Add in that I have been brought on board to babysit some loose television stars who want to go parading around the countryside in the context of 'Ugly Americans'. Maybe these people I'm with are about to embarrass our government and destroy Arab relations. Then, maybe not." Holmes, the inquisitive, in the job of pumping for information, dribbled out fake nonchalance and asked, "I assume the chatter between our field ops in country and Langley has picked up in recent weeks?"

"Well, yes, much of the incoming from along the border."

"What specific city?"

Kane showed reluctance.

"We are out of the loop for most of the satellite encrypted communication, but we get our fair share of ubiquitous questions, weather, known troop redeployments that sort of thing.

Must mean something to someone."

"What city seems to be the focus, Hank?" It was a mistake for anyone to think all within the CIA family knew what the other office across the hall was doing. Kane had been stationed in Islamabad not because his talent was exceptional; no, he was a desk jockey on rotation, capable but limited, a passing agent of dispatches. Keep eyes and ears open. Holmes, the traveling nursemaid, nothing more, wanted to make his assumptions correct, to validate himself for just himself. He had this sneaky suspicion so any info sifted might yield nuggets.

"Bilal Town, a suburb. A lot of retired military officers live in the area. We've had a surveillance team up there for the last three months. Farmed the job out to local talent, I heard."

Not what Holmes was thinking, but wait...

"Suburb? Of Islamabad?"

"No, of Abbottabad."

Bingo. Kane did not need to join a spy pact and Holmes would keep what he knew to himself. It made him give Callie Cardoza her due on investigative results. To himself, he concluded this could be the Big Catch: The bin Laden desk had tracked down the world's number one terrorist. And here he was on the outside looking in...a mothballed dinosaur. Kane brought him back from his reverie.

"How are the stars of *King's Retribution* doing? I know they're keeping low profile. Are they here doing some background research, a documentary? Something on the Taliban? Assume they're going over to Kandahar?" Kane did his own prying, more gushing than sleuthing.

"That's the plan but the schedule remains to be seen. Its part junket for the troops, no big story. You know, USO sanctioned. The main people, the trip's sponsors, they're into save the world's wildlife and presently are on a morning tour at your local zoo. The rest are hanging around the hotel. But perhaps," and Holmes gave his voice a serious bass tone, "maybe you can help me on two small items, no big deal."

"If it deals with *King's Retribution* I'd be glad to help. I have Season One on CD. Would enjoy meeting Colonel King, if that can be arranged? I'm a big fan."

"Don't see why not?" How easy was this going to be, Holmes mused. He still had the touch; he could do his spook boogie act with a clandestine zing.

They continued their walk in the garden while Holmes told the embassy staffer that he wanted to send a coded diplomatic message to Ronald Givens in Washington, a.s.a.p.

From a top floor window of the hotel, Callie looked down on the two men. That government jockey, their official escort, Wendell Holmes, was up to no good. She just knew it.

52.

May 1st 5 p.m.   Serena Hotel   Islamabad

Holmes savored his light early dinner, a local dish, Lahori Beef Karahi, with freshly made wheat bread, tandoori naan. The day had brought about earned hunger as he saw his objective fall into place, awkwardly at best, nevertheless successful.

Callie, after breakfast, had been pushing everyone for an afternoon sortie to Abbottabad, about 30 kilometers distance, and with her computer equipment set up, wireless activated, and her data programs humming, she wanted a strategy session right after lunch, before launching everyone on her Range Rover expeditionary force. Reconnoitering the terrain, she described the road trip.

Just before lunch, the first setback to her plan flew down the hotel hallway in gushing tears. Samantha Carlisle fresh back from the trip to the Islamabad Zoo, wailed, stormed into her room, leaving Hugh in anguished pursuit. Before he rushed in to give her further comfort, and through heaving breaths, he spit out Samantha's tale of distress to the task force who had rushed to discover the source of woeful crying.

"They had to put down a baby rhinoceros," explained Fox, "some sort of throat blockage.

Sam was yelling she had seen the same sort of illness in a larger rhino on the Sergetti. And if they poured a soupy liquid broth down the throat it would relax the interior muscles, and the baby would stop hyperventilating and would catch a normal breath. The vet on the scene just didn't have a clue, said it was a restricting inflammatory cancer, and the rhino was in distress, and death the easiest solution. She was yelling at the doctor, 'you barbarian witch doctor', but it did no good. After the rhino died, one of the vet assistants reached up into the baby's back throat and pulled out a piece of plastic with a nail stuck in it. We all thought it might have come off a feed pallet. Both vet and Sam were wrong in diagnosis, but it was apparent the baby might have been saved with more testing. Samantha was short of hysterical, kept yelling she could have saved the animal. And, I think with the grant she was bringing them, they might have purchased an updated X-ray machine for larger animals might have indeed discovered the obstruction. But too late."

Fox turned to Callie.

"I've got to go to her. Sorry, but we might have to postpone our logistics meeting until the morning, the trip to the town also." Fox tried to give Callie some positive word, a further excuse seeking her understanding, but lost for words, he went back into Samantha's room. They all heard her sobs before he shut them out.

"That's a bummer, all around, but tomorrow's tomorrow," intoned Clayton, walking back down to their newly established hotel conference War Room.

"At least we have more time to develop some lead concepts, maybe track down the relatives to a closer proximity," from Bennie, likewise trying to make Callie accept the change in plans. She just stood there, looking like she was running on empty fumes. She and Holmes exchanged a stare and he walked away without seeking to make her feel better. What could he really offer?

No, he had nothing to do with the death of a baby rhinoceros, but later in the day, just for the sake of icing on the cake, Holmes accompanied Henry Kane and friends up the elevator to knock on the suite door which Storm King shortly opened.

"Some admirers of yours, Colonel," said Holmes, and immediately brought the group into the television star's room.

"Indeed a pleasure," offered Kane, and when they were all inside, and Holmes shut the door, the American Embassy covert agent made the introductions; of himself as just an embassy staff officer, but the other two men were media, a pool reporter from the *Associated Press*, and a staff reporter for the *London Times*. And with the shaking of hands, King recognized these men as important conduits to the public who, with the right finesse, could assure his further rise in international stardom.

To salute like-minded worldly men of action, to establish a sense of instant camaraderie, Holmes pulled from a large grocery sack he had brought along two bottles of Scotch, knowing the label was King's preferred cask peat sipping choice. No mini bar to slake one's thirst, a flow of the good stuff would do the trick.

"Are you here because of your announcement to bring bin Laden to justice," questioned the *AP* reporter, pencil ready in hand, a man quick to the point, his trademark.

"Will you take bin Laden, when you capture him, to the World Court in The Hague," inquired the *Times* man, more in tune with international protocol.

"How in *Episode 6* did you know the drug dealer was hiding with his sister-in-law," asked Hank Kane, a stalwart fan. And King puffed up his chest, forgetting he had been warned not to draw attention to their real reason for being in Pakistan and began to respond to each question.

Wendell Holmes, in time, with no one noticing, exited the hotel room. King, by tomorrow morning, would be in no shape to bounce along Pakistani roadways in search of his elusive prey that could bring him unimagined glory. The trip when it occurred, Holmes now felt confident, would be on May 3rd, or even the 4th, just as he had been ordered. Mission accomplished.

As he sought the dining room for his victory dinner, he again glanced at the response from Ronald Givens that Kane had handed to him before they exited the elevator to King's suite.

Holmes's morning message had been brief: "K and friends going to A this afternoon."

Given's matching response, an implication of curtness, but unsaid: "No. Cancel trip to A.

Imperative. – R. G."

Smokescreen semantics in sending his message to the Agency, just to tweak the snooty nose of Ronald Givens, give him a moment of jangled nerves, petty yes, but now more than ever suspicions confirmed. *Abbottad. Osama Bin Laden was there. And the American government knew it. Good for them. Even sitting on the sidelines of probably the biggest show of the year, Wendell Holmes was still a team player.*

His dinner dishes cleared by his waiter, Holmes decided a celebratory tea was called for, and he placed his order for a Kashmiri chai, a pink, milky tea with pistachios and cardamom. As he was enjoying the relaxation a warm drink brings to a man's thoughts, he viewed into the hotel lobby and across to small alcove where they had created a type of Persian garden with ferns and miniature palms and festooned with several ornate hanging cages of assorted colorful parrot species, a squawk now and then. Samantha Carlisle stood alone, talking to the birds.

He did not mean to intrude into her quiet, reflective mood. Something drew him.

Inquisitive most certainly, wondering how you talked to a classy multi-millionaire, where class might be an impediment. More to truth, he had a heart and understood another's pain and the need for comfort.

"How are you feeling?" As lame as one could offer and he felt stupid.

She looked at him. Her eyes were still moist, puppy dog eyes. She gave a light smile as she bravely stroked a parrot with its bobbing, darting head.

"Much better, thank you. I tend to wear my heart on my sleeve. Too sensitive when I know nature is straight forward with its random consequences." Momentary silence between them.

In a low life Mafia voice he said, "I can make the zoo veterinarian disappear, if you wants?"

She gave him a quick stare of shock, and then a releasing light laugh.

"That was a major effort on your part, thank you. You're always so serious."

"As underneath are you. You are a woman driven, exampled by your success. " He had rushed out his words and again felt foolish for it.

Samantha turned to him, regarding Wendell Holmes, finding something about him, curious, since the first time he had walked into the conference room in Santa Monica. She almost wanted to say that word again, 'alluring.'

"You seem to have drawn a personal conclusion about me without much research."

"Dossiers. Psychological profiles on all of you before I stepped in. One must know the habitat before traipsing around with the wild creatures, correct?"

"You had us investigated?"

"As, I suppose, you had your people check out *King's Retribution*, and dare I even conclude, you did a background on Hugh Fox."

She did not get mad for such intrusion. He was right though slightly rude by his candor.

Before any investment, for business or emotional commitment, nowadays good research avoids wasting time.

"And what did your 'profile' conclude about me?"

"I'm sorry if I misled you. Others did the gathering; my specialty, I guess, is to interpret the acquired information. Make field decisions for an appropriate response."

"And?"

"And outside my traveling with you these last several days my current visible analysis remains: you are a most attractive and intelligent woman, your dining habits are refined, you hold your fork in the proper manner, grip your wine glass by the stem, and you are outwardly, physically in good health."

She did not think with her hard exterior shell, her business brusqueness that she could color in the face, but she did, to a mild blush. That she found somewhat unnerving.

"You said, and whoever you work for, did psychological observations of us: what is your personal interpretation when you read my file? Am I too prone for emotional outbursts as you saw this noon? Brittle inside?"

He found they were exchanging intent stares, her question sincere, not a sarcastic threat.

"You mean that one might interpret your human emotions of caring as a weakness? No, I do not see that. Trying to achieve in a man's world and yet still being a woman has always been the conundrum, the testing of the inner self. As I see it, a strong woman to the world is not necessarily your flaw but your challenge. Still, you do have one or two issues you wrestle with."

"Ah, now we get to it," and she teased. "And I thought I was perfect."

He could only be serious, and truthful, two of his flaws. He could lie as a spy but not when sincerity was the best medicine.

"Your push for success is a good driving force, but now, this crusade to the far corners of the world to mete out justice? I am guessing this is less for you as it is for Hugh Fox's needs.

"Like your African animal hospital, trying to save the world's defenseless animals from extinction by the ravages of mankind. I sense your basic desire for caring, which is a good trait, has become an ideal that might've pushed you to the extreme of your actions. You want to be the doctor, nurse, a savior to all you focus on, man or beast. Hugh Fox or baby rhinos."

She tightened, arms crossed, stern, back to the stone face, not contempt but an anger of someone probing where they should not be.

"Very perceptive, Mr. Holmes. You are suggesting I want to be 'God'? An absurdity in your conclusions. You should watch carefully where you tread."

He did feel he had stepped into sensitive quicksand and was going to apologize, then reconsidered, he had nothing to lose. He did not report to her. She was tough enough to take any crap someone could throw at her. Maybe that was it; he held this inward respect for her.

"Tell me this," and he said this gently against her sternness. "What one emotion, going back to your earliest youth; what one loss in your life was the most traumatic, that you did not necessarily cry out, and say I want to be 'God', but I want life restored, or I want my special happiness back, like it was."

She had been edging away from him, ready to turn her back on him. She paused to his words, and gave thought. Damn, he was good.

A bittersweet expression from her.

"My first pet, a baby kitten; Snackers, I called her. One day she was in my lap, she coughed several times and died. I didn't understand death, too young. I cried for days wanting breath to come back to Snackers." He saw in her eyes the reliving of the tragedy, his heart went out to her, to retain such an impression all these years, to have it significantly mold your life force, he could understand where that part of being a 'rescuer' evolved out of. She could also bear the weight and he viewed the re-transformation, saw her restore the mantle of her inner power, and watched her shoulders arch back and upright.

"It took my shrinks five years to get that out of me, Mr. Holmes, and you read a report, talked to me, and it's out in less than five minutes. I am impressed."

"As wise old man, I have seen and lived all aspects of human nature and have a good idea on what makes us tick."

Her look wry, again appraising. She too could be analyzing, take a statement and suggest other interpretations.

"You are not *that* old, Mr. Holmes." And she turned and walked away.

53.

May 1st 1:22 PM   Washington D.C.

The Director of the CIA put the final call into the Admiral who from the very beginning was in charge and the primary creator of *Operation Neptune Spear.*

"No last minute change on this end. You may proceed, by the President's order."

"Yes, Mr. Director. They'll be in the air in ten minutes."

"Good Luck."

"Yes, sir."

May 1st 11:25 PM   crossing the Afghan-Pakistan Border

From the outside in the boarding process he did think these new design helicopters, with their fancy hood wrap cowling, did sound less *pocketa pocketa* noisy, but inside, all of them scrunched together, Pacheco felt the noise pounding down on them instead of outward, or maybe it was his nerves. His body jostled with this constant reverberation.

The two helicopters whirled and shot through the night sky, not up in the sky, thought Pacheco, barely off the ground, darting down through canyons over hillsides barely a hundred feet above rocks and oblivion. He hoped the pilot's night vision systems were sharp. It was all coming together. His mind burned intensity. What he was trained to do, what he existed for. The military in him started the mantra in his mind of each step of his sole mission, not his participation in some great historical tapestry that would be recalled in books and film. Real life; a time to fight and survive.

Next to him a fellow SEAL pissed in his pants, not for fear, Pacheco accepted that, probably forgetfulness in the rush to combat prep his equipment; bodily functions were the last a SEAL prioritized in his check off list, working equipment came first. The urine smells merged with odor grease of oiled gun slides and black face make-up on silent and poised zombies.

An hour later, "Weapons check," the yelled command, also blaring over the com headsets. "Hooyah!" a charged-up reply from all. Target sited. Next, in a minute, Pacheco would hear "Lock and

Load"—the call back: "Hooyah!" He would sense more than feel the helicopters reducing speed, then the swoop pointed drop down, hovering, and finally "SEALS deploy!"

"Hooyah!"

54.

11:30 PM Serena Hotel Islamabad

The knock to his door.

Holmes had just finished checking his emails, junk mail, nothing personal for him. A caller this late at night? Hotel staff? One of King's group? In the old days, his familiar Glock 17 would be at his side, his back to the wall as he would ask, 'who's there?' easily expecting the door shredded with automatic weapons fire. Yes, it had happened once before, many years back, in a far and distant empire, long since vaporized by political machinations from lowly citizens wanting their voices to be heard.

He opened the door face-to-face with a Pakistani in a dark English Burberry weather coat. A military cap under his arm.

"Hello, Wendell, dear chap, it's been a long time." The voice accented pure British, a product of England's Royal Military Academy at Sandhurst.

"Brigadier Jamshed Khan. An unexpected pleasure. No, I apologize, *General* Khan.

"Congratulations on your appointment; what was it, four years ago, someone told me? Do come in."

He made his way over to the dresser where a bottle of Scotch lay, unopened.

"May I pour you a small one?"

"No, you are most kind, dear fellow. But my driver is waiting around the block, and I can only stay a few minutes."

Holmes went back to his bottled water and sat on the edge of his bed, motioning the General to the only chair in the room, his accommodations not as opulent as the rich and famous down the hall.

"How may I be of service, as I may presume, to the future head of the Directorate of Military Intelligence?" The cordiality was one, not so much of a friendship of the past, but that at one time Holmes was Khan's handler, and though he was no longer active field service in this area of the world, he expected that Khan's current intel overseer, Hank Kane, would have maintained the very special relationship that Holmes had first developed.

"Well, I must say, it is a surprise to find you back in the field. I thought they'd retired you to greener pastures. Or do they shoot old war horses."

"It's coming, I am assured. But I am not on any covert job. Believe it or not, the State Department made the request, and I have been assigned to act as field liaison for a travelling group of television stars."

"Ah, yes, one of Mr. Kane's favorite heroes. I once watched one show of this *King's Retribution*. Found it, what would you call it, 'artificial tripe'? So, you are not sneaking around my country, up to no good?"

"General, I am escorting wealthy people on a tour of zoos of the Middle East, with the television stars tagging along."

"Yes, I have heard that. But I just don't believe that this would be the Wendell Holmes I remember. What did the Syrians call you, "The Magic Assassin"? A man who could by stealth, never be seen, his skill to cajole or induce others to remove thorny opposition or terrorists they might harbor. Never pulled the trigger himself. It is sad to see those days are over for someone so talented."

"I have no idea what you are talking about."

The General enjoyed the banter of old times and said so. "Kane is not you, Wendell. Wherever the term 'foggy bottom' came from, he personifies it. This last week he has been highly agitated, totally unprofessional for the trade he represents, and those at MI, do seriously believe you chaps are up to something."

"Can't help you there, just a tourist." Holmes saw forehead furrows in Khan's expression.

"But assume I could help you? Like the old days?" Vagueness a part of the protocol.

The General liked to be a thief not a beggar. This was hard for him.

"As you may recall, I have expensive tastes."

"You mean your friend Achmed?" The General shifted uncomfortably.

"Wendell, you are so out of touch. At least Kane doesn't know, or he would have spilled the beans to you, probably make it all seem dirty. Well, as you foresaw back then, Achmed instigated a little blackmail. Sad to say that relationship ended three years ago with an unfortunate accident. Poor Achmed. Drive by terrorist shooting, you know. No suspects. Today, my times are quite pleasantly spent. Brian at the British Embassy, height of discretion, and the young man is quite besotted over me."

"Seeing you happy was always my selfless objective."

"Don't patronize me, Holmes. Through me your people learned out how we think, how to push the right buttons. Like allow your drone flights over our sovereign airspace not become political flashpoints for the leftists or the imams."

Holmes put his contrite face on.

"You are quite right. You are still very important, even if others don't appreciate you.

What is the issue, straight and simple?"

"Brian wants a sports car. I want to buy it for him but don't want to dip into my 'escape' fund, you know, the one you convinced me to set up, in case a change of government kicked me out, or worse, my situation became known."

"Which I have always protected."

"Yes, you have. I am still here, and God willing, still with a career future. And though it is an invisible sword you hang over my head, and the ghost of your connivance keeps me supplying tidbits to the unappreciative people like Kane, and like that asshole who came through here muddling up the whole Taliban cesspool. You recall the man?"

"Ronald Givens. Power on the brain, more ambitious than you, General. If I recall, as station chief here, he boasted at an embassy function on who the U.S. was banking on to run Afghanistan once the Taliban were defeated. His loose mouth precipitated, as you recall, the assassination of anti-Taliban leader Ahmad Shah Massoud on September 9, 2001. Givens is the poster boy of how to stumble into war. Next to 9/11 he's the second reason we had to come to the 'rescue' of Afghanistan and commit troops to this ten year battle to seek 'peace in our time' stability."

"A peace you will never find. Vietnam once more, just with a new generation of arm chair generals without a clue on how to fight religious fanatics who fund their war with opium sales. And Afghanistan is made up of tribes with no desire to form a central government. Leave them alone, besides, we need a neighbor where we can send all our own extremists to kill themselves."

"Thank god, your other secret is safe with me."

Khan look perturbed at Holmes's need to bring up the unsaid.

"Why don't I just have our people remove your head?"

"Not so much but I do keep recorded transcripts of my past field work. But, for old time's sake, perhaps I can be of use to you. How much are sports cars going for these days? Any around you have your eye on?"

"We are not backwater third world; we are very international. And we talk in American dollars. $45,000 will make him a slave to my desires."

"Don't your current stipends from us help?"

"A pittance these days. You've got an economic meltdown back home, so your budgets are cut. And you've so many operatives running around here, most we know about, wasteful spending; it is as if I am considered unimportant."

"Never to me, General. I will honestly see what I can do, but it may not be much."

"And perhaps I someday can do you a favor."

"In this part of the world my power is waning. My political enemies list runs for several pages and there are those who don't want to see me retired, but rather pushed over a cliff."

At the door they shook hands, not friends, not adversaries, but respectful of each other's professionalism. The General had one final question, as he pulled up his collar on his coat to make sure his medals and insignia on his uniform were well concealed, "You are sure you aren't up to something? Just before you got here, your Embassy started acting like a closet full of howler monkeys, and when I heard you were around, I said to myself 'Holmes is back, and there will be a bloody mess, something the Directorate will have to clean up'."

"I am up to nothing," affirmed Holmes, the truth within a lie. Some things never would change. When the General had departed Holmes did his usual maudlin reminiscences, recalling the value the then Colonel Jamshed Khan had brought into the Agency, a protected source, Holmes the only contact, and protector of the soldier's secrets. Holmes would take those to his grave, shocking truths that gave him sway over Khan, leverage, to be a productive snitch. In a Moslem country, and high ranking military man to boot, it would be death to the General for the discovery of his proclivities for beautiful young men. Worse, it would be summary execution on the spot, on any public street in broad daylight, for anyone to find out General Jamshed Khan of Pakistan Military Intelligence was in the closet as member of the Church of England.

As he put his head down on the pillow, Agent Wendell Holmes had not heard the last of General Khan as the yelling through the telephone receiver attested to, when Holmes answered in his hotel room at 4:15 a.m. in the dark morning hours of Monday, May 2nd, 2011.

Episode 8

"I can hear you, the rest of the world can hear you and the people who knocked these buildings down will hear all of us soon."
—U.S. President George W. Bush

55.

12:55 am May 2nd Abbottabad

After a day filled with positive snippets of activities, visiting with nearly everyone important in the compound, not the women and children of course, Khalaf settled on his mattress to read the American novel he had brought back from his last courier run.

Earlier in the morning he had surprised bin Laden's son, Khalid, with a travel guide on France, three years out of date, but accepted with excitement by the young man, who immediately went off into a corner and starting flipping through the colorful pages. 'This year', said Khalid, 'with approval from my father, I will accompany you on a mission and when successful, we shall visit Paris as one of our return stops.' Khalaf agreed, and said he would look forward to also seeing Paris, although he found the city pretentious and over-priced and too Catholic for his tastes.

Khalaf spent the afternoon exchanging gossip with the brothers, Ibrahim and Abrar. The two men were not in the inner circle as Khalaf, knowing only the general concept of Crimson Scimitar, so the time was spent in animated discussion, perusing headlines in the Pakistani newspapers and wondering if certain suicide bomb attacks reported were the work of an al-Qaeda cell or merely Islamic sects with their own agendas against the central government.

They exchanged opinions about the problems that their Leader was having internally with the al-Qaeda branch in Iraq, where underground commanders were pushing for a more virulent strain of thinking, behead Westerners first convert later, and were demanding more autonomy.

On another main subject, all three of the men felt the Afghanistan war proceeded favorably as a religious war should, with perseverance and patience. The Americans would leave soon. 'They tire too easily of long wars when faced with enemies they cannot see', said Ibrahim, 'besides the Zionists control the government and want the American's foreign aid spent on them against our Hamas comrades'.

The conversation ended with each discussing their next trip out of the compound. Khalaf knew that both of the brothers would be going separate directions to deliver bin Laden's latest long-paged missives, one to al-Rahman; another would be the important directive announcing the creation of the 'peace' delegation to the United States, upon the success of Crimson Scimitar.

Abrar, would go out day after tomorrow, his assignment as usual, to visit the internet coffee shop, and receive the incoming news via email.

The sanctioned al-Qaeda website alone received nearly 10,000 hits per day seeking the latest spiritual tomes from their leaders, The Sheik, bin Laden, and The Doctor, al Zawahiri. The brother Ibrahim, had a more dangerous trek, going into the disputed tribal lands of North Waziristan to seek out Atiyah Abd al Rahman also known as Atiyah Allah, the al-Qaeda regional commander in that district and as Khalaf knew, a long-time favorite of bin Laden's. Atiyah, by this new decree still in draft form, was to send his delegate representative to accompany Khalaf to America, as was another a planned appointee from Yemen by the Supreme Council of al-Qaeda, expected to be the choice of Anwar al-Awlaki. Khalaf did not like the idea that the American al-Awlaki would impose his will into the negotiations with the U.S. He hoped, in planting seeds with bin Laden, the delegate selected would not be Shahin, once he returned from his victory in the U.S. If and when that occurred then Khalaf would be overshadowed. He could not openly complain to bin Laden, as his own position was tenuous until he demonstrated his own leadership to stand up to the Great Satan.

His day ended upbeat and blessed as he was asked to have a meal with bin Laden, served by his leader's wife, Amal. She beamed and made shy eyes at Khalaf. He knew the reason. A week before she had been allowed to leave the compound with another woman, Abrar's wife, Bushra, to travel and visit Amal's sister who had arrived from Yemen. After several airport delays, and bus breakdowns the women met finally at one the town's more well-kept hotels, a luxury for Amal to enjoy before returning to strict conditions of the compound. Khalaf had heard the reunion had been joyous and tearful, and when bin Laden mentioned it, Khalaf could see Amal's happiness. If only the world allowed Sunni family unity to rule not governments, then certainly there would be peace.

"I will finish the documents tomorrow," said bin Laden, as the evening's last pot of dark tea emptied, signaling the close of the meal and the conversations. "That will create for you the position of our 'Ambassador at Large', my direct negotiator. You will show those documents to whomever to establish your presence and all will be required to give you immediate support to contact the Americans, but again only when Crimson Scimitar has been executed. Abrar brought news from the Scientist. Because of the meltdown at the nuclear reactors in Japan last month, the Americans are moving up their timetable. We shall act when they do and do so decisively but only by my command. Understood?"

"Yes, Caliph."

"I am putting the final dabbed brushes on canvas for our masterpiece. Crimson Scimitar will set the name of the caliphate in history, so when they think of jihad, Crimson Scimitar will be the name that comes to mind, and our followers will shout it strong as they rush into battle.

"It is late. Go and rest, my son. Tomorrow, we will go over the paperwork for your mission. Besides..." but did not finish the sentence as he looked at Amal, his fifth wife, putting away linens on the other side of the room, and he gave a rare, mischievous smile.

Khalaf accepted this as a silent dismissal, and reverently bowing several times backed his way from the room. Even great men must have release from the pressures of leadership.

In retiring for the night Khalaf's bedroom was not a bedroom, but a closet on the second floor. His narrow mattress filled the floor space and a book shelf ran up one wall, filled with books and magazines. Not a library for all others in the compound to use, but his own restricted research materials for al-Qaeda business. This closet when shut disappeared into the wall as a hidden access, one of two in the compound. The other hiding spot, identical, but on the first floor, held the weapons and ammunition.

Within this cramped space, and from all his reading off the shelves, his ideas when conveyed to bin Laden, over the period of a year and half, had been used in the most surprising fashion. And it was this help to bin Laden which brought the Courier Khalaf to the attention of the al-Qaeda leader, seeing in the young Egyptian, a nobler purpose.

Such heady thoughts kept Khalaf awake well past midnight, his breathing the only noise he could hear for all residents of the compound were at rest. Laying on his mattress under a dangling light bulb on a wire cord, throwing off dull brightness, a translated American book lay on his chest unread for the last hour, his mind racing to what all the benefits and glory had befallen him.

He must rest, be prepared, and he put the book aside, and reached up and clicked off the illumination into engulfing darkness. He even slid the closet door somewhat closed for better privacy.

Silence.

No, a noise. Humming on the wind. Closer, louder.

He sat up, and listened hard. Louder, a whizzing buzz.

Helicopters! Now approaching; here, now!

12:58   Nearby, in the early morning hours, S—A--, an IT employee working from his Abbottabad home tweeted:

Helicopter hovering above Abbottabad at 1 AM (is rare event)

1:05 AM   Tweet S--A--

Go away helicopter – before I take out my giant swatter :-/

1:09 AM   Tweet S--A—

A huge window shaking bang here in Abbottabad. I hope its not the start of something nasty :-S

56.

The Compound

http://www.defense.gov/DODCMSShare/briefingslide/359/1
10502-D-6570C-006.JPG
12:57 AM

Something's wrong!
Pacheco feels the helicopter suddenly start to oscillate, shaking them, a whipsaw effect, throwing a few of the SEALS into each other. Only a few of the rappelling ropes for descent have been thrown out when Pacheco hears the grinding noise crunch—he hears the helicopter tail shear off as it hits the concrete wall.

The pilot must have executed a hard landing because that's what came next. Jaw slamming hit. There is no time to wonder what happened. The lead elements are already out as the helicopter leans at an odd angle.

The firing begins. Chatter from Heckler & Koch 416 carbines with attached suppressors.

Pacheco's line of sight, surreal green with the night vision goggles, catches a glimpse of the other helicopter, hovering above, sniper SEALS covering the compound floor area. He does not need to blow the main gate; they're already within the house grounds. He scampers behind two running SEALS, heading towards the house wall, his secondary objective. Headset talk snipes with action commands. "Hostile Target." Another voice: "Acquired." From a small house a man appears with automatic rifle but is blown backwards, his dying trigger finger arching up a stream of bullets into the dark sky. "Hostile Down." A flash bang goes off in the small hovel. No time.

Pacheco and the two SEALS pass through a gate through another gate. They are in front of the building at the base of the triangle compound. Three other SEALS are rushing behind them. He knows who they are: the Kill Team, find and eliminate. A man and woman appear at the building's front entrance. "Target." Both civilians are armed, one with an AK-47 machine gun, so they are the enemy. Pacheco with the explosive satchel has moved to the left to reach the side of the building. He barely hears the *phifft-phifft-phifft* of automatic rifle fire. The man at the door fires back, barely missing him, before he is hit. The woman standing behind him screams and she too falls, her chest stitched and splotching with a dark mass against a white night garment.

He's at the wall. The plastic explosive charge placed. The three of them move quickly away, flush against the building near the back wall. "Whoosh!" The loud detonation shakes the ground, and before the dust is cleared, the Kill Team enters from the front, Pacheco's two SEALS enter through the blown hole. Pacheco scurries to the other wall and through the gate into what seems to be the garden area, nearly running into a cow as scared as he is; the animal desperately trying to pull its stake rope from the ground.

Pacheco runs along the wall, against the building, covering as he was instructed to, only carrying a side arm, his pack of remaining explosives still heavy on his back and he moves out of sight of the down helicopter on the other side of the building, and he can't see the covering helicopter and where that went he does not know. They must have given up on rappelling onto the roof and have landed outside the compound. He quickly looks to the garden gate and sees no SEALS entering. Everyone must be on the west side of the compound. Gunfire reverberates coming from the building, that draws his attention, and as he is turning towards the sound, prepared, about ready to say in his commset, 'East side Secure' when he senses something in his peripheral vision and glances up. He is hit full in the chest.

57.

The Compound

Helicopters! Above the building!

Khalaf jumped to his feet and by instinct closed his closet door. He was naked except for black boxer shorts. He started for the stairs anxious to get to the weapons downstairs. Khalid is running up the stairs. He holds two Russian PP2000 submachine guns, one he hands to Khalaf. "It's an assault. I must protect Father!" He rushed up to the third floor before Khalaf could ask the all important question: from which Army? It cannot be Pakistani; they have an understanding, an accommodation with certain military officers to keep them informed of such a raid as this. Americans! SEALS! Army Rangers!

Khalaf heard gunfire, from the sky, from the compound grounds and started toward the stairs, raising the machine gun into firing position. What of his future. Of his glory? To end like this, dead, ignominious, in his underwear.

Bin Laden's son rushes back down the stairs.

"My Father says you must escape. Launch Crimson Scimitar! This is his command. Here are the orders." Two USB thumb drive sticks for computers are thrust into Khalaf's hands. "Go now, I will guard the stairs for both of you!"

Bullets ricochet into the stair well.

The window is his only exit from this floor, too small like a large mail box opening but his only chance. He pushed it open, wriggling, scraping his chest as he edges out. He puts the two data sticks into each side of his mouth, but can't pull the PP2000 with him and get out the window simultaneously. He throws it to the grounds outside but it hits the wall and bounces back down inside the compound. He was willing to fight his way out killing soldiers as he flees.

He is barely clothed and now unarmed. If he jumps the two stories down he is certain he will break or sprain a leg and be killed or captured, but there is a small ledge around the building, he is standing on. He glances back in the window just as he sees bullets tear through Khalid, like a rag doll he collapsed on the stairs. Three helmeted-type spacemen, brown-black camouflage, two with goggles, one without, all carrying automatic rifles advance upward, stepping over the dying Khalid.

Khalaf eases the window back into place, hoping they do not look this direction. Above him a large helicopter, all black, no insignia, descended into the field on the far side, away from him. They are being over-run. He looked to his left and right, and saw one helicopter had crash landed into the main yard and leaned against the wall, another helicopter sat, blades still rotating on the other on the outside of the wall. The third and much larger helicopter was just coming in to land. A glance at troops inside and outside the wall, all moving in quick coordination, several were pushing the women and children into the yard, all of them with their hands tied. He heard the curses and screams of the women, children wailing. Infidel Barbarians, damn them!

Khalaf moved in the opposite direction, edging himself around the wall. He was now out of sight of all the soldiers as he turned the corner on the building's ledge. No choice and must take the chance. Jump to the wall, and again jump into the garden, and flee. He grabbed a breath.

Taking the first leap, his feet landed on the top of the wall, and a sharp pain followed and he realized he cut his foot. Awkward, he can't regain his balance. *I'm falling*. His forward momentum flings him out, his arms flailing and he lands with a thud on something that breaks his fall. He has landed on top of a soldier who will now kill him.

SEAL Shawn Pacheco gasps for the wind that was knocked out of him. Dazed, his pistol was knocked from his hand, but senses there is a man rolling off of him. Trained reaction he rolls back on the man, and went for his knife. The man, he sees is without clothes. The naked man grabs at his knife arm as the weapon cleared the scabbard. Pacheco yanked his hand back to stab, but the terrorist head butts him, bringing out brain stars , and he feels a bite to his arm causing him to jerk and the knife exchanges hands, and the man stabs it into Pacheco's chest—and Pacheco knows he is a second from death.

Khalaf stabbed again, but his face registers shock that the knife for the second time bounces off. What? Of course, a Kevlar vest. Then, he is kicked in the groin with such force and he falls back as a deep pain racks him.

"Cairo! Cairo!" The soldier shouts. Khalaf is surprised. Why is he yelling my country's city? *Cairo?* It is code, calling for more soldiers. He cannot forget bin Laden's command: escape. *Launch Crimson Scimitar.* He hovers over the soldier for a second, spits the UBS sticks into his hands and yelled back at the prone man, "Khalaf!" Remember my name, infidel.

"Khalaf!"

The knife will not help him now, he flung it aside, and ran to the gate. He does not open it, fearing an ambush. *They will be waiting outside to shoot me.* He scrambles onto a barrel and hoists himself up to the tin roof of the stable in the corner, glances over, no one there, darkness before him, and back at the soldier who's rising to his feet. Khalaf rolls himself over the wall, in a fall to both fours, to the ground outside the compound, away from the carnage left behind, and the death. The Americans probably have massacred all the women and children. No witnesses to their barbarism. Khalaf hopes, *Let us pray they have taken bin Laden prisoner so al-Qaeda could launch attacks to capture hostages as bargaining chips in a ransom.* Khalaf is thinking such distressed thoughts as he runs low, hobbling in his stride, his left foot pained to the deep cut. He runs through the open fields, escaping, praying he will not be seen.

His prayers would be answered. He could not know the men in the house, the observers, who knew him as the Gardener over many months, had vacated the premises only fifteen minutes earlier. No one saw him. No one shot at him. He ran past the curious who stood in their doorways or stared from behind windows. No one opened their doors to him, no one gave him shelter.

Pacheco scrambled to his knees and stared at the empty part of the compound. He had looked into the terrorist's face, both his night vision view and then when the goggle mask was pulled from the his face in the tussling struggle. He would never forget the terrorist's face, as streaks of lights from the helicopters, from flash bangs illuminated the night in spurts of brilliancy. The man had turned and ran as Pacheco went looking for his lost pistol, anger at himself, growling that he had been disarmed in a fluke attack, had been stabbed with his own knife, and the perpetrator escaping over the wall before he could respond.

With his headset back on, the chatter of the com returned, and he was surprised, the Static talk was in the mode of operational clean-up. Two SEALS came running into the garden area and signaled to him.

"Anything of value?" Meaning intelligence, weapons.

"No." He hesitated, started to tell them what happened, but then saw how the story would be viewed, so he blurted.

"I thought I saw someone go over the wall, in the corner."

They looked and saw nothing, and one of the SEALS grinned. "Shit."

"Yeah."

"No, I mean shit, you smell like cow shit."

You gotta be kidding, Pacheco inhaled. It was all over his knees. He stank.

Over the com, came his name, "Pacheco, back to Razor One."

He headed back the way he came, the two soldiers doing a scan of the garden, seeing nothing, and followed behind.

Back in the main compound, ordered chaos reigned. For the first time, Pacheco saw the main gate open and another helicopter squatted near to the stealth Black Hawk. An Army Ranger stood in the open copter door and manned a heavy machine gun as SEALS were taking orders from two 'intelligence gatherers' and loading the larger helicopter with black garbage bags of 'stuff', computers, an armload of weapons. Over in one corner, a SEAL leaned over one of the dead terrorists, inking his hand of fingerprints, while another snapped photographs of the face, then turned and shot stills of the Compound. About twenty children and four women huddled in a corner, guarded by the two SEAL designated guards, an interpreter trying to communicate with the women, but children screamed, and the feisty women shouted at them all, in a language he did not understand, the tone definitely curses he could guess at. He hustled by the dog and handler, both on alert, and griped aloud at the dog, "Cairo, where were you when I needed you?"

Brief direction from his Team Leader, "We have to blow the chopper. You set it, use additional ordinance from Razor Two."

Running over to the down copter, he found the pilot bagging up documents from the cabin, while the co-pilot pounded on the instrument panel with a tool wrench.

"Don't worry," yelled Pacheco, "I'll make a hot fire." And he started to unpack his C-4.

The pilot kept excusing the crash. "It was a vortex ring, stopped my rotor wash from diffusing, not a malfunction. Couldn't know, couldn't be helped."

Pacheco ignored him and focused on his job, and when he finished on the last of the explosives, having to string contact attach wire to more explosives on the outside of the helicopter, he looked around to find himself nearly alone, and for the moment, he thought he had been abandoned, left for his failure to fight an enemy and prevail. He shook the fear as he saw two SEALS herding the prisoners off towards the building, away from the coming explosion.

Those two ran back to gather him up and the three of them sprinted to the lone helicopter, overloaded with SEALS from both helicopters. The black op helicopter had disappeared. Shawn had never heard it take off yet knew that chopper would be far noisier than the stealth copter he was about to blow. Spooks are spooky.

He stood on the ground, turned and with the electronic detonator, set off the charge, and watched the night sky become a fiery day of flame. Well, thank god, he did something right. He did not realize he was the last American to exit the battle scene. He flung himself into the open door of the Black Hawk, falling against a plastic garbage bag, and when he got his senses, as the helicopter fled towards Afghan air space, he shifted to realize he had fallen instead onto a body bag.

He heard the Team Leader shout into a radio: "For God and Country—Geronimo".

Geronimo. "Geronimo—E.K.I.A." *Enemy Killed In Action.*

1:44 AM Tweet S--A—
All silent after the blast, but a friend heard it 6 km away too...the helicopter is gone too...seems like my giant swatter worked!

Of *Operation Neptune Spear,* in action on the ground, no more than 45 minutes between touchdown to liftoff.

But of that night, May 2nd, 2011, what Pacheco found burned into his soul: a brown man's angry face lit by night explosions, the man shouting at him a threat, a challenge: 'Calif or Caliph.'

Something strange like that. And worse, as a SEAL he had not effectively responded, and coupled with his recall of Montoya's not-meant-to-be death, from that night on, a disease of self-doubt to his adequacy began eating away inside him.

58.

**May 2ⁿᵈ   6 p.m. Washington, D.C.
3 a.m. Pakistan**

The Chairman of the Joint Chiefs of Staff put a call into Pakistan's army chief.

"Sir, I am sorry to disturb you, but I must inform you that the President of the United States asked me to contact you. At this moment the President has also placed a call to President Zardari to inform him of recent events. I am to report to you that the United States conducted tonight a military operation against terrorists around the city of Abbottabad."

The phone line held silence for a few seconds, before the Pakistani military man commented.

"I was earlier awakened and informed we scrambled jets to intercept your incursion."

Another silence. "But our aircraft arrived late to the scene. And did your operation succeed? I am getting conflicting stories of a fire fight, a drone plane being shot down. I assume it was Taliban terrorists you targeted and not Pakistan nationals?"

"As we are both allies against the same cause to stop world terrorism," said the Chairman, "and I am sure you have always supported our cause to bring the perpetrators of the attack on the World Trade Center to justice, I have been asked to inform you and your government that our troops apprehended Osama bin Laden, but he resisted capture and was killed."

Another lengthy silence as a throat cleared.

"Near Abbottabad?"

"Yes, sir." The Chairman could hear voices in the background all talking at once.

Several phones ringing and being answered. "General, I appreciate your formal news and I shall relay such events. You certainly are aware that we will object strenuously to your violation of our country's borders."

"I will be happy to let the State Department discuss the proper responses our governments might craft to maintain our need for mutual alliances. But between you and I, sir, I am damn glad we got the son-of-bitch, wherever he might have been hiding. Good night."

The General in Chief of Pakistan's Army looked to the distraught room full of officers, summoned from their slumbers or late night clubs. Ramifications, that's all he could think of.

However we might spin the story, the Pakistani general considered, *the fact remains the world number one terrorist hid in a military town under our noses. It was a slap in the face to the government, to the military, to our intelligence network, who either knew, or was totally and negligently ignorant. And if they knew, they should have hustled that man out of our country.*

The military man grimaced knowing that al-Qaeda killed more Moslems than Christians, and he too, in his final judgment was glad bin Laden met his doom. But that's not how he would play it in public. And he turned to his staff and demanded a full investigation, and picked up the telephone to call the one man he could now shout at and feel a whole lot better.

59.

4:30 AM Serena Hotel Islamabad

"You bastard!"

"General Khan, good morning to you." Holmes from a sound sleep, awoke by the shrill ring on the phone, and shook his head of cobwebs. Not good news, he presumed, and he was right.

"You murdered him! He was unarmed. Shot him right in front of his wife. Shot her too but she'll survive."

"Wait. Slow down. Who, what are you talking about?"

"Osama Bin Laden. He's dead, killed by your commandos landing on his roof. Killed all the grown men in the compound. One woman too. I have seen the bodies. And you knew this, Holmes. Lied to my face."

"Jam, that's untrue. I knew nothing."

"I don't believe that, and it's General Khan. I have already dispatched a group of my men to keep you in your hotel until I decide what to do with you 'spies'."

Holmes sat upright on the edge of his bed, fully cognizant of what was going to come down on his people, those under his protection. A crisis was at hand. Easily, he could see organized mobs sacking the hotel and the American Embassy, killing them all. Think straight, man. "Okay, General. Here is what my assignment was, God's only truth. I was instructed by my government to keep the *King's Retribution* cavalry from going in country until the 3rd of May. And now I can see why the delaying tactics. But General, I had no operational details. Do you think this New Administration is going to let me, an old schooler, into the full plan? Please consider."

He could hear a brain wheel grinding gears. When the voice came back, the old calmness of the man he knew had returned. The rashness out of his voice, replaced with exhaustion.

"What you said is just so preposterous, I actually can see the truth. It would be like your government to do something right for a change and yet farm out one of its best assets to latrine detail. You were being punished, laughed at behind your back, by your own people."

Holmes did not like that assessment of his assignment but could agree the General hit the mark.

"And we will not be arrested?"

"That remains to be seen...maybe...No, no, but you are all to remain in the hotel for your own protection. The office of our president has informed me your President will be speaking to the world in an hour or so. Bragging rights, but I can tell you Holmes, the natives here will be quite restless. And our government is definitely upset."

"You think the hammer will come down on you?" Holmes understood where Khan's priorities lay, to his own personal needs, and safety.

"The entire Military Intelligence apparatus will be under scrutiny and complaint, from the world, for letting bin Laden hide in our country, from the U.S. for us not catching him in the first place, and then from the radicals who let your killers harm a beloved revolutionary. For the next month or so, this office will not be pleasant to work in, when any of us might be arrested by the ISI and disappear."

"General, you need to do something glorious for the cause to take advantage of the situation."

"You think like I do Holmes. Adversity is opportunity. I have suggested suspending NATO supply shipments into Afghanistan, but that will take time to wind its way through the bureaucracy."

Holmes had no urge to argue in favor of America's continued need of Pakistan roads to fight the Taliban. He needed the good graces of the General, specifically to get his tour group safely out of the country.

"If I can think of anything for your benefit, can I get back to you?"

"Use our old code; come to me as Canadian press. Ask for an interview which I will reject, but will return the call."

"Sounds good."

"Holmes, bin Laden dead is not an advantage for me...yet. Think of something. At this moment you do need my protection. Your life in fact might depend on it." And he disconnected, leaving the threat, serious and sarcastic, hanging in the air.

Holmes rose, used the bathroom, splashed cold water on his face. He glanced out the window. A military truck was stationed outside the hotel, troops not alert but loitering, the news on bin Laden not yet public, but General Khan's action made Holmes accept that the world today had turned very dangerous.

60.

May 2nd 5:30 AM Serena Hotel Islamabad

"Hank Kane." His voice brittle, stressed.

"And you were going to tell me when?" Holmes decided the hurt façade would work well; act needy.

"Holmes, I knew little. Some agency people showed up last night, and we were closeted with the ambassador the whole night. Pretty fucking amazing though, a coup for America and for us." Kane meant glory for the Agency, and for him that could mean reward as part of the team, perhaps even translate for Kane an upward posting to some Caribbean island without any local conflict.

"Hank, I need to call in favors, old times' sake or whatever. You kept Colonel King from driving up to Abbottabad yesterday. They will probably give you an inner agency medal if I spin it right in my report. But right now, I got to get these folks out of Dodge City, before the crazies take to the street."

"The President's speaking at around 8 a.m. our time. I don't know what I can do to help, the Ambassador has us all getting ready to tell U.S. citizens to stay inside, something I think you should have your group act upon."

"Hank, I need Exit Visas immediately. All the paperwork approved, the airport called to clear our jets, all the right palms greased. I don't need an Islamic baggage inspector going through all the camera equipment believing they were part of the operation. What did they call it anyway?"

"*Operation Neptune Spear.* Dammit, Holmes, I wasn't supposed to blurt that out."

"Sorry, an old habit. But do tell me was this *Neptune Spear* as successful as General Khan said?"

"Khan, are you talking to that asshole?"

"Who do you think is threatening me with a dingy dungeon?"

"Just like him. Probably asked for a 'fee' to let you out of the country? That man would sell his grandmother for a bag of silver."

"Or a sports car."

"What?"

"Never mind; did the operation achieve its goals?"

"From what the scuttlebutt circulating, almost total success. Beyond our wildest expectations, especially for the agency, a trove of documents, videos, some of his speeches yet broadcasted. A year of analysis and I bet, with this intel, we bag a few more al-Qaeda goons before the year is up."

"You said almost successful? What went wrong? Any of our boys killed?"

"No, they all got home safely. No, seems there was some helicopter malfunction.

It is a new model, some secret design that keeps noise down. The U.S. Military is already screaming at us to make overture to Zardari's government to get all the non-destroyed parts back.

I heard the silent technology was up in the blades and that survived. Our Ambassador said he would make the call but in a few days. Pakistanis probably don't know what they got."

I wouldn't count of that, thought Holmes. The Pakistan military will be all over the attack site, collecting evidence, processing the area like a crime scene. Preparing themselves to arrest someone, even the innocent. Holmes had to play the obsessed fan card.

"Hank, I bet if you were to expedite King getting out of the country, I bet he could reciprocate, maybe even find a bit part for you in one of the shows."

"You're kidding?"

"Hey, we've gotten close. I know he was impressed in meeting a real in-the-field agent. Get him to the airport and out of here and he will owe you."

"Okay, but we got to wait out today, too much crap hitting the fan. Day after tomorrow is best I can promise."

"That will have to do. Stay safe, Hank."

"You too, Wendell." *Yes,* worried Holmes, *I have this rat-knawing in my stomach, either a need for breakfast or my prophetic acid of worse news to come is working up.* He dressed for comfort, and for any emergency exit, and around 7:30 am brought all the King's Retribution contingent into their hotel suite War Room, where he had ordered in a breakfast buffet. For the most part, the atmosphere was upbeat as they thought today they would go in search of their quarry. Storm King had prepped to look his best, knowing the cameras would be shooting much of him looking intent and determined.

All appeared for breakfast, except Callie Cardoza. She did not answer a call to her room and no one knew where she might be. That worried Holmes because he knew what was coming down. And he also noted that Hugh Fox showed concern. Did Fox know what the President of the United States would be saying within the hour? No, certainly not. Fox had a real concern for Callie's welfare, Holmes could spot the vibes. Samantha was unaware, munching on a bagel, in discussion with King on one of his past show episodes, asking how they usually set up the scenes to shoot when on location; were there any famous words King would utter when he drew down on Osama bin Laden?

"Remember 9/11, you muthafucka!" said King with uproarious laughter, wanting to see the censors' faces as they bleeped him. It would be worth it.

61.

May 2nd 8:00 am   Streets of Islamabad

If there could be warning undercurrents in the air, Callie felt them blow across her face and picked up her jogging pace. She would not make the usual five miles today and turned herself around back towards the hotel. She could see for herself the changing atmosphere for each block she covered military trucks bearing armed soldiers raced down streets and started taking up positions at major intersections.

Callie had started her run 30 minutes early, hoping to take side streets and avoid the morning traffic. To be seen as demur, or less Western in dress, she wore a makeshift variation of a shalwar kameez, a traditional dress for both men and women, basically a pant suit, wide at the top, narrow at the ankle and then over that a long shirt or tunic. Instead of the tunic she felt she could get by with an extra-large USC sweat shirt, her alma mater. Most logo shirts she had seen in the Arab world bore colorful branding and trademarks, from Gucci to The Terminator. To round off her ensemble, she hid her hair under a pull over cap, and thought herself totally devoid of femininity, though she did pick up several catcalls as she passed groups of men opening their shops and putting out merchandise. She sought to avoid this attention but if the Islamic Fashionista Police tried to accost her, speed would leave them in the dust.

This increase in military presence gave her wonder. A coup in the making? Was this something that *King's Retribution* should be filming as background? Heightened tensions from the citizens as she ran past them. With that thought she came around to thinking about Storm King, with mixed feelings. Their relationship was at an end and that gave her a sense of relief.

He had made no move on her since the trip began and they exchanged coolness between them, not hatred, merely non-interest. All that had been the passion of the bed seemed an empty voyage, now being replaced with a caution about the man. Storm leaned more for the attention of the bottle. He seemed oblivious to his star-quality charms and she saw him in Cairo slobbering over two lady flight attendants who first found the star intriguing, accepted his mild pawing as part of the conversation, but later eased away from him as he began to slur his words. Callie did not feel their own break-up led to his increased drinking. No, this had been building. She guessed, and it was a good guess, that he found himself unable to match the hero status his television personae had to radiate weekly. Storm King perhaps was hitting the wall of his own limitations. Unfortunately, instead of overcoming such deficiencies and rising above, back to the star pedestal and fans he had grown accustomed to, he found solace in the liquor glass which seemed to be leading him down a road where no heroes should travel.

Callie saw the hotel up ahead. Suddenly, from a side street, three young men, started chasing after her forcing her to sprint towards safety. Quickly, she outran two of what she assumed were attackers, only to glance over her shoulder, to find the third boy gaining on her.

Who was this kid, Pakistani Olympic track and field? Ahead she saw the hotel entrance, and saw the troops in front. What goes on? Could she get in? Would they stop her, roughly frisk her?

Suddenly, a tomato sailed past her. Guy was a lousy shot. Abruptly, she stopped, bring it on punk, if tomatoes were all he had as a weapon, she'd bust him bad.

The kid was laughing, pointed to her, then to his own shirt, and then ran off, back the way he came.

His logoed red shirt: *Stanford.*

After that, she thought, everything else of the morning would be anticlimactic and with her head held high she walked past the ogling soldiers into the hotel lobby.

62.

May 2ⁿᵈ   8:25 am Serena Hotel Islamabad

Callie walking the hotel room corridor on the way to a shower was surprised to find the entire contingent in the suite they had designated as their central headquarters, and caught off guard to see a pleasing welcome from Hugh Fox, even a smile from Wendell Holmes, who busied himself fiddling with the room's television, changing channels.

"What are you all doing here? And does anyone know what's going on outside?" CAM ONE was at the window, camera pointing down on more troop trucks moving along the roadways. Two jets flashed the horizon, their rumble shriek trailing seconds behind, there and gone.

"Here, quiet everyone, I think I got it," said Holmes, turning the sound up, stepping to the side.

On the screen appeared the President of the United States, walking the hallway of the White House to the podium.

8:30 am May 2nd Pakistan
11:30 pm May 1st Washington, D.C.

"Good evening. Tonight, I can report to the American people and to the world that the United States has conducted an operation that killed Osama bin Laden, the leader of al-Qaeda, and a terrorist who's responsible for the murder of thousands of innocent men, women, and children.

"It was nearly 10 years ago that a bright September day was darkened by the worst attack on the American people in our history. The images of Nine-Eleven are seared into our national memory -- hijacked planes cutting through a cloudless September sky; the Twin Towers collapsing to the ground; black smoke billowing up from the Pentagon; the wreckage of Flight 93 in Shanksville, Pennsylvania, where the actions of heroic citizens saved even more heartbreak and destruction.

"And yet we know that the worst images are those that were unseen to the world – the empty seat at the dinner table; children who were forced to grow up without their mother or their father; parents who would never know the feeling of their child's embrace; Nearly 3,000 citizens taken from us, leaving a gaping hole in our hearts..."

Within the ten minute speech, Holmes heard one truism stand out, one the American people were going to forget in their celebrations.

The President said, "For over two decades, bin Laden has been al Qaeda's leader and symbol, and has continued to plot attacks against our country and our friends and allies. The death of bin Laden marks the most significant achievement to date in our nation's effort to defeat al Qaeda.

"Yet his death does not mark the end of our effort. There's no doubt that al Qaeda will continue to pursue attacks against us. We must -- and we will -- remain vigilant at home and abroad..."

The speech ended, and a Pakistani newscaster, in English, starting to talk in generalities, talk-speak since he knew nothing as did the people in the hotel room. Wendell Holmes shut off the TV and for seconds no one had words to comment on the historic moment.

"Shit," said Storm King, dropping himself on a couch. "I gave an interview to the Associated Press saying how I was here to bring in bin Laden."

"You did what?" Callie had heard Hugh and Samantha's admonition that secrecy of their presence must be maintained, or Samantha might lose creditability to her zoo visits, and what if they did not find anything worth televising. Her eyes cut into King.

"Hey, he was alive, then." King realizing what a pathetic excuse he had just offered.

Callie turned to Bennie.

"Check the computer for any online stories on our 'star'." The last word said in derision.

"Well, what do we do next?" Clayton Briggs shrugged his shoulders. "I get the feeling this is going to cancel Season Three with the Network."

"Probably," agreed Abbas, pulling off the jacket to his colorful outfit, feeling defeatist.

"I'll start working on my resume for the trip home."

"I think our first step is to get us all home safely," Fox absorbed the news, compartmentalized the issues, and arrived at the first priority.

"I put an earlier call into the American Embassy," said Holmes. "To start the paperwork."

"You knew this before the President spoke?" Callie turned on him.

"Yes." Nothing more.

"And how did you know? And did you actually know several days ago. It works out swell for whoever you represent that we didn't get up to Abbottabad over the last two days. Just fate, or was it planned, so we didn't get in the way of this attack."

"First, I heard about it was two hours ago. In and out of channels."

"I don't see how you can accuse Mr. Holmes of interference," Fox came to the rescue as if the secretive man needed rescuing. "I see nothing he did to slow down our progress. We are victims of fate, pure and simple."

Callie blustered. "He's...he's devious."

They all heard this sound, indescribable, like an approaching flood, a noise building from a background to a rush of jumbled human voices, shouts, chants.

There was a rush to the suite's windows.

Marching down the street, sidewalk to sidewalk, were thousands of angry Pakistanis, the flow of the human tide passed the hotel and continued down the street.

"There probably marching on the U.S. embassy," said Samantha, guessing their destination, likewise deflated, confused at what had happened to their own crusade, what was going to become of their project?

"No stories out this morning on *King's Retribution*." said Bennie, looking up from the computer. "But all the news blogs are going ballistic on bin Laden's death. I'll try and pull out the hard facts."

"Old news to us," said Callie, at the window, feeling depressed. With the chase cancelled, She watched the street crowds appearing from nowhere, raising clenched fists, angry. "These protestors already have well printed signs denouncing the U.S."

"There will be a run on American flags at the stores for burning," said Clayton, and King gave him a dirty grumble.

"The government, I am guessing," explained Holmes, wishing to abandon this whole mess. His assignment was over. It was not a pleasurable ending. "They must have had a few hour's notice to call out their hired mobs. Control the mob, you avoid anarchy. I would be more worried when the fundamentalists who support the Taliban take to the streets. And I suggest that today everyone stay inside and just watch TV or DVD movies. I'll work on the visas."

"Call the American Embassy, and say you have hysterical American women, having breakdowns who must flee." This from Samantha gained a pursed smile from Holmes.

"Let me call them again and take their temperature on what we can and can't do."

Holmes used the excuse to exit, glad to be away from people who'd you think just found out they all contracted incurable cancer.

It took five minutes and several re-dials before Henry Kane answered his cell phone. In the background, Holmes heard glass break, a loud buzz of swarming wasps, human wasps.

"Opening champagne in celebration," teased Holmes with his question, knowing the mobs had arrived at Kane's place of work.

"Were being bombarded with rocks." Kane definitely worried. This was not in his job description. "The staff marines are on the roof and the place is locked down."

"I know you're busy, but just to let you know my tour group does want to leave, today if any way possible, tomorrow a must. If you can prioritize, I would appreciate."

"Paperwork is somewhere on my desk. If they don't set the place on fire, I'll get it going.

By the way, another wire came for you."

"Oh, really? Can you fax it over to the hotel? Don't think you or I taking a stroll will be healthy."

"It's an "Eyes Only" transmission."

"Go get it and read it to me."

Silence from Kane.

"Don't think that's a good idea."

"Means you read it. No, secrets between us Kane. It's probably sitting right in front of you."

Silence.

"Well, yes. Okay, Wendell, here it is and I am sorry, truly sorry."

'*Attention: W. Holmes Services no longer required. Retirement contract clause invoked. Report to Home Office Personnel for standard release procedure.*'

Brutal, but not unexpected to Holmes; just a lousy bed side manner of notification.

"Bet it is signed or confirmed by the initials. R.G."

"Again, sorry, Wendell. He really wanted you to know how the pecking order was, he signed it: *R.Givens.*"

"Hank, what's my real status? The termination paperwork for this forced retirement can't move that quickly. He's mean with a long memory but this can't be pure vendetta. I did my little dirty job to their satisfaction; they're pushing me out but I'm a bureaucratic afterthought in this *Operation Neptune Spear.*"

Kane spoke, reading: "'*Immediate Termination. Revoke Pakistan visa. 24 hours to leave country. Oversee personally. R.G.*' That was my message."

"And you are doing *what?*"

"Like a good employee, doing my job. But right now watching thugs climb our fences and being beat by the Pakistani police. I think R.G. and the Personnel Department at Langley can cut me slack."

"Thanks, Hank. I will leave peacefully but I need all my people to exit safely with me."

"All I can do. But tomorrow, if I'm still here." Another sound of breaking glass. The call ended.

Wendell Holmes knew fervently he had served his country well. For the good ol' U.S.A. he had taken a few bullets into his body (one still in there), beaten up and thrown into the sea, a lot of good stories to look back on. It was time to leave. But not like this. Not with a bang, but a whimper. And this was not forced retirement; this was being cashiered out, like he had committed some grave offense, had been a traitor to the cause, all because of one man's desire for petty retribution.

He opened the bottle of Scotch. Looked at it, avoided inhaling the enticing fumes. After a long minute of temptation he put the cap back on and then found a bottle of ginger ale in the mini bar. Cold bubbles on his throat. One good point to all this; he had prepared for such eventuality. He did not leave the Agency tied to a pension as his only income source to pay the basic utilities. In truth, Wendell Holmes was well off, no, be factual, wealthy, not in the Fox and Carlisle category to achieve the *Forbes* list but enough to buy, if he so chose, good size fishing boat and sail the world; a ski chalet perhaps; or even purchase a business to keep his mind sharp. You don't work for twenty five plus years in the hot spots of the world, seeing political fortunes change hands, laundered money move quickly from unnamed source to unnamed source; even money haphazardly discarded when palaces are overrun. His hidden bank accounts gave him such a comfort level.

His true issue, as it had been months ago, what does a retired government intelligence officer, a field spy, do to keep the adrenalin flowing? He had no idea. No absorbing hobbies except occasional stress-relief creative writing, his many discarded short stories. No love life except brief relationships with women passing through his assignments. Sitting on the dock and fishing wasn't him.

The streets below surged with those violently aggrieved, who saw a mass murderer as a hero. Instead of uneasy inner turmoil, Wendell Holmes shifted into General Khan's way of seeing such events: Adversity creates opportunity.

An idea came to him. And he made the call.

Episode 9

In a brave new world, a post-September 11 world, anyone is going to make certain mistakes. The mistakes that have been made on homeland security, on protecting our Nation from another terrorist attack, are mistakes of omission. We are simply not doing enough.
--U. S. Senator Chuck Schumer

63.

3 pm   Islamabad

A News Alert morning moved into a Talking Heads afternoon and created frayed nerves as the 'hotel prisoners' absorbed gossiped rumors, watched television and internet news with its conflicting reports, interpretative by those who ruled the media waves. On CNN, jubilant Americans were waving flags in front of the White House. Al Jazeera television, viewed from their web site, brought out the wailing critics, decrying the murder of Moslems. TV clips showed reactions around the Islamic world, with five known dead in Sudanese riots. Pakistan television showed grainy coverage of the killing field at the compound in Abbottabad, blood (presumed bin Laden's) next to a bed, more blood on the stairs; soldiers standing next to the rotor blade of the destroyed helicopter; while outside the walls curious locals mingled, aware of the identity of the former and now deceased resident. Would this place become a tourist site or a shrine, or both?

When they all had re-assembled in the late afternoon, Hugh Fox, with a lot on his mind and pre-schooled to the agenda, sought to lead the meeting.

"We are all painfully aware that our original task of locating and capturing Osama bin Laden has been usurped by our own country," explained Fox. "I assume for television production values this looks negative."

"Assume?" King spoke, a familiar glass in hand. "It's a fuckin' disaster." Not his first drink of the afternoon.

"Please, let me finish. Perhaps I have good news. We've been offered a second bite of the apple, but we should discuss the ramifications and risks. How do I say this: *we have been offered a chance to get inside bin Laden's house for a private tour, who's up for that?*

He held their undivided attention. Everyone stared at him, then their eyes shifted over to Wendell Holmes, the man seeming oblivious, reading a local newspaper, and a realization swept over them, that they might have underestimated this man, or never gave him the value he deserved, the two, most particularly re-appraising Holmes, were the women, Samantha and Callie.

"I don't know if I am ready to jump at this," continued Fox, "but it should be considered as a *"King's Retribution"* decision, and I will abide by the majority. But it seems for you all in the business, an inside filming of the bin Laden death house should gain the high viewer numbers you are looking for to open Season Three of *our* show. Considering the mood of the crowds outside, and what we might expect up in Abbottabad this will be quite dangerous. There are some logistic problems. Only a few can go. We can take only one camera person, but additional hand held cameras are okay." Fox paused, collecting his strength for the next statement.

"Storm, if we do this, it's best that you do not go."

"What, the hell---." King struggled to his feet.

"You are a known quantity. Your face would be recognized."

King burned with anger.

"You need me. I am the only military man here, who has fought and bled for his country!"

"And being an American soldier, even retired, is a negative, especially on this day, when nearly every Pakistani has a low and violent opinion of America's 'invasion' of their country.

Don't you see that?"

King didn't see it like that and huffed around the room; here was a new opportunity for glory, and he was no coward.

Callie, still reeling at what had been offered, the possibilities of such a visit, her participation, yet seeing Fox about ready to enter a violent argument interspersed with spiced curses, felt she needed to offer a solution. Turning to their field sound man and part-time get-away driver, she asked, "Bennie, on any night footage that is shot, can't we use Storm's voice-over, do some later close-ups of him in similar light settings, and no one the wiser that he wasn't there."

Bennie ran with the suggestion, understanding the players and their need for stroking.

"Sure we can. Did it before; if you recall our show going after the bank robber hiding in the Everglades? Studio Insurance wouldn't take the chance of Storm being eaten by gators. It was all second unit shooting. Probably just like this. Just a few hundred more guns pointed our way."

King thought on the business he was in, an actor, a star, no longer a foot soldier, and the bottom line came into focus. Slowly mollified, he acquiesced but in doing so, now shifted to military leader mode, General Eisenhower before D-Day.

"Okay, maybe that's smart, but before we decide if this is worth the risk of anyone, how do we get there? Do we have a cover story?" Callie gave him credit; Storm could be good at tactical command.

Fox looked to Holmes, following a pre-established script, but went on.

"A military truck will pick the three of us up at 10 p.m. We will get there, go in with CAM ONE, if CAM ONE wants to tag along; we run around, under close, watchful eyes, and be rushed out. Three hours max, up there and back."

"Wait," Samantha jumped up. "You said three are going? Let me guess: three men, I presume." She put her hands on hips. "I don't think so."

"It will be extremely dangerous," Holmes looked directly at Samantha, a steady stare. "I cannot guarantee what pissed off soldiers might do if they got out of hand, or if any terrorists or their supporters are lurking near the compound."

"I'm going," affirmed Callie. Not a chance that she'd be left out. This was historic, her career had been touted as dangerous before the cameras, and she was born to play this role.

"As am I." Samantha walked over, to stand near Callie. She turned on Holmes, giving the man a smirk of the victor.

"Don't play with me---us," said Samantha, a hard stare at Holmes, resolute. "You thought this out, the minute you got clearance for this adventure from whoever the high up muckety muck is, and way before Hugh gave us the news, you knew Storm couldn't go, and you knew that we women are the strong willed types, explosive to the bitch level, and used to getting our way. I bet you got all the angles figured. So, 'fess, up Holmes, how are *we* going to break into the most watched house in Pakistan?"

Holmes folded his newspaper. While Storm King knew military strategies for massive ground force deployment and Fox might know how to energize creative people sitting in work cubicles, the now *ex*-C.I.A field agent understood sleight of hand.

He spoke even with a crisp check-off, as if the plan came from some game play book he had personally authored.

"Foreign journalists. Miss Cardoza will go as Spanish press for *El Pais* daily newspaper, Miss Carlisle as French correspondent for *Le Figaro*. Laminated documentation forthcoming from a one hour print shop."

"French, how do you know I speak--." Samantha caught herself, knowing the man's penchant for reading secret dossiers.

He continued, "Hugh will come loaded with still cameras as a press photog. As previously stated, CAM ONE will be there (CAM ONE nodded in agreement), with that camera running constantly for immediate real time spontaneity, and you all can edit to your heart's delight. Clayton and I will look conspicuous as personal guards to the women to keep the macho military men at arms' length, so no questioning can take place."

Holmes keyed on the politics in the room, for harmony, no one should feel slighted.

"And Colonel King will run the whole show from here, with CAM TWO. Bennie will be on the computer and perhaps Abbas can work the streets for information, even scout the safest back way to the airport tomorrow.

"We will use I-phones to stay in contact with your War Room, and when we can, Iphone downloads of any photos we can take without being observed just in case all cameras are confiscated." From around the room nods of approval if not admiration at the staging instructions.

Fox jumped back in.

"Now, we need to take a vote. I don't want this forced down anyone's throat. I don't know the military truck that's picking us up, don't know what we will find when we arrive.

"Ambush? Would we be taken hostage? When I say risks, I mean it seriously, I won't put anyone in harm's way just to gain a headline or win an Emmy."

"That's sweet of you, Hugh," said Samantha, patting his shoulder. "But our original trip was going to be, and you would agree, a naïve run-up into hostile country, all of us with no idea what we were really doing, or what danger we would stumble into. At this point, I have a little more faith that a well-drawn out roadmap is before us. Definitely an exciting one, so who, ladies and gentlemen, could say 'no'?" She looked to Holmes. Fox looked to Callie. All eyes searched the room for a sign of reconsideration.

"It's a plan I can live with," said King, speaking for *King's Retribution*, and all. Of course he could, thought Callie, his butt isn't being hung out there to be shot off.

Holmes spent the rest of the afternoon and early evening in prep work for the night's foray. He had been surprised how it had all come together, almost like planning a road trip to a vacation spot back home. His first call that morning had been to General Khan, dialing in as a Canadian newspaper stringer seeking an interview on the bin Laden raid. Sorry, but no interviews, said the military clerk. Minutes later the return call.

Seeking to defuse any latent anger, Holmes moved quick to set the tone.

"Sports car still that expensive? I might have a willing buyer?" Vagueness in case telephone calls were being monitored, believing a full blown finger-pointing investigation was or would soon be underway.

The General took the bait and likewise expected prying ears.

"Yes. Now, it should be more, just because of circumstances. But the sticker price remains the same. What are the specifications?"

"I have a group of friends who would like to see the garage where you were this morning.

"Spanish and French journalists are car enthusiasts."

Khan balked, and for good reason.

"No, that would be impossible. I am in charge and do have access, but—"

"I might be able to help you out as we earlier talked, make you the hero beyond my buyer paying for the car."

I am listening."

"I hear you have an old wreck up there, went flying into a wall. Can we have that?"

"Certainly not, and that comes from even higher sources."

"That's okay, I understand. What if I bring you another buyer, only to look at the condition, take a few photos, and get back to their bosses, who might up the purchase price with your bosses."

"Mr. Holmes, you do sound like a Canadian used car salesman, not a journalist. And what are you asking for, to have these other friends of yours, just look and see? Are they from your same news organization?"

"No, my ties with that dealership have been cut as of today. These buyers are from the Beijing newspaper syndicate. Very motivated buyers."

"Oh, I see. That is intriguing."

"I see two prices here to quote; the first look, and I equate that to half the price you and I are settling on for the sports car purchase, and on the second value you hook their bosses up with your bosses, and you take the glory for the sale."

Silence, and then General Khan responded.

"Yes, I think the car could be acquired for that pricing." And, sounding even more obtuse, like two mobsters knowing the F.B.I. were bugging the phones, worked out the details of the trip to Abbottabad.

"I will be there tonight, as I believe you Canadian car people say, 'watch that you kick the tires properly.' And Wendell, I am sorry to hear you are going to be unemployed. I am sure you would be welcomed to stay and enjoy our hospitality."

Holmes begged off the invitation, not taking the schmoozing as sincere.

Next, he sought out Hugh Fox, and pulling him aside, pleasantly asked.

"I require U.S. $60,000 cash as soon as possible."

"Geez, is it going to cost us that much to bribe our way out of the country?"

"Something entirely different, and when I have the funds, and work out the details you will be the first to know, and it will be you only who will have to decide if my plan merits bringing it to the attention of your other fellow travelers. Yet, I think you will approve."

Hugh Fox earlier had taken the measurement of this on-loan government representative.

Thinking 'intelligence agent' or 'spy' might be correct, but Fox saw more, viewed the character to the standards he sought himself. Holmes spoke only when he had something to say, and when he did, the comment was well thought out and succinct. When silent, the man must be always thinking, analyzing all scenarios, a puzzle worker, like Hugh himself, and in that he found genial admiration.

"Okay," said Fox, only the way people of confidence have in making a decision and having faith in the person, who in turn, must have strong self-assuredness in the outcome.

As darkness fell, with meals completed, so began the nervous waiting for the truck rendezvous in front of the hotel. Holmes made a last preparatory stop.

Callie opened the door to her suite, mildly surprised. Holmes handed her a wooden box, Which, walking over to her room desk, she opened. A beat-up Smith & Wesson 642, a snubnose revolver, with two small boxes of .38 caliber ammunition.

"Oh, you shouldn't have." Callie said in a flat voice, nearly snide.

"Sorry, couldn't get your favorite piece. My street vendor contact had a limited selection, but said this was 'airweight', perfect for purse concealment."

"Looks like it's gone through several wars and revolutions." She inspected it closely and saw that the revolver was loaded. "Everyone get a popgun?"

"Only you and I. Range qualified over hobbyists."

"And are we going into trouble? Something you haven't told the group?"

"As far as I know we are paying for an open house tour nothing more."

"So, if someone knocks on the door with guacamole and chips and an AK-47, I have your permission to blast away?"

"My sort of girl."

"No, I'm not." They exchanged judgmental looks.

"Yes, in that you are correct." And he left, wondering what was in store for them all.

After he had paid the 'fee' over to General Khan would he gain access to the compound house, take the photographic quickie tour, and head to the airport in the morning? That simple?

No, he sensed that would not be the case. He made a mental note to bring along extra ammo.

64.

May 2ⁿᵈ   5 pm   Abbottabad

Khalaf's nightmare revealed futility, a vision of tracer bullets flying past his head as he ran across an open field in broad daylight. He felt himself panicked. In turning, Khalaf saw the face of an American soldier firing at him, snarl laughing, yelling at him above the rattle of gun fire. "Cairo! Cairo!" A round fired hit him solidly in the back, flipping him up in the air, landing hard, his face in the sand, his eyes opened, searing pain that burned into numbness. And he could see the soldier walking towards him, reloading, and laughing. And in a descending darkness that bore death...

His eyes burst open, startled, wondering why death left him with senses. Regaining his surroundings, he discovered his face and clothes drenched with nightmare sweat. He found himself sprawled across a small frame bed noticing on the wall musical posters of the singing star Atif Aslam, another of the band, Roxen and pinned to the wall near a small desk, a yellowing newspaper clipping of a photograph of bin Laden and the Doctor, al Zawahiri, at a Taliban press conference. He remembered time and place. Khalaf was in the student's house on Iqbal Road, the student who attended Pine Hills College, a loyal follower, though the boy's parents were apolitical and not enthused with their son's rabid outspoken beliefs.

Khalaf lay back into the mattress and let the waterfall of emotions return and pour down.

His Sheik was dead. It was late afternoon on the day of that death, but he had been awake at the other house, his first out-of-breath stop, watching the television, as the results of the raid were made known to the world. His tears were all gone now but they had been profuse, sad for his leader's killing, expressed relief he had made his escape.

The man who had first harbored him, who heard and saw a barely clothed man pounding on his door at 2 am in the morning, could not at first contain his annoyance, even though his house had been designated as a hiding place for any al-Qaeda member on the run, those fleeing local police roadblocks or army raids. Later, after the terrible news was heard, the man's opinion changed, overwhelmed as Khalaf was with the slaying of their spiritual leader, their caliph, but now awed that in the same room with him was the last person to see Sheik bin Laden alive.

Celebrity status was not something Khalaf was ready to accept, because it was awkward: to him, notice gained by a tragedy had no redeemable worth.

At this new safe house, before he had dropped off to an exhaustive sleep mid-morning, he had sent the student out to find certain cell leaders of the local al-Qaeda militia. Even now, fully awake, Khalaf lay in the student's bed and sought to overcome his distress by concentrating on revenge and retaliation, and what came to mind was a poem by his mentor, bin Laden's poem of the U.S.S. Cole bombing.

A destroyer: even the brave fear its might.
It inspires horror in the harbor and in the open sea.
She goes into the waves flanked by arrogance, haughtiness and fake might.
To her doom she progresses slowly, clothed in a huge illusion.

This is America personified. More than ever Crimson Scimitar must succeed. He reached under his pillow to clasp the security of the two data port sticks bin Laden's son had thrust upon him, before rushing unknowingly into the slaughter. Khalid would never see Paris. May Allah bless them all for such sacrifice.

The data and information Khalaf had been entrusted with was invaluable and yet what wasn't there was deeply disappointing, more than Khalaf dare to admit to himself. On his arrival, he had inserted the computer sticks into the student's laptop. Folders appeared with all the operational information on Crimson Scimitar, so where, for protection, each element of the campaign was imparted in bits and pieces to those who would undertake the attack in the U.S., Khalaf could read on the computer each participant's role, and more importantly how to contact them. The other work stick provided more details on Crimson Scimitar but this one specific to the financial side and its importance, defining the role of London banker Taher Abboud, and stockbroker Zia Johnson, the latter, who would be making a trip to the U.S., as his part of Crimson Scimitar. Both of these men Khalaf had met on two previous courier trips.

Within his hands he had all information on Crimson Scimitar and its breadth and audacity gave him a sharp pain of sadness on the military genuis of Osama bin Laden as a brilliant general, now gone. As a mentor and friend, his opinion of bin Laden became tinged with disappointment. Certainly, in the midst of an attack by the Americans everything was rushed, hectic, bin Laden waking from a deep sleep did not have time to prioritize the most important commands, not knowing they would be his last.

What Khalaf did not see from bin Laden's computer folders was his own elevation in the al-Qaeda command hierarchy, his blessed new rank as an al-Qaeda minister at-large. And not having that written promotion that bin Laden must have completed, perhaps even signed, drove Khalaf to agitation and to his first decision of leadership in a war lacking a supreme leader.

By 3 pm, three of the local al-Qaeda city militia leaders finally showed up for an impromptu meeting, all in grief, yet regarding the haggard young man as a living martyr.

They were a chorus of questions: who would now lead? What must we do next?

Those were meaningless to Khalaf and he said with deadly seriousness, "We must go back to the house and secure our secrets, recover whatever the Americans might have not taken. We must gather up our papers to protect the cause." Khalaf's thoughts were not only on the papers that might still be around in bin Laden's bedroom, as in his own promotion document, or what might lie discarded elsewhere in the compound, but he had concern of his own closet room. Definitely there were secrets there, perhaps not overt, but collectively they should not be gathered up by the enemy.

"The Army has control over the building," said one of the al-Qaeda soldiers, "It is hard to get even close before you are ordered away."

"Let us use our contacts and soldier brotherhood. It is imperative I get back in. Isn't there someone in the Army that can gain us admittance?"

Said another, "Yes, we have built relationships. I have heard that one of our cells has developed a contact with a high ranking military officer that they have approached in the past for accommodation. But truly, it will cost us."

"I have the money, but can't get to it until tomorrow." Khalaf was thinking that one folder on the database held information on several regional bank accounts, to be used for al-Qaeda activities, and coded so that they could be used by anyone with these passwords, now at his fingertips: open sisma, open sesame the bank vault. Khalaf controlled over $200,000 but understood little what he had been entrusted with.

His mind burned for retaliation and the power to accomplish such.

"Go, and establish this contact, make the deal, do not pay too much to gain entrance, but above all, I must get back into the compound tonight."

He felt better, he would take action. Action could allay grief, and in a positive mood, a belief in himself that he could approach the al-Qaeda leadership and let them know what the Sheik had promised to him, he would gain his place in the sun. And he recalled a line from another of bin Laden's jihadist poems.

A youth who plunges into the smoke of war, Smiling, Stains the blades of lances red.

65.

May 2nd   10 pm   Abbottabad

The military personnel carrier, carrying the 'journalists' and their bodyguards, bumped and swerved over the rutted highway, gear grinded between fits of slow and fast, traffic still busy this late. They entered Abbottabad and headed toward Bilial Town the location of bin Laden's compound. The human cargo hid from the public's curious eyes all sitting on bolted wooden benches in the bed of the truck, gaining pounded, bruised butts, and all nervous as hell to what lay ahead. The convoy consisted of a jeep in front, an aire of official importance, while the trailing jeep bore four heavily armed assault Pakistani Rangers, suggesting a do-not-mess-with-with-us attitude.

The first mystery to this entire trip was what in the hell were two Chinese men doing sitting with them, saying nothing, occasional smiles responding to the stares. Around their necks dangled press credentials, quite similar to those that Callie, Samantha, and Hugh Fox wore. They wanted to ask the obvious question of what's going on to Wendell Holmes, but for each, they knew they would get some sort of run-around. Holmes would have told them if it had any bearing on their own job to do. And that's what Holmes did focus on. He passed out a grainy Google satellite of the compound and explained the layout, detailing where they should first go and what to do. CAM ONE toyed with camera preparation. Clayton Briggs would follow carrying the camera bag of back up spare parts. Nothing better fail.

"We will start from the top floor down. Hustle to that location first, that is the killing floor. Take wide shots, then close-ups, and then further close-ups. Do so in a mental grid of the room. Everyone stay behind CAM ONE, and then Hugh you follow with your camera, snapping away. If you can do it with low light resolution do so, but if you use lights or flashes, do it with the camera pointed away from the windows, if that will matter much. Samantha and Callie have perhaps the hardest jobs. Memorize detail. I would like you to visualize it all, recall each part of a room. I will ask you to write separate accounts of what you see, and we will compare.

Insignificant items will have importance by someone else's interpretation."

"Seems you have done this before, ever been a film producer?" asked Fox, seeking levity to all their worries.

"Crime scene investigation. Machete massacre of civilians in Uganda; they were just leaving church." So much for a light-hearted frame of mind as they entered the backyard of known Islamic terrorists. Holmes went back to the operation.

"Clayton, you follow last, always guard our backs. Stand at the door, nicely keep out any military chaperones. There are three floors, and two to three locations of ground floor living quarters. Second and third floors are first priority."

"And where will you be?" Callie seemed intent on pining him down.

"I'm the floater. I'll be around."

The brakes screeched and the truck lurched to a jagged stop. The tarpaulin cover thrown back and they stared into faces of intent soldiers, not police, all brandishing weapons. Beyond them, a green gate, guarded but opened, and the compound of Osama bin Laden.

In a hustle fast-walk, they were escorted inside, two soldiers leading the way as they crossed the compound, quickly taking into focus, a large canvas cover against the wall, with bright halogen lights shining, lighting up the interior, also under guard. They passed through two gates to the main building, and without waiting for directions CAM ONE with Fox did a rapid ascent, rushing past the soldiers who seem to be unsure of what their orders entailed.

As Samantha passed, she gave a lovely smile, and said to the escorts, "Merci beaucoup."

Callie, with notepad and pencil out, but hugging onto her shoulder bag, followed the group, passing the hesitant soldiers, with a "Gracias, señor."

Two steps at a time they arrived at the third floor.

Holmes hung back from the group as General Khan walked out from the compound.

"And these are your Chinese correspondents?" He gave a snort of a chuckle, eyeing them with suspicious, as they gave grins back at him.

"Their embassy would like them returned in excellent health."

"And you have something for me?"

Holmes pulled a folded envelope from his overcoat, the evening chilly.

"I hope Brian appreciates not only his new sports car, but your generosity."

The General tucked the envelope into his inside pocket of his military jacket.

"And the Chinese contribution also included?"

"As we agreed. If they are satisfied these men will notify their superiors who will in turn contact you, and let you initiate the high level discussion between governments. And what you have is a cashier's check for both amounts, $45,000 US total. $100 bills in a paper bag is so passé these days."

"I would agree. Very unrefined. I am still somewhat surprised Wendell, that being dumped by one intelligence agency, you would adeptly go shopping to another, without missing a step."

"Let's say I am now open for business as an independent contractor. But enough said, would you be so kind as direct your guests to the ill-fated secret stealth helicopter, or what's left of it."

"Yes, indeed." Patting his breast pocket where the envelope was snug and secure, the General smiled, motioning as would a congenial host to the two Chinese 'journalists', ushering them into the compound. "I can't wait to see Brian's face when I show him the car keys and ask if he wants to take a slow spin."

CAM ONE had to put the camera light on, there would be no sneakiness. The lights in the building had been turned off, or more probably the attacking Americans had cut all wires leading in. After passing dark stains on the stairway, they found the third floor, and began as Holmes, finally catching up to the group, directed a cataloging of the interior.

Samantha could not help but notice the darkened stains on the bed sheets and floor, two to three blackened pools, coagulating, not totally dried. She wanted to gag and fought the urge.

In this place, a man, no matter how terrible, had died violently. She was used to the accepted deaths found in the natural order of jungles and zoos, even the bedside passing of an elderly aunt gave her understanding that all life eventually shall cease. But harsh death of bullets shredding apart a man's skin and tearing asunder vital organs, the heart silenced. The image required a rationale that this action had merit. Her jumbled thoughts were broken by Callie's observation.

"Take note. This place is not only trashed, it has been stripped."

Samantha could see that no papers seem to be where a desk was, nor a television or computer. Holmes had said to observe and not pick up anything or take anything, as there was a good chance they would be searched on departure. She began to do what was asked of her, detailing, taking mental notes of the usual and unusual.

Fox snapped away with his camera, the flashing adding to a surreal strobe effect. Callie wandered to the room's edges, peering down at the minutae of discarded trash. Clayton hung at the doorway, blocking, his back to the room, talking idiotically about football nonsense to the two soldiers who tried glancing around him to see what the others were doing inside.

The signal that the bedroom had been intensely photographed was when CAM ONE clicked off plunging the room back into darkness, except for the flashlight shone by Callie, and a random camera flash by Fox likewise doing last minute angles from the doorway. The group moved to the next floor down, passing the soldiers, more confused than ever and the process repeated.

The discovery, like uncovering the first step that led to King Tut's tomb, happened when in the narrow corridor outside one of the small bedrooms, Clayton inadvertently nudged into Callie, and as she stumbled her hand went up against the wall to catch her balance. The wall bowed inward.

Fox came to her side as she studied the indentation.

"This is not solid," he said, inspecting, borrowing the flash-light to check each corner, and there he found the corner wooden molding, running up the wall, when usually one found it at the ceiling or along the baseboard. Using two hands, he pushed it back and found the wall telescoping inward. Callie instinctively found her hand going to her purse, clicking it open, her hand sliding inside, feeling for security, prepared for a split second response.

"A closet," commented Hugh.

"A hiding place," half-warned Callie peering into the darkness. The flashlight revealed a small library, a mattress on the floor.

"A major find. The SEALS missed this altogether."

"Congratulations." The voice of Wendell Holmes, over their shoulders, coming out of the stairwell darkness. "Photograph it in detail, but take nothing. Have CAM ONE get it all."

Holmes pulled out his I-phone and took his own quick shots. He moved on to the other rooms.

Samantha saw Holmes pass by and wondered if he had taken his own private macabre tour of bin Laden's killing ground. Did the man get his jollies off reliving the shoot-out?

Fox photographed a series of close-ups of the graffiti wall above the mattress and at the book case, stood back when he finished, and made an interesting observation.

"All those book titles, many of them are in English. Some I recognize as best sellers."

When the second floor was documented, they came down to the ground level, but not before at Holmes insistence that the hidden closet be restored exactly as it was, hidden. "Let's see if Pakistani Intelligence is really intelligent." And although they were strictly told not to take souvenirs or remove any article from the compound, one of the King's Retribution team, when not being observed, did slide a small wrapped package with pink stripping into his camera case.

After twenty minutes of a quick documentary coverage of the ground level, basically in a fast pace swing, they all collectively were at the front entrance gate, to make a startling realization.

"Oh shit," said Clayton, looking up and down the roadway.

Their military ride home had disappeared. So had the Chinese.

"A long walk home," Callie gave Holmes her evil eye. "What did you pay for? A one-way ride?"

"Think whatever, but we should move on," Holmes thought General Khan's little joke not particularly funny. "The word will probably be out that more foreigners, meaning we, are in the neighborhood."

Fox saw every calamity from rose-colored glasses. "Let's start the hike to the nearest bus station or find a late-night taxi." He started the trek and with no other recourse they trudged behind, looking from side to side into the shadows of the night, knowing at any moment dire consequences might spring at them.

Khalaf, with his jihadist militia were in two cars and approached the compound from the opposite direction, missing the Americans by thirty minutes, arriving to the schedule set by the military officer that through a series of communication had granted them chaperoned access, no one knowing, except his people, that a high-ranking (Khalaf's implied position) al-Qaeda would be among the visitors, returning home, so to speak.

This was not a tour of the curious. One carload of the militia stayed outside, warily watching the guards, one soldier, definitely sympathetic, striking up a conversation. Khalaf and three others entered the compound to be confronted by a military colonel. One of the militia members stepped forward with a paper bag, marked with the printed name of *Euro Mart*, a local store.

"I hope this is what was requested?"

"Yes, but at such late notice your payment for entrance came from one of our mosques, their donation fund for the poor. Small bills, almost all US $10 and $20 bills. I hope your recipient appreciates the sacrifice of our people for his greed."

"Please be quick. You are the last to visit tonight."

"Oh, and what, you have had other souvenir seekers?" The militia member, as well as Khalaf, were incensed at the desecration.

"Watch your tongue. Important foreign journalists came tonight who will tell the true story of the murders." And the military man turned away, the paper bag secured under his arm. He had the important job to deliver it to the General first thing in the morning, less his own cash fee for handling.

"Let's go," Khalaf's quick command, marching off.

They made two quick stops. The third floor confirmed what Khalaf feared, all of bin Landen's correspondence: videos, computers, all stolen. Damn Americans! His own promotion now in the hands of the enemy, with no chance of return, and what was worse, Khalaf realized if bin Laden had indeed put his name down for this recognition, for him to be noticed as an al-Qaeda sub-lieutenant, a proposed diplomat, that the CIA would add his name as marked for assassination.

On the second floor, with the proper push on the wall, his sleeping work area was revealed. Nothing, it seemed had been disturbed. That, in itself was a blessing. The SEALS had no idea what they might have learned if they had seized his library. He breathed a sigh of relief.

Crimson Scimitar remained undiscovered, that he was assured by his quick inspection.

He turned to the men around him, who were in awe, dazed at the whole scene of seeing what a war zone within a residence looked like, and wondered why the only al-Qaeda survivor looked upon these strange books as if they were a treasure of gold.

"The soldiers won't let us remove anything, I am sure of that. Let me show you something what we must do." He took two of his most important books, and walked back to the window, to the one he had crawled through. When was that? Almost 24 hours ago. He edged up the window and flung the book, across the wall into the field beyond.

"I want you to gather all books up and do what I just did. When we leave we will go around and pick them all up and take them with us."

Giving his orders, he supervised, and as he did so, a shock hit him. Someone, SEALS most certainly, had been there for he saw something missing. But why just take that? Why leave everything else? Why make it look like nothing had been disturbed? The uncertainty of not knowing raged within.

Soldiers watched the al-Qaeda depart, not paying much attention as they drove around the side of the compound and began quickly loading up the thrown books into the car trunks. Men in the other car were excitedly talking and one of them finally came up to Khalaf.

"One of the soldiers is one of us and said that there were foreigners touring the compound earlier taking lots of photographs."

"They were journalists, I was told."

"The soldiers heard they were that, yes, but our brother soldier, overheard them talking when they left. They were talking in English, but not British English, they were talking like Americans."

"Strange, they were here. But considering we gained entrance, I would not be surprised the corrupt government let the CIA and their trash back in to gloat, to post more pictures of this tragedy across the internet."

"That's what we think."

"Too bad they're gone. I would order that they all be executed."

The militia member became ecstatic.

"Yes. Yes. They did not drive away. They walked. What it
means I don't know. But we may be able to catch them!" The
other men crowded around, all talking enthusiastically about
their chance at gaining revenge for their fallen brethren and for
their supreme leader. 'Blood for our leader, for the faith' they
began shouting, and Khalaf had to shout at them to quiet. And
believing that Khalaf endorsed their enthusiasm to exact punishment on the infidels, the first car rushed away, and Khalaf
barely jumped in when the driver of his car sped off.

It was not what he wanted. His life should not be caught up in
a misadventure, of running around the city chasing the invisible
group of spies and killers. His main goal was to reach the southern tribal regions and make contact with al-Zawahiri, both to pay
homage to whom he expected would be the next leader of al-
Qaeda, but more importantly to continue launching Crimson
Scimitar, and bringing to al-Zawahiri's attention what bin Laden's
last desire had been, Khalaf's ascendency. The first militia car
raced far ahead of them, eager young warriors with no sense.
"Catch up to them," he said, really wanting to say, 'Enough'. This
would be a ridiculous wild goose chase, but he would feed their
ardor. A good leader sometimes must be led by the rush of
events.

66.

May 3rd   1 am   Streets of Abbottabad

From the SEALS raid, now the night before, the government must have clamped on a curfew as they found, as they walked, tiring and cold, few cars on the streets, especially no public conveyance. Up ahead they could see more concentrated lights of a downtown shops area and their hopes grew that this adventure might soon be ending.

The old model Suzuki sedan flew past on the street, then began a long screeching brake stop turning sideways. Armed men jumped from the car and began randomly firing their direction.

"Run," yelled Holmes, pulling his market-stall acquired Glock pistol from concealment under his jacket. Everyone took off down an alleyway of refuse, knocking over boxes, scurrying towards another darkened street. He could only guess on how they were discovered. General Khan certainly seeking more fees would not have given them away. Khan liked Holmes as a deal maker who brought cash. Most likely a soldier at the compound ratted them out, identified who to look for. "Keep low and to the sides!"

They had sought to blend in, the women in Pakistani long dresses and head scarfs and men with ball caps. You could not hide the bulk of Clayton Briggs, too abnormal for a late night saunter, too much like an American.

Gunfire rippled down the alleyway above their heads. The most dangerous type, amateurs. 'Crack!' The shot had come in front of him! Callie crouched behind piled crates, her revolver extended in a two hand grip stance. The gunfire chasing them suddenly stopped.

"Didn't hit anyone, but they damn well know now we can fight back."

"How many?" Samantha came to Holmes's side. In her hand she held a small cigarette size derringer.

"What the hell is that? A Cracker Jack prize?"

"A .22 tickler for muggers."

"I count four of them," said Callie from across the alley, seeking a target. "One with an Automatic short machine pistol, two with hunting rifles, one unarmed, I think."

From where the attackers were concealed, another car drove up, distant yelling could be heard, and the car sped away.

"Damn, more to join the party," said Holmes. "They're going to start flanking us, come around the block, we need to keep running to the next block, try to lose them. Callie you take point, I will bring up the rear."

Rapid fire resumed, laying down a stitching carpet of thuds and ricochets, but the quarry was already in motion sprinting across the street, into the next alley, just as the second car turned the car and rushed towards them. It would be a long alley, very little cover.

"Get behind those boxes." Were they trapped? There were houses on both sides of the alley.

Holmes turned and prepared for new attackers from the second car to enter the fight.

This driver must have had experience in military tactics or in gangsta drive-bys. He pulled up to the alley, looking down, to see if they had found their targets.

Callie's shot hit the driver side window, and car edged slowly forward without control, a foot removed forever from the brake, as three car doors flew open, and men fell to the ground, scrambling away.

"Let's go," Holmes called out to all of them, and again at various sprinting speeds they chased after Callie. At one point, Fox yelled in a loud whisper, "How about here?" Whispering did no good. Neighborhood dogs were yipping, a few home lights going on but no one at the windows. Fox pointed to a garden area behind a house, and he opened the gate and rushed in. His thought was to get out of the direction of where a new round of bullets were flying, and close at that. His posse followed. Hugh went to the back door and began a steady pounding.

"No, I don't think so," and Clayton's foot slammed in the back door, his drug bust version of the Welcome Wagon. All went rushing in, Callie doing her room clearing swing with her gun, but kept them all moving, past screaming children, people rising from floor mats, out the front door into a larger street. Their position was not an improvement. They were parallel to the attackers, and Car One could send their people easily to this next street, as could Car Two going to the end of the alley, and they could be boxed in between two fields of fire.

"Another house," said Holmes and they crossed, and he made a choice finding another home with garden on the side, this time rushing through dead plants and pulled up vegetables. A chained dog at the back of the property starting howling, lunging their direction. Clayton hit it solid in the nose, probably breaking its jaw, sending the dog flying dazed and whining.

"Well, if they don't like Americans now..." observed Samantha running past, not ready to debate animal injuries over saving one's life from human beasts.

They were onto the next street, quiet in a relative way of night noises, but void of gunfire.

Several blocks away they saw a market center, more lights, nightlife they could hide within.

They took off running, Callie in the lead, then Fox, Samantha, Clayton lopping along next to out-of-breath CAM ONE. Damn, realized Holmes, the videographer has been recording it all. Don't they know this is real reality, and in real death you don't go into syndication.

In the quarter second as the window shattered brain gore and blood from driver's head splattered over Khalaf, speckling his face. Most merciful Allah, am I hit? He fell out of the car onto the pavement, shaking, looking to his body, feeling his face, not his blood. Merciful.

He had no gun, why should he? And the others with him held twenty year old Russian rifles pulled from the trunk.

"Pull him out," Khalaf instructed to one of the men, "You drive." The other began firing aimlessly down the alleyway. When Khalaf hesitantly put his head around the corner to look, he saw nothing. "Stop."

At the moment, the first men in the chase raced from the alley, their car slowly trailing behind. They did not continue to pursue, no one fired. They all walked over and looked at their dead comrade. These were militia volunteers from the universities and the cities slums, their mindset was broadly smeared idealism offering religious fraternal brotherhood and that bound them, more than a promise of wealth or a heavenly condo of virgins. In shock that their cavalier attitude of chasing down infidels had resulted in the death of one of their own, they sought anger in their shame and loss.

"They are no longer down there. They must have gone to another street. Back in the cars.

You all go that direction, we'll go this way. Call immediately when located. Do not fire unless you have a positive target. We cannot have al-Qaeda condemned for killing any residents. Death to the Americans! Death to the non-believers!" Affirmed shouts, new pledges in faith to enact punishment: to disembowel, castrate, behead their enemies.

It was Khalaf who, in a surprise to himself, brought about the revenge.

He directed the driver, oblivious to the wetness he sat in, no time to clean the seat off.

Intently, he scanned the side streets as they slowly drove, looking one way then the other. The other two men, each held a cumbersome rifle at odd angles, poking from the open windows.

They would have to stop to sight a target and squeeze the trigger.

Frustration of the search built. They had lost them, except Khalaf felt he knew their direction. The market square. Late night produce deliveries were being made, a few private coffee clubs were still open. Perhaps an arrangement had been made, perhaps the C.I.A. army would be there to save them, perhaps this was a trap? Again, Khalaf had to remind himself this was not his true mission, it would be an unholy ghastly error if he were to be killed. It came to him, the right decision, he must find an honorable way to break off the engagement.

Then he saw the group of spies emerge from an alleyway, walking down the street, beginning to cross the wide street towards the maze of market stalls. Headlights off, he yelled at the driver to accelerate the car. Why stop? His men with rifles would not know how to shoot running men and women. But a car was a weapon, backed by a plethora of deadly statistics. The hurtling metal projectile aimed at the middle of the group, they could not miss.

"Watch out!" Their hearing had been impaired by the night sounds of the market workers unloading produce for the morning sales, the motor noises of delivery trucks backing up, backfiring sounds like gunfire. The car was upon them too late.

Samantha looked up to see a man's demented face, one of glee, evil satisfaction, and seconds before the car's bumper plowed into her, she felt a rough shove and went up in the air, off her feet, landing with pain as she felt her ankle twist in the slam to the roadway.

Callie and Fox turned just as Clayton Briggs went up onto the car hood, slammed against the window, smashing it, and rolled up and off to the side, where he hit the road with a hard smack. He lay silent, no movement.

Callie reacted instinctively, and fired at the rear window of the hit-and-run fleeing auto.

The first shot shattered the glass, but the car careened at that moment into a bicycle rack, humping over several bikes popping the trunk open, scattering contents, deflecting her next two shots. Around a corner, the car peeled out of sight, and Callie's footrace to catch it quickly ended, and she turned to find those of *King's Retribution* standing over Clayton Briggs, her bodyguard.

"I'm sorry, Callie, he's dead." Hugh Fox opened his arms to her, but she walked past and looked down at the inert body, blood, seeping from Clayton's ear.

What had she done? Callie wondered, an agony of grief. Why, by her actions of the chase, had she brought them here? To all die? For what purpose? For a damn television show?

To make her a star?

She kneeled and held Clayton's hand, desperately trying to recall all memories of the living man, so many times taken for granted as just being there on the set as supporting background.

Clayton, I am so sorry.

"Let us go back and kill them all," yelled the jihadist from the back seat.

"You fool. Did you not see the ISI police running out to them? They are reinforced. We would be the ones greeting Allah tonight, not those Americans going to hell."

"No, I did not see that. I am sorry, my leader."

Khalaf let the lie do its work. He needed no more of such risk. At his direction the car pulled over to the side of the road and he inspected the damage, both front, back, and driver's side windows demolished. He glanced in the car trunk filled with the thrown-in books from the compound, picking up one thick volume, noting a bullet had pierced the cover, going all the way through, to exit. Allah's miracle, if not simple fate, even with tonight's fiasco of inept men playing gunmen, he began to believe he might indeed be omnipotent, and these books continue to serve their holy purpose.

Slamming the car's trunk tight, they drove off. After a few moments of silence, his commanding presence reestablished itself against earlier trepidation of a bullet ending his life.

Not tonight, nor ever.

"Call your brothers. They can continue to search, and may Allah be with him. You are now tasked, as my bodyguards, under edict from The Sheik's last will and testament. We need another car. You must drive me south. I must make contact with Doctor al-Zawahiri."

The two men in renewed awe looked at Khalaf's hardened visage as he drove on towards the black horizon. How honored were they to be giving homage and duty to such a man, such a friend of our late Sheik. Yes, Khalaf thought, yes they must be thinking that.

67.

May 3nd 7 am Serena Hotel Islamabad

Callie lay in her bed, the sedative numbness wearing off. She thought last night her cop training would let her rise above the personal tragedy, bring out the coldness required to swiftly act in crisis. Instead, the death of a friend, took Callie to a far place of her inadequacies, and she let the born leaders take charge, and she became a mere robot of following instructions.

She could recall all the events, even if in a haze of quick jerked scenes.

Damn that Holmes! He got us all into this! No, her ambition did, she accepted that guilt, but still Wendell Holmes had been the catalyst and we were led to bin Laden's compound for some additional mysterious purpose that Holmes deemed important for himself. But damn Holmes, he did have quick reflexes to the attack.

She remembered him going over to a fruit truck, a dilapidated pick-up. He did not commandeer it at the point of a gun, as much as he haggled, like buying a trinket in the market.

Dickering, he struck a quick deal, and a weathered man, the truck owner who had no political views, could care less of world views, but who understood money and contract handshakes, dumped the remainder of his boxes into a pile at the market.

Callie did not help to lift Clayton's body, she still held his hand. Fox and Holmes accomplished this sad task, easing Clayton's body gently into the truck bed, covering him with a tarp, not a worthy shroud, she knew, for such a good person. Fox and Callie crawled into the back of the truck, and hunched down.

Quick snapshots of oddities came to her mind. She remembered turning to CAM ONE, and saying, plaintively, 'Please turn off the camera.' But Fox said as gently, 'we must remember all, if anything, now for Clayton. But, I promise, it will be ours, and not be seen on any television screen." She nodded, not really there, and she saw him take the gun from her, that she had been holding all the while, the same time, she held Clayton's hand, both cold, both of death.

What had Holmes said to Samantha, she had not heard. But had seen Samantha take

Holmes's Glock and approach the growing crowd of curious, shouting at them. Callie caught the drift if not the waving gun attention grabber, something like: "Stay away! We are I.S.I.!

Security Police! Chasing and killing bandits!" Holmes must have conveyed a similar warning in Pashtun, and everyone drifted away, back to their marketplace jobs, not that eager to find out what really was going on, at least knowing a man, the big man who had died had very white skin.

She heard a siren in the distance. She found herself pushed up next to Hugh Fox in the back of the pickup, across from CAM ONE, a covered body in the middle. Samantha sat in the truck cab between the fruit delivery driver and Holmes.

The fruit truck started off, but after only going half a block, it stopped and Holmes jumped out and picked up something off the street. He threw it in the back of the truck, next to Callie.

"Take care of this," he said to no one in particular. She glanced down, hardly seeing the title in the darkness, the pages flipping back and forth, but finally under highway lights as they entered Islamabad, she could read: *Dead or Alive* by Tom Clancy.

An American novel discarded on a Pakistani suburban street.

What was that all about? As the truck sped closer to their hotel sanctuary, against the biting wind she found herself leaning into Hugh Fox, less snuggle, more burrowing desire to escape this miserable world.

Episode 10

*We will be safer from terrorist attack only when we have
earned the respect of all other nations instead of their fear,
respect for our values and not merely our weapons.*
- -Theodore C. Sorensen

68.

May 4th *Associated Press* News Release (Editorial Sidebar story)

As the world of decency cheers the death of the terrorist leader Osma bin Laden it might be ironic to note on that same May 2nd day that SEALS were attacking the hide out in Abbotabad that an American television crew and its stars of King's Retribution were secretly in Islamabad, only 30 miles away, on their own hunt to capture bin Laden, and do so on camera.

They missed their quarry, and the SEALS got their man. So, King's Retribution returns empty handed today to Hollywood without the fame and fortune they sought. If they had stayed around perhaps the Taliban or al-Qaeda would have furnished more potential primetime moments.

TMZ Television

Host Commentator: Guess the vacation King's Retribution cast and crew took to Pakistan didn't pan out. They wanted to surprise us with bringing bin Laden back wrapped in one of their spiffy TV specials, but the American cavalry, our SEAL boys, beat them to it. Next, we hear Storm King is going after Hitler's ghost.

Commentator #2: Their best seasons are behind them. With that egg-on-their-face farce they will be lucky that the network will let them apprehend overdue parking violators.

Variety **Newspaper** Headlines

[May 6] ***Retribution Flops in Packy, SEALS are Hit***

[May 8] ***Obits: Retrib Star Clayton Briggs – Car Accident in San Fran***

Private Services Set May 11th

[May 24] ***Bigelow-Boal 'Hurt Locker' Team to do Bin Laden Op/Sony Signs Up***

[June 12] ***Relative Media buys in-can real SEALS Flick for $13 million***

Friday May 6th   11 am   Washington, D.C.

Head of the Foreign Intelligence Analysis Section, Matthew Brady, found what he held in his hand awkward and explosive, and worse yet the materials had been addressed to the man whose office he entered, after a slow knock: Ronald Givens, Assistant Deputy Director of the Central Intelligence Agency. Brady considered Givens a limited man, consisting only of being an asshole and butt kisser, but with ranked privilege, and himself desiring a long career Brady knew the system enough to put on his mask of being a lowly, though executive, worker bee in the spook hive.

"Yes, what is it? Did you have appointment, Brady?"

"This came into our Section this morning, with a request to review and verify which we just completed, but what was unusual it was addressed to your attention for an immediate delivery once we confirmed background."

"Well, let's see it." Givens held his hand out, demanding not requesting. Brady complied.

Givens gave off a superior attitude huff at being interrupted, ripping opening the large folder marked: 'Confidential'. A large photograph, black and white, grainy with night features, fell into his grasp, and he glanced at it with a quick dismissive study. He froze, suddenly sat upright, startled and upset.

"What the fuck?!"

"Yes, sir." Brady, seeing his superior's discomfort, realized he could have fun with this.

In masked innocence, he replied, "We were quite surprised when I showed this to *everyone* in our section for their input."

Givens, snapped, flustered.

"You showed this to others and did not bring it to me directly."

"Protocol required our vetting. You can see it shows two Chinese men, both holding cameras, who we suspect must be intelligence agents from the Chinese embassy, standing in front of our stealth prototype Black Hawk, the one that crashed during the *Neptune Spear* Operation. Notice the distinctive hub look around the blades."

"Yes, I see that."

"And do you recognize the man standing off to the side. He's smiling, you can see."

Givens hesitantly glanced again, and then threw down the photo.

God damn it, Givens thought to himself, almost apoplectic.

Brady maintained his faked benign detachment. "I believe that is Agent Wendell Holmes, isn't it?"

Givens could not admit to what he saw.

"When did this hit our Middle East desk?"

"Oh, it didn't sir. As you can see by the envelope this is Inner-Departmental circular. It was put into the Langley mail system early this morning, around 0830."

"Holmes is here? Get me Security to find the bastard; he'll be on his knees before me within minutes."

Brady fought back the buried guffawing laugh seeking release.

"I am sorry, sir. I did think the method of delivery somewhat odd; you would expect it to come through our bin Laden desk, so I made inquiries. Seems like he was here to sign all required paperwork for his retirement release, then left our facility, but not before dropping off several of these memo mailing packets."

"There are more? Damn it, find out who got them, go around and collect them all. This is highly sensitive material, not meant for others."

"Oh, you mean the Director should not receive this photo?"

"The Director received this photo?" Givens, stumbled, then caught himself. "Well, I guess, that is okay."

As if on cue, the phone rang, Givens answered, and his voice immediately shifted to humble subservience. "Yes, sir, I did receive a copy. No, only a few moments ago. Yes, I will be right over." He hung up and Brady thought he could see a tinge of perspiration ooze from the man's forehead.

"That will be all, Mr. Brady."

"Oh, one other thing, I don't know if you saw the small detail surrounding Agent Holmes."

"He is no longer an agent of this agency."

Brady handed over a magnifying glass, and Givens squinted at the photo.

"Damn. Damn him to hell."

Ex-C.I.A. agent Wendell Holmes stood to the side to the rotor component of the downed helicopter, away from the Chinese 'agents', his arms folded. Only on close magnified inspection, could it be seen both of Holmes's hands were 'flipping off' the camera, and the world beyond.

May 9-16th

Three days later, May 9th, U.S. Senator John Kerry, Chairman of the U.S. Senate Committee on Foreign Relations, announced he would lead a delegation to meet with Pakistan's Prime Minister Yousuf Raza Gilani and President Asif Ali Zardari.

Asked, if on his visit, would he push the Pakistani leaders on whether they knew that bin Laden was in hiding for years next to their military academy, Senator Kerry replied, "We have a huge agenda, we have huge interests that are very important to try to be on track, and there's a lot to discuss."

The next day, on May 10th, *ABC News* reported that an unnamed Pakistani official, thought to be a military general, said that the Chinese were 'very interested' in having a 'formal second look' at the helicopter wreckage at bin Laden's compound. That same day in a Senate hearing, Senator Kerry was quoted as saying, bin Laden's death was "a potentially game-changing opportunity to build momentum for a political solution in Afghanistan that could bring greater stability to the region and bring our troops home."

On May 16th, after his initial meeting with Pakistani leaders, Kerry spoke to reporters: "My goal in coming here was not to apologize for what I consider to be a triumph against terrorism of an unprecedented consequence. My goal has been to talk with the leaders here about how to manage this critical relationship more effectively."

Later in the day, Senator Kerry, smiling, informed the press "that Pakistan will return the pieces of a U.S. helicopter that went down during the operation that killed Osama bin Laden."

A U.S. delegation official said at the time that he would be "shocked' if the Chinese hadn't already been given access to the damaged aircraft.

69.

Friday, May 6th   Ft. Campbell, Kentucky

Pacheco sat in the bare room, with its metal desk and chairs. A quasi conference room turned interrogation center, at least that was his view.

He was into his third debriefing. The first one had been as everyone else's a quick interview analysis on their return from the mission, one-on-one at Bagram Air Base. It was here he spoke the qualified truth which was causing so much trouble up the ranks. His verbal and taped report followed his actions upon his rushed exit from the crashing helicopter until embarkation and liftoff. What stood out were two salient points: one of assumed truth and the other a question to which he had no specific answer.

Recorded Testimony:

"I am pretty certain that I saw an undressed individual, wearing shorts, underwear, run across the garden, scale the lean-to stable roof, and jump over the wall." No further elaboration.

He did not mention the struggle, of his nearly being killed, of his failure to kill his enemy. That lie of omission to him was a dogging canker sore.

Recorded Response to Question: "And why did you not put a satchel charge around, what we have called the 'hubcap tail rotor'?"

Caught off guard, when this came out of nowhere in the second interview, he had moved from an 'I don't know' to an answer with a little more thought, but it sounded like an excuse for his failure.

"The crashed helicopter was at an angle up against the wall and to reach the tail rotor section would have required a ladder. I assumed the charges I had set and the resulting fire would have been hot enough to melt all vital components. Perhaps a thrown charge might have done more damage but there was no assuredness it would catch and hold on, and it might have prematurely exploded setting off the remaining set charges [killing me, he did not say]. Plus, as I was putting the charges within the helicopter the withdraw command had been given."

A weak excuse. For him, there was no acceptable explanation. He had failed twice.

Three times if you count Montoya's death.

A man and woman entered the room. By their business attire, coat-tie for him, dark skirt and jacket for the woman, he sensed his previous debriefings were not satisfactory. The first had been his own unit's officers, basically to analyze the operation, compile for the history books, and then to seek further eyes-on-the-ground intelligence. From his comment of the compound escapee, if that really happened (skeptical looks at him), this led to the second interview, with what he guessed were the regional spooks, and their suggestive accusation that he could have done more to destroy the helicopter.

Today, more prying, maybe the lady taking notes was a psychological profiler. He could use one. He did feel he was going nuts, no, more that he had lost his SEAL fighting edge, and internal doubt was fatal on a battlefield.

They began the routine, the repetitive questions, and he thought by their asking in different sequences, they were trying to trip him up. What? Gain a confession? Okay, yeah, he screwed up, big time, as he saw it. But it was not coming from his lips. This was something he knew he had to find answers to.

Outside, he could hear the military bands booming over crowd noise. The President of the United States had entered the base. He was going to give a speech of 'job well done' and then as Pacheco had been told, all those who had participated in *Neptune Spear*--from the Rangers of the 101st Airborne, to the 160th Special Operations Aviation Regiment, the Night Stalkers helicopter strike force to the Fifth Special Forces Group that housed SEAL Team Six— all were going to a private hand-shake moment with the President. Pacheco already had decided if this investigatory tribunal of giving him the fifth degree dragged on, so much the better. He had no desire to receive a pat on the back from the Commander-in-Chief. He didn't deserve it.

The session was an hour, some questions asked several times, and when he finally felt they were at an end point, another man entered the room, and handed over a file folder. The man and woman both reviewed the contents.

He stared at Shawn, seeking by his serious, narrow eye expression, that he could extract the truth by mind games.

"Do you have any Chinese friends?" What was this, wondered Pacheco; where in left field did that come from?

"No." Both of them stared at him, as if he had just lied.

The man in the black suit took what seemed to be a paper photo, like a faxed photo, and folded it in half, and pushed it across the table at him.

"Do you know this man? Ever meet him?"

Night shadows encased a vague man standing in front what Pacheco could see was the rotor section from the helicopter he had failed to destroy.

"No. I don't know who that is." And the interview ended.

Pacheco struggled through the crowd, hardly blending in, since he was in his field dress uniform, his only clean one left. The people push was to the hanger where the throngs were breaking up yet hanging around, waiting. He had missed the President's rah-rah speech. It would have not made him feel any better. He sought out the mess hall room where he, along with the rest of his SEAL Team, had been told to report this morning. He had probably missed the President doing a personal High Five to his buddies.

An MP stopped him.

"And where are you going?"

"SEAL Team Six. I'm suppose to be in there."

"Yeah, go ahead and try, but they got it locked up tight. The Commander-in-Chief is visiting with you boys. By the way, great job."

Pacheco nodded, and made it a few more yards, and at the hall door, before two men, both in black, very similar to the suits he had just left, but these were Secret Service, with their ear buds and lapel pins.

"Sorry, no admittance."

"I'm in SEAL Team Six."

"Yeah, that's what everyone's coming up to us is saying. You should have been cleared a couple of hours ago. Just wait, he might be passing by."

"It's not a big deal." Pacheco deadpanned, and realized the president's bodyguard was giving him the once over inspection of a potential threat.

Applause. Multiple shouting of "Hooyahs". And the door opened and out walked the President of United States, beaming, leaving the men who had just accomplished the impossible.

Like a good stump vote-getting politician he began working the crowd of soldiers, surrounded, in these close quarters, by more Secret Service agents. Pacheco could see television cameras jockeying for position. The crowd pressing him against a rope barrier and in an instant of handshaking, the President of the United States held his hand out to SEAL Shawn Pacheco.

Both men looked at each other. Pacheco did not extend his hand. And the political President took momentary regard, then flawlessly, not skipping a beat, moved to the other soldiers, handshaking, standing buddy-buddy for digital photos. The Secret Service agent who had stopped him at the door, and was in the passing procession, gave a quick stare.

"What's your name, sailor?"

"It doesn't matter. I'm not important." And he let the jostling crowd swallow him up as the President of the United States moved on, very pleased of the day, forgetting the refused empty hand. It didn't matter. It wasn't important.

Others did not think so.

Pool television coverage caught the brief moment. The one second of awkwardness between a soldier and his commander became interpreted, to some, as a refusal to respect the office, to others, the dissing of the man of the office, perhaps dislike of the President's politics, even to some as implied racism, it was Kentucky, the South, after all.

As a small item in news coverage where balanced news was required formula the refused handshake act of the unknown soldier made national news snippets and universally became exampled as an act of disrespect to the country during this glorious celebration in killing of the mastermind of 9/11. To his comrades, once they saw the clip, but not knowing the mental circumstances for his rebuff, as Pacheco would agree he himself did not understand why he had not reacted as he had, Pacheco once again became an outcast to his military family.

To retired Army Captain Russell Mosswood, watching television in his home in Cleveland, Ohio, with his daughter Janet, he said in disgust, "I don't know what you see in that man?"

Janet had to admit Shawn, over the video phone calls the last several months, he did not seem himself, but very distant and morose. She loved that man she had last held and kissed good-bye before he left on his travel orders, but with a disapproving father, and actually seeing her betrothed's metamorphous, including what she had seen on television with the President, this was not the man she knew. She was confused in her emotions, and these were to be only further strained by the immediate ignorance of the situation. Because of strict military orders of secrecy the Mosswood Family continued to believe Janet's fiancée, Shawn Pacheco, still served in the SEAL Team Four unit and did not participate in the bin Laden operation. Captain Mosswood, a Bronze star veteran from Viet Nam, expected any man worthy of her daughter, and a soldier at that, ought to have that character of higher standards, insert himself into the action, not just sit on the sidelines of the battle. Captain Mosswood began his own campaign to separate his daughter from this ungrateful loser.

70.

May 11th   Forest Lawn Memorial Park Hollywood Hills

Remembering the good in a good man should have been the over-riding sentiment that brought them to the grass hillside dotted with grave stones. No, sadly, *collective guilt*, in various degrees, bound them briefly together as they watched the coffin lowered into the ground, and listened to a solemn minister speak, who had never met this Teddy bear personality once alive as Clayton Briggs. Those who knew the real story, that Clayton sacrificed his life to save a life, could not tell the world, not yet, perhaps never.

The only outflow of visible grief, of hiccupping sobs, came from Clayton's secret male lover. He was being consoled by the man's sister who was at a loss to understand the depth of the man's bereavement, accepting that a strong friendship between them both had existed, and nothing more.

Everyone from the *Pakistan Folly*, as the recent overseas trip was being called by many, friends and enemies, already had expended their sorrow, accepted their share of guilt, and parceled out blame, right or wrong, as they felt it justly deserved.

The two private jets, in fact became the funeral procession with the returning travelers on board, depressed and exhausted, and they either slept or read, with very little exchange of conversation.

Placing himself in charge of Clayton Briggs body, Holmes accepted that it was his partial responsibility. He should have stopped this whole wild goose chase from even entering Pakistan's airspace. He stayed a day behind, handling the red tape of placing the deceased aboard a commercial airliner, and he came later on that flight. His job had ended, he was no longer part of the *Retribution* team, and knew aboard the Fox or Carlisle planes he did not want to face maudlin tears, and more so, expected frigid and angry resentment.

For Hugh Fox, he felt sick to his stomach. He lived in an artistic non-real world of vampires and space monsters where you could kill thousands and become a winner on a high point system, or if bored with repetitive violence, just turn off the machine. Being shot at, which he had never experienced, and seeing men violently die should not be dismissed as a novelty. He had been standing right behind Callie as she fired and saw first-hand the terrorist driver's head explode, and for her to rise and turn and walk past him as if, killing another human being, did not phase her at all, found him inexplicably empty in his comprehension.

To the side of the grave, Samantha Carlisle, held a red rose, soon to be tossed into the dirt grave with the wooden coffin. Such un-imagination is death, she reflected, such drab rotting. She paid for all the funeral expenses, hoping that this could be some sort of penance, knowing it would be very little. Clayton had exchanged his life for hers. He knew Callie better than her, and Callie would be a person he could relate to, know she was worth saving. Samantha had barely spoken to Clayton, mere smiles when he opened a door for her, or helped with her luggage. And, he saved her life with his. She had succeeded at all business endeavors she had undertaken, made millions, multi-millions, but this bodyguard to the television show she had power over, he never knew her personally, she never knew him. A stranger saving a stranger, without debate, an instantaneous decision made on the value of life. And her guilt? Could she have made the same choice, could she have sacrificed herself for another? She did not know the answer, and that bothered her conscious.

From the night of Brigg's death, and the days that followed, Callie Cardoza floated, acting as if she was dealing with it all, but not really. She dealt as best she could with the loss of a very close friend. Hurt, yes, that was part of her malware psyche. More so, hurt fed into anger, and she, of them all, stayed silent, using her mind to pass out blame. Could she have made a quick shot and killed the driver who ran down Briggs? Why did Holmes take us to Abbottabad?

What had he been up to? And, then there's Storm King. Fox wisely had put him in the second jet, Samantha's, and let Bennie and Cam One babysit him. King's guilt in all this was in *faking* guilt, that none of this would have happened, he explained, if he had been there leading the troops.

And later, just before they boarded, he had seen the *Associated Press* news story, reviling and ridiculing their presence, and none of that would have happened, he had told them, lecturing, if they had all stayed home, and for not being strong enough to make them do so and he felt that was his error. Callie saw him standing there at the gravesite, slightly swaying. She wanted to be far from this drunk.

Callie's worst guilt was a silent wish, a very wrong one, that the car should have hit Samantha Carlisle instead of Clayton. That would have solved several problems, and she cursed herself for being so low to think like that. And only, when she looked across the grave, and saw

Wendell Holmes, his head bowed in some form of silent prayer, did she dismiss that sacrilege and let another evil arise in her soul: she wanted to kill someone, and she knew who that was.

What happened next was remarkable, but maybe not so unexpected. The service ended, dust-to-dust in the form of dirt sprinkled in the grave by some, roses dropped by others, and they all turned, and saying nothing, walked to their individual cars and limousines.

They, the survivors of Abbottabad and bin Laden's compound, all went their separate ways and would not again meet for two months. But when they would finally gather, all hell would break loose, and the foundation of America would hang precariously in the balance, and *King's Retribution* would have a featured role in the outcome.

71.

May 9th   Tribal Lands, Southern Pakistan

Five days of everything going wrong in his transportation
choices brought Khalaf to Lahan, a small village, a few miles from
the Tribal Agency town of Wana in Southern Waziristan. While
back in Abbottabad he enlisted if not drafted his two youthful
zealots, those car passengers with him in the firefight with the
American spies. He gained their blind allegiance by intoning bin
Laden's final command for him to go and meet with al Zawahiri.
He did not tell them that he knew to reach the Doctor he had to
go through Ahmed Abdul Rahman, son of the 'Blind Sheik', who
was imprisoned in the U.S. for the first attack on the World Trade
Center in 1993. Rahman, the son, a senior al-Qaeda operative,
acted as a layered in-between, a gate keeper to the securely
hidden al Zawahiri. With bin Laden's death, Khalaf had to reach
them quickly, foremost to gain his new appointment, and second-
ly, to see who he eventually would report to, someone had to
assume the mantle of al-Qaeda leader. Khalaf feared the passion
for establishing the caliphate would dissolve into regional guerrilla war, with random acts against NATO forces, no mighty strike
at the heart of the beast. Crimson Scimitar was at risk.

His two disciples had gone forward to make travel arrange-
ments, still nothing went right.

For safety reasons he could not go directly west into the
northern federally administered areas and then go south. It was a
pure war zone, almost all travel by night, and the higher smuggler routes would require donkey travel, and from his Yemen trip,
he despised riding on the back of any four-legged animal that
smelled and had mind of its own. Instead, he would take the train
south to Pezu, and then west to Kazur. The trains broke down
twice, requiring an overnight stay, and the final leg of his rail trip
reminded him of cheap commuter travel in India, crammed and
overflowing with human cargo, smells of sweat and excrement.

Things looked up when his two men greeted him at the rail-
way station with three used BMW motorcycles, not in great
shape, but dings of durability. This he could enjoy, the coolness
of the air streaming past his face, his eyes soaking up the landscape, apple orchards and goat pastures shaded by Neem trees,

wide leafed, their bark suffused with medicinal powers. Once when they had stopped along the road for afternoon prayers, a small animal called a Pangolin, like a miniature scaled armadillo scurried past them, a good omen, and good eating if you capture an adult.

Before they began their ascent into the mountainous area of South Waziristan, very likely where they might meet bandits or rival tribes who, by blood feuds, had no love for al-Qaeda factions, the three travelers stopped in Manzai. Here, a local shopkeeper received a hefty payment from Khalaf and they purchased automatic pistols, stuffing them into their side saddlebags.

From this point on, they were in the midst of an area of Pakistan that the central government admitted they had no control over, a land of lawlessness and extremist religious fataws many placed against another's neighbors. In this part of their trip, they would cycle through two Pashtoon tribal lands, the first, Mashsud, and the second, Ahmadzai Wazir to reach the town of Wana. All this territory fell under the control of the warlord, Mullah Nazeer Ahmed, who hated the U.S.A. and could not tolerate the Pakistan government, and had a spotty history with any loyalty to the Taliban, but on this day, this month, he served as a member of the Central Council of the allied Taliban groups in Pakistan.

Khalaf and his men sought to ride only when darkness arose or descended, the best protection against the high-flying Predator drones. He had never heard of an air strike against fast-moving motorcycles and the decision to travel in this mode brought them up to the roadblocks. The first, controlled by a ragged group of Burkis, an ethnic group, assimilated into the Pashtoons were equally armed as Khalaf and his men and when he saw that they wanted only a 'road passage fee', he understood they only sought enough money to buy themselves their next meal. The descending face of rural poverty had been evident the last twenty miles. To save face, they dickered and haggled and he finally paid them a few rupees, whining, as they expected he would complain as formality, that they had stripped him of all his money. His men, as they drove on, rode up to him to extol his skill, the art of a chameleon, 'you are such an actor' they yelled at him and said he was as good as the famous film star of the '60s, Waheed Murad.

The Pakistani soldiers manned the second roadblock, more a slowing than stopped inspection, soldiers eyeing them carefully as they passed. It dawned on Khalaf, perhaps the word had gone out before that he was expected. His own worth rose in his mind. Yes, that is why we weren't hassled.

Evening dipped over the ridge lines as they drove down onto the Wana plain, circled through the military district town, and a few miles more came to the village of Laman. Most of the locals, seemed to keep to their small homes which were made out of Pucca bricks slathered with mud. The village had no electricity and eyes peered out with concern. In curiosity to identify the strangers, Moslem hospitality soon ventured out and the weary travelers were nibbling on maize bread, followed by small bowls of rice and mutton, all soon devoured.

When Khalaf wondered what was the next step to his journey, on how to make contact, he was surprised to face armed men, menacing as they entered the small house where they had been led as guests. He had not expected to see Ilyas Kashmiri, a handsome bearded Pakistani, wearing shaded eyeglasses though darkness outside dipped into black ink. Around him stood a cadre of fierce al-Qaeda fighters, ready to growl and lash out, as if they had just come in from a vicious battle with the enemy.

Kashmiri addressed him loudly in recognition.

"Maulawi Abd al-Khaliq Jan." Khalaf felt uncomfortable being addressed by his formal name which only a few within his organization knew. For the last year he had been promoting all to call him 'Khalaf', which meant 'Successor'.

"You are alive and the Emir is gone to Allah, do you not think that unfair?" Khalaf who had met Kashmiri once before on a courier run decided on the spot he did not like the man, but this leader of many attacks was his tactical superior, the best strategist and the best chief military commander of al-Qaeda. Khalaf had his response prepared, for he expected this question to come often: why did he not die gloriously alongside bin Laden?

"It is Allah's Way, and I would have died to save him, if it was not for his command to come to see my brothers and bring my Sheik's last command."

Kashmiri stared for a moment and then nodded to the words, accepting the answer.

"Crimson Scimitar. Yes, it will be our revenge for the Sheik's martyrdom. Yes, perhaps there will be a journey to heaven for all of us, taking as many Americans along with us as possible."

"It is my wish to speak to the Doctor." Khalaf could mince no words and must make it sound important.

"Rahman shall speak for him. There will be a meeting in one week with regional commanders to discuss the ramifications of this tragedy and to seek Allah's inspired guidance.

"And you must of course be present to tell us the tale of the Emir's last hours. And the Doctor says, we all must exercise caution especially after what has happened not only in Abbottabad, but in Karachi yesterday."

"What? We have been on the road, racing to reach you all with my report."

"Yaqub was taken."

"Killed?" Abu Sohaib Al Makki was the fourth courier that bin Laden used between himself and others, most notably up along the Pakistan-Afghanistan borders, and interchangeably with Khalaf's assignments.

"No, arrested by the I.S.I. in Karachi on May 4th. There is no doubt by all the public relations they put out the Pakistanis wanted to show their masters, the Americans, that they too, are still fighting us, and not hiding us in Abbottabad."

"What was Yaqub doing in Karachi? I last heard he was up here meeting with our brother Rahman."

"He was awaiting a ship from Yemen, the arrival of one of his fellow countrymen, Shahin and his attack force."

"Shanin?"

"He was not captured and should be here within a few days."

Khalaf felt the opposite would be better for the man, yes, if Shanin had been killed honorably in a shoot-out, but he swallowed his prejudices. Crimson Scimitar came before all other pettiness and Khalaf must come to accept that Shanin would most likely become the international hero of the jihad when the attack succeeded.

"Praise to Allah for such deliverance," said Khalaf, seeking to sound sincere.

"Well, it leaves you with a great honor?"

"I am sorry I do not follow, honorable commander?"

"You are now the last of Sheik bin Laden's personal couriers, and the Supreme Council after they select a new leader, must decide what to do with you."

And with that, Illyas Kashmiri, turned and left with his bodyguard. Khalaf did not know what to think? He had to recapture the high ground and tell this shura when it met of bin Laden's last command to him, his new position. Beyond that he sensed this gathering of al Qaeda leaders would have those present who did not support him. He must be wise and shrewd. As he prepared to sleep that night, exhausted, his body still vibrating from the day's bumpy ride across pocked roadways, one thought came to him, and he could not fathom if it was a positive revelation. He knew al Zawahiri, ever wary, would be close by, but would not make an appearance, instead using Ahmed Rahman, a fellow Egyptian, as he himself, as the Doctor's spokesperson. Rahman derived his power from being both an al-Qaeda commander, and a facilitator between the warlord Haqqani family network of the area who aided and abetted the al-Qaeda with the tacit support of the Pakistan security agency, I.S.I., on a secret agreement that they must stay near the Afghanistan border.

And then, from tonight, on the scene, was Kashmiri, the most violent of them all, founder of the feared 313 Brigade and the brains behind the Mumbai, India attack in 2008 and effective suicide attacks on many Pakistani government institutions, boasting many civilian casualties with the plan to destabilize central power and in the anarchy to follow bring about the rise of the caliphate. Zahwari, Kashmiri, Rahman each wore a US$5 million price on their heads for capture, dead or alive. At least Khalaf was in good company with men judged by their enemies to have great worth. It was his goal to stand among them as equal but that would require great deeds.

72.

May 22   United States

The consensus, though no vote taken, was that they had made a run at a great cause, went on a dangerous chase but trying had failed, and that was that. It was time to move on. In the subsequent weeks priorities shifted, though never far from their minds had been the intrigue of the chase.

Samantha Carlisle attended the opening of two Sammy C boutiques, one in New York, the other in West Palm Beach. She skipped over a slew of charity fundraisers that were the height of the Summer Season and without fanfare or want of publicity her foundation had shipped, to the surprise of the Islamabad zoo director who received the shipment without prior notice, a portable X ray machine able to check the stomach contents of elephants, or the throat obstructions in rhinos. In a second shipment, the Pakistani zoo received from the Sammy C Wildlife Preserve, two pigmy hippos that had been saved from illegal trappers bent on capturing exotic species for unlicensed wildlife parks. She did not acknowledge their profuse 'thank you'.

Her relationship with Hugh Fox cooled as expected with long distance relationships, where mutual interests had parted. Cordially they exchanged the obligatory emails on a weekly basis, more or less what are you up to; how are you doing type missives? She missed the steamy exchange of bodily fluids, one of his finer points, so to speak, but she could, and did, focus her mind into constant projects. There was one day on a Manhattan street, as she exited her limousine, she witnessed a purse snatcher make his grab yank from an unsuspecting woman and take off, amidst shouts of 'stop', with other pedestrians shoved out of the way in the culprit's getaway.

Instinctively, she reached for the small derringer in her purse, but stopped, what could she do, run down the perpetrator in high heels, kneecap him? For a sudden moment, she wondered and knew: Wendell Holmes would have stopped the thief, somehow he would; how she did not know but she knew he would have. And it surprised her to think of him in that odd way.

Across the country, with fierceness, Hugh Fox fell back into running the Skilleo Empire.

He held good memories of Samantha and, in his mind, wished her well, and not the ordinary man, wondered if he should have done more in the relationship, but if it were to be, it would have happened, she would have been the one to give him a signal, but she did not, and he moved on...back into game play.

Upon his return, Fox found his glass top desk piled high with unresolved decisions. That the ever efficient J-Q could organize was apparent, but crossing the line to sink millions of dollars into funding prototype games that might be obsolete by the time Research moved it to manufacturing was too great of burden. J-Q was quite happy to make the shop hum with directional memos and he bubbled with relief on his boss's return from what the administrative assistant considered a lark, or the first mid-life crisis that must happen with youthful tech entrepreneurs; hitting the mid-twenties had to be a mind-blowing mid-life crossroad. J-Q saw some subtle changes in the returning Hugh Fox. One of the directives he got from On High was to set up a rifle range in one of the outer buildings, and to establish after-work, free and optional, martial arts training for anyone who would sign up, with the suggestion, usually meant compliance, that all female employees take a basic course in self-protection, which rapidly and enthusiastically gained full classes for a series of weeks the program was offered. 'Scream' and 'Kick the guy in the nuts' seemed to be the mantra the instructors taught. JQ found it somewhat disquieting that Fox reduced his company gym regimen and began training in the arts of Kung Fu and Ju Jitsu when not practicing American kickboxing moves.

Another aspect of the 'enhanced' Hugh Fox was more daily trips to the Research and Game Development Departments, checking on what was in the works, encouraging more innovation, thinking outside the box. J-Q, overhead Fox one time ask his Head of Research, a nonchalant question though J-Q felt otherwise. "Does this concept," inquired Fox, "have any military applications in a real world?" J-Q did not register what the answer had been. In another uncharacteristic act of market share positioning, a team was created to study and generate ideas on what worked in the war gameplay market, a highly profitable arena to enter but where Skilleo had been pegged as anti-military since they offered no games series with battlefield themes.

These moves might seem toward the strange, but raised no suspicions to the company employees nor to the world outside, and the machine of success which was Skilleo Games continued to manufacture and release fascinating products of role playing delight to which the game world hungered.

Like nothing had happened, as best they could hide their feelings, Callie and the rest of *King's Retribution* went back to work on scripts that had been left hanging out in pre-production.

Clayton was no longer there though the coming season would be dedicated to him in the show credits. Bennie, the chase driver added to his duties the role of supporting muscle though that wasn't his strength, literally. Well, he rationalized, he could when confronted he could Taser with the best of them. Abbas filled in the gaps beyond his special effects role. All looked like it would go back to the normalcy of search out the crook and capture him, except the issues surrounding the two main stars.

In the filming of the capture of a serial child molester, hiding out from federal warrants, and discovered leading a unassuming life as a small town postal delivery man (the more opportunity to scope out young children at home), the *King's Retribution* team let the snatch and grab get away from them. King showed up at the shoot, tipsy, and when making the demand for the pedophile to come along peacefully the mailman took off in his truck, and a high speed chase ensued, more comical if risking other motorists and pedestrian lives on the street could be seen as such. But it was a small electric mail delivery truck and its get-away most of the time was curb jumping, weaving through flowerbed yards and picket fences. When finally, the vehicle hit a tree, Callie jumped out, and instead of handcuffing the jerk, ended up beating him senseless, requiring his hospitalization. An ambulance chasing attorney of the lowest dregs was talking a multi-million lawsuit against the network, the television show, and casting Callie as the true criminal. And even though the tabloid newspapers and television media like *Entertainment Tonight* – scandal sheet type television shows crucified the guy with X-out photos of all his under-age victims, the word coming down was the show's insurance company might just have to settle on a small sum to make the story go away, which infuriated Callie even more. One of the aspects of the settlement was that she would have to go through an anger management course.

What came out of this additional attention and notoriety surrounding *King's Retribution* is that the media, had to subtext the story with recalling to its viewers-readers the recent 'scandal' of trying to capture bin Laden, now the story slant, two weeks later, suggesting American taxpayer dollars might have been wasted, getting *King's Retribution* safely out of Pakistan before angry mobs were going to tear them apart. This incensed Colonel King and with his reputation being challenged, a major component of his ego, he could not let a false story go unchallenged, plus he could garner free ink with his name attached.

On May 20th, from CAM ONE he demanded all the footage of the trip to Abbotabad, more specifically that film segment from the tour of the bin Laden compound be sent to Production. He had studio editing grab snippets of the inside of the compound, shots of the bloody bed and floor, and King did a voice over, with the finished product sent to their Public Relations Department, for release, without gaining any Studioz Five Aces head office clearance.

King's blind focus was that this visual teaser would tout his continuing stardom and guarantee the precarious future of Season Three. Who should object? As he saw it, *King's Retribution* might not have captured bin Laden, but they were in his home the day he died, and that ought to have some heavy Nielsen Ratings weight from viewer interest for a kick-off show for the season.

King's Voice-Over on the 10 second video release.

"And here I am in the bedroom the night after bin Laden was killed. The SEALS have departed and you can see the destruction they caused. What else did we find, that no one else, including the C.I.A. is talking about? Tune into *King's Retribution*, this fall."

[May 24] <u>Los Angeles Times</u>, Weekend Section: *Surprise to us, but King's Retribution may have indeed pulled off a coup that even our best foreign journalists could not have gained. A private tour inside bin Laden's home the day he was killed. We all will have to wait for the season's opening show to find out the rest, and no doubt Colonel Storm King will keep reminding us to watch. I, for one, will be interested in what they did find.*

The good news: King had regained favor with the fickle public. They would watch the show. The Network realized they had been boxed in, understood they could build hype around bin Laden's death and the tease King had left hanging out there and they again reconfirmed they would renew for another season. Bad news: King had made no effort to craft a well-thought out, and enticing one hour show. All the raw footage, all that he had, lay around on copied digital in a studio editing bay. No one knew what to do next.

73.

May 27   off Catalina Island, California

"You look like death."

"I think my insides are coming out."

"I don't think buying this boat would be your best decision."

"Do you think?" Said Holmes with pained sarcasm.

He had once run the Marine obstacle course at Paris Island. Nor would he forget freefalling into Venezuela to meet with opposition leaders, pulling the parachute cord at 1,500 feet. The gusting winds and the high wave swells mixed his breakfast like a blender, shortly to be his undoing. This had been the second of his 'trial' New Life experiences. Golf ended at Pebble Beach when he found the ocean or the bunkers more than the fairway. What did they say of the sport, 'an endless series of tragedies obscured by the occasional miracle'. Buying a 2011 26 footer Skip Jack sports fishing boat for a hundred grand was going to be his Hemmingway moment—catch (and release) blue marlins, sail off to an island, drink mojitos, dance with the native girls. Now, he might never make landfall alive.

He leaned over the railing. God, there went breakfast!

"I think we ought to put into Avalon, let you get your land legs back." The boat charter captain, and sales agent, knew after the first mile out of Long Beach that this landlubber would not be buying the boat and changing his life style to a Captain Ron. It took Holmes, as the prospective buyer, past the point of no return to realize the weather conditions were not even severe, modest at most, and this was not the best idea in contemplating a change in his priorities.

"Yes, I agree. I will sleep in a hotel tonight, and if you don't mind, I will take the ferry back tomorrow." The daily ferry being a larger ship with a deep draft to cut the waves, more life jackets to grab for.

And here he was, mid afternoon, sitting at an outside restaurant, enjoying a club soda, still calming his gurgling stomach. It was time, he thought, to take stock of himself. He was not *that* old, mere rocking chair retirement on the porch did not suit him, and as he was finding, idle time did not keep his mind functioning as he wished.

Before him was today's copy, May 26th of the <u>L.A. Times</u> and one article stood out, just two small paragraphs, under the fold, at the bottom of the International Section but the headline said it all "*C.I.A. To Search Bin Laden Compound.*" He chuckled wondering if King's puff piece several days earlier of 'revealing' what he had seen that night in bin Laden's home had set the Agency into reviewing their operation; did they leave anything behind? It would be like the government to rush back and see what they might have overlooked, forcing them to defend their efficiency. Holmes had seen the C.I.A. publicity gristmill milking their intelligence coup to the max of positive goodwill in the public's eyes. The headlines the last week spoke volumes.

--bin Laden tape on new uprisings
-- 39 Terror Plots Foiled Since 9/11
-- al Qaeda minus bin Laden still deadly
-- bin Laden knew of European plots

Didn't the public understand that the intelligence community was engaged in subtle propaganda convincing the public to accept that spies are more needed now than ever, and oh, by the way, tell your Congressman, to maintain our appropriations, if not grant us more.

Holmes wondered, with good reason, if Givens was behind this screen of currying more favors with Congress, a skill that Holmes conceded his ex-field partner excelled in, banal schmoozing.

As he watched the tourists cavort around shopping for Chinese made souvenir trinkets that Wal-Mart back on the mainland was selling for less, and taking photos of the idyllic harbor with its water parking for day tripper sail boats, none of them realizing that the water slapping expensive hulls was rated yearly as one of the most polluted harbors in the nation. What looks photogenic on the surface can be deceiving.

Clicking cameras brought his mind to tumble back through the night of May 2nd into the 3rd, still upset that this last operation of his went so terribly wrong. Poor Clayton Briggs; to be another unheralded statistic in the War on Terror. Maybe *King's Retribution* could redeem themselves, as King was trying, and do something constructive with all those photos and video shot in bin Laden's compound. At least do a Hollywood public service announcement and alert the public as the headline warned, al Qaeda is still a dangerous threat to America. He mused at his own jingoism: our culture waves the flag only on the 4th and all other times we slip into a stasis where only a Pearl Harbor or 9/11 will awaken the Sleeping Giant. America has never fought a 24/7/365/forever war which it is right in the middle of.

Holmes with his loyalty still firm to the Agency, even if he considered a few in the upper leadership were pricks, understood the intelligence gathered in the bin Laden raid would lead to more operations, definitely an increase in targeted missile launches from the drones. He felt a little envious to be missing out. But did they have all the information? He picked up his cell phone and made a call to central switchboard, and gave his old code check-in.

"Sorry, sir, but that number is not active."

"Oh, yeah, it was a good try, though. Could you do me a favor and leave a message for the bin Laden desk?"

"I'm sorry, sir, we do not have anything like that. If you would like to send us a letter perhaps it might be directed to the right party." Gee, obfuscation continues to reign.

"Okay, let's try this."

"My message is this: the Chinese ask-- do you have any more Black Hawks to photograph? Here is my name and number. Have someone on the bin Laden desk call me back." He hung up. All incoming calls he knew were taped and his message, could only be interpreted as suspicious, definitely would get a quick assessment analysis.

Five minutes later, as he expected, the call came in.

"Wendell, is that you, trying to get the Espionage Act thrown at you? Want to see Guantanamo this time of year."

"And this is?"

"Matthew Brady."

"Oh, Matthew, right, you are a new Section Head? Thought I would get some tech grunt dealing with me, read me the riot act, and shuffle me out the door."

"I caught this as it was going across my desk. You realize, you are persona non grata."

"Still taping all interesting conversations?"

"Of course."

"Well, I will guard my vapid tongue against cursing certain employees using his family's anatomy as a reference point."

"Most helpful."

"My greater fear is that I hear Director P. is being tapped for Defense. I would hope the President looks to a successor from beyond the Agency, instead of promoting bad apples from within."

Brady skipped the social visit knowing the unstated animosity between Holmes and Givens. "And your call pertains to, what?"

"Just like you boys, sift the general bull for the hard crap. And how is the bin Laden desk going these days?"

"You know very well, there is no more bin Laden, so no more desk."

Oh, please, let's not have Wild Bill Donovan roll over in his grave. So, now it is the al-Qaeda Desk, am I close? But here's my reason for calling. I note you boys are going to take the same tour myself and a few of my *closest* television star friends took a few weeks back. The Agency P.R. planted it in today's Times. So, when your folks climb to the second floor, there is a hidden closet in the hallway. Push on the side wall moulding, and it will open. What I want to know, only in a general sense, what you guys find in there. I am waking with these nightmares that I saw something in the dark but just can't get my brain to click the light bulb on."

Silence. "If you can hold, let me get back to you in a few minutes."

"Okay." Seals frolicking in the harbor kept him amused until the connection came back.

"Tell me what you saw." A new light bulb from a part of his brain he had planned on unplugging beamed to brilliance.

"Matthew, I am impressed, so, you guys already went in there. When? Probably on Senator Kerry's visit on the 16th. Am I correct? The press release was just safety wall paper to deflect any possible leakage. Keeps with your improved good guy image."

"Holmes, what did you see?" Brady knew his side of the answer, and in this regard, Holmes accepted they were on the same team.

"Books. A kind of bookcase, three shelves and they were filled with books and magazines. Also, some graffiti on the wall, not much, no 'Kilroy was here', more doodling, reminder to-do-this notes, maybe."

Silence.

"Give it up, Brady. Quid Pro Quo, and all that."

"Door was open. No books. Grafitti still there. Looks like Pakistani army came back in and did a cleanup, or a cover-up."

"Maybe, maybe not."

"Holmes, you know something?"

"No. And I am retired, remember? Thrown under the bus. No one to bounce my ideas off." And that was the truth. What could he really deduce from that empty closet? But he could not lose this door opener.

"If I do come up with something, is there a faster way to make it through to the proper decision makers, I wouldn't want to be shuffled around on a merry-go-around, after all the Agency is a part of the Washington, D.C. mindset, that's why I always tried to stay in the field."

"You were a good agent, Holmes. That's the word from some of the other old mastodons around here. Anything you got, someone will listen. Let me give you some numbers. By the way, your hands in Abbottabad were quite photogenic." The flipping off photo. Holmes chortled aloud that someone appreciated the inside joke, Brady, being recorded, could not laugh.

Holmes jotted down the numbers, the call ended. At least all bridges weren't burned.

Books in a secret closet and two weeks later they're gone. Why?

He leaned down and pulled *the* novel from his overnight bag. At least I brought something to read on the trip home tomorrow, thumbing the pages, noting several words written into the margins, *in Arabic*. But maybe I should wait, I'll probably get seasick reading, and besides, I'm out of work, plenty of time on my hands. Maybe in a few days I'll start it. Maybe download it as an e-book. No, I like the feel of this one, hefty, good paper, hard cover. Tangible worth. It's seen a lot and I need it to talk to me. He dropped the book back into his bag, unread.

Episode 11

The suicide bomber's imagination leads him to believe in a brilliant act of heroism, when in fact he is simply blowing himself up pointlessly and taking other people's lives.
--*Salman Rushdie*

74.

June 1st, 2011 New York State

"They have set the date for the shipment, October 4th."

"Plenty of time for us," answered Brahma Singh. Plenty of time to get the Crimson Scimitar team in place, thought the Scientist.

"Yes, but I want to have secondary plans in place to leave earlier if need be, just in case.

After talking today with the staff working with the Nuclear Waste Alternative Task Force, I get a sense they are a little freaked out, and running in place without a roadmap."

Singh, The Scientist, as al-Qaeda hierarchy gave him this cover name, was responding to his immediate superior, the Operations Manager at the Indian Points Nuclear Plant.

"What makes you think that?"

"Have you read the series The New York Times has been running on our industry?" The manager did not wait for a response but pulled from a file folder and handed over a faxed copy of an article, the headline reading,

[June 1st] *Changing Nuclear Picture After The Tsunami*

Singh assumed this article arose from the decision last week by German Chancellor Angela Markel to end the country's nuclear program, making Germany the biggest economy to abandon nuclear power.

"Well, I don't expect a tsunami inland New York State."

"Don't count out Mother Nature," corrected the Ops Manager. "Just recall that the 5th largest grossing film last year was *2012*, filled with earthquakes, volcanoes, tectonic plate shifts, and the climax with the largest continent destroying tsunami in the universe."

Singh was always reminded by his boss that the man was a movie trivia freak, less the scientist, more the generalist data absorbing bureaucrat who could, as he had been enlightened, list all movies that teamed Veronica Lake with Alan Ladd, and still on the side have the time to operate a nuclear facility.

"Grant you that. But I would guess, the first Times article was really what set off the Task Force."

"Indeed." And on cue, he pulled out that article.

[May 11th] *A Dangerous Fusion: A Crack in the Safety of Nuclear Reactors*

Singh refreshed his memory by scanning the article, shaking his head at the fearmongering teaser sentence, '*Since the Three Mile Island accident, at least 38 nuclear power reactors have been forced to shut down for a year or more because of safety problems.*'

He handed the article back.

"At least this time we were not mentioned by name." He donned his 'them against us' editorial positioning. "Why don't they write something positive we are doing, like supplying all the electricity the public is demanding?"

The Operations Manager nodded in agreement.

"Well, with this shipment we are being proactive and disposing of nuclear waste into a program that might just be the answer to our overflowing stockpile problem."

"Yeah, but the government doesn't want to let everyone know we do have an answer."

"Unfortunately, the State we are sending the waste shipment to doesn't want it, even after $1.5 billion spent there to build the repository. U.S. Senator Reid is Majority Leader and has clout with the President who's facing his second term election next year, so the Task Force has deemed this a 'National Emergency Priority' and 'Top Secret' and everything is being couched as an 'incomplete transit shipment', just being stored temporarily the public manifest will state, until it moves on to the final waste destruction facility."

"Which plant the government hasn't built yet. So, the shipment may sit years waiting for its final destination."

"When we succeed with this test shipment, and let everyone know after the election what we've accomplished, I think we'll have the votes in Congress to reopen the repository. I hear a bill will be introduced tomorrow just for that purpose, but it will take a year or so to be veto proofed, at least until after the election."

But you won't succeed, thought the Scientist, we will. That evening, at an office store with computer rentals, he emailed out an invite-gram, 'Aunt's Birthday, October 4th. Please arrive month early to visit old friends and family.' He knew *The Profes-*

sor would receive this message, but on the other end he wondered, who in the al-Qaeda network, would step in to run Crimson Scimitar?

The same day, a coded email from the NRC came across the computer screen of Assistant Deputy Director Givens at Langley, and he read, "October 4th Shipment Date Set, any changes in conditions?"

"No." Givens typed in the simple response sending it back to the Task Force Chairperson without even glancing at the Daily Briefing Reports from other security agencies, but knowing the CIA had no high interest international traffic interested in a domestic strike within U.S. borders.

75.

June 1st, 2011 Village of Lahan, outside town of Wana, South Waziristan, Pakistan

Khalaf hated rudimentary democracy. For the last week, he had been trapped in the village, listening to various sides put forth their tiring arguments, and stump for preferred candidates to take over al-Qaeda to fill the vacancy left by bin Laden's 'murder by the Great Satan'.

It was apparent two camps were forming, those of the old guard, a conservative wing that favored al-Zawahiri as being the logical heir, after all did not bin Laden defer to the Doctor's direction and input on the 9/11 planning? To the other side, a young Turk revolt seemed to be building strength, with the candidate being Kashmiri, with planks in his platform being for more aggressive war taken to the enemy within Pakistan. More quick surgical thrusts into the belly of Pakistani government, carried out by greater number of suicide bombers. Destabilize and conquer, and to Khalaf's horror, Kashmiri began shifting away from total enthusiasm for Crimson Scimitar, not openly negative, just more circumspect. The plan ought to go forward, his supporters said he said, if only to keep America paranoid, and let them know al-Qaeda still could deliver a far-reaching blow. But whether such a grandiose plan had any chance of success [a backward slap at bin Laden's strategy] the war had to be first won on the local ground where we live, this said by many al-Qaeda within the village, and Khalaf noticed those starting to show up for the shuria, the political gathering, were coalescing in this opinion.

The shuria was set for the 4th of June, and at that time it was expected that a new al Qaeda leader would be chosen, and by then Shahin would be on the scene for his final briefing on the Crimson Scimitar attack, gain everyone's blessing, and began the process to put the wheels in motion, the first priority to have the attack team make a safe and unchallenged entry into the U.S.

The grand council meeting would be interesting. Khalaf believed Shahin would again fire up the nay-sayers to support bin Laden's final plan of attack. Would Kashimiri oppose Shahin's role and go into an open play to take over al-Qaeda?

Towards this important meeting, al-Rahman appeared yesterday on the scene, and like Kashimiri, brought with him an escort of scraggly yet lethal bodyguards, and more important news directly from al-Zawahiri.

To those gathered, he said, "After our beloved leader's martyrdom, the decision was made that if the CIA found anything compromising upon his body or in his home, that the Doctor ought to seek another location, and taking no chances, that is what he did. While he is incognito, I have been delegated to speak for him."

At the appropriate time, when they could be in private conference, Khalaf gave his report in more detail than what he had been outlining to Kashmiri and his followers, including the command from bin Laden that Khalaf be appointed as one of the chief al-Qaeda delegates to the United States to participate in the negotiations after Crimson Scimitar's success. Rahman had no love for the United States. His father, the blind cleric, would spend the rest of his life in a U.S. prison, for coordinating if not blessing the first attack on the World Trade Center. When Khalaf finished with his report, Rahman spit out, "They should all perish."

"There should be a few left to surrender. Remember bin Laden's plan is a good one, to have America withdraw is a great defeat in itself and allows us to arise to power."

"Yes, you are right, the Sheik could see the greater vision while we only could see the haze of the battlefield a few steps before us."

In a gesture to mark his obedience to al-Zawahiri as the leader he would be now wish to follow (instead of Kashmiri), Khalaf made a great ceremony in handing over the computer thumb drive, consisting of all the plans, contacts, participants, and codes to Crimson Scimitar.

"You have done our cause a great service to rescue this information," said Rahman holding tight the gift received. "Crimson Scimitar has many disjunctive parts kept separate to protect everyone, and here is the key. It would have failed had you not brought this out safely. I will convey to the Doctor all that you have said. I do not know if those in our meeting will wish to give you so much power as an envoy, and unfortunate from your perspective that the Sheik did not set such a high commission into writing, but I will be your advocate and make a case for you when I next talk to our future leader."

There it was, a little camel trading. Rahman gained Khalaf's support for the Doctor to be the anointed successor to bin Laden, and Rahman would present Khalaf's petition. If Khalaf were going to move up the ladder within al-Qaeda, he accepted he would make choices, and doing so meant taking sides, and that translated into fresh enemies. He had now done so.

Khalaf did not tell his fellow al-Qaeda compatriot, or anyone for that matter, that he had made copies of the information on both thumb drives; that Rahman and the Doctor would only see one, that of Crimson Scimitar, and Khalaf, protecting himself, would keep the other data stick to himself, the original on him, a copy hidden back in Abbottabad. This data stick contained the banking information for certain secured al-Qaeda accounts, those accounts once under bin Laden's control, no more. The amount in question being $US 200,000 and in terms of Pakistani worth Khalaf could believe himself a wealthy man, but he saw the money not as his to covet, but his to apply towards his goals. For all he had recently been through he sincerely believed what he wanted was best for the jihad and he took the position he was a trustee of these funds, to use as he saw fit, and such personal confidence begat by ready cash continued his forward momentum.

But these final days before the *loya jirga*, the grand council meeting, made him impatient, restless. He could not stand the petty politics of impoverished zealots brandishing guns while arguing before and after prayers, even during the meal hours. Nor was he appeased with entertainment from the gathered men who extolled their war stories or sang ballads of close calls and sacrifice in battle.

Khalaf began to take long walks from the village, limited in exploration, all the while clearing his mind to again study from memory the computer files bearing all nuances of Crimson Scimitar. He felt this attack even if completed by others, in some way, there must be a way he could attach his star... but only if he could convince Supreme Council that he would be the spokesperson for al-Qaeda when they sat to negotiate with the Americans.

There they were again, the four women. Days earlier he had seen them on a trail leading out of the village but attached no importance to them. He took other trails, including once the roadway into Wana to buy coffee from a vendor, and sit under a shade tree, and listen to old men talk about the weather and how poor the harvest that fall might be, as he surmised, old men had done so for several millennium.

In his third sighting of the women, he noticed there was a pattern. Two women would walk out of the village from one direction and run into the other two women, all four in a single file possession. One woman carried on her head a large clay jar, with a wide mouth, another woman, balanced a small crate with some sort of cloth wrapped package. The next time, they carried the same, yet he sensed they switched who was carrying what. That seemed odd. In their manner of dress, all four wore the niqab wardrobe, with their faces completely covered, all in black, except one of the women, the tallest of the group, who wore deep blue. An imbalance to a set order and with nothing better to do, Khalaf followed them, out of curiosity, hopeful, for variety, they might know another route he had not traversed before.

After about a half mile of walking through a rocky terrain, the path barely visible, where he thought they might be doing a circuitous route into Wana, they branched off another direction.

Soon, he could see they were approaching what looked like a large ruin, what he deduced was some sort of British Raj era military outpost, most of the place reduced to rubble with several remaining walls standing in various forms of weathered erosion.

He hung back not to be seen and when he moved forward again he caught a glimpse of the last woman treading over a crumbled wall, down inside, out of sight. Ready to turn around, his eye spotted a rusted sign and he went forward to read the wording, both in Pashtu and English: *Warning! Mine Field!*

Instinctively, he quick-stepped backward, fearful of where he stood. Before the outpost, he surveyed a large open area, and as he saw most of it had strung barbwire, aged and broken in many places. Indeed, a mine field must have existed, either emptied of explosive ordinance, or the good chance a few unstable devices had been forgotten ready to take a leg, or a life. Yet, here, surely the women had crossed unhurt, but no man, as himself, would take such a risk just to be curious on what lay beyond the wall. In this dilemma, he spotted a few black threads, caught on a metal barb. Here is where they entered, and bending, as a tracker after mountain sheep, he studied the ground seeking the mark of a footprint on rock. No tracks. But what's this? A colored pebble, hand colored, not natural rock, every few feet he could spot them, the gait that might be the length of a woman's step. To step to the side, right or left, or step on the stone, was a life-death decision and with trepidation he chose the latter, the first step with a catching breath.

Nothing happened. Next small step, and another after that.

Near the wall, he heard a rare sound: laughter.

Securing a hiding place, he moved himself over the fallen wall stones, accepting he had passed through the abandoned mine field, agreeing it was a good ruse to keep people away.

Carefully, he peered over.

Football. Soccer it was called in the West.

The four women were in gaiety, not loudly, but eagerness in the play of kicking an old soccer ball around on the dirt of a small enclosure. Khalaf soon enough figured out their deception. The large jar had carried the ball, the small balanced crate hid tennis shoes which they now wore, their sandals off to the side. Stimulating something deep inside him, a perverse reaction, he saw they had hiked up their skirts, wearing white pants underneath, loose fitting pants, and removed their face veils, still covered but more modestly by hijab scarfs And as she turned in a parrying, rapid kick demonstrating she was the most talented of the other three, in fact, probably a teacher-coach, Khalaf saw her face and found it beautiful. He watched transfixed, the motion, a gracefulness in making her ball strikes artistic, like it might be set to music as a frenzied quick-step folk dance. And dance throughout time conveyed sexual innuendos, invitation.

One of the untutored kicks of another woman bounced into the rocks, and the woman in blue, walked over to retrieve, and when she did so, and glanced up, her eyes locked into Khalaf's gaze from his hiding place, her entrancement overwhelmed him. Both reacted by not reacting: what should he do? He recalled his Qur'an:

O Prophet! Tell your wives and your daughters and the women of the believers to draw their [jalabib] veils all over their bodies that is most convenient that they should be known (as such) and not molested: and Allah is Oft-Forgiving Most Merciful.

First stern at their discovery, she froze and waited, but when he did not jump up and shout Qur'an scripture, or try to stone them as heretics, likewise she said nothing, finally placing a smile of mutual conspiracy between them and returned to their game. Khalaf, only last week believing he had the courage of a lion, having been in a running street battle that killed an infidel with a car, fled in utter cowardice from four women, mostly shamed that his spying had been discovered.

What he had seen must have broken some sharia law, which one he did not know, but women in competition, in athletics must be forbidden, since he had not known of any other such examples in Afghanistan or in Pakistan. Yes, Moslem women he knew in Egypt were more progressive to mimic Western women dress and say they were equal to men. As he was taught and must agree he still accepted, by Mohammed's writings, men's actions only sought to protect a woman's virtue. He had heard rumors that some Saudi women wanted to participate in Olympic Games. Such knowledge of a perceived sin, as playing soccer, had at this moment no influence on his morality, for Khalaf's mind focused only of the uncovered beauty in the face of the Woman in Blue. He must learn more about her.

Truth is not a friend of happiness, he concluded soon enough, by his later discoveries.

76.

June 2nd   Village of Lahan

Shahin's entry into the village, to Khalaf, seemed more like a Roman conqueror returning to receive laurels of victory. Rewards not yet earned.

The attack leader for Crimson Scimitar arrived with his squad, and most noticeable, all the men were clean-shaven, beginning to shift into their role to look unassuming as they were expected to look as they entered America, coming in somewhere out of Mexico, according to Khalaf's reading of bin Laden's plan.

They arrived with a great deal of uplifting buoyancy for all, as al-Qaeda in Yemen had scored a major victory and had captured Zinjibar, the regional town of great import. The war there was going their way, and Shahin made sure that all of the Supreme Council members on the Arabian peninsula --- including al-Wahishi, Saif al-Adel, even al-Awalki received Shahin's praise of great leadership. So apparent was his boasting it became apparent that another slate of candidates was now in the running, but from which of those, might be offered up as bin Laden's replacement. Not al-Awalki, prayed Khalaf, not the American.

Both Shahin and Khalaf exchanged mutual greetings in cool courtesy. Maybe he was just an ethereal reminder of the ghost of bin Laden that Khalaf found himself, which he deemed nevertheless as his rightful due, to sit in private council when Shanhin updated Kashimiri and Rahman on the outline of his planned travels, kept general to avoid the ears of spies.

"I received word today that October 4th will be the beginning of our operation, with October 7th, the anticipated date of our major attack."

"And what do you need from us," asked Rahman, in sincere differential respect to someone who might not be returning.

"With our Sheik gone, I made this trip for a final ratification from the rest of the Supreme Council based here. Yemen still remains in support of the operation. And while I am here you have a certain landmark that would assist us in our final training exercise."

"And you feel, even with our Sheik in heaven, this Crimson Scimitar will succeed?" This from Kashimiri, unafraid to show his skepticism, certainly positioning himself if failure were to come.

"More than ever, dear comrade. We have no word that they suspect us. All others in our plan are preparing. My men and I are ready."

"As we will confirm at our meeting on the 4th," stated Rahman giving off every confidence that this would be the supportive decision.

"Yes, we shall see, when everyone gathers." Not a rebuke from Kashmiri, but putting such matters in the proper perspective of the larger assemblage having the last word.

"Our late and beloved leader wished that Khalaf, here, be elevated from his important position of Council courier and act as one of the representatives to our delegation when we treat with the Americans...after our brother Shahin's great triumph."

Khalaf was stupefied. He assumed that Rahman would speak to al-Zawahiri and behind the scene lobbying would gain his post. This was too open, he too defenseless from scourging attack, and such began.

"Khalaf is one of the best of our couriers and to lose him would not be best for all our interests." The backhanded compliment from Kashmiri was too transparent and from this quarter there would be no support for his advancement.

"Khalaf does not even like Americans, he has said so," said Shahin, sensing from Kashmiri which way the winds would blow for the young Egyptian. "To negotiate with an enemy by first grabbing at their throat is not my idea of tact." Shahin laughed at his joke.

"I have seen Khalaf any many disguises," Rahman came to his defense, "and he has a skill to mask his face from the emotions he really holds inside, as he does now."

"The Jirga on the 4th will certainly offer many choices and consequences," said Kashmiri, and they said nothing more, drank tea and ate wheat cakes, and let Shahin tell glorious stories of al-Qaeda's battles in Yemen.

Quite later, when Khalaf and Rahman walked alone, with only two bodyguards trailing at a discreet distance, he had to ask, "Why did you mention our Sheik's wishes for me? Was the time appropriate?"

"Khalaf, if you are to be an ambassador at some point in time, it is important to know that as you guard your front, you must keep eyes in the back of your head to watch out for your supposed friends. And please, Kahlaf, if I can be frank, by putting you into play as a pawn, you can be offered for sacrifice, not literally of course, but the only move at this time is to have the king crowned. When the king is enthroned on the chess board, we will all be glorious under his banner."

Khalaf felt the analogy weak and wanted to say the Queen was the strongest of all chess pieces, but he nodded his acquiesces, and thinking of a female chess piece brought him to a far more serious question, one to be asked with the delicacy of a future politician. He looked to his surroundings.

"I have noticed all the new people who have been arriving over the last weeks, and seek to put names to faces, but I have seen a woman walking through the village, taller than most, and her dress does not seem to be of this territory. In fact, of finer cloth. Is she here to join a future martyr brigade?"

"Ah yes, I know exactly of whom you speak. *Sabz.* The green eyed woman-child. No, she will not be strapping on any bombs and fling herself at government leaders." Rahman thought and laughed at his private joke coming. "Yet, she will be strapped on, and explode with babies. Her uncle brought her here and acts as her guardian. Her father was brother to the Emir Tahir Yuldashev of the IMU [Islamic Movement of Uzbekistan] who was killed in 2009 in this very region, by a missile strike. His deputy Abu Usman has taken control of IMU. Usman and al-Zawahiri decided one positive way to rebuild the strength of IMU and give a closer relationship to the al-Qaeda of Pakistan is through a blood marriage."

Kahlaf did not like the way this conversation was going. Rahman, a consummate story teller, continued, oblivious to his listener's mood change.

"She is married, then?"

"No, not yet, they are still haggling over the dowry. The ceremony will be a rushed one, war time conditions as you can expect. The engagement is scheduled to be several days after the Jirga. She is to marry Gupta."

"Gupta? He is Pakistani, but from Punjab. And he is a lieutenant to Kashmiri. That marriage will give Kashmiri...extensive connections, a stronger power base."

"I do not disagree, but the Doctor, feels he can control all the tentacles that we have out there, again if he is chosen to lead." Rahman thinking Khalaf's mind was worried about the outcome of these strange internal politics put his hand on Khalaf's shoulder.

"Do not fret, my young brother, such a marriage, if it does happen, will be miserable for both. And if a failure there will be shame on both families, and no power will be consecrated.

This Sabz will be a hellcat. I heard among the women, she has voiced her opposition to her own father's wishes, though he himself did not have much say in the decision. A forced marriage sinks to its own doom. One of her male cousins attends her, more the guard to keep her from running away, or killing herself. What's worse, she is educated, sent away to a university in Kyrgyzstan, would you believe, a degree in mathematics, and knows several languages, including English and Russian. I ask you: what's all that have to do with birthing tomorrow's heroes?"

Trying a tactful way to move away from his dismay, Khalaf offered a supportive answer, "Yes, a smart woman for an uneducated soldier will bring ill luck, may Allah protect our brother Gupta."

Rahman gained a notion, seeing the conversation offered another perspective and an opportunity.

"Perhaps you may be of service, sooner than later. Tomorrow night, Kashimir and Sabz's cousin and the prospective groom will be meeting to discuss the dowry, hopefully a small celebration to follow, perhaps a few crude Sitthniyan songs. If you were to show up, perhaps offer to be a witness, and offer congratulations, that might disarm such antagonism that you are an outsider, or better yet, those who harbor suspicion on why you did not perish with our martyred Sheik." He gave Khalaf a serious look. "As we who believe in you, know you saved yourself to help further our cause."

Khalaf tried to recall: that bridge once crossed, where there is no turning back, what is it called: the Rubicon, that's it. He had crossed his own Rubicon.

"If you feel it helpful I will attend."

77.

June 3rd

He made it through the next day, concentrating his mind on all bustling activities around him, as if this meeting of al-Qaeda leaders would be some sort of colorful festival.

After lunch, Shahin took his men, with a curious fan base of another ten men, to travel twenty miles to a highway bridge flung over a mountain gorge, where they would do mock attacks all day long, coming back well after dark. Shahin in mock grandiosity invited Khalaf along, both knowing his proper refusal would be interpreted as weakness on his part. He bore the low voiced derision behind his back as Shanin and his men departed. Khalaf's felt belittled that his task of war was to attend a party.

Preparing for tomorrow's important and critical meeting and with the inflow of attendees and visitors, a goat was on a spit roasting in a communal fashion, and those hungry were allowed to cut slices from the cooked flesh, and tasty it was. He heard a voice near his head, *English*, and his whole countenance felt immobilized.

"Thank you." He heard the words repeated, English with a Russian accent, he was sure of it. And from a side glance he looked into deep emerald pools.

"Thank you for not betraying us. It was only a simple game for our health." And she was gone, carrying a large plate of meat and vegetables to a group of men sitting a ways off, lounging on the ground, one of them Kashmiri's man, Gupta, the future husband of this girl named Sabz.

Her voice child-like but strong in such brashness to talk to a non-mahram man [not of her family/tribe]. Her cousin could beat her for such breach of etiquette. Kahlaf placed that voice, replayed her words, to a face he had briefly seen, happy in kicking a ball, how did she say it, 'for our health'. A woman who thought for herself, about her needs; remarkable, and such a waste to have her legs opened to such a lout as Gupta. Yet, it was Gupta, in his anticipation at marital and conjugal bliss, who had later walked over to him and made the invitation to Khalaf directly, perhaps a seed planted by Rahman, a need for many dowry witnesses, or that the foreigner might want to enjoy the local customs of the neighborhood, or a sly hint of making the foreigner, the Egyptian, jealous of Gupta's good fortune. The latter much closer to the truth, Khalaf reasoned, and properly accepted the smiling offer to join the men later in the garden behind Kashmiri's house.

An hour later, Khalaf made his toilet of preparation. He accepted his own body smells as being a part of the heritage of field service where no baths were easily accessed. For this approaching gathering, he made a wet rag cleaning of his upper body, and put on his best, his only floral silk coat. He felt relaxed. As the customs dictated he knew he would not see her there, so would not have to avoid looking at her.

He walked out of his small house, inhaled the night air, not for freshness as smoke of banked cooking hearths still rose with seasoned aromas. No, the air intake was to push his chest up, his back straightened, and hearing men's jovial voices coming from behind Kashmiri's house he walked to his duty, straight into the brilliance of a thousand stars exploding, and found himself floating through the light into a dark world he had never seen before.

78.

June 9th Los Angeles

A faulty $25 light bulb fuse, not Fate, would start the inextricable movement towards their reunion.

Holmes had spent the last week of his California vacation, New Life Experience #3, travelling up into the Los Olivos – Solvang wine country behind Santa Barbara, touring vineyards, and staying in a trendy B&B. In Los Angeles he became the tourist visiting the La Brea tar pits, sympathizing with prehistoric animals sucked to their deaths in asphalt, and later following a ribbon of modern asphalt he drove the I-405 up above the smog to visit priceless works of art at the Getty Museum. Spending all his free time exploring did not resonate well with him, a lacking of exhilaration from not direct participation, he found himself being unsatisfied even in the midst of fascinating education.

At the airport prepared to return to his condo in Virginia, he discovered his airplane on a five hour delay, something about a cockpit light not functioning and maintenance without the correct fuse replacement, the cost being a mere $25, as he overheard. Holmes accepted this stoically, placing the blame squarely on his shoulders, for without his government credit card to expense such business class flights, he had sought the most economical fare, bringing him to a cut-rate airline, who to make such ticket costs so low must have scrimped on all parts, without a back-up inventory of spares, including this $25 fuse. The ticket counter clerk gave him a limp apologetic smile, but then all service people did that when your world had just been made miserable, but theirs had not.

With time to kill, and lunch forthcoming, Wendell decided to grab a cab ride over to Santa Monica and have lunch on the 3rd Street Promenade. Coincidentally, as he well knew, only a few blocks from where Hugh Fox and his Skilleo team had opened up the War Room for the bin Laden search and escapade.

Poking around the old stomping grounds, he was definitely surprised to find the door to the War Room's office unlocked, and more so, that there were people inside. Four of them to be exact, each to their cubicles, and they seemed to be busy at work, no sloughing off, even if there is no further end objective.

He looked into the nearest office cubby hole at a young man with purple-slashed dreadlocks, large earlobe plugs, and wearing a band shirt, some group called Maroon something.

Feeling good to get back into role play he introduced himself as a friend of Hugh Fox, and that he had accompanied him to Pakistan, downplaying that he had only gone as a favor, nothing more.

"What are you all doing?" he asked. "I would have thought Hugh would have boarded this place up, and taken the door key with him."

All youth is innocent, or expects the world to be so, and so why hide anything.

"We all thought that too, and as you can see he did downsize to the max. But, no worries, everyone went back to the campus, no one lost their job."

Good ol' Hugh, thought Wendell. The boy genius can do no wrong; no one hates the guy.

They exchanged name introductions and firm handshakes. The geek kid's name was Gizmo, saying with pride, "Everybody calls me that."

"Yes, you are, I'm sure, but what specifically are you doing? Bin Laden is kaput. Maybe dancing with a hundred virgins, but as I hear it, not so pretty to look at, after taking a round to the face."

"Definitely a bummer, man, but as Mr. Fox said to us four, 'the war ain't over until Armageddon'."

Gizmo waved around the room. "All four of us do different tasks. Bridget over there, the blonde, she just enters all the news, worldwide, everything about terrorists, wars, all this Arab Spring shit, who's who, who's killing who. Mark, next to her, takes the news and runs scenario programs, all those simulations of potential outcomes, using variables. You know, like war games, assassination probabilities, you know?"

Holmes did not know, but found it fascinating that Fox was not letting go of this 'catch the bad guy' obsession, even if he was no longer day-to-day hands on.

"And what do you do, and I assume your partner there?" In the cubicle across the way, another young man sat hunched over his keyboard, rapid fire typing. A part of his costume of rebellious independency was that he wore a braided pony tail and a multi-colored tattoo down the length of his arm,that Holmes might take a wild guess and say, it was a lavish display of comic book heroes. He could spot Wolverine gracing the young man's shoulder.

"Lars and I are programmers. We've been asked to design a 'kill the terrorists' urban combat game." Holmes had been correct on an earlier assumption about Fox being anti-war, anti-military. A real war zone is a great eye-opener to a preconceived West Coast Richie Rich group mentality. Holmes guessed that Fox's recent in-the-field reality check made a convert out of him, redefining his interpretation between good and evil, no longer that evil was just misunderstood, or that America was the real bully in the War on Terror. But to reconstruct his beliefs into a video/mobile game, what does that say?

"Fox told me that there was strong competition out there already?"

"Yeah, don't know why Skilleo didn't jump into the field earlier, but hey, we'll catch up.

"With bin Laden dead, games with SEALS or Delta Force shooting up the landscape, those will be the next generation of fad. We just need to be ready with the next hot ticket item."

The geeky programmer was a fount of info, definitely seeing other adult humans in near proximity had launched his tongue to chatter. That brought up a new line inquiry that had resonated with Holmes since the tour of Skilleo's Research Labs.

"And I assume this new game will have all the high tech whiz bang stuff, and pardon the joke, but all 'the Gizmo high tech, like Wii Game meets *Futurama*."

Gizmo was honored to be identified with a TV show like *Futurama*, that this man even knew about it. Holmes didn't know, never watched consumer TV, had just threw out associated wordplay off the top of his head.

"Yeah, like, from the mall or from across the country, I could say a code and my computer thousands of miles away, could log me in, and start a game mode, and I could play it in my head, or with remote sensor glasses."

"You're talking about the jaw implant?"

The kid was impressed, to have that inside scoop, Mr. Holmes must be a really close friend of the super boss.

Holmes gave a quick glance to the kid's work station.

"What's that?" Holmes thought he knew, in fact, he did know.

"That's a bad night shot inside bin Laden's compound. We've been asked to pixel enhance and make the shot look like it was a daylight photograph. More resolution for a sharper image."

"Looks like you're getting there. That's quite remarkable, night into day." He pulled his own cell phone out of his pocket. Went to 'Camera' app and scrolled back passed Renaissance paintings, reconstructed saber tooth tigers, and up-close snapshots of wine labels. He offered his camera-phone to the programmer.

"Do you think you could do the same with these? I think there are five shots."

"Wow, man, you were there?"

"Just a tourist, tagging along with buddy Hugh."

"Well, sure, won't be a problem."

"Can you download these and can you email me the do-overs?" There came a look, the one separating youth from age, where without saying anything this zit-faced, IQ dudester, had thought, 'what planet were you born on, old man. That's kinder-garten play for me.'

Holmes let the jibe expression slide and thanked him, paying kudos to such brainiac abilities, and then, almost as an after-thought, said, "Could you include in what you send me, what you did for Hugh, so I can compare, and can you send him a copy of mine and his together.

"I think he would appreciate your special talent, give him a great souvenir to review. Oh, and while you are knocking out copies, there were a couple of other people on that trip. I'm sure Fox's office has their contact information. Send a copy to Saman-tha Carlisle and Callie Cardoza."

"Yeah, sure, don't think that would be a problem. After all, that's a pretty historic souvenir, for them to have."

When later that day, with Wendell Holmes seeking comfort, crowded into his economy class seat, the metropolis of Los Ange-les shrinking in size, and then slipping behind him, over the western horizon, he pulled out the book. Finally, he decided, he would give a proper amount of trapped time in reading; best-selling author Tom Clancy's 2010 published *"Dead or Alive"*, his latest techno-thriller. Maybe, this will be my Life Experience #4, an author's research expert on espionage, or better yet, a book critic.

79.

June 10th Los Angeles

The next day, when Hugh Fox received a computer disk from the Santa Monica office, with the note: "Mr. Holmes said you would like this as a souvenir", he did not readily pull up the contents on his computer. In fact, he could guess what the disk might hold, Wendell Holmes's photographs from Pakistan. He went over to a cabinet, punched in a code, and a file drawer opened. He looked inside at the souvenir he should not have brought back from his trip, but at a loss at what to do. The sudden reappearance of Holmes, his name, brought back all the guilt, of Clayton's death and stealing, if that's what you called it, of the small package in the pink wrapper. Wendell Holmes would be the perfect person to deal with this matter, but every once in a while, when procrastination can do no harm, postponement is inevitable. Hugh Fox shut the cabinet, and secured the combination. Some other time.

Everyone tried to let go, but couldn't, in some twist and turn, they were drawn back in.

For Callie, the moment was a call from the Editing Department.

"What are we going to do with all this footage from your trip to Pakistan? The way Storm built it up to the public we gotta start work on it soon, to make any sense of it all."

No one in production was really talking to King, he just wasn't fun to be around, if and when he showed up at the *King's Retribution* offices.

Callie empathized with their dilemma.

"Get CAM ONE and CAM TWO in with you, and cut out all the superfluous garbage. They have a feeling for the good stuff. Next week, I will come down and start working on a story board, and make sure they send me over a script writer, preferably Halley, he knows Storm's turn of phrase and pacing, since this primarily will be his voice-over in the show." She gave a momentary thought, inhaling, as all the memories of that trip ripped through her emotions. Damn it all.

"How much of the bin Laden compound night shooting do we have?"

"Not a lot, maybe 30 minutes, really like you guys were running through the place."

"Well, we were. And, let me make this perfectly clear, when I show up, I don't want to see any footage of what happened after we left the compound. Understood?"

"We don't have anything like that."

"What?"

"CAM ONE told us that Mr. Fox, who was paying for the trip, took all the footage of that camera work, once you guys left the compound; nothing on the return to the airport or covering the flight home, or arrival. He has it all."

That was interesting. Hugh was keeping the public, keeping her, from ever having to relive Clayton being killed, murdered, in front of her. There could be no other reason, and she could only feel, and did feel, a sense of wanting to thank him, somehow. But she had not seen him since their return. Only yesterday, a disk with photos of bin Laden's compound came over by regular mail, no note attached. Probably an afterthought coordinated by his Admin Assistant, his ever present J-Q. She accepted that *King's Retribution*, in Fox's thinking, was now only an investment for the Skilleo accountants to fuss over. As B.B. King's song went, 'the thrill is gone'.

A sliver of an idea came to her, probably would lead nowhere, but the only gesture she could offer, letting him know, she was out there...

"Ms. Cardoza." Reminded, she was still on the phone with Editing.

"You do have CAM ONE's footage of the compound tour?"

"Yes, rough as it is."

"Clean it up, the best you can. Make a copy, two copies, no four copies, yes, four copies and send them to me posthaste. Got that?"

"Your wish is our command. Good to get something going."

"Don't hold your breath. We've time to create the season opener. I'll take a look at everything else in a couple of weeks. Ciao." The call ended. Four copies. She knew the list: one for herself, one sent to SammyC Fashions only as the proper courtesy; and hell none for Storm King, let him get his own. Another copy for Wendell Holmes, but she didn't know how to reach him, and expected him off on some exotic adventure.

The fourth copy she would express deliver over to Hugh Fox, no personal gift note, simply—*thought you might like this—Callie.* He would get it, he would remember she existed, that was the real message.

80.

June 14th New York City

"Any other man would consider this a bribe."

"Moi? Bribe the New York City Police Commissioner? Don't be absurd."

"There's something you are after, Ms. Carlisle?"

"See that's why you are the policeman and I, the simple dressmaker."

"Hardly." And they both laughed.

"When I sold my company, one of the small contractual stipulations to my benefit was that I got a monthly dress allowance, befitting both rank and need to personify my own label when I went out in public. It is not my fault I am thrifty in choices, and not a clothes whore, so I have this huge surplus of clothes credit, and no caveat that prevents me bestowing some of my good fortune on my friends."

"As I was saying, what are you after?"

"I bet you always got a confession out of your suspects?"

"A good rubber hose without witnesses helps, but in your case, I am sure you would never confess to your ulterior motives, correct?"

"I am more transparent than most believe. A month ago, I ran across a gentleman, who worked, I believe, for the federal government, in law enforcement. I was impressed with both his attitude and the job for a friend of mine I saw him perform. He's left government service, seems to be out of touch, his office not willing to give out his home address or phone number let alone acknowledge his existence. My people have already tried going through the normal channels of inquiry. I have something that recently came into my possession that urgently I would like to discuss with him, of a personal nature."

"If it is blackmail with compromising photos, extortion, or your company has clothing design espionage that would be a police matter."

"*If* only compromising photos; that would add spark to my dreary existence; no, nothing like that."

"If your job is private investigative work, I know of several ex-detectives now in private consulting."

"That is most kind, but this is of more an international flair. I just need to track him down, so we can have a sociable meeting, lunch at Le Cirque perhaps. There, would that request that be so hard?"

"I do have contacts in Washington, up in the Justice Department. I could---."

They were distracted. A woman entered from behind a curtain, not a model, nor a matron, but dressed to exquisite taste and her smile well suited to her fashion, a teased hint of naughtiness which had the Police Commissioner ogling the woman with blatant lust.

"I will find your man. You can count on me," said the Police Commissioner his eyes fixed on the woman coming towards him.

"Your wife looks spectacular, doesn't she," cooed Samantha Carlisle, accepting she had not lost her touch, with men, or the fashions she had created.

81.

June 15th suburban Cleveland, Ohio

It was awkward. She was waiting for him to drive up in the rental car. When he arrived, she hurried down the steps and gave him a deep hug, but not with a passionate, longing kiss; no kiss at all.

Shawn felt cool civility in Jane's touch, the fondness but at the same time a holding back.

"I think it best you not come inside."

Shawn looked up at her house, and there was her father, the Captain, glaring from the window; ready to do what?

Shawn started, "I want to try and explain myself from all these months. It is difficult.

"And much I want to say, I can't."

"We're you on a mission, we're you hurt?" The concern still there, and that made him feel better.

"See what I mean. Strict silence by orders. I thought you knew that when I went off and couldn't call you." It came out sounding like he was putting her down, but if she were to be his wife, there were certain limitations she would have to come to accept.

"You seemed to have changed." There she said it. Shawn even knew that would be the observation at some point.

"Yes, I think, I have. I don't know if it is bad or not, and I am working on it."

"Over the phone, it was a distance, like some wall between us. And in the Skype calls your eyes were wandering, like you didn't want me to see you."

"This last deployment has been very hard."

"Were you upset that you couldn't go on the bin Laden mission?"

There it was; the crux of it all, that she even believes he was a no-show at the greatest *publicized* victory in SEALS history. He almost exploded at her, and wanted to say, 'I was there, I helped carry bin Laden's body from the helicopter.' But his silence let her draw her own unfavorable conclusion and that led to the next condemnation.

"My father says you disrespected the President."

Of course he would, anyone would say that whomever saw the multi-replayed television cut.

"What do you think? Do you feel I'm that sort of man?"

She paused. "I don't know...No, I don't think so. But all my friends..."

"Jane, it's not what your Father or your friends think, it's what you believe inside, what you believe of me. I still love you, but..."

"But...what are you saying, Shawn?"

"I'm on medical leave."

"You were wounded!"

"Yes, and no. I have to go to San Diego and see some Navy shrinks. My problem is me, not us. I want to come back to you, I want to marry you."

"What are you saying?"

"What I think you wanted to say, the pressure you're Father lays on you that perhaps we both need a break, just some time off."

Tears welled in her eyes.

"I don't want that, but..."

"Yeah, those 'buts' are relationship killers. I think we both need to get our priorities straight. I need to bring back the old Shawn, it's there somewhere. And you need to separate yourself from your Father's control. I never really understood it, when I see you and he together, it's a bond I can't compete with, nor do I want to live up to his *Go Army* standards."

"And our engagement, the wedding?"

"Ah, Jane, you are the realist, the best part of you." He raised her head with his fingers to look into her eyes. "This will be the hard part. I will try to stay in contact with you as much as they will let me. You will have to have strength for both of us. Anytime you can't wait, I will try to understand. Devastated probably, but you will know what's best for your happiness. That is important for me to accept. My goal is to come back to you. Will you try for me, to wait?"

She was crying now. The front door opened, and her Father stood there ready to intervene, to throw a punch to prove something.

Shawn hugged her, kissed the top of her head, and left without looking back. Only when he turned the corner, did he pound at the steering wheel, and let his own tears escape. He did not want to lose her, would not, but he had to find himself first. He was lost in spirit, inner confidence, but the good news, he knew it.

Episode 12

No desire to open my mouth
What should I sing of...?
I, who am hated by life.
No difference to sing or not to sing.
Why should I talk of sweetness,
When I feel bitterness?
Oh, the oppressor's feast
Knocked my mouth.
I have no companion in life
Who can I be sweet for?
No difference to speak, to laugh,
To die, to be.
Me and my strained solitude.
With sorrow and sadness.
I was borne for nothingness.
My mouth should be sealed.
Oh my heart, you know it is spring
And time to celebrate.
What should I do with a trapped wing,
Which does not let me fly?
I have been silent too long,
But I never forget the melody,
Since every moment I whisper
The songs from my heart,
Reminding myself of
The day I will break this cage,
Fly from this solitude
And sing like a melancholic.
I am not a weak poplar tree
To be shaken by any wind.
I am an Afghan woman,
It only makes sense to moan
Nadia Anjuman
(1980-2005)

82.

June 17   Wana, Pakistan

"So, what are you waiting for? Save yourselves and your chil-dren, because the opportunity is here."

The voice; he knew who that was, it was his beloved Sheik speaking to him. He must open his eyes. But wait, bin Laden is dead. Are we speaking in heaven?

"Let the truth ring out. Remember those that go out with a sword are true believers, those that go fight with their tongues are true believers, and those that fight in their hearts are true believers."

Dry lips mouthed his mute cry, 'Yes, yes my Sheik. I am your devout follower." His eyes fluttered open and he saw the world around him was that of the living. He lay in a small room, bare of everything, a small table with nothing on it. The smell was strong, of disinfectant, of medicine. He sniffed, the smell came from him, and he realized that a swath of bandages covered his chest, a bandage covering over one side of his head. He now felt the pain, constant throbbing. Frightfully and slow, in ordered concern, he moved a hand to feel if he had been deprived of his manhood, and thankful, went on to wiggle his toes.

"Back from your conversation with Mohammed?" An elderly woman, with a red crescent insignia on her dress, moved to his bedside, and offered him a glass of warm water, the glass dirty.

"I heard my Sheik's voice," his voice raspy. "He was in this room."

"The radio. I turned it off. Your people have released a video tape our most beloved leader made before his martyrdom. The Americans are releasing their own tapes from where they stole all his possessions and murdered him, trying to show him as an old and enfeebled man, concerned more with his vain appearance. But they can't fool us; he was strong until the end.

"Wasn't he? We saw a quick glimpse of you in one of those videos. We are honored to have you here, and have you back from the dead."

"Where am I?"

"A small medical clinic, inside Wana. We are funded to take care of our injured fighters.

This is as far as she decided to have you moved."

"She?"

"Your wife. She has been at your bedside daily. A truly remarkable young woman. You are quite lucky."

"My wife?"

"Yes, rest some more. I must inform the leadership you are recovering. They said they must visit when you awoke."

My wife? He did not understand but closed his eyes, and remembered his Sheik's words, asking all his followers to act immediately. Yes, that was it. *"A delay may cause the opportunity to be lost, and carrying it out before the right time will increase the number of casualties."*

Crimson Scimitar. For that, he must recover his strength, but what happened, how did I get here? His eyes closed, next to open and see angry eyes staring at him.

Abu Hafs al-Shari, divisional commander of al-Qaeda, operational coordinator between al-Qaeda volunteers and the Taliban in Afghanistan, another man with a U.S. million dollar plus award on his head, stared intently at him, before speaking.

"This has been ill fortune for all. But, once more, you are the only survivor. First at the Sheik's house in Abbottabad and now the drone bomb on Kashmiri; I wonder if you are a bad omen, sent by the Devil to test our resolve."

"Kashmiri?" But what was al-Shari doing here; he's based in Afghanistan. Oh, yes, a memory flooded back, the Jirga. Was it held today?

"Everyone dead at the man's house when the infidels struck, stinking body parts still being found, after nearly two weeks."

"Two weeks! I've been here that long?"

"Concussion. Shrapnel in your chest. When the doctor said you would survive, it was decided you must get back on your feet. Al-Zawahiri wishes to command you personally. He must hold great stock in you." The last was said with mild distain. "You must be prepared to leave for London by July."

"London?"

"The C.I.A. They are making use of all the intelligence they took from Abbottabad. I assume you and our Sheik were taken by surprise" – he squinted at Khalaf—"because you all left around a lot of computer information and files." And books and movies,

Khalaf did not speak up to mention, but at least he had retrieved and destroyed his materials.

Al-Shari continued, "Seems like there were several plans for future attack operations in Europe, and they have been warned. But in England, they arrested a young man, al-Zawahiri informed me through Rahman, that you had seen of recent. You are to go there and re-establish contacts, to follow through on this part of the plan of our Sheik's, what Rahman called, 'Crimson Scimitar'.

Good, the containment of the plan is still safe, if an operational commander like al-Shari has little knowledge.

"Rahman, he is safe?"

"Yes," he said, "he was fortunate, that he felt only you should attend those festivities, and he was spared, thank Allah. As well as that fellow called Shahin. He and his people came back to the village, searched the rubble for any other survivors, and sent all our key people away to better safety. I was coming to the Jirga, only a day away...if I had come a day sooner, so I too am fortu-nate. It was cancelled but a proxy vote was taken by those de-parting, and with Kashmiri killed, no one was in opposition to al-Zawahiri. The Doctor is now the head of al-Qaeda. I assume that will please you, since you are both Egyptians?"

"Praise Allah for some good news. I am pleased, Commander al-Shari, because our plans go forward, and America will suffer for what they did to the Sheik."

"Well, it is important to continue a battle, even if generals are lost. Fazul Abdullah Mohammed also killed this week in Somalia in a roadblock gun battle. Dedicated soldiers win most battles, but we are taking losses of gifted fighters."

Khalaf knew of Fazul, a reward of $US 5 million to capture or kill him, a man with over 18 identities to escape but all such measures failed him. With a quick thought, he wondered if the soldiers who killed him would share in the reward? Do Americans with their missile attacks, do they split up such millions of U.S. dollars when they kill us? By now, if that were true, there would be many millionaires among the American soldiers who oversee the drone program.

Al-Shari took notice of the wounded man's glazed look, and waited a moment until he again had his attention.

"For myself, I have been tasked with taking over Kashmiri's goals to strike back at the heart of Pakistan government. But first, there is one plan in Kabul I was working on. The Taliban and we of al-Qaeda are going to go after NATO tourists and their press lackeys, catch them were they sleep, so to speak." He said no more, definitely distrustful of the man in the bed.

"Power to your success, my brother," Khalaf made his comment sincere as he could.

"And to you, heal. I will send your wife to you." He left the room, and Khalaf felt he had been tired by the exchange, bluster and suspicion aimed at him. And he would sleep again, except, a strange anticipation kept his mind seeking... his wife's appearance.

Covered in blue cloth, only her emerald eyes were visible. *Sabz.*

"You."

"Yes, my husband." He started to speak, but she put a finger to his lip. "Nurse, will you give us time alone?"

"Yes. Yes. A good wife's care is better than antibiotics."

When they were alone, she sat beside him and said, "Let me tell you my story and you tell me if I did correct."

Sabz's story:

"I blame my curse for all that happened. I did not like this arranged marriage. My father is a weak man and basically sold me for his own honor. This Gupta was a mountain pig. I would have had to keep my eyes closed if he put his body on mine. And my body is precious to me. It is a gift from Allah and should not be wasted. So, I cursed Gupta, and prayed that some divine act of Allah would save me, and Allah sent the Americans and their bomb. But you want to know why you are here?

"I was across the village, waiting to be summoned. Once the dowry was set, I would be paraded in front of everyone as a great catch for Gupta, but then I heard the explosion. All the women ran out of the village, but I knew what had happened, of the death from the skies. I had been in the same circumstances when the missile killed my other uncle, Yuldashev, leader of IMU. One missile, never more than one, that is all they need. They seem to know on whose head their missile must fall.

"There was great death when I arrived. And not very pretty. It was too bad, Allah's will, that one of the young girls to assist with my wedding was serving them food and chai. She died.

"They all died swiftly and there were few whole bodies to be recovered. Gupta's head was found on a roof. Kashmiri they identi-fied by a ring on a hand in the wreckage.

"I was the one who found you a short distance from the destruction, covered in blood and metal shards. You were alive and I recognized you. Yes, I admit, I had seen you around the village. I remember that you did not betray us for playing our game. You were the important man, the one who escaped the Americans when the Sheik was killed. It must have been a feat of great daring you must tell me sometime. I must admit I did not run to your side and begin to take care of your wounds. I thought only of myself, and such an opportunity. I found one of my friends, one of the girls I was teaching soccer to, and I asked her to get you medical help. With her help, I fled to the old fort, and for two days hid among the ruins."

"It was craziness in the village, no one knowing who had been killed; all your brothers fleeing the village for safety. They all thought, because of women's parts found, I was dead in the blast. After three nights my friend and I got some villagers to take you to this hospital here in Wana. That is when I made my next major decision, a smart one, I think. I told them I was your wife. Who was there to say otherwise, so I hid, right at your bedside. I have no wish to go home and be sold off again, and for what? That my children might someday die in these mountains. I am not a peasant woman, Sheik Khalaf. I would make you a very good wife.

"And it is even better that we travel to London. I can speak fair English, much in a Euro-Russian accent not Arabic sounding. You need me. It will look less suspicious if you travel with a woman, who is taking care of her invalid husband."

Those green eyes, deep of the Spring grasses, held him. He was overwhelmed, with his pain, the tiredness of his body, the news of all that had happened, and now this, a woman imposed into his bachelor life, where his own dedication had been for only one to share, himself.

"How old are you, Sabz?"

"Seventeen. But I matriculated early and have three years of the university into two years, almost a degree, which I would like to complete. And I am still a virgin, though if you know such life, you would not expect me to be ignorant of flirting and stolen kisses, which should not shame me, as I feel no shame in being totally educated. Wouldn't you agree?"

"As much as I would like, Sabz, I can't take you with me. It is dangerous where I go. Those Predator drones may find me some day."

"Not in London."

"But the police or the C.I.A. might kill me."

"Then, you would have a widow who would cry every day in your memory."

"I live and travel as a pauper to go unrecognized."

"In London, you must look successful. In the West one gains respect by money. And that you have, my Sheik."

"What?" He groped to his clothing, realizing he was wearing an entire new vestment, the other certainly destroyed, rent from his body by the explosion. "Where, Where—."

"You mean this?" She held up the computer thumb drive. "They gave me your clothing here in the hospital. And I remembered how the American news reports boasted that they discovered your leader bin Laden had sewn into his clothing money for a future escape. And I looked through your nasty, torn clothes, as any wife concerned, and I found this. I was hoping, I must admit, that if you had died, that there might be money sewn in your clothes, so that I might go somewhere, far away from here, Karachi or Mumbai. But this told me that you are a wise man to have made this much money, somehow, in the fight against your enemies."

"You opened these files?" He was mad, or thought he should be, but something in his mind began to work, a plan, that as she spoke, he realized they were speaking and thinking along the same lines. And after all, she was beautiful, and she was offering herself, in her own design, to him. What sane man would forsake a golden apple?

She sought to close the deal.

"You have money, you are to go to London, and it will be hard to move around for several weeks. You need to concentrate on all your secrecy, which I could care less about, but I know duty and

I am smart. In a few days, a good car, an SUV, will come to take us to wherever you wish to go. And it will have a strong body-guard to protect us, worthy of the Sheik who fought at Abbotta-bad to save bin Laden, and was ordered by bin Laden to carry the truth to all the rest of your jihadist army. I don't know if that is the truth, but the men I hired were very eager to serve Sheik bin Laden's memory, and thus you."

"You paid them?"

"Of course not, you will pay them, as I told them, only when we arrive safely. When we are in London you can plot and scheme and seek revenge against the Americans. I only want a better life, of my own choosing." She paused for effect, and put her hand on his arm, and gave him a coquettish smile. "My beloved husband."

83.

June 22 Washington, D.C.

Today, the President of the United States, gave a major policy address the primary emphasis was to live up to his political campaign pledge of withdrawing all U.S. troops from Iraq, and to begin in 2011 the slow disengagement of U.S. presence in Afghanistan. In his delivered remarks he said, "We have broken the Taliban's momentum, and trained over 100,000 Afghan National Security Forces. The U.S. will withdraw 10,000 U.S. troops from Afghanistan by the end of 2011, and the 33,000 'surge' troops approved in December 2009 will leave Afghanistan by the end of summer 2012."

The President was in a favorable position as his poll numbers indicated that he could make this policy decision citing as supportive evidence which he put forth in his speech:

"We are starting this drawdown from a position of strength. Al Qaeda is under more pressure than at any time since 9/11. Together with the Pakistanis, we have taken out more than half of al Qaeda's leadership. And thanks to our intelligence professionals and Special Forces, we killed Osama bin Laden, the only leader that al Qaeda had ever known. This was a victory for all who have served since 9/11. One soldier summed it up well. 'The message,' he said, 'is we don't forget. You will be held accountable, no matter how long it takes.'

"The information that we recovered from bin Laden's compound shows al Qaeda under enormous strain. Bin Laden expressed concern that al Qaeda has been unable to effectively replace senior terrorists that have been killed, and that al Qaeda has failed in its effort to portray America as a nation at war with Islam – thereby draining more widespread support. Al Qaeda remains dangerous, and we must be vigilant against attacks. But we have put al Qaeda on a path to defeat, and we will not relent until the job is done."

"Well, that about sums it up," said an elated Roger Givens listening to the speech played over the C.I.A's internal video feed, "we got them running with their tails between their legs." He said this to no one in particular in the small social after-work gathering, a subdued celebration, except for Givens who basked in conceit with his new found promotion.

The word had come down that the President was moving the C.I.A. Director over to serve as Secretary of Defense, effective July 1st, and on a temporary basis, everyone in the upper echelon shifted, and Givens found himself as Temporary Deputy Director of the Central Intelligence Agency, as the Deputy stepped in to a holding pattern position as Acting Director, either to be confirmed, or deflated, and if the latter, probably leave government service for a lucrative private sector job, leaving Givens locked in to be confirmed as Deputy Director, his political aspirations finally achieved.

In his position, as he was informed, he was rewarded with oversight of all intelligence dealing with potential terrorist threats within U.S. borders, and as such he would serve as the Agency's primary contact to the head of Homeland Security, a prestigious platform by which he could establish public esteem as he testified before Congressional committees, and become a quoted go-to 'unnamed source' to certain friendly media contacts. Further advancement was at his fingertips and set his mood as ebullient.

The only thing that could go wrong was another 9/11 on his watch.

84.

June 27th Fort Calhoun Nuclear Plant Nebraska

Flooding from the Missouri River surrounded the nuclear plant with two feet of water, six feet more and the potential of contamination might occur. The good news in accordance with safety plans the plant had shut down anticipating the flooding. Yet it was the fear of a major accident, as demonstrated with Japan's tsunami destruction this year back in March, that sent a tremor throughout the nuclear industry, pressured by anti-nuclear energy activists raising horrible specters of what climate disasters like tornadoes, earthquakes, and floods might do to cause unimaginable human tragedies, leaving surrounding countryside abandoned radioactive wasteland.

To this headline fueled and multiplying paranoia, the Manager of the Fort Calhoun Plant contacted the Manager of the Indian Point plant, where The Scientist worked, and made the request to allow them to join the planned convoy with spent fuel rods as their storage facility would be threatened throughout the long summer. The decision coming down in July and approved by the Nuclear Waste Storage Taskforce Committee, of which Roger Givens was a member, would allow one trailer designed for radioactive transport to meet and accompany the Indian Point vehicles in Denver, before proceeding south to Albuquerque, New Mexico, and west through Arizona, into Nevada.

Again, Givens scratched his initials to an inner-governmental memo once more stating his Agency *had no evidence that would substantiate a reason for the caravan not proceeding.*

85.

July 4th New York City

"I once asked a young man, 'should not *creativity* be used for a higher moral purpose', and it got us into a mess of trouble, and I now question that premise, but with you, I think I should rephrase, 'Should *experience* be wasted when it could correct great wrongs?'"

"And, Ms. Carlisle, whom should I infer that question is addressed?

"Mr. Holmes, I have discovered, as best I can, is that you are a skilled professional, in what should we call, interpretative analysis of facts and one who then takes the appropriate action. Would that be an acceptable generalization? And yet, when I track you down, I find you skydiving over the Virginia countryside, at what I was told was your new hobby."

"Not a hobby, call it a Life Experience investigation. I was seeing if a person could get sea sick at 5,000 feet."

"I don't understand."

"Private joke. But definitely a parachute tonight would be in order, if required. In receiving your strong, very firm invitation, I did not expect to be standing on a New York City skyscraper at the end of Manhattan, looking down on the Hudson River, with our Lady of Liberty brightly shining on this auspicious patriotic anniversary. So, why do I get the feeling that I am going to get more than I bargained for?"

"Patriotism, nothing more Mr. Holmes, and it is best appreciated with a sky full of Fourth of July fireworks as the City is about ready to provide. I thought this vista would remind you of what your past government service has brought to your fellow citizens, I being one of them."

"And that is?"

"A sense of security taken for granted and that you are unappreciated. And I am here tonight, setting the stage, to let you know you are indeed appreciated." She gave him a look, smiled, and then handed him a bottle of champagne, the custom of opening still relegated to the man. "And why don't we skip certain formalities, please call me Samantha, if I can call you Wendell?"

The champagne cork popped, not a single drop bubbled forth in waste. He filled her glass, and both leaned back in very expensive lawn furniture, brought in for this specific event.

This was not her apartment balcony. This atmosphere of the night festivities came from a friend of Samantha's who owned a major stock brokerage and investment banking firm, the offices situated under the rooftop where they now lounged.

"Let me ask you a question, based on your years of being out there, in seeing the darker side of human nature."

In courtesy he sipped, when she was not looking he would find a way to dispose of the fluted contents. He had not had a strong drink of alcohol in ten years. Every so often, he would test himself with an open bottle in front of him, his internal battle, maintaining willpower had to be closely regulated, to keep his edge. Two months ago, witnessing Storm King in the process of liquid disintegration, reminded himself of how close he had once come to such depths.

"Ask away...Samantha."

"How are we, political governments, we the people, how are we actually going to settle our differences and find a general peace without wars or these terror attacks, the killing. I mean yesterday, in Kabul, terrorists attacked a hotel, the same hotel chain we had stayed at in Islamabad. Twenty killed. Wendell, don't give me canned platitudes or spouted jingoism.

"Somehow, from you, I think I might discover a basis to believe in."

They exchanged glances. As since the first time they met, there existed in him a subtle charisma of understatement, she still sought to define. From Wendell's view of her character, he had come to be impressed with a serious thinking woman beneath the sophisticated beauty; she really did want a solution that had viability, a real possibility of true implementation. She sought to be a savior, whether kittens, animals or, as he had seen recently demonstrated, young men seeking definition.

He did not take another sip, instead gave several seconds of thought, and drew in his breath.

"We shall always have wars because we are tribal. Though we are a human species of the mammal genus, and blessed with a thinking mind, we have filled our brains with the need to form associations in which we can seek supremacy over others. Over eons two fundamental conditions have contributed to our failure to cohabit with our neighbor peacefully."

"Two, I would expect many issues of faults within us."

"Two at their extremes are over-riding. The first is to seek the best advantage and comfort to ourselves; translated in the extreme that is the search for economic wealth. The Discovery of the New World was in the search of the gold of China. In planting crops seeking the lowest level of expenditures to increase a better return on the harvest, led to the business of providing slaves to tend the field. The collective tribal stress of seeking and obtaining wealth leads to coveting the resources of your weakest neighbor. This will not end, and you and I can do nothing to prevent the rise and fall of world economies."

"I better ask about your second extreme. I need hope that there is hope. It bothers me I can do so little."

"Saving wildlife from poachers is a very honorable quest, and I admire you for that.

"Sincerely."

"Why, thank you, Wendell. I do think you mean that."

He felt suddenly uncomfortable, cleared his throat, and launched into the hardest of all discussions, the threat of religion.

"Again as the thinking animal and more so with the truth of science available to our understanding we should have achieved a sense of peaceful enlightenment. Unfortunately, we are limited with a very prehistoric trait we have been unable to purge, and that is 'superstition'.

In the basic sense, it is that false belief there is more sort of magic to the unknown, and if we can't understand it, then through superstition what we can't understand must be more omnipotent than we mere mortals, either accepting the existence of a 'Creator' figure or to rationalize why bad events happen the blame must arise from an evil spirit."

"I don't know your religion," said 'Wendell'. Everyone called him 'Holmes', but for her...He caught himself from wondering. He continued his thought. "Nor am I here to argue how we create religions, but I would say religions are sustained by an unknown no one can repudiate, 'faith'. If you have faith, all things imaginary exist, all questions have answers, and when all else fails the unknown Creator understands what we don't and can forgive us for human errors, including genocide. But let me get back on track, and apply it to a real situation as I see it.

"Islam and Christianity have always been at war against each other. It is one big tribal slugfest feud. Who cast the first stone is irrelevant, as is the second person who had to retaliate with equal violent force. Each side of these faiths believes the other is the infidel, destined for hell, unless, one can wipe out the other before the End of Days when the Creator takes all the non-repented non-believers, which of course will be everyone on the other side."

"So, you are saying, even though the most religions preach goodwill there can be temporary peace, but not lasting? Then, we are doomed to wars without end, how depressing."

"Not necessarily. I think if someone could bring new change to one side or the other of the embattled faiths, present an altered perception in their beliefs there may be a chance, slim but possible."

Samantha leaned over and let Wendell fill her glass. "Indeed?"

"Let's look at the currently most violent; the Islamic fundamentalist with a gun. The moderate Moslem can see a cooperative position with Christians of 'each to their own' but the jihadists cannot, and we kill them as they try to kill us. But, what if they were to gain a new interpretation of their religion. Stay with me on this for a second.

"What if we found a new all-knowing Prophet. Jesus came out of the Jews, Martin Luther, a Catholic, changed fundamental dogma of the papal church. Even in the last two hundred years, Mormonism rose to suggest a better life for 19th century Protestantism."

"But do we want take orders from a ruling Scientology mage or find holy forced mass weddings under Reverend Moon? I don't see that bringing world peace."

She laughed lightly, remarkably impressed with the depth coming from the man she knew was a former spy. Of all the surprises. He continued,

"This is a modern world where movies create believable zombies and vampire lovers.

"Advertising preaches and convinces that whatever we buy is something we need desperately. It would not be, I believe, so hard to define a Newer New Testament or a 'heavenly revelation' of a

Revised Qu'ran, perhaps the same lesson but repackaged, something like, 'rise above tribal thinking and love thy brother and sister and put down your AK-47.'"

"You want a new religion for Islam?"

"No, never disrespect the good of Mohammad's teachings, but could we not have another perspective vision from a New Prophet? Or even a new burning bush vision that updates Christianity. Hey, even Hinduism of Buddhism could stand a 21st century make-over."

"And you want to be the leader of this, as you call it, 'spirtual make-over?"

Holmes, ready to tilt at windmills, got off his eager high horse. He sighed, and relaxed back into his chair.

"No, that is the problem. I am a speck of sand on the beach, quite unnoticed. Society will not let an ex-government worker become a visionary. Great ideas must find viable platforms from which to launch."

"But when this new manifesto comes about, can I have a hand in it, rid the world of male macho chauvinism, give women the right to make their own decisions. Wear a veil or not, have babies or not, but their choice. Not interpretive words written by a monk or imam from three thousand years ago."

"It shall be called the Book of Samantha." They exchanged glances. Sometimes serious truths must simmer behind a cooling smile.

"Before we go writing a new Bible, and you mentioned the jihadists a minute earlier.

That brings me to back to a real reason for this invitation."

"I did wonder."

"I received in the mail two separate correspondences, one from Hugh, a disk of the photos of the inside of bin Laden's compound, and perhaps coincidental a day later, a copy of the video shot by Cam One under Callie's signature."

"Any messages on why they were sent to you, and why now?"

Samantha seemed confused, slightly sad.

"No, not really. J-Q sent it; said Hugh was in the middle of a new game release and would call me soon. He has not. Oh, well. Callie did say she had a copy for you but did not know how to reach you, meaning you had not been in further contact with

King's Retribution, and I felt I had better resources to locating the mysterious Holmes."

"I am not a mystery, hardly a closed book."

"Perhaps, not closed, but no one has read properly."

Holmes again shifted his body uncomfortably.

"Speaking of books, I read an interesting one recently, dealt with Islamic jihadists and an attempt to detonate nuclear weapons. And one feature of it that perked my attention."

"And that was what?" She felt at ease in his presence. No airs, no pretense. Not a manufactured man of society, no snobby upsmanship in playing mind games; he was not even trying to come on to her, and that absent expectation seemed to her a letdown.

"I found this book on a street in Abbottabad, and believe it came from bin Laden's house."

"Now you have my rapt attention." A loud boom reverberated through the steel canyons.

"Maybe not tonight," her eyes moved skyward. "Let's do lunch tomorrow. I will show you mine, if you thrill me with yours." The innuendo in her tease left hanging.

The first salvo of fireworks arced the night, reflecting off the river, and Samantha leaned over and turned on a disk player, and the martial strains of John Phillips Sousa paraded out.

They enjoyed each other's company, laughing with oohs and aahs, watching the sky dance in exploding floral and starburst designs. It would have been the perfect night for a couple to sit close and hold hands. Unsaid, they both thought that, but did not do so.

86.

July 10th Claridge's Hotel London

"But I do not like America."

"You must go", said banker Taher Abboud, sweating, wiping his forehead. "I know I will come under the scrutiny of MI 6. It is only a matter of time, and their persuasive measures, that Ziad will give me up. Probably, there is already a hold on my passport." He pushed back the copied disk of Crimson Scimitar, the financial aspect of the attack. "Our Sheik, may Allah hold him close, entrusted the entire operation's secrets to your safekeeping. That suggests to me that you were to become an integral part of Crimson Scimitar. As I see it, you are now the facilitator of this operation, not some guerrilla fighter in the Solomon Mountains. And what you told me to do does demonstrates leadership.

"To protect us from Ziad's confession, I have changed account names but not to my name as you asked but to your passport cover and moved out the last funds we deposited from the Islamic charities, and ran them through the Cayman bank, and back as new investment accounts at several brokerage houses as it has been planned. Ziad's role has always been limited, courier and collector. I was to go with him for the paperwork on the final trades. You now must do that

Abboud's appeal went directly to Khalaf's base desires. After all the germinal idea for this part of Crimson Scimitar had come from his late night reading and movies he watched at the Compound. Sheik bin Laden must have thought highly of him to include his idea in the operation that in itself spoke of great trust. Besides, above all others, he not only knew the intimate details of the plans, he was on the scene to carry them off, even travel to America, and that held added importance. He would be in the belly of the beast, seeking its heart.

This task if he undertook it would be as important as Shahin's attack, though he still himself hungered for military action. At least he would be in North America when Shahin carried out the violent part of Crimson Scimitar and if his team achieved victory and crowned themselves with garland laurels of victory to wave to the world, they must say he was there, and give him his share in the glory. And if Shahin failed and Khalaf succeeded his membership up from courier onto the Supreme Council was assured.

"Yes, I will go, for the sake of the mission and retaliation for Sheik bin Laden." Yes, that had a nice nationalistic ring to it, thought Khalaf.

"Then, this is yours." The banker deposited the suitcase next to Khalaf. "This is the last of the monies we have collected from the charities. The monies are secreted behind tear away leather."

"And again, I am to do what?"

"Here is the address of our Islamic Benevolent Foundation contact in the Bronx. His name is Nidal. He knows very little and is looking only for a payment, no questions asked. He will convert the cash into cashier's checks for deposit to the bank accounts, the lists in your hand. He will assist you with the planned investment strategy. To our secure email address the Crimson Scimitar leader in the U.S. will text a 12 hour notice before the first attack.

"And I must say, I do like this new cover, the businessman, traveling with your wife.

"Very smart of you, Maulawi Jan."

"No, I am now Sheik Khalaf bin Zayed, oil trade negotiator from the United Arab Emirates, advisor to the President of UAE. If I am going to the U.S., then my cover would be I have been chosen to meet with American commodities trading firms. Traveling with his bride."

Not yet, but very soon, she said so.

"And she is here? I would like to meet her."

"Oh, I am sorry, I believe she is napping. But on our return, there will be a dinner for all of us to toast our success."

"A pity, I may not be there to enjoy such fruits."

"Oh?"

"If the police come knocking at my door, for the success of Crimson Scimitar, to protect its secrets, I must take my life." He stared at Khalaf. "As I assume you have such an oath?"

Another test of loyalty? Khalaf would not fall for such games. No one seems to think he is capable of such great accomplishments.

"As once a courier to the Emir bin Laden I took a blood oath to die to protect al-Qaeda."

"Even a man with a new bride can have second thoughts about sacrificing all?"

"She will accompany me to heaven."

"A dedicated man is to be shown great respect."

"My allegiance is to the memory of my Sheik and to see his last command secures his immortality."

"Then, indeed, Allah willing, perhaps we shall celebrate again soon. May He go with you."

"And with you, Taher Abboud." The banker bowed slightly and made his exit.

Khalaf, travelling under the passport of Khalaf bin Zayed of the UAE, put the suitcase from the banker on the desk near the window. He and Sabz were ensconced in the Victorian decorated Davies suite at Claridge's Hotel, one of the finest in all of London. Sabz's idea; she had Googled the top ranked accommodations, and chose this one befitting a UAE emissary.

Actually, the whole itinerary planning had fallen to her as Khalaf nursed his wounds, and caught up on world news as they traveled. Not that he minded her travel maintenance, her hovering to see his bandages changed.

In their stop in Islamabad, he found himself being measured by a tailor brought to his hotel room, and before flying out, destination the U.K., he had undergone a transformation into the proper Arab businessman, clean face with a proper mustache, acceptable to Western customs.

He had traveled widely in Europe in his college days, even studied in England, but found himself, as he watched Sabz, likewise devouring their surroundings, inhaling all that was different. Wherein these past times, he merely had tried to get between here and there, negotiate airports and local languages, ever wary of secret police who might pounce on a young Islamic revolutionary. In this travel he saw the enthusiasm of a young girl transfixed by all that was new, giddy with a world outside the poverty of Central Asia. Whether it was good or not, he felt her influence provide a lightness in his heart. behind him came her voice, and not a *light* voice.

"So, if you fail, you are going to kill me; for what, your mistakes?"

She had been listening from her bedroom. He turned and found her standing, irate, hands on hips, and absolutely divine, beautiful in blasphemy.

"What are you wearing? It is sacrilege."

"What, that I am not covered head to toe, hidden where you cannot see my expressions, judge my temperament, either to see in my glow your wisdom, or notice my evil eye and to protect yourself from my wrath. And this fashion you see, is completely demur, maintains proper shyness, and at the same time is what any Muslim woman who is married with a husband of rank should be seen in public wearing, to show through these styles"— and she twirled showing off her outfit—"the value the husband places on his married property."

"But the colors? They're so..."

"Vibrant? Yes, do you want your 'bride' to be wrapped in a black funeral shroud? Do you like? The head scarf is Hermes. The coat design, if you have not realized, is from the latest Egyptian fashion magazine, though the pants, I bought here locally, they are from a boutique shop called SammyC Fashions, very, what do they say, 'hip couture', the latest. But my looking the best for my husband means nothing is if he is going to kill me in New York?"

"What? You are not going to New York? This is the beginning and..."

"And I know, it will be 'dangerous'. But what will you do with me? I know your mind.

"Give me a few pounds, stick me in a lesser hotel room than this penthouse—and you like my choice here, I know that---and then expect me to fend for myself, in lesser style, having to use my womanhood to survive, just like back in Ubekistan and Pakistan. No thank you, I would rather follow you and your stupid project."

He was on her in a second, his hands grabbed her arms and shook her violently.

"What I am doing is not 'stupid'!"

She looked him hard in the eyes, fierce.

"Isn't it your option if all fails then death is the appropriate measure. The Japanese in fighting the Americans, they killed themselves after every small failure, but they could have been a lot more victorious if they had stayed alive to win future battles. And what of your al-Qaeda?

"Every day in the newspapers and on the television I see where they are killing your leaders. You just have to wait your turn, you will be the last one, eventually their leader, and then they will kill you." She did not laugh at him, her lips pursed. "I do not want that, your death. And I do not want to die."

He let go of her arms, frustrated, tired at her back country logic.

"I will not fail. And I...what I said about you was for an old fanatic's ears, I did not mean it."

She smoothed the fabric of her outfit, shook off the wrinkled anger, and reposed her smile.

"I hope you do not fail." She went over to a coffee table and picked up a guest guide.

"You control the bank accounts. And I would like to shop in New York."

"New York is out of the question. I may go out beyond there." A plan had been formulating in the back of his mind, percolating since learning of this trip. He would try to join Shanin in the attack in Nevada. He believed with timing coordinated he could accomplish his part in New York and then go to the battleground. He wanted to fight, to be a warrior hero, to prove his merits to himself, to al-Qaeda, and yes, to Sabz. She would want him if he were a true hero of the cause.

She looked up from the magazine, noticing his attempt at sternness, believing she understood what drove his needs.

"I will give myself to you." Casually said as if a comment on the weather.

"What?"

"You were planning on taking my virginity at some time. You are healed well enough to perform the sex act. In some ways, you have been the proper gentlemen expecting at your call my eager willingness. I would rather give my purity to you than you getting angry and like a ruffian raping me and believing I would like such beast brutality. I have seen women who have been raped by soldiers from both sides, soldiers who believe they are the righteous army; these women's souls are damaged, their spirit for life extinguished. So I have decided you may have my body...but in New York, in a nice a hotel, a king size bed like we have here...

and not in our separate bedrooms"—she gave him that child-like come-hither glance at him, her eyes to the floor, the female tigress offering submission to the docile male lion, but not so fast—"and we will have the night you so well deserve—after you return from whatever success you seek. But to have me you must come back alive."

He did want her, their few nights in close proximity, he had thought about kicking in the door to her bedroom, and found himself hard and excited with dreams of ravishing her, and here it was, handed to him, she to be in his own bed...her rules but his dream fulfilled. He could live with that, after all, the ending to Crimson Scimitar was in sight. His belief in its ultimate outcome had not wavered. He had no plans to sacrifice himself.

"New York," he stated in a firm voice as if he were the one in control. "We will leave in a week."

"And I shall have an allowance there." Not a question.

"Reasonable yes, no foolishness."

A notion struck him, odd and unnerving; he had made no plans beyond Crimson Scimitar. What of Sabz and himself? What fate would follow, what did Allah have in store for him, and worse, he wondered if even Allah knew what was coming.

"Let's go out for dinner," she bubbled. "The guide says 'Amaya Restaurant' has top star Indian food. And Khalaf, my dear husband, do you think we could go to a soccer game this weekend? Act like normal people, cheer for a team?"

Could he deny her anything? And in her innocence, which he knew was a lot more calculating than her purring sounds, this young thing had great insight, she offered an alternate choice in perspective to his narrow mindset, and what cause of Islam was to tell him that he must suffer and be stoic and not enjoy life to its fullness before the epic battle began. So, why not with a beautiful woman to be with and to show off, to show to all that he was a man of impeccable taste. Taste he would soon savor.

"Yes, we could do that."

There was some yip of joy, and she ran to him, hugging, kissing his cheek, and skipped away to the window, looking at the wide world beyond the suite's glass and balcony.

"Oh, one other small thing, my dearest Khalaf," she paused for his attention, then patting the suitcase on the desk, she gave that devilish smile to him, and in a whispered kitten voice, "Do you have to give up all that money for this Red Sword project of yours? Don't you think it wise to put some aside for the next battle?"

87.

July 18th Santa Monica, California

"Our work may not be finished."

"And by this reunion you are referring to all of us?" Storm King sneered at Wendell Holmes, not happy on joining the alumni group of terrorist hunters in the War Room, and knowing he would be more pissed off to be left out.

"What Wendell is asking for is a little of your time," piped up Samantha. "We have had a chance to review all the materials, the photos and video of the bin Laden compound, sent to us, and interesting questions arise, that we want to present to you, gain your input, and decide if the next steps are taken by *King's Retribution,* or just send our findings to the Federal authorities."

Callie found it interesting that Samantha said 'Wendell' and 'we', no 'Hugh and I'. You would think she would have gone to Hugh. What was going on?

"I have no problem," agreed Callie. "We still have to make a show come together since the public is now demanding one." She glanced to the end of the table where the morose King sat in a grumpy mood. "Something new as a lead into the storyline would be helpful."

Everyone around the table, one way or the other, gave approval. The conference room was filled, besides those who went to Pakistan, added were J-Q, and the four Skilleo workers who had been left to man the databanks in the War Room. CAM ONE and CAM TWO were back at their jobs recording all that was said, for posterity and future show footage.

Hugh Fox considered the meeting from another disconcerted angle: he was not in charge.

Ever since the failure of the bin Laden chase he had felt a lacking. Always task centered, a goal escaped him. He could do better. Maybe he would have another chance. He glanced to Samantha as she readied the presentation. Ever the take-charge go-getter, well, let her have this moment. He had no feelings, one way or the other, and that was the problem. If he, if she had the time maybe they would hook up again. Maybe this momentary look back at their adventure might spark something, maybe not. His eyes caught Callie's glance, and they smiled. Maybe she thought as he did. Maybe something was here today, some discovery of import; she for revenge, for Clayton, her friend; Hugh for the lost chance to use his creativity to save the world. He smiled back.

Callie's smile had nothing to do with what Hugh thought.

Wendell turned off the lights and started the Power Point slide show against a large screen in the War Room.

"I have taken out the entry, and tour, and the exit. Nothing stands out, in my opinion.

Most of what you will see are the brief shots from the videos and then still photos from our individual camera phones. First, bin Laden's bedroom where he died. Unless, you all can see something Samantha and I missed, and please make the assumption we overlooked a valuable piece of evidence (and we will supply you with 8x10 blowups for your later study), then the conclusion we can make is that this was thoroughly ransacked by the SEALS and anything of probative value long removed."

"Except the bastard's dried blood," a turgid comment from King, ignored by Holmes.

"Next the second floor, which will hold our interest is the discovery of the hidden closet library slash mattress bed. Since we all found this unusual and a true discovery by *King's Retribution*, overlooked by the SEALs, a lot of photos were taken and we have many different angles. Later, we are told, that this closet was stripped and left bare, either by Pakistani military or by al-Qaeda, or both in cahoots.

"Let's do a role playing game, a little Sherlock, a little Columbo. Before you are paper and pencil as I go through the next ten views, write down what you think you see. The last two shots are close up provided thanks to our friends here at Skilleo."

"This is stupid," said King, ignoring, and not picking up the pencil.

In the five minute drill, staring and scribbling went forward in fervor.

Like a quiz master, and on the last view, Holmes told them time up, and please put your paper pencils down. He started around the room.

Ladies first, with Bridget, one of the geeks, honored to be part of the illustrious group.

"Scribbling on the wall, Arabic which I don't understand. A couple of art drawings, red ink maybe, but it's too dark to tell, of looks like a sword, curved. Three shelves of books, several titles in Arabic, but and this is crazy the rest are all English or American books."

Said Holmes, "We will have the Arabic translated. The few I could read were al-Qaeda slogans seen on mob posters at rallies."

From Callie, "I can recognize the names of some major bestsellers." She read off a couple of names: "Tom Clancy, Clive Cussler, someone called David Baldacci, another is Robert K. Tanenbaum. A few more. Like Brad Thor."

Samantha passed down a sheet of paper to everyone.

"Here is the list of author names we could read on the spines. Some we can't make out."

"Maybe our main laboratory could try further digitizing," said Hugh. Gizmo, the geek programmer that Holmes first had met, looked affronted but said nothing.

"Anything else?"

"Well, if you consider the mattress, and look at the photos," said J-Q, "then what I see is someone staying there, but not living there. I don't see extra clothes hanging up. One toothbrush in a glass, nothing else medicinal, no shaving cream, probably wears a beard."

"We can assume he is a man," snorted Callie. "No woman would live in such conditions unless she was a sex slave in bondage."

A few of the men raised their eyebrows. Hugh recalled as a cop she may have seen something as terrible.

"Could you get any close up of the magazines, know what they were?" The question from Bennie, the show's driver, now supposed elevated to security, Clayton's position, and feeling uncomfortable in the role.

"A couple are folded, as you see, and we believe they are jihadist tracts, another is by the writing, and the head of blonde female, probably, Dutch porn."

"Our mystery man is lonely," suggested Samantha.

"A man into self-love is never lonely," intoned King, then caught himself, and quickly added, "That's what I've found in inspecting barracks."

Abbas, of Special Effects held up and pointed to his sheet of paper. "There is another pile of what, over in the corner, holding up some books on the shelves? Smaller books?"

"I think they are old VHS tapes," explained Holmes, pointing. "Only two or three names on the ends. More digitizing, close-ups required to see what's there. I am sure Gizmo here can handle it." The kid smiled at his new-found friend.

"Okay," Holmes getting people back on track. "Ready for the first analysis?"

"Here comes the Sherlock part of the Holmes," Fox lightening up, seeing some postulations where this might be going.

"1. Our closet guest, let's call him 'Ali Baba', knows how to read English, and thus should be able to speak it.

2. If he can read novels with American or British slang chances are he had a college education. From the newspaper reports—and yes, I don't have access to private channels anymore—none of the couriers or bin Laden's son had that sort of study of Western pop culture; in fact Pakistan universities certainly do not teach the lifestyle of American writers.

3. As J-Q observed, the man did not live in that hole, so...

"Someone want to take a stab at the first deduction of facts?"

From nowhere, Gizmo's game partner, Lars, dutifully raised his hand seeking permission to speak. This would be the first time anyone had heard the Silent One respond.

"Ali Baba was a traveler, a visitor, passing through and since it seems he read a lot and having a mattress, he came there a lot, but he was a rank higher than the rest, staying on the second floor, close to El Supremo."

"Very good; a star for that man. Ali Baba might have been either the third or fourth courier bin Laden used, or maybe more so he was a military commander, a strategist for al-Qaeda, who had come to consult with his leader and take back their battle plans to the field commanders to implement. And now, the Slumdog Millionaire question: do we know what plan or plans did bin Laden hand to Ali Baba to give out to the field army?"

Negative shakes of the head.

"I think," started then corrected, "We think the answers are in these books. Sadly, many titles we can't discern."

He pointed to the last PowerPoint image of the book shelves up close. Callie could see Samantha positively beam as he continued. "Think on this hypothesis which came to me as a revelation recently when the night sky was exploding with fireworks." Callie watching Samantha saw the woman laugh under her breath. Something was going on between them, and Callie wondered if Hugh, the genius he was, could see fireworks happening in the room, mostly from Samantha, nothing she could see reciprocal from Holmes. Gads, he probably didn't even realize he was being stalked. Samantha Carlisle, Callie concluded, again being the woman detective, wanted both men. Ménage a trois or at least the fashion designer as the femme fatale ménaging un and deux at her leisure. She turned back to Holmes's lecture.

"...after 9/11 al-Qaeda certainly can't go to America and start planning the next attack.

"No, they have to wait until our guard is down again, let years go by, maybe believe the best attack date would be the 10th Anniversary of 9/11...wouldn't that tell the world that al-Qaeda had not been weakened and could attack at their pleasure. And maybe this attack will be even be bigger, more a doozy than airplanes crashing into buildings."

Even Storm King was listening. He understood long term military strategies. The North Vietnamese suffered through twenty years of guerrilla war, proxy through sacrificing the Viet Cong, and aerial bombardment to prevail against the South Vietnamese and the Americans.

Holmes continued the analysis, "Where would al-Qaeda go to gain research and intel to develop the most thought out audacious attack plan to be launched in the United States since 9/11?"

Pregnant pause for the dramatic effect; he was enjoying having an audience who thought his experience still had value, and to Samantha he was grateful for this second chance, to be assured he was correct, and damned, if he was correct.

"Drum roll," said Gizmo.

The answer. "Why, from the best-selling authors of terrorist thrillers."

"Oh, come off it." King thought the man the silent kind of megalomaniac when they first met, now to grasp out so foolishly.

"Again, here me out. Ali Baba starts reading these American pot boilers where they usually kill the foreign, usually Islamic fundamentalists, or the crazed army seeking world domination, but for our strategist they do more: they conceive plans where one of them might actually have a chance of succeeding. What do bestselling authors have these days but their own investigative teams who do all the research on all the minute detail, to make the plot realistic. In some ways, the American author has done all the leg work for al-Qaeda without one of the real bad guys having to step into the country.

"Samantha, if you please."

She stood, and advanced the PowerPoint to the cover of the novel, "Fury" by Robert K.Tanenbaum, an orange-black cover featuring the Brooklyn Bridge. "2005," Samantha began, "This novel deals with terrorists trying to blow up Times Square on New Year's Eve. I read this on the flight here. Strong plot, but a lot of carryover characters from books going back to 1993. In 2008, in his thriller, "Escape", a terrorist character called *The Sheik* is introduced, and ends up in subsequent plotting in two separate novels.

"New projected book. *Dead or Alive* by Tom Clancy. "2010 in which C.I.A. and Jack Ryan, Jr., our protagonist, are trying to capture the terrorist called the Emir. Wendell read this book."

Tag teaming, Holmes stepped in., more taking his cue to add in.

"The plot is fascinating," he explained. "The terrorists go to Nevada and shoot their way into the nuclear repository at Yucca Mountain, with the intent to explode a bomb, cause an earthquake, and let the nuclear waste seep into the groundwater. That plot is flawed since there is nothing at Yucca Mountain, yet. But we have to ask ourselves, what if Ali Baba read a book and took it with him to do more intense research, or hand it off to a conspirator to double check the plot's accuracy. What would worry me more is that Clancy's 1991 techno-thriller called 'Sum of All Fears', has Arab terrorists finding a nuclear bomb lost by the Israelis and they detonate it in America, using non-Arabs."

"Yeah, man," said Gizmo, "Ben Affleck starred as Jack Ryan, and it was a scary scene the bomb blowing up in Denver, and almost starting a war between us and the Russians."

"Here is our problem, folks." Holmes had to bring the whole presentation back into a reasonable focus wrapped into a challenge.

"I think al-Qaeda is planning another strike against the United States, aimed at the 9/11 anniversary or around that date. The answer is in these books, maybe in a VHS movie Ali Baba and bin Laden watched together—from public media photos, the TV seized upstairs in the Compound had a VHS system built-in or was attached. And as you can see from the list in front of you, there are twenty American and British authors, and I am guessing, each one has some sort of terrorist plot. Many of these authors like Flynn, Thor, LeCarre have multiple books dealing with some sort of bad guys planning an unholy act of terror. And one of those plots has been thought out so well by the author's research team, in actuality, it can be duplicated and with minimum effort."

"If you believe like we do," Samantha gave off a light plead, "We need you to read over all the books you think you can devour. And no Cliff Notes summary write-ups, a paragraph unread might be just as critical. We would meet back in, say, ten days, and compare notes."

"We should contact the Government, give them a warning." said the fourth geek guy, the one partnering with Bridget.

"And what would we say?" said King, still a non-believer. "Hey, we have a list of fiction plots that will lead you to saving America from Islamic bookworms?"

"For once," said Bennie, "the Colonel is right. We are lacking hard evidence." King scowled at his lesser employee.

"Read the books," said Samantha. "We have a staffer securing all the ones on the list.

Let's meet in ten days, and see what we have."

"I'll watch the movies that were on that list," said King, setting the tone and standard for non-expectations that this literary exercise would lead to any great discoveries of immediate threats.

88.

As the group broke up, several post-meetings occurred, each involving Hugh Fox.

Samantha, in passing, put her hand on his arm. Awkward time.

"I am sorry that I have not talked to you in a while. What we are doing now I feel is important and hope we can continue to be professionals and business partners."

"Regrettable but understandable. This was a no-fault relationship. Last week I checked my schedule and was surprised that not one minute could have been carved out for personal time."

"A true commitment would have found the time." Malice not intended, she quickly added. "The same sort of restraints prevented my communicating more often."

"Maybe I am just worried about what a commitment means." What he meant to say is, 'If I gave this deeper thought, I'd realize I blew it.'

"My issue is still not knowing what I really want. What she meant to say, 'You would be a great constant at one-night stands, but I am still unfulfilled.'

"Doesn't seem like it. You have the good-bad habit of wanting to save everything, from animals to rain forests to people. I think I was more of a project for you, but at least it was full service."

They both laughed. She moved back to safer ground.

"I would ask you to glance at the books that Tom Clancy wrote; he is very techno, something you would appreciate."

"I will do so. And see you at our next meeting, unless a late night romp is in the cards?"

"Sorry, no deal. I'm becoming a nun again, and this new project is my catechism. But the invitation recalls great memories, ones I will sincerely treasure and recall on cold, lonely nights."

"For myself as well."

A few minutes later, Callie stopped by a cubicle in the War Room where Fox had Googled the books of Tom Clancy, recalling his first published work, *The Hunt for Red October*, 1984, was very military technical that had the U.S. Government officials wondering where he had gained all the restricted off-limits information, specifically about a Russian stealth nuclear submarine and America's top secret ability to use deep water sonar buoys to track subs cruising off U.S. shores. That was interesting, thought Fox, all books so far mentioned on Ali Baba's list contained nuclear plotting as the base threat.

"This is for you," said Callie, handing over two CD disks. "A present I hope you would appreciate, plus I have ulterior motives."

"And, should I guess what's on them? Let my imagination wander?"

"If only." She smiled a smile with a lot of interpretive nuances attached. "No, for your creative staff's viewing are the last two seasons of *King's Retribution* shows, including outtakes. I had heard, from one of the crazies here, Gizmo, I think, that you are mocking up some Warcraft type games, and felt you might just consider a shoot-'em up bounty hunter game, and if you are interested, I am sure the Five Aces Studioz attorneys could work out the licensing."

"Ah, that's right, I am part owner of Five Aces Studioz; so I have to out-negotiate myself.

"A definite challenge. Does Storm support this direction?"

"I don't talk to Storm very much, unless it's scripting dialogue on set."

"Cooling down between co-stars? Should I fear for my investment?"

"I am a professional, and Storm is the main star, as he keeps telling us. The show will go on."

"Good to know. What about all this book stuff? You think there's merit here?"

"As much as I never have trusted Wendell Holmes for his loyalties, I can't hide the fact the man is one of the best I have seen as a 'field operative'. He could cover my back anytime.

"What he is starting to suspect is a good path to follow."

"And good for *Retribution*'s third season?"

"Can't be ignored, but there is something more sinister that rises above, at least puts my own vanity in check. I mean, what would you think if you ran across an al-Qaeda strategist who only reads best sellers with terrorist plots? Yes, something is there. And I've got this concern, we need to hustle."

"Why's that?"

"If I were planning a super major attack, and as Holmes suggests the best publicity angle would be on the anniversary of

9/11. I would have all my people in position well ahead, so nothing would go wrong, and that's a super worry."

"Meaning?"

"They're already here." That comment had them staring at each other, the seriousness of her statement pervasive, but something more existed, and Fox turned his view back to the computer screen, where Clancy's 'Sum of all Fears', plotted the explosion of a nuclear bomb in Denver. When he glanced back, Callie Cardoza was gone. Some signal vibrated in his mind undefined; he mastered such a high I-Q there came moments of ill-timed brain farts where basic human nature eluded his thought processes.

Fox recalled Callie's worry of an attack plot already in motion. Who could they warn?

They had Holmes's speculation, Callie's acceptance, but nothing more. Key and reliable information was desperately needed and Fox knew he had one piece of the puzzle.

This had been bothering him since Pakistan, and believing baring your soul to correct a mistake would give him feel-good redemption, or some bullshit like that, He went searching for Wendell Holmes, who was still on premise.

"I have a confession to make," said Fox, sitting down next to Holmes, who was going through a stack of Vince Flynn novels. Fox had read a few of them. Mitch Rapp, Flynn's main hero, is an unsanctioned assassin of terrorists, usually of Middle Eastern ethnicity, having nothing nice to say about the perversion of Qu'ran teachings to fit fundamentalist dogma. Fox considered that Holmes indeed had several Rapp characteristics, one being an immovable credo: good is good, and there are no grey areas when it comes to bad.

"The confessional stands open," said Holmes, giving his attention to the games inventor.

"You said when we were in the compound in Abbottabad, not to take anything. I sinned.

"I saw something that could be used against innocent people in the future and did not want to leave it just lying around."

"Sin to prevent sin; this is why mankind created rationalization. And what is your sin, my son," giving a mock beatifying gesture of folding his hands into a temple.

Hugh Fox placed on the desk a small package wrapped in brown paper with a printing design that resembled pink ribbon.

Holmes gave a started reaction.

"A mighty sin, indeed. You know what this is?"

"Plastique explosives. C-4. French origin by the writing. I just couldn't let it sit there and be used later as a roadside bomb, or something."

"Where did you find this in the compound?"

"At the foot of the mattress, under a bed cover, where Ali Baba read and slept."

"Your sin is forgiven. You have been wise and we've been fortuitous. I have seen this similar brand before...and recently."

"Where, Pakistan?"

"No, here...in Florida...in a bombing."

89.

July 20th San Diego, California

The door creaked, opening with caution. In his hand the gun felt comfortable as it readied itself, poised and aimed. On the other side of the door, several guns pointed at his chest.

"Buenos Dias, Luis," cordiality from Razzor Hassim, always a faked emotion from The Enforcer. "Did you bring me some important gifts?"

"Si." Luis Delgado stood aside as six men climbed the stairs from the tunnel, all unsure of their surroundings, wary, prepared for a trap set by undercover agents, but no shouts to surrender greeted them.

Razzor said, "Welcome to the United States of America, may your stay here be fruitful."

The leader did not smile, instead looked at the olive-skinned man, noticing one of his ears missing. He had no time for cordiality.

"On the day of victory no one is tired."

"Ah, yes, quite correct." And Razzor replied in Arabic, "Days will show what we were ignorant of, and news will come that you have not sent. In the name of Allah, the Benevolent, the Merciful."

Only with the final words of code, did Shahin lower his weapon, and a twisted smile appeared on his face.

Keeping fit, his private therapy, to offset the two daily psychological talk sessions, Shawn Pacheco jogged the sidewalk leading from the Marine military base where he was housed to make a hard-impact run alongside San Diego Bay, near Lindbergh Field. In the distance, he could see the aircraft carrier, *U.S.S. Carl Vincent* anchored; an ironic circumstance to Shawn, as this naval vessel when on station in the Arabian Sea was where bin Laden's body finally ended up, and later laid to rest in the dark depths, over which his watery grave no followers could erect Mecca type mosques.

Where irony could be recognized, sometimes coincidence, however fated, bypasses the onlooker, and as Shawn gazed to the beauty of the bay and the sailboats on tacking courses against a mild breeze, he looked away from the street where taxis and cars hustled to and fro at the airport terminal. A van with seven men passed by him, six of them staring out the windows like first-time tourists, as they were, their destination to drop off one of their comrades, who in turn, had a flight to catch to Florida.

Crimson Scimitar was slowly being tugged from its scabbard, to be blooded by its sharpness.

Episode 13

The cost of freedom is always high, but Americans have al-ways paid it. And one path we shall never choose, and that is the path of surrender, or submission.
--John F. Kennedy

90.

July 22nd Miami, Florida

"And what do we owe the pleasure," asked FBI Agent Harry Curtis, his hand extended business like to welcome a fellow of the law enforcement fraternity.

"Let's say I'm on a whirlwind tour, going through my recent cases."

"I heard you were no longer with the Agency. A pity."

"Greener pastures, they're telling me. Cleaning out the desk, so to speak. My real reason for showing up is somewhat serious in nature. Where do you stand on that biker's weapons cache bust—?"

"Which we never did put together with our intended witness vaporized. Everything quiet, just a repair shop with bike repairs. Two weeks ago we pulled surveillance."

"I don't know if that was a good idea." Holmes gave the lawman his hard no-nonsense stare.

Even for a Fibber on the front end of his career, Agent Curtis locked eyes with his own tough guy stance.

"You, and your former employer, know something we don't?"

"Not the Agency, just a hunch on my part. Do you have the files? I want to look at the bomb scene photos again, and then will be happy to share."

The two men flipped through the photos from the case file: Coroner's Inquest verdict: 'death by misadventure'.

"Here, see, this coloring, very faint, mostly scorched."

"Yeah, we determined that was part of the covering for the explosive charge."

"Take a look at this." From his pocket he pulled out a photo, folded in half.

The F.B.I. agent compared the two photographs.

"Yeah, similarities, pinkish lines. I could make the stretch and say it was the same type.

What? Same manufacturer?"

"C-4 plastique explosive made exclusively by a French company, mostly used under special contract by French Special Forces. Some, however, must have slipped through the cracks and gone missing."

"Where did you get this?"

"This small brick of C4 was discovered two months ago in a known terrorist hide-out in Pakistan, an al-Qaeda base."

"Jeez. What are you saying, Holmes? That these Waco-whacked bikers are in league with foreign terrorists?"

"Hey, I wish I had more, but this link being so recent gives me pause, but I might suggest your office needs to ramp it up again. At least through 9/11 if you get my drift?"

Curtis felt himself unsettled. No threat as crazy as it might sound was that crazy.

"You really think something might be coming down?"

"I have some other intangible evidence that I am trying to veri-fy." He could not very say: 'we're reading books'.

"Well, I know your background; you still have the rep you left office with. What do you think we should do about it?"

"Surveillance, wiretaps, if you can get them. And keep me in-formed. And, believe it, any smidge of a hot wind that I hear about blowing in from the Arabian Desert, you guys will be the first on my speed dial."

"We can handle the home grown guys, usually they trip up with a snitch, or we get them with a sting, but if there are fanati-cal nuts out there, they're going to be hard to identify, especially if they don't wander far from their cell group."

"If the agencies around here are on alert, we might gain an edge on whatever might be out there. Again, it might not be anything."

"It would be nice if you could put your own Agency into the local mix here, every bit will help."

Holmes gave a shrug. "That might be hard for me, again hav-ing lost my Double Zero rating and license to kill. But consider this; if you hear from Washington, can you voice my concerns as yours? Sometimes, the second opinion becomes the substantia-tion."

"If you stand by your 'guesses', yeah, they certainly would be a valid concern to us."

"Final question, and don't go ballistic on me and think I'm the kook. I'm just fishing here, but do you have anything nuclear around here?"

"My God, you think that might be the target?"

"Never said that, part of the general background investigation."

"This will kick up my peptic ulcer. Well, there is the Turkey Point Generating Station here in Dade County. Out of four electric generators I think two of them are small nuclear reactor units."

"You might find a way to let them know your concern, at least through 9/11."

"Wouldn't hurt, I suppose."

They talked socially for the next thirty minutes, interesting cases, budget cuts, family life at the Curtis household. Holmes said little of himself; what was there to offer? He was a mere unemployed nomad on a questionable quest for answers. When the agent offered him a ride to the airport, he declined. It would be the wrong signal to be driven to the private aviation terminal to board Samantha's jet, on loan for the project's quickie tour de force. Next stop, change of clothes from his Great Falls condo in Virginia, plus by hitchhiking on her jet, he could return to California with greater firepower from his private arsenal. Just in case. And on his arrival in the Washington, D.C. area, he needed to make a new acquaintance, work on building new friendships.

91.

July 23rd Washington, D.C.

"Studebaker?"

Matthew Brady of the C.I.A., on his day off, looked away from washing his car in front of his Georgian-style home, situated in a quiet neighborhood of Alexandria, Virginia, and turned the hose nozzle off.

"Studebaker 1941 Commander and President."

"Classic for the war years."

"And what brings Mr. Wendell Holmes to my house on a beautiful Saturday?"

"Office calls are monitored, and I'm off the clock; hell, I'm out of work, unemployed."

"Thought maybe those TV stars might want you around, you know, consultant pay?"

"Would be nice, but no, just trying to make sense of what I saw in bin Laden's hideout, that you guys missed." He showed up to be friendly, but thinking of his forced exit from his job, his only career work, his voice tinged with seeping bitterness.

Brady ignored the tone, accepting the ex-agent had not received the best treatment.

"And what do you, and I know you were a good agent, deduce by what we did not find, specifically in that closet that you said was full, and we found, on our return, completely empty?"

Holmes did not like the statement with an emphasis on the words *were a good agent*.

Does ending the term of employment end the skill, he did not think so, and an urge in himself wanted to prove his worth. Like a good poker player he ran a bluff.

"Tell me about the guy who got away?"

Brady reacted with surprise.

"How did you know about that?" Holmes hadn't but by deduction of who had been identified as being residents of the compounded, who survived and who did not, there was one unaccounted for sleeping space. Who then used that closet for a sleeping accommodation? And now Holmes confirmed his suspicion of the unknown guest, and that individual was present the night bin Laden died. *Interesting.* So, Holmes gave up some free analysis.

"I think the guy came back to retrieve his belongings because they would have led us—I mean you and the Agency—to the real bombshell success of that raid."

"And that is what? Wasn't killing Osama the high water mark of the op?" Brady could not let water spots form on his car and once more began rinsing it off.

"I think a major attack on the United States is about to be launched by al-Qaeda."

Again, the hose turned off.

"I don't know where you are going with this, Holmes, but be careful. Scare mongering can be a federal offense; the boy who cried wolf, and all that."

"What if I am right? And if I am not right tell me so now and I will happily shut my trap and not call the New York Times."

Brady chuckled at the weak effort in a threat from an ex-government man who certainly must have always despised a media that had a rep in slamming all U.S. clandestine operations.

"Okay, you are still family, if now alumni. All I can say is that we have no intelligence of any immediate threat within the United States."

"What if I could tantalize you, what if you could take it up the ladder, and look like a hero. Maybe not uncover any bad guys, but better safe than sorry."

"I'm listening but don't expect much from me."

By Brady downplaying his management role in intel-gathering, Holmes knew he had found his 'inside' contact.

"One: explosives found in bin Laden's compound were similar in make to those used in a bomb killing in Florida. Two: Your mystery man who escaped the compound was studying terror attack strategies against the U.S., within the U.S."

"How do you have those facts? Where's your evidence?"

"Contact the Florida F.B.I. on the bombing. Did someone escape from the bin Laden compound that night? Answer that, and I can give you more."

Brady did not like playing these games, he was a chief CIA analyst, but he was starting to realize was that Wendell Holmes must have been regarded more than a simple field agent.

"A SEAL said he saw a man escape over the wall. At the time, the claim was discounted.

The SEAL had been diagnosed with battle fatigue and after the attack those symptoms seemed to have heightened. No one assumed he might have actually seen what he said."

"From my side, I am still looking at the evidence. But what was in that closet, that was later stripped clean, seems to suggest to me some sort of attack involving a nuclear plot."

"Nuclear?"

"Maybe."

"*Maybe* led to WMD which led to invasion of Iraq and led to no WMD. *Maybe* doesn't cut it."

"Better than raising a banner on the bin Laden hit 'Mission Completed'. I am working with what I have, but I do urge preventative caution. You have the 9/11 ten year anniversary coming up. I'm sure the terror alert will be heightened, but you just might start the paperwork now."

Brady likewise decided he had a source; and in the intel business that was your gravy train.

"What can we do for you?"

"Nothing yet, but someday when I am surrounded I may call the cavalry and I don't want to have to fill out request forms in triplicate."

"Agreed." He gave a second of thought. Use the code word 'Retirement Benefits' to reach me.

"Appropriate. By the way, if I recall, the Studebaker Corporation, failed because of poor management decisions. Let's hope no one up the ladder at your 'corporation' is dense to the risks we still face against our security."

92.

July 25th   Washington, D.C.

Density, as head in the sand, existed in one bureaucrat's office.

"I'm not going to recommend raising the terror alert just because of unverified evidence."

For ten minutes Brady had sought to make his case, based on his recent call to Florida and his conversation with the F.B.I. agent, but Acting Temporary Deputy Director Givens, would have none of it. His casual defense: since there is no incontrovertible proof of a threat then no need for undue alarm.

"But the F.B.I. Miami office seems to think there is a valid threat worth further checking, and the need for us to maybe put out a Pink Sheet Notice of Concern."

"The relevant phrase is 'seems to'. No, let them keep their concerns local. If I can't see it, and recall, Brady, I have had field experience. We don't need to be spooked at any little twig snapping in a gigantic forest. Remember prior to Pearl Harbor there were so many false signals, no one believed the actual warning signs."

"Pearl Harbor still happened."

"Be that it as it may, I don't want to see us go off stampeding. I will grant you this, around September 5th, in precaution to 9/11 then and only then we ought to remind people to be watchful; it will go well with any presidential comments on the anniversary. Yes, that sounds right. In fact, I myself will write the text, a press release announcement to raise the terror alert in anticipation of the 9/11 anniversary."

When Matthew Brady returned to his office, like the dutiful, yet wise, bureaucrat he was, he drafted a recollection of the just held meeting with Deputy Director Givens, a cover-your-butt memo. From his perspective, he now believed Wendell Holmes, whatever his sources, had better analytical insight than Givens, but Brady prayed that Holmes was wrong in his worries.

Brady placed a long distance call on a roundabout strategy, and left a phone message.

"Agent Curtis, I would like to recommend you calling Homeland Security's headquarters directly. Here is the phone number that takes you to the top. Please convey your concerns as we discussed. Thank you." He made a notation to have this call highlighted in the telephone logs, self-preservation habits essential in the shark-infested back halls of government.

July 26th Washington, D.C.

Without sufficient hard evidence from the intelligence community, Homeland Security, even after talking with a local office of the F.B.I. in Miami, Florida did not see the necessity of putting out any press release of possible internal attacks within the United States. During this time discussions of potential terrorist activities did make its way within the beltway of Washington, D.C. and at least one action was taken in a cautionary tone.

On July 26th, 2011, the U.S. State Department issued an update to its Worldwide Caution Report of places where Americans should and should not travel. The warning amendment stated in part, "There is an enhanced potential for anti-American violence given the death of Osama bin Laden in May, 2011. Current information suggests that Al-Qa'ida and affiliated organizations continue to plan terrorist attacks against U.S. interests in multiple regions, including Europe, Asia, Africa, and the Middle East. These attacks may employ a wide variety of tactics including suicide operations, assassinations, kidnappings, hijackings, and bombings."

No warning alert was issued for Americans living or traveling within the borders of the United States. Most Americans, by polling numbers, believed with bin Laden's death the threat of another 9/11 type attack within the United States was less than 15% probability. A comfort zone they could live with.

93.

July 27th New York City

Samantha's smile, genuine and fresh, greeted Holmes, the guest bearing gifts, when the door opened at her penthouse condo. "I wondered when you might appear." She walked back inside and he followed. She did not wonder how the concierge doorman failed to call her on his arrival in the lobby; she assumed Holmes had this character flaw of skirting even limited authority.

He saw that she dressed comfortably in a slacks and wearing a hip length dragon-design silk shirt, which to Holmes looked like a man's pajama top, though he quickly decided it must be some hip couture mini kimono. As was his inbred training, he gave a quick, all-encompassing scan of her residence, finding a well-furnished condominium overlooking Central Park, where outside the floor to ceiling windows the day's brightness faded over a skyscraper horizon. As to furniture styling and art on walls, he saw she lived to higher tastes but not flaunting ostentatious.

Samantha expression asked for an answer to the large shopper's bag he was carrying.

"Homework and dinner," he replied. "I had to run down some of the books and movies off our Ali Baba list. In two more days our team meeting resumes in Santa Monica. You are attending? You have not abandoned your friends for a fashion show?"

"Of course I will be there." That came off snippy, and she recovered somewhat. "I did think I would hear from you when you returned from Washington." She did not want to sound peevish, she was glad to see him.

"You are correct in chastisement if that's your direction. A man borrows a woman's executive jet, and when he returns it, he should express his gratitude immediately." He held out the shopping bag he had been carrying.

"And so?"

"Movies and popcorn, to be interspersed with Italian salmon pasta salad and a bottle of mid-priced Pinot Grigio. I was hoping your evening might be free."

"You presumed my calendar would be open just for you?" Her reaction more startled at his brazenness. She did not know if she liked this take-charge sort of approach, from this mysterious Spy Man. She had always been the one in control.

"I sleuthed. A couple of discreet calls using boldface lies and you will be surprised how information can be quickly gleaned. Last night you were busy, tonight open, tomorrow night some charity kowtow, and the next night we are off to California, if I can bum a ride."

She smiled, and took the bag from him and walked to the open kitchen.

"What's this?" After a jar of popcorn, food boxes and the wine removed, she found a gift wrapped box at the bottom.

"A gift; for the woman who has everything."

He enjoyed seeing her in a delightful glee rip off the paper, absorbed in the anticipation.

"Wendell, you shouldn't have." In the beryl wood box nestled a small handgun.

"It's a Ruger LCP, stands for 'Lightweight Compact Pistol'. 9.4 ounces unloaded, but a lethal punch to put a bad guy down. Far more practical than your dainty derringer popgun."

"I love it. You are so thoughtful." She looked at him, almost in a new light of appreciation, seeing a sensitivity, male though he was. She grew more serious.

"Do you think there is a chance, all that we are looking at, the possibilities you are alluding to, all that could put us in danger? That I might really use your gift?"

"'Preparedness only' should be the motto. Chances of finding us surrounded and fighting a pitched gun battle with hostiles is remote. However, you do live in New York and you do travel to strange destinations like the wilds of Africa. I hear Hugh Fox has installed a target range at his Skilleo complex. I am sure he will welcome practicing fire arms with you."

An invisible wall of unsaid complications descended, tempering the congenial atmosphere. She could not tell if he imposed Fox to quell the possible urges beyond tonight's business 'date' of investigating movie plots. And she was unsure of what she wanted from him; was it to maintain the arm's length acquaintanceship, or something more? Certainly, she assented to herself, her seductive powers would manipulate down any defenses. They had never failed her before. Samantha accepted she found Holmes desirable; he looked in top physical shape, and was he not a man of the world, traveling among the exotic locales where women made love through teased, rutting rituals of animal dominance or subservient bondage. She began to create her own eroticism of what he might be like undressed, hard before her, ready to stroke, to thrust inside her.

"Samantha, want me to open the wine or heat oil for the pop-corn?"

Pop...corn.

Almost a disappointing sigh, she said, "You, the wine, I feel like boiling scalding oil."

When later seated before her wall-sized TV screen, she in-quired. "What's our headline feature for the evening?"

"Double Feature, but we can fast forward any lame backsto-ry." He laid out several blown-up photos. "Here and here are the titles we are going to view." The close-ups were of the interior of Ali Baba's hide-out, and visible and circled on the shelves were two names on what must apparently been VHS tapes.

They munched on fresh popcorn and watched "The Taking of Pelham One Two Three", filmed and released in 1974, starring actors Walter Matthau and Robert Shaw. The plot unfolded to where four armed men hijacked a New York City subway and demanded one million dollars, which must be delivered in one hour, or passengers would start to be executed.

One hundred minute running time later, both Samantha and Holmes, dissected the plot.

'Good thriller for the times'.

"You don't seem that enthusiastic," she asked. When the film had started he had sat on the couch, and she on an adjacent deep chair, quite proper. When she returned with a refilled glass of wine for herself, ginger ale for Holmes, she moved over to the couch, and sat near him, her feet tucked up underneath her.

"I am trying to put Ali Baba's mind into adapted this script into a terrorist scenario, and it doesn't seem to fit with the al-Qaida template."

"For example?"

"Al-Qaida would not take prisoners and bargain, especially for ransom. They'd kill outright for the publicity value."

"Hijacking a subway car, even if to blow all passengers up, seems like something they might do."

"Yes, I grant you that. And it is New York City, home of 9/11, the poster child of all terrorist wannabe targets. But, if we are to presume, al-Qaida wants to make a statement, even more diabolical than 9/11, just bombing a subway doesn't work. They did that in London, backpack bombs in the tubes and on busses. Lots of fear and confusion but negligible disruption of the transportation system."

"Shall we go to the next movie, and see if the puzzle is solved?"

"Let's: if this is not boring to your highbrow idea of cultural stimulation?"

"To me, boring is only found among people who talk about themselves."

During the course of the next movie, body language on the couch sought ease, and midway, Samantha was leaning on his shoulder, and without import, he put his arm around her, and she snuggled. Both though were odd to their respective thoughts.

Samantha felt encased in a mantle of warm protection, and said to herself, 'So this is what stay-at-home comfort is all about.'

Wendell Holmes could only keep his eyes glued to the screen, and wonder, 'What the hell is going on?'

"Rollercoaster" (1977) tells the story of a young terrorist who is blackmailing companies by placing home-made radio controlled bombs at amusement parks, specifically on the main attraction roller coasters. George Segal, Richard Widmark, Henry Fonda, and Timothy Bottoms the stars, and Samantha pointed out actress Helen Hunt in one of her earlier roles.

With movie ended, Samantha put in her critique.

"Fair. Stop the bad guy before he kills more people, race against time sort of thing. But you are right; if al-Qaida was plotting they would hardly just blow up a roller coaster for attention."

"Perhaps I am reading into these movies too much; maybe Ali Baba only wanted to be entertained on cold Pakistani nights?"

"You don't believe that? I certainly don't." Holmes had taken the movie's end as an excuse to rise and walk the living room thinking, unsaid but obvious to move away from her warmth.

"Maybe, like any well thought out project, you have to begin with research. The only VHS movies in the local al-Qaida Blockbuster are the old ones. Maybe they offer ideas, maybe they are ideas to be rejected. Not so flamboyant. Or, on the other hand, ideas to be sent out to the training camps for the Lone Wolf infiltrators who indeed could take a bomb to an amusement park, reek some havoc, undermine America's confidence of security."

"Where do we go from here?"

"For me, for the evening, it is time to go. Santa Monica next, and learn what your stalwart *King's Retribution* task force uncovered. Maybe all heads are better than one."

She took the plunge; why not, the evening had been enjoyable.

"You could spend the night here." A lot said in the statement, and his glance to her did let her feel that she had torn something inside him, a wavering of his confidence.

"Samantha, you are in a relationship."

"And, I said earlier it had ended, the issues being distance and commitment. I am not looking to start anything long term. If you can accept bluntness, I need companionship, for tonight...only."

His eyes eased over her. "A beguiling invitation. And tomorrow, the one night stand is over, no regrets and everyone moves on? Tempting. More than you know. But Samantha, not for me. I am not around for the bounce back from a broken relationship or just pure sport fucking with someone I admire. Perhaps someday when you can see yourself clear from the thrills of short term gratification, your perspective might be enlightened. And while I go home, and take the proverbial cold shower, we have to refocus on our little quest. Something is going on bigger than we can imagine. I thought these movies would have a 'nuclear threat' subtext, they don't.

"One of my hypotheses fell to the wayside tonight. Truly, I thought al-Qaida had graduated to a nuclear plot, I was sure of it. But not anymore."

"It was a wonderful evening."

"Yes, it was." She had nothing to be ashamed of, she asked for something, and it was refused. He did not make her feel small, no man could do that. He had just stated his own position. She could accept that, and think in terms of 'other fish in the sea' sort of thing. Why then did she have this emptiness in her body, somewhere above her stomach? The upset gurgle must be a repugnant fear, that the man might have accepted her offer if 'monogamy', or 'domesticity' was the endgame and to her current lifestyle settling down invoked horrid, unspeakable thoughts like losing her independent nature, like sharing emotions, like losing her heart.

Resuming her composure, she sought to make the parting neutral, all business like.

"Oh, there is one thing I thought of."

He turned to her, with the door opened.

"*The Taking of Pelham One Two Three.*"

"Yes?"

"There was a remake. I don't know when, a couple of years ago. Starring John Travolta and Denzel Washington."

"I didn't know that. Probably I was out in the field, below radar somewhere in the bush.

"I'll track it down see if there are any variations."

"Our friend Ali Baba could have picked up the new version of 'Pelham' when he was on the road, what if he saw it on a hotel movie channel. There could be other movies or books out there, he picked up and discarded. Ones we didn't find in his room. And what about those on the shelves we couldn't read. Maybe they had the nuclear bomb plots."

They were back to even keel, discussion among associates, so they thought.

Wendell Holmes gave off a slight head nod of serious sadness.

"Yes, that's what I am afraid of, that we have no clue on what's coming down." And he was gone.

Samantha Carlisle, in the silence of her home, before her the lights of a city where eight million people were settling down for the night, as she would do so, alone, and she could only think, 'I would like to have slept with him, if only to know him better.'

Wendell Holmes, flagging down a taxi to take him back to his hotel, kept muttering to himself, 'What did I just do? What did I let slip out of my grasp? My scruples can't be that noble.' He began to think of yoga positions that might allow him to kick himself.

94.

July 30th Hollywood, California

The old World War slogan: *Loose Lips Sinks Ships* more accurately in today's climate of buzz-saw media frenzy would be so apparent when Colonel Storm King, showing off his new public 'date', took to the red carpet at a movie premiere of a romantic comedy.

Storm had moved on from his tempestuous relationship with co-star Callie Cardoza without missing a beat, as there were so many young things in Tinsel Town that would give their virginity, if any true purity still existed, to be seen in the limelight, even with a reality show TV Star, with mixed credentials of moral fiber and lucidity. Storm gleamed as the cameras and reporters interviewed strolling stars, while utmost in his mind with its alcoholic buzz of the night, is that he would get laid.

In the Q & A while passing among the reporters, one well-known gossip interviewer, after complimenting his date on her revealing, breast extrusion and hip-cut dress, turned and pushed the microphone into King's face.

"As you told the world, Season Three will debut with a tour of bin Laden's hide-out. Do you think looking into empty buildings will move your show up in the rating battles?"

King never liked the reporter, never liked any of them, but also accepted everyone here on tonight's red carpet had to make kissy-kiss face. King knew he had to give more of the tease to attract viewers and the microphone was the tool, too addictive to ignore.

"Well, there was more to our Pakistani trip than people are aware of. From our on-site investigation we intend to reveal what the items discovered in bin Laden's compound told us."

The reporter, following the glam trail of this premiere, had the smarts to recall no one had mentioned *King's Retribution* found anything. Quickly, the question was asked: "What items did you find? We thought the SEALS removed all the secret stuff?"

King basked in the glory of having the upper hand.

"Our team believes bin Laden was planning a new attack on the United States, and that attack still will happen, but only if--."

His buxom, ditzy date paying no attention to the interview

dragged him away to gain camera time with a fashionista mother and daughter tag team who gushed over his date's choice of a minimal see-most sequined wardrobe.

King felt he had done no harm, satisfied he had planted another show teaser for the eager public. He gave it only a passing thought to have the production crew splice together 'what if' video vignettes of terrorist hypothetical plots, intersperse them in the Pakistani footage. And with his date, he entered the theater and snored through the last half of the film.

The fallout from King's casual comment had greater repercussions than the television star could foresee, from the top to the bottom.

July 31st Washington, D.C.

The President of the United States when informed fumed and cursed aloud.

"What do they know that I don't?"

"We have no intel to suggest any attack within our borders," said the C.I.A. Director, having already yelled at subordinates down the ladder, including Assistant Deputy Director Givens, demanding assuredness from his staff: he wanted their certainty of no foreign plots before he met with the Commander-in-Chief.

"This King is a drunkard and his TV show is tanking," assured the head of Homeland Security. "It's all last ditch showmanship. My people have no evidence to collaborate his off-the- cuff remark."

The President spoke to the top officials in the Oval Office.

"We don't need to have our citizens living in a constant stage of fear. Let's nip this in the bud." He turned to his Press Secretary.

"Don't turn this from rumor into panic. Laugh at it in the Press Room; suggest what was just said here, that though all government security agencies are vigilant, there is no fact to this comedian's wild guesswork. Laugh him back into the hole he came out of."

"We are planning on a 'cautionary' warning for the 9/11 anniversary," affirmed Homeland Security, gaining likewise a 'yes' from the C.I.A. Director.

"Good, but make sure these two, the TV star's mouthings and any anniversary statements are held completely separate. Sometimes, and I am half-way kidding, for national security, and the peace of mind of our citizens, I wonder if the FCC couldn't find a rule to shut down fear mongers. And for the sake of all our intelligence, unplug reality television."

95.

August 1st Los Angeles

The Attack Leadership had assembled in a small warehouse in the industrial side of East Los Angeles. Shanin, Razzor, and *The Professor*. The morning newspaper's was being passed around.

"What do we do about this?" The question from *The Professor*, who found himself nervous and intimidated by the power of the other two men who had stone-cold eyes, frozen hatred in their faces.

The L.A. *Times* newspaper headline, from the National Section, read: *'TV Star Says Bin Laden's Ghost Seeks Revenge'* followed by a short story speaking of unknown evidence found in bin Laden's compound that the TV Show would reveal with the season opener. The final sentence in the article from an unnamed government source belittled the source, a television star, and assured the public, all the proper people had the situation of guarding the nation's security under control.

"It is that damn Khalaf's fault," grumbled Shahin. "If he were here, I would execute him on the spot." They were all talking in English, a part of the over-all disguise of being perceived as shopkeeper Americans. "It may have been him and our beloved Emir who conceived Crimson Scimitar, but it was he who abandoned bin Laden during the attack, and both must have left incriminating evidence behind."

"Will it affect our attacks?" *The Professor* was the outsider looking into the plans of the operational leaders. He had played his part in creating the sleeper cells, accepting he had to payoff the Mexicans to gain that cell's loyalty, but he now wished to step back and let the attack team accomplish their goals.

"As I see it, and have since understood," Razzor Hassim spoke in calmness, sounding more sinister by his slow deliberative voice. "This television show, *King's Retribution*, does not air until October. I do not see them revealing any more details. And I don't see how they could have uncovered all our plans. We have broken each segment into smaller attacks. I think we should be cautious but there should be no stopping. We have come too far."

Shahin did not like loose ends that might threaten his attack.

"It would be better to blow them all up, before they stick their nose further under the tent."

"Such could be accomplished," said Razzor, with an aire of confidence, thinking back to a situation in Florida he had cleanly taken care of.

"No," piped up *The Professor*. "Crimson Scimitar, focus on that. After that, you can blow up whomever you like."

Both men smiled back at The Professor. They both knew something he did not.

Conveyed separately, directly from bin Laden, even side-stepping Khalaf's input, was the last order for the operation. There would be no survivors of the attack teams, except Razzor and Shahin. No one would take the glory but al-Qaida; no one would be captured who could compromise the organization's future abilities.

Razzor's smile was the most insincere for he had been chosen to eliminate *The Professor*, whom he thought was weak, too Americanized.

Shahin's point man, now attached with the Florida cell, would remove the bikers after their task had been accomplished. The man assigned, extolled himself as a rabid Islamist, who once had volunteered as a suicide bomber, now blindly dedicated to renew that vow for al-Qaida's glory, but only after their target was destroyed. Another 'volunteer' would be spun off from the main attack team to accompany Luis and his cartel gang members on their side show distraction operation.

As if the discussion had been settled, all three men rose, and went to a low table, covered with cloth.

"Good, invite in our fellow brothers." Shahin opened the door and with jovial comradeship invited in four members of the attack team who had been assembled in Yemen. The room soared with an air of anticipation, all training, planning, had come down to this. The cloth was pulled back to reveal a topographical model of their attack objective.

The bridge.

96.

August 2nd   North San Diego County

Not the dream vacation he supposed. The doctors had given Shawn a clean bill of health; he even believed them, felt he had conquered his demons, though still felt a necessity of proving his worth, to someone-- a call to duty to remove once and for all his previous lack of confidence.

They told him he would report back to his unit, but being the medical people they were, proud of themselves, omnipotent after allegedly curing a patient, believed he deserved an R&R reward of thirty days furlough, to visit friends and family. Part of the healing therapy, they told him.

His call to Janet, brief without satisfaction as she told him the time was not right for him to visit. He accused her of being a daddy's girl without a mind of her own. She hung up on him.

That did not go well.

So, for thirty days, what to do? Daily he kept in physical shape, more satisfaction to his career specialty than a sport. Still he did deserve to do something decadent for himself.

Unfortunately, he mused, a chocolate overdose did not seem appropriate for SEAL elite.Shawn Pacheco, in the end, decided what the heck, he would visit every amusement park in Southern California; none of these parks had this Ohio native ever visited. Discover the kid within. Sea World first, Lego Land, San Diego Zoo and by the fourth day he was at Safari Park, with roaming and grazing animals, from giraffes to gazelles in a large park-like setting, and in his travels jostling the too many park visitors enjoying the near end of summertime. People abounded like the wild beasts, defined best, as in a mass of families. Being alone yet amidst carefree children made him miss Janet, visualizing all that might be, like having children with her, settling down. With her, he could find happiness. He was not going to lose a good thing.

With African type heat swirling up the temperature, he was sitting on a shady bench near the gorilla enclosure, inhaling a rare treat of cotton candy, watching an ape female suckling her baby, feeling vexed he could not even escape images of family life when staring at the wild. He scanned headlines in the San Diego

Union newspaper, seeking news on the Afghan war, wondering where his next deployment might take him, when the article on King's gabby riposte from the movie premiere caught his attention.

My god, as he read, they are right. He vividly recalled the night in the compound, everything that went wrong, his allowing one of bin Laden's inner circle to escape. He knew the fugitive existed even if military did not believe his story. He knew what the terrorist looked like.

Someone should be told. Of course there would be revenge against Americans for Osama bin Laden's death and the man who escaped him, that is the man who is going to attack America.

In his newspaper reading of this day, Pacheco had skimmed over a capsulated small news article, obscured in the back pages that seemed not important as it might affect his life and choices, like most all Americans today. A warning only to be recognized in hind sight, yet, beneath the surface, infecting a nervousness within the nuclear energy industry to rush along its plans for nuclear waste disposal.

Workers find ultra-high radiation levels at Fukushima Daiichi plant

Tokyo (CNN) 8/2/11
The operator of Japan's crippled Fukushima Daiichi nuclear plant has detected the highest radiation levels at the facility at the facility since the initial earthquake and tsunami five months ago, a company spokesman said.

The radiation levels – 10,000 millisieverts per hour—are high enough that a single 60- minute dose would be fatal to humans within weeks...

97.

August 3rd New York City

Khalaf sipped at the black tea just offered him on a silver platter by a perky young girl.

Decadent America, he thought smugly, and their bold provocative population of very attractive females. From his London stay he had acclimated to the sight of women traipsing the streets unprotected from public stares, even his own eyes constantly strayed, much to the humor of Sabz who many times in accompanying him on his outings teased him at his double standard. But, thanks to his prodding, she looked the proper Arab woman, though of the modern times, dressed colorfully, her head wrapped, face uncovered, striking in its clear-lined smoothness, there for him to cast his eyes upon at any moment. Khalaf did not understand why he felt upset when other men cast their eyes on her, he knew, urging their beastly imaginations to guess what lay beneath the garments.

And here they were in New York, at the final stage, to create history. Far different from sedate jolly old London, he was unprepared for the menagerie of people, mixed races and cursed Jews, in constant motion, seeming to rush, as if they had no time, yelling not speaking, as if no one could hear them. Hell must look like this, he believed, and he felt satisfaction 9/11 had come to this city of the damned.

In his uncertainty of his new role, from courier to key player, he went on his assignments by taxi, where he could sit in relative peace, and at all other times secured himself in the suite at the Waldorf, two bedrooms as they had agreed, for the time being, as she suggested, until the mission was successfully completed, as he now prayed, not for the Islamic cause but for very selfish reasons of fulfilling personal gratification.

Sabz did not know of the mission in New York, nor of his plan that he was going to expand upon his responsibility and go beyond, traveling West into America's belly, to add his support to Shahin's brigade. Sabz, in ignorance, held the role as the wondering child, taking in all around her as a festive dream of happiness. When confined to the suite, she could be satisfied with fashion magazines and speechless at the voyeurism antics of reality celebrity television.

She did not accompany him on this day's appointment. With him, in the next chair in the richly decorated office of the head of the stockbrokerage office, sat his new contact Lawrence Nidal, a greedy little man, more interested in the commissions he would generate from Khalaf's transactions. He was sympathetic to Arab causes in general, was unaware of Crimson Scimitar, and believed he was a mere middleman in doing currency exchanges and securities trading for the several benevolent charities which Banker Abboud had set up to assist refugee assistance. He knew there was a plan but not of the plan. Dreams of great wealth from his guiding advice held the man's silence.

"Your account is completely in order and activated, Mr. Rasil." The paperwork and new account information was slid across the desk to Khalaf, a.k.a., *Rasil,* one of three false identities that he would use in establishing accounts at other stock brokerage accounts in the city's financial district. All business mail addresses went to the same post office box, and any trading funds could be wired to the same bank account, his account back in London, which then had instructions to make simultaneous transfers to very secretive off-shore banking locations, once more under Khalaf's direct control with a specific access code.

"Thank you," came Khalaf's response, seeking to heighten his normal English-Egyptian tone with a more Edwardian lilt, speak in an upper class brogue, suggestions of his Oxford education and more to this meeting, the voice of wealth.

"Here is the list of stocks Mr. Rasil would like invest in with the funds he has deposited."

Mr. Nadil, a stockbroker in his own right, acted as the facilitator to all the paperwork and nuances of the stock exchange inner-workings. "Mr. Rasil or myself, under Mr. Rasil's power of attorney, will be calling you in the near future to make several initial trades, buys, sells, maybe even some short sales, dependent on market fluctuations. Is that acceptable?"

The head of the stockbrokerage firm, who dealt with millions of dollars in trades, still knew when to give deference to any new client who opened up a personal account with $1 million cashier's check, verified and deposited.

"Of course, at yours or Mr. Rasil's pleasure. You are aware of the new SEC rules on short sales?"

"Yes, of course," affirmed Mr. Nidal, with confidence, knowing that trading mechanism was the featured part of the financial attack plan on Crimson Scimitar. Short selling involves the selling of a security that an investor does not own or has borrowed against. When shorting a stock, the investor expects he or she can buy back the stock at a later date for a lower price than it was sold for, and cover, making a profit on the spread. The Securities and Exchange Commission, the SEC, to avoid driving down market prices on bad news, had created an 'alternative uptick rule', where covering on short sales might be frozen if a stock dropped more than 10%.

The stock brokerage president reviewed the list of his first purchases on behalf of his client, and gave a wry acknowledgement to the hefty commissions they would generate.

"I see you are going to be a player in the entertainment industry."

"Yes," said the fake Mr. Rasil. "One cannot do wrong in investing in American entertainment. I enjoy watching movies, and my children like visiting amusement parks."

Outside, the brokerage house, Mr. Nadil beamed.

"That went extremely well. Two more such meetings today, each with $1 million orders placed and everything will be in place. When will you place your short sale order?" Meaning, on information the stockbroker did not have access to, when would the first attack of Crimson Scimitar begin?

"Soon." His actions, separate from Shahin's attack on the bridge, was to be coordinated to occur a few days earlier, the date tentative to October 2. Khalaf decided, though not astute in this capitalistic system, he might have a little fun playing with the stock market, buying and selling, just dabbling, only enough to show account activity, and whet the appetite of the greedy capitalist stockbrokers who would later jump to his command when the real play began. After all, he was playing with other people's money.

"I am sure the Benevolent Association will do quite well," Nidal's comment of hope.

They sought out a taxicab for their next appointment, something he dreaded. He could not stand this man he must work with. Khalaf's primary dislike was Nadil's aftershave, too fruity to inhale within close quarters. He would be pleased when this operation would be completed, and whether successful or not, and it had better be success, Nadil would receive his payment and be gone. From reading through bin Laden's battle plan against Wall Street, and in his discussions with banker Abboud, Mr. Nadil would be compensated in a separate transaction, that Khalaf would have no part in. A courier with Mr. Nadil's commission would be sent to make the final pay-off. Khalaf seemed to recall the courier's name, Hassim something.

98.

August 4th Santa Monica, California

The War Room.

Once again the place was jammed with what could be called the 'Hunt and Discovery Teams'. Instead of joviality, singleness of purpose, the meeting began quickly acrimoniously, with Callie snapping at Storm King.

"Can't you just keep your mouth closed when you get out in public?"

"It's not like I said anything profound," King bit back. "There's nothing here. You are all playing a game where there is no game."

"One way or the other you aren't helping. If there is no terrorist attack planned, then you are making us look like the laughing stock; and if one occurs, and you've told us to dismiss the possibility of an attack, we will be labeled non-caring fools and klutzes. Just let everyone here try their best, so we can go home satisfied we gave it our best shot."

With the silence in the room uncomfortable, Hugh Fox sought control.

"Okay, from what everyone has submitted, here is a matrix of all the plots and subplots."

He motioned to Gizmo, who pulled a curtain back from a wall, to reveal a large graph layout of author and movie names, central plot feature, primary target, and action taken to thwart the bad guys.

"Very impressive," said Holmes, admiring the work that had gone into the informational analysis.

"Yes," agreed Samantha, "A great deal of thought into this." She smiled both at Hugh, and then so as not to suggest he was her focus, gave Gizmo, the computer nerd, a friendly acknowledgment, when she added, "Is there some sort of consensus of where we think this Ali Baba might had been concentrating on his ideas for a good attack concept."

Fox stood and went to the walled chart.

"Let us agree on a few 'non-starters'. Ali Baba is not going to discover any religious icon or extraterrestrials that could destroy this country. Agreed?"

Several voices in the audience nodded, a few saying 'Agreed'. Fox wiped off the chart two movies, *'Raiders of the Lost Ark'* and *'Independence Day'*.

"And I previewed," offered the special effects coordinator Abbas, "that Bollywood film where a master thief and his gang sing and dance while robbing a train of museum treasure. That certainly would not, as Mr. Holmes has pointed out, create a maximum 9/11 effect."

Fox erased the Bollywood film and train robbery as being an idea generator, while Abbas added, "Dancing routines weren't half bad and I liked the costumes," a statement which brought out laughter and moved the Teams back into a more pleasant affectation.

"I think we all see what the preponderance of evidence is pointing to," said Holmes, making sure they all felt what seeing the truth meant.

"Something nuclear," spoke up Fox's assistant, J-Q. Silence again, at the ramifications of what this might mean, if true.

"There are however," said Samantha, pointing at the matrix graph, "some of these that are either too far-fetched for what our reality is, or if they are conceivable, beyond our reach and out of our pay grade. For example, 'The Hunt for Red October' is definitely nuclear, but I don't think Islamic terrorists would be able to hijack a nuclear submarine and explode the missiles.'

"A good point," said Holmes. "There is so much redundancy built into arming a missile it would be near impossible. Even sabotage might cause an explosion, perhaps like the *U.S.S. Cole*; they might try to sink a sub, but radiation, if any, would be contained and thus not catastrophic.

Fox instead of wiping out 'Hunt for Red October', drew a line through the line item, with his opinion.

"Improbable but not impossible. 'Least likely' is my vote when we get to prioritizing the final list."

"From looking at the photographs blown-up," said Gizmo, pointing in the photos to several books on their side. "There are a pile of magazines, at least four books we can't identify.

There is one book, on its side, the spine perhaps sun faded, where all we got out of the title and author was a partial, 'Spring' and 'Hawk'. I am still trying a computer search algorithm for matching possible word combinations. Nothing yet to report."

"'Hawk,' with an 'e' on the end of it, might be 'Alex Hawke' the main hero in the Ted Bell spy adventures." Everyone in surprise turned to look at King at the end of the table. He merely shrugged, but continued, 'Bell has, I think, written seven Alex Hawke thrillers. In 'Tsar', a killer known as Happy the Baker wipes out an entire Midwestern town with sabotaged computers. A little far-fetched but, hey, you guys are flailing away. There's my two cents."

"Not bad, Colonel," and Fox added the author's name Bell and the hero Hawke to a new line in the matrix, and instructed J-Q to find all the appropriate novels, and they would be parceled out to the Team members for quick reads and summations, stressing to his listeners, to seek out what looks possible with a nuclear plotline.

"And now," said Fox, "Let's have a report from what everyone read or watched, and ask the question: what is reasonable to be turned into a real attack? And yes, we don't know, if the bad guys have stolen a nuclear bomb, which seems to be a central thread in several of these works, like George Clooney in 'The Peacemaker', but it may have occurred and we might not even know it. That's when we have to call the government if we remotely think we have hard evidence."

For the next hour, they went back and forth, listening to storylines, discussing if such fiction could be turned into a real-life threat. At one point, Callie leaned into Samantha and whispered, "Wendell Holmes comes off like Brad Thor's hero, Scot Harvath, ex-SEAL, ex-Secret Service, just more mature, hopefully less lethal." Samantha did not know how to take Callie's comment; deciding it was a good spirited observation. Extremely curious she would have to borrow a Brad Thor thriller, and compare a Scot against a Wendell.

At the end of the session, they were all brain-drained. Several more books and a movie had been crossed off the chart, but too many remained, meaning indeed such possibilities with dire consequences seemed patently feasible.

Fox finally, throwing his hands up, felt the dejection among the Team members. "Okay, which plot do you think it is?"

A new voice.

"It could be one strategy, but more than one plot." They all looked to the door and the young man who stood there, sheepish and awkward.

"9/11 was not one event but three separate attacks carried out."

Sailor-Soldier Shawn Pacheco had joined the conversation.

Episode 14

Each year, enormous quantities of radioactive waste are created during the nuclear fuel process, including 2,000 metric tons of high-level radioactive waste and 12 million cubic feet of low-level radioactive waste in the U.S. alone. More than 58,000 metric tons of highly radioactive spent fuel already has accumulated at reactor sites around the U.S. for which there currently is no permanent repository.
--Physicians for Social Responsibility

99.

August 4th Santa Monica

Pacheco had first tried Five Aces Studioz, the production office, seeking to locate the central star, Colonel Storm King. He was told at the receptionist's desk that the stars might be up in Silicon Valley, outside San Francisco at Skilleo Game Technology, where they were working on production scripting for the next season. An aside from one secretary to another at Five Aces led Shawn to overhear that co-star Callie Cardoza was the better of the two, and Storm King never showed up before noon because of his 'snootfuls'. Shawn Pacheco had heard of *'King's Retribution'* but had never watched a show, agreeing with his fellow troopers, that the show never could measure up to SEAL combat qualities of stealth and technical prowess, so why waste the time.

He telephoned the Skilleo offices, and learned of Hugh Fox (he knew of him and even played his space killer games for eye-hand coordination) and that Fox was the owner of Five Aces and indirectly the main man over the television show. That Mr. Fox might be in Santa Monica at a Skilleo field office, working with *King's Retribution* cast and a Ms. Samantha Carlisle, his business partner. That location was close enough so he drove that direction.

A SEAL is not just a mere mastiff brute with a capacity for tolerating intense pain or for dispensing it. Self-survival training also honed a SEAL's intelligence and upon his arrival at The War Room, Pacheco as any good recon soldier might, gained a lay of the terrain, noting a meeting in progress with a large following of spectators in animated dialogue, and felt it the prudent strategy to ease quietly within earshot and to develop an understanding of what was going on, an adaptation of the tenet, *know thy enemy.* At a point he had heard enough; they were friendlies, except maybe one.

"And who are you?" King's voice was commanding and arrogant. He thought a reporter had discovered their lair, and Callie would be right; he would be portrayed as a buffoon.

"Shawn Pacheco. And I was there." He played his trump card up front, he needed them.

"Where?" King voiced confusion.

"Abbotabaad."

King assumed the worst: a reporter.

"Yeah, you and the whole world has been there." He laughed in put-down disbelief.

"Yes, but the night before you all went there."

Everyone seemed confused, until what was said soaked in, and Samantha put it into perspective, the ah-ha moment.

"The night bin Laden was killed?"

"Yes, ma'am."

"Yeah, right," scoffed King, knowing his first assumption must be the right one.

"And you are…" Fox put forth the question, dangling, letting the answer fill itself in.

"Specialist E4 Shawn Pacheco of SEAL Team Six. And you are correct, I mean that gentleman over there [nodding towards Holmes]. I believe there is going to be an attack on us. I saw the gook, the one you are calling Ali Baba escape. I was there."

Conversation erupted from around the room. Discrediting doubt from King to palatable fear from the younger people who now realized this role playing of a presumed mock game was no longer imaginary; real terrorists were fomenting a real plot somewhere in their own backyard.

"Executive Committee Meeting", intoned Fox with hard command in his voice. "Right now." Pointing to their 'guest', Fox emphasized, "You, stay."

Within a few minutes Pacheco understood the hierarchy of who was who as the room emptied, and introductions made from those remaining. He was surprised that King did not stay, not because he wasn't invited, but that he mumbled that they were all being 'hoodwinked' and 'off on a wild goose chase'. In the same motions of offering a seat to him, Pacheco saw Hugh Fox scribble out a note and pass it to a young man who then left. Wise move, they were going to check him out.

They all looked at Pacheco and he at them, no one knowing where to start until Holmes initiated the inquisition with a wide grin. A minute into the conversation, Pacheco had a hallelujah realization of who was talking to him, the man in the photo, the one standing beside his own downed helicopter, the man his own government might be in fear of.

"Can't tell us too much about what happened, can you?"

"No, sir."

"Under orders of complete secrecy?"

"Yes, sir."

"But you did tell us that you did see someone leave the compound, one of bin Laden's comrades? But that would be against the edict you were given, correct? So, why did you tell us?"

Pacheco did not know anything about Holmes and his background, but accepted if he made Pacheco's military inquisitors concerned he was therefore a very smart and yet dangerous man who indeed had perhaps practiced field interrogation—ex military? The SEAL remembered back to a course he had once gone through, where he had to react as the captured prisoner in front of shouting tormentors. Today, the truth, would release a great burden from him, not all the story for he would never mention he was the dunce that allowed this 'Ali Baba' to escape his grasp.

"No one believed me when I told them."

Holmes remembered back to his conversation with Matthew Brady of the CIA. Well, surprise of surprises.

"And this would be because of what...your mental condition?"

Pacheco's jaw dropped open. Who was this guy? He saw various forms of awe among those around the table, especially seeing the fashion lady, Samantha Carlisle, exhibit like a devilish look of idol worship to her expression. Not at him, but at this Mr. Holmes.

His words came out slower, now cautious.

"Yes, sir. The doctors called it battlefield stress. I have just been released with a clean bill of health."

"What caused the stress, Specialist Pacheco," asked Holmes, no sympathy to his voice.

"Having traded places with a buddy and seeing him blown up, instead of me." There he had said it to strangers, and he could say it, and no depression welled over him. Was he really cured?

"Yes. The conundrum of all fighting service men and women: why did I survive and others, my friends, died? No one here will condemn you for having a human heart. But, why indeed, are you here?"

"I have leave until November 15th when I have to report for assignment. I believe you all are on to something, and I want to help in any way I can." Then, Pacheco did the one thing he felt would put him on equal standing: he folded his arms across his chest, imitating Holmes in the photo, hoping no one caught him and would take offense.

Pacheco caught a glimpse at the young man at the window of the conference room, giving thumbs up to Hugh Fox. At least the Google search revealed he wasn't a fraud, but would they---.

"He passes muster with me," said Holmes, chuckling at the inside joke between the two men, he had deciphered.

"That's good enough for me," said Samantha.

"We could use an upgrade in military intelligence," this from the Spanish-looking lady, Cardoza her name, that Pacheco felt had a something of military bearing about her, and then realizing her comment might have been aimed at Colonel Storm King. What was he getting into?

"Welcome, Specialist Pacheco," said Hugh Fox, offering his hand to the young military man, "Welcome to the *King's Retribution* Team, or what I now believe is the 'Stop bin Laden's Revenge'. And you come at an opportune time. I want to show you all two surprises but as they so wisely say here in California, 'Let's do lunch'. Oh, and the surprises are up at the Skilleo campus, and our chariot awaits at the Santa Monica airport."

100.

August 4th Silicon Valley, CA

Actually three surprises, one unanticipated.

With all the key team members re-assembled at Skilleo, they ate, in a garden like setting, box lunches, simple and definitely healthy with organic overtones. King chose not to accompany them, and Pacheco overhead someone say the television star was somewhere drinking his lunch.

Pacheco found himself immediately part of the group's sociality, though as much the center of curiosity. They peppered him with questions which he could not answer, and several thought the secrecy shtick was ultra cool. Eventually, among the younger set, they found they all appreciated video games, and found a common denominator for discussion.

After lunch, Fox walked them down a path to the back of the property, to discover a large and long Quonset hut type building, recent prefabrication.

Inside was a target practice range, along with an instructor, who demonstrated targets that were not made of paper but 3-D holograms which could record the rounds fired as they crossed lines of invisibility within various moving scenarios of bad guys running, or firing back.

"I am a techno dinosaur," commented Holmes, with Samantha standing next to him.

"No, you aren't, Wen," laughed Samantha, "merely vintage wine requiring a good screw...opener."

Pacheco heard the exchange and wondered, but his mind had been amazed at the inside practice range and before he could ask a question, Fox gave him the answer.

"I want everyone to know how to handle a firearm. Be comfortable with the weapon and be accurate."

"Are you expecting trouble? For all of us?" The question came from Callie Cardoza, who Pacheco learned from the others, was ex-cop.

"If we uncover a plot and no one believes us." He cast his eye at Shawn. "Then we may have to take action into our own hands, though I am relying more on the U.S. Government to come to the rescue." And for that he looked at Holmes. Pacheco not understanding knew he had to learn everything about his new found friends, learn their talents, their secrets. Someday, that might come in handy, like save lives, his. One thing he did discover in watching the happy bunch of weekend warriors was that Callie Cardoza seemed to have her eyes focused on Hugh Fox, a lot.

"One more thing I want to show you," said the Skilleo president, and from the Quonset hut, he took them to the side of the building where was parked a delivery sort of truck. The vehicle had no markings.

"This looks like the field production truck we use," said Bennie, the show's driver, who knew his road equipment.

"From the same company, the same set-up." Foxed opened the back doors to reveal sets of shelves on either side of the interior, all empty.

"Yes, what you might suppose, for field operations. What if we get a call to stake out a suspect's location; what if you get a chance to capture a real terrorist in true *King's Retribution* fashion?"

"We'd win an Emmy, hands down," said Callie. And they all laughed, not comprehending she was quite serious.

"I have bought two of these," explained Fox, "to be on the spot 24/7, to be stationed and waiting on the East and West Coast, the action most likely be in the New York City and L.A. areas. What I have in mind is to stock these vehicles for any eventualities. If after six months nothing has happened maybe I will donate our crime busting trucks to respective police department as SWAT command centers, or maybe we can use one of them with *King's Retribution* ops. What I have in mind—"

Holmes cell phone rang and he excused himself.

"What I have in mind," Fox continued, "I want to fill this truck up so it becomes our S.W.A.T. and Command Center, all the bells and whistles. CAM ONE and CAM TWO will create amini TV production studio with the right equipment. Abbas you put together special effects that could be used for subterfuge." Fox turned to Pacheco. "And now that we have a military man who is current in his field experience—which he won't tell us". And there were appreciative grins among the group. "I would like to ask him if he would like to volunteer to be our Armament Specialist. Give us the firepower to stop bin Laden's ghost and all his demon minions?"

Pacheco thought he had stumbled into a madhouse, the inmates running the asylum, but what the hell, what else was he doing with his life in the near term? This looked fun and in a couple months he could return to being a better SEAL and even perhaps marry the woman he loved. When he had the time, he would show them all Janet's photo and tell them what he was really fighting for.

"Sure, why not."

Holmes returned to the group, as they were inspecting the truck in more detail. He looked grim faced, and brought sobriety to them all, until Callie asked, "What's the matter?"

"Remember, I told you about the Florida bombing, and that the Fibbies had several White Supremacy bikers under surveillance?"

"Yes," answered Fox, "there was a connection between them and the room in the compound." Fox did not mention the explosives, only Holmes and he knew about the pink wrapped package's deadly contents.

Pacheco's antennae went up; what was this all about?

"Anyway, they just had a visitor show up at the repair shop and talk to the biker owner for over an hour. And a visitor you would think not welcomed among skinhead racists...an Arab-looking gentleman."

"No shit," said someone.

Fox was all business.

"Okay, folks, whatever is going on, let's try and get these trucks tricked out as soon as feasible. And start your target practicing tomorrow. I doubt we are going to Florida, but as our latest team addition informed us, there may be more than one attack in motion."

No shit, Shawn echoed to himself, maybe the world is going crazy, and the crazies in the asylum are the sane ones.

His call from F.B.I. Agent Curtis began in the same way.

"Shit, Holmes, you are not going to believe this."

"Try me."

"Some towelhead just visited Gator Donaldson's repair shop."

Silence from Holmes, so Curtis added.

"And he didn't ride in on a Harley."

"Do you have a wire inside?"

"No, we thought they were paranoia enough to sweep the place."

"Probably a good call. The pricks are getting wiser these days."

"Well, Holmes, you know what this fuckin' means, is that something big is coming down, just like you thought. My bosses already want to pull the plug, bring the guy in. I told them 'no'; we have nothing."

"Keep that thought, Curtis. You got squat right now. He's an appendage, one leg of a poisonous spider. We need the body, or at least pull all the legs, make the spider immobile, and dead. Track the guy, bury him in surveillance."

"We're on that. This Middle Easterner's staying in a cheap motel over off the I-95."

"Above all, you need to get an idea of their target. You guys rush in on him, and my past employers will want to step in and waterboard him, by then it will be too late. This guy is a bin Laden pick, a son of 9/11, he's top of the al-Qaeda class, he's not going to crack for a month and by that time you will have a nuclear incident spreading across the Okeechobee."

"We've already put the nuclear plants on high alert. And the call went out to our D.C. office but nothing came back, they don't seem excited, except for us to keep them in the info loop."

Holmes felt derision at the incompetency of a bureaucracy that is suffocating in on itself.

"Homeland Security is the culprit, with too much layering like the old Soviet appratuschetiks. And I am guessing the C.I.A. is not waving red flags to the public, think if there is fire where there's smoke to them it's a small blip on the radar, not worth their time; so they think you guys can handle it. And Curtis, you J. Edgar boys have the cojones, but I know this is a national thing, bigger than we ever conceive, think 9/11 to the Tenth Power. We need to discover Mr. Evil and where the Big Show will be playing."

"If so, you better hustle. The hammer is going to drop on this al-Qaeda dipshit sooner than later, regardless of where they are going to take their pretty pink bombs."

"Hey, I want to be there. Give me a heads up."

"You brought the party, you're on the list."

101.

August 23rd 1:15 p.m.   C.I.A. Headquarters at Langley, Virginia

Acting Deputy Director Givens fell out of his chair, literally, on his ass on the floor of his office.

"What the --?" What was going on? Did he misjudge, had they attacked? Had a plane hit his building? How could they? The military maintained an anti-missile rocket battery on the roof for just such a threat.

His secretary rushed in, holding the door frame, swaying. She yelled at him, her face flushed.

"Earthquake, sir. The alarms are going off; everyone's evacuating." She rushed away without waiting for him.

Earthquake, of course it is. He considered himself a brave man, but to go up against the power of Mother Nature, he quickly deferred, and found himself scurrying out onto the Langley manicured grounds. By the time he exited the front door with the rushing crowd, the ground's vibration had subsided. He milled around with other CIA employees, most he had never seen before, such was the place. They were all in the same wonderment. An earthquake on the East Coast was a rarity. And to think, he thought it was a terrorist attack, when all his daily briefings spoke of the quiet out on the grid. Well, except, if you consider the blip down in the Florida that the F.B.I. had their eyes on. It's just speculation, he told everyone who would listen, a single sighting of an unconfirmed olive skinned person does not constitute an assault by foreign elements. Hard facts, he said, would receive hard response.

Within half an hour, along with the others, they returned to the building, everyone chatty to the excitement of the ground shaking beneath them. Instead of going back to the drudge of his office paper shuffling he walked down the corridor to a section of intelligence gathering which they classified as 'loose chatter'. He saw Matthew Brady standing at a desk, reading over the shoulder of an analyst who specialized in the National Desk and both were reading the incoming wire reports. Brady walked over and handed Givens a print-out.

The earthquake measured a magnitude 5.8 and lasted only 30 seconds. The epicenter, and this was a surprise to Givens, was centered in Mineral, Virginia only 84 miles southwest of Washington.

"What are the incoming damage reports?" He questioned Brady, in a snappy, bossy tone.

"So far, very little, dishes rattled off shelves sort of thing, though no one is taking chances. Amtrak stopped its trains, and several airports have diverted planes or put those flying in holding patterns. Homeland Security, through FEMA, asked the public to refrain from using text messaging and cell phones to clear up congestion on the networks. Negligible aftershocks; one was magnitude 2.8 about three minutes ago, but no one felt it."

Givens turned to go, considering, nothing much at all in the scheme of things, yet a needed break for him.

"Did you get my memo," asked Brady, "On that explosives tie-in between a bomb explosion that killed a man in Florida and similar bomb making materials over in Pakistan?"

"Yeah, I glanced at it," Givens spoke dismissively. "But thought it was a reach. The only tie-in seemed to be similar wrapping paper which probably is a common manufacturing style and widely sold. Need harder evidence to make a case for me. Besides the F.B.I. has jurisdiction and I hear they're on it."

The man at the desk handed another print-out to Brady.

"Anything else?" Givens stopped at the door.

"Reports that a tourist saw a crack in the Washington Monument. And the Dominion Virginia Power shut down their North Anna nuclear generating station, which is located only 20 miles from the epicenter. Said their units tripped offline automatically as planned and no damage to the plant reported."

"The Washington Monument damaged?" Givens reacted as if in alarm. "Now that is quite serious. What if it toppled over; what about our national pride?" And he exited with a flourish already formulating in his mind a plan to assess damage to the monument, make whatever repairs, and to do so he would, from behind the scenes, orchestrate the creation of a V.I.P. committee of Senators and Congressmen, movers and shakers, and he laughed at his own wit.

Sadly, Givens had given his attention to the wrong news report.

The North Anna Nuclear Plant had been impacted by the earthquake, violent by the undulating roll of the land on which they were so closely sited to the epicenter. But why alarm the public? There had been structural damage, not severe, and the report about the power generators being undamaged stood correct, but unreported was the critical damage to the waste storage facility which remained shut, and already full to capacity, several storage containers when tested for stress signs of vibrated metal fatigue, showed leakage. Indeed, critical concerns in their findings and a disaster in the making unless something wasn't done immediately.

102.

August 25 New York State

"They want us to do what?"

"There has been an emergency at the North Anna plant in Virginia. NRC [Nuclear Regulatory Commission] has asked us to add another truck to our convoy and to move up the transportation date from October 4th to next week. They will have several other trips required in the foreseeable future."

"Impossible." Brahma Singh's negative reply might have been him speaking out as the Assistant Operations Manager of the Indian Points facility but his thoughts were tied to the timetable dictated by the al-Qaeda plans for Crimson Scimitar.

"Inconvenient, but not impossible," said the Plant Manager. "You've had plans for a hurry up transfer out of here in place for months. Okay, activate it. You will be getting their truck here in three days, plan to leave the day after, say, on the 29th. When would the transport trucks arrive in Nevada?"

Singh, 'The Scientist' in the Crimson Scimitar plan, found his mind reeling. Are the other members of this operation in country? Can they be in place in time, when the trucks reach the targeted ambush spot? He calculated quickly for his supervisor's question.

"The trip will be taken slow, four days, with secured stops at military bases along the way. If everything goes on schedule we should be at the Yucca Mountain storage terminal on the afternoon of September 2nd." But not if Crimson Scimitar is successful, he thought. The attack would now take place sometime in the afternoon of the 2nd, four hours before their expected arrival at Yucca Mountain.

"No, we must use the term as in 'temporary holding at the in-transit terminal'".

"Yes, of course, our trucks are merely stopping on their way to their final destination."

"And such a halt might turn into years." And they both laughed though Sing felt his heightened nerves beginning to fray.

"Will you need to add any additional personnel to the transit team", asked the Manager.

To The Scientist this meant more security.

"No, there's our truck, this newly added truck from the North Anna generating station, and the Fort Calhoun truck that will drive down from Nebraska to meet us on I-70 near Ft. Leavenworth, Kansas. Maybe I will put one more mechanic into a truck cab for any emergency repairs, but no, I think the less we look like a military convoy and more like three trailer trucks perceived as general carriers, the better.

"By the way, will their manifest likewise be spent fuel rods?"

The manager hesitated, not anxious to complicate matters with details that they could do nothing about.

"No, much worse, I presume. Highly concentrated tritium, the highest I have ever heard. 5 million picocuries per liter."

"You're kidding," said The Scientist with a shocked expression, but to himself, 'This is wonderful news, a blessing from Allah. This is the first truck that must be targeted, the highest priority.' "What radioactive isotopes are in this batch?"

"High readings of Cesium-137. They've used the new magnetic concentrator on the tritium, so we can expect more requests to ship after this first test run."

"Wow, I remember when we had our own tritium leakage readings here at Indian Point.

That was Strontium-90 but the releases were at such low levels."

"That's why we have been asked to expedite this specific transfer. Not only put it in a safe place for a thousand years, but the Virginia Power people say they have ten more truckloads of this stuff that need to be taken away and safeguarded. They've found stress corrosion in the metal holding containers, and one major spill, and our industry would be set back a hundred years, let alone most of Western Virginia evacuated. The sooner the better."

"Yes, sir, I will start hustling." Singh turned back to his work desk, and made the necessary calls to activate his transportation plans. It could be done, both the transit of the radioactive waste and the hurry up of Crimson Scimitar. He was still amazed that lethal dosages of tritium would be given to him as a bonus. Beyond merely causing radioactive damage with his original truck shipment of spent fuel rods, he now had two additional truck trailers, and the havoc would be multiplied exponentially. If Crimson Scimitar now succeeded and all three trucks compromised, then millions of people would be unable to drink their water, or eat their produce, and if they did eat or drink, most certainly the incidences of cancer would spike beyond reason and with that result, the U.S. medical and insurance industries would be overwhelmed and collapse. Governmental anarchy and dying and death for countless of untold nonbelievers, a proud moment for al-Qaeda and a proper revenge for their leader's recent assassination, and The Scientist smiled and thought, the sooner the better.

That evening, The Scientist, went on the computer rental at the office store, and sent a bubbly email about his cousin's triplets had arrived earlier than expected and a revised baptism was now scheduled on the 2nd of September. Like the earthquake which triggered the advance in the schedule, this simple notice of multiple births would stir up aftershocks. By being focused on the transportation as his only task, as Crimson Scimitar operations were highly be compartmentalized. The Scientist had no knowledge that the first part of the plan would actually happen two days before Shahin put in his team for the attack at the bridge. Crimson Scimitar would be launched on August 30th.

103.

Friday, August 26th New York City

Khalaf read his email from The Scientist. Now it begins, he considered. His life would turn on these momentous events. He picked up the phone and called his contact Nidal.

"Liquidate our present holdings into cash."

"You just invested in the markets; many of your stocks have even moved up quite well. A tidy profit if indeed you were a player."

"Listen to me: our short selling strategy will begin in three days, the 29th. I will fax over a list of stocks I wish to short."

"Yes, of course." Commissions for the stockbrokers, increased fee remuneration for himself, thus Nidal would follow these orders to the letter.

"I will also send over additional instructions but remember specifically, put a cover order on these stocks, to a level where the price drops 9.75 per cent."

"I see, well under the ten per cent that would trigger the trading freeze."

"Exactly. And you will have a second list to turn and buy back in on the lowest stocks which have dropped. And I will have a sell ceiling put on these. And I want my instructions followed even if I am unreachable, as I might be travelling."

"Yes, Mr. Rasil."

Khalaf ended the call pleased with himself, felt the power of leadership, and all things considered, indeed it was he who was in charge of Crimson Scimitar. He felt elated.

He looked over to Sabz watching him, a fashion magazine in her lap she had been reading.

"I will be leaving town on the 31st, and should be gone only a few days."

She said nothing and returned to her reading.

He returned to his computer, downsized his page of stock market news and sent out his own coded email and wished he could see the expression on the recipient's face.

Friday, August 26th Los Angeles

"Curse the Infidels and our own incompetents!"

"What is it?" Razzor asked of Shahin, as they sat in the kitchen of the dingy apartment, while the rest of his attack brigade watched senseless television.

"They are sending the shipment out a month early. Not October 4th. It will arrive at the bridge on the 2nd of September."

"Your men seem prepared. Waiting to October is a long time and could make them lazy and tempted by American filth."

"Yes, but the strategy was to attack when everyone was complacent, after the 9/11 anniversary. They would have said, 'see nothing happened, so we are all safe', and they would be made foolish."

Shahin looked back to his email, and Razzor could see the disgust.

"I thought such news would please you."

"It is the add-ons to the message which disturb me. There are now three trucks, three babies born, instead of just one, and we are told to target all three, but most specifically, one particular truck (baby), an industrial tanker truck carrier with two tanks, which is to have a red 'birthmark' on its rear end. That seems strange. All three must be destroyed, but the message must imply we have to prioritize. And then, there is the final part, our new leader, Doctor al-Zawahiri, is sending a representative to be made part of our attack team. I don't like it. I know this man. He is neither a soldier nor a leader, merely a messenger boy. Most assuredly, he will think high of himself and do no good in our plans. We are a tight team. We don't need outsiders who could wreck the mission."

"Do you wish me to 'babysit' him? Keep him out of your way."

"If he were to stumble in front of a stray bullet, I do not feel the cause would lose a tear."

"And we would gain another martyr."

"True enough."

Both men rose from the table. Shanin walked to the TV and shut it off. The lazy men of the Attack Brigade, bored from inaction, looked to their leader.

"The schedule has changed. The time is at hand. The first phase begins on 30th, in three days. I will alert Florida and *The Professor's* people." He pointed to one of his men, a man named

Mustafa. "You go to Luis and tell him to put his people together and bring them across the border." To his group, "The rest of you, we will leave for Las Vegas this afternoon.

Tomorrow, we will be tourists and go to the dam."

He turned to Razzor, with a questioning expression. The man had never said what his role was to be, and Shahin never pressed. They had, in the last several weeks, become close companions with the same sort of radicalism in their blood, understanding brothers to the cause, that Islam should rule the world, and all others, the unbelievers, must convert or be exterminated.

"I have places to go," said Razzor, heading to the door. "One of them is to look in on those interlopers from that television show. With your timetable moved up, we don't need any publicity drawing attention to our objectives. They need persuasion to refocus. And then I must make a quick trip back East."

"May the wisdom of Allah be with you."

"And with you. But I will be back quick enough to stand with you on the bridge."

"Your presence will ensure our success."

104.

Friday, August 26th Silicon Valley and Los Angeles

For the *King's Retribution* team from their meeting on August 4th with the decision to 'be prepared for any eventuality' to the end of the month they were all in motion where each action taken acted like pebbles tumbling, gathering speed to where not one but the culmination of all initiated the avalanche of discovery.

Hugh Fox, who had a regular scheduled session at the target range (which any good detective or ex-police person might learn from his desk calendar) ran across Callie Cardoza there with her pistol in practice mode. After a few minutes of congenial banter, she took it upon herself to give Fox a private lesson. Where the instructor gave him the stance and the breathing exercises in previous lessons, she spoke of the need of emotional calmness of decision-making when only a second might be required to make a life-death choice. Fox said nothing when Callie wrapped her arm around his back to steady his posture, and did not laugh when, in running through a series of surprise action targets, she flung herself to the ground and unloaded her gun's chamber in rapid-fire hitting all the pop-ups. Fox scored less than fifty percent when his turn came, but Callie said nothing, did not chide him for a poor performance, merely said, 'let's both do it again.'

When the firing session reach a conclusion, Fox invited her to a more personal, behind the scene tour of Skilleo. She saw how his employees were not awed to his corporate power but talked to him as an equal, asked him questions as to his opinions, and he gave ideas back to them, which Callie realized in several instances, the worker had not thought in that dimension of a possibility. Fox, in his own observation, realized that though a former policewoman, she had a quick grasp of the computer world and could talk their language, his language. Where he had this shyness of the geek who did not grasp with ease the limelight, he smiled to see she used her 'star power' when recognized to make them smile and not flaunt an arrogance of ego, he had seen many times in Storm King.

The tour turned into dinner but a group affair, perhaps a disappointment to both, or a shield of sorts, when F/X Abbas, Bennie the driver, and SEAL Pacheco joined them, with most of the conversation, when fortified with great Napa reds, turned boisterous concerning the ongoing equipment stocking of what those involved were now calling the 'BeenLadenNoMobile' while Five Studioz Executives to rationalize the project, called it the 'StormWagon' to satisfy the production accountants and one of the stars. Abbas laughed that Pacheco placed parachutes into the truck's inventory, and Bennie worried that an entire cabinet of medical supplies did not speak well of confidence in future assignments.

It was during this dinner that Callie offered an opinion, and everyone thought it was a tremendous idea, and with Fox agreeing, he made the notation to move two of his employees on a temporary basis down to the Santa Monica War Room; employees who spoke Arabic.

During those same days, down in Santa Monica, in this very War Room, Holmes had been given his own little office, and this is where Samantha found him one afternoon, watching him scribble away on a yellow pad, before she let her presence be known.

"What now, writing your memoirs?"

"Someday, when National Security and the Freedom of Information release the CIA archives, and I am assured women who bent to my magnetism won't sue for my explicit remembrances, perhaps."

"I will be the first in line at the bookstore. But, no really?"

"Don't laugh at me. Recall our serious 4th of July conversation about how I thought if one could modify and change the course of religious interpretation the world might stand a better chance at harmony."

"Yes, and sincerely, I thought it was a noble sentiment, though close to impractical with such a hotbed of extremist among every faith."

"This is going to be one of my Life Experience experiments, seeing if I can crystallize grains of truth towards an enhanced new testament. Sounds farfetched, I realize, but it fills in the time while we wait for answers on the terrorist objectives.

"By the way, would you like to join me for dinner? I can promise it will be quite boring."

Samantha felt the invitation sounded promising and had not she be an intelligent person with an inquisitive nature, she would have indeed been bored out of her gourd. They did not dine alone, much to her disappointment.

It was a first class dinner, and she wondered somewhat that Wendell could afford such luxury and extravagance, but then he might be smarter than even she thought, that he would be able to deduct such a meal if this was research leading to publication.

And, in a way, it was research, two professors from separate California universities, both doctorates in religious studies, one for Islamic and the other Christianity and in Talmudic scriptures. She found it fascinating because it opened up a new dimension to her perception of Wendell Holmes. Not as an intellectual but as a person who looked to investigate every nuance of life, to see how other people thought, therefore their reasoning for actions taken, good or perceived evil. And she found it extremely funny watching him scribble out notes from the friendly exchanges between the professors on the back of napkins, ten of them in hand, when they left the restaurant.

The limousine would drop him off to his hotel first. She would not invite him to her suite for the night. Any invitation was in his hands. She knew she would not decline if he invited her to his place, but knew such an offer would not happen. She still had not figured him out, or even her own feelings, of why she wanted to bring him into her passionate world, into her bed. It was as if, without trying, he was above her and that she was not worthy. That was not the case, she knew it. He was still only a man, a dime a dozen, to enjoy in various flavors, slurp a few times and discard. Her life called for the fast and furious, and still...

She sought the even ground of light conversation or an attempt at it.

"So, have you gone up to Hugh's private gun club for a practice round?"

"No, I found there are similar such places around L.A."

"I presume you are a crack shot, never miss at what you aim at?"

He gave her a look, half-smile, at her prodding for more of him.

"Are you about to ask me how many men, women, and small children have I picked off either by sniper rifle, hand grenade, or hand-to-hand combat?"

"Something like that? Never been in close quarters with a man who has taken a human life?"

"And you find that what? Exciting or disgusting?"

"Actually, I don't know, you are a charming man, but..."

"But a charming man as a killer might put you off your current intrigue in my character?"

She took slight umbrage at his cavalier assumption of her motives, as right as he might be.

"I am not intrigued with you. We need to work together and I just want to understand who you are and what choices I might face by your actions."

They were at his hotel, and the limo stopped, and the driver opened the door for Wendell's departure.

"I welcome your inspection of me. I am not such a distant nor mysterious person, Samantha, but I do choose carefully how much of myself I am willing to reveal, what I wish to gamble and invariably lose. And to your earlier question, I have never killed a person directly, nor planted a bomb and stood off to watch it kill guilty or innocent. But I have spent my life, fighting for and bleeding for this country, as corny as it might sound, and as we are finding, she is still vulnerable and requires my protection, in whatever role I might play. And, yes, in my past employment I have directed other people to kill for what was considered a just cause. In future such circumstances, I would act in a similar manner."

He exited the car, but turned back to her.

"Miss Carlisle, I find you beautiful and brilliant, and I am attracted to you. But I might ask of you more than you are willing to give, and that is the gamble of expectations I mentioned I am not willing to chance. Good night."

Praised and rejected in one lovely statement of sentiment was not in the best interest of Samantha's karma.

105.

Saturday, August 27th Santa Monica

They all gathered in the War Room for their second data gathering session of the month, the first being where Shawn Pacheco made his entrance and thereafter joined the team. And it was Pacheco's military sense that felt the strange vibrations in the air within the conference room. Obvious was the downer feeling among most was that nothing concrete had so far been forthcoming, no skywriting in the sky pointing to lurking terrorists, who would be quickly identified and dispatched to their ancestors.

The personnel aspects within the room, hard attempts hiding emotions, could be viewed through Pacheco's dispassionate skill at observation. Hugh Fox and Callie Cardoza exchanged quick, furtive glances at each other, while they stationed themselves strategically across the table and at either end. Another couple, non-couple, as Shawn viewed them, were Wendell Holmes and Samantha Carlisle, they ignored each other even when one might be talking to the group; Holmes with seeming indifference, while Ms. Carlisle smoldered. If he were the team leader he would have had had tough scolding to all four of them, 'think only of the mission' and shut away the personal issues in the farthest recess of your brain until this all over.

When 'what' was all over? That was the central question as various team members gave verbal reports. Storm King played the devil's advocate and Shawn found him brusque and offensive, yet he was scoring points. The entire hypothesis of a terrorist attack by al-Qaeda could be distilled down to only gut feelings, that of Wendell Holmes and of Shawn Pacheco, both with less than transparent credentials. And if nothing happened soon, the interest would die off and old lives would be resumed.

Pacheco and Abbas reported on the completed 'Storm Wagon', emphasizing the name so King would accept the homage paid. The vehicle was downstairs for later viewing guarded by the building's security, they not even knowing an arsenal of weaponry locked up and under their watchful ideas contained machine guns, phosphorous grenades, riot shotguns, even a miniature bazooka, all per Holmes's specs, that is, unregistered and where possible serial numbers removed with acid. The cast of *King's*

Retribution were highly impressed; so this is how a real 'covert operations' would be readied.

Gizmo and the Skilleo geeks kept the meeting upbeat in going over their continuing book-movie search of Ali Baba's cache.

"We finally figured out that Hawk title," said Gizmo, a very laid back, mellowed by recreational chemicals sort of young man. "It turns out it is an obscure eco-thriller going back to 1975—man, that is so prehistoric. Called 'Wellspring' by Ed Hawkins."

"And I presume there is a loose nuclear bomb in the plot?" King's continual skepticism.

"No, Colonel Storm, just water pollution stuff in the Colorado Rockies, I think. None of us have had a chance to read it, we can't find a copy. Brigidt is out now rummaging through all the used bookstores. There's one copy on the internet we sent away for. Should be here today or tomorrow."

"Water pollution of sorts was in Tom Clancy's "'Dead or Alive'," recalled Holmes, "an attempt of nuclear pollution."

"If any of these plots were in play, it still doesn't give us a place or time," said Callie, feeling the dejected spirit of all. "Near hopeless."

And on that note, they broke for a working lunch, a buffet catered in, and tried to move off into social chatter of no significance.

In one exchange, Bennie jokingly asked of Pacheco, "Well, now that we're armed to the teeth, thanks to you, but nothing to shoot at, what are you going to do in your spare time."

"Oh, nothing much. When there's the chance, I have been going around to the amusement parks doing the extreme rides."

"What's your fave?"

"Last weekend, I rode the 'Silver Bullet', the longest inversion ride at 3,000 feet."

Callie walking past, added, "Space Mountain is still the all-time classic."

"That's on my list," said Shawn, "But if nothing is going on tomorrow, I am going to take on twelve of them at one park."

"What are you clowns talking about?" Samantha questioned moving their direction, nibbling on cheese and crackers, self-conscious in realizing Wendell was walking right behind her."

Shawn laughed.

"Why, 'The Riddler', the tallest and fastest stand-up; 'Super-man' that goes from 0 to 100 in seven seconds; twelve varieties of rollercoasters."

"Rollercoasters?" As if struck by a freight train, Wendell understood with clarity. He spoke to Samantha, "The movie, 'Roller-coaster'. Ali Baba's movie." His paper plate of food was tossed unceremoniously to the table and he rushed back to the conference room. Everyone had stopped mid-bite.

'Rollercoaster', said Samantha and she followed him, and in a wave like motion all followed.

Wendell was punching in numbers on the conference desk telephone, putting it on the speaker box, as everyone crowded in.

"Agent Curtis, Holmes here. I am with a bunch of my investigative cohorts talking to you and we think it may or may not be nuclear, but we now have a lead that the attack might be aimed at...amusement parks."

"Amusement parks, Holmes? You gotta be kidding? What proof do you have?"

"Let me ask it this way: has your suspect under surveillance taken any road trips in the last two weeks?"

Dead air in the conversation.

"Yeah, I have a general report he took two long drives with Gator Donaldson, the repair shop owner, but the agents said it seemed fairly aimless, like the biker was giving his buddy a day out, but mostly, I recall, it was just a drive, nothing that seemed like they were casing any specific target."

"Where did these trips take them?"

"Hold on let me read the field reports." Silence hung in the room as they all waited, listening to shuffling papers over long distance; even King wanted an answer. They could hear Agent Curtis returning to the phone.

"Shit, Orlando, two trips. Drove right past the major amusement parks, but didn't stop, not even slowing, so it wasn't logged as 'of interest'. Damn. Why would that be the target?"

Callie Cardoza spoke up and introduced herself as ex-San Diego police, to give herself better creds to the FBI agent.

"We're dealing with terror to generate mob hysteria. Like the two Washington, D.C. snipers that paralyzed that whole region until they were caught. Think of it, amusement parks are part of the psyche of fun-loving Americans. Make them afraid to go and enjoy themselves, and you do mental damage as much as physical, let alone the catastrophic hit to the economy when free-spenders stay home."

"You all may have something. I never did see this 'nuclear' angle. The al-Qaeda bunch are not that smart to go out and find a nuclear weapon, even a dirty bomb; we've never heard of them having that sort of expertise for constructing any radioactive device."

Several heard Gizmo mutter under his breath, '9/11 was a pretty brilliant plan.'

"You may need to bring the Arab joker in and see if you can sweat it out of him and his new found biker buds."

"I'm starting to agree."

"I want to be there, Curtis, when it goes down."

"Fine, but there is something else that might be an expedient factor; yesterday, our Arab visitor to Florida, received a ten second phone call to his motel room. Not enough time for a trace but we gained point of origin. You ready?"

"Let me guess," scoffed King, "a pay phone in Abbottabad?"

"How about the call coming from California, the Los Angeles area?"

"Rollercoasters", said Pacheco.

"There are two groups, two attacks," said Samantha, deeply concerned.

"And the Florida cell yesterday must have got the launch code date," Holmes with his serious assessment. "Curtis, can you notify your California office, inform them of our thinking?"

"I will do so and put them in contact with you."

"Tell them to check out their local skinhead covens and see if any had any foreign looking guests recently visit. Put area amusement parks on alert. Have your counterparts contact Mr. Hugh Fox. I will be with you by tomorrow."

The conversation ended with in a disconnect and all in the room chewed over in their minds trying to guess the sick strategy of unknown killers.

"If all true, you still don't have a solid lead on time and place. That was said before and hasn't changed." King could not let all the high IQs in the room dismiss the obvious lack of verifiable intelligence.

Fox would have none of the negatives. He now put explicit trust into Holmes inner gut.

"Let's take a break and start thinking of a surveillance strategy we might be able to impose on the amusement parks in Southern California. The budget will be unlimited, on my nickel." He turned to Pacheco. "You're the military man, scope out a plan of reconnaissance.

The least we can do is assist the local F.B.I., give them more boots on the ground."

"Hey, wait a minute," King visibly sat straight in his chair. "You don't expect a private to run a battle. I have the experience, and it is my team, my people. If anyone heads this up it's going to be me." His face turned towards the ever present CAM ONE, jutting his chin, knowing that conflict drew more viewers.

"The problem is," said Fox, having had enough, his eased voice carrying the sting of rebuke, "Is that Colonel, from the very start you have not believed in the possibility of another terrorist attack in the United States, and the evidence has been mounting towards this conclusion."

"You just don't believe, or can't see what's coming down," said Callie, trying to be tactful but not so artful at it.

King bristled. "And you all think Mr. Holmes here is the Almighty General in Chief. My god, the man has been canned, not retired, from our own government. They must know more than we do about him. And what do we know?" King, agitated, was standing. "That he can get our people killed."

"That's unfair," said Samantha.

"And what of you both, the new owners of Five Studioz. This has just been a lark for you bored people. We had a good television show going before we started running around on these wild goose chases. And what are we now, the butt of all late night comedians. Well, count me out. I don't believe any of this. We are wasting time and will now be wasting government resources, our tax dollars down the drain. And for what, chasing this imaginary Ali Baba," and looking directly at the SEAL, "all on the fact of being seen by someone who probably is going to get a medical discharge from the service."

With that King stormed out. Those in the conference room said nothing for a full minute, until J-Q, who had said nothing for the entire day, as the scribe assigned to take meeting minute notes, put down his pad and pen, and said quietly to the group, most now shaken and morose.

"Anyone interested in looking at our mobile firepower wagon? I feel the urge to hold a gun and consider where it might best be used."

With nothing better to do for the moment, and like the walking dead, they all adjourned in silence down the stairs to the streets of Santa Monica, and began a quiet walk to the alleyway where the weaponry truck could be seen, closely guarded. Ahead of them on the street stalked the angry star of *King's Retribution* heading towards his SUV, a ticketed vehicle which only infuriated him more. They watched him, turn on them with dagger eyes, and tear up the ticket, toss it to the ground, grinding it into the road. It had come to that final realization, seeing in that act of a former military officer disregarding and abusing civilian authority, that an uncertain future of King's Retribution was at hand.

Samantha stood beside Holmes, ready to let her emotions take a back seat.

"I think I have another thought on 'Rollercoaster', she said. "We need to stand back and look not at just one Ali Baba book or movie, but if various plots might have been spliced together."

"Like what?"

"*The Taking of Pelham One Two Three*, the latest version, 2009, the one you did not see, but I did. I think--."

She did not finish the sentence.

In front of them, King's vehicle exploded.

Episode 15

Video Game Perspectives

"Everything is teetering on the edge of everything." **(Spec Ops: The Line)**
"I need a weapon." **(Halo)**
"The President has been kidnapped by ninjas. Are you a bad enough dude to rescue the president?" **(Bad Dudes)**

"It's time to kick ass and chew bubble gum, and I'm all out of gum."
(Duke Nukem 3D) *(taken from "Rowdy" Roddy Piper in movie "They Live")*

106.

28th Sunday   Los Angeles

Like a television drama set in a hospital emergency room and played out with an ensemble cast, vignette scenes heightened the tension.

Hugh Fox looked through the glass at Storm King swathed in bandages, hooked up to a myriad of machines which could monitor the weak pulse and other vitals. Yesterday into this morning, the doctors had a touch and go time of it but the prognosis after a lengthy repair on the operating table was at best 'critical but guarded'.

Fox could not see King's face and his gaze more intently fell on trying to decipher the meanings in Callie's tear-streaked face. He had thought the relationship between co-stars had ended but with the bomb's explosion and Callie's distraught reaction, he felt that between Callie and Storm a fractured bond had been re-forged.

Not that it mattered to him, he thought, or tried to believe so. In the last several weeks, when he was with Callie, the times were enjoyable, an ease of their being able to talk, and yes, laugh. That's what Hugh thought was unique, he had not really laughed in his lifetime, his pleasure derived from a satisfaction of hard-working creativity. Laughter, he found, with Callie gave him a new dimension of appreciating the world around him; his universe he found was larger than a laboratory, more colorful and animated than a mere computer screen. Callie, and yes this band of funk warriors called the *King's Retribution* Team, had made his journey worthwhile, but now it was at an end.

Callie looked up and saw him, offered a weak smile, but Fox, not noticing, had turned away. He was confused and depressed. He now believed he was getting everyone killed, or at least placing them in danger. Storm King had been right after all, this terrorist hunt game, was self-indulgent, letting Fox play cops-and-robbers for real out of the comfort zone of his game world, while using his own money, the risk element was with other people's lives. It was time to call it quits before anyone else got hurt.

Storm King stirred, and opened one eye. He was pretty well drugged up and enjoyed the numbness, though he could feel someone hard squeezing his hand. Callie was in the room, next to his bed, looking down at him. He whispered barely, 'Okay, bad guys do exist.' And then, added, 'Some water please.' Callie fed him some ice chips, praying he was back from the brink, and began chattering aloud.

"Storm, you did it, you big lug. All the press in the world is out on the hospital grounds tracking every single doctor's report they issue. How's that? The rumors are that you were targeted because of what the fall show might be about. Can you believe that? It will probably be the most watched season opener. And don't worry; you are going to pull through. You better.

"We are partners; you are King of *King's Retribution*. Those big bad terrorists forgot that the bomb they stuck under your car would not disintegrate you into nothingness. Didn't they comprehend your car is a Hummer, just like what they drive around in war zones, and with your stupid bravado and being a star with military background you went out and had the damn thing jazzed up with all the military gadgets, including armored plating every-where, especially under the body frame."

King sleeping again, no longer was hearing Callie's rambling.

"And Holmes says the terrorists think you are the body and the rest of are just the supporting legs, meaning you are the center of our Team, and we need you; I need you back. Please."

She had lost Clayton Briggs, now a close call for King. Her distain for him lapsed into the concern with a person who had been so close, so recent in her life. The tough shell she had always wrapped herself in felt brittle. Within was a wanting; a desire for immediate revenge, a hard need for someone to hold her. But no one was around, to love, or to kill.

107.

August 28th, Sunday Anaheim, California

He stared to the heights, at the ribbed edifice and heard the screams of the people high above, screams where fear and joy mixed with the rush of air as bodies are thrown towards death and then pulled back, to repeat again.

"I don't want you to leave," a voice from behind him. Samantha Carlisle.

"A personal request, or otherwise?" He turned to face her, as the rollercoaster made another pass, his voice muffled against the mechanical grating swoosh.

"Perhaps both, but I think we are all on our own emotional rollercoaster, some of us even more so, rushing beyond the tracks."

"You mean me?"

"I don't know you all that well, Wendell, …yet…those genetics, as you told me, which make up your drive to save the world…so now rushing off to Florida to do battle, might not be the best use of your talents. Besides, personally, I don't want you anywhere near a terrorist cell, especially after what happened to King."

"We at least know where one of the son of bitches is, and I am going to make him regret the day---. Hey, wait a minute, how did you get here? How did you find me?"

They were standing in the parking lot of the amusement park, against the fence, below the rollercoaster structure. Holmes had sought out a place to think by himself, to try and separate the events of yesterday; the King attack, the latest War Room data that moved them away from a nuclear plot to something to do with targeting public gathering spots like Florida amusement parks. He had told no one of his destination but here she was. What did he feel about that?

Samantha replied, "After last night, and waiting for King's surgery to be completed, Hugh said we were at war, or at least someone had declared war on us, so he activated the 'Storm Wagon'.

"Activated?"

"Abbas had installed into the van a bunch of monitoring electronics so he went around making sure all of us were GPS connected."

"GPS? Like planting bugs? Why, that sneak."

"In your car and on your person, don't ask how he did it. You can compliment him personally or beat him up." She pointed past several lines of parked vehicles, and Holmes could see Bennie and Abbas sitting in the Storm Wagon waving back at him.

Holmes turned to Samantha, actually glad to see her, but still set in his mission.

"I have to fly out today."

"Your Agent Curtis and his troops can handle the Florida show. Go interrogate the creep when he's in custody. Yesterday, I didn't even have a chance to advance my theory; you were in such a tizzy to run to Storm's aid, take control of the scene for the police, get us all away safely.

"God, I am surprised I didn't see you wearing a 'S' on your chest, and flying around with a cape."

"Samantha, please, you are trying to tell me something."

"If you recall in the movie 'Rollercoaster', the bomber was extorting money from the amusement park owners."

"Right, and that's been checked out. These owners are multinational conglomerates, publicly traded companies, who would have been required to report such threats to the police and the FBI."

"Exactly. But what if our Ali Baba took plot A and added a little from plot B?"

"Okay, I can accept the possibility, but we saw so many, the variations might run to a hundred."

"Yeah, but going back and removing all the nuclear threat books and movies, it limits us significantly. Personally, I can see only one working that fits with your guess that Florida might be targeted to amusement parks."

"And that is?" They began walking towards the Storm Wagon.

"*Pelham One Two Three*. This actually fits with the extortion of 'Rollercoaster', but modernized. At the end of the 2009 version of *Pelham*, the bad guy, played by John Travolta, uses fear of subway killings to cause panic in the stock market thus making a financial killing, so to speak, and does a stock transaction called 'selling short' to make millions."

"You think al-Qaeda terrorists are trying to steal rather than kill?"

"Well, think on this, their main money source from the wealth of the bin Laden family was cut off with his death; so many al-Qaeda leaders have been killed so their rogue state sponsors like Iran or Syria don't know who the new checks are to be sent to. I could see very easily bin Laden himself in his last act, unknowingly of course, wants to hurt America as well as rob a capitalistic system, the height of radical Islamic hutzpah. But now, the terrorists, post- bin Laden, need cash and his plan will create a tidy nest egg for them."

Holmes started thinking. Samantha had made millions herself, she knew Wall Street, and with her smarts she certainly oversees her own investment portfolio, and thus is looking at the scene in the larger landscape versus his narrow view, that an evil plan usually functions under the most simple of conditions. Holmes sought to see the diabolical and never thought of bombs exploding being 'investment related'. His own financial advisor had him conservative in mutual funds, while the rainy day fund under the mattress was actually in an unreported offshore banking account stuffed to seven zero figures, earning little interest. So, he gave her thinking the credit due.

He mapped out the strategy. "So, they will attack the amusement park? In doing so, adverse publicity drives the stock of the parent company down; yes, that would happen. And the bad guys know the news beforehand so they basically have insider information? The market is rigged."

"Correct. There could however be a twist to that plot, and back to my original statement that is why 'we' want you here."

"And that is?"

"Let your mind wander on this one. What if, merely attacking one company in the East doesn't do the trick? The entire stock market would not necessarily drop even if they attacked two public companies in only Florida, and two of the amusement parks in Orlando are tied to the two largest trading entertainment companies in the world. A bomb exploding on the East coast, doesn't make it as visible as al-Qaeda might desire, it does not make the impact 'national', does not put fear into everyone across America to avoid going out to entertainment facilities."

"So, you believe one attack will take place in Orlando, and the other...?

"Here, in L.A."

Adding that scenario into his mulling equation, he pulled out his cell phone and put a call into the Florida FBI. Instinctively, so she could hear the conversation, as it was her hypothesis, he pulled Samantha close to him.

"Agent Curtis, you have to follow your perps all the way to the gate of the amusement park before rushing them. First, you need to determine if they all stick together. If they split apart then one set of them is going to go to another amusement park, one with a rollercoaster. If they stay together, then my people here..." Samantha at this point leaned into his embrace. "...and your people here need to go on alert that at the same time, the terrorists will be targeting an amusement park in the Los Angeles basin."

They could hear the agent yelling his own stress, warning of the risks to civilians, questioning where Holmes got his information, begrudgingly agreeing in the end, when Holmes simply said, "Trust us."

"You're right, Sam," said Holmes. "Looks like I will be staying here."

She kissed him lightly on the cheek.

"Why, does that not make me feel any better?"

108.

28th Sunday New York City

Khalaf clicked off the computer. All was in place. The short sale orders would be placed in the morning into the marketplace, transactions into several entertainment companies, masking any chance of a computer program spitting out anomalies. The first phase attacks were to begin when the parks first opened on Tuesday, early enough to allow the news to have impact across the stock wires.

On the other fronts of the Crimson Scimitar operation, the Scientist had reported to him that two trucks would be departing tomorrow on schedule, with one more truck joining up along the way. This would be fortuitous for Shahin's assault team.

On Wednesday, the 31st, Khalaf would fly to Las Vegas to join the attack. There could no longer be any doubt of achieving success for if they missed on one truck, there were two other windows of opportunity. If they destroyed all three, Southwestern United States would become a wasteland and uninhabited. Khalaf would share in this glory, his name etched in history books.

The overhead light in the living room went dark, and he turned to see Sabz in the shadows, she was holding a newspaper in her hands.

"Come sit with me on the couch, my husband." To him it was an odd command. Indeed, he was exhausted; it was late, and tomorrow there would be anxiety in the waiting. Over the last several weeks he had become use to being called 'her husband' in public, less the teasing lie, more recently spoken as an endearment he silently enjoyed.

He sat on the couch, and in another oddity she sat right next to him, a show of closeness she never gave easy. He tried to make light of it.

"You found another clothing sale in the newspaper?"

She leaned over him to turn on a side lamp next to the divan and handed him a section of the Sunday *New York Times*.

"My sheik," her voice was breaking. "I have bad news. Your friend, your comrade, the Libyan, Atiyah Abd al-Rahman, has been killed."

His eyes blurred in trying to read the headline. He knew immediately. Predator drone strike.

Of the story he read certain parts stood out. "Thousands of electronic files recovered at Bin Laden's compound in Abbottabad, Pakistan, revealed that Bin Laden communicated frequently with Mr. Rahman." Many of those messages Khalaf had couriered between them. The article continued, "They also showed that Bin Laden relied on Mr. Rahman to get messages to their Qaeda leaders and to ensure that Bin Laden's recorded communications were broadcast widely." Again, the inference to Khalaf's role in being the go-between.

At this moment he did not curse the Americans for their death from the sky, such lethal happenings were becoming commonplace within the tribal lands. He did mourn for the soldier al-Rahman, but more numb for himself, having no idea on where his standing was. Would he report directly to al-Zawahiri or would another take Rahman's place, and would he be pushed aside? Khalaf gave wonder to what was not said in reading the story, for he heard if the *Times* got any leak on a good story they would run with it, regardless of consequences to American security. Mentally, he did a check off. First, he was convinced the treasure trove of gathered documents bin Laden was unable to destroy before the SEALS killed him had most likely led them to Rahman's hide-out and his horrific death. Second, in reading between the lines of the Times story, Khalaf found no suggestion that Crimson Scimitar had been compromised, the national terrorist warning level had not been summarily raised. If otherwise, it did not matter, they all must go forward, martyrdom would await and he would die at the bridge. Finally, in the previous weeks, he had read no news article suggesting there had been a third courier at the compound, himself thankfully undiscovered, and he could somehow find ease that as others died, he had no bounty on his head, nor believed he was in the crosshairs of a missile strike.

Nevertheless, he mused, if he were in charge, going outside on a clear day should be taboo for all al-Qaeda leaders. His prayers henceforth would be for overcast weather.

Sabz sat listening to Khalaf's heavy breathing and believed it to show the extreme grief he held within. She felt a pang of tenderness and set aside her own selfish motives for a higher cause, turning instead to comfort a distraught man, but she could not do that so easily without speaking her troubled mind.

"I don't want you to go. Don't you see; *you are* the only one left? They are killing all the others. You must stay here where they cannot find you."

Khalaf did not see this, himself as the rare breed, one of the few surviving members of the al-Qaeda echelon. He again saw himself as having no future, unable to reach and embrace his personal goals. This conjured up the specter of fatalism, as if he were being drawn to Allah's command, not his, to a unknown destiny in the Nevada desert.

"I must leave on Thursday. I believe it is written and out of my hands."

She leaned over him and turned off the light, and eased onto his lap, whispering, "Nothing is written that you cannot erase. But if that is your decision, then I wish you to have me. If you are facing danger I do not want to tease you anymore by putting a reward out of your reach." His mind moved away from his worries to what she was saying, a purring voice, "If you are so determined to leave, then do so with my body smells on you, let that be the perfume to remind you to return safe to my arms."

Her lips met his, the small moist tongue searching. She pulled her robe apart; naked beneath. Sabz placed his hands within, on her breasts, while moving herself in a gentle motion on his lap.

In the early morning hours for the first time in his entire life, he opened a hotel room door and hung out the sign reading 'Do Not Disturb'.

109.

29th August, Monday Washington, D.C.

Matthew Brady and his entire section were swamped, for once with too much Class A –Prime intelligence. The plastic bags that Pacheco had seen carted from the Abbottabad compound were now giving up their secrets with positive results. A bomb-making cell in Germany had been broken apart with the radicals detained. A stockbroker in London had been arrested nearly a month back with damning Islamic manifesto treatises in his possession, while last week one of his associates, a banker, committed suicide rather than face interrogation.

Brady's desk cluttered with leads to assign to his analysts, this was going to be his excuse for not taking former CIA agent Wendell Holmes telephone call, except he did need to ask him one question, clarify a point on the hidden alcove with the mattress and bookshelves found empty.

Something the SEALS uncovered in bin Laden's bedroom, a name that meant very little in the data searches was bothersome to him.

"This is my obligatory call," said Holmes, and went on to explain how the shift was being made from fear of a nuclear plot to that of the minor, if one dare call it that, bombing of amusement parks, and somewhat good news the F.B.I. had one Arabic look-ing suspect under close surveillance. Holmes had to ask, "To be sure, you've heard nothing about the Russians losing a nuclear bomb or the Iranians or North Koreans selling fissionable materi-als to Mideast terror groups?"

"Not a peep. And stolen nuclear bombs are no longer your prime scenario? Amusement parks the real plot?" Holmes could visualize the CIA analyst smiling in debunking mirth.

"Not that you guys don't run the real Google Search of the War on Terror, but our preliminary research –."

"Meaning your bin Laden empty closet analysis?"

"Okay, don't shoot the amateurs. Yes, we had the itchy feeling something was leaning towards a nuclear type incident. Even more so recently, the imaginary plot got a lot more farfetched.

"How's that?"

"Open a weird file and call it, 'Wellspring', from an old novel I finished reading last night. Here's where al-Qaeda would have to be ultra genius-types. Somehow they take a nuclear bomb, or perhaps radioactive chemicals, make some sort of poisonous brew and dump them into the streams at the Continental Divide in the Rockies."

"Continental Divide?"

"Mountain waters from snow melt run to the east and west; we're talking about al-Qaeda trying to poison the Western United States. But, this breaks down into pure fiction; you would need to haul in a lot of radioactive junk to the top of the mountain, locate the right streams into which to dump, but even a handmade dirty bomb would consist of solid components not liquid based. And beyond that, dilution would cause the poison to go inert. As I said, that was our latest stab at guessing. Attempting to blow up amusement park roller coasters with C-4 seems to be where we are heading."

Brady felt the conversation had lasted too long as it was. "Sorry, I can't give you a roadmap leading from bin Laden to his American target, if one really exists. Nothing you have is solid. Stick with the F.B.I., I have been told several times already, it's their jurisdiction anyway. Oh, by the way, Holmes, did you ever see or hear the Arabic phrase, 'Crimson Scimitar'?"

Two seconds of consideration from Holmes. "Not really. Any importance?"

"Confidential?"

"Oh, come on, Brady, I have been the saint of cooperation."

"Well, not much to show from you, just rattling our chains. Crimson Scimitar? No? It popped up twice on our radar but nothing definite. Our people do feel like it could be the name of an operational plan that was being considered, but never went anywhere, except..."

"'Except'...don't torture us retirees."

"Crimson Scimitar was by itself scratched on a crumbled piece of trash paper in bin Laden's compound, found in fact in his bedroom and the name was found again only a few days ago in the study of a banker who committed suicide in London. The local constabulary was looking into fraud among some Islamic Benevolent Charities the man ran. Seemed like he absconded with their funds, and then killed himself when the Bobbies closed in. We did get some scuttlebutt that he might have been a front, channeling funds to Middle Eastern terrorist groups. But we are only in preliminary investigation. Coincidently, from what the Brits have been uncovering from the SEAL raid, MI-6 had earlier picked up a stockbroker associate friend of this banker, who did have radical Islamic literature in his flat. They think it could be a sleeper cell, put in place years ago. And the stockbroker did have a flight ticket to New York."

"Stockbroker, you say. That is interesting."

"And, why so?"

"Let me get back to you on that. I need to dig, but now that I put aside all these hair brained schemes I see strange linkage of sorts?

"What sort?"

"In our secret hide-away in Abbottabad, if you go back to the photos you took, those we took, among the graffiti on the wall there was a sword-like drawing; and if it wasn't so dark, I would now surmise it was drawn in red, maybe even in dried blood."

"Damn. The London banker; the report I read with crime scene photos, showed a sword doodling on a message pad on the man's desk, where they found his body, his brains blown out first obscured it. Isn't a scimitar an Arab sword? What's this all mean, Holmes? Give me your on-the-spot field op opinion."

"I think our Ali Baba, he with American books and movies at his disposal, and buddy buddy with bin Laden, is maybe a co-creator of this Crimson Scimitar, and it's an active plan.

"Al-Qaeda isn't going to launch it on the anniversary of 9/11. They'll launch it whenever they can as revenge for us wasting bin Laden. And you have interconnected plots as in plural: Florida and California with amusement parks and something to do with money and a London connection.

"Thank God, it's not going to be a dirty bomb in Times Square or a Wellspring nuclear poisoning at the Continental Divide."

Later, as he pondered, Brady could have filed his conversation with Holmes away in a dusty drawer and gone back to the euphoria permeating the intelligence section of the Mideast Department. After all, the military just erased Atiyah Abed al-Rahman from the ledger of killers.

If only bin Laden's intel could lead them back to Anwar al-Awlaki and Doctor al Zawahiri then the ghosts of 9/11 might be appeased.

He could not dismiss so easily Holmes and his TV cowboys. Sure, they were prospecting leads and some sounded promising, especially since it seemed someone was trying to kill off the show's stars. Most likely local police would check out the car bombing and discover a disgruntled fan. And this hype of a Florida attack being imminent had his interest, but if home grown terrorists were around, the FBI wouldn't want the Agency sticking their nose into their domestic shit.

Crimson Scimitar, whatever it might be, rankled his mindset requiring systematic order to all things, and although Holmes dismissed the notion for any lack of evidence, it was Matthew Brady's job and obligation to make sure a 'what if' did not turn into his greatest fear of 'why did we miss it' as the intelligence community itself had let occur in not preventing 9/11. So, it would only take a few telephone calls to dismiss this line of reasoning as a false alarm.

His first call went internally to the National desk, with the question: "Any problems at the nuclear plants?" The reply, after scanning the data links: outside a few short term closures from the earthquake in Virginia, nothing out of the ordinary. "How is security at the plants?"

And found it was heightened in preparation for the 9.11 anniversary.

He did not relish his next call, and expected the result. NORAD, buried under Cheyenne Mountain, Colorado held tracking control of American missiles and the running inventory of nuclear weapons locations. He made it sound routine, but the question tumbled out all wrong, "May sound strange but is all your ordinance accounted for?" He got the expected dismissive laugh, then a few moments of silence, and he knew that call would come back on him. Most certainly he just initiated a massive double-check accounting of their entire nuclear inventory.

Damn you, Holmes.

His last call was to the National Regulatory Commission, the government's nuclear industry oversight organization. Brady found himself passed off to a sub-manager, where he shot the breeze for a moment, then following an earlier cue, asked how their protective preparation was going in lieu of the approaching 9/11. As expected, he received a lecture on the security systems in place for the country's highly secret enrichment program, the stuff big bang bombs were made of. Just as he was ready to sign off, he asked, "So sounds like everything is secure?"

"Yes, everything will be on lock down," came the official reply, "a week before and a week after the anniversary. Taking no chances. Of course, the stuff in motion that's under a separate NRC division."

Brady's mind blinked. "*In motion?* What do you mean?"

"Nuclear waste by-products. There's always some disposed centrifuge or spent fuel rods off to secure locations. They have their own security detail."

"How is this 'waste' taken to these locations?"

"Depending on size, shipment either by train or truck."

Brady made a redial to NRC and asked for the Chairman's office. Acting as if he was merely verifying what he already knew he asked if any transit shipments were 'in motion' this week or next, part of the required check-up on 9/11 anniversary preparedness.

The response was not the answer he wanted to hear, ever.

"Yes, we have a transit shipment going out by truck. Destination unknown, highly classified, but then you people know about it."

That news surprised him, so he played along. "Oh, yes, we do. Just doing, as I said, this protocol verification. If I send a form around, again, who is the person in our shop that's on your need-to-know list?"

He heard, "Your Deputy Director, Ronald Givens; why, he even sits on our ad-hoc task force committee on nuclear waste with our Chairman, the Homeland Security people, F.B.I. representative, you know, all the oversight agencies."

Even though he had only assumptions, a bad premonition sent a cold chill down Matthew Brady's spine. He intercom buzzed the duty officer at the CIA's central input-output desk. "Get me anything on the world net dealing with the word 'Wellspring'."

110.

August 29th Monday New York State

The Scientist was quite pleased on how the day had gone. All the overtime effort resulted in his crew seeing the two trailer trucks leave the Indian Point station. They were non descript looking trucks, one a tanker truck, the other a closed container, marked with temporary signs stating, *Eagle Freight*, a design of a screaming, plunging eagle with a captured trout in its talons— but, no warning signs affixed of 'Dangerous Chemicals'. The Anna Generating Station's truck load containing the concentrated trillium bore one additional tag. Singh very simply had taken a spray paint can and placed a slash of red against the back of the tanker, odd-looking, like graffiti, but nothing to draw anyone's attention to, and that was the point. A red slash, but to his people, the suggestion of a red scimitar.

As to the truck convoy details, in front of the final three truck caravan would be a black Hummer, matching the lead pace, a half a mile ahead. Within, were two armed guards, not military, but private hire under government contract, each one with a concealed side arm, and one automatic rifle in the vehicle and as Singh noted, not really in placement where it could be reached easily, but they were not expecting emergency usage as this would be a long, grueling but otherwise routine trip. An identical guard-Hummer configuration would travel behind the tractor trailers, again far back as not to draw attention. The whole plan was to make the trucks look invisible to the whizzing traffic along the interstate roads they would travel.

Singh, the employee at Indian Point, was heading home for the evening, relieved his part of the operation went off without a hitch. No longer 'The Scientist'. He knew nothing more of Crimson Scimitar operation but was smart enough to want to be glued to the television, knowing the attack on the trucks would garner major media coverage. For himself, he was not worried at all that his cover might be blown when the trucks were destroyed and the government would come looking for the leak, on who might have told of the truck's planned cross-country trip and eventually the transit across the bridge. Singh felt inner strength that he could weather any sort of interrogation. They would have to kill him first before he would betray his fundamentalist brothers.

With deepening shadows and clouds bringing on early dusk, Singh's car rounded a curve on the country road a mile from his home, and in a sudden response, he was alert, his car's screeching brakes, to stop in front of the auto accident, a car halfway off the road, at an awkward angle on the graveled shoulder strip. Singh could shake his head knowingly. This curve had seen many such swerved accidents, most usually, when the roads were rain wet. This evening, the road was dry, but still dangerous as the accident bore witness. He could see a man slumped over the wheel, probably unconscious. Singh pulled in front of the car, put on his emergency blinkers and got out to offer assistance.

The car did not look that damaged. He reached in the opened window and gently shook the injured man's shoulder, "Mister, are you alright? Where do you hurt?" Only then did The Scientist note the oddity, the driver's ear was missing.

111.

29th Monday   New York City

Idyllic was not a word that Khalaf would usually bring to mind to describe his feelings.

Yet, here he was, Sabz by his side taking a pleasant stroll in Central Park, close to the entrance, across the street from the Plaza. And though romance was not sex, as most of his efforts over the last two days were animalistic pumping away, he sensed the rising urge to be romantic, to hire one of the horse and buggy rides through the park to extend the happiness of the moment. Yes, it was happiness, but these times must now end.

Nidal had placed the short sale orders this morning, the trucks from Indian Point had departed for their journey and the attacks on the amusement parks, the first phase of Crimson Scimitar, would be launched tomorrow. After that, he would need to begin packing the day after for his trip. That thought gave him mixed emotions. He was a committed man to the Islamic cause, but he did not want to leave Sabz. Instead, selfishly he wanted to, as he had done the last two nights, hold her close, and listen to her breathing as she slept, wipe the light perspiration from her forehead from their strenuous coupling. The girl was who she said she was, a virgin.

That excitement, to see her give up her maidenhood for him, her brief pain, then widened eyes, as his rhythm within moved her to respond, warily at first, eager next with wrapping legs, and finally the insatiable cub tigress, who could moan and scream among the best of the beasts of the jungle. It was apparent she had found a new outlet of her bubbling enthusiasm for life, that is, beyond her shopping sorties. It was he, who would have to admit that one part of jihadist philosophy must be revisited. To die for the cause and in heaven be rewarded and serviced by 100 virgins, if all like Sabz, would destroy him all over, from nub to soul.

"You are happy?" asked Sabz. "Your telephone calls, the emails today will bear fruit?"

"It seems so."

You are happy with me?"

"Yes."

"Then we should marry when you return."

At that he coughed, surprised, but did not want to cloud his future.

"We shall see."

"Are you going to take other women for your wives?" She said this with a childish possessive pout.

"Only if you bother me too much." He smiled at her. Allah protect me against two women such as her.

"I saw on the television that they have, what do you say, a pornographic channel. You have to pay for it to watch. I hope I please you but I am not experienced. Can we watch how other women perform that I might learn to do these strange things that make men crazy with desire."

Khalaf recalled the few tattered porn magazines that had been circulated among the men at the Compound in Abbottabad. To watch western women naked and cavorting, that could be interesting, and if it were to give Sabz ideas for physical exploration, that might be acceptable to the end benefits.

"We shall see." The statement not being negative was taken as an affirmative by Sabz, and she grabbed onto his arm, in a joyful hug, then skipped over to watch squirrels chasing each other around the base of large tree.

Khalaf for the first time was going off to do battle and would leave someone behind that he now understood he cared about. Before he left on Thursday, he must set her up with her own bank account, enough in it, that if he did not return, she could go wherever, live modestly, if she could possibly do that which he doubted. He pledged his self to return. I have responsibilities, he considered: the transferring of the money made from the trading account funds to al-Qaeda operating accounts; to reap the laurels of the attacks to gain him favor, to follow the wishes of The Doctor, to gain new, more prestigious assignments.

But he faced gyrating inner debates. This world of comfort was enticing, for around him instead of the whipping hellish desert wind, he had started to relish the sounds of the urban city, men and women of all looks and faiths, temperaments tested daily, yet moving on. They all had political opinions but he saw no one caning a person in public because they did not follow another's religious scriptures. How strange it all seemed to him on his arrival and today, civilization teemed around him and having an attractive woman beside him gave him a new perspective, like a new blasphemy, that perhaps people living together in toleration was a religion unto itself, greater than those from blessed books. Such a thought he quickly shook from his mind, mad at himself for even conjuring up such speculation.

"Let us return to our hotel room," he said. Sabz smiled back for she knew someday, if he survived, she would have Khalaf as her champion and someday by her wits she would gain control over her own future. Maybe she would leave him then, but then maybe not. She enjoyed his touch, recognizing in that first passionate embrace he was as much the novice as she was.

"Yes, my sheik, and I shall endeavor to figure out how the television pay system works."

112.

30th Tuesday   Florida and California

"They're on the move," said Curtis in his hurried phone call. "We are mobilizing. Chopper is in the air. And they are heading north in a six passenger utility type van, something was viewed hidden under a tarp in the back.

"We have about two hours before they reach Orlando. They should be in the area around noontime."

Holmes glanced at his watch. "That will make it at 9 a.m. here, just when the parks open. I bet they will coordinate strikes, just like 9/11. Please keep me informed with any breaking news. We'll get going on this end."

"I have put our L.A. office on alert. There will be an undercover presence at all the amusement parks."

"Yes, but I think it might only be one park, depending on the one they hit in Florida."

"So, you say. But keep your people out of the way. This is our job."

"Another couple of eyes won't hurt. I will coordinate with your office; we will be in stake-out mode only."

"You do that."

The *King's Retribution* Team did their own form of mobilizing. They had two trucks available, one the fully armed Storm Wagon, the other a production truck used for the show.

They were in radio contact with each, and positioned one at each of the amusement parks that Holmes felt most logical to be attacked, one in Burbank, the other in Anaheim. And, he thought ruefully, he could be totally wrong, but that's not what made Holmes Holmes. To survive, you had to work off of little fact and inbred instinct and there still could be total error in judgment or risk if you were proved right.

Before they headed out, Holmes sought to dissuade everyone from going, as did the hesitant Fox. Let law enforcement handle the operation, they said. When all said no, then Holmes tried to get the most professionals to be the only ones in the field: Cardoza, Pacheco, and himself. No way, said Fox, reluctantly not wanting to be the one left behind, if we are committed we are in this from start to finish. Cardoza even emphasized the need for

CAM ONE and CAM TWO to be present, to record all the events, so Storm could see the results of his Team.

Holmes, in resignation, only shook his head; he was in a damn reality show, after all.

They were all crazy, believed Pacheco. Why weren't the police and National Guard brought in? This called for military intervention. But he knew the answer. They were operating on hunches and to put fear into the public would only set off mob panic. What he found not so much humorous but a sign of the times was when Holmes said, "It would be easy to do racial profiling and believe every Arab-looking person was a terrorist, but keep in mind the Florida suspects are skin heads with an Arab, so you have to believe we are probably going to see a mutt-jeff mixture of bad guys. Keep your mind looking for a facial tic of nervousness or people wearing long jackets in this heat. If you see something you will have a radio and frequency to notify your nearest FBI agent."

Curtis's call came close to noon. He named the amusement park where the van was headed to. The dice had been thrown and the Storm Wagon (Holmes, Cardoza, Fox, Carlisle) with CAM ONE, not the utility truck (Pacheco, Bennie, Abbas) with CAM TWO lucked out, if that was it, to be nearest to the amusement park expected to be targeted. When in closer position, they couldsee the rollercoaster above the park's landscaping.

"We should probably join the FBI at the entry gates and start eyeing those coming in."

Callie and Samantha filtered through the crowd. Fox stood near the ticketing office, while Holmes took up a position at one of the gates, which required personal bag checks, as it was his opinion if there was any hardware to be smuggled in then this would be the most likely port of entry. Too easy did he spot the supposed discreet FBI agents, talking to no one, yet doing so. Likewise, the Hunt Team had their own ear buds and hidden mike coms, but it was the cell phone which vibrated and he answered. The number reflected was FBI Curtis.

"Damn mess here."

"Say again," He was watching a Mexican family group entering the park for some birthday occasion; three men carrying balloons, wrapped presents, and a large flat box with the cake (white icing he viewed as the gate guard inspected the pastry box), within the group must be the lucky birthday recipient, a woman carrying a small boy, and a man with a ball cap and jacket, dragging along a crying child. How could that little boy being forced along be unhappy to have a whole day of frivolity, plus cake and gift unwrapping?

He turned back to Curtis's out of breath shouting.

"We were set up to nab them at the parking lot entry but they i.d.'d us and rammed their way through, trying to crash in the main entrance. We blocked them, surrounded, and the bastards blew themselves up. Took out about a dozen cars, injured about five tourists, no one critical. But confirms all you said. I've notified our people out there to call in reinforcements. If anyone confirms a suspect near or within the park, call it in and we will evacuate. We have locked the park down here, keeping everyone inside so we can do a safety sweep."

Samantha walked over to him.

"I am seeing nothing standing out. All look like happy families ready to enjoy all the rides."

The FBI agent in his situation mode hung up. "Agent Curtis said the Florida creeps blew themselves up."

"Hell, you say."

"That's where they went, hell. So long, Gator. I have a feeling the surrounded al Qaida goon did the self detonation and the skinheads were as surprised as the FBI."

"We have to be very cautious, Wendell."

"Yes. If cornered, it's a one way ride; they will detonate their explosives, become suicide bombers, could be much worse than just destroying one rollercoaster to make news."

Holmes's eyes were still scanning the crowd. He watched the birthday mother and two children walk by, exiting the park, at a fast pace, leaving, the smaller child in her mother's arms still bawling. That was unusual. Skin color and texture, he recalled of the supposed 'father', a baseball cap hiding eyes and features. Spanish looking and Arab looking could be misidentified, especially if the Arab was tugging along a screaming brat, everyone would look at the unruly child. And the birthday presents, even with colorful ribbons, were wrapped in varieties of pink paper. Weird, both children, were boys; wasn't pink for girls, and some of the smaller pink packages...

"They're already in the park." Holmes began squawking into his microphone gathering his forces, speed dialing his FBI counterpart. "There are four of them. Brought the explosives, probably guns, hidden in presents and a cake box. We're heading to the rollercoaster." He heard the FBI agent yelling at him to stay where he was. Sure thing, buddy, and ignored the advice.

Holmes did tell Fox and Samantha that when the terrorists were spotted that their job would be to help coordinate the evacuation of the park, safely and without scaring anyone. The al-Qaeda terrorist would definitely blow himself up and try to take a large number of innocents with him.

No heroes, please.

Callie Cardoza merely gave him her patented, 'oh, yeah', and her hand moved into her shoulder purse, no doubt her finger firm on a trigger housing.

The park was filling quickly, parents grabbing at wayward children, dabbing on sun block, hydrating them, letting them scurry in front to jump into the ride lines. The rollercoaster was in the process of making practice runs, but the line of families anticipating entrance to the ride extended into a several rope turns. Holmes scanned the crowd. He did not see anyone, and then he did. Three of them bunched together off to the side, near the barricade, over which someone might be able to scramble and climb up the siding to set an explosive charge. Three Hispanic men, tattooed and gang-looking, were providing security. Ball cap guy nowhere to be seen.

The FBI agents found the birthday party gangbangers at the same time the trio spotted them, two seconds of stare back, and weapons pulled and a firefight exploded. Bedlam. The crowds screamed, and fell to the ground, while others scrambled, sprinting away.

Holmes needed to find the bomber. If he drew his own firearm, he would probably be picked off in friendly fire by over-eager Fibbers who did not receive the memo on who were the good guys. He moved around to the side, keeping his eyes to the structure, feeling Callie Cardoza near his side.

"There." She pointed.

Ballcap guy had climbed the barrier and was working his way into the center of the ride's structural lattice work.

Holmes motioned.

"Go around, don't let him out that side, and if his hand goes into that jacket, duck. I'm betting he's not only carrying explosives, he's wired with a vest." Callie darted away.

The gunfire around them had trailed off to an occasional ping of single fire, and Holmes glanced back to see a prone body not moving, one of the Hispanic attackers. Feeling a little old, Holmes grabbed the top railing of the fence, and pulled himself over, and plopped down on the other side. The bomber must have used the structure of the rollercoaster to conceal himself.

Holmes guessed the explosive charge had to be affixed with a timer and knowing the troops were closing in on him he would set it for a quick sequence, so Holmes had to reach him before he set the device, and to make his getaway, which meant running to another spot in the park, one with crowds, and blowing himself up and those around him.

Holmes could not take that chance and pulled his Glock and through the steel work, in spotting the darting ball cap, fired, an expected missed. Make the man jumpy, if he could not stop him, then blow himself up away from the people. By the shot's miss the bomber now knew it was all over except for him to meet his perverted version of God. In a blind craze, he pulled a revolver and let off a blast of gunfire back at Holmes forcing him to duck. The bomber threw his gun away, shifted his stance, stepped up and into another steel girder, and wrapped one arm around a central leg to the rollercoaster's famous upside down hairpin turn, and yelling what most probably was a cry of 'Allahu Akbar!' reached into his jacket--only to stop and look up, startled. Holmes saw the red hole materialize in the man's forehead, a mist floating in the air behind him, no sound heard beyond the rollercoaster's noisy tumult as the hurtling cars rocketed by. The man toppled from his perch, but in his fall jammed in the crossbeams, lodged upside down, a Dalisque crucifixion.

Hugh Fox, panting, ran up to Holmes.

"I didn't mean to hit him. I wasn't trying, I swear, I was just trying to give you more covering fire. I am not that good a shot."

"Good enough," said Callie, arriving to the scene, removing the fired weapon from Fox's shaking hand.

Holmes took in the scene with swarming FBI agents in clean-up mode kicking weapons away from the dead, one agent being tended to with an arm wound. "Best we all get out of here without fanfare; it's better we not get caught up in this; there are ramifications." Holmes looked around as the Team re-assembled with Samantha joining as they blended into the fleeing throng of park visitors. Over his shoulder, Holmes added, "And Callie, tell CAM ONE to shut off the damn camera. You don't want the world to know that your billionaire boyfriend just killed someone."

"What?" Both Callie and Hugh looked at each other, reacting simultaneous in embarrassed denial.

113.

30th Tuesday
12:30 p.m. East Coast Time   New York City

Khalaf followed the Associated Press stories as they came across the newswire in real time on his computer trading program.

12:30 p.m. – *Explosion reported at - - - - Amusement Park, Orlando, Florida.*

The stock of this entertainment company dropped two points on the NYSE. Very good, just as planned, thought Khalaf, but minutes later a different story started to materialize.

12:45 p.m. – *Propane explosion in motorhome forces park shutdown. Five people injured, three fatalities reported. Fire Marshall promises full investigation of park safety.*

What's going on? An anonymous text message should now be received to the media outlets announcing al-Qaeda's revenge attack. The stock dropped another three points, a slight shift downward across most other entertainment securities.

12:55 p.m. (9:55 am West Coast)   *Gunfire reported at amusement park.*

1:20 p.m. (10:20 am West Coast)   *Gang warfare breaks out at amusement park, first of its kind. Two dead. Park closed as police investigate.*

The funds, with their computer programs of anticipating trends, start a sell-off as investors become wary of entertainment stocks. After —- Company loses 10% of its value, the Stock Exchange calls a halt in trading in the stock, and by its new regulations puts in place the freeze on short sales.

2:15 pm Congressman L.D. Sheftel of Missouri makes a public call for an industry wide review of safety procedures at all entertainment facilities. The two companies effected directly by their park shutdowns, and loss of substantial revenues, issue separate press releases stating 'that the incident in question had nothing to do with park operations, and were occurrences not controlled by us, and with police approval, the park would be open for business tomorrow as usual, and all customers who were inconvenienced by the day's event can either gain a full refund or be issued a free ticket for another day, provided you have previous proof of purchase.'

2:45 pm Congresswoman Laura McCombs, representing the hardworking entertainment workers in her Florida constituency speaks to a reporter from CNN, saying, 'it is sad tourists lost their lives when their vehicle caught fire but such a tragedy should not undermine or call in question the exemplary record of safety by all businesses in Florida.'

When the New York exchanges closed for the day, Kahalf heard from a pleased Nidal.

"Congratulations, Mr. Risal. We covered and you did quite well. Are we buyers tomorrow?"

"I expect another day of concern. On Thursday, let us check the openings and then I will make a decision. Also I will be leaving town for a few days. Nothing is to be done until I return.

My wife has further written and notarized instructions if you require further direction.

Understood?"

"Yes, of course, Mr. Risal." Nidal knew him only as Risal, not knowing he stayed at his hotel under his UAE alias. Khalaf felt insulated by these false identities but today he was not a happy person.

It seemed apparent that this phase of the Crimson Scimitar operation had been out foxed.

Law enforcement was in conspiracy to expunge all attempts to paint this with a terrorist brand.

He knew why, the 9/11 anniversary. As al-Qaeda wished to demonstrate their omnipotence to strike anywhere, anytime with no opposition, the American Government had to show that al-Qaeda was not a threat, that the obese and lazy population could go about their lives and enjoy their sense of complacency.

He saw this quite clear when someone unknown emailed the Los Angeles *Times* informing them that the California attack at the amusement park was the work of al-Qaeda. Most probably sent from Shahin himself, upset at whatever occurred at the park. Undoubtedly, Khalaf mused, it wasn't a major news story of a rollercoaster exploding and riders falling to their deaths.

As he expected, by early evening, a brief news release was issued by the F.B.I., 'preliminary investigation by local police are able to report a turf battle between local gangs resulted in two deaths. We have no indication that such shootings were in anyway related to a terrorist act; however, we do ask citizens to be mindful and alert as the 9/11 Anniversary approaches and to report anything unusual.'

Khalaf looked at the big picture. The first phase of Crimson Scimitar achieved half of its objectives: al-Qaeda received no credit and the American people were not again in fear for their lives, but on the brighter side the plot from that subway movie did actually result in several millions of dollars being gained in Khalaf's trading accounts. This part of the Crimson Scimitar plan was over. He was easily tempted that he might take some of the profit and play the futures of stock market gyrations especially on the future news of the destruction of the trucks at the bridge and the devastating implications to millions of Americans. He did feel a growing knowledge on how to play the market, but, now he hesitated in giving Nidal that direction to make untried investments. In the back of his mind, there was a shuddered tinge of worry: what if Shahin's attack failed and American stock exchanges would not react and he would lose all he had gained? No, he would wait, play it safe; rather be the wise investor than an uncertain speculator.

His mind turned to more pleasing matters. As he had discretionary funds (from bin Laden's personal bank account) at his disposal and considered himself proud that his stock market efforts were the only success so far, he decided, "Tonight, I will take Sabz to an expensive restaurant. I would like to show her off in these new garments she buys. Besides, tomorrow night is my last night before I travel. I will not wish to leave the bedroom."

114.

August 30th Tuesday   5 p.m.   West Wing, White House

In the hastily called meeting, the main players of American intelligence were there: the heads of Homeland Security, the F.B.I, C.I.A., and the meeting run by the President's National Security Advisor. Several supporting sub directors were in attendance including Ronald Givens and unexpected in the invitation to attend, Matthew Brady, who felt his presence might be as the sacrificial lamb to be thrown to the lions.

"And in fact, this was an al-Qaeda operation, not some home grown loony?" The President's Advisor looked around the room, settling on Givens, who in turn looked for help to Brady, so he responded.

"We had no intel from our own Mid East sources; the F.B.I, Florida office, gained information on a totally unrelated case they were working."

The F.B.I. director spoke up, not sure if to take the credit or if his Agency was going to be a scapegoat, so he did a little blame spreading. "Our local office actually got a lead from one of your former employees." He gave a glance to the Acting C.I.A. Director and at Givens, and then glanced at a paper he held. "Former C.I.A. Agent Wendell Holmes."

"Holmes," cried out Givens in surprise, so this is where the trouble is coming from, "The guy is a rogue, totally not a team player."

"And yet," said the President's Advisor, "He uncovered a plot to attack our institutions, even if they were amusement parks."

"It is imperative that we maintain the charade," offered the Homeland Security, who earlier had developed the strategy to present at this anticipated meeting. "Downplay these incidents as being totally unrelated and having nothing to do with terrorists, especially al-Qaeda."

"I am in agreement," concurred the F.B.I., "There could be other attacks in the making and we need time to search them out, perhaps meanwhile cause division in their ranks to where they might make a mistake. If we let the press know, the public would inundate us with thousands of false leads. Racial profiling would be an unimaginable witch hunt. Behind the scenes investigation is our best hope at uncovering any other planned cell attacks."

"Are we expecting more?" The top leaders of the intelligence community in the nation looked at each other and gave hesitant nods of 'I don't know'.

"Should we bring in this Holmes fellow, as Mr. Givens characterizes him, a 'loose cannon'?

"I have no problem if you arrested him," Givens smiled that such a chance was possible.

"It may be best if we let him operate outside the box, develop his own independent research. He did uncover the amusement park attacks." Brady did not mean to step up to the defense of Holmes, as much as he did not want Givens to gain his way. He accepted the glare from Givens.

"And what makes you think, this former agent, out there by himself, can develop better leads than all of our departments combined?" Homeland Security knew he was on the top of the heap, as most others in the room reported to him.

"Because he sent a photo showing himself on a private tour of bin Laden's home the night after his death. Isn't that correct, Director Givens? He sent the photo to you directly."

Givens found himself in a corner, cleared his throat and squeaked out, "Yes, that's right.

To me, and others."

"And, Mr. Holmes," continued Brady, "uncovered intelligence that we missed when the SEALS swept through the Compound, no fault of their own; as it was secreted away in a wall?"

"What intelligence?" The Acting Director of the CIA was not in the loop.

"We aren't really sure, Holmes has not revealed much. Seems he has some bitter taste in his mouth on how he was dismissed from the agency." Brady did not make eye contact with Givens.

"So how did he end up believing the amusement parks would be attacked?" The F.B.I.

Director needed the information to develop his own background story if the press ever put two -and-two together.

"Books and movie DVDs he found in Abbottabad that were later destroyed by the enemy.

From what he saw, I believe he notified the F.B.I. of his finding, his guess, and we should be thankful the guess was the correct one."

"Al Qaeda books and movies? Sounds ridiculous," Givens was not giving Holmes any credit, if he could help it. "Plus you should all know he's running around with those TV people of *King's Retribution*. No creditability at all, if you ask me."

The President's National Security Advisor now recalled the interference from *King's Retribution* just as the bin Laden operations were being launched. He had to agree with Givens they had no need for a bounty hunter TV show personalities.

"Let's hear no more of Holmes. Well, where do we go from here?" And they all came to the consensus that the announcement of warning to the public in the approach of 9/11 anniversary should be issued forthwith. That all the intelligence agencies would go on quiet alert and sift through past data to glean if any other plots were being fomented. The 9/11 timeframe seem to be in all their minds as when another attack might be scheduled.

Ronald Givens, not to miss an advantage, and having received an earlier call from U.S. Senator Crandall of California, offered the suggestion, "If the President could be scheduled to visit an amusement park and shake hands, take a ride, that would make a favorable and subtle impression on the public's confidence." They all thought the idea a sound political move.

Outside the meeting, Givens braced Brady, angered.

"You certainly didn't help me in there."

"Actually, Director Givens, I thought I did. Holmes's latest brainstorm is that some al-Qaeda plot is aimed at attacking nuclear plant or nuclear waste shipments."

Givens visibly was shocked.

Brady said, "If I had brought that up, you would have laughed at it, and if it turned out to be true, you might have been caught in a vise. *You are* overseeing a truckload of waste byproducts delivered to an undisclosed location?"

"Yes, but it is totally secure."

Brady playing the detective, had confirmed a truckload was 'in motion', He hoped Givens would give up more information.

"Holmes made up some story that the nuclear waste would be hijacked and dumped into streams at the Continental Divide in the Rockies."

"Absurd. Wherever he's getting his ideas are off-the-wall. Our truck group won't be going over anywhere close to Colorado mountains; they will swing south in Denver and go through New Mexico. And besides, the NRC and all the other agencies approved the route. My signature required only for the formality. I think Holmes should be arrested for fear mongering."

Brady without launching clandestine spying within his own agency, tantamount to getting himself prosecuted, had gleaned enough information from the Deputy Director. But what to do with it? Who within the American government would believe him? They would only say he was crying 'Wolf', but what if Holmes was one per cent correct in his assessment. As farfetched the whole plot sounded such an eventuality meant a nuclear disaster, environmentally catastrophic.

Matthew Brady, a good man, not a great man, facilitated between self-courage within and self preservation of his Washington employment future.

He returned to his own office, closed the door, and quickly wrote another one of his cover-your-ass memos which he was becoming proficient at, basically laying all future blame to the feet of Ronald Givens for being bias against giving credence to a possible threat. With the memo completed and placed in his personal and secure safe, he picked up the phone. Maybe Holmes and *King's Retribution* could save America from al-Qaeda, and itself.

Episode 16

"Gentlemen, you can't fight in here! This is the War Room!"
--President Merkin Muffley/Peter Sellers in **Dr. Strangelove**
(1964)

115.

August 31st Wednesday Santa Monica

Shawn Pacheco waded through a mini media circus in front of the War Room offices, dodging questions asking who he was and what did he know about the gang shootings at the amusement park. Two burly guards at the door checked his driver's license, checked him off the list, and let him pass into the building. Here, he met Callie Cardoza waiting herself for the elevator.

"What's going on out there?" He pointed to the hungry press.

She gave off a wry grin. "A tourist said they thought they saw TV star Callie Cardoza running through the park with a drawn pistol. At today's meeting, I guess, we are going to be told how to spin this whole episode."

"Well, I certainly wasn't there." Pacheco's response reflected his frustrated demeanor.

He had been in the *King's Retribution* van at the other amusement park, missing all the action, a downer for any battle-honed SEAL. They were giving him a consolation prize of sorts. Holmes said he would try to get a breakdown on the timer elements found on the bomber's body and the recovered IED strapped to the rollercoaster base structure. Pacheco would then be able to do a comparison to see if there was any uniqueness in the bomb creation, disturbing if so. On the other hand if there were similarities to what the Taliban or al-Qaeda used on the Afghan battlefield, then law enforcement bomb squads could react with more confidence on how to diffuse a future explosive threat. The Team at least gave Pacheco his due, he was the expert in explosives, now requiring his involved presence.

Upstairs, Callie and Shawn found the Team gathered. The mood of chattering gossip quickly descended into a gloomy mood as Fox spoke.

"It is my opinion that we should shut down our offices," said Fox, his voice strained, his eyes showing little sleep. "We rose to the occasion, you all gave 150%, and I believe we made a difference." They all knew he was still reeling from killing a man, even if a terrorist.

"I don't know why the government is keeping a lid on this," said Bennie, "Calling it a gang turf war. That doesn't help us using it in *King's Retribution* and telling the whole story."

Abbas added, "We would lose creditability going up against their present storyline."

Callie said nothing. She knew something they did not.

"They can't admit the general citizenry got wind of a terrorist plot," surmised Samantha, "and all their billions spent on intelligence gathering missed all the road sign of clues." Fox agreed.

"They have egg on their face and are pissed and they have the power to react and cause us all misery. The Studioz office has already been put on notice the F.B.I. and the C.I.A. want formal sit downs with all the principal stars and management."

"Speaking of which," Samantha turned to Callie, asking gently,

"How is Storm doing today?"

"Much improved, though the doctors think he may be crippled in his legs. Rehab will tell.

He's a fighter."

That brought silence to the conference room. Beyond the genuine concern for his recovery, the underlying message was clear: a bounty hunter who could not chase the bad guys signaled the death knell to *King's Retribution*. Fox looked with empathy to Callie, seeing that she might face the hard facts of life: possible unemployment. He still wondered on how her relationship with Storm would weather his handicap.

Fox brought them back on track, after all he was co-funding this strange adventure.

"We set out to capture bin Laden, we failed. We gained access to his house, but had one of our own killed, murdered before our eyes. We played this game of clues and stopped irrational killers from hurting others, American citizens. I don't care if all we did ever becomes a television exclusive. To hell with pandering to a fickle public audience; real life is sometimes not in our destiny to create it as we see fit. Now, we just need to pack it in, and resume our day jobs."

Depression descended at the thought of breaking up the camaraderie of the Team.

"What do you think, Wen?" asked Samantha, and all turned to him. In the midst of everyone's genius, skills, and talent, this mysterious silent man had become their solid anchor, centered stability.

His cell phone buzzed. He answered, listened, and then put the phone down on the table and pushed the 'Speakerphone'.

"Please repeat," said Holmes, "And do so very succinctly."

The voice on the other end, enunciated with clarity, as if to convey the import.

"Three tractor trailer trucks are heading west, your direction. Each are carrying nuclear waste by-products. I know they are going to Denver, then south to New Mexico, and then west from there. They are not crossing the Rocky Mountains. I do not know their destination. I don't know how potent their cargoes are but I've been told they have adequate security. There will be no reaction on our end. We don't have any confirming chatter this is a viable threat."

"*Wellspring*," said Samantha, knowing and fearful.

"Crimson Scimitar was a multi-attack operation," affirmed Holmes. "Small feints at amusement parks, then the knock-out punch when we're not expecting it. Damn bin Laden's ghost. He's out for revenge."

"When are the trucks leaving?" queried Fox, all thoughts of dismantling the Team no longer a subject of discussion.

"They left the nuclear generating station on Monday, the 29th."

"Ay Dios mio," exclaimed Callie. "Wherever they're going, they're almost there."

116.

September 1st Thursday   Las Vegas, Nevada

"Brother Khalaf, Allah blesses you on your timely arrival."

"And may Allah bring you and our cause much success."

Khalaf, tired and worn from his cross-country flight, accepted the stilted formal greeting as Shahin motioned him into the large warehouse room, their staging area, situated close to Vegas's McCarran International Airport. Khalaf would say nothing about the failed amusement park attacks. He knew Shahin's temperament would be explosive for he had lost two of his men with no publicity gain for al-Qaeda. In the compartmentalization of Crimson Scimitar to protect each element from discovery, Shahin was unaware of the stock market manipulations tied to the bombings, and to learn that Khalaf held a role in that part of the operation would only foment the man's wrath.

Khalaf was informed that the attack force was present. Shanin did not make introductions. Names did not matter. Khalaf walked with them over to the model which had been brought in from California and set up. Any stranger looking at it would see a model landscape, a miniature layout of the Hoover Dam and a bridge arching the surrounding canyon.

The attack would be located 30 miles northeast of Las Vegas.

"I was just about to do our final rehearsal," said Shahin. Stepping up to the layout Khalaf watched the stern faces who likewise were giving the table their concentration, except for one man, who seemed to inspect him. The stare left Khalaf uncomfortable. He accepted that some would not like his late arrival and his desire to be a participant, but he could live with such minor aggravation.

"Our current update is that we expect the trucks crossing the bridge sometime tomorrow morning." The man who spoke Khalaf knew was the *The Professor*. He stood within a group of four young men, who gave him deference that a learned man might come to expect, a leader with his cadre of followers. One of the former students was absent, they were told, somewhere on the highway, having traveled and met up with the trucks coming their way, now tracking, unobserved, with cell phone updates.

"There are two blind spots on either side of the bridge," began Shahin, using a laser pointer. "Force One [part of the Professor's cell], on the Arizona side, will have posted construction slow down signs a mile back to have the trucks reduce their separation. By the time they reach the bridge, we want them close together. After the last truck goes past, Force One will close the road for a construction delay, hopefully blocking out the last escort vehicle. They, and any other auto traffic, will be told it will be a twenty minute delay. That is when our time clock will begin. Twenty minutes to hijack the trucks and depart."

Khalaf found Shahin's explanation interesting. He knew the truth, knowing the scope of the entire operation, from bin Laden's computer thumb drive. They were to destroy the trucks on the bridge, not steal them. Khalaf guessed the reason for such subterfuge. The Professor's cell, those who were going to block either end of the bridge, to keep traffic away, were not privy to the entire plan. Younger without battlefield experience, they were better as programmed robots, blinded by enthusiasm for whatever private motivation. Just like most of the 9/11 hijackers. All were not informed. They carried out a hijacking, not realizing Atta and the selected al-Qaeda pilots were on a suicide mission. Khalaf had no reason to say anything. The plan was to destroy and escape. Shahin would not kill himself, believed Khalaf, knowing the man's ambition, equal to his own, the reason for their competiveness among al-Qaeda. He must have a good tactical reason for this lie.

Force Two, as the attack groups were named, *the Professor* and two of his cell members would block traffic with similar construction delays on the Nevada side of the bridge.

Shahin mildly laughed imparting this directive.

"As of yesterday, the Americans are so ignorant to what is about to be brought upon their heads. We drove across the dam on the old road which is now a dead-end turn-around. They still have police with a checkpoint believing someone like us would drive onto the dam and blow up such a formidable place with near 7 million tons of poured concrete. And yet, there is no slow down or police surveillance on the bridge, their weakest point."

By the scenario to this point, the road was blocked. Any stray auto traffic would be allowed to proceed by one of Shahin's personal team, part of Force Three, dressed in a facsimile Nevada

State Highway Patrol uniform. Only the trucks, with both convoy escorts blocked to either side of the bridge, out of sight, would remain. Their fate would be left to Force Three, the professionals from Yemen.

Khalaf was told he would be in a honored position with Force Three and that he would partner with a man introduced only as Razzor, who would instruct him as to his position. Beyond that, he heard nothing of his participation in the plan. Nor did they offer him a firearm. It seemed Force Three, as Khalaf himself had seen in Southwestern Pakistan where they practiced on an abandoned bridge, were prepared and confident and they did not need a refresher. Was that over confidence or again hiding their plan from the others?

A few minutes later, they broke into subgroups, to quietly discuss each Force's assignment. Khalaf, Shahin and The Professor, along with the man called Razzor, went off to the side to talk in general terms.

"And where did you fly in from," asked Shahin. "And when do you plan to depart?"

By his tone Khalaf knew Shahin was unhappy at his appearance on the scene, so he lied to inflate his value to the operation.

"I recently came from London to New York, and will return the same way. I have been asked to report directly back to our new leader Doctor al-Zawahiri on your success." The first lie. "I have been asked to stay in London to handle any international ramifications of your attack.

"To see if it can gain us further believers out of the Britain mosques." His second lie. In truth, he had stepped beyond his mission and was on his own.

All three men listened without comment. Hopefully, they saw him as valuable to what was going to transpire, of that he still had no idea what his role would be, so he asked.

"And what do you ask of me tomorrow."

"Very simply," said Shahin, twisting his mouth to a low snarl. "You and our brother Razzor will kill the driver and guard in the first truck."

Later, when *The Professor* left taking Khalaf to his motel accommodation for the night, saying he would be at his door the next morning at 5 a.m. for the drive to the bridge, Razzor had asked of Shahin.

"He must be of some importance if he is speaking to al-Zawahiri."

"He is merely a messenger boy. Leave him as a martyr on the bridge. I will tell our new Leader of our success, as it should be."

"His martyrdom is assured."

117.

1st Thursday Washington, D.C.

Acting Deputy Director Ronald Givens initiated the call to the head of the National Regulatory Commission, who served with him on the nuclear waste taskforce committee.

"I have been giving some thought to the convoy on the road. With 9/11 approaching Homeland Security has put out the appropriate 'Alert' warning, perhaps it might be a good idea that we beef up security along the route."

"You have heard something?"

"No, nothing at all." Meaning, he had no verifiable evidence; rumors as he saw them.

"Well, that's good. We can't turn the trucks around. We have no place to put them. It would be a logistical nightmare, especially with the death at Indian Point of their main transit manager a couple of days ago."

"Death?"

"Auto accident. Ran off the road, broke his neck. We're kinda in the fix we have to finish this one trip since Singh put it in motion and prepared all the routing.

"Too bad. Well, yes, I agree, it must be completed. Forget my request."

"Well, we don't want to draw attention to our cargo; that's the way it was planned."

"You said the man who died, his name was 'Singh'? Is that a..." Givens wanted to say, 'was the man a Moslem; was Singh a Moslem name?'

"Singh is Sikh, immigrated from India. His family is back there," said the plant manager; "but they can't seem to find any of them to let them know of his passing. Probably will have to do the funeral in New York, and send his ashes back to be poured into the Ganges."

Givens ended the conversation somewhat relieved. He felt his call had been ill advised, that he was only on edge from his White House meeting, and what Brady had said of Holmes's wild theories. He needed to think of a solution to put the ex-CIA agent out of everyone's reach.

Too bad he had no say-so over the Black Ops division. Like the dead Hindi, a simple car accident would rid him of an intrusive thorn.

How true to the times; religious ignorance had pervaded the conversation. Singh was not Hindu. Hinduism cremated their dead and placed their ashes in the Ganges River, home of the Ganga maa (the goddess who removes sins). What Singh had purported to be was of the Sikh faith, a monotheistic religion of 30 million followers, the fifth largest religion in the world. It did not matter. Singh, in truth, had been in secret an Islamic radical, murdered as part of a greater scheme, and his body lay in a funeral home, against all tenets of his hidden faith, awaiting instructions as to his final place of burial, wherever, and under whatever religious mantra the final choice would essentially be wrong, all except the 'ash to ash, dust to dust' part.

118.

September 1st Thursday Santa Monica

Wednesday into Thursday saw a frenzied rush, each hustling to their assignments, all without a clue of where the ending might lead.

Bennie serviced both the TV show's film equipment van and the lethally armored Storm Wagon. Pacheco worked with Abbas inventorying the various equipment, moving duplication of weapons from the Wagon to the Van. Pacheco, with an unlimited budget, made the point to add gas masks, even a couple of glide parachutes to both vehicles to the humor of both Abbas and Bennie, until they wondered if they were expected to be the jumpers if the circumstances presented themselves.

At 10 a.m. on Thursday the *King's Retribution* van with Bennie and Abbas departed, along with CAM TWO, with the strange directions to take I-15 east to Las Vegas and then continue on Highway 95 into Arizona. They were to keep their eyes open for three trucks escorted by either military or unmarked vehicles in convoy fashion. They were to drive into New Mexico until these trucks were located.

Later in the afternoon, Pacheco would follow in the Storm Wagon, with CAM ONE. He was to meet in Las Vegas, Callie, Fox, Samantha and Holmes who would fly in. Callie and Holmes would join Pacheco and then begin to proceed east following the route *King's Retribution* van.

Meanwhile, Fox and Samantha planned to take to a private helicopter and fly from Vegas along the Highway 95 Road and to act as spotters, looking for anything unusual.

To these decisions they had taken a circuitous journey, and the dialogue between the principals revealed their struggle.

"So, we are in agreement that another attack is going to occur, and against this truck shipment?" Fox again found himself as the designated chair person.

"Yes." A collective consensus.

"Beyond, Holmes's contact at his old place of work, we have no more information," said Callie. "And it seems we can't go out and scream warnings. What if we got it all wrong?"

"Let alone looking like fools to a predatory press," agreed Samantha, "I think there must be a dozen Federal laws we would break interfering with a government shipment."

"If my contact is correct," began Holmes, his mind juggling, "then the assumption doesn't jibe the trucks will be driven over the Rockies up I-70 and their radioactive cargo dumped into streams on the Continental Divide. And I just don't see that as the flash and flamboyance that al-Qaeda uses as its signature attack.

"However, if they go south to New Mexico and then west, I see too many opportunities."

"Like what?" Fox could wonder but he preferred to have a visual reference.

"Let's say the trucks reach Las Vegas. They can go north into Utah, west to L.A., or south to San Diego. If I felt those trucks carried a 'dirty bomb' that al-Qaeda could detonate we might presume they would try to explode it in Las Vegas, courtesy of Stephen King."

"The author?"

"Ali Baba may have picked up a copy of *The Stand* by Stephen King. In the end the bad guys explode a nuclear bomb and destroy Las Vegas."

"That's what they call an oxymoron, isn't it?" Weak smiles at Fox's humor.

"I don't see wasting a nuclear incident on Sin City," said Holmes, dismissive to the possibility, "Even though a million people live in the metropolitan area. L.A. would be a more dramatic target. But if they have the makings of a bomb, their targets should be New York or Washington, D.C. Seats of power."

"Well, let's revisit Ali Baba's books and movies. He mixed the disaster themes of a roller coaster and a subway high jacking. What if..." and she looked at the board list of all they had seen in Abbottabad. "How about Clancy's *'Dead or Alive'* and that old copy of *'Wellspring'*. Both have water elements, one a poison dumped into Rocky Mountain rivers at the Continental Divide, the other, a nuclear incident at Yucca Mountain that impacts groundwater."

Callie weighed in each hand, "Nuclear waste products and water pollution." They watched as she clasped her hands as in a fisted prayer, her elbows on the table. "You bridge these together, and what have we got?"

Holmes stared at her gripped hands and heard her last words.

"That's it. *Bridge.* A bridge, not just any bridge. That new bridge that spans the Colorado River at the Hoover Dam."

Fox quickly Googled on his laptop. "The Mike O'Callaghan—Pat Tillman Memorial Bridge, second highest in the U.S. after the Royal Gorge Bridge. It carries Route 93 over the Colorado River between Arizona and Nevada. Opened in October, 2010."

"Plenty of time to be developed into this Crimson Scimitar plan," said Samantha, starting to understand what might be the target. "Look up The Colorado River."

Fox did so, and read, skimming, "The principal river of the southwestern United States and northwest Mexico...The Colorado's steep drop through its gorges is utilized for the generation of significant hydroelectric power, and its major dams regulate peaking power demands in much of the Intermountain West...The river is a vital source of water for agricultural and urban areas and furnishes water for irrigation and municipal supplies of almost 40 million people both inside and outside the watershed."

Holmes summed up the growing truth. "Blow up one truck or all three and drop the contents off the bridge. Poison the river with radioactive pollution. Destroy crops, make tap water undrinkable. Perhaps not instant death but the panic, a massive fleeing population eastward would overwhelm all services, collapse our entire economy. It's diabolical, and all out of the creative minds of our own best writers/directors, instigated by crazed zealots." He concluded somberly. "The attack will happen on the bridge."

The rest looked stunned.

Finally, Samantha asked the all-important question: "But when will they strike?"

Fox called in Gizmo, the computer nerd of the War Room.

"What is your estimation of arrival? We think the attack will come at the Nevada-Arizona Border."

Gizmo pulled his hand-held P.A. and reconfigured all the assumptions he had been given; departure time he knew; speed of trucks to stay near the speed limit; definite stops for tired drivers, anticipating they were union drivers with required breaks.

"Best guess; sometime on the 2nd, barring unforeseen delays."

"Shit," said Fox. "That's tomorrow."

"We should notify somebody, the authorities, everybody," suggested the practical Samantha.

"Full circle to our earlier conversation: who's going to believe us?"

Holmes offered the compromise.

"I will let all the authorities know what we believe will happen. I will make it from me, and assume all the blame. Gitmo is probably lovely this time of year. But until we identify an Arab-looking terror group heading towards government trucks carrying radioactive materials do I believe we will be taken seriously."

Fox put forth a reality check. "And if we're wrong and it's not at the bridge, but they strike somewhere else, as bad?"

"America is in for a nuclear winter," said Holmes. No one was smiling as the ramifications sank in.

119.

September 1st   Los Angeles, Las Vegas, Arizona

By the end of the day the King's Retribution's two vehicles were on the road heading out towards I-15, heading east to Vegas, and points beyond. The TV production van still had to locate the convoy somewhere on I-40 coming from Albuquerque. When discovered Abbas and Bennie were to give the trucks an unobserved escort. The Storm Wagon with Pacheco, Holmes, and Cardoza planned on being situated near the bridge's Nevada crossing. Hugh and Samantha, with Gizmo a last minute addition for computer logistical command, from the helicopter, would see the larger picture and could direct forces. Their problem, so far they could not find a last minute private helicopter lease with a pilot.

To the anticipation of what events might unfold the next day, September 2nd, 2011, there was a gravitational pull between the main players, into new coupled grouping, unexpected but perhaps not.

Hugh gave Callie a lift over to the hospital to check on Storm. The prognosis for recovery still guarded, with the doctor surprising them with a new setback. *Delirium tremens.*

"Did you know he was alcoholic?" the Doctor put forth the question, light in condemnation, knowing those closest usually never comprehend the signs.

"I knew he drank a lot, and a sloppy drunk," answered Callie.

"He must have hid the fact he was constantly ingesting alcohol. With his injuries, we can't put him into a cold turkey withdrawal. The sudden changes in his system could lead to a heart attack. We will need to keep him longer and try and wean him off this addiction. But to accomplish that he will a network of support. It is always a battle to walk away from the bottle."

Callie nodded, accepting Storm King had a disease that she had only responded to with anger.

Fox tried to offer her comfort, to say Storm's actions were of his doing.

This did not help, and Callie felt the guilt, which put her in a piss poor mood, and they said very little as he drove them back to her condo.

"See you tomorrow, early flight to Vegas."

"Yes," she said, exiting his car, somewhat numb to her emotions. Then, she stopped, and turned to him. "Hugh, you have been absolutely the best in what you have done. Without your drive and goals these assholes would have hurt a lot of people. Whatever happens tomorrow..."

She let the words hang, and turned and went in the building.

Hugh Fox, with his mental brilliance, could not in time splice together the proper response of his emotions. It was too far from his heart to his mind to his mouth.

Samantha Carlisle and Wendell Holmes had an entertaining dinner at a French restaurant on the 3rd Avenue Mall, as if the weight of 'whatever happens tomorrow' was indeed tomorrow, and those problems would be dealt with at that time.

Their conversation consisted of small talk, each exploring the other's history, listening to stories of how they became who they were. Samantha pestering to hear some of the agency secrets, Holmes gently declining talking more about what he should do in retirement, which brought a scoff from his dinner companion.

"Retire? You're too young. Why should you? Look at the troops you have mobilized, the confidence you have given all of us. I can now fire an Uzi without messing up my makeup."

They both laughed.

He heard her rags-to-couture biography, of her interest in the Save the Animals Foundation, and sensed when 'tomorrow' was over, she would be too eager to find a new thrill.

She asked him how his religious writing was going; was that going to be his retirement hobby?

"No, a mere exercise in applying my thoughts to solve a problem, creating a basis for tolerance among Medieval dogma. I have been a traveler in that world where violence has become a faith. I feel I could create a better utopia, one where we could actually live comfortably and safely."

"Again, I am impressed in seeing the deeper man."

He laughed at himself.

"Well, it helps to soothe my spirits, a release of sorts. Probably will go nowhere, but I am having our two professor friends you met give me critique, offer suggestions, and actually turn my prose, not into Western propaganda, but written from the eyes of someone, you know, like a person preaching in the wilderness. It will allow me perspective."

"I assume you will let me read it?"

"I would be honored."

The meal excellent, they talked on, like a couple, that both were coming to realize was a very pleasant experience, trying to ignore their barrier, she of society, bored by lacking purpose and he, as described by others, the cowboy, untethered, now unsure in a world he had avoided.

Perhaps they were more compatible because of their incompleteness than they yet realized.

Finally, as dinner ended, and over brandy, they came back to what had been avoided all evening, on all the Team's mind: the morrow.

"Do you really think the terrorists will be at the bridge?"

"One can't bet the farm, but if we believe Ali Baba plots come out of American books and movies, and pray they have no access to their own nuclear weapons, then, yes, dumping the trucks into the Colorado River, will be the last of the components of Crimson Scimitar, and we must stop them."

They sat in silence, understanding the daunting task before them, seeing this craziness as being Citizen Soldiers, as Minute Men rushing to, so to speak, the Concord Bridge. The answer they saw before them on the street—other couples, shoppers, families out for an evening stroll, listening to the street musicians, and with all urban freedoms, avoiding the beggars or in kindness proffering a token dollar so to the less fortunate for solace in food, shelter, even cheap wine escapism. All they asked for was peace and happiness and some cretins wished on them the worst.

"Let me ask you something," said Holmes, "about the first part of the Crimson Scimitar operation."

"Yes?"

"Do you have good contacts in the New York financial industry? I mean like owners of stockbrokerage houses, even officials on the stock exchanges?"

"Why, yes, of course. I have been a major charity maven." She didn't want to tell him the president of the largest investment bank in the country personally handled her portfolio. "Why, do you ask?"

"I think we might have been remiss in not using our talents, your talents most particular in this situation, in tracking down who might have been selling those entertainment stocks short against the amusement park attacks."

"Wendell, you're right. I forgot about that direction. I think we might be able to do that.

As they say, 'Let's follow the money.'"

They were both silent for a moment. "Back to my al-Qaeda spider analogy," Holmes spoke, with deep voice determination, "If we are lucky the authorities, or us, are going to locate the Spider's legs and chop them off, but in the end, we need to sever the head." He paused in his thoughts. "Or graft on a new head."

Lost in these thoughts he told her he would forego her limousine invitation and walk back to his hotel, to enjoy the warmth of the night and to think. No doubt, she considered, like a spiritual monk, he would be seeking his center of calm, preparing, sharpening his senses. She now knew him better, expected him to understand they were connecting and let him work out his own feelings.

Where the Team had all interpreted the character of Wendell Holmes as being this governmental action-hero spook, Samantha knew it was only a part of the whole. She had come to discover a man introspective of life, methodical in his observations, consuming when in participation. Tonight, he had opened himself up just enough for her to look in and she liked what she saw. In that revelation, within her own core, she gained a new insight, a feeling of deep attraction towards Wendell Holmes, a desire to be with someone, not for the credentials, nor bank account but for the individual's inner worth, a valuation unique in her world. Samantha dare not define her feelings, for if tomorrow would bring disaster, losing him would hurt deep; and if they survived, then, it would probably become the worst of all passions, *unrequited love.*

120.

Friday, September 2nd   somewhere in the United States of America

In the Storm Wagon as they approached the bridge, Holmes placed his telephone calls, several of them anonymous.

To Matthew Brady [8 a.m. in Washington, D.C.] he explained what *King's Retribution* believed was about to occur. Brady would make his calls but still expected a disbelieving response. Holmes asked if Brady would place a call to the Nellis Airbase in Las Vegas, speak to the commander, and put him on notice that Federal Agents might need some help on a planned bust of a weapons stash. That they would understand. Brady said he would.

In his own form of Holmes's Retribution, he left a voice message with Ronald Givens:

"Hi, Wendell here, since you did not take my previous call [a lie] about the attacks on the amusement parks as serious, I wanted to give you a heads up, that terrorists will soon attack a government shipment of nuclear waste. You know all about it [another lie]. Have a nice day."

If what might occur occurred, that recorded call ought to do the trick for his own personal zinger...if Holmes was correct. If not, what could they do to him?

An anonymous call to the Las Vegas Metropolitan Police Department, a tourist passing by who thought he saw two suspicious people, Middle Eastern near Hoover Dam. He did not expect a SWAT team to show up, but he was hoping that some police witness would be sent to the bridge and in position to call in back up. No big deal if nothing materializes.

8 a.m. Abbas and Bennie radioed in. They were pretty certain they had located the convoy on the west side of Kingman, Arizona. In the early hours they had neck strain jerking around at all the different tractor trailers travelling the early hours on State Highway 93. What separated the final acquisition of target was the observation that these trucks had minimal signage, Eagle Freight, while all other trucking firms were plastered with brand advertising and most visible to confirmation, no gasoline tax

stamps nor multi-state license tags. Also noted were the two Hummers, darkened windows, one in front, one trailing the three trucks, both going right at the speed limit, not the usual modus operandi for tourists getting close to the neon destination of Las Vegas.

"The three trucks are strung out with a half mile of separation on each," said Bennie. "Two tractor trailers, the cabs both silver, and a tandem chemical truck in the center with a two tank hook-up. They look too pristine, we're pretty sure we got the right ones."

The Storm Wagon texted the message to Samantha in the privately hired Tourist helicopter. She responded they would be on top of them in half an hour. The helicopter had been rented, at a hefty price, from a Grand Canyon tour company, based in Vegas, so she and Hugh could make the pilot do a wide turn over the Hoover Dam and gain an open view of the O'Callaghan-Tillman Bridge.

Fox called into the two Teams on the ground. Reception was bad.

"Looks beautiful, quiet, and I see nothing unusual. Some construction crews working on the road. On both sides and near the bridge."

The helicopter pilot oblivious that he was in Command Central, ready to show them the sites, with the special tip on the side he was promised, blithely added his tour director comment.

"The bridge is the first concrete-steel composite arch built in the United States, and it incorporates the widest concrete arch in the Western Hemisphere. It is 840 feet above the Colorado River."

"Good to know," Samantha shouted back through the headphones. The pilot might be gaining the surprise of his life, not to be found in the tour guidebook.

Abbas and Bennie were trailing the convoy and not seeking to stand out placed themselves a car behind, not knowing the auto clunker in front of them, was a driver from The Professor's cell, appearing to be a college student heading back to his university, blending in with UNLV Rebel bumper stickers.

Shahin wearing a construction hard hat and an orange colored road vest swigged at a cup of water from the pickup truck. The heat, even this early in the morning, moved into the upper 90°s heading to the early fall norm in the desert of 110° range. He glanced at his watch. The first truck would be at the bridge in forty minutes. The duration of the attack no more than twenty minutes; the explosives to be timed out at 27 minutes, allowing escape, but only for two.

He and Razzor would be the only ones to leave the bridge alive. There would be no witnesses, no members of the attacking Force groups would survive to give up information. Razzor would handle the Professor's cell, he would dispatch his own comrades after the bomb detonations, when the trucks and their contents spilled into the river. His men had pledged to Crimson Scimitar to give their lives, not expecting death would come from a friendly hand. That was what was so funny and ironic about the bridge. He had read where the bridge's namesake, this Pat Tillman, played U.S. football, but quit to join the Army, only to be killed in Afghanistan, and by friendly fire, killed by his own fellow soldiers. Friendly fire today would anoint this bridge with martyr blood. He only wished he would be in a good viewing position to see when Razzor dispatched the troublesome Khalaf; but no mind, the trucks were the priority.

121.

9:10 a.m. Detective Chase Taggart of the Las Vegas Metropolitan Police Department, nibbling a sprinkled donut and drinking her second cup of coffee from a thermos received a computer message in her unmarked patrol car: *Please check and advise on report of suspicious behavior on 93 bridge.* Shit, if it couldn't get any worse, she thought. Please not a jumper. The bridge highway traffic had been opened less than a year, and with a scenic walkway attached on the eastern side, with a spectacular view of Hoover Dam, the bets were on when the first suicide would take the plunge.

She rolled down her window, and shouted to the two U.S. Bureau of Reclamation officers manning the tourist checkpoint access road leading to the dam.

"Everything okay here?" When she got a thumbs up, she replied, "Making a routine run on the bridge, will be back."

The Metropolitan Police Department covered all of Clark County which included Las Vegas, Lake Mead and Hoover Dam. Within the Federal boundaries of the Hoover Dam usually Nevada State Patrol and Metro Police steered clear of overlapping jurisdictions with the Feds, but in this case, Detective Taggart had been assigned to a solitary outpost as part of her trip in purgatory. Caught up in an officer involved shooting three months back, she being the shooter, Chase had been thrust into the middle of an tug-of-war between Internal Affairs and the Sheriff's political fortunes, and while not calling it a suspension, since to some she was still the department's first female heroine (another story), to others her exile to the boonies was not punishment enough.

Bored, and perspiring from a strained air conditioner spitting at her, she turned her car up the dam access road towards its junction with Highway 93 and the O'Callaghan-Tillman Memorial Bridge.

9:20 a.m. Text message to Shahin from tracking car behind the convoy: *1st Target @ bridge--two minutes*

Nevada side: Receiving a hand wave from Shahin Attack Force Two consisting of *The Professor* and two of his men jumped from a State Highway pick-up truck and threw up the barricades across east-bound side of the highway, with a printed sign:

Construction Delays: 15 – 30 minutes. In State Highway vests the Professor's men begin waving a Slow/Stop sign at the slowing traffic. Near their feet under a tarp were two submachine guns. The Professor returned to his pick-up and watched as a State Highway Department marked van carrying Shanin, Razzor and Khalaf moved on to the bridge.

Khalaf was uneasy. He has been handed a 9 mm Barretta. Razzor looked to have armed himself with the same weapon, plus a submachine gun rested on his lap. Shahin was armed with a large caliber .45 Smith & Wesson. In the van were the pre-packaged C-4 explosives with attached timers. On the Arizona side, a pickup with three of Shanin's team move onto the bridge.

The pickup positions itself half way on the bridge. In this vehicle is the ordinance specialist with the task of setting and arming all explosive charges. Another terrorist in a Nevada Highway Patrolman disguise gets out and starts directing the few vehi-cles moving across after the roadblocks have been put in place.

9:22 a.m. *The Professor* texts a message to those on the Arizona side the make and model of the last tourist car crossing behind the barricade going west to east. They immediately exit their phony Highway Department truck and begin erecting barricades on the west side of traffic redirecting the flow into a congested one lane.

This occurred because a large concrete median, chest-high runs the length of the bridge.

Another concrete short wall separates the highway from the tourist walkway. Shahin and his team would have had to blow up both of these barriers with unforeseen consequences and too much time would have been expended. Answer: re-route the ongoing trucks into a one lane which in turn would bunch up the trucks, placing all three onto the bridge.

9:23 a.m. The lead escort vehicle crosses the bridge into Nevada and when he passes the road barrier, the barricade is put in place across all four lanes of traffic. From the drop and curvature of the highway the escort vehicle can no longer see the bridge, and it will take three critical minutes before the Hummer driver realizes the lead truck is not behind him. The driver of the Indian

Point load of spent fuel rods slows down seeing a construction worker [Shahin] standing in the middle of the bridge waving a yellow flag.

122.

9:24 a.m. All hell begins to break loose simultaneously.

Fox with binoculars from the helicopter which is stationary high above the Colorado River with view of both bridge and dam calls into the Storm Wagon.

He yells over his phone: "Construction crews are shutting down the bridge, re-routing traffic."

"It *is* the bridge," whoops Pacheco, an awed glance to Holmes, and as the driver of the Storm Wagon, Shawn pulls on Highway 93 from the road shoulder near the access road. He does not realize that as he picks up speed he is catching up to Detective Taggart's unmarked police vehicle.

Samantha, passenger in the front helicopter seat turns to the computer nerd. "Light up the switchboard, Giz." Gizmo sends out a pre-arranged wi-fi email to Metro police and FBI, with *"This is no drill. I repeat this is no drill."* A modification on the Pearl Harbor attack news-to-the-world.

From Holmes: "Do you see the trucks?"

Fox: "One is stopping on the bridge, the other, the tanker is a quarter of a mile from it."

Holmes: "And the third?"

Fox: "Maybe in the distance, yes, a good mile away."

Holmes: "You need to stop that truck from going on the bridge."

Abbas: "We're on it."

Samantha turned to Hugh. "They may need some help. At least a show of force to make the driver think about stopping."

The tour helicopter pilot asked, "What are you all talking about?" And then went into near shock watching the lady next to him pull out a machine pistol from her Gucci bag.

"We need you to head down to the highway now! Please do so immediately or I will try and fly this meat grinder myself and you won't get this bonus." She dropped two packets of hundred dollar bills into the pilot's lap.

123.

On the bridge--

Shahin shot the guard in the first truck through the front window. The driver panicking jumped from cab and started to run and from Razzor he received two bullets in the back, sending the man's body sprawling onto the highway.

Trained to the mission, Shahin's ordinance man, arriving in their pickup truck, grabs from the back of the van two parcel satchel charges, running to the side of the bridge on the river's downstream side, and affixing one of the satchel charges, setting the timer for three minutes, the other charge would be affixed the undercarriage of the truck's trailer, enough explosives to blow the cargo into the canyon below. That charge was set twenty minutes, to detonate when all of them have left the bridge.

Khalaf followed behind, not knowing what to do. The slaying of the guard and driver did not unnerve him as he had seen battlefield death, yet he felt out of place. Yes, that was it. They brought him along, armed him, but gave him no assignment. He found this strange at the same time was caught up in the excitement of the attack in progress.

Suddenly, from across the highway he looked into the eyes of a group of Asian tourists on the scenic walkway, frozen like deer in the headlights, paralyzed to the sounds of shooting.

Razzor turned their way, beginning to shift from his pistol to the submachine gun. Khalaf knew instinctively this man held no morals, was a stone killer, who would see the tourists as collateral damage worthy of wiping them up for a better headline. To Khalaf, this was not about a body count tally but about the trucks, about revenge for America's foreign policy against Muslims, about al-Qaeda achieving world supremacy.

Khalaf fired at the tourists, aiming low at the concrete, the gunfire achieving the effect of scaring them. In crouching screams along the catwalk pedestrian bridge they ran, but not before two of them snapped photos at him. Crazy.

Even crazier, a shock came to Khalaf, his missed firing did not throw up in flying rock chip from ricochet against the concrete. He looked down at his pistol, a shock of dreadful comprehension-

-he was firing blanks. Razzor was the one who handed him the gun before the operation had begun. He was defenseless.

Arizona side of the bridge—

Bennie accelerated the van into the passing lane, pushing the speed up to 85 mph.

Quickly, the van overtook several cars, including the trailing escort car, who stared back at them, with concern. Abbas, who is Arabic, smiled at them, not the best time to do so.

In his driving Bennie forced an oncoming car to squeal into the shoulder gravel. That alerted everyone on the road. Passing the trailer truck, the last one in the covoy, which was now coming up on the bridge, he began one of his patented TV show daredevil, slamming fishtails, finding himself in a reverse position facing the truck, with the driver standing on his brakes, as Bennie did the same.

The smoke of burned rubber floated the air. Abbas and Bennie jumped out and raised their hands in warning. The guard in truck cab only saw the Middle Eastern resemblance of Abbas, pulled his gun, leaned out the window and began firing. Bennie retrieved weapons for both he and Abbas but did not start firing; this was for self-protection, and just in time. The two guards from the escort vehicle ran up to the truck trailer and with the other guard began unleashing a wild fusillade at the *King's Retribution* van.

A moment later two simultaneous events occurred which changed the field of battle. One of the men guarding the trailer truck pitched over, grabbing his shoulder. The shot had come from behind him, from the one cell member who had been following the truck caravan.

A bullet dinged into the van right above Abbas's head. The construction crew members, again from The Professor's squad, had been startled when this van had screeched in front of the truck trailer, halting its progress onto the bridge. They had no time to understand what was happening; the men grabbed their weapons and began firing, one with machine gun, the other with an automatic pistol. Perhaps they hoped the two and his other companion could gain control over the truck and still have time to drive it to the bridge with the other two trucks.

Abbas and Bennie ran to the front of the van returning fire towards the bridge.

The driver and guards, carrying their wounded comrade, taking rapid fire from behind them, while watching their Hummer blow up, moved to a secure position ahead of the truck cab.

Abbas smiled at one of the guards. Abbas was not shooting at him, but someone was shooting at both of them, from different directions. He gave a quizzical smile of 'what the shit' and began firing back at the rear attacker. All of them came to the same conclusion--the truck and its contents must be protected with their lives.

124.

On the Nevada side—

Detective Taggart had just pulled onto Highway 93 when she saw the eastward line of cars, backed up, bottlenecked.

Shit, she sighed, it was a jumper.

Just then, a large white truck van raced past her car. Must be Emergency Medical volunteers, she considered. Instinctively, she turned on her own flashing lights and put the mobile light on her car's roof and turned on the siren.

Quickly, racing to catch up, she saw an unprecedented action, the van blew through a construction barricade, smashing it to bits, sending a worker jumping to the side. *What the---.*

She could only follow and her real shock came when once she drove past the destroyed barricade, her back window blew out. *Holy---*. A quick glance saw one construction worker in a yellow vest and hard hat firing a machine gun at her.

Trying to keep her head low, beneath the dash, avoiding a bullet to the head, she grabbed at her radio and shouted out in a hurried quick breath. "Shots fired at the Tillman Bridge!"

Deranged construction worker armed and shooting. Approach with extreme caution."

She gave one second in consideration she should stop and deal with the armed man, but something was not right. This was not about a jumper. Whatever was happening, the answer was with the speeding white van.

On the bridge –

Shahin saw the tanker trailer slowing down and began his approach, his gun hidden behind his back, which did not matter. The two dead men on the highway would be noticed within seconds, and they were. The Highway Patrolman, slowing down this truck, pulled his service revolver, dropped to his knee, took careful aim and put a bullet through the glass into the brain of the truck guard, the driver instead of being shocked, ducked. So, Shanin moved forward to dispatch the driver, when he heard...what...a siren.

A siren, it could not be.

His phone rang out a text. *'Third truck stopped. Guard shooting but not at us. Will try to capture.'*

What was going on?

A white truck raced onto the bridge, and spun to a halt blocking the roadway. Three people jumped out, firing...at them!

Shahin turned his head back to the driver of the trailer truck who had not waited to be shot dead, but was taking off, running in a zigzag over the middle concrete barrier, following over the walkway concrete. The Highway Patrol terrorist fired off several harmless and ineffectual shots. The truck was in their hands, but Shahin found himself crouching in protection, as bullets began to ping close by. Crimson Scimitar, his operation, was starting to unravel. But why? And then he knew...the attack on bin Laden's compound, captured secrets compromised Crimson Scimitar.

The Americans knew but why did not they attack sooner? Was this a trap? Did those vehicles really contain radioactive waste that could poison the entire Colorado River watershed?

He gained control of the truth. No, there had been surprise. Americans did not let their own people, drivers and guards be slaughtered. He must go forward and destroy the trucks.

Shahin spied Razzor heading toward the tractor trailer with the liquid cargo. Yes, that was the primary target. The occupants of the white van were close to the first truck and besides it was already wired. These unknown attackers would only discover they were too late when the bridge railings would explode and the truck blown into the river. He began a slow retreat, firing as he could.

Panting, now near Razzor, he asked, "Where's Khalaf?"

"He ran back to our truck."

"Right into their arms. With their torture he will give it all away."

"I will go kill him." And Razzor ran to the other side of the trailer truck and began a stealth crouch walk towards where had last seen Khalaf, cowering at their van.

Shahin's ordinance man reached him with two new satchel charges.

"What of the third truck? Where is it?"

He shouted above the increasing gunfire. "Forget it. Concentrate on this truck, and make sure you set the strongest charge on the back container. We have to angle the front over the edge, so it will all fall into the river." The man nodded, and ran off to set the charges, as he had done at the first truck, one against the bridge siding, the others on the truck. This time with the two tank trailer configuration, each unit would receive an explosive package.

Shahin did a sweeping spray of his weapon towards the white van, not believing he would hit anyone. He glanced at his watch. If he could keep them under cover for at least ten minutes, Crimson Scimitar would succeed, in some part.

125.

Sean jumped from the driver side, Holmes from the passenger side, and Callie out the back. Holmes laid down a covering fire as each took a protective position. They were receiving returning fire but it seemed haphazard.

Before them, they could see the field of fire. Two Highway construction trucks, one pick-up, one side-slide door van were to their front, behind that, what Holmes knew was the government waste carriers, with unmoving forms on the ground. Damn, if he could only have known with more certainty the bridge was the target, they could have stopped all three trucks earlier. His milisecond reverie broke as Sean Pacheco, rose from a crouch, and with a tight formation of concentrated shots killed a man who tried running from the front of the second truck, his pistol firing at them.

"You just shot a Highway Patrolman," yelled Holmes.

"He was shooting at us, if that matters. Ours or theirs, we'll sort it out later," said Pacheco. Holmes could respect under fire decisions. Besides he knew all on the bridge were assuredly the bad asses.

"Good shot. Guess they train our military boys well," a yell from Callie, pot shotting toward the trucks.

"Please aim at men not at the two trucks." Holmes admonished knowing the silent radiating killer which could be unleashed with an errant bullet or explosion.

Though keeping their focus ahead, they heard the approaching siren and saw uncontrollable skid braking as the car became an attracting pegboard of automatic fire its front end going from smoke into a burst of flames under the hood.

Scrambling from behind driver side, came a woman, dressed as police officer, a fire arm in her hand. She caught her breath then ran to the Storm Wagon, crouching behind Callie.

"What the fuck is going on?"

"Al-Qaeda's attempt to outdo 9.11" said Callie casually as if they were girlfriends at cocktails, still sighting her aim down the roadway. "And you are who, that's joined our *bridge* game?"

"Detective Taggart, Metro Police. Stay where you are. We should half back up in about thirty minutes."

"Afraid not, ma'am," Holmes shouted from the other side of the van. "We are dealing with bombs and timers. They're trying to blow up the trucks, toxic chemicals we don't want to see go into the river."

Detective Taggart moved to the man behind the voice.

"And who the fuck are you people anyway?"

"Wendell Holmes, ex-CIA, at your service."

Callie called out, "Carlita Cardoza, ex-San Diego Police. Got your back, Detective."

A third voice of the posse. "Shawn Pacheco, Seal Team Six, on medical leave. I am spotting an IED tied to the bridge."

Damn, must be insubordinate misfits, like her, and hunkering down, Detective Taggart smiled. "Okay, what's the plan?"

Could be no plainer to Holmes, "Shawn, I need to get you to the bomb, ASAP."

"Roger."

"Hold a second," said Callie. She saw this man running between trucks, and reaching the pick up door through it open and aimed his gun inside, saying something at the same time, she took careful aim and fired. The truck window blew out and the gunman dropped to the ground, scrambling for safety. "Damn, missed."

"But you flushed out more quarry," said Detective Taggart, watching another man bail out the pickup driver's side, and run up the road, and throw himself over the concrete median wall.

"Time's a wasting. Ladies, clear a path from around all those trucks. Shawn, we will give you covering fire and I will follow."

On the bridge—

Khalaf sat in the pickup and tried to gather his thoughts, to decide what he must do next.

He had been set up. Shahin had no need for him, and Razzor was to execute him. He could have been of help. Instead they gave him a pistol with no real ammunition. He began to understand Shahin wanted no one to receive glory for Crimson Scimitar except himself. Yet, now the entire operation was caving in, and more so the leader of this expedition wanted no one to put the spin on failure except himself.

He must flee that was certain. Just as he turned the key in the ignition, the passenger door was thrown open, and he looked down the machine gun barrel at Razzor.

"A coward ready to flee."

"I would die as a worthy jidhast, not to be shot in the back by scum like you."

"No, I am going to shoot you in the front." The window blew out and Razzor screamed and disappeared, Within the seconds of falling glass Khalaf was in a heightened frenzy, throwing himself from the truck, racing to mid highway, and tumbling over the wall there. He began to run to the Arizona side. The Americans had charged in from Nevada so it was no good trying to that way. Twenty yards up the road, he glanced over the barrier at the firefight. He was now parallel to the first tractor trailer. He could see that Razzor must have responded quick enough to take his place as the driver since the construction pick up he had fled had been driven up close to the second truck, the tandem tanker, what must contain liquid radioactive waste. One of Shahin's men were returning fire, while another prepared explosives on the truck. For the cause, that boded well that Crimson Scimitar might yet be salvaged.

He saw Razzor talking with Shahin, and Razzor had cloth wrapped around his hand. He had been struck somehow by the Americans firing at them. Screw him, thought Khalaf, realizing he was a spectator and had no idea how to get off the bridge, alive.

In his position, peeking over the barrier, he saw a young man, definitely of soldier physique, run toward the first truck, armed and wearing a backpack. If this was military response there would have been more firepower, choppers overhead, though he had seen a tourist helicopter minutes ago. No, this man had purpose. And realization hit Khalaf. Bomb disposal.

They knew what was going to take place, they were prepared. Crimson Scimitar would fail if this man succeeded. Khalaf's loyalty was to al-Qaeda, although it seemed part of them had betrayed him. His desire to demonstrate his prowess had arrived. He had to stop the soldier, and it meant his certain death. He made his mind up. Without a weapon he would sprint across the highway and with the man's focus on dismantling the bomb, his weapon at his side, he would tackle him, and kill him. Such an idea came to him with such clarity and he understood what suicide bombers saw in that singular moment when they depressed the triggering mechanism. Before he charged to his questionable chance of being the hero, he glanced at the two people who were firing down the highway, pinning down the Attack Force, including Razzor and Shanin. He opened his mouth in the only way a devout Moslem might do, when he saw those defending the bridge were both women. And then he saw another, with a weapon within the white van. No, not a weapon...What is this? Allah, it cannot be so. That is a shoulder mounted camera being aimed through the window. They will be filming his death.

Khalaf took off running towards the man fiddling with the bomb both now knowing only minutes remained before its detonation.

Episode 17

"If you can kill a disbelieving American or European – especially the spiteful and filthy French – or an Australian, or a Canadian, or any other disbeliever from the disbelievers waging war, including the citizens of the countries that entered into a coalition against the Islamic State, ...kill the disbeliever whether he is civilian or military, for they have the same ruling."
--excerpt from Dabiq, ISIS/ISIL magazine

126.

On the Arizona side—

From above, in the tour helicopter, Hugh and Samantha could see the good guys below were pinned down. Two construction workers firing on them from the front, and one gunman who had moved up behind the burning escort Hummer and was firing at the guards and Bennie and Abbas from the rear.

"We need to take out the guy at the back," Fox's assessment. "Similar strategy in Level Eight -- Skilleo's *Attack of the Undead.*"

Samantha pointed down and spoke to the helicopter pilot, "Swing around, and come in behind that truck."

"I don't think I ought to. FAA rules. This is not my sanctioned flight pattern. I could lose my license."

What a wuss, she thought. "Today is your chance for 15 minutes of fame, or to make the tabloids as the biggest asshole in aviation." She turned to Fox. "Give me two of those fireworks we brought." He reached into a duffle bag and pulled out two flash-bang percussion grenades.

Samantha took both of them doing small flips in her hands.

"Now do you want me to activate one in here, or let me drop them on target?"

The gunman at the convoy's rear was ready to make his spring toward the trailer truck. If he could not kill the drivers and guards then he would try to angle a shot at the fuel tank and see if he could burn up the entire vehicle, truck and trailer. Behind him he could see the confusion and logjam of cars on the highway when angry drivers would pull up, see the gunfight, and turn to flee. At least no Highway Patrol element had tried to interfere. He threw a glance into the sky at the Grand Canyon tour helicopter circling. He should fire warning shots but they were a mere mosquito and he affirmed the truck had to be his own goal of destruction.

He felt he was in position to go for the gas tank when he heard the increasing rotor thumping of the helicopter, reducing altitude in its hovering. Dust blew into his eyes. He heard something plop at his feet. Looking down he saw the grenade, turning to flee, his foot hit a second one. Two explosions, a deafening noise, flung him into the roadway, away from his cover. Samantha's first shot took him the chest, spun him around. And one of the guards on the ground laced up the gunman with a staccato of dancing flesh shredding rounds.

"I see you have improved with practice," said Fox.

"Holmes offered me suggestions about accurate quick fire under non-ideal conditions."

Gizmo added in his own kind of compliment, "Gee, ma'am, you blew that man away."

"Yeah, life's not fair, is it?"

The helicopter landed behind what they perceived was the gunman's vehicle. One of the guards came running up from the truck to the helicopter. Fox jumped out.

"Thanks," said the guard, "they send you in as back-up?"

"You might say that," Fox could go along with that interpretation. "Listen, you know the truck you have been following carries highly radioactive materials?"

The guard agreed. "I guess you guys are cleared, huh?"

"You might say that. You need to take this truck turn it around, and give it close protection back to Kingman. Notify the local police to help meet and secure it. There's a fire fight going on the bridge and you all need to clear out and protect this truck."

Back in the helicopter, as it climbed upward, Fox radioed to Abbas, "You need to cause a distraction. They're going to try to turn their truck around and get out of there."

"I can do that. There not trying to kill us any longer. It is apparent they just want to pin us down to give their buddies on the bridge more time."

"We'll back you up, if you need us."

"Naw, this is my department: the art of scaring the hell out of people with fakery."

The helicopter passengers watched as Abbas rigged an enormous rubber band, a giant slingshot. The first launched missile, made up of non-lethal 2 pound black powder canister with a ten second fuse, hitting to the right of the roadway. The explosion as it was supposed to produced something like a whistling incoming howitzer round.

"They're definitely nervous now," shouted Bennie with glee, "Ten degrees left and another 5 degrees in arc."

The second round landed in front of the orange barrel barricade the men were firing from, pushing them back from cover.

"I think that did it. They are making a run to their truck." Bennie signaled at the helicopter which landed nearby. Everyone met in the middle of the highway in elated cheers and hugs. Abbas, Bennie, Samantha, Hugh, Gizmo, while CAM TWO filmed. All except the helicopter pilot who took the celebration as a diversion to power up and disappear into the sky.

"Remind me," said Hugh to all, "To buy that tour company and fire his sorry ass."

"What next?" from Abbas, pleased with his catapulting antics.

"Good question." said Samantha. At that moment they heard a large reverberating boom in the distance and saw smoke rise from the direction of the bridge. Fear entered their hearts, thinking only the worst.

127.

9:30 a.m. On the bridge

Piece of cake, Shawn said to himself, not trying to be cocky, just part of his constant SEAL training.

The IED was of standard configuration. It was the bomber who was too confident, believing since there would be no discovery standardization was best and no need to booby trap the wiring circuitry. They weren't even going to use a cell phone detonator, probably fearful they could not get service out in the desert. Old fashion timer with five minutes left. Piece of cake, until he felt the collision against his body.

For a half a second he thought the bomb self-detonated but took in he was alive and found by his reflexes he was rolling on the ground with someone trying to grab at his side arm in his holster. The man had retrieved the gun, but Pacheco held it firm and away from his body. He body punched the guy in the face, and slammed the man's hand down on the pavement breaking the gun away from their grasp, still within reach.

Hold on, there was something familiar about this. How this terrorist fought, the same choking neck hold he found himself in, the man trying to bite him on the arm to distract. Jeez, that night, the fight he never told anyone about. He pushed back and looked the man deep in the face. He was clean shaven but yes, this was...what did he shout at me?! Remembering, Shawn shouted in vehemence at the terrorist.

"Caliph! Calaf!"

Khalaf in the moment made the same recognition, a shock in realizing the SEALS knew about Crimson Scimitar. And this man, the soldier who--.

"Cairo! Cairo!" In crazy recognition he screamed at the soldier, his free hand grasped the soldier's gun and brought it up towards the man's head. He had won, the bridge would explode, he would die, but Crimson Scimitar was assured.

Khalaf's world went black.

Afraid of killing the SEAL where his sensitive trigger firing might send several bullets through the terrorist with high power velocity Holmes brought the butt of his submachine gun down on the man's head. He bent over and picked up Pacheco's firearm as the SEAL pushed the unconscious man off of him.

"Don't kill him," gasped Pacheco, turning back to the explosive charge. One minute left.

He snipped two wires, then pulled out the connection timer and threw it over the bridge.

"You know this guy." Pacheco pointed to the man, but Holmes saw no familiar face.

"I believe this is your friend, Ali Baba."

"You're kidding. Hey, it computes. Here is the creator of Crimson Scimitar. It figures al-Qaeda would have him lead the show."

"I bet the CIA will make this guy squeal. The biggest catch since Khalid Shaikh Mohammed."

Holmes did not like that scenario of relinquishing such a prize, but said nothing, except, "I'll plastic cuff him. If this bomb had exploded there would have been a big hole but nothing would have happened to the truck that makes me believe the truck has been rigged."

A bullet pinged near them, letting them know they still had their work cut out for them.

"I'm on it."

An explosion wracked the bridge into shaking and swaying. Holmes and Pacheco picked themselves off the ground, but kept in a crouch.

"Because we're here they're moved up their timetable."

Pacheco ran to the first truck and started his inspection.

Callie and Detective Taggart reached Holmes, eye darting at the tied man on the ground, while searching out targets. Callie put the barrel of her pistol against the terrorist on the ground, but saw Holmes shake his head to the negative. "We need a live one," he said, trying to defuse Callie's anger at seeking outright revenge for Clayton's murder. She pulled her gun away still seeking personal vengeance.

Detective Taggart regained her voice as the serious, inquiring detective.

"What did they just blow up? The bridge is still standing."

"They want to blow up the trucks and dump their contents into the river, but first they need to make an exit point in the side of the bridge."

"What'll that do?"

"Poison everyone downstream, make all crops uneatable for a hundred, if not a thousand years."

"Jeez."

To both women he said, "Shawn's going to try and defuse this truck, but it is the next one I am fearful about. The bad guys we need to take out quickly since I feel they moved up the detonation sequences."

"Shit. Well, this beats my recent life of doodling crosswords in the middle of the desert."

Callie fired off a braced shot into the head of one of the terrorists who had just moved out from in between the tanker units. "Now, I am feeling a lot better," and she took off with Detective Taggart following, both leapfrogging, covering each other, into a better firing position. Holmes moved to cover Pacheco at the first truck.

128.

9:35 a.m. on the bridge

Razzor looked down at Shanin's dead ordinance man.

"Did he complete his tasks?"

"Yes, though somehow the first bomb against the bridge abutment should have detonated by now, so we have a misfire. Still the truck will explode, a part of the spent fuel rods will go in the river, some may be left on the bridge, and if the winds are right, Las Vegas will receive a strong radiation dose."

"Did you kill Khalaf?"

"He ran." Razzor looked down to his hastily bandaged hand. "And I lost a finger in the process."

"Protect me for one minute." Shahin jumped in the cab of the truck, started the engine, pushed the truck in reverse, backed up twenty feet—there was little maneuver room for doing a speed run-up and no time -- and then he pushed gear driving towards the jagged opening, chugging the truck up over the bombed rubble, its front wheels, edged off the bridge, tipping downward. As he expected, the truck had high centered, wedged. The exploding bombs would do the trick of dislodging and sending the truck's liquid cargo into the canyon and river below.

Shahin edged carefully out the door and around to the back of the cab then jumped to the ground. He ran to the back of the truck, but stopped short, when a voice, a woman's, yelled at him.

"Hands up, behind your head, on your knees. Now!"

He turned to see a gun aimed at him when Razzor rose from behind the construction pickup and shot the woman.

On the Arizona side—

As soon as Shahin and Razzor exited off the bridge in the pickup truck they met up with the racing construction truck and the two young men from the barricade, and as Shanin saw, these 'boys' being the Professor's protégé wannabes, proved such, babbling in distraught immaturity.

"They attacked us, stopped the truck, and turned it around." Said one.

"The Professor never told us we would have to fight back. We were almost killed," Said the other.

"You are wrong."

"What?"

"You were killed." And Shanin shot one, Razzor the other. And they drove on, taking the turn-off road seeing in the distance a van racing towards them. This escape route was one of several planned and Shahin felt secure they would make their escape. One question however had just been raised, that led to a bothersome mystery. What happened to The Professor? Where was Khalaf? If both lived, as the original plan dictated, Razzor would take care of The Professor, and Shahin swore to Allah he would eradicate the boil called Khalaf .

129.

They were all stuffed in the *King's Retribution* S/FX van racing toward the bridge.

Bennie pointed out the pickup truck with highway department markings making dirt clouds as the vehicle spun under the highway and up a gravel road, strangely, going back toward the dam, on the old and closed road.

"We don't have time for car chases, Holmes asked us to rush to him." That settled that.

Gizmo inspected the spider marks of bullet strikes on the windshield, the window however not shattered.

Bennie gave him the answer.

"After King's car bombing in the Hummer, I reinforced this mother with steel plating and bulletproof glass. If you saw the grill work, we took ten direct hits but did no damage, that's why we can still hustle."

A bad omen, slowing, they passed the pickup truck from the barricade with the door open, one body leaning out, the other man in the passenger seat, his eyes open, his mouth agape from the surprise of the hole in his forehead.

"Fleeing from us and not dying for the jihad cause must have been cowardice to the boss man," intoned Fox. All of them, watching gathering flies circle the dead, understood they were not before a game console.

At the bridge they came upon a miniature Armageddon. Two vehicles were burning.

Bodies lay on the ground. The chemical tandem truck, with a red painted slash on its back, hung precariously off the bridge.

Armed and cautious, Fox and Samantha exited, followed by Bennie and Abbas. Gizmo had had enough excitement for a lifetime remained stuck to his seat. CAM TWO shot video out an open window.

They approached Callie on the ground...cradling a woman.

"Hurts like hell," groaned Chase. "You forgot to tell me: kill terrorists first, read them their rights later."

"You're lucky," said Callie trying to give comfort. "It's a through and through. Hey, Abbas, pull out the medical kit, I got a patient for you." Abbas returned to the van.

"Where's Holmes", asked Samantha definitely showing worry.

"He's fine; he's over there with Shawn, doing nothing much except trying to diffuse two bombs. We have about fifteen minutes to evacuate the bridge, in case it goes wrong." Callie saw more worry to Samantha's face, her concern for Holmes too obvious. Then, Callie noticed Hugh Fox staring at her with almost an identical mask of concern, leaving her wondering.

"What's that noise?" asked Bennie.

"Gunfire, what's new?" Callie's tired idea of a weak joke. "I think the first crossing escort guards...and maybe the Metro Police are taking out the terrorists blocking the bridge on the Nevada side." Still holding Detective Taggart, Callie turned to Bennie.

"Holmes has a present for you to pick up. He's over there all packaged up. Considering you can't go to Las Vegas, he wants you to drive all the way to Kingman. Hopefully, Ms. Carlisle can have her jet waiting there."

"I'll make it happen," Samantha went for her cell phone and walked away, towards where Holmes might be found.

Abbas returned with the first aid kit.

"And you can take Detective Taggart with you and get her to a hospital."

"No way. I want to use my police insurance at our University Medical Hospital, best knife and gun club in the West. Patch me up. I bet you have great drugs." She was starting to get a little pain punchy. "Our boys will break through any time. Did I tell you I got into this today because I thought we had a jumper. If there is a suicide on the Nevada side, your body gets to a Coroner in an hour, but if you high dive from the dam or the bridge on the Arizona side, takes them three hours to do a pick up, does no good to your squished complexion in this sun."

Abbas brought out the hypodermic needle and Chase gave him a Cheshire Cat grin, "My man."

Abbas took Callie's place as the healing Samaritan.

130.

Callie and Hugh walked over and into an argument in progress between Samantha and Holmes, the latter turning to them
with a plea.

"I've asked Samantha, and am asking everyone to clear the
bridge. No one is safe here.

There's about 15 minutes left, and Shawn has just started."

"And I told him 'no'. We started this together and we'll finish it
as a team."

Fox tried to intervene. "Sam, it would be best..."

Her anger was not sharp, but still pointed.

"No, not until he really tells me why he wants me to get out of
harm's way. Can you honestly do that, Mr. Holmes?"

The ex-CIA agent who had faced battle field death many times,
held a curse under his tongue, then gave his head a shaking
smile of defeat.

"Because I care about you, Samantha, and I do not want to
see you hurt in anyway."

"See that wasn't so hard."

Holmes heard Fox chuckle, and turned on him.

"Okay, your turn, Mister. I've just opened my heart in front of
'friends'. Time to step up to the plate, bite the bullet, be a real
man."

Such being on his mind for a while, Hugh Fox conceded to an
emotional risk worth taking. "Callie, I don't know how to say this,
but I think, no, I would like to see more of you."

He stumbled the words out like a shy boy asking the girl for
their first dance.

"You mean like a date or like playing one of your games." Surprised, happy, she put the tease on him.

Hugh wondered if he could handle her.

"More like seeing if we have 'passionate compatibility'." No one
saw the tweak smirk from Samantha Carlisle knowing by personal experience Hugh could bring heat to a bed, but still satisfied
with her choice; she would see if an old war horse could compete
and win the Triple Crown.

"I'm game," said Callie, giving him a quick hug.

They heard a yell from between the truck.

"I know they have a drink called 'Sex on the Beach'....Shawn poked his head out, 'But they have not yet invented 'Sex on the Bridge'. Will all of you kindly stand way back until I call you...or until I don't call you." His head disappeared back to work, time running out.

The two new couples gave a relieved smile to each other and accepted that was the best course of action, when the pavement beneath them moved.

'*Crack*'! A muffled earthquake-like noise followed by a moving snake-like break appeared in the roadway, and with a shutter of the entire bridge the tanker truck suddenly lurched towards the precipice of falling into the river.

131.

On the Nevada Side—

The Spirit of the American Way of Life had as much to do with Professor James Rogers abandoning Crimson Scimitar as did events at the Bridge.

The Professor likewise had been deluded that his cell would be put only in charge of blocking traffic, and after the quick and tight 30 minutes for the attack on the bridge, they would all depart safely and without harm with three high-jacked trucks heading to an undisclosed location. So, no real thought was given to the weapons given to his five charges, all received to provide further courage, seen more for bravado show than for actual use. Thus, a mistaken belief that no response from the outside would be forthcoming in time, led to horrendous consequences.

The Professor had been sitting in one of the fake highway construction pick-ups, hydrating with water against the blistering heat, when the white van truck crashed the barrier, followed by a siren-screaming car. One of his men started firing shots at the escaping vehicles.

Thinking at first only to the operation, he shouted to the other two of his cell manning the barrier.

"Fix the damn thing and defend it. Keep everyone away from the bridge!" He drove his pick-up up the hill and around the curve and came to witness the firefight between Force Three, Shanin's cell, and the armed occupants from the mysterious two vehicles. Very easily, he could have gotten out of his truck, and flanked the attackers. Maybe kill one, maybe all, but he was a university professor and though he had great grievances against a government who had indirectly been responsible for the killing of his parents, and blood revenge was strong, so was a desire to see his own family again, and see his children grow up. He had been enlisted in Crimson Scimitar to block the bridges, to send a man to find and follow the trucks, no more.

He returned to his guard post to find his two men under attack. Down from them in the traffic snarl, behind a SUV, a man was firing back at the roadblock protectors. He could see his companion dragging himself along the ground beside the Hummer, gravely wounded. The Professor saw the details of how it all must have unfolded. The lead escort Hummer returned to locate the convoy, to find a roadblock and his nervous, trigger happy American-grown jihadists, fatally reacted to the threat.

It was too much for The Professor. The stifling heat bore down on him, salt sweat stinging his eyes. Either way he went he would become immersed in the shooting and most likely be slain when their positions were overrun. Had not he already completed his responsibility as they were given; was not the bridge blocked? It was now up to Shahin and Razzor Hassim to complete their tasks. The trucks would explode and dump their cargos.

America would be punished; he so rationalized, his parent deaths would be avenged. Thoughts of the future, of life, gave him resolve to his next decision.

He drove his pick-up off the road and down a steep hill, rattling, bouncing, missing boulders, to reach, not too far away, the dam's access road. He surprised a few tourists as he swung the pickup back onto the narrow paved road and sped up onto Highway 93 heading back towards Las Vegas. Hearing the pop of gunfire fade, catching his breath and wiping his forehead, he felt much better, and the methodical man he was he re-prioritized his life, remembering he had to prepare his curriculum studies for the fall semester and this weekend his son's soccer game to attend.

Razzor and Shahin, by coincidence were travelling only a mile behind him.

They had abandoned their pick-up at the blocked old road, and walked down to a parking lot overlooking the dam where tourists were snapping postcard photos. They found the vehicle that best suited their needs and the timing could not be better as an official vehicle drove by informing over a loudspeaker to all the dam had been closed and they were to exit the area immediately.

Driving, expecting no one to stop them, since who would consider a 'Rent This Travel Home – See the Wonders of America' to be suspicious, they began to relax. Only when three siren-blasting police cars whizzed past them heading to the bridge did they feel the tenseness that had been with them all morning.

For some time they said nothing, then Shahin, looked at his watch.

"The bombs have exploded. Not a total success, but enough for us to claim a victory."

"Yes, congratulations." Razzor turned on the radio seeking a news station. He wondered if any clean-up was required before heading south with Shahin to enter Mexico and return to Pakistan or Yemen for his next assignment. In thinking in terms of clean-up, like one might check off a grocery list, he would have to abandon this rent-a-vacation van, and looking back at the older couple on the floor, their throats slashed, Razzor knew it would have to be sooner than later.

132.

On the Bridge –

There could be only one leader, and no questioning of command. Wendell Holmes who in earlier months wondered what in retirement he would do to keep himself engaged stepped easily into the role.

"Put everyone into Retribution van, including our prisoner. Sam, you and Callie, can sit off the bridge on the Arizona side, and if Taggart wants a local hospital she can stay too." He gave a deep, plaintive look of care. "Please."

"Yes, Wen." And she hurried off.

"Callie, call the local police, tell them there are only friendlies on the bridge. We don't need complications from our allies. Ask for Medevac helicopter for Taggart, tell them where you will be. Here's my cell phone. Punch in Brady ask him for two heavy lift helicopters to scramble out of Nellis Airbase, something like a Russian Mi-26; tell them they may be picking up a large truck out of the river. Tell them to wear HazMat gear."

Fox and Callie exchanged glances, realization of the impending disaster. They understood his concern in sending Samantha away from this news.

"Even if the bombs are deactivated," Holmes looked around scoping out his limited options, "the bridge at least at this junction might not hold. Stress fractures are undermining the concrete beams. Hugh, drive up the *Storm Wagon*. It has a winch on front."

"That wouldn't hold a falling truck of that size."

"Probably not, but it might break the fall, so the tanks won't split apart when they hit the water." Fox ran off with Callie trailing working the phone.

Holmes ran to the truck.

"How are you doing, SEAL?"

"Would you believe hanging by a thread," came the strained reply.

Holmes moved over the rubble to the side of the truck. Pacheco was working on the IED affixed to the end unit located between both tank carriers, but the way the truck was twisted from the last movement to the edge, Pacheco was now working from the top down, upside down.

"Time left?"

"Ten minutes."

"How are you doing? Can you just rip them off?

"Little slower, hopefully five minutes to spare. And no, these are locked on with sensitive glue strips and tightened with pressure clamps. Have to fiddle with more wires with my magic fingers."

"Be safe."

"Yeah, but if the bridge shakes any more I may go down with the ship, or rather, the truck."

"We cannot let this truck burst open."

Both men exchanged knowing looks. Shawn Pacheco, either by bomb or fall, the SEAL would not survive. He must stay with it to whatever end...doing his job.

Fox ran up the Storm Wagon close to the twin tanker truck. Bennie jumped out and began pulling out the winch cable, and hooking to the under carriage of the Eagle Freight chemical truck. Holmes walked with him giving an explanation of what Pacheco was facing, what might be a partial solution. Bennie nodded and ran to *Retribution* production van jammed with its refugees.

The bridge shuttered again and the truck trailer jerked forward.

Holmes shouted to Fox.

"I will take the Storm Wagon. You take the van out of here."

Abbas came running up carrying several interesting pieces of equipment. Samantha followed hefting a folded up two-man raft, and a paddle.

"You gotta be kidding, Wen? Up the creek already?"

"Taking no chances. Have to support the kid. I thought you were going. Please, you need to get out of here, please. I think this span is about ready to break apart."

She, threw her arms around him, and kissed him hard.

"I'll be waiting for you."

"Look for me, probably downstream."

She ran off, following Abbas and Fox to the van, and Bennie burned rubber towards the Arizona side of the bridge.

Holmes watched them drive away. Damn, he thought, just when I find something special, and realize it, I might have blown it, literally.

He walked up to Pacheco.

"I am going to give you a choice."

"What the--? You're crazy."

We both are, so let's do it together. We have women to get back to."

"You can say that again. Pretty sure I have the wiring on the last one figured out."

"Well, this may be a burden, but please put it on."

Holmes heard the pavement crumbling before he saw multiple cracks appear beneath his feet.

"Shit." He ran to the *Retribution* van, got in and eased the van back, bringing the cable taut. He ran a lot of *what if* strategies of bridge failure but couldn't compute them all before the bridge split along the concrete beam and one section tilted and the large truck, tilted, slid and fell off the bridge.

133.

In slow motion, the truck fell, but not really.

By the concrete pavement tipping downward, the truck started its slide over the edge.

The *Storm Wagon's* tires scorched the pavement as, Holmes accelerated the truck in reverse, but the opposite slowly was drawing Holmes forward in the Wagon, following the tandem trailer truck.

At the point of no return the truck began a faster tumble. Holmes caught a quick glance of Pacheco holding on for his life. Whatever it would do for him, the small oxygen tank was strapped on Pacheco's back.

Holmes had his own equipment strapped on his back, a quick release parachute. He knew he would have one second of decision: jump to safety from the van onto the bridge or follow Pacheco down and see if he could be of help, if he first survived the jump, and help either as rescue or body recovery, at the same time—if the truck broke apart-- taking in heavy radiation doses that would leave him suffering a horrible, agonizing death. Within those few seconds, he did not see his life flash before him, but only of Samantha and wondering what she would be doing tomorrow.

Pacheco felt himself in a mix blender, the truck gyrating so much. He could not easily work on the bomb's wiring. He thought he understood which wires had to be cut apart and was about to do so when he was flung upward. He grabbed a steel ladder rung, found himself dangling, looking down 800 feet to the water below, marvelous in its beauty, ghastly in the distance down to meet the bottom.

And the truck suddenly dropped, fast but not free falling, and then lurched to a stop.

Pacheco felt a pain as his arm and his body jerked. He held on, fingers slipping.

Above, the *Storm Wagon* had lodged sideways in the bridge's torn opening, halting the truck's fall but straining the winch, pulling on the concrete, holding back both vehicles, the weight too much to hold it long.

Holmes would have had more seconds to decide to jump, but in the screeching pull of the Wagon, when hitting the rubble, the van turned sideways, and fell over on its side. Holmes was trapped, momentarily...the concrete opening crumbled, at the same instance a section of pavement broke free and both trucks fell away.

Physics aside, the trailer truck broke Pacheco's fall, sort of. The front end part of the crashing truck sent up a water geyser that cushioned Pacheco hitting the river. When he rose to the surface, he bobbed in a moving current, and within a few strokes, was beside the truck trailer, in the process of sinking below the surface. To Pacheco's surprise the truck caught in the flow and no longer was being pushed downstream. He did not realize the *Storm Wagon* had acted as an anchor when it became lodged between two rock pillars at the river's bottom.

Good news, bad news. The trailer truck was underwater but would not sink further or be pulled downstream; bad news: the pressure of the river's current made it almost impossible to gain a traction for Pacheco to reach the last explosive package.

The mini oxygen tank he held strapped on his back was for on-land accident resuscitation purposes, now he could grab snatches of air as he was pulled underwater, making his way back to the bomb's location, fighting the pressure of the river's flow against him. Brute strength, determination of purpose, urged him on.

Three minutes and counting down.

Right behind the falling trucks came Holmes, his parachute deployed immediately as he fell away from the van but barely caught enough air to give him buoyancy. Knowing he could make only one glide turn in close quarters, he did not aim at the bobbing truck, the top of the two tanker units just breaking the river's surface. He swung instead back toward the bridge to an outcropping at the water's edge which met him on landing too fast with a painful hit to his shins.

He was too old for this shit. He took note that the trailing package attached to his leg made the trip, the wrapped, compact raft, with portable paddle, which he began to unfold. He glanced at his watch and scanned the river. He held his breath, but there was silence in the canyon except the singing from soaring aerobatic swallows. He should have seen the explosion or at least a plume of water to mark the grave of one young man, the grave of America. He saw nothing but rolling water and began to paddle out into the current an angle intersection where he last saw the tanker disappear beneath the roiling turbulence.

135.

September 2Las Vegas, Nevada

Channel 8 News Alert:
"We interrupt our broadcast to report that the F.B.I. has announced an apparent attempt by unknown person or persons to explode a truck laden bomb on the O'Callaghan-Tillman Bridge, near Hoover Dam which separates Nevada and Arizona.

"Some sort of explosive device was detonated but did not destroy the bridge.

"From the sketchy reports we have coming in, initial reports inform us that when the Las Vegas Metro Police arrived on the scene they discovered one of their fellow officers wounded by the assailants. The name released to us is a Detective Chase Taggart, who had been assigned to the Hoover Dam's security team. Detective Taggart in a routine traffic stop had confronted the suspects and in the ensuing exchange of gunfire killed two of them while receiving a non-life threatening injury to herself.

"We have been told that the two dead suspects were identified as U.S. citizens and students from Idaho. Protest signs against using the highway to ship wild mustangs from Utah and Nevada to slaughter houses in Texas, were found at the scene.

"There has been slight structural damage to the bridge and it will remain closed to traffic as the investigation continues and until highway repairs are completed. The State Patrol is establishing alternative routes. We will bring you up-to-dates as we receive them.

"In other chilling news of the day, a Wisconsin couple were found slain in their camper off Blue Diamond Road. We will be right back with more details after these announcements."

September 3rd   Arizona desert east of Hoover Dam
The behemoth military helicopter, Sikorsky CH-53E, fifth largest in the world which could carry 73,500 lb, gently lowered the final tank unit of the truck trailer to the ground. Men in hazmat uniforms approached the tank holding Geiger counters and more sophisticated reading devices. With concentrated air-floating trillium, there were carcinogens that would evaporate, unseen

but present, prolonged death still the outcome. But the readings gave relief, there had been no breach of the containers (which in fact were containers within containers) even after being at the bottom of the turbulent Colorado River.

The remaining two trucks of the convoy sat off to the side and were being minutely inspected for bullet holes or other structural damage.

When approached by one of his colleagues, and asked, "What are we now supposed to do with these cargos now?"

The scientist in charge looked over all three battered trucks, shook his head negatively, and merely said, "Afraid we will refer the dilemma back to the committee in Washington."

136.

September 5th Las Vegas

The Professor could not endure the waiting to face his killer. Two days after his escape from the bridge he knew by the press and media reports the attack had been a debacle which he knew would incense Shahin, and the man would want to clean up loose ends before using the border tunnel escape route.

He had taken measures but would they be enough. He had planted the seed with his wife that he thought some burglars might be casing the neighborhood; he placed a call to the police of his concern; to his worry he encouraged his wife to allow her sister take the children for a couple days of late summer fun, which she did so hesitantly. To avoid being murdered in his sleep, he added a chain lock to the bedroom. To the rest of the house he bought a few high tech gadgets and installed them himself. Yet, if he and his family were marked for execution beyond three days he could not maintain his vigilant paranoia which already began to take a toll on his health.

To the expectation for something, anything, to happen, it did so, almost on a schedule, on the second night of his apprehension.

He was working at his desk in the family den. He had the light on over his desk, and the window shades open, so that anyone from the street could see him sitting there. He did not expect a bullet through the window glass. If they shot him from the yard, through the sliding glass door, it would be a just punishment, Allah's will, for having gotten himself caught up in such a scheme. No, his death would be personal.

A small red bulb illuminated on the device on his desk. Someone had breached the security and entered into the house. He did not wish to set off the home burglar alarm which would bring the security company, little good they would do, and too late. No, it had to end now.

He pushed a button on a garage-door type remote he held in his hand, and he waited.

"Professor, good to see you again." Shahin had sent Razzor Hassim to do his dirty work, walking into the den from the kitchen.

"I guess I should have expected it would be you."

Razzor held a large serrated knife in his hand.

"You left the attack and did not die on the bridge; that was most unfortunate."

"You mean run like you and I presume as Shahin did? I plead guilty, but with me survival wins out over martyrdom every time." He needed to stall for time.

"But I guess I would have to ask: was there an al-Qaeda attack on the bridge? The press does not mention your glorious deeds so I presume there is no leaked radiation. And the F.B.I. today released only two wannabes killed on the bridge, calling them a Timothy McVey type American terrorist. No mention of al-Qaeda."

"The American government is hiding the facts. But their press is predatory and the truth will eventually come out."

"But why was their security on the bridge immediately? Crimson Scimitar failed from the onset. I can't be blamed for that." That rattled Razzor, from his killer control to defensive anger.

"We were betrayed."

"It did not come from me."

"Does it matter?"

Everything was in place, thought The Professor, and beneath the desk, he pushed the pre-dialed 911 on his cell phone. Giving a second for a connection, he spoke loudly in a scared voice to his attacker.

"I can pay you money and you can leave wealthy, no one knowing you entered the Painted Desert neighborhood. And please don't kill my wife, she's innocent."

"As I told you, once I take care of you, then it will be your wife and children. And your wife will be after I pleasure myself."

The Professor put on a slight wail.

"You can't kill my children, they are not here. Don't make the Roger children orphans."

"I will hunt them down.. You can count on that." And Razzor took a step forward, menacing with the knife.

"I don't think so," came the voice from behind Razzor, a woman's voice, and he turned in surprise. "You will never touch my children," and The Proffessor's wife fired the Remington 1100 shotgun, purchased only yesterday. The 12 gauge shell impact threw Razzor up and back through the sliding door leading to the patio, shattering the glass into body-slashing shards.

The shotgun's recoil knocked The Professor's wife to the carpeting, the shotgun dropped from her grasp.

"My God," she screamed. "What have I done, Jim? You told me the shells were loaded with rock salt. They would scare him, sting him. I have killed him." She was in hysterics.

He tried a calming voice, "The sporting goods store must have given me the wrong shells. But don't worry, dear, please, you saved us all. You heard him. This was a home invasion, and he meant to rob and kill us. And most certainly he would have raped and tortured you. Don't worry, everything will be all right."

Under Nevada's laws of self-defense and right of protecting one's home, The Professor, knew his wife would have no fear of prosecution. The 911 call recorded Razzor's lethal threats and there was his knife lying on the floor. All would be right again; he would go collect his children tomorrow, and call the family doctor for advice. Of course, his wife, for some time to come, would need psychiatric help.

Outside the Professor's home, Shahin heard the boom accompanied with the breaking of glass. In the distance he heard sirens of approaching police cars. He moved over into the driver's seat, turning the car on, putting it in gear, slowly moving off, giving Razzor if he were to come running, a few seconds to catch up. In one minute, and with no text response, he knew Razzor must be incapacitated or better yet, he was dead. Everything had gone wrong and this was no different. He would drive all night and be in San Diego in the early morning hours, and enter Mexico, closing out the Crimson Scimitar operation behind him. It was time to go back to Yemen, home territory and to wars he knew how to fight.

A day later, the San Diego Union Tribune, reported the discovery of a major tunnel under the border, when an undetermined explosion collapsed it. One of the most professional and modern tunnels yet uncovered, officials reported. U.S. Border Patrol and Mexican Federal Agents were able to recover quantities of drugs including meth; guns and C-4 explosives. One of four men killed in the explosion was the building's owner.

137.

September 11th, 2011 New York City

Sabz, agitated and fretful, knew today would not be good news. The telephone call had come two days ago to the hotel suite. She was asked if Mr. Rasil lived at this residence. No, she said, this suite was registered under the name of Sheik Khalaf bin Zayed from the United Arab Emirates. Did she know a Mr. Rasil? She clutched. Yes, she lied, he was an associate of her husband, knowing full well Rasil was one of Khalaf's several passport aliases. Someone would be by at 10 a.m. on the 11th to visit with her and her husband, a matter of Mr. Rasil's stockbrokerage accounts.

She did not know what to do. There had been no word from Khalaf since his departure.

She knew some operation of al-Qaeda was in play, but every day she watched the television news and no alert of al-Qaeda presence in the United States. She still viewed plenty of American violence—from domestic dispute shootings, to robberies that went wrong to gang warfare. By her constant watching she found herself caught up in the movie star drama and politician indiscretions and sought out those television shows where they talked about such events in empty chatter.

The only news item close to an attack was two young men who tried to blow themselves up on a bridge somewhere out West but were killed by police instead.

Meanwhile, as she watched the news, on the international front, governments continued, especially in the Middle East, to crash inward under the rhetoric of seeking democracy, finding anarchy instead, what American officials labeled in blind optimism, 'Arab Spring.' Sabz had seen firsthand such futile violence but cared little for radical politicians as they never seem to make life easier. Iraq and Syria were falling back into anarchy, religion and tribes at each other's throats. Seeking peace and comfort had become her only priority, that and this happiness she shared with Khalaf, as much the naïve child he acted. Could he not see his jihad beliefs outside tribal borders were so irrelevant against the daily lives of billions of people? As much as she subtly tried, he did not see the better world that surrounded him, the freedom to act as one pleased.

She was watching television when the doorbell to the suite rang. Certainly, they were here to announce Rasil's [Kahlaf's] death, then to arrest and deport her. Her dream had ended.

When she opened the door, an Arab, an American Arab, asked to see her passport. He sounded official and she complied. He studied her face against the English passport she held.

"You live in London?"

"Yes. My husband travels a lot but we are temporarily staying there."

"And you will be returning to Great Britain soon?"

"As soon as my husband returns."

"Oh, he is not here?"

"He has been travelling. I really don't know his itinerary." She paused, in his conversation he had made no police-like threats, and as young as she was she overcame nervousness to regain her strength. "And this questioning is in regard to what?"

"There has been an accident."

"Oh, no." The blessings on her life and Khalaf's were dashed. She caught herself before her tears began. "My husband, he's dead?"

"No, no. It is his friend, Mr. Rasil. He was in a serious auto accident, but he shall recover. He just needs a place to regain his strength, and it was thought your husband and you might help nurse him back to health."

"Rasil?" She was confused.

"Excuse me, one moment." And the man stepped into the hall returning with a stretcher, and another man holding one end.

Khalaf lay on the stretcher, covered in a sheet, one side of his head and jaw bandaged.

The joy in her expression brought a humpf grunt of displeasure from the other man.

"Where do we put him, Abbas?"

"The bedroom of course, Bennie."

Once they had eased Rasil/Khalaf on top of the bedcovers, they departed but not before the man that had been identified as Abbas, spoke seriously to Sabz.

"A doctor will drop by daily to check his injuries. It is our recommendation that as soon as he is able to walk that you all return to London."

"Who are you?"

"His new friends. We have left a packet for him to open and read when he is feeling better." Abbas stepped to the wide window overlooking the balcony. Later today, rain was in the forecast. He turned to the small Arab woman. She was quite attractive though her face bore exhaustion.

"Do you know what day this signifies? No, probably not. Ten years ago, this day, 3,000 people were murdered in this city and elsewhere in the country, a tragedy to make us all realize how lives can be controlled by evil people. It will not happen again. We have made an investment with Mr. Rasil and we expect our profit. Please take care of him. He is destined to become an important man."

Abbas and Bennie left, closing the door behind him.

Sabz ran to the bed and stared down at the bandaged Khalaf. Tears came. She lay next to him, held his hand, and watched the rising and falling of his chest. When this Abbas man appeared she had been watching the television in the living room and the set remained on, now she was too tired to turn it off. She tried not to hear the programming but it was so repetitive like Khalaf's steady breathing: a name spoken, a different name stated, a new name, another. Even after Sabz closed her eyes to sleep, the names continued until 2,753 names were read and marked, a somber repetition of warning, containing the same message Abbas had repeated in Wendell Holmes's speech to be told to the terrorist's bride.

Episode 18

"Islam is the religion of the sword, not pacifism."
Dabiq *[the ISIL/ISIS magazine] heartily rejects the statement often repeated by American statesmen that "Islam is a religion of peace." Instead, they cite the linguistic origin of the word to mean sincere submission. Based on a fundamentalist interpretation of Sunni Islam, ISIS does not even consider the Shia, followers of the other major sect of Islam, to be Muslim. Shia Muslims, including Syrian Alawites and Iranians, are referred to with religious slurs, and ISIS cites Koran verses to urge its followers to kill these supposedly false Muslims.*
--'Quotes from ISIS' by Patrick Martin

138.

September 15, 2011 The White House

"I don't want to know, do I?" An entirely rhetorical question as The President of the United States indeed did not want to know. If the entire story became public exposing the failure of the government's intelligence community to ferret out threats within the U.S. heads would roll, and with the election next year, his up poll numbers from taking out bin Laden might suffer a setback, and he could find his political neck on the chopping block. At least with this 'understanding' reached, any heads rolling in the future would be further down the chain of command, and damage control could be initiated and what had transpired at the amusement parks and on the bridge would be seen as a long ago event, befuddled in a mix of storytelling, diffused and mitigated.

"No, sir, it is better this way. We have reached an accommodation with all parties," explained the Head of Homeland Security. "And nothing was put into writing."

"Actually, we have had to give up very little," said the new C.I.A. director (there had been a shake up within the Agency) mostly future accommodations which we can live with."

"No money exchanged hands," said one of the officials as an afterthought, as if to imply money might have been required to buy silence.

"Well, if you all are comfortable then I will accept your direction and wisdom," said the President, ready to move on. "We shall look on these events as having been concluded in a positive light. A national disaster was averted. You have told me, in not so many words, that proper punishments have been meted out, and deserved rewards tendered. Gentleman, I do not want this possibility to ever happen again, not only on my watch, but in years beyond my Administration."

Around the room, there were nods of concurrence, from the four individuals in the Oval Office who would be in that tight circle of knowing the truth and taking it to their graves: the Head of Homeland Security, the Director of the F.B.I., Director of the C.I.A., and the President's National Security Advisor.

To these four powerful government leaders he said, putting a newly manufactured smile to his face, "Now, ladies and gentlemen, let us set aside our country's close call and let us bestow a just reward to the truly courageous." And the President rose, as did the others, and as if on cue, the visitors were ushered in.

Recently promoted to E-9 Rating Shawn Pacheco came first in full dress Navy uniform, followed by his fiancée Janet, and her father former Army Captain Russell Mosswood (retired), definitely awestruck at the majesty of this well-known odd circular office. Pacheco saluted the President and the President extended his hand. The grip between them was solid. The President made small talk, with the emphasis to his fiancée, "You should be very proud of him." "Yes, I am," replied Janet, feeling more confident than ever in her life, ready to be a SEAL's wife.

In a short formality of ceremony and among the remarks made by the President of the United States, Janet remembered a blur of the President's words.

"The United States is in a continuing battle to protect our citizens from those who have no morality and desire only the total extermination of our way of life. Many in uniform rise to the occasion when there are times of crises. In recent events that have transpired, and because of issues concerning National Security, the actions of Ensign SO Pacheco may never be known to the public and we would hope your respect in such confidences as being essential. But I can tell you both, since he wanted you to share this historic and special occasion with him, that he exemplifies the best in our men and women of the Armed Forces."

With that the President opened the small case, and placed the Congressional Medal of Honor around his neck, which Janet assisted proudly in the fastening.

"Navy SEAL Shawn Pacheco, the United States and all its citizens owe you a debt of gratitude that can never be repaid. I proudly award you this decoration, the highest in the land for our military heroes, for exemplary courage and decisive action in facing extreme danger in the saving of countless innocent lives." Brief, vague, and well said.

Again, sailor and Commander-in-Chief shook hands. Shawn turned to Janet and gave her a kiss, and she tingled in the excitement that there would be many more. Even Janet's father knew this was more than a momentous occasion. There were no cameras, no press in the room, and the four witnesses to the ceremony were among the top officials of the Administration.

What his future son-in-law must have been involved in had to be so dangerous and so critical to the security of the country total secrecy had to be invoked. Obeying orders and duty he understood, it was part of his own fabric of past military service. He was so proud and at the same time so ashamed he ever doubted the young man's character and he knew he would spend years in atonement, and pledged to himself, hopefully in the not so distant future, to be the best grandfather ever.

As the ceremony ended, and the good-byes were being said, the President casually asked Pacheco, what were his plans, was he going back to his SEAL unit for reassignment.

"No, my commander, gave me an open-ended extended leave, and has approved my being assigned as a military technical liaison to the television show, *King's Retribution*."

As they say, the surprise on the face of the President of the United States: 'priceless'.

139.

September 18th Islamabad, Pakistan

He signed his name to the two documents.

"Here you are folks. Temporary passport replacements. Please remember next time do not leave your travel documents lying around in your room. The hotel safe would be more secure."

The tourists departed grateful for the embassy's quick response to their travel distress.

Governmental Affairs Director and Senior Attaché, Ronald Givens, looked up from his desk in the U.S. Embassy and saw the man approaching him, the military bearing obvious, the dress coat in this warm weather a poor attempt at being discreet.

"Mr. Givens, I heard you were back. Welcome."

"General Khan. How unexpected."

"I presume your new posting was for great service rendered back home."

Givens sought to put his demotion, the 'take this exile position or leave' offer, in the best possible light.

"Yes, it was decided to put me back into the field, they call it a 'refresher course', in preparation for future advancement." Not true. He knew his career had stalled for good. He would now only hang on, do the required, wait out his pension.

"Well, then, allow me to extend once again my friendship. Let's do lunch next week at my club. Perhaps, if you will allow, let me help you integrate yourself back into our country's wonderful society."

Givens's face brightened.

"Yes, that is very kind." Perhaps this place might have diversions to keep him from utter melancholy.

"Good then, my secretary will call you for our luncheon date. And again, welcome."

As General Khan walked out of the U.S. Embassy, he could only laugh, and wonder.

'How did this perfectly plump pigeon get placed on my table for carving? It would be only a matter of weeks,' he bet himself, 'before I would start extracting all the gossip and news from the goings on in the Embassy. Why did they send such an ineffectual louse? Or did they? No, it couldn't be. He shouldn't have such clout, he's retired. But if he was behind this man's arrival, he must know the incompetence that has been unleashed. It is certain such a contrived gesture is tit-for-tat. As I gain all the access to U.S. State Department secrets and C.I.A. loose chatter, the same will be expected of me. Well, such are the games we must play.'

Outside, the General eased himself into the passenger side of the shiny new Mercedes Roadster.

"Like your car?"

"Of course, haven't I shown you my appreciation many times over?"

Yes, you have, smiled the General to himself, and will again and again, accepting the odd irony that all his intertwined benefits were due to Mr. bin Laden, and his timely demise.

140.

September 20 London

He was a wealthy yet a very disturbed man. Daily, he tried to sum up and recount what he knew and guess at what he did not.

He knew he first awoke in Sabz's arms, warmth and tenderness. A doctor showed up at the hotel and removed stitches from the top of his head and jaw from his 'auto accident', as he was told, giving him a bottle of pills, offering to prescribing more pain medicine if required. He spent thereafter a week recovering in full confusion.

Sabz recounted as best she could his arrival in the litter and her conversation with the American Arab called Abbas. Whether by his suggestion or their fear of imminent arrest they decided to leave for London when he felt he could make the trip, and did so.

From the London hotel suite he stayed in seclusion working out thoughts he was too afraid to speak aloud. He remembered little of the bridge battle, except that Shanin desired his death by Razzor's hand. Crimson Scimitar had been a failure as no announcement of a radiation cataclysm appeared in the press, and if the disaster had occurred, everyone would know. What had really happened? As his past reading of spy thrillers suggested, the Americans had 'sanitized' the attack site.

What started growing in his consciousness was the shock that al-Qaeda, specifically the Supreme Council, must have sanctioned Shanin to kill all participants in the attack. To kill true Moslem patriots seemed a damnable sin, and tainted the cause. He began to doubt his base beliefs.

In such a quandary, and angry, he did his first 'treasonable' act, both in distrust and towards self-preservation. Through middle man Nidal in New York, always energized for more fees, he liquidated his nearly all of investment portfolio but wired only half of the initial investment capital back into the al-Qaeda laundering accounts, the remainder of funds found safe haven in Switzerland and the Grand Caymans, with a token management account in London. To anyone asking, and they would, he could rationalize, that with the failure of Crimson Scimitar without any market-shattering news the short sales were a loss, when he had to cover the stock positions.

His investment program in the American stock market actually made a sizable profit; first, the short sale was effective when entertainment stocks dipped slightly on the amusement park news; second, covered on that, he repurchased into a small portfolio that did well on the short term market correction, and though prepared to go short on the bridge attack, he held back, a wise decision as no particular American company would reel and falter from the bridge attack. The stocks he left in place unaffected because there was no crash from bad news of a national disaster and within a week the stock market ticked upward on reports of strong quarterly earnings of major bell weather stock indicators. In short, Khalaf, the stock market playing novice made a quick killing that would have brought envy from the likes of Jay Gould and the Robber Barons.

All in all, $US 2 million dollars went back to al-Qaeda accounts, and the balance, $US 6 million fell to Khalaf's personal ownership. Totally mercenary, he believed his and bin Laden's Crimson Scimitar had value, assured of success, and when undone by Shanin's bungling, Khalaf deserved to exact a penalty against a failure to perform. Trying to kill him to shut up such failure made any niggling guilt at perceived thievery negligible.

He did leave one trading account open in New York for several miscellaneous stock holdings Sabz had found interest in. While waiting for his return, she had begun to delve into internet communities where she could learn more about America and the world without revealing herself. She told Khalaf when he had sufficiently recovered that many people in the chat rooms she visited were upbeat on what was called 'social media'; so to appease her, to let her know he did appreciate that she waited for him, that she wanted him, and he had his stockbroker invest in a few of these internet companies where masses of people, without prejudices, interacted; one of them in particular he bought in a private market sale, a 'restricted' stock where insider talk was in launching an IPO the middle of next year. Though satisfying to continue to play in the investment world, his current mind floated in limbo at the unknowns.

His greatest agony was in not deciphering who his unknown 'angels' were. He concluded they could not be the C.I.A., or he would be in Guantanamo at this moment being tortured with sleep deprivation or near drowned by waterboarding. Sabz made the suggestion that this Abbas might be part of an Arabic crime syndicate like she saw on TV, like the Russian mobsters who shared control of any lucrative criminal enterprises in New York with the Zionists.

Most bewildering, was the packet that they had left for him. It contained three cellular phones which he assumed allowed anywhere international use. And, mystery of all mysteries, also included in the packet, a five page document, an essay, written in Arabic, a note attached with two parts. He had read the transcript over twenty times, amazed at its premise. To the note's demands, though they seemed minor, he was afraid to follow the instructions.

Now, safely, he hoped, ensconced in his hotel suite in downtown London he faced hard choices.

When he re-established his presence in a certain Islamic chat room, he received a coded back-door communication from Doctor al-Zawahiri: *What happened to your sword? What happened to your allowance?*

Khalaf responded, warily, no longer assured of who his friends were, even at the top.

Sword broke in desert, ask S on details. – Our banker died. His crimson investments failed without sword; remaining money returned.

After a day, where the recipient of this response probably was engaged in high level discussions, Khalaf received a message he was not expecting.

With sword broken, must concentrate our strength at home. Our uncle, al-Shari fell and died. You are one of my few loyal friends. I am choosing you to join our business. Proceed to visit our friends in Yemen to confirm and receive instructions.

It was powerful news in its interpretation.

Bin Laden's schemes of attacking the United States were to be shelved. From now on, The Doctor and al-Qaeda would focus on weak governments where their attacks might sway control into their hands. The uncle in the code who had been killed was Abu Hafs al-Shari, chief of al-Qaeda operations in Pakistan, and as Khalaf believed al-Shari would have been the logical choice to take over the Number Two role left by the death of al-Rahman. He could now see why Doctor al Zawahiri was consolidating his forces to only mount attacks in Pakistan, Afghanistan, and

Yemen. Sabz was right, he was among one of the last in the organization's hierarchy.

Osama bin Laden's ideal for the caliphate was no more; al-Qaeda operated numbly under siege, its leadership decimated, power ebbing; soon, those of al-Qaeda would be made up of only impressionable suicide bombers, and such fanatics don't conquer governments. Khalaf noticed he did not think in terms of 'we' of al-Qaeda. Still, a position in the Supreme Council was his goal achieved. For several days he fought his doubts against his ambition.

Two surprising sources of comment tipped the scale to his decision.

"If you go to Yemen, then you go. I will not try to stop you. And yes, I will wait for you for you say we are to be married before Allah. But I will not sit in this room and do nothing. I am going to work, to find employment."

"What?" He now had money; she could do anything, within reason.

"It will be for our benefit. While I was shopping the other day I met another Arabic woman, from Tunisia, but a British citizen, who said she was working at a bank, and they were looking to hire Arab-speaking employees for their local and international business. I am smart with math. I could learn and help you with your investments. Would you rather trust me or some stranger?"

He had grown to trust her. She had her own interests but at this time they coincided with his, and she enjoyed the trappings of success, a role he also had easily found to his liking. Bin Laden should have used his money out in the open to chase his political dreams, instead he got caught up in waging a guerrilla war, and see where it has brought him and his al-Qaeda. Again, Khalaf did not use the words 'our' al-Qaeda in his thinking.

"And what should I do with these writings and this note left with me?" He asked of Sabz, ready to consider her opinion.

"Did not this Abbas, and his companion Bennie, did they not save you from death?"

"That is so."

"And if you do what they ask, how can it harm you? I would rather you do it, than find them at our door threatening, or worse."

"It all seems innocent enough, but they are using me."

"I do not see how; in truth it all seems to your advantage. Let's look at what they ask, and take one step at a time." She picked up the note and read:

Sign this writing and mail to the following address. The address seemed to be a postal box in Mayfair. "The essay is positive, asking for a consolidation of Sunni and Shi'ite beliefs into one Islamic voice. To me, it is merely an opinion without teeth."

"I do not want to put my name to any such paper."

"Well, then sign with a different name. Did you not say we need to re-invent ourselves.

Neither the name you use as the messenger or from the Emirates or the investor Risal. Tell me what my married name shall be, my future husband?" She gave him a light laugh which in turn gave him the strength for his first decision. He took a long moment. "_alā_ ad-Dīn Yūsuf ibn Ayyūb."

Sabz gave him a loving smile.

"The Unifier. Yes, that would work with such a document. We are nomads ourselves between the Western and Eastern worlds. Saladin, is the name they called him in the West."

"It is only for this one document. I shall sign it Yusuf Sala ad-Din, and be done with them."

"Consider it for all time. I would be married to Sheik Yusuf Saladin, and people will know me as Sabz Saladin." She handed him a pen. "Sign it and throw this back in their faces."

She looked to the note again.

Turn on the red cell phone. "I would not think this is a bomb." But she was not sure.

Khalaf...Saladin with his future wife's help had regained his courage, agreed to what the Abbas fellow had told Sabz, that someday he would be a man of distinction. With wealth he was half way there, now for the recognition of his peers, to rise above the status of messenger.

"The Israelis Mossad might make this phone a bomb, but who am I? Do you see a reward upon my head? Not yet at least. No, these are Americans, they like to talk, to play silly games." Holding his breath, Kahlaf turned the phone on and let it power up. Both he and Sabz stared. Nothing happened.

He laughed and put it down on the table. The phone buzzed a silent vibration. A text message in Arabic, he read and with wide eyes said, "By the beard of the Prophet." Sabz read. "I am now in fear for you, my sheik." They looked at the text again understanding Khalaf, or this new Yusuf Saladin, was no longer in control of his destiny.

Go to Yemen. Take two of these phones with you. Follow instructions. May Allah bless your journey.

141.

September 30th London/Santa Monica

Samantha woke up to find it was late afternoon and she was staring closely at two feet.

Oh, yes. Afternoon delight. She kissed Wendell's heel, and worked her kisses up his leg to his—

"I am definitely awake," he said. "In all departments. What time is it anyway?"

"What part of the world clock do you wish to track?"

"Three time zones today. We are about to test out what I am calling the Skilleo Effect Caper."

"It has worked so far."

"Today is most critical. All systems must work to perfection."

Realizing there would be no immediate repeat of their marathon love-making, she rose and stood naked before the hotel room's full length dress mirror and with clinical touching studied her body to see if it survived a classic roll in the hay, and glancing in the reflection accepted Wendell Holmes admiring her from a destroyed bed.

"Why do I have these red splotches down here?" Samantha pointed between her thighs on both sides.

"Whisker burn, perhaps."

"That must be the culprit. I will remind you to shave before we romp again."

"Tonight, after our mission." He rose to go to the bathroom and she in turn admired him.

"You know, lack of endurance is not one of your weak points. I have been quite impressed."

She went over to the bed and took his place, and like a giddy young nubile smothered her face into the sheets, inhaling his musk scent. She spoke again with candor, from the heart.

"I could get to like this. We both have this freedom, no restrictions, few complications. I find your male chauvinistic idiosyncrasies tolerable. You pick up your underwear off the floor, and always put the toilet seat down." She giggled. "Even your stream is strong and your aim true, no after use mess."

He returned, sat next to her, and began to rub her neck and shoulders. She continued, "And I don't want to know how long it took you to develop the habit of making sure the woman was satiated and near languorous comatose before letting her take care of you. And that is not a complaint."

"Your pleasure is my pleasure." He drew her face to him and kissed her gently, tenderly.

"Time to go to work."

"Oh, yeah, thanks big boy. Just a quickie one night stand and then go off and save the world."

"If I am recalling, it has been a two week stand." He started to rise and she grabbed his arm, and gave him all her sincerity.

"I am quite happy, Wendell, wherever this ends up."

An inquisitive snarl-smile from him.

"Are you leaving?"

"Do you want me to?" A concern.

"Ye Gads, Samantha, just like a woman, insecurity when it is so good, and it is good, right?

"Absolutely. And your insecurity over performance is touching."

"My dear, as they say, ride with the tide, go with the flow. Up for another joint shower— you wash mine, I wash yours?"

"Read my mind. And I can certainly see yours."

In a leased posh London penthouse condominium, Samantha and Wendell had set up their own mini-War Room in one of the extra bedrooms Against one wall, four large television screens were mounted and tied into his and her computer systems.

Holmes looked at all the electronic bells and whistles and said, "Time to boot up the show; where's the on-off switch."

"Such a cave man." Samantha worked the keyboard and within a few minutes four wall screens were illuminated in real time, and Sam and Wendell said their hellos.

"Hugh and Callie, are we ready?" The back-forth viewing was like a Pentagon version of Skype. The pixel faces of the Hugh and Callie smiled back from California. Samantha noted Callie's hair looked out of place and wondered if their tele-cam system like hers was set up in Fox's boudoir versus Skilleo offices.

"Yes," said Fox, "Gizmo is going to walk us through as it goes down." Gizmo sitting in the Santa Monica War Room offices seemed to have several worker bees punching away on cameras, and in turn they had a large wall mounted screen full of words and oscillating swirls.

To the another face staring back at them, Holmes gave a welcome, "Deputy Director Brady, glad you could join us. Are your people in place?"

"Considering on how you saved our bacon in Nevada you have gained a carte-blanche to call us up anytime and use our resources—of course it would be helpful if we knew what was going on today."

"And Matthew," said Holmes, "Congratulations on your new position with the agency. I heard the former agent who occupied the office of Deputy Director is brushing up on his Pashtu."

"Enough of the feel good moments," said Brady in a heavy voice, everyone accepting they were being recorded. "You have the best of our Joint Special Operations Command. I have a satellite in place, my military field counterpart standing by, an eye-in-the-sky communications bird circling above Yemen, and an armed drone has just taken off from a secret military base, no one knows about."

"Works for us," agreed Fox, moving his eyes to a screen on his end. "Gizmo clock is ticking. Might as well bring all our new found friends up to speed, and please observe the little secrets we must omit."

"Ladies and Gentlemen and Spooks," Gizmo enjoyed his role as the ring master.

"We have in place a gentleman of al-Qaeda persuasion who at this moment is meeting with the Supreme Council of al-Qacda on the Arabian Peninsula and..." He puffed up his chest.

"We have this guy wired for sound and with an imbedded GPS tracker. We know right where he is. We can hear him speak, listen to who he listens to, and a few other choice tech apps."

"Good God," arose an unseen voice on the C.I.A. side.

"No, Good going Skilleo," said Gizmo proudly, "and our tech is not for sale, nor can we be coerced. However, for any torture contact the Skilleo front office for an appointment."

"Gizmo," admonished Fox.

"Ok. Listen in. The gentleman in question and we are listening in now, is having his clock reamed by several of the speakers. We have two Arabic translators who know multiple dialects doing real time translation. Care to listen in."

Voices came in, fast and definitely furious. On the screen in which everyone could see from Gizmos input, came the written word of the conversation. Everyone who heard the dialogue could read closely the moving translation. The man called Khalaf was seeking to defend his conduct about an operation called Crimson Scimitar.

"He did say 'Crimson Scimitar'," asked Brady. "Isn't that's bin Laden's last messenger.

"He's a high value target."

"Off limits," said Holmes. "Part of our agreement. We've turned him...in a way."

"You've turned him? He works for us?"

"Not quite, but I'm working on it."

Another Arabic voice came into the conversation, and when it could be seen on the screen the C.I.A. team listening in on the feed showed noticeable excitement.

"What's up, Mr. Brady?" asked Samantha.

"We've just identified the voice belonging to al-Qaeda's most dangerous recruiters and mouthpiece, Anwar al-Awlaki. American-born, Yemen ethnicity, ties with the powerful Al-Awlik tribe that gives sanctuary to al-Qaeda fighters. I'm sorry, Wendell, but al-Awlaki trumps all. We're going to drop a big one on that gathering."

"Matthew, you gave your word, I would have operational control."

"I would be derelict in my duty, brought up on insubordination charges, if I did not stop the greatest threat, next to Zawahiri."

"It doesn't matter," interrupted Gizmo. "They're on the move, meeting over; probably have to stay one jump ahead of your spy cams."

"Can you track al-Awlaki? We need the GPS coordinates for our eye-sky surveillance."

"I will have to ask Mr. Holmes, he's in charge on our end."

"Wendell, give us a hand here. For old time's sake. For the Agency."

"Don't press my good side. If I can I will get you a bead on al-Awlaki, but on my terms.

"Let me put you on hold and get back to you in one minute." The C.I.A. screen went dark.

Holmes turned his attention to the Hugh/Callie and the Skilleo/War Room screens.

"Okay, we don't have much time. Callie you heard the conversation with our Ali Baba, I mean his new moniker, Yusuf Saladin, not bad choice by the way—but what is your investigative read in tone?"

"Definitely, that was a kangaroo court. One guy there accused our buddy of al-Qaeda treason, blamed him for every mistake of Crimson Scimitar, even said he had abandoned bin Laden and ran like a dog like he did at the bridge. His accuser probably is one of those two assholes who shot Detective Taggart and killed their own people. Boiling it down, Ali Baba, walked into a trap, they're looking for a fall guy, and if they're moving Ali Baba is getting a one wayride."

"Gizmo," Fox pushed. "What do you have for us?"

"They went in two cars. Your man Khalaf is in one, with his accuser, and two other men.

The other vehicle, a matter of deduction, contains al-Awlaki and three men, not sure if they are VIP."

"Okay, going back on screen."

Samantha put back the C.I.A. into visual.

"And?" Asked Brady, somewhat miffed in being held off.

"I need fifteen minutes. Here's the GPS of their location in motion. Let us in on your visual."

Thirty seconds later.

"We have them," said one of the C.I.A. intel techs and the screen showed a high-level grainy view of two cars on a dirt road, dust trails billowing.

"Need fifteen minutes."

"I can't lose the chance, Holmes."

"They're going to execute my man. I need fifteen minutes."

"You can't save him from there."

"I need to make a telephone call."

"He's not going to get a signal from London to Yemen."

"I can if you patch me through your flying com control."

Stare down. Brady between Holmes "*King's Retribution* can accomplish anything." Added Hugh Fox and put his arm around Callie. Samantha squeezed Holmes's hand. There is more at stake, prayed Holmes, than just the body count. It reminded him of the assignment a long time ago, in the darkened Khartoum streets in Sudan, knowing the cruise missile was incoming, that the innocent watchman had run back in and died; Holmes could not save the man. Was this Khartoum all over again? Was he helpless?

"Our drone is ten minutes out," said Brady. "You have ten minutes. Make your call."

142.

September 30th Yemen

With the Jirga of top regional al-Qaeda leaders in full swing, he felt elation. He had presented his credentials that Doctor al-Zawahiri had requested his presence on the Council. He offered that from his past experience he could help bridge the divergent philosophies of the wisdom of Yemen leaders and those in South Waziristan within Zawahiri's circle. He assumed, in a few minutes, he would be selected as a leader within al-Qaeda and be able to help direct the future of the organization. To his on-going inner debate, he held uncertainty that such elevation was what he now sought; that he did not see the end plan of what he would become. Amidst the desert world of men sitting on carpets discussing the next bombing, he had this longing for the optimistic advice of Sabz. Should she not be proud of him in such an achievement?

As if his hesitation signaled his weakness, the world of his expectations came crashing down. Shahin walked in accompanied by two rough-cut men, slinging rifles, appearing to be his bodyguard, and they seem, by costume dress, to be from al-Awlaki's tribe. Both Khalaf and Shahin exchanged hard looks, each seeing betrayal in the other's eyes. In his grand entrance, definitely staged, thought Khalaf, Shahin immediately was given the right to speak. His speech was one of angered accusation against the failure of Crimson Scimitar, not because of how it had failed in being carried out, but because the whole battle plan had been flawed, created by those who knew nothing of true holy war. The last indictment was pointed at Khalaf, and indirectly cast aspersions on bin Laden himself.

Khalaf, to himself thought of the Jewish expression, that he saw the handwriting on the wall, the changing sand of power politics, an adept art he still was not proficient in. Murdered Osama bin Laden would remain the poster martyr to the masses, but his policies must be rewritten to give new and tight control to the next regime. Instead of the caliphate or any confederacy, those remaining in al-Qaeda were dividing up the spoils. Anwar al-Awlaki, a man Khalaf had never trusted as to his own ambition believing he sought to gain equal ranking to bin Laden, dominated this meeting, and certainly Shahin spoke as his right hand hatchet man. Khalaf understood. In this new order al-Awlaki would have the fiefdom of Yemen; Doctor Zawahiri would become the dominant dictator of Pakistan's tribal regions, and a puppet master over an infiltrated conservative Islamic Pakistan. In the course of the conversation new men, he had never met before, stood and asked for their piece of the basboosa cake. Iraq and Syria were divided and given to the New Turks, who promised the current governments would be attacked and undermined, through fomenting rebellion in each state, would al-Qaeda gain renewed strength.

The underlying conclusion of the Jirga was this: the ghost of bin Laden must be purged, and to Khalaf this meant him, the only reminder of their failed quest for Islamic world domination; and he felt what it must be to be like the prophet Jesus, his own people casting stones against him, but invisible here, condemning him of his cowardice, believing he ran from bin Laden's compound and pushed an inept plan which could not possibly work against the formidable America. At this moment, faced with such denunciation, Khalaf lost all faith in the cause he had embraced and to which he swore fealty.

"Enough," said al-Awlaki. "We will take all this into consideration. It is time we moved on to Ma'rib." He looked between Khalaf and Shahin. "Both of you have served our cause well.

"We must seek a solution to end this disharmony." The meet-ing ended and Khalaf felt himself being herded to one of the cars by Shahin's men, and shoved inside. Shahin sat in the front with the driver, Khalaf in the back with one of the bodyguards. Travel-ing in the second following car was al-Awlaki, his bodyguard, and an American born in Saudi Arabia, Samir Khan, editor of al-Qaeda's English-written web magazine, *Inspire*.

As they drove the desert dirt roadway Shahin leaned over the front seat at him, with a false sympathetic voice.

"My words were perhaps too strong. You should be able to convince al-Awlaki to place you in a position of importance. It has always been your wish, is that not so, my brother?"

By such obvious pandering, Khalaf realized he would be executed before they reached the Ma'rib Governorate meeting. This would not be a public spectacle to reveal the rifts within al-Qaeda ranks, instead, a bullet in the head, abandoned as a white-ribbed skeleton in the wasteland. He would never see his true future, as he believed Allah wished. He would never see Sabz again.

A few minutes later as he was contemplating his impending death, he felt a vibration against his leg, and to his shock comprehended that one of the two phones he was asked to carry by his 'angels' had activated. That is not possible, he thought, not out here. He eased it out of his inside robe pocket, masking its presence in his hand, alert that the other three men did not discover this stealth. Pretending to look out the window at the drab nothingness, he threw a quick glance at the text message.

In Arabic, it read: *Move away from car—NOW!*

"Please stop I am going to be sick," groaned Khalaf. "The food today must have been spoiled."

"You can wait," growled Shahin.

"If you want vomit smells in the car for the next hour."

Shahin stared, despising such weakness, then motioned the driver to stop. Behind them, al-Awlaki's car came to a halt.

Khalaf bending over, hugging his stomach, groaned and walked from the car. The message gave a command but did not specify what would happen next, but Khalaf began to have an idea, a searing memory of the night in the village near Wana came back to him. He must get as far away from the two cars as possible. He started to walk towards a bus-sized boulder.

"Do not go far." Said the driver, obviously knowing Khalaf was a 'prisoner'.

"I feel diarrhea coming on, I must hide my embarrassment."

The driver walked back to tell the others in the second car of Khalaf's sudden illness. He was laughing to the others, probably telling them how a condemned man wanted to cleanse his bowels when death would easily release them.

Standing next to the boulder, having no idea on what might come next, Khalaf first pretended to vomit, and then made a show of squatting down next to the rock, his robe pulled up, relieving himself, which he took advantage of in his nervousness. Peering around the rock, he took in the two cars, the impatience of the passengers in the second car, and looked to Shahin to see him checking the slide arm of his automatic. For whatever to happen would come too late, Shahin had decided this was as good as place as any to hold an execution.

Shahin walked around the car and talked to the one body-guard. A laugh of conspiracy between them, Shanin, with the pistol to his side, a menacing sneer on his face, turned towards Khalaf and took two steps before he paused. A momentary thought. A glance to his right and left, back to Khalaf. Knowing. Jerked glances to the sky, and there he saw it: a microscopic reflection, of sun against metal. Surprise panic doused with horror came to Shanin's face and he yelled, "Predator!"

A second later came obliteration.

When the noise and falling stray shrapnel subsided, Khalaf picked himself up off the ground and looked at the two destroyed vehicles, smoldering wreckage, metal and body parts.

Khalaf grimly recalled the code of the Al-Awalik tribe: "We are the sparks of Hell; whomever interferes with us will be burned." Such irony.

He looked around having no idea on what he should do next. No, he should depart the scene as quickly as possible. And an idea came to him. Everyone around him, all that knew him as 'bin Laden's lowly messenger' were no more: Osama Bin Laden, those of the compound, al-Ramen, Shahin. Yes, Doctor al-Zawahiri knew him but not well and not with intimacy of friend-ship. He would believe he had been killed along with Shahin and al-Awlaki. And the Doctor could never leave his mountain hide-out to discover the truth. As Sabz faked her own death in Wana to avoid a bad marriage, so too would he reinvent himself and al-Qaeda would not be part of his future. But what of his future?

The phone gripped in his sweaty hand vibrated.

He screamed out a relief of salvation. Allah would see him through this new danger, as he laughed at the text.

Are you alive, Yusuf Saladin?

Yes, I am, texted back Yusuf Saladin, *Thanks to angels.*

How did they know of this new alias? Did it matter?

His spirits lifted, courage building from twice escaping death from the skies and being a survivor, yet he still wondered about the two remaining phones, one of them back in London.

One of these remaining phones he guessed was to be deployed if he ever met up with al-Zawahiri to call in another drone to the scene and bring plummeting death. Would that be true of the phone he now held? He started laughing. Not today. All this would be for another day, his angels wished him to live for the time being.

He heard a noise, a bell, and turned to see a lone villager coming over the hill, in curiosity of rising smoke, the smell of burned flesh in the air—the yelling and joyous dancing of a strange man. The villager walked a path holding a rope to a beast of burden, the bell around the animal's neck.

Yusuf sighed, what does fate hold for me if I must enter a new life on the back of this donkey?

143.

October 1st Gatwick Airport, Great Britain

The disembarking passengers clearing customs surged around them. There were hugs of new found friendship among the four alumni of *King's Retribution's* unsung adventure.

"Good to see you both, and arriving with the common people versus your jet, how did you manage?" Holmes gave Fox a pat on the back.

"First class helps."

"Well, it is a business deduction," added Callie. "I went the length of the plane and counted three children and two adults playing Skilleo Games."

"Well, welcome to London," Samantha locked arms between Callie and Hugh. "Wen wants to show you our little experiment. It should be happening soon."

"You are staging a flash mob for our benefit."

"No, but a surprise nevertheless, and then we will wine and dine you both and spend the next several days discussing Five Aces Studioz and the future of *King's Retribution*."

Callie response was sad.

"With King still in therapy I don't see much good for the show's continuance."

"Well, I have a few ideas to bounce off you both."

Wendell halted them off to the side, next to a boisterous group of anxious members of the Fourth Estate, a small mob of English and international press.

"I tried to coordinate this all for your benefit, but it's hard to initiate delays and extra baggage checks to have one airline a little late to match your arrival."

"Isn't he just the best 'fixer' you've ever met," beamed Samantha, "And he's all mine."

They could see the press gain excitement and crowd around one of the exiting passengers.

"Mr. Saladin, are you aware the amount of interest your essays are having within the Moslem communities?"

The target of the reporters' microphones thrust in his face seemed surprised.

"Essays?"

"Your second essay was published yesterday by *The Sun Times*. 'Islamic Faith in the 22nd Century'."

"I have just arrived and certainly will pick up a copy." Several of the media people laughed.

Another question: "In your first essay, you say that Sunni and Shi'ite should put aside differences and join in a new Islamic union. Do you feel that's possible?"

"Yes, that was written...by me." He paused. "Yes, I believe peace among our brothers and sisters should be the highest priority. A combined society of faiths is possible."

A few more questions were lobbed at him, and he answered cautiously and awkward.

Another reporter had her opportunity. "Can we look forward to seeing your thoughts in a book soon?"

The young woman garbed in Moslem dress pushed her way through the throng.

"Yes, he is working on a book," said Sabz, demurely, with lowered eyes, respectful of her husband-to-be in public, "but please give him a chance to recover from his trip. Contact us through the new Madrasah school he will be opening. His press secretary will be happy to set up interviews with you all."

The working press never accepts an ending dictated by others.

"A final question. Al Jazerra Television, here. Do you consider yourself *The Mujaddid* for this century?"

Yusuf Saladin reacted, taken off guard, but seeing a potential road map of the direction he must follow, the first, understanding the pitfalls of grabbing too quickly at the prize.

"I am a simple man, a messenger, you might say, who hopes his words will bring all my Moslem brothers and sisters into a new Islamic harmony." He used his hand in a traditional thank you and farewell, that some took as a blessing, for all those present, and to those who saw it again when the interview was played over and over on television.

Sabz led him by the arm towards the exit and an awaiting limousine. Holmes noted the newly patented celebrity pulled a cell phone from his jacket, looked at it, reacted disappointed in seeing no message, and put the phone away, and turned to hug his wife-to-be with the ardor one sees in a soldier returning from war, and to ask many questions of his absence, and to tell none himself.

Fox turned to Holmes showing his surprise.

"That's our Ali Baba? You stage managed this whole affair with the reporters."

"Can never dismiss good press and yes, indeed our Ali Baba, reborn as Sheik Yusuf Saladin, to be a philosopher and teacher in Islam on how the modern Moslem should exist within modern society."

"Who is a Mujaddid?" Callie asked.

"A planted question, well placed," smiled Samantha.

"A Mujaddid is a person who comes once a century to revive Islam, bringing back to its purity; such could be a prominent individual, a teacher, scholar, and yes, a caliph. I think Sheik Saladin's brain is churning right now on the ramifications of that possibility being himself."

"Of course, our Sheik doesn't have the full story," explained Samantha. "Wendell still hasn't completed the working script."

"And you expect him to do exactly what you say," Callie a little more skeptical.

"No, at a point he will become his own man, perhaps more the pragmatic politician, at which point he will hopefully have the savvy to compromise with liberals, moderates, and conservatives in all Islamic beliefs, hopefully finding the common ground..."

"Which by the way," Samantha interjected, "will be based in love for the fellow man, peace among your neighbors, and stop killing each other."

"That's a big order," whistled Fox.

"To give him the courage to try and bring his faith into an acceptance and toleration of other's beliefs, I have one further card to play?"

"And that is?"

"The Skilleo jaw implant inserted during his 'auto accident' phase. When activated, he will start hearing voices, literally in his head...a voice from above...the burning bush of motivation, so to speak. He will move from teacher to prophet to leader. We know what his ambition is; he has mentioned it before to Sabz in pillow talk. It will be up to us to help him achieve his goal, if it restores peace and stability among nations."

"And what is that goal?"

Holmes began leading the delegation of 'angels,' the Team of *King's Retribution*, out the airport doors. As one might expect, the

English day was filled with a light rain. Each couple drew close to their mate, heartfelt smiles all around.

"We are going to take the Arab Spring and mould it into the Pan Arab Caliphate ruled by Sheik Yusuf Saladin."

Epilogue

Four years ago, I promised to end the war in Iraq. We did. I promised to refocus on the terrorists who actually attacked us on 9/11. We have. We've blunted the Taliban's momentum in Afghanistan, and in 2014, our longest war will be over. A new tower rises above the New York skyline, al Qaeda is on the path to defeat, and Osama bin Laden is dead.
U. S. President Barack Obama

144.

One Year Later, 2012 Southeastern Kenya

The poachers, three of them carrying automatic rifles brought over from Somalia walked with silence along the brush path, many miles within the boundaries of the Tsavo Conservation Area, near the Galana river. For the last half hour they had been listening to the trumpeting of the bull elephant, and guessed he was in the stand of acacia trees just ahead. There, they spotted the largest land mammal in the world, its gigantic head swinging back and forth displaying enormous tusks worth a fortune on the Asian markets. Running forward the lead man dropped to a knee, took careful aim, and spit out a burst of rifle fire. The poacher's face went quizzical as his compatriots laughing at his apparent miss unloaded their weapons, each knowing they had struck the beast, but the animal did not collapse, but continued the calling, the shaking of its head again, and again, the same movement, over and over.

Sirens screamed and from hidden blinds Park Rangers with their own firepower stepped into view, the barrels of their rifles aimed at the three men. A loudspeaker blared: "Throw down your weapons and put your hands in the air." Another voice made the same command in the local district dialect. A jeep bowled through the underbrush and pulled within feet of the criminals as they complied and surrendered to the overwhelming force.

From the jeep, leaning heavily on a lavishly ornate and decorated cane sculpted in African mahogany, stepped Colonel David 'Storm' King (ret.). "I arrest you in the name of the decency to protect our wildlife heritage. You will now face King's Retribution." He paused for a moment, his face a malevolent grin, sweat leaking from under his pith helmet, he then yelled, "Cut."

A small bus came up to him and the mini production crew alighted.

"Abbas, sorry, old fellow, but it looks like they peppered up Jumbo, this time like Swiss Cheese." They both looked the animatronics creature still doing its routine. Abbas pushed a remote and the fake elephant went into stasis.

"I'll get on it. We have a pacing lion ready for the next episode."

"Good." Storm wiped his brow with a wet towel handed to him by a staff member, a young cute thing, where Storm's eyes wandered on for a second too long, but obvious to all.

Storm being Storm.

"This heat is getting to me. A gin and tonic would do the trick right about now."

"Here's a cold ice tea," replied Bennie, handing over a thermos. "Remember your contract."

"Yes, yes, I do, but considering everything, a little libation might add some edge to my character."

"Storm, you are the top show on The Animal Planet. *King's Retribution – The African Campaign* is renewed for another year. And you don't have to worry about playing up to advertisers. Sammy C Wildlife Foundation underwrites the program costs."

Storm's eyes followed the attractive young intern snapping background publicity stills.

"And," added Bennie, to put King back in his reality check. "You are a father figure to all nature loving children around the world; National Geographic wants to do a documentary on your saving African wildlife from extinction. Remember the image, remember the large paycheck that comes with the image. A soldier's duty, Colonel."

"That's right, duty. And, the fact, we are one of the top shows on cable." He returned to business, always the main man on battlefield logistics. "CAM TWO, get a close up of them carting off our suspects. The viewing audience must be made aware: Our planet and its creatures must be protected."

Bennie and Abbas rolled their eyes behind Storm's back, but accepted their own duty, stipulated in their contracts, a generous bonus by Five Aces Studioz as glorified babysitters, 'combat pay' as they reminded each other many times during the Kenyan production season.

145.

2012 Silicon Valley

"Can I read you this article out of the *Hollywood Reporter*?"

Callie put down the book that Holmes and Samantha had mailed to them, the one just published and released by their friendly terrorist from the bridge, Ali Baba, though the author's name on the book's cover read, Sheik Yusuf Saladin.

"Sure. Feel-good philosophy with a dash of world politics was about to put me to sleep.

"Where's a good Michael Connelly, even Elmore Leonard for some hard-boiled dialogue. So, what do you have?" She curled her legs under herself on the couch. They were at 'their' place, once Hugh's, now her things were moved in. Still, the décor said minimalist and not fru-fru. Callie never was a House Beautiful sort of girl.

Hugh read:

"'Reviews are positive over ABC's debut show, *Queen's Revenge*, put out by the Five Aces Studioz, and starring Carlita 'Callie' Cardoza, the former co-star of *King's Retribution.*"

"The show also features former SEAL Shawn Pacheco who some are calling the Young Stallone."

"Premise of *Queen's Revenge*, similar to the bounty hunters of *King's Retribution*, but with a new twist, *cyber crime*. Independent testing says *Queen's Revenge* may have scored among three strong demographics; Cardoza, a steaming bombshell ex-cop, pulling in the male audience; women drawn to Shawn Pacheco, especially when he takes off his shirt, reminiscent of Storm King's antics (sorry girls, Shawn's married); and creating top suspense in the cyber hunt for white collar criminals which seems to have attracted the geeks away from their I-Boxes and Play Stations. Congrats to *Queen's Revenge* towards your upcoming second season.'

"Steaming bombshell is that my soul-mate?"

"You want me to show you my interpretation of, 'steamy', as an adjective?

"Yes, but later." He handed her an oblong small box the cardboard sleeve in familiar design of pink paper with 'C-4 Explosive' markings.

She looked at it warily but saw his smile. "When they called me a bombshell you shouldn't take it literally. Besides I don't need any more gifts from you; the ring expressed what you sometimes can't. But I'll get you there to say the 'L' word someday." She flashed the diamond, not extravagant, but noticeable to the message given, the emotional turf staked.

Fox spoke with inventive excitement something Callie relished as a good trait in him.

"Holmes suggested the paper, for old time's sake. We will test market it, but I think the buyer will understand the significance of packaging once they're into the game."

"A new game?" Out of the covering sleeve, she looked at the cover, like a classic motion picture poster of the 1940's, all action, depicting four people running towards the camera, their guns blazing, explosions surrounding them, a truck tipping over a bridge.

Terror on Demon Bridge

"Hugh, you can't be serious?"

"The understanding agreed to by *King's Retribution* and by each of us, is never to speak of what happened in Abbottabad, at the amusement parks or the bridge; how American authors were used to foment one of the most diabolical terrorist plots ever unleashed on our soil. I have said nothing, only a game plot that tells an interesting story of trying to stop a terrorist plot.

Green screen characters, some animation. With Level Six some of the terrorists melt into zombies."

Callie frowned. "One of the women on this cover looks a lot like me."

"Who you, *the steaming bombshell?* I find you more the firecracker type." She gave him a disbelieving look. He continued, shrugged his shoulders, an effort to extract himself, "In the game there are standardized characters if you don't want to build your own avatar."

"The others on the cover look a lot like Wen, Sam, and you. Let me ask, what's the name of my 'standardized' character?"

He gave an impish grin. "Viper'. The one that might look like me is 'Wolfe'."

"Okay, Wolfie, come over here, and let's play this game and see who can kill off the most terrorists and save America. But let's do it different: 'Strip Video Game', the loser will end up naked."

"No fair, I tested the prototype against the engineers and won every game."

"And the point, Wolfie, is what? As I see it, lose or win, I still win."

"Oh, yeah," Hugh Fox, president of Skilleo Games Technology finally caught on.

Callie smiled as a devilish Viper might; sometimes with genius you got to lead them by...

146.

2012 London

The banker held out her hand and the other woman shook it and sat down.

"And you want to open an account, Miss...."

"Carlisle. Samantha Carlisle."

"You wouldn't happen to be, and pardon me for being rude, 'Sammy C'.

"The same."

The young girl flushed.

"Oh, I am a big fan of your fashion. Have several outfits, and wear them when I can."

Samantha regarded the nameplate on the banker's desk which read, "Sabz S."

"Nice to find someone who appreciates quality design. Do I call you Sabz, or what is your last name if we are going to be banker and customer?

"Saladin. Sabz... Saladin, Head of New Accounts."

"Saladin? You aren't related to that famous author are you?"

Embarrassment from Sabz.

"Yes, he is my husband."

"Why, my dear, you should be so proud. An immediate best-seller throughout the world everyone is talking about '*A Modern Moslem Life*'. For a non-Islamic person it opened such a new world of possibilities between world religions, and that one part of bringing all Moslem countries into their own style of a United Nations, very progressive intellect."

"I am impressed you read it. There have been critics, those I know who have not read the book, and said it was trash, like that German book by Hitler."

"Oh, you mean, 'My Struggle'; in German, '*Mein Kampf*'. Rubbish. Nothing like it at all, I'm sure. Any public figure will have envious naysayers," and Samantha paused with a little of her own inside humor, 'until all truths are self-evident'."

"Yes, the Sheik, my husband, is being recognized for his wisdom."

"To imagine he wrote with such insight. He did not have help in writing this book, did he? Such a gifted work."

Sabz stumbled. "No, he worked very hard; it is all his own words."

"Well, much congratulations to you both."

Sabz picked up the bank account forms. "What sort of account do you want to be opening?"

"I should ask you. On one hand, I am thinking about opening a small boutique where I can create new designs under another brand. My non-compete runs out this year, so I will start over, but for the fun of it. So, a business account. And, then I want an account where I can draw on funds for some speculation in the stock market."

"Stock market? I should not talk personally, but I do the same thing. My husband has been generous and allows me a small account to pursue growth companies, mostly American high tech."

"Really, exactly what I do. In fact, my stockbroker put me into Facebook before it went public."

"That is a remarkable coincidence. I was able to talk my husband into making a similar purchase. We are quite fortunate and look forward to holding the company long term."

"I agree. You know, we should talk sometime soon, maybe over morning coffee. I would be interested in your opinion on some of my other investments."

"I would like that very much. I don't believe it would be against bank policy."

"No, of course not, I'm sure. And perhaps, you and your husband might wish to join me and my boyfriend and a few friends for a small social gathering next week."

"Oh, I'm sorry, although I would my husband is spending a lot of time working on his presentation when he goes on his book tour."

"A book tour? How exciting. I am sure the crowds will be thick; he will be mobbed with fans."

"That is what I am afraid of. More so of the religious zealots who cannot consider the suggestion of change as positive for all."

"My exact sentiments. Yes, you do have reason to worry. Fame brings out the unhinged. I should give you my boyfriend's business card; he is in the security business. He provides bodyguards and security systems for some of the top celebrities in the U.K, movie stars, even soccer stars."

"Soccer stars?"

"Oh, yes, European football. We get free tickets all the time to the major contests. You seem interested? Let me know and I will arrange some tickets. Oh, here is his card; please call him, or have your husband or his publisher call Wendell's office. One can't be too careful in this crazy world, especially when it comes to someone who has become as famous as your husband."

"Oh, yes," agreed Sabz, eager to place the business card of *Sherlock Holmes Security* where she would not lose it.

"Shall, we start doing the paperwork? I have been so lucky in meeting you, Mrs. Saladin."

Outside the bank, after two accounts were open, and an invitation firmed up to have coffee with Sabz in two days, Samantha met up with Wendell Holmes, sitting on a park bench, scanning his copy of *"A Modern Moslem Life"* inspecting how the writing from his clandestine cabal of professors with him as executive editor had translated into print by author Sheik Yusuf Saladin.

"A very nice girl," said Samantha. "I truly believe we will become close friends. And you did overhear correctly, on her advice, her husband made several millions of dollars in an early buy into Facebook, and gave her a mil to play the market. I may have met my analytic match."

"What of Sherlock Holmes Security?"

"The bait is dangling and they should take it. She is afraid for him and he knows his old comrades might want to set an example against this 'modernizing moderation'." I will take very good care of him. Keep him alive and hope hc amounts to something positive for us all."

"Well, if he doesn't prove out, don't have him assassinated. I don't want to see Sabz a widow, she'd never recover."

"You mean have Brady fly a drone over him. No, we are setting this in motion, planting the seeds of what we believe is the right course. He must grow himself, nourish, find wisdom; then harvest, good or bad, will be his own fruit of conviction. We can only pray that his ambition is refocused on this better path. Here is where we must have faith in a higher authority, whether God, Allah, or Zeus." Holmes put his arm around Samantha, happy to be with her. They should go home, make love, and then he would go back to his ghost writing.

Samantha had a thought.

"Saladin, writing best sellers, and proselytizing to small groups, is one thing, but multi media marketing would reach a wider audience. Maybe film a documentary."

"Yes, reach for the less literate masses, better yet, then why not a reality show?" Holmes caught a glimpse of the person following them. Over his shoulder, not missing a step, he shouted, "Did you get the bank meeting with Sam and Sabz, and what we just said; all of that?"

CAM ONE nodded, and spoke, "Yes, a good beginning."

The End...Not Quite...Let Author know which Next Chapter you might choose to be written.

[Roll Credits: insert vignette closings]

Three Separate Unfinished Threads

2014   Brussels, Belgium

Hans Luber ('Lubbie') hated everything and everybody, and if they had tested him, certifiably, he would be found mentally incompetent, but he hid it well.

The bookstore sales clerk only saw a customer.

"Can I help you?"

"I have a reading list of books." He handed it over. "Do you have these?"

"Why, yes, I think we do. Some are now out in paperback, less expensive. Two of your titles are actually movies."

"Yes, I know."

"We should have those in our DVD and Audio section." The bookstore sales clerk again scanned the list. "You seem to be a fan of action thrillers. You like those sort of cliff-hangers-- the world about ready to be blown up, where at the last minute the good guys come to the rescue."

Said Lubbie, his eyes bouncing, glancing around, nervously, "I like to wonder what would happen if the good guys didn't show up in time."

The sales clerk had no witty response, but noticed the young man was carrying a dog-eared copy of a book, filled with yellow post-it notes, for page marking. With friendly customer service in mind, he asked, "That must be a great story. Is that a book like these on your list?"

"Yes, said Lubbie, his face showing what could be a smile, or not. "It is my Bible. One must learn from mistakes and make improvements." He showed the clerk the title: *with Revenge comes Terror.*

2015 Washington, D.C.

In the hallowed halls of Congress, after sitting in the hearing room audience of the U.S. Senate Environment and Public Works Committee, two governmental aides who worked for very important people made small conversation before they headed home for the weekend.

"Robert, how do you think the President's nominee to the National Regulatory Commission will fare for confirmation?

"A battle royal like usual between parties. If she goes on the NRC, probably will be the death knell for Yucca Mountain."

"Speaking of which, Charles, like before, I'm putting you on verbal notice, we have received a request for another shipment to be sent out. Almost two a month these days. Do we handle it the same way?"

"Yes, as before, Robert, call that telephone number I gave you, give the particulars, and the people on the other end will take it from there. No questions asked, by you or them. No fuss, no muss."

"You don't think these shipments are still going to Yucca? Like we tried year before last?"

"Not after that flare up when they had that truck accident out in Nevada, and as you saw today any new NRC appointments have too much uncertainty about underground storage and will tilt towards closing Yucca for good; there goes our only 'sanctioned' national nuclear waste depository."

The mid-level official called Charles looked left then right down the empty hallway, most fellow government workers already having left for the day. "I am even out of the loop but I can guess they found a new location, top-top secret. Not even my clearance. At the highest levels this time around they want to avoid all politics of 'yes, we need to dump it, but not in my back yard.' I think I heard somewhere in the grapevine, they got the idea from a movie. You remember the one, *Raiders of the Lost Ark*.

"The best was always the first *Raiders*."

"In the closing scene, the crated-up Arc of the Covenant is placed in a huge government warehouse, and the heroes are told it will be safe and sound, when the irony is it will be lost in the bureaucracy, no one ever knowing its worth or danger. That's what I think; they have this huge facility, and all the excess and most toxic nuclear waste in America is being stored there, and over time we are all going to forget it exists."

"Good analogy. So, Charles, what are you doing for the weekend?"

"Early round of golf; I take it as my medicine for a week of stress listening to Hill doublespeak."

"Then, hit a hole-in-one for me."

"That would be glorious. Life should be so kind."

Charles and Robert headed their separate ways. Charles headed home in his car only to find himself caught in rush hour gridlock of Washington's belt highway system. He listened to the radio announcer informing him traffic was moving when it wasn't. He glanced at his surroundings of cars and trucks immobile or inching forward at a snail pace. Across the median, he notice three tractor trailers in convoy, each with two chemical tanks attached, following the other, going the opposite way he was traveling, actually merging onto another freeway, heading south. He found this curious because on the overpass above him likewise in the rush hour traffic jam three similar trucks inched forward in a tail-gate crawl going west, and odd—all of the trucks had the same markings: *Eagle Freight* just like the others which he could see across from him in the rear view mirror, disappearing over the horizon.

Traffic in his lane started to move but slower than in the other highway lane, and Charles looked for a gap so he could pass the truck in front of him, a two-tandem tanker truck, lots of dents in the sides, and with a red graffiti slash on its rear tank; and then after that he would have to pass the two trucks in front of this one, each labeled *Eagle Freight*, with its logo of an eagle swooping to grasp a helpless trout.

2016 Outside Al-Raqqha, Syria

The bomb strike hit the front of the convoy, the line of cars and trucks taking him to the meeting in Mosul. His bodyguard driver swerved the truck he was riding in, bumping off the road, into the side streets of the village they were passing through, seeking out a marketplace or crowded neighborhood to hide within. The sky eyes of the Enemy were forbidden to come after him among civilians. Their policies against collateral damage would protect him and their political fears of 'boots on the ground' would keep their troops from coming after his leadership council, and after him.

Yet, he was tired. Paranoia at the dangers from the sky, frustration against his failure to consolidate their earlier victories, even in-fighting of the various groups that built his coalition seemed to be fragmenting, requiring ruthless intercession to regain loyalties. All these elements, along with the rise of a new apostate spouting his religious mantra of moderation, non-violence to the masses, stoked his anger to retaliate against his Great Enemy, the ultimate of infidels, a distant country which provided false security for all sorts of non-believers. Indeed, the Great Satan.

He jumped from the truck and with a cadre of armed body-guards ran to safety into a sharia school, the boys looking from the doors and windows at the rising flames from the highway, explosions of small arms, smells of burned flesh. He stared at the carnage. Many of his troops had died without a prayer to their lips.

He gave instructions to get the road cleared. He must go on. In the past, in another such attack, he had been wounded. Enough was enough.

"I will have my revenge." He knew the previous attempt, revenge for Osama bin Laden's murder, had failed miserably. He would not fail. Attack the unaware Great Satan. Kill the apostate of Islam.

He would succeed, after all, he was Caliph Ibrahim; in his own mind, he was the mullah of destiny.

--The End--

People of 'With Revenge comes Terror'

Hugh Fox – Founder and CEO of Skilleo Game Technology
Samantha Carlisle – Former owner of SammyC Fashions, head of Sammy C Wildlife Foundation
Wendell Holmes – CIA agent, facing forced retirement
Khalaf, [Yusuf Saladin] a.k.a. Maulawi Abd al-Khaliq Jan – Courier between bin Laden & al-Qaeda Supreme Council—Aliases: Risal and Sheik Khalaf bin Zayed
Sabz ('Emerald') – niece of Emir Tahir Yuldashev of Islamic Movement of
Uzbekistan (IMU) – killed in 2009

King's Retribution **Reality TV Show:**
Colonel (Ret.) David 'Storm' King – Star
Carlita 'Callie' Cardoza – Co-star
Clayton Briggs – Muscle
Bennie – Car get-away driver
Hiram Abbas – Special effects coordinator
Cam One and Cam Two – floating videographers

Crimson Scimitar:
The Professor – American al-Qaeda; James Rogers, Professor, University of Nevada at Las Vegas
Razzor Hassim – Enforcer
Shahin – Field Commander of Crimson Scimitar
Mike "Gator" Donaldson – Miami cell
Luis Delgado – Los Angeles cell

At the Abbottabad Compound:
Osama bin Laden – Founder and titular head of al-Qaeda, a global militant Sunni Islamist group, and the designated future Emir of the planned Caliphate Dynasty
Amal Ahmed Abdul Fatah – Bin Laden's fifth wife
Khalid – Bin Laden's son (by previous wife)
Ibrahim Saeed Ahmed and his brother, Abrar – Couriers

SEAL Team Six:
Shawn Pacheco (his fiancée: Janet Mosswood)

Reyes Montoya – of SEAL Team Four; killed in Afghanistan; Pacheco's friend

U.S. Government:
Barack Obama – President of the United States
Leon Panetta – Director of the CIA until June 30th, 2011
Ronald Givens – Assistant Deputy Director of the CIA
U.S. Senator Lucy Crandall of California
Matthew Brady, Analyst, CIA

al-Qaeda:
The Doctor/al Zawahiri – Successor to bin Laden
Naser Abdel Karim al-Wahishi – Leader on the Arabian Peninsula
Anwar al-Awlaki – American-born Islamic clerical leader & field commander
Saif al-Adel – Sword of the Just
Fahd Mohammed Ahmed al-Quso – One of the collaborators on the USS Cole bombing
Ibrahim Hassan Al Asiri – The "Yemen Bomber"
Ilyas Kashmiri – Regional operations chief for al-Qaeda
Umar Farouk Abdulmutallab – The attempted Northwest Airlines flight bomber
Ahmed Abdul al Rahman – son of 'The Blind Shiek'; 2nd in command to Zawahiri after
bin Laden's death

London al-Qaeda:
Stockbroker – Ziad Mahoummed Barakat (a.k.a. Zia Johnson)
Banker – Taher Abboud

Others:
Pastor Samuel Tate, Church of True Believers
J-Q – Assistant to Hugh Fox
General Jamshed Khan, Pakistan Military Intelligence
Russell Mosswood, (ret.) U.S. Army Captain (Janet Mosswood's Father)

Timeline to date

Mar. 1957 Osama bin Mohammed bin Awad bin Laden born in Riyadh, Saudi Arabia

Dec. 1979 Soviets invade Afghanistan; bin Laden arrives

Jan. 1980 CIA Agent Wendell Holmes meets bin Laden

Apr. 1982 CIA Agent Holmes and Arab Volunteer bin Laden in Soviet firefight

Sep. 1988 al-Qaeda begins operations

Aug. 1990 Iraq invades Kuwait

Aug. 1996 Bin Laden declares war on the United States

Aug. 1998 U.S. Embassy Africa bombings; bin Laden placed on FBI Most Wanted List

In retaliation, U.S. cruise missile strike on pharmaceutical plant in Sudan;

CIA Agents Wendell Holmes and Ronald Givens at scene

Oct. 2000 USS Cole attack in Yemeni port of Aden

Jun. 29, 2001 al-Qaeda creates U.S. sleeper cell

Sep. 11, 2001 al-Qaeda attacks on America

Oct. 2001 U.S. and coalition forces enter Afghanistan to destroy al-Qaeda and capture Osama bin Laden

Dec. 2010 Sleeper cell in Las Vegas activated

Dec. 23, 2010 Newspaper falsely reports bin Laden is dead

Jan. 2011 Hugh Fox meets Samantha Carlisle in New York City; *King's Retribution*

TV Show filming in Sao Paulo, Brazil; Indonesian nightclub bomber

Umar Pate captured in Abbottabad, Pakistan; SEAL Shawn Pacheco injured in Afghanistan

Feb. 2011 Col. King and Callie Cardoza meet Hugh Fox and Samantha Carlisle;

SEAL Pacheco transferred to SEAL Team Six and sent stateside for operational training; On behalf of bin Laden, courier Kahlaf in Yemen to meet with regional al-Qaeda leaders

Mar. 2011 CIA Assistant Director Givens tasks Wendell Holmes to spy on King's Retribution; al-Qaeda Enforcer Razzor Hassim removes a problem with the Miami attack group; SEAL Pacheco training in California; on March

27, President Obama discusses possible action to be taken from intelligence leading to bin Laden

April 2011 4/5 - Al-Qaeda operative Kahlaf is in London on financial aspect of Crimson Scimitar; 4/10 - Hugh Fox meets CIA agent Wendell Holmes;

4/11 - *King's Retribution* in San Francisco for Col. King to participate in legal forum; CIA Asst. Director Givens involved in plan to ship nuclear waste cross country; 4/13 - Professor and Razzor Hassim meet Luis Delgado at the Mexican border; 4/15 - *King's Retribution* decides to go find bin Laden in Pakistan; 4/19 - President Obama agrees to advance

Operation Neptune Spear to April 30

4/22 – Pacheco lands at Bagram Air Base, Afghanistan; 4/28 *King's Retribution* flies to Egypt; 4/29 – President makes decision for attack;

4/31- Operation Neptune Spear postponed one day because of weather;

4/31 – King's Retribution arrives in Islamabad, Pakistan.

May 2011 May 1st--11:52 am – SEALS enter Pakistani airspace; May 2nd – 12:55 am – Attack on Abbottabad compound

1:44 am – SEALS depart from compound

May 1st – Washington, D.C. 11:30 pm – President announce death of bin Laden – 5/2 – 8:30 am -- *King's Retribution* learns of the failure of their mission

5/2 – 10 pm – *King's Retribution* tours bin Laden home; 1 am -- death of Clayton Briggs

5/4 Newspaper headlines on the raid on bin Laden Compound and failure of *King's Retribution*

5/6 Wendell Holmes leaves C.I.A.

5/6 President of the United States at Ft. Campbell, Kentucky to meet bin Laden raid military, Pacheco present;

5/11 – Funeral of Clayton Briggs;

5/27 – Wendell Holmes seeks retirement activities; more news on al-Qaeda events;

June 2011 6/1 -- Planned shipment of nuclear waste across country;'

6/3 – Khalaf injured in Predator drone attack;

6/9 -- Wendell Holmes visits the War Room in Santa Monica;

6/10 – Callie Cardoza creates CD of bin Laden visits

6/14—Samantha Carlisle seeks out Wendell Holmes

6/15 – Shawn Pacheco has falling out with fiancée

6/17 – Khalaf meets Sabz
6/22 – President of U.S. delivers policy speech on terrorism
6/27 – Flooding in Nebraska damages nuclear power plant;
July 2011 7/4 Holmes and Carlisle discuss issues
7/10 Khalaf in London takes over part of Crimson Scimitar
7/18 King's Retribution Team meets – unfinished work;
7/20 Crimson Scimitar Attack Team enters U.S. from Mexico;
7/22 Holmes visits Miami FBI agent;
7/23 Holmes meets with CIA contact Matthew Brady;
7/26 State Department issues international terrorist warning but not one for the U.S.;
7/27 Holmes and Samantha watch movies;
7/30 Storm King gives up gossip on *Retribution's* terrorist hunt;
7/31 President of U.S. reacts;
August 2011 8/1 Crimson Scimitar Attack Team go over final plans;
8/3 Khalaf in New York to implement part of attack plan;
8/4 *King's Retribution* meets SEAL Pacheco;
8/23 Earthquake hits Washington, D.C. area;
8/25 Timetable moved up to ship nuclear waste;
8/27 War Room—discovery of attack plan location; Storm King injured car bomb blast;
8/29 CIA Brady investigates nuclear threat; waste shipment trucks leave;
8/30 First Phase of Attacks of Crimson Scimitar; Khalaf waits for results; White House meeting of national security heads;
Sept. 2011 9/1 Khalaf arrives in Vegas to join strike team; King's Retribution prepares;
9/2 Attack on the Bridge
9/3 Clean up from attack
9/5 Attack on The Professor
9/11 Injured Khalaf returns to Sabz in New York
9/15 The White House; Pacheco meets the President
9/18 CIA Givens meets General Khan in Pakistan
9/20 Khalaf and Sabz in London
9/30 Anwar al-Awlaki killed in Yemen, Khalaf at scene
Oct. 2011 10/1 Gatwick airport; press conference
Epilogue 2015-2016
Three Separate Unfinished Threads

Author's Final Note

In writing a contemporary political action thriller the issue sometime arises at what point is the story's timeline set firm with whatever occurring in future current events becoming, by your plotting, either prophesy come true or anachronistic improbabilities. Halfway through my first draft manuscript, Osama bin Laden was killed by U.S. Navy SEALS. In my then story I had him captured and tried in a U.S. Court (and acquitted!). My 2012 finished e-book produced a race against a ticking time bomb climax coinciding with the tenth anniversary of 9.11, now passed on by several years.

Now, at the end of 2015, we have more terrorist attacks across the world, a distorted and evil radicalization of a religion by just only a minority of adherents who believe if you do not think as they do, you, as the non-believer, must be killed. Only a few decades ago, the world called this the Holocaust. And every intelligent and rational person said, "Never again."

The many political *what-if* premises of this edition retains merit as historic fiction. Luckily, I have discovered it is quite easy to edit, revise and refresh the E-novel to not only correct grammatical errors discovered by readers as well as re-weave today's headlines within and improve with those news stories that are of concern to us in the present day. If a fan base is acquired, a sequel containing current events needs to be written with our cast of characters.

If your gather in any wisdom here, know for certain the tendrils of world terrorism are spreading and what occurs and what is thwarted, may be closer to your own home. Maintain vigilance.

S.P. Grogan
2016

For more information visit author's website: www.spgrogan.com

And buy today soft cover or Ebook: ***Captain Cooked***, ***Vegas Die***, and ***Atomic Dreams at the Red Tiki Lounge***.

If you enjoyed this story, please inform your social media friends. Thank you.